D0458556

Regards from The Dead Princess

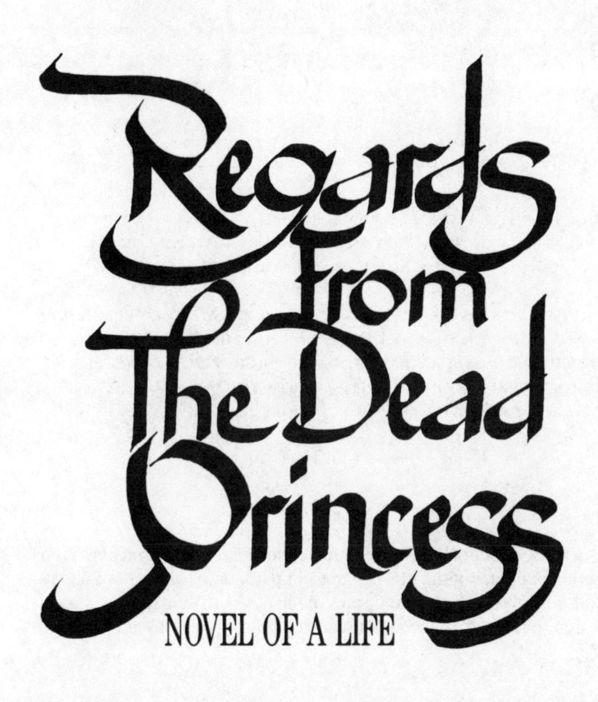

NOVEL OF A LIFE

KENIZE MOURAD

Translated from the French by
Sabine Destrée and Anna Williams
in collaboration with the author

Arcade Publishing · New York
Little, Brown and Company

FIRST U.S. EDITION

This is a work of fiction. It is based on the life of a real-life princess, Selma, the granddaughter of the last Ottoman emperor and daughter of Sultana Hatijé. Many of the events and figures in the book are drawn from historical research, but they have been fictionalized for the purposes of the novel.

Library of Congress Cataloging-in-Publication Data

Mourad, Kenizé.
[De la part de la princesse morte. English]
Regards from the dead princess : novel of a life / Kenizé Mourad : translated from the French by John Brownjohn, Sabine Destrée and Anna Williams, with the collaboration of the author.
p. cm.
Translation of: De la part de la princesse morte.
ISBN 1-55970-019-X
1. Selma, Princess, granddaughter of Murad V. Sultan of the Turks, 1911–1941 — Fiction. I. Title.
PQ2673.09467D413 1989
843′.914 — dc20 89-15096
CIP

10 9 8 7 6 5 4 3 2 1

HC

Published in the United States by Arcade Publishing, Inc., New York, a Little, Brown company

PRINTED IN THE UNITED STATES OF AMERICA

To the children of Badalpour

ACKNOWLEDGEMENTS

Many friends have helped me put this book together – friends in Turkey, the Lebanon, India and France. Their advice and their memories have enabled me to reconstitute not only thirty years of history – which often differed markedly from the official record – but also all the small details of daily life.

To quote them by name would risk embarrassing them, but I would like them to know how very grateful I am.

I would like to thank also Marina Urquidi and Aamer Hussein for helping me to revise the Anglo-American translation.

PREFACE

The story I am about to tell begins in January 1918, in Istanbul, capital of the Ottoman Empire, which for centuries had been a threat to Christianity. The Western States had finally crushed its power, and were fighting over the spoils of the old Empire, known for a long time as "the sick man of Europe."

Over a period of forty-two years three men, all brothers, had come to the throne: first Sultan Murad, who was deposed and held in captivity by his brother Abdul Hamid, who eventually was himself overthrown by the "Young Turk" revolution and replaced by Reshad.

Sultan Reshad was to be no more than a constitutional monarch. The real power lay in the hands of a triumvirate, which led the country into World War One on the side of Germany.

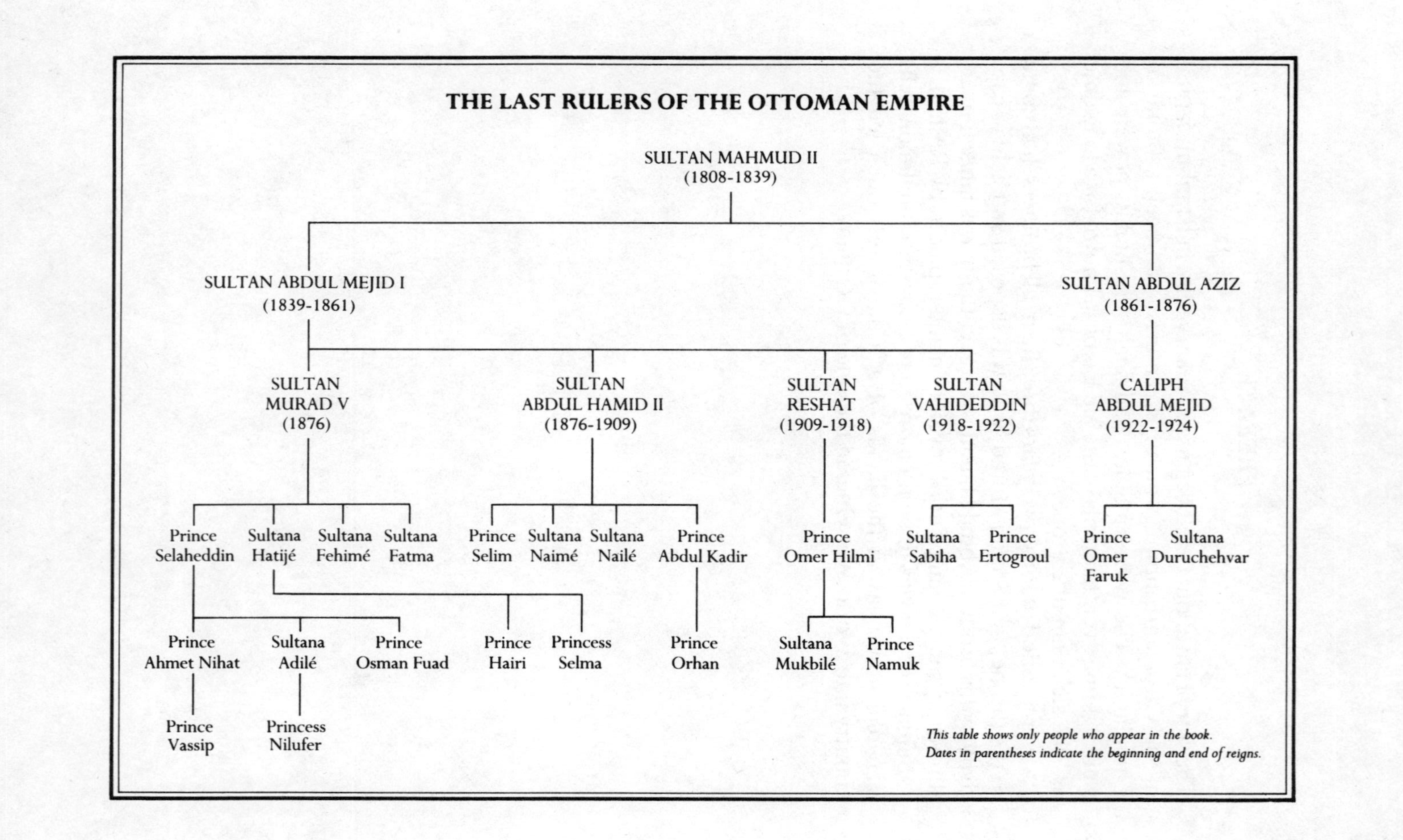
THE LAST RULERS OF THE OTTOMAN EMPIRE
SULTAN MAHMUD II (1808-1839)
SULTAN ABDUL MEJID I (1839-1861)
SULTAN ABDUL AZIZ (1861-1876)
SULTAN MURAD V (1876)
SULTAN ABDUL HAMID II (1876-1909)
SULTAN RESHAT (1909-1918)
SULTAN VAHIDEDDIN (1918-1922)
CALIPH ABDUL MEJID (1922-1924)
Prince Selaheddin
Sultana Hatijé
Sultana Fehimé
Sultana Fatma
Prince Selim
Sultana Naimé
Sultana Nailé
Prince Abdul Kadir
Prince Omer Hilmi
Sultana Sabiha
Prince Ertogroul
Prince Omer Faruk
Sultana Duruchehvar
Prince Ahmet Nihat
Sultana Adilé
Prince Osman Fuad
Prince Hairi
Princess Selma
Prince Orhan
Sultana Mukbilé
Prince Namuk
Prince Vassip
Princess Nilufer
This table shows only people who appear in the book.
Dates in parentheses indicate the beginning and end of reigns.

PART ONE

TURKEY

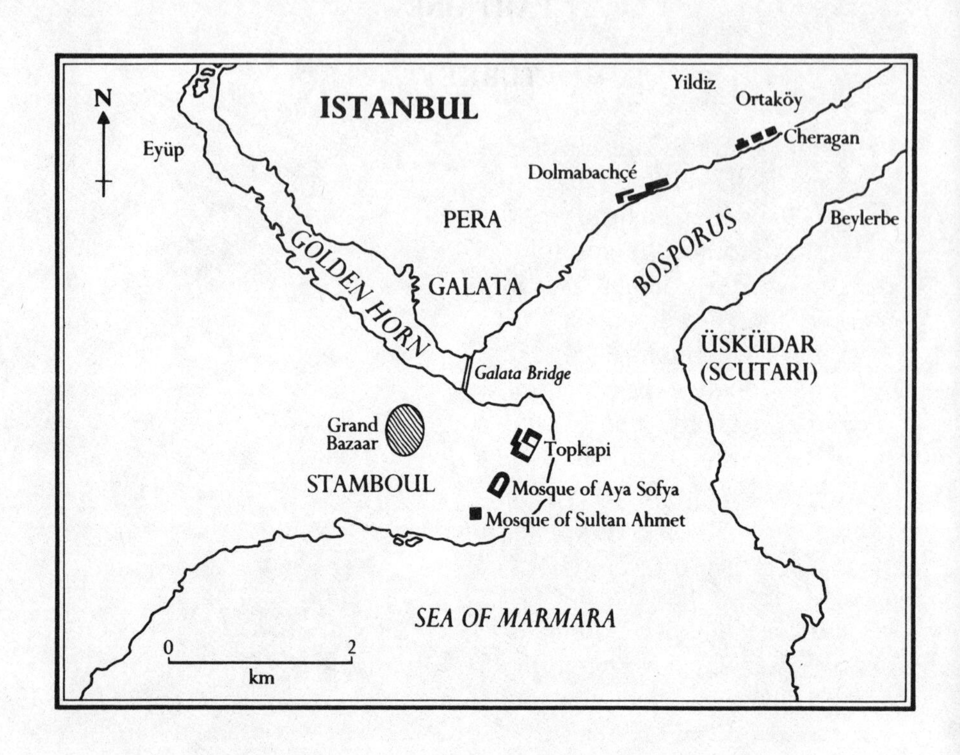
N
ISTANBUL
Yildiz
Ortaköy
Cheragan
Eyüp
Dolmabachçé
PERA
BOSPORUS
Beylerbe
GOLDEN HORN
GALATA
Galata Bridge
ÜSKÜDAR
(SCUTARI)
Grand
Bazaar
Topkapi
STAMBOUL
Mosque of Aya Sofya
Mosque of Sultan Ahmet
SEA OF MARMARA
0
2
km

CHAPTER 1

"Uncle Hamid is dead! Uncle Hamid is dead!"

In the white marble entrance hall of Ortaköy Palace, lighted by crystal chandeliers, a little girl was running. She wanted to be the first to tell her mother the good news. In her haste she almost knocked over two elderly ladies, whose aigrettes and jewelled headbands marked them as persons of wealth and rank.

"What impertinence!" fumed one of them.

"What do you expect?" her companion chimed in. "The Sultana[1] spoils her to death. She is her only daughter. A delightful child, of course, but I am afraid she is going to be a handful for the man she marries. It is time she learned how to behave. A girl of seven is not a child any longer, especially when she is a princess."

Far from worrying about the disapproval of a hypothetical husband, the little girl ran on. She was out of breath by the time she reached the massive double doors of the haremlik[2], the women's apartments, which were guarded by two Sudanese eunuchs in scarlet fezzes. There had been few visitors today, so they had sat down and were chatting. As they saw the "little Sultana," they jumped up and half-opened one of the great bronze doors, and bowed with particular deference for fear she might report their indolence. But the child was too preoccupied even to glance at them. She hurried in and paused briefly in front of a Venetian mirror to check her light auburn curls and make sure her blue silk gown was tidy. Then she pushed aside a brocade curtain and entered the small boudoir to which her mother customarily retired after her late afternoon bath.

Unlike the dank palace corridors, the room was pleasantly warm, thanks to a silver brazier tended by two female slaves. Reclining on a divan, the Sultana was watching her grand coffee mistress ceremoniously filling a cup on an emerald-encrusted salver.

1 Princess of the blood royal and daughter of a sultan. A sultan's wives were known as cadins.

2 A Turkish harem might be occupied by several wives and concubines, or by one wife only and her maidservants, as was often the case during the nineteenth and early twentieth centuries. To avoid confusion, the one-wife harem is here referred to by its Turkish name, *haremlik*.

The little girl paused, momentarily overcome with pride at the sight of her mother in her long caftan. In the outside world Sultana Hatijé complied with the European fashions which had been introduced into Istanbul in the late nineteenth century, but in private she insisted on dressing *à la turque*. No corsets, leg-of-mutton sleeves or hobble skirts for her, not at home; there she gladly wore the traditional robes that enabled her to breathe freely and recline in comfort on the soft, yielding sofas that abounded in Ortaköy's reception rooms.

"Come here, Sultana Selma."

At the Ottoman court, familiarity was frowned on, and parents addressed children by their titles to instil in them as early as possible an awareness of rank and responsibility. While the maidservants were performing a graceful temenna, a profound obeisance in which the right hand touched the heart, lips, and brow in turn, Selma quickly kissed her mother's perfumed fingers and put them to her forehead as a mark of respect. Then, too excited to contain herself any longer, she cried out: "Annéjim[3], Uncle Hamid is dead!"

The little girl thought she detected a spark of triumph in her mother's grey-green eyes, but the voice that promptly reprimanded her was cold as ice.

"You mean His Majesty Sultan Abdul Hamid, I presume. He was a great monarch – may Allah welcome him to paradise. Where did you hear this sad news?"

Sad? . . . The child stared at her mother in amazement. Saddened by the death of that cruel great-uncle, the man who had deposed her own father, Selma's grandfather, on the ground of insanity?

Her wet nurse had often told her the story of Murad V, a likeable and liberal-minded prince whose accession had been greeted with universal rejoicing because the people had expected him to introduce far-reaching reforms. But Murad V reigned for only three months. His naturally nervous disposition had been so affected by the palace intrigues and assassinations that had accompanied his rise to power that he lapsed into a state of extreme melancholia. The distinguished Austrian specialist Dr Liedersdorf assured the court that a few weeks' rest would restore His Majesty to health, but his advice went unheeded. Murad was deposed and, together with his entire family, confined to Cheragan Palace.

For twenty-eight years Sultan Murad had lived at Çerağan, constantly spied on by servants in the pay of his brother Abdul Hamid,

3 "Dear and respected Mother."

who feared a conspiracy to put him back on the throne. Only thirty-six when he entered captivity, he did not leave until the day he died.

Every time Selma thought of her poor grandfather she felt like emulating Charlotte Corday, the heroic assassin whom Mademoiselle Rose, her French governess, admired so much. And now, today, the tyrant had died peacefully in his bed!

It was impossible that Annéjim felt sad, she who after twenty-five years of being sequestered in Çerağan had regained her freedom only by accepting the frightful husband imposed on her by the Sultan Abdul Hamid. Why was she lying?

This blasphemous thought jolted Selma out of her reverie. How could she for a moment have imagined that a mother as perfect as hers would stoop to a lie? Lies were to be expected from slaves afraid of punishment, but not from a sultana! Upset, she finally managed:

"I was walking through the garden and I heard the aghas[4] talking about it."

Just then a rather portly eunuch appeared in the doorway, wearing white gloves and the traditional black tunic with mandarin collar. Having bent almost double in three successive temennas, he straightened up and decorously folded his hands on his paunch.

"Most respected Sultana –" he began in a falsetto, but Hatijé cut him short.

"I already know," she said. "Sultana Selma has been more diligent than you. Go at once and tell my sisters, the Princesses Fehimé and Fatma, and my nephews, the Princes Nihad and Fuad, that I shall expect them here this evening without fail."

Sultana Hatijé, who was now forty-eight, was the eldest of Murad V's children. Since the death of her brother, Prince Selaheddin, she was also, because of her intelligence and willpower, the undisputed head of the family.

The seeds of her inflexible personality had been sown on that terrible day forty-two years ago when she thought the gates of Çerağan Palace had closed on her forever. The little girl nicknamed *Yildirim*, or "Lightning," because she so delighted in tearing around the gardens of Kurbalidere, her father's palace, or sailing the Bosphorus in a caique with the wind buffeting her cheeks – the girl whose dreams were all of freedom and heroism – had found herself a prisoner at the

4 Eunuchs whose seniority entitled them to respect. Until the Ottoman Empire was abolished in 1924, every princely or aristocratic household employed eunuchs as a medium of communication between the women's quarters and the outside world.

age of six.

Hatijé had wept and hammered on the bronze gates until her knuckles were raw, but in vain. Then she fell ill – so ill that everyone feared for her life. A doctor was summoned urgently, but Abdul Hamid kept him waiting three full days for permission to enter Çerağan.

He had applied leeches to Hatijé's body and made her drink a potion of bitter herbs. Whatever it was that saved the little prisoner, the physician's learned medications or the two old kalfas[5] who told their amber beads and recited the ninety-nine attributes of Allah night and day, she had recovered consciousness a week later. The first thing she saw when she opened her eyes was her father's gentle, handsome face. But why did he look so sad? Then she remembered. . . . It was not just a bad dream. She curled up in bed and started sobbing again.

Sultan Murad looked stern. "Sultana Hatijé," he said, "how do you think our family could have ruled such a great empire for six centuries if we had wept each time we ran into some minor problem? You are a proud little creature. Let your pride teach you dignity."

Then, with a smile, as if to mitigate the severity of his reprimand, he had added: "If my daughter refuses to laugh any more, who is going to bring any sunshine into this palace? Do not worry, Yildirim, we will leave here sooner or later. And when we do I will take you on a long journey."

"Oh, Baba[6]," she had cried ecstatically, "will you really?" No imperial princess had ever been far from Istanbul, let alone Turkey. "Could we go to Paris?"

Sultan Murad chuckled. "Quite the little woman already, eh? Very well, my blossom, as soon as we get out of here I promise I will take you."

Had he believed it himself? Without hope he could not have gone on living.

Living? The Sultana's eyes clouded at the recollection of her father's twenty-eight years in captivity. Day after day throughout that time, Sultan Murad had endured his living death.

Dusk was falling when two phaetons came clattering into the inner courtyard that led to the women's apartments. From the first of these ornately gilded carriages stepped a graceful figure in a mauve silk

5 Ladies in the service of a palace.
6 Papa, Daddy.

charshaf, or voluminous cape. The plumpish woman who alighted from the other wore a black charshaf of classical design. The two charshafs exchanged a cursory embrace before hurrying into the palace, with eunuchs ceremoniously preceding them and bringing up the rear.

Like most royal residences, the palace was constructed of carved wood – a wise precaution in a city prone to earthquakes. Painted white and set amid gardens abounding in fountains, roses, and cypresses, it overlooked the now twilit Bosphorus. The festoons and arabesques adorning its balconies and staircases, verandas and terraces, made it appear a mansion of lace.

Sultana Hatijé's chief secretary was awaiting the visitors at the foot of the double staircase leading to the first-floor rooms. Dressed in a high-buttoned satin gown, she wore the traditional muslin toque – no respectable woman went bareheaded, even in her own home – and carried her symbol of office, a long cane with a gold knob.

She had scarcely bowed to the sultanas before together they folded her in a warm embrace. In noble houses, elder kalfas of her seniority were treated almost like members of the family. Although they would never have violated protocol, of which they were fiercely protective, they regarded the esteem lavished on them by their royal mistresses as a well deserved tribute to their devotion.

The old kalfa looked on, tremulous with joy, as the sultanas divested themselves of their bulky capes with the help of two slave women.

"Allah be praised!" she exclaimed. "My lionesses grow lovelier each day."

She bent an approving gaze on the ivory taffeta that set off gentle Fatma's superb dark eyes, then turned her attention to Fehimé, her ebullient sister, whose slender figure was enhanced by a gown sprinkled with butterfly bows – a creation straight from Alder Muller, the finest couturier in Vienna. Paris, alas, had ceased to be a source of modish marvels ever since Turkey had made the mistake of declaring war on France in August 1914.

The sisters linked arms, laughing, and had just started to climb the stairs when they were almost knocked over by a little blue hurricane who hurled herself at them and smothered their hands with kisses.

"Djijim[7], you'll be the death of me yet!" exclaimed Fehimé, giving her an affectionate hug. The old kalfa, outraged by Selma's lack of decorum, muttered indignantly.

7 Darling. Term used in addressing children.

Following in the hurricane's wake came a fat, pallid little boy, who greeted his aunts with a self-important bow. It was Haïri, Selma's brother. Two years older than his sister but her devoted slave, Haïri constantly disapproved of Selma for her mischievous behaviour but never dared to oppose her.

Sultana Hatijé appeared at the top of the stairs. Taller than either of her sisters, she carried herself with sinuous, majestic grace. Even the most rebellious members of the family bowed to her authority, and when they spoke of "the Sultana" it was her they meant, even though the title was given to all three of Sultan Murad's daughters.

Fatma stopped short and gazed up at her eldest sister with undisguised admiration. Fehimé, who by conventional standards was the prettiest, was clearly irritated and hastened to break the spell.

"My dear sister, what made you summon us at such short notice? I had to cancel an invitation to a soirée at the Austro-Hungarian Embassy tonight that I was looking forward to."

"Why? Because our uncle, Sultan Abdul Hamid, is dead." Hatijé's tone was all the more portentous because she had not quite yet decided what attitude to take.

Fehimé raised her eyebrows. "And why should that . . . that tyrant's death ruin my evening?"

"Bravo, Aunt! Well said!"

The booming voice made them jump. A corpulent man in his thirties had just materialized behind them. Prince Nihad, eldest son of Prince Selaheddin, was accompanied by his younger brother Prince Osman Fuad, handsomely attired in the general's uniform he never took off. The "General Prince," as Fuad liked to be known, for he valued a title earned on the battlefield more highly than one acquired by birth, had been badly wounded on the eastern front some months before. He was now spending an enjoyable convalescence in Istanbul and brazenly making the most of his heroic reputation with the ladies.

Having bowed to the sultanas, the two men followed them into the green drawing-room, where some youthful kalfas had almost finished lighting the hundred and thirty-seven oil lamps in a crystal chandelier. Haïri and Selma tiptoed in behind the grown-ups.

Smiling, Sultana Hatijé waited for everyone to sit down. She knew that this contest could be difficult to win, but she relished the challenge.

"I have called you together this evening so that we can all decide whether or not we should attend the ceremonies to be held tomorrow in honour of Sultan Abdul Hamid. Tradition demands that the princes should follow the funeral procession through the city. As for the princesses, they are expected to call on the wives and daughters of the deceased and offer their condolences." The Sultana injected a note of solemnity into her voice. "I am asking you to disregard your personal feelings and instead only think of our public image."

Fehimé was the first to break the silence. "I find this whole situation melodramatic," she said. "But as for me, I have no intention of going. Our beloved uncle ruined twenty-five years of my life, and he is not going to spoil one more day of it!"

"But isn't this an occasion for forgiveness?" Fatma ventured timidly. "The poor man atoned, after all – he himself was deposed and imprisoned for years. Can't we forgive and forget?"

"*Forget?*"

Prince Nihad's face was so flushed that for a moment Selma thought he would choke. He glared at his young aunt, his eyes filled with fury.

"What about loyalty? Loyalty to my grandfather Sultan Murad, who was vilified and buried alive? Loyalty to my father, who was carried off by neurasthenia? To attend that funeral would be to vindicate our persecutor. I say we should stay away; that would be a public statement about the irreparable injustice done to our family. That is what our dead expect of us."

"Please, Brother. Let's not speak for the dead."

All eyes turned towards Prince Osman Fuad, who was savouring his cigar.

"Being the youngest here, I must beg your pardon if I seem to be offering advice to my elders, but my years at the front with my men – simple folk from Anatolia, Izmir, and the Black Sea – have taught me one thing: despite our failings, the people love us. They simply will not understand a public show of disunity. To them, Murad's replacement by Hamid and Hamid's replacement by his brother Reshad seem merely quirks of fate. The main thing is, our family has always rallied around the throne. Especially now, during this war, the people need a firm focal point. For six centuries that focal point has been the Ottoman family. Unless it remains so, we may live to regret it bitterly. . . ."

At that moment a eunuch came in to announce that a messenger from the Sultan had arrived.

The messenger was a Sudanese of imposing build. Although he was a slave they all rose, not in deference to his person – in their eyes he did not exist – but to convey their respect for the message he bore.

"His Imperial Majesty Sultan Reshad, Commander of the Faithful,

Shadow of God on Earth, Master of the Two Seas, the Black and the White, and the Emperor of the Two Continents, advises Their Imperial Highnesses as follows: on the occasion of the death of Our well-beloved brother, His Imperial Majesty Sultan Abdul Hamid II, We invite the princes and princesses of the house of His Imperial Majesty Sultan Murad V to mourn his passing as custom prescribes. May peace be with you, and may Allah the Almighty preserve you from harm."

They all bowed. It was not an invitation. It was an ultimatum.

Prince Nihat scowled at the messenger's receding figure and shrugged. "Well, I am not going whatever happens," he growled.

"Come, Nihad," the Sultana said reproachfully. "Fuad has a point, I think. The situation is serious. Family unity must be preserved at all costs."

"Family unity? All right, my dear aunt, let us talk about that! A family that for six hundred years has been endlessly killing one another for the sake of power. How many brothers did our ancestor Murad III, the 'Conqueror of the Persians,' have put to death? Nineteen, if I am not mistaken. His father was more modest: he limited himself to five."

"They killed for reasons of state," Sultana Hatijé cut in. "These dramas are common to all royal families, the only difference being that European monarchs have fewer brothers. . . . Personally, I no longer bear Abdul Hamid any ill will. In those difficult times, when Britain, France, and Russia were planning to carve up our territories between them, we needed a man like him at the helm. For thirty-three years he managed to preserve the empire from those who wanted to dismember it. My father – being too honourable and too sensitive a man – might have failed to do so. In any case, doesn't our country take precedence over our own petty considerations?"

Fehimé and Osman Fuad glanced at each other and smiled. Hatijé had always been a woman of principle, but who cared about principles these days? Fehimé's main ambition was to have fun, and she pursued it with a zest intensified by the feeling that she had wasted the best years of her life in captivity. Her frivolous manner had earned her the nickname "Sultana Butterfly," and all her gowns were adorned with the butterfly bows that had become her symbol. She was an artist; she played the piano well and had even written some music. But there was nothing she detested more than solemnity and responsibility.

Her nephew Prince Osman Fuad resembled her. He had the same lust for life but a keener sense of reality. Very conscious of his own interests, Fuad knew how to give an inch in order to steal a mile, and he relied on his charm to extricate him from awkward situations. At this point he could not refrain from teasing his Aunt Hatijé.

"If I understand you correctly, Efendimiz[8], not only should we attend the funeral but even shed a few tears for good measure."

"Simply be there," Sultana Hatijé told him. "But remember this, Fuad, and you too, Nihad: if either of you succeeds to the throne, model yourselves on Sultan Abdul Hamid and not on your grandfather Sultan Murad. One cannot have a child and preserve one's virginity as well."

She burst out laughing at their expressions of amazement – they had never become used to her forthright language – and brought the meeting to an end by rising to her feet.

8 *Your Grace*. Used for members of the imperial family.

CHAPTER 2

Almost as soon as she awoke the next morning, Sultana Hatijé was seized with an urge to go shopping for some ribbon in the bazaar. It was considered unseemly for a princess to frequent public places, even in a closed carriage that shielded her from inquisitive eyes, so Greek or Armenian merchants usually brought their frills and furbelows to the palace. Today, however, the Sultana decided not to await their next visit.

She sent for Zeynel, her favourite eunuch, a tall Albanian with very white skin. Zeynel was nearing forty, and she noted with amusement that a recent tendency to stoutness had lent him the dignified appearance of a pasha.

She could well remember the timid youth who had arrived at Çerağan Palace twenty-five years ago, when she and her sisters were sharing their father's captivity there. Zeynel had been sent by Sultan Abdul Hamid's chief eunuch, who found it a convenient way to get rid of him. Although he was a lively, talented youngster who had distinguished himself at the palace school attended by children being groomed for service in the imperial court, Zeynel later had shown himself ill suited to the strict discipline of the harem.

Çerağan soon tamed him. Did he feel freer among those prisoners? The Svetana remembered that he used to follow her everywhere, attentive to her smallest wish, and ignored her two sisters. It was she whom he had chosen to serve.

Touched by Zeynel's devotion, she came to rely on him more and more. She valued the tact and discretion that set him apart from other eunuchs, most of whom were as garrulous as old women. At Ortaköy she had made him her eyes and ears, regularly sending him into town to glean rumours and eavesdrop on coffee-house conversations. He reported the complaints and concerns of the ordinary folk of Istanbul, who were exasperated by the never-ending war and the difficulties of everyday life.

Thus, though confined to the haremlik, Sultana Hatijé was more in touch with public opinion than most other members of the imperial family, whose appreciation of her perspicacity and sound advice often led them to consult her on political matters.

In recognition of Zeynel's unfailing loyalty, she had recently promoted him to "chief eunuch," a prestigious appointment that gave rise to many malicious remarks on the part of the older eunuchs.

She studied him thoughtfully as he stood there with downcast eyes, patiently awaiting her orders. What did she know of this slave apart from his exceptional qualities as a servant? What sort of life did he lead outside the palace? Was he happy? She had no idea, and anyway, she felt it was no concern of hers.

"Agha," she said at last, emerging from her long reverie, "I want you to hire me a carriage as soon as possible."

The eunuch bowed, concealing his surprise. The two calashes and three phaetons in the palace were all in perfect order, but they naturally bore the imperial coat of arms. Could his mistress really intend to leave the palace incognito, just when her husband, Haïri Bey, was out of town? Zeynel was no stranger to feminine whims, having served in the imperial harem until the age of fourteen, but his sultana was different. Chiding himself for having suspected her motives, even for an instant, he hurried out.

Hatijé, assisted by one of her kalfas, had donned a dark charshaf and was on the point of leaving when Selma accosted her.

"Annéjim," the little girl said imploringly, "please take me with you!"

"What about your piano, Princess? I thought you had to practise your scales."

"I will as soon as we are back, I promise."

There was such a look of anguish on the child's face that the Sultana did not have the heart to refuse. She had suffered so from her own cloistered childhood that she was determined to allow her daughter as much freedom as possible within the limits laid down by convention – and sometimes, so malicious tongues asserted, beyond them.

The hired phaeton, its windows screened by fine wooden trelliswork, emerged from the courtyard at a trot with Zeynel, looking the very picture of dignity, seated on the box beside the driver. It was a fine winter's day, cold but sunny, and the clouds of pigeons were circling the mosques and palaces along the Bosphorus.

"My glorious Istanbul," murmured the Sultana, feasting her eyes on the view like a mistress long deprived of her lover. Selma, sitting open-mouthed beside her, vowed that when she grew up she would go for at least one drive a week even if it did set tongues wagging.

They crossed the Golden Horn, the narrow inlet separating the capital's two waterfronts, by way of the Galata Bridge. The bazaar was in the old city not far from Topkapi Palace, a majestic building deserted by the imperial family sixty years earlier, when Sultan

Abdul Mejid, to his own greater glory, had built the palace of Dolmabahçé. As a result, the sultanas and princes imprisoned within the dank walls of the seraglio no longer died of consumption.

The streets were unusually crowded – in fact the turmoil was such that the carriage pulled up after a few more yards and Zeynel's face appeared at the window.

"We cannot proceed any farther, Highness. The funeral procession will be coming this way."

The Sultana smiled. "Oh, really?" she said calmly. "Very well, we shall wait till it goes by."

Selma glanced at her mother. Just as she had thought: the ribbon was only an excuse. Annéjim did not care all that much about her wardrobe. Since women were forbidden by custom to attend funerals, she had devised this way of watching it.

The Sultana was astonished to see such a large crowd. *Oh well*, she thought, *in wartime people are so starved of entertainment that it takes very little to bring them into the streets*.

A sudden silence fell as the procession appeared at the end of the avenue.

Preceded by a military band in black tunics, the coffin was slowly borne along on the shoulders of ten soldiers. The princes followed on foot in order of age and seniority, their chests encrusted with diamond-studded orders and decorations. Behind them came the damads, or princesses' husbands, then the pashas in their ceremonial uniforms and the viziers in gold-embroidered tailcoats. Last of all, equal in status to a minister on such formal occasions, came the Kislar Agha, chief of the palace black eunuchs, the Custodian of the Gates of Felicity.

Soldiers in full-dress uniform lined both sides of the route from the mosque of Aya Sofya to the mausoleum where the Sultan was to be buried, a distance of nearly two miles. The Young Turk government that had deposed Abdul Hamid ten years earlier and now ruled the Ottoman Empire's destinies under the aegis of Sultan Reshad seemed intent on giving the late Sultan an impressive funeral. One could afford to be magnanimous toward the dead.

Magnanimous . . . the man whom Istanbul was honouring today had never been magnanimous. Tears blurred Hatijé's eyes as she recalled the bitterly cold night, fourteen years earlier, when her father had been buried in unceremonious haste on the orders of his jealous brother. Sultan Murad had been escorted to his grave by only a few faithful retainers; his loving ex-subjects were denied any public display of grief. The Sultana shivered, her hatred of the man rekindled by the pomp attending his burial. Had Abdul Hamid been humiliated she might perhaps have forgiven him, his long detention having partly redeemed him in her eyes. But all this pomp and circumstance was giving him back the glory he had stolen from his brother. Even in death, Abdul Hamid was supplanting Murad. After ten years of obscure captivity, this ceremony had resurrected his memory.

A sour taste filled Hatijé's mouth. Could she really be jealous of a dead man? She now understood what had prompted her to flout custom and attend this funeral. It was not simply curiosity, as she had wanted to believe, but a desire for revenge. She had come to savour and relish the death of the man who had killed her father by slow degrees, day after day for twenty-eight long years. She would never have believed that her heart still harboured so much hatred. . . .

The procession had now drawn level with the carriage. She scanned it in search of her nephews. Nihad had stayed away, but young Osman Fuad, resplendent in his handsome uniform, had taken her advice and was representing the family to good effect. The Sultana, who always knew what was right and proper, now wondered if she had been right after all.

There was a sudden surge of shouts from the crowd. Hatijé suppressed a smile. So that was why they had turned out in such numbers: forgetting the convention that said one could not malign the dead, they were giving the tyrant the send-off he so richly deserved!

Then, as she listened more closely, she thought she heard wailing and lamentation. No, that couldn't be – she must be mistaken! And yet. . . . She stiffened and turned pale: what she had presumed to be cries of hatred were actually cries of grief. She was overwhelmed with indignation. Had these people forgotten the dark years when the police and the secret services were all-powerful? Had they forgotten their joy when the Young Turks' coup d'état replaced Sultan Abdul Hamid with his brother Reshad? Hatijé shook her head. The memory of man was indeed a short-lived thing. . . .

"Father, why are you deserting us? We had bread in your day – now we're starving!" The voice, a woman's, came from the window overlooking the route, and other voices took up the cry: "Where are you going? Don't leave us alone!"

Alone? The Sultana started. What did they mean? Didn't they have a worthy ruler in Sultan Reshad? Had they lost faith in him? Had they guessed what the whole court already knew: that their Sultan was merely a puppet in the hands of the country's true masters, Enver, Talat, and Jemal, who had not even consulted him when they took Turkey into the war on Germany's side four years ago? Since then they had done their best to disguise a whole series of blunders and defeats, but with diminishing success. Every day hundreds of wounded soldiers were streaming home from the front, and the lines outside the bakeries were growing longer, while beggars began to swarm the streets.

The Sultana sighed. That must be it: in mourning Sultan Abdul Hamid, these people were bewailing the disappearance of the last remaining symbol of a strong and respected Turkey. She felt filled with nostalgia. Her determination to maintain the pretence of a visit to the bazaar waned abruptly.

"Home, Zeynel," she called.

The eunuch looked at her in distress; he understood his sultana's feelings. He knew how badly she needed a few words of comfort at this moment, but his status forbade him to utter them. He bowed and curtly transmitted her order to the coachman. The carriage slowly turned and headed back to the palace.

The sun was going down over the Bosphorus. Sultana Hatijé gazed through the tall bay windows at the waterway and, beyond it on the Asiatic shore, Beylerbey Palace. She could not help smiling at the irony of the situation: it was there, just across the water from Ortaköy, that her former jailer, imprisoned in his turn, had lived out the last few years of his life. Gossips had it that she had deliberately chosen to reside here because it enabled her to gloat over his downfall, but they were mistaken: she had moved into Ortaköy well before it. She had taken her revenge, yes, but in another way. . . .

Zeynel came to tell her that the caique was ready. It was time to offer her condolences to the dead Sultan's relatives. Discounting official ceremonies at which the two branches of the family pretended not to notice each other, this would be their first contact for many years.

Followed by her sisters and her daughter, the Sultana walked through the palace grounds to the little wharf of mossy stone slabs. All four were dressed in white, the colour of mourning. Black, being considered unlucky, was forbidden at the Ottoman court.

They stepped aboard the slender craft, assisted by eunuchs and respectfully saluted by ten oarsmen attired in the loose cambric shirts and scarlet breeches that had been traditional since the time of Suleyman the Magnificent. Ten was the number of oarsmen permitted to princes and princesses. Viziers were entitled only to eight, whereas the Sultan's personal caique had a crew of fourteen.

While the boat glided across the water the sultanas raised their veils to make the most of the breeze. They were safe from observation because the oarsmen had to keep their heads down on pain of dismissal. In the old days they would have been put to death.

Selma, seated in the stern, was fascinated by the fish that seemed to be following in their wake. It was an old custom to tow long blue ribbons embroidered in silver with lifelike representations of carp or trout, and she loved the effect it created.

The princesses landed in Beylerbey, slightly drunk with sea air, and were conducted by eunuchs to the great hall. The ceilings were decorated with geometrical patterns in green and red, the walls lined with Damascus mirrors encrusted with mother-of-pearl. Beylerbey had been built in the last century by Sultan Abdul Aziz, who wanted its splendour to be wholly oriental and uninfluenced by European fashions in design. It was even said that when Eugénie de Montijo had stayed there on her way to the opening of the Suez Canal, the Sultan, who was much enamoured of the Empress, had commanded that the mosquito net around her bed be embroidered with thousands of seed pearls.

Preceded by the grand mistress of ceremonies, the princesses entered a room draped in scarlet velvet. This was the drawing-room of the Validé Sultana, a title bestowed on the mothers of sultans. Abdul Hamid's mother being dead, his last wife Musfika Cadin was presiding in her stead, a frail, erect figure enthroned in a massive armchair of gilded wood. The Cadin had remained with the royal captive to the end, and this day of mourning was her day of glory – the day on which she was at last to be rewarded for all her devotion.

Seated around her on cushions and brocaded footstools, women of all ages lamented the dead man's passing and recalled his virtues and good deeds. Some of them wept noisily, pausing only to watch the arrival of each new visitor.

The appearance of the three sultanas was greeted with a murmur of surprise. The Cadin smiled. Too intelligent not to divine the political motive underlying their visit, she was nonetheless appreciative of its magnanimity. She hurriedly rose to greet them, for even on this, her greatest day, she would never have neglected to show the respect due to princesses of the blood. Like all the Sultan's wives, she was merely a woman of the harem who had been singled out for favour by her all-powerful spouse.

Selma, bowing repeatedly, kissed the hands of various ladies of quality. She was just about to do the same to an ugly woman seated on the Cadin's right when she stopped short, transfixed by the hatred in the eyes looking down on her. What on earth had she done wrong? Not quite sure how to handle the situation, she glanced over at her mother, who gave her a little push.

"Selma, pay your respects to your aunt, Sultana Naïmé, daughter of His late Majesty Sultan Abdul Hamid."

To everyone's surprise and disapproval, the little girl shook her auburn curls and backed away. Her mother thrust her aside and bent over the princess.

"Please excuse the child. Grief at the loss of her great-uncle must have given her a touch of fever. . . ."

Naïmé disdainfully turned her head as if unable to endure the sight of the woman who had addressed her. Then Hatijé drew herself up to her full height and, with a mocking glance at the others, accepted the Cadin's invitation to sit on her left. She glowed with triumph. No one present could be in any doubt: her cousin's discourtesy was a form of homage. So, even after fourteen years the wound still had not healed!

Listening with only half an ear to the widow recounting, for the umpteenth time, exactly how His Majesty had died, Hatijé immersed herself in recollections of the past. . . .

It was true that Kemaleddin Pasha, Naïmé's dashing husband, was a handsome man. . . . The two cousins had married in the same year, but whereas Sultan Abdul Hamid had chosen a brilliant young army officer for Naïmé, his favourite daughter, born on the day of his coronation, for his niece Hatijé he had elected an obscure civil servant as ill-favoured as he was narrow-minded.

Marriage was Hatijé's only means of leaving the palace-prison where she had been confined since childhood. At the age of thirty-one, she was desperate to see something of life. She welcomed any opportunity to gain her freedom but had not foreseen that it would entail such a degrading match. For weeks she stubbornly refused her husband, who went and complained to the Sultan. At last, wearying of the struggle, she gave in. Even after all these years, her skin still crawled with distaste at the memory of that first awful night. . . .

The palace the Sultan had bestowed on her, as on every newly-wed princess, was next door to that of her cousin. Hatijé made a habit of visiting Naïmé, whom she treated like a younger sister, giving her friendly titbits of advice and sending her little gifts by way of Zeynel. They very quickly became friends. Naïmé was madly in love with her handsome husband. Hatijé could think of no sweeter revenge than to steal him from her cousin. What surer way of wounding her persecutor, the persecutor of her beloved father, than to drive his favourite daughter to despair?

Coldly and deliberately, in the firm belief that she was fulfilling a sacred duty, Hatijé set out to seduce Kemaleddin. This proved all the easier because Naïmé had unwisely insisted, contrary to custom, that her husband and her best friend should become acquainted. The Pasha not only fell in love with Hatijé but declared his passion for her in fervent letters which she carefully preserved.

Mortified by her husband's indifference, Naïmé refused to eat and wasted away, to the despair of the Sultan, who could not fathom the reason for his daughter's mysterious illness. Hatijé, being the unfortunate young woman's confidante, eventually decided that the game had gone on long enough. Kemaleddin had become so indiscreet that Vassif, her husband, daring to be jealous, was berating her unbearably. She bundled up Kemaleddin's letters and told Zeynel to take them to the Sultan, pretending to have found them by chance. A scandal of this magnitude would inevitably spell divorce. She looked forward to her revenge and her freedom.

Even now, fourteen years later, Hatijé was amazed at her own naiveté. How could she ever have believed herself capable of outmanoeuvring Abdul Hamid?

She recalled the day the Sultan had summoned her to the palace and greeted her with the Pasha's letters in his hand. The fury in his little black eyes was plain to see, but so was the derision, which perturbed her a good deal more. The whole court awaited his verdict with bated breath. Kemaleddin Pasha was packed off to Bursa, the former capital, some sixty miles from Istanbul. What was to become of the object of his adulterous passion? Would the Sultan banish her too? Anyone who thought so did not know Abdul Hamid. Not a word of reproof escaped his lips; he merely smirked and . . . sent her home to her husband.

It was not until the revolution of 1908, which deposed Sultan Abdul Hamid and replaced him with the benevolent Sultan Reshad, that Hatijé finally got rid of Vassif. The new Sultan, who could refuse his niece nothing, permitted her to divorce her husband.

Everyone expected this romantic story to culminate in the marriage of Kemaleddin and the Princess. As soon as he was released, the Pasha, more smitten than ever, hurried back to Istanbul. The Sultana received him coldly and told him that she had never loved him.

The following year, during a riverside excursion near Istanbul, Hatijé met a handsome diplomat whom she fell in love with and decided to marry. That diplomat was Haïri Rauf Bey, the father of Selma and little Haïri.

Night was descending on Beylerbey Palace. Chill, damp air drifted in from the Bosphorus, and the shadows in the Validé Sultana's drawing-room were lengthening. The women had instinctively begun to whisper.

Slaves tiptoed in to light the candles in four green crystal candelabra resembling big, broad-leaved trees, one planted in each corner of the room.

It was time to go home. Sultana Hatijé slowly emerged from her reverie and glanced at her sisters to signify that the visit had lasted long enough. The dowager Cadin swiftly rose and insisted on escorting them to the door.

Sultana Naïmé did not even lift her eyes as they left the room.

Selma never understood why her mother, whom she had expected would scold her on the way home for refusing to greet her aunt, suddenly drew her close and kissed her.

CHAPTER 3

A melodious but gently insistent sound roused Selma from her slumbers. She opened her eyes and smiled at the girl seated at the foot of her bed, who was stroking the strings of an oud[1] with a feather. It was an oriental custom to avoid waking someone too abruptly because the soul went roaming in other worlds during the night and had to be allowed to return to the body by slow degrees.

Selma loved these musical awakenings, which seemed to give promise of a happy day in store. This morning she felt a special thrill of happiness. It was Bairam, the great Islamic festival commemorating Abraham's offer to sacrifice his son to God. Everyone had to dress up in new clothes and exchange gifts. The whole city resounded to the music of carousels and the cries of tumblers and sweetmeat vendors, and every street corner was thronged with people watching puppet and shadow shows. The festivities were going to be particularly elaborate at Dolmabahçé Palace, where the Sultan would spend the next three days receiving courtesy calls from senior dignitaries and members of his family.

Selma refused her morning glass of milk, which was supposed to beautify her complexion, jumped out of bed, and ran straight to the little hammam[2] where two slave women were busy preparing her rose-petal bath – a luxury reserved for special occasions as her mother had no wish to encourage any precocious interest in her personal appearance.

The big silver ewers tilted, and lukewarm water cascaded over the child's pale skin. After carefully drying her on a white muslin cloth, the slaves sprinkled her body and hair with rose petals and gave her a lengthy massage. Selma, inhaling the delicious perfume, felt as if she herself were turning into a flower.

Half an hour later, attired in her new broderie anglaise dress, she hurried to her mother's apartments. Her father, who had returned

1 Oriental stringed instrument resembling a mandolin.
2 A hammam was a suite of domed rooms, maintained at different temperatures, with steam baths, and fountains containing cold water. Bathers could move between cooler and hotter rooms as they chose, and might spend several hours in the hammam.

the day before from a trip to his provincial estates, was already there. He greeted his daughter with a smile and gently stroked her hair, as it was considered bad form for parents to kiss their children. Selma blushed delightedly and gazed at him wide-eyed. He looked so splendid in his pearl-grey frock coat and vermilion fez. But how, she wondered, did he ever manage to keep the ends of his moustache tilted skyward all the time?

Very slim and of medium height, Haïri Bey cultivated the bored, supercilious manner common to all the Turkish upper class. An indolent man accustomed to success with women and entirely devoid of personal ambition, he had drifted into marriage with the Sultana rather than sought it. Being far from stupid, he disliked the flattery which his damad's[3] status brought him, but he was too idle to carve out a career for himself. Once a self-confident and ambitious youth, he was now a world-weary man. He took little interest even in his children. At best they were a source of amusement, especially Selma, who already knew how to exploit her natural charm. As for his wife. . . .

The Sultana had just entered the boudoir. Haïri Bey rose to kiss her hand. Then, in accordance with custom, he handed her a velvet jewel case. Every husband was expected to give his wife a present at Bairam and on the Sultan's birthday. Failure to do so was a sign that the marriage was in danger. The Damad breathed a surreptitious sigh of relief: his secretary had thought of everything, fortunately. Hatijé opened the jewel case to reveal a magnificent necklace of deep-blue sapphires.

"What beautiful stones," she murmured.

Her husband bowed gallantly. "Nothing is beautiful enough for you, Sultana."

Yes, his secretary had done well, but how the devil was he going to pay for this bauble when the civil list[4] had been cut back so drastically to help finance the war effort? Haïri Bey brushed the thought aside. The Armenian his family had dealt with for so long would give him credit. Anyway, at his age it was too late to develop miserly habits.

Reaching into his pocket, he brought out another, smaller jewel case – he had chosen the gift himself – and presented it to Selma. It contained a brooch, a dainty piece of jewellery in the shape of a peacock with an emerald tail. Although he was expecting gratitude, the extent of the little girl's enthusiasm puzzled him. Did she really

3 Title reserved for a princess's husband.

4 Sum granted to members of the imperial family for their personal needs.

appreciate jewellery so much at such an early age, or was she merely imitating her mother?

Since the question did not really concern him very deeply, he failed to notice that Selma's shining eyes were focused not on the brooch but on him. It was the first time her father had given her a grown-up present – a woman's present.

The Sultana was growing restive. "My dear, you will be late for the selamlik[5]."

Haïri Bey cut her short with a gesture. "Who cares? These formalities bore me to death. I'm not even sure I'll go."

He knew he would go, and so did she. Yet he could not resist provoking her. He found his prince consort's role more and more intolerable as the years went by. There was no question of divorce, however. One did not divorce a sultana. She alone had that right, and then only if the Sultan agreed.

In any case, Haïri Bey had no grounds for divorce. Hatijé, he told himself, was a model wife but every inch a princess and deadly boring. He was loath to admit, even to himself, that he felt crushed by a personality so much stronger than his own, which made him feel nothing but a shadow.

For a long time after her father left, Selma wondered why he had seemed so moody. Swinging her legs as she sat on a window seat waiting for her mother, she reproached herself for not having tried to cheer him up. But what could she have said? He would almost certainly have laughed at her.

The Sultana was ready at last. Her gown, which was embellished with fine pearls, had a sable-trimmed train, and precious stones sparkled in her hair. She wore the diamond star of the Order of Compassion, an honour reserved for a few great ladies of the Empire, together with the heavy gold and enamel collar bearing the imperial coat of arms, to which princes and princesses alone were entitled.

Selma's red-golden curls bobbed with delight: there would never be anyone more beautiful than her mother.

Assisted by kalfas, they boarded the ceremonial carriage, which was driven today by a coachman in a silver-braided cape of midnight blue. He cracked his whip, and it slowly set off on the one-mile journey to the imperial palace.

*

5 Friday prayers at the mosque, where all present had to take their places before the Sultan's arrival.

Dolmabahçé Palace, built entirely of white marble, sprawled lazily along the Bosporus in an opulent confusion of styles borrowed from every period and land. It was all Greek columns, Moorish ogives and Gothic or Romanesque arches drowning in rococo ornamentation that smothered the facades in bouquets, festoons, rosettes, and medallions delicately engraved with gilded arabesques. Purists found it horribly ugly and called it "the wedding cake" but its luxuriance, extravagance, fanciful elegance, and naive ignorance of the canons of architectural propriety made it as endearing as a child who dresses up in all her mother's finery in an incongruous attempt to look lovely. That was the sort of thing only poets understood, and the Turkish people were poets.

On entering the palace, Selma paused, spellbound for a moment by its cascades of gold and crystal. She had often been there before, but every time its sheer magnificence took her breath away. The chandeliers and candelabra tinkled with thousands of sparkling drops, and the grand staircase was of baccarat crystal, as were the enormous fireplaces, whose diamond-cut hoods reflected a blaze of iridescent light that changed colour at different hours of the day.

The little girl loved all this splendour. It confirmed her belief that the empire was invincible, its wealth inexhaustible, and the world was a good and happy place. True, there was this war which her father's friends discussed so gravely. There were also those hollow-eyed men and women who thronged the palace gates every day, begging for bread, but to Selma they were as much creatures from another planet as the war was only another grown-up word among many.

The Sultana and her daughter were ushered inside by a cohort of eunuchs, then surrounded by a swarm of beautiful young slave girls – ugliness was forbidden in the palace – who helped them to remove their veils. Meanwhile, a Circassian kahveji[6] dressed in baggy trousers and a little embroidered bolero served them coffee scented with cardamom to refresh them after their drive.

Carefully shielded from all outside influence, the imperial harem was a jealous repository of ancient custom where the upbringing of the young was supervised with merciless rigour by venerable kalfas. Its occupants, who still wore traditional costumes, eyed the gallicized attire of the visiting sultanas with curiosity and a touch of amusement but felt no desire to emulate them. After all, wasn't the palace above the vagaries of fashion?

The grand mistress of ceremonies appeared, an impressive figure in

6 Female servant in charge of coffee-making.

the long, gold-embroidered coat that was the mark of her exalted office. She had come to conduct the princesses to the Validé Sultana[7], the sovereign's elderly mother, for all visitors to the court had to begin by paying their respects to the second most important personage in the empire.

The validé Sultana sat enthroned in a drawing-room hung with mauve silk and furnished with heavy Victorian armchairs.

She was said to have been very beautiful, but advancing age and the sedentary life of the harem had turned her into a prodigiously fat old woman. All she retained were the superb blue eyes that bore witness to her Circassian blood.

Selma and her mother bowed respectfully to the former slave girl.

Like most inmates of the imperial harem, she had been sold to the palace as a child because her parents, being humble folk, wanted their daughter to have the best possible chance of social advancement. Rumour had it that slave girls received an excellent education at court, and the glamorous careers of certain slaves who had risen to become grand viziers or first wives had so fired the imagination that it was no longer necessary, as it had been at the beginning of the empire, for children to be snatched from their grieving parents; nowadays, parents begged the palace to accept their offspring.

The validé Sultana had never seen her family again. Selma wondered if she sometimes had missed them, but the truth was, she had never had the time. Taken in hand by the grand mistress of the kalfas as soon as she had entered the harem, she and her companions had been taught to play the harp, as well as poetry, singing, dancing, and, most important of all, refined manners. Once a girl was considered sufficiently accomplished, she was admitted to the sovereign's service.

The old lady liked to recall the day when the Sultan had noticed her and she became *gözdé*, one who had caught her master's eye. As such she was entitled to a room of her own and new silken robes. Luckily, the Sultan had not tired of her and sought her company often, so she acquired the coveted title of *ikbal*, or favourite. She then moved into much more spacious quarters and was given three kalfas to wait on her. It was time for her to bear a son.

Selma had often heard the old ladies of the court tell how, when her son Reshad was born, the beautiful Circassian was promoted to the rank of third cadin. Beauty alone was insufficient to set a girl apart from the other concubines and earn her such a coveted position; she

7 Mother sultana.

had to be intelligent and tenacious as well. For the higher her status in the harem hierarchy, the keener the competition and the greater the dangers. Merciless rivalry prevailed at this exalted level, because every cadin's son was an imperial prince and, thus, a potential sultan. Custom dictated that the throne should pass to the eldest of the family, but in the six centuries of Ottoman history many of the eldest had met with accidents or succumbed to mysterious ailments. . . .

The Cadin, being acquainted with too many cases in which wet nurses or eunuchs had been bribed by ambitious rivals, never entrusted her son to another's care. She had sworn to herself that he would be Sultan and that she would become the Validé Sultana. Her whole life had been devoted to that dream, but she was seventy-eight before it came true. Now, having fulfilled the ambition that had sustained her throughout sixty years of manoeuvring and intrigue, she was no more than a weary old woman.

The Validé Sultana patted Selma's cheek with her milk-white hand, a mark of great favour, and told Sultana Hatijé how well she looked. Then, taking a long pull at her gold narghilé[8], she closed her eyes. The audience was at an end.

Now was the time to call on the other cadins, all of whom received visitors in their own apartments. These were miniature courts-within-a-court staffed by whole retinues of eunuchs, secretaries, stewards, and kalfas of varying degree, and etiquette demanded that each should be visited before the main ceremony commenced.

This year, for the first time Selma was to undergo her test in protocol. Her heart pounded as she made the rounds of various august personages under their coldly appraising gaze. She carefully adjusted the depth of her temennas to the importance of their recipient. This procedure was the result of a complicated equation that took account of birth, rank, and age, and required of the little Princess an accurate knowledge of the subtleties of the court and its customs. She breathed a sigh of relief when she saw the faces around her break into smiles: she had passed the test.

A sudden hubbub signalled that the Sultan had returned from the Friday selamlik[9]. The hand-kissing ceremony was about to begin.

Gossip and sweetmeats were promptly forgotten. As fast as dignity permitted, all the women hastened to the circular gallery overlooking the throne room. From there, hidden behind the moucharabié, a

8 Hookah; a pipe with a long flexible stem which runs through a container of water. The smoke is passed through the water to cool it down.

9 Friday prayer attended in the mosque by the Sultan and all his male entourage.

pierced wooden screen, they would witness one of the most sumptuous and entertaining spectacles of the year. Selma, wedged between two very stout ladies of the court, could hardly breathe, but nothing in the world would have induced her to abandon her vantage point.

She saw, a hundred feet before her, a forest of vermilion fezzes and black or grey frock coats interspersed with the splashes of colour provided by military uniforms. Dazzled by the thousands of lamps in the throne room – the biggest in Europe, it was said – Selma took a while before she could recognize a few faces.

The Sultan, an imposing figure on his throne of solid gold encrusted with precious stones, was seated at the end of the room. On his right, wearing full dress uniform and arrayed in order of age, stood the princes of the blood.

Standing on tiptoe, Selma looked for her favourite cousin Vassip, who was two years older than she, but at this distance she could not find him. Nor could she pick out her father, who must be among the damads and viziers glittering with medals on the Sultan's left. Facing him, also in ceremonial garb, were field marshals, generals, and other army officers of senior rank. The raised galleries were occupied by members of the diplomatic corps, looking like vigilant ravens in their black coats.

One by one the grand dignitaries approached the throne and bowed low three times in succession. They did not kiss the Sultan's hand itself, which no one was entitled to touch, but the emblem of his authority, a broad red velvet stole adorned with gold tassels and held by the grand chamberlain.

Next to pay their respects were the frock-coated senior civil servants representing the various ministries. Last of all, wide-eyed at the sight of so much splendour, came the notables who were being rewarded for their particularly faithful service. Stirred by the honour being done them and anxious not to infringe the sacred rules of protocol, they kissed the stole devoutly and withdrew backwards, stumbling occasionally to the amusement of those looking on.

A sudden silence fell and all the court held its breath. The Sheikh ul-Islam, the Empire's supreme religious authority, had stepped forward in his long white robe and brocaded turban, and the Sultan, in a special mark of favour, had risen to greet him. Behind him came the great ulemas, the doctors of Islamic law, in their green, mauve, or brown robes. They were followed by representatives of the empire's various religions: the Greek Orthodox patriarch and the Armenian primate, both clad in black, and the Grand Rabbi of the Jews, who had enjoyed a privileged status in Turkey since the sixteenth century, when the Ottoman Empire had constituted itself the protector of the persecuted Jewish community in Europe.

Throughout the ceremony, which lasted over three hours, the members of the imperial orchestra, in their red and gold uniforms, played an alternation of Ottoman marches and uplifting Beethoven symphonies under the baton of Lange Bey, a celebrated French conductor who had fallen in love with the East.

A ripple of feminine laughter issued from behind the moucharabie. General Liman von Sanders, whose stiff and haughty bearing made him look like a caricature of a Prussian officer, had appeared. Close behind him came Marquis Pallavicini, the ambassador of Austro-Hungry, whom evening strollers in Istanbul often saw out riding on his chestnut mare. Pallavicini was said to be extremely well-informed, but, like the consummate diplomat he was, he cultivated an air of innocent surprise.

In fact, it was the three masters of Turkey whom the women were mainly eager to see: Talat, the crafty Grand Vizier, built like a bull and endowed with a pair of huge red hands that betrayed his humble origins; Jemal Pasha, the Minister of Marine, a short, pallid-looking man whose affable manner was said to conceal a harsh and merciless nature: dispatched to Syria in 1913, he had put down the brewing war of independence there with a brutality that earned him the nickname "The Butcher of Damascus". . . .

But the undisputed star of the assembly was Enver Pasha, the Minister of War. Slim, graceful, and handsome, he captivated every woman in sight. Of enormous courage and equally enormous vanity, he considered himself a military genius. Now in the early months of 1918, however, the Turkish forces were retreating on all fronts and the reputation of "Napoleonik," as some sarcastically called him, was on the wane. The voices that once sang his praises were now raised in criticism.

"It is disgraceful, the receptions he gives in these days of wartime shortages," whispered one lady.

"This minor civil servant's son is so happy to have married a princess that he has lost all sense of proportion," commented another.

The hero of the Young Turk revolution had, in fact, married Sultana Nadié, Sultan Reshat's niece. Enormously proud of his imperial wife, he loved showing her off and continued to throw ostentatiously lavish parties in the middle of the war. His table always groaned with delicacies, whereas even the imperial palace had had the decency to cut down on its menus. But the Sultan's family would have forgiven him everything had he refrained from playing the emperor: by dictating to the elderly monarch and humiliating him, he humiliated them all.

"See how ill and unhappy His Majesty looks," the princesses told each other ruefully, still indignant that Enver Pasha should have compelled him to welcome Kaiser Wilhelm II at the railroad station a few months before. They were far less disapproving of the fatigue to which the Padishah[10] had been subjected than shocked by the way his War Minister had humiliated him: never since the dynasty's foundation had a sultan left his palace to welcome any foreign ruler, be he king or emperor.

Above all, they could neither forget nor forgive the execution of Salih Pasha, the handsome young husband of Sultana Munira, one of Sultan Reshat's favourite nieces. Enver had accused him of plotting against the Young Turk party and demanded his head. Munira threw herself at the Sultan's feet, and he himself implored Enver to spare the young damad's life. In vain. Heartbroken, Sultan Reshat was forced to sign the death warrant himself. He succeeded only at the third attempt, it was said, because his eyes were so misty with tears.

Selma, all ears, was listening to these comments and criticisms when the orchestra abruptly stopped playing: the Sultan had terminated the ceremony by rising to his feet. He slowly left the throne room followed by the princes and accompanied by the ulemas' traditional cry: "Padishah, be humble and remember that Allah is greater than thou!"

The ladies were already hurrying toward the Blue Room, where the Sultan would come to pay them a ritual visit. The mistresses of ceremonies firmly marshalled them into line according to age and rank while the harem's orchestra of sixty-odd female musicians settled in the adjoining vestibule. When the sovereign appeared, preceded by his grand treasurer, it struck up a song of welcome composed especially for the occasion.

Her eyes lowered, Selma covertly inspected the white-haired, amiable-looking old gentleman with the china blue eyes and thick lips. Smiling serenely, he invited his mother to sit down beside him.

First to step forward were the sultanas and their daughters, the so-called hanum sultanas. Their long trains rustled across the silk carpets as they performed three graceful temennas and took their places on the Sultan's right. Then came the cadins and ikbals, who arrayed themselves on his left. Finally it was the turn of the ladies-in-waiting

10 Synonym for sultan.

and the oldest kalfas, who, after prostrating themselves, humbly retired to the back of the room.

Once these salutations were complete, the slaves appeared bearing a velvet cloth filled with freshly minted gold coins. Scooping them up by the handful, the grand treasurer threw them to the musicians and the younger kalfas, who gathered them up, all the while loudly blessing the Padishah for his generosity.

Now was the time for conversation. His Majesty, having invited his relations and wives to be seated, inquired after their health and said a few gracious words to each. However, conversation soon languished as etiquette did not permit anyone to address the sovereign first or do more than answer his questions. While the ladies sat waiting, perched stiffly on the edge of their chairs, the Sultan took refuge in a minor fit of coughing. Selma, furtively glancing at him, saw to her great surprise that he seemed embarrassed. After a protracted silence he began to speak of his pigeons. He had a passion for these birds, which he imported from Europe, and appeared to think them a subject that might interest the ladies. They actually all seemed very interested. Then he spoke of the beautiful roses he picked when walking in the grounds of the little palace of Ilhamur, stressing that no more than one should be picked from each bush, never two or the bush would be ruined.

This was typical of Sultan Reshat's gentle disposition. The only thing that ever aroused his ire, it was said, was the sight of a foreign ambassador crossing his legs in his presence. "That infidel stuck his feet up my nose again," he would complain on such occasions. But he kept his temper by reciting a sura[11], for he was very devout. He belonged to an order of religious mystics, although he never talked about it.

At long last, when His Majesty felt that the pigeons and roses had exhausted all the conversational topics appropriate to such charming company, he rose, bade the ladies an amiable farewell, and withdrew to his own apartments.

Everyone relaxed. Gaily mingling in the smaller drawing-rooms, the princesses greeted one another joyfully, happy to renew old acquaintances, congratulating each other on their gowns, and exchanging confidences. Some of them had not met since the last Bairam, so they had hundreds of important things to tell each other. In one boudoir a young sultana played fashionable mazurkas on the piano while her cousins, in fits of laughter, tried to dance; elsewhere,

11 Chapter of the Koran, the sacred book of Islam.

a keenly contested game of backgammon was in progress. The senior Cadin had organized a poetry competition on a specific subject. Poetry was held in high esteem at the Ottoman court, and some of the greatest sultans had devoted themselves to it with talent and success.

But the most crowded drawing-room of all was that presided over by the miraju, or storyteller. She was the finest in the city, and no festivity was complete without her. Selma, seated on the floor with her chin cupped in her hands, stared at her: she must be a hundred years old! Little by little, though, her wrinkled face grew smooth, her shoulders straightened, and her eyes burned with dark fire. No longer was she an old miraju; she had become the lovely Leila for whom young Majnun had died of love. Hers was the melodious voice and gazelle-like gaze, hers the beauty that bewitched generation after generation of lovers who dreamed and wept for her.

At nightfall the whole company went down to the gardens to watch the display of fireworks traditionally given by the Sultan for his subjects. The lawns had been spread with carpets and cushions, and female slaves served supper on silver gilt trays while the orchestra softly played a Mozart concerto.

A sudden cry made everyone jump. A young princess, deathly pale, pointed to some clumps of hydrangeas advancing on her from out of the darkness. Then they tilted to disclose that the court dwarfs, concealed behind enormous bunches of flowers, had come to present their compliments to the ladies.

This joke was variously received. But there was no disagreement about the rosewater sherbets and honey and almond pastries prepared by the palace chefs, who were unrivalled anywhere in the Near East.

And when, at long last, fiery fountains gushed into the night sky and the star and crescent, those emblems of eternal Turkey, stood outlined in flame against a pall of smoke, everyone agreed that never – no, never – had they attended a more successful festivity.

Gazing out across the moonlit Bosphorus as the phaeton bore her home to Ortaköy Palace, Selma relived her happy day and reflected that life was sweet indeed. How could anyone believe those birds of ill omen who predicted the downfall of an empire so rich and powerful?

CHAPTER 4

It was hot in Istanbul during these early July days when the Bosphorus sent no cool breezes to refresh the city. The night before, a messenger had come from Dolmabahçé Palace, and after he had left Sultana Hatijé sent for Selma.

"Tomorrow," she told her, "you and Haïri are to go and play with your cousin Princess Sadiyé. His Majesty's grandchildren, Princess Mukbilé and her brother Prince Namuk, will also be there."

Selma tried to hide her feelings. She heartily disliked Sadiyé, who, for a child of six, had a very inflated idea of her own importance. Her father, Prince Abdul Mejid, bragged to anyone who would listen that his daughter was the loveliest of all the imperial children. He would line them up at every family reunion and proudly announce that she was also the tallest for her age. Annéjim was well aware of this, so why should she be forced to play with Sadiyé? Fortunately, there were certain compensations. Prince Abdul Mejid's garden, which overlooked the Asiatic shores of the Bosphorus, was perfect for playing hide-and-seek. Besides, there was never a dull moment with Mukbilé around. . . .

What on earth was keeping Mademoiselle Rose? Selma paced the corridor outside her governess's room. She did not understand how anyone could spend so long primping, with such meagre results.

In spite of her little failings, though, Selma was very fond of her "*demoiselle Française*," especially as the poor woman's authority over her was nil. Being ignorant of Turkish social conventions, and even more so of court etiquette, she swallowed Selma's tall stories and let her do as she pleased.

Mademoiselle Rose had arrived in Istanbul before the war, at a period when relations between France and the Ottoman Empire were still quite good. An avid reader of the novels of Pierre Loti and Claude Farrere, she was bedazzled by Turkey and its inhabitants and thought she understood them. She had answered an advertisement placed by the nuns of Notre-Dame-de-Sion, where she had been educated. Their order's prosperous house in Istanbul was looking for an art teacher. No one else applied for the post, so she was hired on the spot.

It took courage for a provincial spinster of twenty-eight to exile herself in this way, and she would never have embarked on such an adventurous step had she not regarded herself as the victim of a tragic love affair. A handsome young cavalry officer on garrison duty in Beauvais, her home town, had courted her and promised marriage. She allowed him to kiss her (several times) and fondle her (a little) until an anonymous well-wisher sent her a photograph of the vile brute with two small children at his knee and his arm around the waist of an attractive blonde: his wife. Mademoiselle Rose wept bitterly and – as her mother had so often advised – vowed never to trust another man. As soon as the opportunity arose, she left her family and her country as though taking the veil.

But Mademoiselle Rose was an incurable romantic. At Istanbul she fell in love with a Frenchman on the staff of Galatasaray College. He, though unmarried, was fickle, and when she discovered that he was simultaneously courting two of his female colleagues she began to pine away.

It was Fehimé, the Butterfly Sultana, who saved her. Meeting Mademoiselle Rose at a reception at the French Embassy, one of the big parties that preceded the summer vacation, she told her that she was looking for a French teacher for her niece. Mademoiselle Rose seized on this unexpected opportunity to consort with the refined society to which her prematurely old-maidish nature had always aspired, and that was how she became the little Sultana's French governess.

It was already three o'clock. Selma had almost given up hope when her governess emerged wearing a broad-brimmed violet hat adorned with canaries that matched the fields of buttercups on her muslin gown.

Zeynel, impassive as always, was waiting for them at the wharf with Haïri, who looked very spick and span in his sailor suit, his black hair impeccably parted and reeking of brilliantine. "He must have smeared a whole jar over his head," Selma thought irritably. "If he thinks he is going to impress Sadiyé that way. . . ." Her brother's crush on their cousin was one of their many bones of contention.

The oarsmen helped them into the caique, which was soon speeding toward the Asiatic shore. There, to Selma's great pleasure, they found an open calash awaiting them. She was condemned to a closed phaeton when out driving with her mother, but that was doubtless considered unnecessary in the case of a Christian governess and a prepubescent girl, so they were free to enjoy the sun and breeze as they rattled up the stony road to Prince Abdul Mejid's summer residence.

Sadiyé was waiting for them, poised in a pink lace dress and blonde ringlets. She was coming down the steps to welcome her visitors when a plump little girl with sparkling eyes pushed past her towards Selma. Mukbilé was too delighted by this reunion with the cousin who shared her love of mischief to stand on ceremony. She rushed up to Selma with Namuk, her younger brother, trotting along behind.

After some minutes' animated discussion, it was decided to play Conquest of Constantinople[1].

Namuk, being the youngest, naturally had to be the prisoner, but who was to play the coveted part of Sultan Fatih? They drew straws for it, and Selma won.

"That's impossible," Sadiyé objected. "You can't play the Sultan – you are't even a sultana!"

"What do you mean?" snapped Selma. "I'm just as much a sultana as you are!"

"No," her cousin said in a schoolmarmish tone. "My father says *your* father is not a prince, so you're only a sultana's daughter, a hanum sultana."

Selma would have strangled Sadiyé with pleasure, but was reduced to tongue-tied, impotent silence. Her stuck-up cousin was right: her father was only a damad. Everyone at Ortaköy called her "the little Sultana," but she had noticed – though no one had ever alluded to it – that protocol at ceremonies in Dolmabahçé Palace gave preference to some princesses younger than herself. She had sensed all kinds of minor differences in status without understanding them, but Sadiyé's insult had abruptly brought them home to her.

The sky had clouded over and the trees were shivering in a stiff breeze. All of a sudden the future seemed terribly drab. She was only a hanum sultana: no matter what she did, she would always be outranked by the others. It was as if someone had clipped her wings. . . . She thought of her mother, whom people called Jihangir, or "conqueror of the world," because of her majestic presence, and all of a sudden the injustice of the situation enraged her. Sultana Hatijé was superior to most of the imperial princes, yet she could not pass on her nobility of blood simply because she was a woman. Selma found the idea not only absurd but intolerable.

Raising her head, she glared at Sadiyé with all the disdain she could muster and searched for a suitable retort, but none seemed suffi-

1 Constantinople, now Istanbul, was captured in 1453 by Sultan Mehmet Fatih, the Conqueror.

ciently withering. At a loss, she turned to Haïri, only to find that he had sneaked away. She eventually spotted him at the far end of the path, contemplating a rose bush. *Coward!* she thought. Her brother's attitude did not surprise her in the least: he always disappeared as soon as an argument arose. But what surprised her was that, instead of being enraged by his behaviour, she found it merely depressing. Mukbilé, who had remained at her side, did not know what to say. She had never been so embarrassed before. Finally she ventured, "How about a game of hide-and-seek instead?"

Everyone accepted this compromise with relief.

It turned out to be a lively afternoon. Wearing plain cotton dresses, Selma and Mukbilé sought out the most unlikely and inaccessible hiding places. They climbed trees and hid in nooks and crannies where their cousin, afraid of ruining her elegant gown, could not follow them. "That's not fair!" she kept complaining bitterly. "Princesses do not act like that!" That only made them laugh so hard they cried.

Eventually, however, the hostilities ceased and the atmosphere lightened as they sat down to afternoon tea. The veranda rang with their happy cries and laughter and their quarrel was forgotten.

It was growing late when Prince Omer Hilmi, Namuk and Mukbilé's father, appeared in full dress uniform.

"Why is Baba all dressed up like that?" Mukbilé exclaimed. "It is not a special day, is it?"

"You mean you do not know?" Sadiyé said scornfully. "Your grandfather Sultan Reshat is dead. That makes *my* father the Crown Prince!"

Mukbilé started as if someone had hit her. She stared at her cousin in disbelief, and tears began to trickle down her cheeks. Furious, Selma turned on Sadiyé.

"You are a pest! Go away!"

Sadiyé gave a sarcastic shrug and turned her back on them.

The gentle Sultan Reshad was buried at the little mosque of Eyüp, far from the sumptuous mausoleums where his predecessors lay. He had chosen this peaceful, shady spot because he wanted "to hear the birds chirping and the children laughing. . . ."

The accession of Sultan Vahiddedin, the last of the four brothers who between them had occupied the throne for the past forty-two years, was celebrated a few days later. Enver Pasha, head of the ruling Young Turk party, insisted that the coronation and its attendant military parade should be more elaborate than usual, to impress a war-weary populace.

The people were certainly impressed, but more by the bombs which the British chose to drop on the Ottoman capital just on that day. Were they meant as a warning to the new monarch? In any event, he cherished few illusions about the real extent of his power. He wore a mournful expression throughout the ceremony and gave his relations a gloomy reception when they called on him at the palace the next day.

"Why congratulate me?" he said bitterly. "The throne I sit on is a throne of thorns!"

No one took him seriously. Vahiddedin was a notorious pessimist – in fact the children called him "the Owl" because he always seemed about to make some ominous pronouncement. He was exaggerating as usual: the army was having problems, to be sure, but they would pass. The empire had known worse. And besides, their German allies were so strong. . . .

The army was indeed having problems. The authorities might play down the fact that hundreds of thousands of men had deserted, but there was no ignoring the thousands of casualties crowded into Istanbul's hospitals and the numerous public buildings requisitioned for their benefit.

Sultana Hatijé paid weekly visits to Haseki Hospital, in the centre of the city, to comfort the wounded and bring them little treats. Till now she had refrained from taking Selma along for fear of upsetting her, but her daughter was now seven and a half and very perceptive for her age. Besides, the Sultana was a believer in stoicism. Having undergone some very harsh experiences in her own childhood and survived them unscathed, she felt that emotional ordeals were character-building. She had too often observed the disastrous effects of a sheltered upbringing on Istanbul's charming but childish high-society women not to wish to preserve Selma from them.

Yet when she told her usually easy-going husband of her intention he lost his temper. "You'll upset the poor little thing," he said angrily. "She'll learn the meaning of hardship soon enough – who knows, she may even experience it herself. Let her enjoy life while she can!"

Where her daughter's education was concerned, however, the Sultana considered herself the sole good judge, just as she did in all domestic matters. Although she let her husband handle the upbringing of their son Haïri – Islamic custom dictated that a boy be reared by his father from the age of seven – she was doubtful of his success. Her firstborn's cowardice was a wound to her vanity. She had often tried to jolt him out of his apathy and appeal to his pride, but she had given up when she saw that she only drove him a little farther into his shell each time.

Could it be that her son was afraid of her? Reproaching herself for being too severe, she had tried gentleness instead. She began to think that what she had condemned as lack of character was really extreme sensitivity: perhaps Haïri was an artist! The only thing that interested him – apart from himself – was the violin, so Hatijé had engaged the best teacher in Istanbul, a Viennese, to give him lessons. However, she had soon been compelled to face the fact that, although Haïri had a delicate touch, he lacked the inner fire essential to a virtuoso.

Happily, in Selma the Sultana found all the impetuous daring that had been her own as a young girl. Haïri, she felt, had taken after his father, and she had ended by regarding them both with the same disillusionment. It was not that she had not adored her handsome husband: her love for him had been as fervent as an eighteen-year-old's and as demanding as that of the thirty-eight-year-old woman she was when they met. Perhaps she had expected too much of him. The dreams she had cherished as a lonely adolescent and a woman ridiculed by a first husband whom she hated – all these had been transferred to Haïri Rauf Bey. Before long, however, she lost faith in everything he did. It was as if, having credited him with every gift, she could no longer see any talent in him at all. But when she told herself she was being unfair and made an effort to get closer to him, he received her overtures in astonished silence, his manner somewhat quizzical.

Now she no longer demanded or expected anything of him. Even their physical intimacy had ceased after Selma's birth. She did not think he was unfaithful to her, but instead of welcoming his fidelity she despised it and attributed it to sheer apathy. Their relationship had all the flavour of a glass of lukewarm water. Although Hatijé was long past feeling nostalgic, she did occasionally look at her husband and wonder who it was she had actually loved.

It was a hot July morning when the Sultana and her daughter set off for the hospital. Selma had spent the previous day wrapping presents for the wounded. A kalfa had cut up some squares of pink gauze, and into each went a packet of tobacco, some candy, and a few coins. Then they were tied up with a nice blue satin ribbon. Roomy baskets, also trimmed with ribbon, overflowed with hundreds of these little parcels and Selma was overjoyed at the pretty sight they made, and the prospect of such an out-of-the-ordinary expedition.

Two carriages were required, one for the Sulṭana and her daughter, the other for the servants and the gifts. To reach the hospital they would have to cross the Golden Horn by Galata Bridge and make their way through old Istanbul.

As they neared the bridge the crowd was so thick that the carriages had to slow to a crawl. Galata, situated on the edge of the harbour, was Istanbul's commercial centre and its liveliest district. All the banks, shipping companies, and major industrial firms were based there, but so too were money-changers and shopkeepers of all kinds. Standing at the intersection of the old Muslim city and the "Frankish" city where the Christians lived, Galata was the crossroads where all the empire's races met and mingled.

Black-robed Greek Orthodox priests rubbed shoulders with long-haired Jews in embroidered caftans, old Turks in baggy trousers and turbans shared the streets with elegant young men-about-town wearing European frock coats and red fezzes with black tassels. Selma, watching through the phaeton's blinds, did not know where to look first. Seated at the mouth of the bridge, a big Albanian in a bright blue costume stroked his moustache with a bellicose air as a pair of beautiful Armenian girls with milk-white complexions went by. Bulgars, recognizable by their massive build and little fur caps, strolled past in groups, while a few Muslim women in coloured charshafs had ventured forth to do some shopping. The whole crowd bustled along, heedless of its motley composition.

Crossing the bridge was an epic struggle. Yelling at the top of his voice, the coachman strove to forge a path through the clutter of vehicles coming the other way, all in the wildest confusion. He could have saved his breath. The smart calashes and luxurious phaetons were squashed between a stream of handcarts, cabs, and ox carts, while porters, bent double under their heavy loads, threaded their way through the turmoil with loud grunts. Water-sellers clinked their glasses, and the vendors of ices and syrups, wearing harnesses stuffed with flasks of alluringly colourful liquids, took advantage of the enforced halt to cry their wares to thirsty travellers in need of refreshment. Selma, who was delighted by all this, and reluctant to miss out on anything, said she would really love a sherbet, flavoured with Smyrna melon, but her mother frowningly lectured her on hygiene and self-restraint. As she watched the children around the carriage regaling themselves, Selma wistfully concluded that being "well-born" was not an unmixed blessing.

At last they reached Stamboul[2]. They might have been in another city, another country. After the frenzied pandemonium of Galata, they appreciated the tranquillity of the narrow streets flanked by pretty wooden houses with closed shutters and high walls overlooked by cypresses. Stone archways and spiral staircases led to shady little courtyards. A kahveji had erected an awning near a mosque, and the men beneath it were silently sipping coffee, engrossed in endless games of backgammon, or daydreaming as they puffed at their narghilés.

Farther on was a little market. Enthroned behind pyramids of vegetables and fruit, potbellied stallkeepers were serving housewives veiled in black. The public letter-writer, with his array of quills, penknives, and inkpots, was gravely officiating beneath a tree while some old women, squatting beside a scrap of carpet, divined the future by throwing knucklebones. Beggars were also in evidence, but they never accosted anyone. They confined themselves to accepting any coins the passersby saw fit to give them, dignified of mien and firmly convinced that, if Allah had favoured some more than others, it was so that they could share their good fortune with the poorest of the poor.

When the carriages finally pulled up in the hospital yard after a two-hour drive, Selma jumped down without waiting for Zeynel to open the door. She could not wait to see "our gallant warriors," as her uncle Osman Fuad called them.

The hospital was a big, greyish building constructed in the sixteenth century by Suleyman the Magnificent. Followed by their maidservants, the Sultana and her daughter entered the lobby, where they were greeted by the director. With a flurry of bows, he insisted that Their Highnesses take tea with him first. To Selma's great relief, her mother declined. The little man, who had bragged to everyone that he was on intimate terms with the imperial family, swallowed his disappointment and proceeded to escort them around the wards.

They had scarcely entered the first corridor when Selma was assailed by a sweetish but pungent smell that caught in her throat and made her nauseous. She gritted her teeth: she could not possibly be sick here! The farther they went, the more unbearable the smell became. "What funny medicines!" she thought. It was only when they reached the second corridor that the horrifying truth became apparent: cloths soiled with blood and excrement filled the bowls that stood in every corner.

Groaning men lay sprawled on mattresses, sometimes only on a blanket. Some were calling for their mothers; others, with their heads

2 Contemporary name for the old, purely Muslim quarter of Istanbul.

back and their eyes closed, seemed to be fighting for breath. There must have been at least a hundred of them in this one airless corridor. A few privileged patients had a woman – sister? wife? – at their bedside, supporting their heads, moistening their lips, and shooing away flies greedy for blood.

"These women remain here day and night," the superintendent explained. "We let them stay because we don't have sufficient staff to look after all these poor devils."

The nurse on duty, a young woman with her hair done up in a nurse's veil as spotless as her long white apron, was in charge of the entire corridor. What with giving injections, taking temperatures and distributing the few drugs still available, she never had a moment's rest, but she contrived to find a smile and a word of encouragement for each of her patients. Selma, whose one desire was to run away, suddenly felt ashamed; she had to keep going!

At the end of the corridor, which seemed interminable, lay a huge room. It was lighter in here; the walls, painted blue to ward off the evil eye, were pierced by large windows and lined with serried rows of iron bedsteads. More groaning men, most of them young, were stretched out on bare mattresses, the hospital's stock of sheets having long since been ripped up for use as dressings. Sometimes a scream would interrupt the macabre recitative, but no one took any notice; each was intent on keeping his strength for the ultimate, desperate struggle against death.

Most of the wounded were lying two to a narrow bed; they were the privileged ones. The dying, from whom nothing could be expected but a last breath, had been relegated to the floor beneath the beds to save precious space. Every morning it was the same inexorable procedure: the bodies of the dead were removed and returned to their families or tossed into a communal grave, and the casualties considered past saving were slipped down under the beds in their turn, while new arrivals took their places.

Selma trembled, torn between revulsion and stupefaction. Where were "our gallant warriors?" She found it impossible to associate the proud soldiers she had admired on parade with these moaning creatures. She wanted to cry, but was it out of pity or disappointment? The "General Prince" was always talking about courage in the face of death and the joy of laying down one's life for one's country. Were all those noble sentiments a gigantic lie?

She felt her mother squeeze her hand.

"Be brave, my little darling, I am here."

Even more thrown by the Sultana's uncharacteristically affectionate tone, she gave her an imploring glance.

"Annéjim, please let's go home!"

But her mother shook her head gravely. "These men are very miserable," she said. "Can't you give them a little comfort?"

Selma wanted to say no, she never wanted to see them again and hated them to suffer in such an undignified way. Like animals! Suddenly she felt neither pity nor fear. She was simply furious with these wounded men, with the General Prince, with . . . she did not know with whom exactly. Yet although the words nearly choked her, she heard herself say, "Yes, Annéjim."

And they proceeded to distribute the little pink and blue bundles. The Sultana paused at each bed and said a comforting word. Those that were strong enough thanked her with a smile; some tried to detain her as if the presence of this serene and beautiful lady in their nightmare world could preserve them from death; others turned their heads.

Selma was following with bad grace, staring fixedly at her white shoes, when a hand seized her arm and a wild-eyed man drew her towards his bed. "Nejla, my darling daughter," he muttered. The Sultana, hearing her cry out in terror, came to her rescue. Instead of moving her away, however, she kept Selma at the wounded man's bedside with a protective hand on her shoulder.

"This poor soldier thinks you are his daughter. Let him look at you. It may be his very last moment of happiness."

His daughter? Selma stiffened. How dare he!

One interminable minute dragged by. Then very gradually, under the dying man's adoring gaze, her hostility melted away until she abandoned all resistance and began to weep with him.

Two months later, on 30 October 1918, news of the defeat came. The Ottoman Empire requested an armistice, following the example of its German and Austro-Hungarian allies. The war was over at last, and the exhausted populace breathed again.

Selma was overjoyed: no more hospitals, no more wounded, no more dead. She would now be able to forget the horrific visions that had haunted her since her visit to Haseki. Life could resume its carefree course.

But why did her mother seem so sad?

CHAPTER 5

Those who had welcomed the armistice – or "the peace" as they called it – were soon disillusioned when on a cold and misty November morning thirteen days later, the victorious Allies' fleet, steaming through the Dardanelles, entered the Bosphorus.

There were sixty warships: British, French, Italian – even Greek. The terms of the armistice made no provision for the latter, but Turkey was now too weak to protest, especially as the country no longer possessed a government. The triumvirate responsible for embroiling it in the war had fled on armistice day itself. An ominous silence reigned as the ships drew nearer with destroyers in the lead. Slowly, they entered the Golden Horn and dropped anchor with their guns trained on the Sultan's palace and the Sublime Porte, the seat of government.

"How low we have fallen," Sultana Hatijé thought as she stood motionless at a drawing-room window, watching. For the first time since her ancestors had conquered the city almost five hundred years before, Istanbul was under foreign occupation. The empire that had made all Europe quake for centuries was now at its mercy. She was glad that her father was dead. At least he had been spared this supreme humiliation.

Selma's voice broke in on her thoughts. The little girl was pointing at something in the distance, over towards Galata.

"What is happening, Annéjim? It looks like a battle – or is it a festival?"

Sultana Hatijé could definitely see some kind of commotion going on. Intrigued, she sent for the powerful binoculars that were a memento of an admiral uncle of hers. She peered through them and froze: the waterfront on the Christian side of the city was thronged with a motley crowd of people waving flags. Hatijé made out the French, British and Italian colours, but the majority displayed white crosses on a sky-blue background: they were Greek flags. Angrily, she laid the glasses aside. The traitors had turned out to welcome the enemy!

Suddenly she felt overcome by a mortal weariness. She simply could not understand it: The Empire's Greeks were Ottomans[1] like the rest of the population. They might be Christians, but they were perfectly at liberty to practise their religion. Their patriarch was one of the Empire's most influential figures – indeed, they were far better off than the Turks who scratched a living from the barren soil of Anatolia. Although they could have emigrated when Greece gained its independence ninety years before, they had not only chosen to remain but prospered. Together with the Armenians and the Jews, they dominated the world of commerce and finance. What more did they want?

In fact the Sultana knew very well what they wanted, but she refused even to acknowledge what were in her opinion such exorbitant demands. They wanted to put the clock back six centuries, drive the Turks from Eastern Thrace and Istanbul in particular, and re-create the Byzantine Empire. What was more, they were counting on the Allies to help them make their dreams come true.

The occupying forces took only a few days to set up a unified command structure. Although the Turks continued in theory to administer the city, the port, streetcar network, and police force came under Allied supervision. The French took control of the old city, the British of Pera[2], and the Italians part of the banks of the Bosphorus.

The Christian districts of Galata and Pera hummed with new life. Inns and taverns were jam-packed with sailors and soldiers noisily squandering more money than the delighted innkeepers had seen in years. Their officers patronized elegant bars where they were served by beautiful Russian refugees from the Bolshevik Revolution. The lobby of the Pera Palace, a fashionable hotel and one of the few to have electricity, teemed with uniforms of all kinds. One could even see pastel-turbanned Sikhs of the Indian Army and French spahis in their brilliant red cloaks.

The management swiftly decided to reinstitute its tea dances on the terrace overlooking the Golden Horn, where handsome young officers waltzed with Pera society girls under the approving eye of mothers gratified that their country's defeat should have bred such an unexpected crop of potential husbands.

In the Muslim city opposite, the atmosphere was funereal. Its inhabitants ventured out as little as possible for fear of being harassed by Allied soldiers, who were often drunk, or simply so as not to have to

1 All the Empire's inhabitants, whether Greeks, Bulgars, Arabs, Turks, or members of other ethnic groups, were known as Ottomans. The designation "Turk" was reserved for subjects of the Turkish race.

2 European name of Beyoglu.

stand aside for the victors, who monopolized the narrow sidewalks. Long accustomed to dominating other nations, the Turks found it bitterly humiliating to be dominated in their turn. Above all, they avoided shopping in Pera, as they used to, among the Christian minority with whom they had always thought they had friendly relations. Now the look of smug triumph on their neighbours' faces filled them with resentment and indignation. Worse still, they risked assault if they failed to salute the ubiquitous Greek flags, and so, if in spite of everything they had to go to Pera, they made long detours around the Greek quarter to spare themselves such an affront to their dignity.

But the future looked blacker still. Considerable unease was caused by the appointment of General Franchet d'Esperey, reputedly a brutal and arrogant man, to command the inter-Allied forces. Rumour had it that he intended to make Istanbul a French city and reduce its Turkish inhabitants to slavery.

Although life went on much as usual at Ortaköy Palace, Selma felt herself imprisoned. The only outings still allowed her were visits to ancient Greek or Byzantine monuments. The Sultana had long sanctioned these "cultural excursions," despite the raised eyebrows of her entourage, because she was determined to give her daughter as full an education as possible. A strange mixture of traditionalism and freedom of thought, she was far too conscious of her rank to worry about gossip. "We are the ones who make the rules!" she used to say.

On 8 February 1919, as on every Wednesday, Selma went on one of her regular outings with Mademoiselle Rose. They had planned to visit the monastery of Akataleptos, the fine seventh-century building constructed by Patriarch Kyrakos II, but this Wednesday was a special one: the French general was expected in the capital. The Sultana had considered cancelling the trip because of the crowds, but Selma looked so crestfallen that she relented. The monastery was in the old city near Şehzade Mosque, whereas the procession was scheduled to follow a route from Galata Bridge to the French Embassy in Pera, so there was no danger of crossing its path.

Selma and her governess duly set off in a phaeton accompanied by Zeynel, one of whose many prerogatives was to escort the sultanas on their outings. Their visit to the monastery was swiftly concluded. Selma, whose usual practice it was to spin out every excursion by asking innumerable questions, seemed impatient to get home. Then, just as the coachman was about to head for Ortaköy, she called to him.

"Take us to Pera, quickly!"

He reined in, looking dumbfounded. Zeynel got down off the box and came to the door.

"It is impossible, Princess. The parade –"

"I know," Selma said imperiously. "That is just what I want to see."

"The Sultana would never permit it."

"What about those other little drives we have taken lately, after our visits to museums? She did not permit those either."

It was true. Selma had two or three times prevailed on her companions to prolong a sightseeing expedition by going for a drive afterwards. The little girl looked threatening.

"I wonder what would happen if I told her. . . ."

The eunuch frowned and Mademoiselle Rose twisted anxiously in her seat. They knew they were at fault for having given in to Selma's demands but the drives had been completely innocent and had been as much fun for them as for the child. Now they felt trapped; they had never imagined the little monster would bribe them. If she tattled about these escapades she would certainly be punished, but Mademoiselle Rose would undoubtedly be dismissed for having abused the Sultana's trust. As for Zeynel, he dreaded to think how disappointed in him his mistress would be. He could not bear to see the relationship which had built up between them over the years founder on a peccadillo. Besides, he knew Sultana Hatijé's vulnerabilities; her life in captivity had been marked by so many betrayals that she extended her trust to only a very few: but from these she expected absolute loyalty. Zeynel had always been too soft with the little Sultana; she was the only child he had ever loved. . . . His anger was tempered with admiration for her cunning, he decided that it would be wiser to give in.

"Just for a few minutes, then," he said, exchanging a glance with Mademoiselle Rose.

"Oh, thank you, Agha!" cried Selma, and gave him one of her most dazzling smiles.

The carriage toiled uphill to Pera, through streets choked with happy crowds, to the main thoroughfare where the procession was to pass. The shops were shut and the handsome stone buildings were adorned with flags. On the pavements – it was the only street in Istanbul to have them – enthusiastic spectators waved litle flags of their own. The Greek colours were in evidence, but so were those of the Armenian minority whose demonstrations in favour of an independent state in eastern Anatolia had often been harshly suppressed in the past. Secretly abetted for years by Britain, France, and Russia, who had aided them as a means of undermining the Ottoman Empire, the Armenians were now counting on the Allied victory to fulfil their dream.

It was wiser not to be seen in a carriage bearing the imperial arms, so the phaeton waited in a side street while Selma and Mademoiselle Rose threaded their way through the crowd followed by Zeynel, who alone grasped the potential dangers of the situation. Yet no one would be able to tell that this little girl with auburn curls walking with this old-fashioned-looking gentleman wearing an outmoded high-necked tunic could be Muslims. And the blonde lady with them looked typically French.

Preceded by a crash of cymbals and a blare of trumpets, General Franchet d'Esperey rode into view on a superb white charger, looking thoroughly majestic in his red kepi and voluminous cloak. Everyone clapped and cheered. The symbolic significance of the white horse was obvious to all: it was on a white horse that Mehmet II, "the Conqueror," had ridden into Constantinople in 1453; and it was now also on a white horse that this Christian general was again taking possession of the city.

The ceremony had been carefully designed to impress an already amenable population. The cortège was led by officers of the military police in full dress uniform. Several yards behind them, with head erect and the reins of his horse held by two soldiers, rode the general himself, followed by his standard-bearer and aides-de-camp. They were followed at a respectful distance by a detachment of dragoons with long lances, a troop of cavalry in blue uniforms, and a company of infantry. Then came the British commander, General Milne, leading his Highlanders, and the Italian general with a battalion of Bersaglieri in hats adorned with pheasants' feathers. Bringing up the rear was the pièce de résistance: a regiment of Greek evzones attired in white kilts and red pompom caps. They could not resist responding to the cheers of their compatriots in the crowd they had come to "deliver" from the Turks.

The procession had just passed the spot where Selma, Zeynel and Mademoiselle Rose were standing when a woman's voice rang out. "Say it, why don't you? Say it – and may it choke you!" A chorus of jeers and laughter followed. To her amazement and alarm, Selma saw a woman in a black charshaf trying to defend herself against half a dozen harpies who had torn off her veil and were hitting her unmercifully. "Go on," they shouted, "salute our flag! Say 'Long live Venizelos!'[3]" On all sides, men were looking on with derision. They would

3 Eleftherios Venizelos, b. 1864, Greek premier. Known as *the Great Cretan*.

not themselves have struck a woman – their sense of honour extended that far – but it was not for them to prevent their wives from teaching a muz[4] the facts of life.

Selma was on the point of calling for help when Mademoiselle Rose gripped her hand hard. "Keep quiet and don't move!" she hissed. "They'll kill us all!"

Transfixed, the little girl obeyed. "Oh, God," she kept muttering, "save her, please save her!"

And God intervened in the shape of some French sailors looking for a bar. Attracted by the din, they rescued the unfortunate woman and sent her on her way, but not without cursing her for having ventured into the district in the first place.

Selma, still trembling, accompanied by her two guardian angels, walked back to the carriage. The coachman, who had been anxiously awaiting their return, whipped up his horses and got them back to the palace just in time for tea.

Although their jaunt had turned out all right in the end, Selma felt ashamed; for the first time in her life she had been cowardly. It was no use telling herself that she had simply done as she was told, and that her cries would have endangered Zeynel. Deep down she knew that she had been afraid.

Natural honesty compelled her to face up to this new and unfamiliar image of herself: a fraidy-cat! Her pride could not stand it. She, who so often imagined herself performing heroic deeds and prided herself on the valour of her royal forebears, had behaved contemptibly. She had nightmares about it night after night. She looked for excuses, but found none.

Finally time and sheer fatigue overcame her anguish, and life and its pleasures regained the upper hand. But she never forgot that a simple woman of the people had shown more courage and pride than a sultan's granddaughter.

4 Contemptuous abbreviation of Muslim.

CHAPTER 6

Just as the more privileged of Istanbul's inhabitants had during the last few months of the war, when defeat was staring them in the face, thoughtlessly frittered away their time, so now that the capital had been occupied they yielded to pessimism and despair. They spoke of nothing but the victors' excesses: of the British trooper who had horsewhipped a passerby for not getting out of his way fast enough; of the Highlander who had obscenely lifted his kilt in front of some Muslim women; of drunken brawls involving French and Italian soldiers; and, above all, of the uncouth behaviour of the Senegalese. To the people of a country where black people had never been anything but slaves, nothing could have been more offensive than black French troops swaggering around and giving them orders. Heavily embroidered tales of looting and rape circulated, and everyone was aghast that Europeans who had always been considered so "civilized" should perpetrate such crimes.

To combat the universal mood of depression, Sultana Hatijé decided to give a "hammam party" of the kind that had always been popular in Istanbul, where people invited their friends to take a bath just as Europeans invited each other to tea. Her sole proviso was that no one should mention current events. In these sad times, having fun was a way of defying the enemy – almost a patriotic duty.

In spite of prevailing shortages, the Sultana insisted that her party be as lavish as in the old days. The entire female staff of the palace, some thirty kalfas of varying seniority, welcomed the guests in the great hall by showering them with rose petals. Then, having helped them out of their charshafs, they conducted them to the flower-bedecked boudoirs adjoining the bath-house. There slaves braided their hair with long gold or silver ribbons and coiled it on top of their heads, wrapped them in a peshtamal, or finely embroidered bath towel, and put slippers encrusted with mother-of-pearl on their feet.

Thus attired, the women betook themselves to the rotunda where the Sultana awaited them. Sipping cardamom-flavoured coffee, they complimented one another on the gold and silver toilet articles that each woman had brought with her. Parties of this kind were really an opportunity to parade the ewers, perfume bottles, and ointment boxes that every bride received on her marriage.

The guests then headed for the steam rooms, each escorted by two slaves whose task it was to bathe, massage, depilate, and perfume her from head to foot. Fountains played in these three white marble chambers, the last of which was so filled with steam that one could hardly see across it. The women remained there for hours before immersing themselves in the cold pool in the rest room, a leafy bower furnished with sofas and couches. As they voluptuously took their ease to the gentle strains of an orchestra concealed behind a curtain, silent slave girls brought them violet- or rose-scented sherbets.

This was the time for confidences and indiscretions of all kinds. Relaxed in mind and body, the guests dreamily surrendered themselves to the expert hands of slaves who slowly massaged their feet or the backs of their necks. In such an atmosphere of refined sensuality, even the ugliest felt desirable.

As for Selma, she felt she was in paradise. A singular form of licence prevailed in the hammam, where the Victorian educational precepts instilled into Ottoman girls of good family no longer seemed to apply. In this intimate atmosphere, the oriental nature – generous and pleasure-loving, free from prejudice and untrammelled by guilt – burst the bonds of an imported sense of modesty that had never been more than a veneer. The happy complicity that existed between these women devoted to their physical well-being was a mixture of eroticism and childish delight. They admired and caressed each other, clasped each other around the waist, and gently, affectionately embraced.

A little bemused by the heady scent of the tuberoses, Selma marvelled at all those beautifully rounded breasts and soft, milk-white bellies. Would she, too, have breasts some day? If she did not, it would not be for want of trying. Every night in bed she stroked and gently pulled at her chest to make it grow.

In the languid atmosphere conversation soon became rather libertine and the little girl made herself as inconspicuous as possible to avoid being sent away by her mother.

A young woman was talking about her husband, a senior official at the Foreign Ministry, who was modern-minded enough to take her with him when he attended official functions. She had once accompanied him to a dinner given by the Swiss ambassador, one of the few neutral households.

"All the other women were Europeans," she said. "They were very elegant, but their gowns were cut so low it made me ashamed for them. What really amazed me, though, was that none of the men seemed to notice. They mingled with those half-naked creatures as if they could not have cared less!"

"Western men have no strong desires," her neighbour observed with a knowing air. "It's an accepted fact. That's why their women can afford to go around half naked."

Everyone burst out laughing.

"Mashallah! You cannot say the same of *our* men, God be praised! The sight of an arm or an ankle drives them wild!"

"Those poor European women," sighed a pretty brunette, "how unhappy they must be! In their place I would die of frustration."

"They don't mind. They think they are emancipated – they say their men are tolerant, when they are really indifferent."

"It may have something to do with their religion," suggested a skinny little woman who prided herself on being an intellectual. "The prophet Jesus, whom they regard as a god – they are polytheists, you know; they worship three gods: the Father, the Son, and the Holy Spirit – well, Jesus avoided women and never married. The main Christian sect, the Catholics, actually believe that chastity consecrated to God is the highest form of perfection. That is why their priests remain celibate. So do some of their young women – nuns, they are called."

"Celibate?"

The ladies echoed the word in disbelief. To them, celibacy was an affliction. Wasn't a woman's first duty to bear children? Didn't the Prophet himself have nine wives? To Muslims, sex was unassociated with the concept of sin – anything but. Every woman present was familiar with the verses of Ghazali, a mystical poet of the eleventh century: "When the husband takes his wife's hand and she takes his, their sins run through their fingers. When they live together, the angels surround them from the earth to the zenith. Sensual pleasure and desire possess the beauty of the mountains. . . ."

It was Ghazali, too, who affirmed that if Mohammed, unlike Jesus, had numerous wives, "it was because he had attained so exalted a degree of spirituality that the things of this world did not prevent his heart from being in the presence of God. The revelation came down to earth in his person even when he was in the bed of his wife Aysha. . . ."

Christian eccentricities were a truly inexhaustible topic of conversation.

"They are cannibals, you know," the intellectual went on.

"Cannibals?"

A shudder ran around the room.

"Yes! Every morning their priests magic their god into a piece of bread. Then they eat him."

The guests stared at one another open-mouthed.

"Perhaps it's only symbolic," hazarded one.

"That's what I thought at first, but no: they swear their god is there, flesh and blood!"

Another shudder.

"And they dare to call us fanatics!"

"It's always the same old story," the intellectual lady concluded sententiously. "The strong impose their ideas as well as their laws."

A kind of melancholy descended on the gathering. How had the conversation turned to politics when they had promised to avoid such a disagreeable topic? One of the princesses quickly changed the subject in a voice charged with mystery.

"Have you heard the latest news?"

All heads turned in her direction.

"Tell us! Don't keep us in suspense!"

"Very well," she said, full of her own importance. "It is about Golden Rose. . . ."

Their eyes lit up. What had Golden Rose done now?

"He has asked for the hand of Sultana Sabiha."

A barrage of exclamations.

"What! Marry His Majesty's daughter? Impossible!"

Offended that anyone should doubt her information, the Princess drew herself up. "It is absolutely true. I had it from Sabiha's mother, the Cadin herself!"

Excitement rose to fever pitch. To think that beautiful Sabiha, Sultan Vahiddedin's favourite daughter, might marry the hero of Gallipoli, the young general who had saved Istanbul from the British invaders of the Dardanelles! Golden Rose was a legendary figure to all present. In defiance of his superiors' advice, he had tackled a European expeditionary force superior to his own troops in numbers and equipment. His daring, coupled with absolute faith in himself and his men, had enabled him to emerge triumphant from a situation pronounced hopeless by all the experts, both at Istanbul and at the front itself. The fame he derived from this brilliant victory was enhanced a few months later, when he recaptured the towns of Bitlis and Mush from the Russians, thereby gaining the only Turkish successes in a whole string of defeats.

The younger generation of Turks, disillusioned by their politicians' blunders and their elderly generals' failures, praised him to the skies, and all the women were crazy about him. He was not only brave but handsome and arrogant. Pale-skinned, with high cheekbones, flashing blue eyes, and a magnificent head of fair hair – hence his nickname – he was a native of Salonika and said to be of Albanian extraction. His father had been a junior customs officer, but he himself, who was firmly convinced of his own superiority, looked like a prince in his perfectly tailored uniform. His whole person radiated an almost savage power and energy.

He had been seen at court since the end of the war. Sultan Vahiddedin, who liked to consult him on the state of the army's morale and listen to his nonconformist views, had held him in high esteem ever since 1917, when he was still crown prince and had visited the Kaiser in Germany with the young colonel as his aide-de-camp.

His handsome appearance and glamorous aura were not lost on the princesses who covertly watched him during his visits to the palace, and more than one of them dreamed of becoming his wife. One young sultana went so far as to write him some innocent but ardent letters and send them to him by a slave. The hard-hearted man had never even deigned to reply, and the sultana had fallen ill, stricken with grief. Was he indifferent because he had his sights on the Sultan's daughter? His origins were humble, but that did not matter. Turkey possessed no aristocracy outside the imperial family, and the highest positions were attainable on the strength of personal merit alone. Princesses were often married off to pashas or viziers on whom the sultan wished to bestow a signal honour. Hadn't Sultana Nadié married Enver Pasha, the War Minister, son of an obscure railroad official, five years before? Golden Rose was every bit as good as Enver!

The hammam buzzed with joyous excitement. The women deserted the couches on which they had been languidly reclining and clustered around the Princess. Delighted by her conversational coup, she made them beg for every crumb of information. No, His Majesty had not replied yet. Yes, he would reply in due course, but – as they all knew – he always weighed his decisions with the utmost care.

"What was his initial reaction, though?"

"He told the Pasha that his daughter was still young, and that he would have to give the matter some thought."

"Sultana Sabiha young? She must be twenty at least!"

The Princess lowered her voice. "His Majesty is hesitant, it seems. There is no denying that the Pasha is our finest general, but he is very quick-tempered and he drinks like a fish. Besides, they say he has republican ideas. . . ."

The very word sent a shiver down everyone's spine.

"Golden Rose a republican? You must be mistaken!"

Selma, unable to contain her curiosity any longer, turned to the young woman beside her. “Excuse me,” she whispered, “but who is this . . . Golden Rose?”

“You mean you don’t know, Princess?” her neighbour exclaimed. “Why, General Mustafa Kemal, of course!”

CHAPTER 7

"'Greek troops have occupied Izmir. After a number of bloody skirmishes, order has been restored.'"

Haïri Rauf Bey sighed and sank back in his mahogany armchair. "If it says so in the foreign press, it must be true. . . ."

Like many of his generation and class, the Damad was a fervent admirer of Europe and had nothing but contempt for everything Turkish, notably Turkish newspapers. Rather than read them, he had half a dozen foreign papers sent him daily, most of them from France and England. They presented the enemy's point of view, admittedly, but he thought them more objective than the local press, which was subject to censorship, conveniently forgetting that the latter had been imposed by the occupying powers, the very nations he admired so much. To Haïri Bey that was just a mere detail because information had almost always been censored in Turkey, not only during the thirty-three-year reign of Sultan Abdul Hamid, but later under Enver Pasha's nine-year dictatorship.

He refused to believe that the press in "free" countries was just as strictly though more subtly controlled, for their governments realized that direct and drastic intervention was ineffective as well as dangerous. In his view, those who claimed democracies were past masters of manipulation were merely slandering them. In Europe, so these maliciously-minded people declared, governments no longer imprisoned newspaper editors; they invited them to dinner, gave them a "full, free, and frank insight into the problems of the day," and flattered them into preserving an attitude of benevolent neutrality.

Haïri Bey was infuriated by such suggestions. In any case, nothing would alter his belief that the key to Turkey's prosperity lay in westernization. "We must pluck Europe's roses," he used to say, "never mind the thorns."

He liked to flaunt the theories of the rationalist philosophers and the ideals of the French Revolution, but if he was prepared to grant the masses certain rights, he would never have stood for their taking those rights themselves.

Thumbing through his papers, he noticed a front-page editorial in the big French daily *Le Journal*, dated 17 May 1919. The journalist Saint-Brice was analyzing the Allied landing at Smyrna[1] and criticizing it severely. "The armistice only allows the Allies to institute martial law if order is threatened. Yet even the most biased sources have not been able to point out a single serious incident. . . . What we have, then, is a deliberate, carefully planned political act which will, moreover, have far-reaching consequences: the occupation of Smyrna is the death sentence of the Ottoman Empire."

"How brave of him to take the side of the defeated against his own government – now that's real freedom!" Haïri Bey exclaimed, neglecting in his enthusiasm to note the article's conclusion: "The death of 'the sick man of Europe' would hardly matter to us if it did not also bring with it the death of French influence in the Middle East. What role will be left for us between the formidable mandates of Britain and the United States?"

There was a tap at his study door and a little auburn head appeared in the doorway.

"Why, if it is not my pretty little daughter. To what do I owe this honour? Come in, come in."

Whenever they were alone together, out of earshot of his wife and the servants, his manner was thoroughly informal and every time his almost conspiratorial familiarity made the little girl's heart beat faster. He sat her on his knee and eyed her quizzically.

"Well, what are you after this time?"

Selma was piqued that he should have seen through her so quickly when she had spent the whole morning working out her plan of campaign.

"Honestly, Baba," she protested, "I promise you. . . ."

He burst out laughing. She looked at him entranced. How different he was when they were alone together – how cheerful, how utterly devoid of that languid expression he wore at other times! She loved him for being so glad to see her. Putting her head on one side, she assumed her most coaxing air.

"Baba, you said the other day that European children are better prepared for life because they are brought up in greater freedom."

He frowned, wondering where this was leading. "I suppose I did."

"Don't you think it is essential for a young woman to understand the world she lives in?"

Haïri Bey chewed his lip. Where could she have picked up a phrase like that? Probably from one of those French novels scattered around her governess's room. She must have learned it by heart.

"Perhaps," he said, "but you are not a young woman yet."

1 The Greek name for Izmir, used by Westerners.

She eyed him reproachfully. "Mademoiselle Rose says it is not age that counts, it is maturity."

Mademoiselle Rose! Just as he had suspected. He strongly doubted if that harebrained old maid was an ideal governess, and he made a mental note to speak to his wife about her.

"Come to the point," he said, a little irritably, instinctively taking a more distant tone. "What do you want?"

"I should like" – she fixed him with her big, imploring eyes – "I should like you to take me to the demonstration in Sultan Ahmed Square."

"What!" Haïri Bey almost choked. "You are mad! There will be thousands of people there, all baying for blood. You are not going and neither am I. I have no intention of mingling with that mob."

Selma's eyes filled with tears. "But Baba," she said, "those horrible massacres at Izmir. . . . Something must be done, Zeynel says."

"*Zeynel* says? Wonderful! So my daughter pays more attention to a servant than she does to her own parents. What does your mother say to this?"

"Annéjim? She is out."

"I thought so! You waited until she went out before coming to me with this – this absurd request!"

"Absurd in what way, my dear brother-in-law?"

Sultana Fatma, Hatijé's younger sister, was standing in the doorway. The eunuch escorting her had been trying for the past half-minute to attract the Damad's attention sufficiently to announce her. The young Sultana had paid the palace an unheralded visit. On being told that her sister was out, she had asked for her niece instead.

"I mean to attend the demonstration myself," she declared, "in a closed carriage. We shall not get out, naturally, but at a time of crisis like this I feel bound to join our people in prayer. It is a religious demonstration, after all."

Haïri Bey rose abruptly and bowed. He was furious that his sister-in-law should have caught him losing his temper, and not too certain why he had lost it in the first place. As a way of asserting his authority over the child, or because he had the unpleasant feeling that the capture of Izmir affected her more than it did him? Anyway, to the extent that it was a prayer meeting, it was a matter for the women. He could no longer feel concerned.

"Are you sure, Sultana, it is a genuine prayer meeting and not another excuse for a riot?"

"I am positive, Damad. Every precaution has been taken."

He cocked his head. "Very well, take the child with you. Just to be on the safe side, though, take Zeynel as well. The illiterate masses are unpredictable. This is not France, remember."

Sultan Ahmed Mosque, generally known as the Blue Mosque because of its internal decoration, was situated near Topkapi Palace in the heart of the Old City. To reach it one had to cross a maze of narrow, noisy alleyways, lined with stalls and booths, craftsmen's workshops and cafés, all of them crowded from dawn till dusk.

On this particular Friday, however, a deathly hush prevailed. The shops were closed and shuttered, and Ottoman flags, their flagpoles draped in black, flew everywhere. From every lane and alley people were converging to form a long procession that slowly, solemnly wound its way through the streets with resolute tread. Old men walking with difficulty limped beside younger men whose steps were brisk but whose eyes were reddened with tears. There were war-wounded veterans covered with medals barely restraining their emotion beside whole classes of school-children wearing black armbands inscribed in green with the name "Izmir." Above all, there were women. Usually confined to the home, they had turned out by the thousands. Many of them had raised their veils and were marching along with the rest, faces pale, eyes alight with defiance.

Without warning, some British aeroplanes appeared. They roared overhead at rooftop level to deter the crowd, but in vain: no one even flinched. All they evoked were a few scornful smiles. Let them kill us – what does it matter, when our country itself is at death's door?

One could see hatred in the demonstrators' eyes, but also incomprehension and despair at having been abandoned by the entire world. They had been betrayed by those whom they trusted. Why were they being attacked? The war had been over for seven months, Turkey had signed the armistice, demobilized, and laid down her arms, and now was patiently waiting for the victors in Paris and London to decide her fate.

The Ottoman Empire was a dead letter, everyone knew. The Turks had lost their last remaining European territories in the Balkans, together with Libya and all the Arab countries of the Near East. Their Muslim brethren had stabbed them in the back. Instead of supporting his sovereign the Sultan, Hussein[2], the old Sheriff of Mecca, had raised the banner of revolt and sided with the British in return for the promise of a kingdom. The disaster was total: seven years had sufficed to destroy an empire almost seven centuries in the making.

2 Great-grandfather of Hussein of Jordan.

The more philosophical regarded it as only fair that the subject peoples of the Ottoman Empire should regain their liberty, if only in name. They would soon discover that life under the French, British, and Italian mandates was no sweeter than it had been under the lax administration of far-off Istanbul.

The Turks resigned themselves with a certain fatalism to the loss of an unwieldy empire whose multifarious peoples, customs, and beliefs had remained alien to them. What they did find intolerable, and what they were ready to resist to the death, was any assault on the integrity of their own Turkish homeland, a country inhabited, cultivated, and developed by the Turks themselves, those tough Anatolian descendants of the great nomadic tribes that had come from Central Asia in the ninth century.

Drunk with victory, the Allies had underestimated the tenacity of this nation in disarray and thought they could treat it as they pleased. It was Lloyd George, the British prime minister, who had overridden French and Italian advice, yielded to the Greeks' entreaties, and sanctioned their seizure of Izmir, Turkey's second-largest city. What the British really wanted was to win over the Greeks and turn their country into a reliable base in the heart of the unpredictable Islamic world, which not only possessed immense reserves of oil but separated them from India, the most precious jewel in the British crown.

The carriage was making no headway through the crowds, so Sultana Fatma decided to continue on foot with Zeynel in attendance. Selma was delighted. She would have been ashamed to sit back and watch all these people marching, marching as if they would never stop – as if they were already on their way to recapture Izmir from the Greeks.

Sultan Ahmed Square was filled to overflowing when they got there, but not a voice could be heard. Flags fluttering in the wind provided the only sound.

Suddenly, from the summit of the Blue Mosque, black-robed imams intoned the call to prayer: "Allah Akbar. . . ." Taken up by minaret after minaret, the cry came back like an echo from the city's seven hills: "Allah Akbar . . . God is the greatest. . . ." The very sky seemed to quake, rocked by the heartfelt prayer that issued from several hundred thousand throats: "Allah Akbar, protect us, O Lord!"

Selma could not see for the tears running down her cheeks. Whether choked with grief or speechless with joy, she did not know; never before had she been so deeply moved. She had the impression she was no longer Selma, but a part of this crowd, in which she felt herself melting, exploding, dying – yet she felt more alive than ever before.

Someone had mounted a makeshift rostrum. Selma, watching in a sort of dream, saw a slim young woman, unveiled and wearing a plain black dress. Her voice rang out across the square, conjuring up a picture of Izmir, that green and tranquil city where Greeks and Turks, despite their differences, had coexisted for centuries. It had taken years of war and foreign intrigues to turn its peaceful inhabitants against each other.

"Passions, my friends, can so easily be aroused by agitators. They burn down a church or murder a Muslim, and all the suspicion, age-old fear, the hatred we thought had been forgotten, renew with terrifying force. Those who recognize the malicious intent and try to avert disaster cannot make themselves heard – they fall silent for fear of being accused of cowardice or treason.

"Make no mistake, my friends: the seizure of Izmir is only a prelude to the dismemberment of Turkey. Venizelos lays claim to all the territories bordering the Aegean and all our islands – even to Istanbul, our capital city. What will be left of our country? An arid expanse in the middle of Anatolia, a wretched province under foreign domination – in other words, nothing!

"Are we going to submit? Answer me, my brothers and sisters: are we going to accept this sentence of death?"

Overcome with emotion, she stretched out her arms to the crowd. Like a peal of thunder, like the growl of some mighty beast, a deep-throated roar travelled from one end of the square to the other: "No, never! We shall save you, beloved, beautiful Turkey, Turkey our little bride, Turkey our mother's milky breasts, Turkey our ailing child. You have our word: we shall never let you die!"

"Who was that lady?" Selma asked, still red-eyed as the phaeton bore them back to the palace.

"That was Halidé Edib," her aunt replied, "a famous writer and ardent champion of women's rights. She certainly knows how to galvanize a crowd. It is a pity we do not have more men like her. . . ."

Selma, curled up in the corner of the carriage, thought hard. So a woman could do that, could she? Gradually, her face brightened: that was what she would be one day. Her country, her people – for them she would live and fight.

Selma had discovered her consuming passion.

CHAPTER 8

Selma had just returned from the demonstration when she passed her brother in the hallway.

"It's settled," she announced portentously. "We are all going off to fight the Greeks, even the women and children."

Haïri stared at her. He hadn't the least desire to go to war, but he was not about to admit it to a girl.

"When do we leave?" he inquired, in an offhand manner.

"Ssh! Nobody is supposed to know. The Sultan is talking it over with his ministers."

It was not a deliberate lie, she simply was anticipating a little. After what she had seen in Sultan Ahmed Square, she took it for granted that the Turks would set off to recapture Izmir within a matter of days. Resolutely, she hurried on ahead of Haïri to tell her father the news.

The Damad was in his Empire drawing-room, entertaining some former colleagues from the Ministries of Foreign Affairs and Finance. They were tickled to see Selma, who was a familiar figure in Haïri Bey's apartments. She often sneaked in to see him, being still young enough to escape the strict seclusion of the haremlik.

"Well, my little patriot," said her father, "how did your demonstration go?"

Selma, conscious that all eyes were on her, proceeded to tell him in minute detail. When she came to Halidé Edib's speech and her call to arms, the men started laughing.

"That meddling suffragette?"

"What about the women – did she ask them to march into battle with or without their veils?"

Selma subsided into hurt silence, but everyone had forgotten about her. The argument interrupted by her arrival resumed in earnest.

"The people are exhausted, I tell you! They will never fight. Do you know how many deserters there were in July 1918? Half a million! You cannot blame them – they were dying of hunger and disease, short of ammunition, even short of boots. The situation is no better today. The harvest has rotted underfoot – there is famine everywhere. I tell you, what matters is not racing off to recapture Izmir like some latter-day Don Quixote, but tending to the crops in the fields. If that is not done, there won't be any Turkey at all in a couple of years, you mark my words!"

"We backed the wrong horse, you have to admit," sighed a diplomat, looking very dapper in his "*bonjour*," the pearl-grey frock coat sported this year by every man of fashion. "So much for the invincible Germans! All we can do now is try to negotiate the best possible peace treaty. Going to war again is a mere fantasy. True courage calls for realism."

Selma listened intently. Her father and his friends must know the state of the country better than anyone, yet that crowd this afternoon had been itching for a fight. . . . Bewildered and weary, she curled up in an armchair and let the tide of conversation flow over her, mingled in her mind with voices chanting "Izmir, Izmir! Allah Akbar!"

Her drowsiness was suddenly dispelled by the sonorous voice of a short, stout gentleman who had just arrived on the scene.

"Have you heard the latest? His Majesty has sent Mustafa Kemal to Anatolia."

Selma opened her eyes. Everyone was looking stunned.

"To Anatolia? What for?"

"Officially to pacify the interior. There's still a lot of fighting going on – or banditry, to be more precise. The occupying powers have allowed our Greek citizens to keep their weapons, so they are holding Turkish villages for ransom. Turkish soldiers have taken to the hills and are doing the same to Greek villages." "What is more," the man grimaced at a young officer in the party, "your friend General Karabekir has gone mad. He is ignoring the armistice, refuses to demobilize, and has set up his headquarters at Erzurum with six divisions. The mountain people have joined forces with him, and so have those loyal to Enver Pasha and Talat. The upshot is, the British are furious. They are threatening to send troops to restore order."

"Can you see those little Brits operating in the Anatolian highlands?" someone exclaimed. "Our Turks would cut them to ribbons!"

"The Sultan is afraid," said the portly gentleman, who was an official from the Ministry of Defence, "that once foreign troops are in the interior, they will never leave. That is why he has personally undertaken to pacify the country. He may be head of state in name only, but he is still Commander of the Faithful. As such, he has promised to deal with the rebels himself."

Scepticism greeted this announcement.

"And the British have agreed?"

"They are prepared to let him try. They have no wish to get their own soldiers killed, it would not be popular back home. After all, the war is supposed to be over."

Selma had completely woken up during this talk on Mustafa Kemal, the Golden Rose who turned so many women's heads. All attention now, she did her best to follow what was being said.

"Exactly what powers has Kemal been given?" her father asked.

"The Sultan has appointed him inspector-general of the northern zone and governor of the eastern provinces. His authority is ill-defined, in other words, very extensive. Kemal is a good choice. With his heroic reputation, he is the only person capable of enforcing the decisions of the central government."

"Don't be so naive, my dear fellow," said a pallid-looking man, a senior court official who had shown no previous interest in the conversation. "Kemal is the worst choice His Majesty could have made. When we submitted a list of generals suitable for the job, we warned him that Kemal was an adroit and ambitious man who might take command of the rebels instead of putting them down. However, the Sultan was adamant."

"That is just what the British are afraid of," conceded the gentleman from the Ministry of Defence. "Their commander-in-chief, General Milne, is furious. Kemal's appointment was endorsed by his deputy while he was away. When he returned he tried to have it rescinded, but Kemal had already left. The commander even sent some torpedo boats chasing after him, but too late – the bird had flown." They all burst into laughter at the thought of the trick that had been played on the damn British.

"Just between ourselves, Mehmet Bey," said the pallid gentleman, "do you think His Majesty may have instructed Kemal to do something other than restore order? If so, it would be a dangerous move. In the event of a revolt, Article 6 of the armistice entitles the occupying powers to take permanent possession of Istanbul and abolish the sultanate."

Mehmet Bey sighed. "The Sultan is so secretive – who knows what goes on in his head? I can only tell you what I heard from his senior aide-de-camp. His Majesty's parting words to Kemal, spoken on the day Izmir was seized, were: 'Pasha, you have already done the state great service, but forget all that – it is past history. Nothing could be more important than the service you are about to render. Pasha, you can save the country!'"[1]

The army officer raised his eyebrows.

1 cf. Lord Kinross: *Atatürk*.

"What does 'save the country' mean? It could be taken two ways: either pacify Anatolia to prevent the occupying powers from stepping in, or rally the rebels there and take command of them yourself."

"The truth, I think, lies somewhere between the two," said Mehmet Bey. "I have the honour of sharing the same dentist as His Majesty, who makes a habit of confiding in the old torturer after his sessions in chair. Well, do you know what 'Tooth Pasha'[2] told me? He says our Padishah is keeping two irons in the fire: on the one hand, he is being very accommodating toward the Allies in the hope of obtaining favourable peace terms; on the other, he would not be averse to a rebellion in Anatolia. That is apparently why he picked Kemal Pasha. His Majesty wants to prove to the occupying powers that the Turkish people are not entirely at their mercy, and that they cannot impose any terms they choose. If the disturbances in Anatolia grow worse, they will be a valuable card in our hand at the conference table."

"What about the so-called sinews of war?" said the civil servant sarcastically. "Even a modest rebellion costs money, and no one is better placed than I am to know that our coffers are empty. Our civil servants have been on half pay for months now."

"Kemal is said to have been given a substantial sum in gold," Mehmet Bey confided, lowering his voice. "General Milne was astonished, knowing how close to bankruptcy we are – he is dying to discover where the money came from. I have no proof, but it's rumoured at court that His Majesty has secretly sold his entire stable of thoroughbreds to raise fifty thousand gold sovereigns for Kemal's war chest. . . ."

They helped themselves to more brandy while a manservant in a long blue kaftan circulated with cigars. Everyone was immersed in his own thoughts. It was a risky venture, to be sure, but worth chancing if only to spite General Milne, whose arrogance was becoming insufferable. Suddenly the gentleman in the pearl-grey frock coat sat up abruptly.

"But if Kemal has left for Anatolia, what of his plan to marry Sultana Sabiha!"

"Ah, that . . ." said Haïri Bey. He smiled faintly. "The Sultan has not said no, but, believe me, he will never say yes. He hasn't the slightest intention of giving his daughter to someone so addicted to the bottle and the opposite sex. In any case, he has been heard to say in private that there is nothing in the world he wants less than a second Enver Pasha dictating policy to him."

2 "General Tooth," Sultan Vahiddedin's nickname for his dentist.

"Poor Golden Rose," thought Selma as she returned to her room, "he will be terribly disappointed. And I was so hoping he would become one of the family. . . ."

Pensively, she started counting on her fingers. Only another five or six years, and she would be of marriageable age. Why shouldn't she. . . . Her cousin Vassip, whom she had always dreamed of marrying, had suddenly lost his appeal. Golden Rose was a far more attractive proposition. He was a great general, a hero! She would help him drive the enemy out of Turkey – she would mobilize the women of the country, she would be another Halidé Edib!

That night Selma fell asleep with a smile on her lips.

CHAPTER 9

Of all the women slaves who adorned Sultana Hatijé's palace, the loveliest by far was Gülfilis. Slim, dainty, and high-breasted, with eyes as blue as periwinkles and hair the colour of ripe corn, she was a Circassian beauty in the classic mould.

Orphaned at the age of eight, she had been purchased by a dealer who banked on selling her to the court at a vast profit, calculating that in a few years' time she would become one of the jewels of the imperial harem. He had reckoned without the revolution of 1909. Once Sultan Abdul Hamid had been deposed and his half-brother Reshad crowned in his place, the sultanate became a constitutional monarchy, and one of the first reforms enacted by the Young Turks, who were anxious to demonstrate their progressive ideas, was the abolition of slavery.

The harem doors were flung wide and families throughout the Empire informed that they could come and collect their daughters and sisters. Not many did so, nor were many young slaves prepared to exchange the gilded seclusion of a palace for the freedom of a miserable peasant shack. Accustomed to a life of luxury and refinement, they shuddered at the thought of the hard work and uncouth existence that awaited them there.

During the few months it took for life to resume its traditional rhythm, the slave-traders' guild grew anxious, and Bulent Agha, Gülfilis' fortunate owner, decided not to risk a direct approach to the imperial court. Being acquainted with the chief eunuch of Sultan Murad's eldest daughter, who had just remarried and moved into her new palace, he discreetly opened negotiations with him. They quickly agreed terms, each convinced that he had done the orphaned girl a great favour.

That was how Gülfilis came to enter Sultana Hatijé's service. She was far too pretty for anyone to dream of teaching her housework or ruining her eyesight by making her study mathematics, so the grand mistress of the kalfas decided to school her in music, singing, and the art of flower arrangement. In the course of time she became an expert at adorning the vases that graced the entire palace, and her skill as a harpist gained her a leading place in the haremlik's orchestra. At seventeen she was even more beautiful than the old dealer had foreseen.

The Sultana, whose pet she was, often eyed her thoughtfully. If she entered His Majesty's service she might well become one of his favourites, and possibly – who could tell? – one of his wives. On the other hand, she might fritter away her youth without ever being chosen, for the Sultan was an elderly man and, in these difficult times, preoccupied more with politics than with women. Yet keeping her here in this exclusively feminine environment would be an affront to nature. A creature as superb as Gülfilis, so obviously made for love, should be allowed to bear fruit. Hatijé resolved to find her a husband.

One morning, as she was leaving her room, Selma came across Gülfilis in tears. She tried questioning her, but the girl was sobbing too desperately to get a word out. Selma sat down beside her and held her hand until the sobs subsided a little and she wiped her eyes.

"The Sultana wants to marry me off," Gülfilis said mournfully.

Selma's nurse had often told her heartrending tales of arranged marriages. "You mean he is old and ugly?" she asked.

"Oh no, he's thirty and handsome – I saw him through the moucharabié."

Selma was puzzled for a moment. "I see," she said sympathetically, "so he is very poor, is that it?"

"No, he's well off – he has a good job at the Ministry of Finance. Your father, the Damad, recommended him to the Sultana personally, but. . . ." She started to cry again. ". . . I just don't want to marry. This is my home, my family. Why should I go to a stranger's house?"

Touched at this declaration, Selma took the girl in her arms.

"Don't be sad, Gülfilis, I shall have a word with Annéjim. I am sure she didn't mean to be unkind."

Like a knight preparing to do battle for his lady, she hurried to the Sultana's apartments.

Her mother was not alone. Squatting in front of her, on a carpet adorned with a pink motif, was Memjian Agha, the Armenian jeweller, with flat velvet boxes of every size spread out all around him.

"Come and help me, Selma," said the Sultana.

Selma adored jewellery. Her eyes lit up. Deciding to postpone the subject of Gülfilis, she went and stood at her mother's side.

"I am choosing a present for Sultana Sabiha," Hatijé told her. "The date of her wedding has been fixed at last."

Although Selma was delighted for Sabiha, whom she liked a great deal, she wondered how Golden Rose would greet the news when it reached Anatolia. For the lucky man was not Mustafa Kemal but, contrary to custom and tradition, Sabiha's cousin, an Ottoman prince.

The affair had caused a great stir at court: to everyone's scandalized delight, it was a genuine romance. Prince Omer Faruk was undeniably one of the Ottoman Empire's most eligible bachelors. Tall and blond, with clean-cut features and wide-set blue eyes, he possessed a style and elegance that every young man of good family vainly strove to emulate. A guards officer in the service of the Prussian emperor, Turkey's ally, he had fought on the Western Front. On returning to Istanbul from Germany he was appointed an aide-de-camp to the Sultan, and that was how he had met the lovely Sabiha.

It was love at first sight. Never a man to do things by halves, Omer Faruk informed his father, Prince Abdul Mejid, that he would either marry the Princess or commit suicide, and everyone knew that he meant it.

The Sultan did not, however, view the match with favour. Under a centuries-old rule designed to avoid the degeneracy afflicting certain European dynasties, members of the Ottoman family never intermarried. What was more, the two branches of the family had not been on the best of terms since the death of Sultan Abdul Aziz, whose children claimed that he had been secretly assassinated on the orders of the Mejid branch. Omer's passion for Sabiha thus had all the makings of a Turkish *Romeo and Juliet*.

For two months the court awaited the Sultan's decision with bated breath. Omer Faruk was Prince Abdul Mejid's only son. The father swallowed his pride and made repeated visits to the palace. The Sultan finally gave in. He wanted his daughter to be happy, but he also reflected that family unity was a desirable thing in troubled times, and that Sabiha's marriage to Omer would set the seal on a feud of over forty years' duration.

Surrounded by all the jewels she knew so well from having seen them worn by her mother, Selma could not make up her mind. She wanted Sabiha to have something really beautiful, but she knew that the young princess disliked the heavy pieces favoured by her elders. She eventually settled on an emerald necklace composed of four-leaved clovers sprinkled with diamonds representing drops of dew. With it went a tiara, earrings, and bracelets of the same design.

"A perfect choice," said the Sultana. "They will suit our Sabiha's delicate colouring admirably. And now, tell me which two sets you like the least."

After a moment's hesitation, Selma pointed to two of her mother's caskets. One of them contained a set of rubies and pearls, the other a long turquoise necklace with matching bracelets and an enormous ring.

"There you are, Memjian Agha," Hatijé said with a laugh. "I should have found it hard to decide, but the finger of innocence has given its verdict. Settle the details with Zeynel."

The jeweller stammered out a few benedictions, picked up the two caskets, and slid them deftly into a black leather briefcase. Then, with a profusion of flowery farewells, he took his leave.

Selma stared at his departing figure in disbelief.

"But, Annéjim, why did he take your jewels away – and where are the ones you have just bought?" Memjian Agha's visits, though lately not so frequent, had always been occasions of extravagance.

The Sultana drew her daughter close and looked at her gravely.

"I did not buy anything, Selma – in fact I have just sold the sets you picked out. What with the war and the occupation, everything has become so terribly expensive. We have sixty slaves to feed and clothe. I could dispense with half of them but where would they go? Many have been with me since childhood, and some grew up in my father's home. They have always been loyal to us: I do not have the heart to abandon them. That is why I sold those jewels. I have more than enough in any case."

"You mean we're poor, Annéjim?"

Selma was dismayed. She had seen pale-faced street urchins selling shoelaces, pins, and reels of thread displayed in cardboard boxes suspended from their necks. Mademoiselle Rose had told her they were "*petits pauvres*," so she had given them a few coins and hurried on, embarrassed by their sad, yearning glances at her pretty dress and well-tended curls. *She* would never be poor, she promised herself – no, never! Afterwards she consoled herself with the thought that people were born rich or poor just as they were born black or white. The world was divided up like that, and she, fortunately, was on the right side of the dividing line.

But now her mother's words had filled her with trepidation. When there were no jewels left, would she, too, be forced to sell pins on the street? The Sultana reassured her.

"No, silly, we are not poor, but there are more and more poor people all around us. That is why I have decided to organize a foukaramin chorbasi, a soup of the poor, from tomorrow onwards."

Selma had no idea what a soup of the poor was, but she did know that a big reception was due to be held at Dolmabahçé Palace tomorrow to celebrate the first anniversary of the Sultan's accession. She had just spent nearly an hour deciding which dress to wear.

"This soup thing, Annéjim," she said anxiously, "will it be before or after the party?"

"There will not be any party. His Majesty feels that festivities are out of place in a bankrupt country under foreign occupation. He has also cancelled the usual fireworks, illuminations, and gun salutes. The money that saves will help to alleviate a little suffering. From now on, only religious festivals are to be celebrated."

Selma hung her head in disappointment. She had been hoping to see her cousin Vassip. She did not want to hurt his feelings, but she felt she ought to tell him of her decision to marry Golden Rose.

"Annéjim," she said, suddenly remembering her original errand, "Gülfilis is very unhappy – she does not want to get married. Can't we keep her here with us?"

"You are the fourth person to raise the subject!" The Sultana sounded thoroughly exasperated. "I have decided to marry her off – her and another two or three of our prettiest slaves. You are too young to understand this, but you should know that a woman's happiness is in having a husband and children. Gülfilis will be given a decent dowry and may visit us as often as she pleases. In a few years' time she will be too old to make a good match. Besides, I may not be here to help her find a husband."

May not be here. . . . Why not? Why should the natural order of things have to change? Selma could not understand what her mother was getting at, but she thought it wiser not to persist. In any case, the Sultana had risen and was making for the hammam with a kalfa at her heels.

The following morning, in the teeth of an icy wind from the Black Sea, a handful of servants set to work outside the tall palace gates. Having slotted some wooden planks together, they placed them on trestles to form two makeshift tables and draped them with lengths of unbleached cloth. More servants arrived in single file, each with a tray on his head, and perched on each tray was an enormous pewter tureen. The tureens were then set out on the tables alongside baskets filled with thick slices of bread.

Word of the Sultana's generosity had spread like wildfire, and the six kitchen boys in charge of the soup had no sooner taken up their positions than the first customers timidly stepped forward. To avoid incidents the Sultana had given orders that men should be served at one table and women at the other. To her own surprise and that of Selma, who had been forbidden to attend the proceedings and was looking on from a balcony, there was no jostling or pushing, only a few anxious exclamations from latecomers fearful that the food would run out before their turn came. They were soon reassured to see that the empty tureens were regularly filled. The "soup" turned out to be a tasty meat and vegetable stew.

Istanbul's eternal beggars had showed up in force, but Selma also noticed a number of men in patched and faded uniforms. Demobilized nearly a year ago, since when they had drawn no pay, these unemployed veterans had become vagabonds roaming a country ruined by eight solid years[1] of war. There were also refugees from the Turkish interior, recognizable by their peasant costumes. They had fled their villages when these were sacked by gangs of Greek or Armenian nationalists bent on convincing the Allies that coexistence with the Turks was impossible.

Finally there were the new poor, identifiable by their scrupulously clean clothes and sheepish manner. These were craftsmen or minor employees who had earned a modest wage before the war. Now that they had lost their jobs because bankruptcy was rife and Turkey's few factories had been devastated, their savings were exhausted. Faced with inflationary price rises fuelled by the ubiquitous black market, they were compelled to depend on public charity. They were the ones whom Selma pitied most of all. Looking terribly ill at ease, they glanced in all directions to reassure themselves that no one they knew was there to witness their degradation.

All the food had been doled out and the servants were already dismantling the trestle tables when Selma saw a man and a little girl approaching hand in hand. The man, who was very tall, wore baggy trousers and a grey military tunic without insignia. Going up to one of the kitchen boys, he inquired in broken Turkish if there was not a piece of bread left.

"No, no," the boy replied without even glancing at him, "you're too late. Why didn't you turn up sooner? You'll have to come back tomorrow."

Selma saw the man shake his head and lean against the railings. He looked as if he was about to faint. Laboriously, he extracted a wad of ruble bills from his pocket.

"Please, it's for my little girl. She hasn't eaten for two days."

The kitchen boy regarded the rubles with a jaundiced eye. "What

1 Including the Balkan Wars and World War One.

do you expect me to do with those bits of paper?" he growled. "I told you, you're too late. Push off or I'll call the guards!"

The man turned pale at this indignity. Mustering what strength he had left, he straightened up and was about to walk off when a child's voice stopped him in his tracks.

"Wait!"

Selma came racing down the steps and across the forecourt. Crimson with rage, she snapped at the kitchen boy.

"Bring meat, and cakes, and cheese! At once, do you hear?"

The terrified boy disappeared in the direction of the kitchens. Only then did Selma turn to look at her protégés. The man was fine-featured, with blue eyes and a fringe of fair beard.

"Thank you," he said, smiling. "Permit me to introduce myself: Count Valenkov, captain of cavalry in the Czar's army. This is my daughter, Tanya."

Selma eyed the little girl curiously. They were much the same age, she guessed, but Tanya looked so frail and timid that she felt years older.

"I am Sultana Selma," she said. "Follow me."

Inside the grounds, a few yards from the gates, stood a white marble pavilion where visitors sometimes took their ease before entering the palace. They had scarcely sat down when the kitchen boy arrived, followed by a manservant laden with food enough for ten. The youngster was clearly anxious to apologize, but Selma glared at him, unwilling to forgive his heartlessness. Her mother always said the weak turned into tyrants once they got a taste of power. . . .

As if he had divined her thoughts, the officer said, "Don't punish the boy – he does not even understand why you are angry. After all, he was only obeying orders."

Selma gave a start. His merciful attitude struck her as the height of contempt. She had always heard that Russian aristocrats regarded their serfs as animals. . . .

"He understands perfectly well, monsieur," she replied stiffly.

They had resorted to French, which they all spoke fluently. The officer told how, when his regiment was wiped out in the Crimea, he had made his way back to St Petersburg, where his wife and daughter were waiting. By the time he got there his home was a charred ruin and his wife had been butchered by "the Reds." The child had survived because an old maidservant had hidden her in safety in her own home.

"It was a terrible shock. I was very much in love with my wife. I wanted to die, but the servant put my daughter in my arms and made me face reality. She disguised us in peasant clothes and that is how we made our long journey to the Turkish border."

Several times the count had almost been discovered, since his white hands and aristocratic manners seemed incongruous. But whether out of venality – he gave out hundreds of thousands of rubles during the trip – or simply because they were tired of all the bloodshed and felt vaguely sorry for the child, the peasants let them go.

He told of hunger, thirst, and fear, and as Selma listened, tears rose to her eyes. She no longer heard him, but instead saw herself in the palace she had grown up in, now in flames, surrounded by men shouting: "Long live the revolution!" She saw herself calling out to her mother and father, terrified, but no one answering. They were dead and now she was alone. She started running, running along an endless path with bullets whistling at her ears, all the time asking herself, even in the midst of terror, why they wanted to kill her.

She began to sob in earnest. Touched at her sympathy for him, the officer broke off. "You have a kind heart, my child," he said. "God will reward you."

Ashamed both of her self-centredness and that he should have mistaken her selfishness for compassion, Selma wiped her eyes.

"But you're not eating," she said, seeing that they had barely touched their meal.

"We have eaten so little in the past month, we have lost the habit."

"Then you must take it all with you."

She signed to the manservant who wrapped the food in white napkins and put it in a big wicker basket.

"What are you going to do now?" she asked.

"God will provide."

God? Selma pulled a little face. Rather than rely on God, it would be better, she decided, to consult her mother.

"Please wait here for a minute."

Sultana Hatijé, who was in her boudoir, gave Selma a frosty reception.

"Well, Princess, what is all this I hear about your entertaining strangers in the pavilion?"

"I was going to tell you, Annéjim," Selma said haltingly, "but they were so hungry. . . ." And she blurted out the whole story. "Oh, Annéjim, can't we help them?"

The Sultana's expression softened. "I would like to, but there are a hundred thousand Russian refugees in this city, and thousands of Turkish refugees are pouring in from Anatolia and the Aegean provinces every day. They have first claim on our resources. I am sorry, my child, I cannot do more than I am doing."

Selma was dumbfounded; her mother had never been known to refuse a charitable request. No doubt about it, things were going from bad to worse.

Silently, she kissed the Sultana's hand and ran to her room, where she picked out her prettiest dress, her shiniest patent leather shoes, and her big Ukrainian doll. Then she returned to the pavilion.

The little girl accepted Selma's gifts with such a sad, sweet smile that it wrung her heart.

Overcome by her inability to help, she stood behind the gates and watched Tanya and her father depart, hand in hand, as they had come.

CHAPTER 10

On the morning of 16 March 1920, the inhabitants of Istanbul awoke and looked out on their home in disbelief: in one night the city had been transformed into a vast military encampment. Armoured cars patrolled the streets and machine-guns covered every intersection. The police stations and police headquarters itself, the Ministries of War, Marine, and the Interior, the Officers' Club – all had been occupied. British soldiers and Gurkhas were bivouacking in the railroad station, in the customs houses, and along the Galata waterfront. Even the public parks and the environs of the Petits-Champs Theatre had been invaded by French infantrymen and squadrons of cavalry. A Senegalese regiment had surrounded the old Saray and armed detachments mounted guard outside all the palaces and town houses belonging to anyone important. Every street was under surveillance by four-man patrols consisting of a British policeman, a French gendarme, an Italian carabiniere, and a Turkish constable hobbling along after them. The smallest gathering was dispersed with swinging clubs while squads of military police carried out house-to-house searches and arrested Turks suspected of having links with the rebels in Anatolia.

"General Tim," Sir Charles Harington, the British commander-in-chief, had finally convinced the reluctant French and Italian authorities that it was time to snuff out the discreet but effective resistance of the population of Istanbul.

Arms and ammunition had been disappearing nightly from Allied depots, and Turkish officers and men were daily leaving the capital in a variety of disguises to swell the ranks of Mustafa Kemal's little army. The rebellious city would have to be subdued. The British high command having allegedly uncovered a plot to massacre all the Europeans in the city, it had been decided that Istanbul should be placed under "disciplinary occupation."

To dispel any doubt that his intentions were serious, General Harington plastered the walls of the city with posters on which the word "DEATH" figured prominently in bold black letters. Death to anyone who sheltered a rebel. Death for stealing weapons. Death to anyone who in any way assisted the outlaw Mustafa Kemal.

Sultana Hatijé's palace was in turmoil. All her menservants were sent to gather information. One by one they returned with ominous tidings: Allied troops were even ransacking tombs in search of arms; sixteen young brass bandsmen had been shot in the erroneous belief that they were soldiers; dozens of members of parliament who had been known for their nationalism had been arrested – among them Rauf Pasha, the former Minister of Marine, and Prince Said Halim of Egypt, an old family friend – and would doubtless be exiled to Malta. The police were also looking for Halidé Edib, whose patriotic writings and speeches were considered dangerously inflammatory.

Selma, who was listening attentively, had a vivid recollection of the beautiful young woman whose impassioned oratory had moved her to tears during the demonstration in Sultan Ahmed Square. For the first time, she felt a positive hatred for the foreigners who were lording it over her country.

A eunuch brought the latest newspapers. Every front page carried a communiqué issued jointly by the British, French, and Italian high commissioners: "Members of the so-called nationalist movement are attempting to thwart the good intentions of the central government. The Entente Powers have therefore been obliged to place Constantinople under temporary occupation." *How odd*, thought Selma, *to persist in using the Christian name for a town which had been known as Istanbul for five centuries!*

"Far from wanting to destroy the sultanate's authority, the Entente Powers want to reinforce it. Although they have no wish to take Constantinople from the Turks, any riots or massacres would be likely to modify this decision. A new Turkey is to be erected on the ruins of the old empire; everyone has a duty to obey the sultanate."

"Obey the sultanate?" Hatijé exclaimed, almost speechless with indignation. "What a farce! As if everyone does not know that the Padishah is the allies' hostage. He cannot lift a finger without their threatening to depose him and hand Istanbul over to the Greeks!"

Selma, who had never seen her mother so enraged, concluded that the situation must be grave. Perhaps her father would prove a source of greater enlightenment.

She found him in his usual haunt, the smoking room, with a handful of friends. They were all looking stunned. Their ministries had been occupied and a number of their colleagues arrested. Like the Sultana, Haïri Bey was being kept abreast of events by relays of servants. The latest one had just arrived with another list of arrests.

"Heavens," said someone, "I had no idea that *he* was a Kemalist too!"

"He may not bc, but the British are so furious at losing all those supplies, they suspect everyone."

"You cannot blame them. Guess what the Turkish sentries at the biggest depot in town told a British officer when asked to explain the disappearance of several ammunition boxes? They swore on the Koran that some goats had smashed the wax seals on the doors by butting them with their horns. I suppose the officer thought it pointless to inquire if the goats had eaten the ammunition as well."

Everyone guffawed.

"The fact remains that these latest measures are only adding to Kemal's popularity. After this morning's developments, I am almost tempted to back the madman myself."

"*Is* he so mad?" Haïri Bey narrowed his eyes. "His Majesty does not seem to share that opinion. The British even suspect our Padishah of encouraging Kemal – while stringing them along to gain time. Their Foreign Secretary, Lord Curzon, is supposed to have said recently that he had not realized how close relations were between the Sultan and Mustafa Kemal."

No one risked going out unless it was absolutely necessary. Selma, confined to quarters, seethed with impatience. It was always the same: whenever anything interesting happened they kept her shut up at home. There was no question of escaping supervision by going on a "cultural expedition" – the palace gates were firmly shut. Even the incessant stream of visitors that usually enlivened the haremlik, bringing its inmates their daily ration of news and gossip, had dried up. Life seemed to have come to a full stop.

Mademoiselle Rose vainly tried to distract Selma by offering to teach her some French songs, but the suggestion was ill received. Selma, having finally found someone to vent her spleen on, bluntly informed her that she detested the French, the British, and all these foreigners who restricted her movements.

One night, while she was irritably tossing and turning on her bed, she heard footsteps outside in the corridor. There was a "Ssh!" as they passed her room; then they receded. She jumped out of bed and opened the door an inch or two. Zeynel, lantern in hand, was walking ahead of a figure in a long overcoat. They were making for her mother's quarters! She consulted the pretty enamelled alarm clock the General Prince had brought her from Switzerland: half-past midnight! Who on earth could be calling on the Sultana at this hour?

With a pounding heart, she left her room and groped her way along the corridor, then paused, torn between curiosity and fear. Better not even think about what would happen to her if she were discovered.

On the other hand, how could *she*, who dreamed of being a heroine like Halidé Edib, tremble at the prospect of a scolding from her mother?

She drew a deep breath and set off again. At the end of the corridor, light was filtering through the brocade curtains. A low murmur of voices came to her ears as she drew nearer. Concealing herself in the curtains' ample folds, she parted them just enough to enable her to peer into her mother's boudoir. What she saw made her gasp.

A young man was sitting in an armchair beside the Sultana, whispering as he handed her various documents which she studied attentively. From time to time he raised his head and darted apprehensive glances in all directions. Selma took a closer look at him. He was not a member of the family, nor did he look like one of her father's friends, with his unshaven chin and crumpled overcoat. Who could he be, then, and what was he doing in her mother's apartments, which no man except her husband or a member of the family was entitled to enter?

Zeynel was standing in the corner with downcast eyes, looking uneasy. All at once the Sultana rose and, indicating the eunuch, told the stranger to go with him. Selma shrank back just in time. The two men walked past her and headed for the spiral staircase leading to the third floor. She heard the heavy attic door creak open. A few minutes later Zeynel reappeared, alone. Selma could not get over it: her mother was hiding a strange man in the women's wing of the palace!

Now the boudoir was in darkness; the Sultana must have retired to bed. Selma tiptoed to her room with a mixture of stupefaction and delight: something was happening at last in this dreary palace! Her over-excited brain buzzed with unanswered questions. If the man was in hiding he must have done something wrong, so why should her mother be protecting him? Would she tell her father about him? Baba would surely disapprove of her entertaining a stranger in his absence.

Haïri Bey had gone to spend a few days with friends at Üsküdar[1] on the eastern side of the Bosphorus. He went there more and more often these days – in fact Selma had heard the kalfas grumbling about his absences. Considering what was going on in the city, they said, it was not right to leave the Sultana all alone.

She looked at her clock again: only 2 A.M. How slowly the time was passing! She could not wait for the night to be over.

She was just dozing off when she woke with a start: someone was hammering on the front door. Running to the window, she saw three

1 Called Scutari by Europeans.

Turkish policemen gesticulating fiercely in the lantern-lit inner courtyard while the palace guards strove to pacify them. Then two eunuchs appeared. Selma caught the gist of what they were saying: the master of the house was away, they explained, and the policemen must leave at once because they were outside the women's quarters. The policemen regretted the intrusion but were undeterred: a dangerous bandit was reported to have entered the premises, and their orders were to carry out a search.

Very pale, the eunuchs stationed themselves in front of the door and prepared to defend their sanctuary. The guards hesitated: their job was to protect the palace, but not against representatives of the law.

"What is all this?"

The Sultana had appeared on the doorstep, her face half hidden by a dark veil. She looked the policemen up and down.

"What are you doing here?" she demanded. "Since when do Muslims try to enter a haremlik by force?"

Momentarily taken aback, the officer in command bowed.

"I couldn't regret this more, Sultana, believe me, but a criminal was seen entering your home and the Grand Vizier, Damad Ferid, has ordered us to search it."

The Sultana smiled disdainfully.

"That puppet? How dare he! No one gives me orders except His Majesty. Bring me a warrant signed by the Padishah and I will let you in, otherwise not."

The officer looked disconcerted. "But, Sultana. . . ."

"Say no more, Captain, it's useless. This is a matter of honour." Then, seeing him hesitate, she turned to one of the palace guards. "Your revolver!"

Selma, watching from her balcony, saw the policemen reach for their guns, but before she could cry out her mother spoke again.

"Do not be afraid," she said sarcastically. "I would never shoot a Turkish soldier, but of one thing you can be certain: you enter this haremlik only over my dead body."

They stared at her aghast as she weighed the revolver in her hand.

"The choice is yours, gentlemen," she pursued with a cold little laugh. "You can either incur Damad Ferid's wrath or risk incurring His Majesty's when he learns what you have driven me to do."

A glint of admiration appeared in the officer's eye. Seldom had he met a man with the moral fibre of this woman. "My apologies, Sultana," he said. "I know our man is in there, but I won't trouble you further tonight, even if it costs me my captaincy."

Then, clicking his heels, he disappeared into the darkness.

The next morning Selma hurried to her mother's room. The Sultana was seated at her dressing table, idly leafing through *Chiffons*, the celebrated Paris fashion magazine, while a slave brushed her hair.

"Did you sleep well, Annéjim?"

"Perfectly, my dear, and you?"

"Not very well. I heard some funny noises."

If Selma thought her mother would confide in her, she was wrong. Having said "Really?" in a tone of complete indifference, the Sultana reimmersed herself in the magazine. Selma lingered on for another few minutes. Then, realizing that it was hopeless, she left the room in annoyance. So her mother didn't trust her. She thought her incapable of keeping a secret. She treated her like a baby even though she was nine years old! Very well, she would find out the truth for herself.

It was eleven o'clock, but the sheikh who instructed her in the Koran had cancelled his daily lesson. She had two whole hours of freedom ahead of her. She told Mademoiselle Rose, who was eager to fill this gap in her schedule, that she would devote it to studying the Islamic scriptures in her room. As soon as the governess had gone, she slipped out and sneaked along the deserted corridor to the stairs that led to the attic. She tiptoed up them, holding her breath, but the more care she took the more the wooden treads seemed to creak.

In front of the attic door, she hesitated. Should she knock? It would be more polite; but did one have to be polite to a criminal? In the end she coughed loudly and pushed the door open as slowly as possible.

The attic was too dark for her to be able to distinguish anything clearly. She was groping her way forward when a muffled voice made her jump.

"Stand still or I'll fire!"

As her eyes became accustomed to the gloom, she made out the dim figure of a man crouching in a distant corner. He was pointing a revolver at her, but his hand was as shaky as his voice had been. Quite obviously, he was even more scared than she was. Cheered by this realization and convinced that he would not pull the trigger, Selma magnanimously reassured him.

"Don't be frightened, I won't hurt you."

The man stared at her. Then, as the absurdity of the situation dawned on him, he started to laugh. He laughed so much Selma thought he would never stop, his body racked with convulsive little hiccups of mirth. Laughter was the last thing she had expected from a wanted man. It seemed misplaced, to say the least.

"Who are you?" he asked, when he finally caught his breath.

Added to the man's insensibility was this obvious lack of breeding! How could he address her in such a familiar manner? Selma drew herself up, saying cunningly:

"I am the daughter of Sultana Hatijé, whom you called on last night."

Instead of being deflated by the revelation that she had seen everything, he greeted it with a malicious chuckle.

"So you were spying on us, eh? I never knew little princesses could be so nosy."

Selma bristled. Their conversation was not going according to plan. Instead of being the accuser she had become the accused. Grown-ups were insufferable – they thought they could treat children any way they liked. It was time to take the situation in hand again. She put on her sternest look.

"The police are after you. Why? Who are you?"

"So I'm under interrogation, am I?" The man smiled even more broadly and his eyes lit up. "I'll be delighted to answer your questions, Princess, but won't you please sit down?" He ceremoniously indicated a heap of old rags on the floor beside him.

He is poking fun at me, thought Selma, but now she could not very well reproach him for being polite. Anyway, she did not want to annoy him – she was too eager to hear his story. He scrutinized her as she gingerly perched on the heap of rags.

"You've turned into quite a pretty little girl," he said. "Odd, considering what an ugly baby you were."

That was too much! Blushing furiously, Selma searched around for a suitably scathing retort. The man appeared not to notice her irritation.

"I've known you since you were a year old," he went on. "I used to be aide-de-camp to your uncle, Prince Selaheddin. After his death I was posted to the Caucasian front. I spent three hellish years fighting a war that wasn't even ours. . . ."

He was muttering now and Selma could hardly understand him. She had the impression that he had forgotten she was there. "We've been defeated and now our enemies want to divide up the empire. They want to wipe us off the map as if Turkey were a monster and they had to crush it completely so it won't rear its ugly head again. But they're making a big mistake. They're going too far and they're going to force us into the last battle we may as well fight, since we've nothing to lose."

Why, oh why, thought Selma, *can't grown-ups ever give a simple answer to a simple question.*

"The police are looking for you," she said crisply. "What have you done?"

The man studied her for a moment. She was so young, how could she possibly understand? "Have you heard of Kemal Pasha?" he asked.

"Of course I have." What did he think she was, an idiot?

"Well, I'm one of his officers. My job is to contact other officers who want to join the rebel army in Anatolia. I help them to get out of Istanbul – I tell them the best disguises to use and the safest routes to take – but someone gave me away. Yesterday the British surrounded the house where I was hiding. I managed to escape across the roofs. Then I remembered Prince Selaheddin's telling me what a patriot your mother was. I didn't think the police would dare to invade a sultana's home, but I was wrong. Your mother managed to get rid of them last night, but they'll be back – they know I'm here. Look."

He led Selma to a skylight and pointed. A dozen policemen were stationed in front of the haremlik.

"There are just as many outside the other entrance," he said. "They're waiting for the order to move in. I must leave here as soon as possible. The question is, how?"

Some hours later a group of women in black charshafs emerged from the haremlik and set off for the local market carrying big wicker baskets. Too busy discussing where to find the freshest vegetables and the ripest fruit even to glance at the policemen in front of the palace, they took the first turning on the right and continued on their way, still jabbering away.

"Allah gave women tongues as long as the Devil's tail and a brain the size of a chickpea," one of the policemen said scornfully.

The laughter that greeted this sally was all the more contemptuous because the men were in a foul mood. They had spent the whole morning vainly watching every exit, chilled to the bone by an icy wind. No one had left the place except a flock of old magpies. How much longer would they have to remain here? A lot longer yet, in all likelihood, for the situation was a touchy one. The strong-willed Sultana was threatening to create a scandal, which the Allied Commander was anxious to avoid. But how could they give way without making a laughing stock of themselves? Teeth chattering, the policemen brooded on the complexity of the situation.

Out of sight by now, the women paused in a doorway and clustered around the oldest of them, discreetly shielding her from the gaze of any male passerby as they helped her to adjust her charshaf. Suddenly, the veiled figures underwent a convulsion and a man emerged in their midst. Without appearing to notice him, the women picked up their baskets and walked off, laughing and talking. The man crossed the street and was swallowed by the crowd.

The pavement was empty again. But on the ground in front of the porch lay a small pile of black cloth – the charshaf of the old woman.

Three weeks later Selma received a mysterious card. It read: "The attic rat is back in his hole again, thanks to his guardian angels."

Bubbling over with delight, she ran off to tell her mother the news. The Sultana raised her eyebrows.

"Who would have sent you such a strange little note? I cannot imagine. Neither can you, of course."

She gave her daughter a meaningful glance. Selma's cup of joy was full; they shared a real secret now – a secret which, if the enemy's threats were to be believed, could have sentenced them both to death. Thinking of Halidé Edib, who had gone off to join the nationalist rebels in Anatolia, Selma fancied that her heroine was smiling at her.

CHAPTER 11

The phaeton lurched and jolted along the dirt road, threatening to overturn at any moment, but the coachman righted it every time by hauling on the reins or plying his whip.

Selma, bouncing around on the seat beside her Aunt Fatma, laughed delightedly. This was a real adventure – even more fun than the merry-go-rounds installed in the palace grounds during Bairam. They were a long way from the centre of Istanbul. If they had an accident in these sparsely populated suburbs they might have to spend the night out here, and possibly to ask for shelter in one of the tiny cottages Selma had only seen from afar but always dreamed of entering. Whenever she tried, during one of their outings together, to steer Mademoiselle Rose in the direction of some poor neighbourhood that intrigued her the governess bit her head off.

"What is it you are so eager to see? Filth, hardship? There's nothing funny about those, I assure you!"

Selma had been taken aback by the old maid's uncharacteristic vehemence. What *did* she want to see? She did not really know. She simply had a feeling that it was there, in the poverty she dreaded so much, far from the luxurious cocoon in which she was growing up, that in spite of everything people really *lived*. Peering through the windows of a closed carriage while out driving, she had often watched half-naked urchins boisterously playing tag and envied them their rough-and-tumble games. They looked a lot more interesting than her cousins – as if they breathed a different and more stimulating air.

When she tried to explain this feeling to Gülfilis, with whom she had become friends, the young slave looked thoughtful and shook her head. "You're mistaken, little Sultana," she replied. "It isn't wealth that prevents one from living life to the full, it's poverty."

Selma remained unconvinced. If Gülfilis was right, why should the eyes of the poor children seem so much more intense than those of her wealthy playmates?

The phaeton was now driving along a paved road shaded by cypresses. Selma resigned herself to the fact that they would not have an accident after all, at least not today. They were nearing their destination, and she was consumed with curiosity. This would be her first sight of thc monastery and shrine her aunt had visited every week for years. For if Hatijé was the intellectual of the three sisters and Fehimé the artist, Fatma was the mystic. As a young girl, she used to spend whole days meditating on the Islamic scriptures, but it was her marriage that had confirmed her religious leanings. Her husband, Refik Bey, was a member of the fraternity of "whirling dervishes" founded in the thirteenth century by Jelaleddin Rumi. The fraternity being open to women as well, Fatma had joined it as a matter of course.

Mystical orders had abounded in Turkey since time immemorial, she explained to Selma. Their disciples were called "Sufis," after the "suf" or white woollen robe they wore to symbolize their purity and renunciation of the world. Not that this renunciation precluded action – far from it. Fatma told Selma of the celebrated janissaries, the soldier monks who had for centuries formed the backbone of the Ottoman army. Sultan Mahmud had exterminated them in the last century because, like the Templars in France, they had become more soldiers than monks, so powerful that they constituted a threat to the throne.

Selma listened attentively. Though not too clear on the meaning of mysticism, she was flattered that Sultana Fatma should think her grown-up enough to explain it to her. In any case, she found it more interesting than her daily dose of the Koran. She did not know Arabic and the old Sheikh's monotonous voice was soporific. But there was no escape: the sacred book had to be read in the original tongue, just as it had been transmitted by Allah to the Prophet Mohammed, for, according to tradition, the weight of the holy Word transcended human understanding, which was limited.

Selma had always longed to see the famous whirling dervishes, who prayed while dancing. Dancing was indecent, she had always been told, and she would never forget the day when her mother caught her trying to learn belly-dancing in the company of a young slave girl. She had paid for it with three days' confinement to her room. . . . Obviously the dervishes were not going to belly-dance! She almost giggled at the thought. On the other hand, the polkas and quadrilles the princesses performed together were considered quite proper. Knitting her brow, Selma tried to picture the holy men dancing the Koran to the rhythm of a polka, and mysticism suddenly quite appealed to her.

The carriage drove through a wrought-iron gateway and pulled up in a shady garden. The Sheikh's modest wooden house was smothered in ivy. In a small cemetery beyond it Sultana Fatma pointed out the tombs of the Sheikh's predecessors, a dozen-odd graves surmounted by finely carved stone turbans. They paused to recite the prayer for the dead, then walked on down a path flanked by rose bushes. At the end stood the tekké, an elegant stone building with a green cupola. This was where the ceremonies took place. Muffled up in her charshaf, Sultana Fatma swathed Selma in a long veil and led her to the women's entrance, a door at the corner of the sanctuary. They climbed some narrow stairs to a circular gallery enclosed by lattice work where white-veiled women of all ages were at their devotions, each on her own little prayer mat.

Selma, wrinkling her nose at the fusty smell of stale sweat, was looking around for an empty space when a pudgy woman bustled up and kissed her aunt's hand. This was the Sheikh's wife, who insisted on conducting the princesses to a box reserved for persons of quality. Sultana Fatma tried to dissuade her, upset to find that considerations of rank still counted in such a place, but her hostess looked uncomprehending. Rather than hurt her feelings, the Sultana accepted their enforced seclusion with a sigh.

With her face glued to the moucharabié, Selma gazed down into the body of the rotunda, whose walls were punctuated by pilasters of carved wood. All around it, behind slender balustrades, the faithful had assembled for prayer. The larger open space in the centre was bounded by the mihrab, the empty niche – hollow like an unfulfilled desire – that indicated the direction of Mecca.

Suddenly the hush intensified: the dervishes had appeared, wearing tall felt hats and white robes under their black cloaks. The Sheikh brought up the rear. Together they bowed before the mihrab while a youth slowly intoned a love poem of great antiquity in honour of the Prophet. There followed a pure, crystalline melody improvised on the flute with cymbal accompaniment.

The Sheikh rapped on the floor and the dervishes stepped forward. Slowly they circled the hall three times, each circuit representing one of the three routes to God: the path of Knowledge, the path of Intuition, and the path of Love. Then, throwing off their black cloaks, emblems of the tomb, they stood forth in all their luminous splendour and began to rotate, right hand raised heavenward to receive divine grace, left hand pointing downwards to transmit that grace to the world.

At that point the Sheikh joined the dance, and its pace quickened. He was the sun, radiant with knowledge, and the dervishes revolved around him like planets communing with the law of the universe. Faster and faster they spun to the limpid strains of the ney, the reed flute believed to impart divine mysteries to those with ears to hear. They were abandoning their entire being and, at the same time, striving for mystical ecstasy – for union with the supreme Reality.

Selma watched them, spellbound by the music and the sight of their whirling white robes. She felt an overpowering urge to join them and lose herself in the magical dance, but her place was behind the moucharabié. Suddenly she wanted to cry: something essential was happening there, from which she was excluded. She looked around her helplessly. God was certainly not up here in this stuffy gallery: he was, she knew, down there among the men who were dancing, intoxicated with joy, in the rays of the setting sun.

Blinded by tears, she gripped the screen hard. They had no right – no right to prevent her from breathing! No right to exile her from life! Till now she had accepted that the streets of Istanbul, its crowds and gardens, had been stolen from her, but today she felt that God Himself was being stolen from her! She almost choked with resentment, unhappiness, frustration. . . .

The music sank to a murmur, the whirling planets slowed, the white robes subsided like wilting flowers: the ceremony was over.

The Sheikh had retired to his room to receive his disciples. To Selma's great surprise, women were admitted with their faces uncovered. The master held that no impure thoughts could intrude upon the atmosphere of joyful innocence engendered by the sacred dance.

Sultana Fatma propelled her niece toward the holy man, who was relaxing on some low cushions while a disciple respectfully dabbed the sweat from his brow. Small and thin, he looked wholly unimpressive. There was no hint of the aura that had seemed to emanate from him during the ceremony. He was just a very ordinary man in a cheaply furnished room, surrounded by disciples with sheeplike faces.

Selma felt cheated, but her aunt signalled to her to go and kiss the sheikh's hand. The girl had to fight to overcome her distaste. After all, she had kissed so many hands in her life: rough, smooth, sinewy or soft, perfumed, perspiring, tight-fisted or generous, sensual, wicked, weak or strong; hands she liked and respected, others she would have preferred to bite. Somehow, though, she felt that paying homage to the Sheikh would be a form of deceit far worse than the social hypocrisies in which she had been schooled from infancy.

The hand awaited her on a velvet cushion, slim, white, and slightly wrinkled. Selma was just bending down when the hand turned over to reveal the pink palm. Disconcerted, she glanced at her aunt.

"Kiss the master's palm," she whispered, "it is an honour – a sign that he has opened his heart to you."

Selma brushed the hand with her lips. Raising her head, she was suddenly struck by the brilliant intensity of the old man's gaze. His eyes seemed so luminous that she could not tear her own eyes away. The rest of the room had gone dark. She felt afraid.

She straightened up with an effort, swaying a little, and clung to her aunt's arm. Sultana Fatma, whom she dimly discerned through a kind of haze, had noticed nothing. But *had* anything happened?

The Sheikh was now regarding her with the benevolent smile of an indulgent, understanding grandfather. He cordially invited her to join two or three other children on a small divan beside him. Sultana Fatma beamed with pleasure at her niece's reception. The master reserved the places near him only for those in whom he sensed a genuinely spiritual quality.

The room had gradually filled with visitors. They all seemed to know each other, judging by their cheerful, uninhibited conversation. Suddenly, without warning, the door opened and four uniformed Turkish officers came in. The others stood aside to let them pass, and Selma was astonished to recognize them as four of the dancers who had been whirling around the sanctuary only minutes before. Having kissed the Sheikh's hand, they sat down on some cushions just in front of him.

The devotees engaged in a lively debate on points of doctrine while the Sheikh's wife, assisted by a maidservant, plied them with yogurt and sweetmeats. One young man expressed surprise at the existence of evil in a world created by a god of infinite goodness. Various explanations were advanced. The officers shuffled around uncomfortably until one of them could contain himself no longer.

"The origin of evil?" he exclaimed. "Is that the real problem? The fact is, evil exists in our midst. What's more, it enjoys the backing of our supreme religious authority, the new Sheikh ul-Islam!"

Everyone had fallen silent and was staring at him.

"Our country is in the hands of the infidels, and our Sultan Caliph, leader of the Muslim world, is their hostage. Isn't it our first duty as believers to release him, liberate Turkey and end the Christian domination of Islam?"

He looked at the Sheikh, who nodded gravely.

"True, my son. That is our first duty."

"In that case," the officer went on, "why has the Sheikh ul-Islam publicly condemned the nationalist struggle led by Mustafa Kemal? Why has he issued that disgraceful fetva[1] proclaiming us traitors and

1 Religious decree having the force of law.

commanding the people to take up arms against us?"

The silence had become oppressive. All eyes turned to the Sheikh, who sighed.

"You say our Sultan is not a free agent, and you're right, but I am sure the same applies to the Sheikh ul-Islam."

"He could at least have kept his mouth shut," the officer said angrily.

"Yes, he could have been more. . . ." The Sheikh hesitated. "More courageous, let us say. But perhaps, like many of our fellow countrymen, he feels that the nationalist cause is hopeless, and that it will only increase the severity of the peace terms imposed on us."

"We shall win, master. We have no choice!"

The oldest of the officers turned and addressed the room.

"Ever since the so-called disciplinary occupation of Istanbul, recruits have been flocking in from all over the country. Even women and girls have left their families to tend our wounded, and some are daily risking their lives by carrying messages or smuggling ammunition to us in their babies' clothing. There are also the patriots who house, feed, and shelter us all along the lines of communication between Istanbul and our headquarters at Sinop. They include the inmates of numerous sufi monasteries, which the occupying powers would never dream of searching." The officer smiled and bowed to the Sheikh. "They are a great source of moral support, master, as you know."

Selma could not believe her ears. So this was one of the centres of nationalist resistance! These whirling dervishes, these humble devotees, this Sheikh with the piercing eyes – they were all . . . she searched for the word she had heard only yesterday from one of her father's friends . . . yes, that was it: "conspirators." It had a daring and heroic ring. Were her Uncle Refik and Aunt Fatma conspirators too? Now that she knew the secret of the sanctuary, did she also qualify for that enviable title? Her spine tingled with delight: life had suddenly become enthralling.

Her train of thought was interrupted by the arrival of a servant who announced that the boxes had been loaded on to hay wagons and the officers' disguises were ready.

"Excellent," said the Sheikh. He turned to the four men. "You will leave at midnight, when the sentries are less alert. A dervish will show you the safest route."

Selma listened as if in a dream. "Boxes" must mean arms and ammunition, and the men beside her were real, live heroes bound for the front! She eyed them admiringly. How splendid they looked!

With these she felt victory was certain.

Conversation resumed as if nothing out of the ordinary had happened. The officers laughingly recounted how arms were being spirited away to Anatolia under the very noses of the British.

"French and Italian soldiers are helping us too. They are furious because the British have grabbed all the spoils of victory for themselves and their Greek protégés. Izmir, for example, which they have given to the Greeks, was promised to the Italians. As for the French, it is dawning on them that the British have not only seized the lion's share, notably Iraq and its oil; they now want to control the whole of Turkey and leave the French with only the province of Cilicia. It seems Clemenceau is so furious that he is studying ways of covertly supporting Kemal. He is determined not to let the British dominate the Middle East. The result is the soldiers obligingly shut their eyes when we raid their arms depots at night. One of the French functionaries has even gone so far as to let us know which nights the sentinels would just happen to be away from their posts."

"But tell us," asked someone, "how are the arms and ammunition transported to the Anatolian side of the Bosporus?"

"By night," one of the officers replied, "in boats lent us by the caique-owners' association. They help us tremendously, even though they are nearly all Armenians."

"What is so surprising about that?" demanded a man with a bushy white beard. "We still have plenty of Armenian friends, especially in Istanbul. The two communities have happily coexisted there for centuries. They know very well that the 1915 massacres in the east were partly the result of Kurdish tribes laying claim to the same lands as the Armenian peasants. But needless to say, since the Ottoman Empire had to be destroyed, the European press played it up as genocide ordered by Istanbul. In fact, it was a deportation order, which was in itself inhuman enough, considering the toll it took on human lives, including women and children."

"But why were they deported?" an adolescent asked, reddening at his own audacity.

"Do you think governments take such measures in wartime just for the fun of it?" the old man said indignantly. "The Armenians were living in a strategic zone along the Russian border. The Armenian extremists, let us say nationalists – for after all what they wanted was independence and that is what the Russians promised them – were collaborating with the Russian armies, against the Turks. Our eastern border was a sieve! That is why Talat Pasha ordered that tragic deportation."

The group fell silent, each lost in his own thoughts. Then the Sheikh's hoarse voice broke in. "You are an optimist, Jemal Bey. The truth is, most Armenians support the occupying powers because they hope they will give them independence. They are deluding themselves, poor things. The Allies are exploiting them. They will drop them as soon as they have no further use for them."

Selma followed the discussion intently. The Armenian drama, which Mademoiselle Rose had alluded to one day, touched her especially because one of her best friends, the granddaughter of a vizier, was Armenian. She had tried to ask her mother to explain the situation to her, but as soon as she had begun to speak the eyes of the Sultana had filled with tears. Selma had been overwhelmed: it was the first time she had ever seen her mother cry.

"Oh, Annéjim, please forgive me," she had muttered, kissing her hands and slipping away, and she had made up her mind never to bring up the subject again.

Only today did she begin to understand that something terrible had happened in her country, something nobody ever talked about. When she was small she used to bury the objects she had broken, thinking that would take care of the problem. Now she realized that adults sometimes acted like children.

The maidservant came around with a trayful of cups containing a honey-coloured infusion of herbs from the monastery garden, known as "the beverage of serenity." But the face of the Sheikh had clouded over.

"One hears it said that Mustafa Kemal is a friend of the Bolshevik government, and that he himself may be a communist. Is that true?"

One of the officers smiled sardonically.

"Kemal is no more communist than I am. Egalitarian ideas leave him cold, I assure you. If he courts the Russians, it's only because he needs their help. We're short of money and military supplies. Well, the Soviet government has undertaken to send us sixty thousand rifles, a hundred trucks, and two million pounds sterling in gold. To save the caliphate with those atheists' gold would be quite a coup, you have to admit!"

Everyone laughed except the Sheikh, who still was not satisfied.

"The Bolsheviks are shrewd," he insisted. "They are trying to convince the Muslims of Russia that communism and Islam share the same ideals. As proof they cite certain verses from the Koran to the effect that all men are equal, that the earth belongs to God alone, and that its fruits belong to those that tend the soil. They have already contaminated the north of Persia, where certain mullahs have started to adopt their subversive ideas, and it seems that the same nonsense is being disseminated in Anatolia by sheikhs close to Kemal Pasha." His tone became stern. "Inform the general from me that no Sufi fraternity will continue to support him, even to save Turkey, if he allows communist ideas to infect our people."

"Never fear, master. If the communists acquire too much influence, I am sure that Kemal Pasha will be the first to exterminate them."

Nodding contentedly, the Sheikh sipped his "beverage of serenity." It was growing late, and no one had yet dared to ask the question uppermost in everyone's mind. At last, the young officer who had castigated the Sheikh ul-Islam took the plunge.

"Tell us, Master, what do you see in your dreams? Are we going to win?"

The Sheikh seemed lost in thought – in fact Selma wondered if he had heard the question at all. It was quite a while before he spoke.

"The struggle will be a long one," he replied in a subdued, weary voice. "Turkey will put the infidels to flight, only to be defeated by them."

A murmur ran around the room.

"Please explain, Master. What do you mean?"

"That is all I know. Turkey will win the military victory, but this victory will mark the beginning of our spiritual domination by Europe. . . ." The Sheikh broke off, looking exhausted.

"But in that case," said one of the officers, "are we right to leave for the front?"

The old man sat up and shook his head impatiently.

"Why ask? Your present duty is to liberate the country at all costs, but a few decades from now our children and grandchildren will have to wage a different kind of war against the foreigners – a war of even more vital importance. . . ."

Sultana Hatijé and her sister Fehimé were arguing fiercely when Selma and her aunt got back to the palace after midnight. The Sultana was incensed that her sister had been attending functions at the French embassy.

"You have no shame!" she snapped. "They are occupying us, or had you forgotten? How can you play the belle of the ball on enemy premises?"

"In the first place, my dear, I am not the only member of the family to go there," Fehimé retorted. "Some of our princes are in and out of the French salons all the time. Where is the harm in it, anyway? Will

Turkey be liberated any sooner if we all live like hermits? Fatma's hobby is praying, mine is dancing. If you and she do any more to benefit the country than I do, I would like to know what it is."

"*We are* conspirators," said a little voice.

Three pairs of eyes converged on Selma. She was so alarmed by her own audacity, she could have bitten her tongue off. Fehimé surveyed the others with a mocking smile.

"Conspirators, are you? That is wonderful! Well, *I* conspire too, believe it or not, and a sight more effectively than the rest of you put together: I do it by diplomacy. I prove to the French authorities who send off daily reports to Paris that the Turks are civilized people and friends of their country, that we regret our past mistakes and our disastrous alliance with Germany in particular, and that very shortly, when we take up the reins of government again, we will be France's most loyal allies!"

Selma wavered – her aunt's line of argument sounded quite convincing – but Sultana Hatijé shrugged her shoulders.

"The French will do whatever they believe to be in their own best interests, Sister. A smile from you will not sway them either way. On the other hand the Turkish people, who see you dancing with their oppressors, may some day call you to account – you and the entire family!"

CHAPTER 12

"Congratulations, my dear, His Majesty has taken a firm stand for once. He has gone and sentenced Kemal to death – Kemal the national hero, the only man to reject the arrogant demands of the occupying powers and rebuild a fighting army! Incredible, isn't it? One would have thought the Sultan more likely to decorate him, but no, he only listens to his brother-in-law, and Damad Ferid is a lackey of the British. It is hard to tell whose interests our government is trying to serve – Britain's or Turkey's."

Sultana Hatijé paled under this verbal onslaught. Her husband had been nagging her for weeks as if he considered her personally responsible for the sovereign's actions. Just what did he want? That she disavow the Sultan? He knew she would never do that, not from blind devotion to the imperial family, but because she was convinced that the Padishah, a shrewd and intelligent man, was playing a double game: the condemnation of Kemal, who was hundreds of miles away and safely out of reach, was a purely symbolic act, just as the caliphate's army, dispatched from Istanbul to fight the Kemalists, was merely a band of undisciplined volunteers whose first few resounding victories had been followed by an unbroken string of defeats. All these measures were so much dust in the eyes designed to keep the British at arm's length. Of course the Sultan would be better off without his grand vizier – he had seen through his sister's husband long ago – but Damad Ferid had been wished on him by the British authorities.

Hatijé, who considered it beneath her dignity to seem stung by her husband's barbed remarks, managed to control her temper.

"Do you know what Sultana Sabiha told me when I lunched with her yesterday?" she began. "When Damad Ferid was recalled to office, she went to see the Sultan. 'Father,' she said, 'I just do not understand – you were so pleased to see him go only six months ago.' 'Ah, Sabiha,' His Majesty replied, 'if you only knew . . . I can do absolutely nothing about it.'"

"I know your uncle is powerless," Haïri Bey answered, "but he could at least disown that puppet government of his."

Selma, curled up in an armchair in the corner of her mother's boudoir, had never seen her father get so heated about politics. In the old days, he had always been the first to laugh his friends out of their political arguments. She had the uncomfortable feeling that his criticism of the Sultan was just a way of getting at his wife. Selma glanced at her mother: the Sultana was looking her husband steadily in the eye.

"Haïri, do you really believe that a sovereign has to justify his actions? In my view, the Padishah is keeping quiet so as to allay the enemy's suspicions and give Kemal time to build up his army. The strength of that army will be our principal bargaining counter at the peace conference. The Allied powers do not want to go to war again. If they are confronted by effective resistance in Anatolia, they will have to moderate their demands."

Haïri Bey responded with a sullen shrug. "You have an answer for everything as usual. The fact remains, the Sultan's conduct is inexcusable."

The Sultana looked at him contemptuously. "But, my dear, if you really feel so strongly, why don't you go and join Kemal Pasha in Anatolia? It would give you a chance to demonstrate your courage and patriotism."

There was a sharp crack: the Damad's well-manicured hands had snapped his slender ivory cane in two. He tossed its remains at the Sultana's feet and strode from the room without a word.

In the heat of the moment they both had forgotten Selma. She shrank even deeper into her armchair. God, how she hated these scenes between her parents, which were becoming more and more frequent. If only they could really argue, but their chill sarcasm was worse than any rowdy quarrel. It seemed to her that a wall was growing up between them, higher and higher every day. She was not interested in knowing which of them was in the right. She only wanted them to stop tearing each other apart – tearing *her* apart.

On the western side of the Bosphorus, Istanbul sloped gently down to the Golden Horn in an alternation of carved wooden houses and gardens. It was drizzling, and the city's mosques and palaces were softly wreathed in luminescence by an indecisive moon.

Zeynel paced to and fro, clenching and unclenching his fists. Heedless of the cool fragrance of the spring night and blind to the beauty of a city that customarily filled him with an odd mixture of pride and homesickness for the rugged mountains of his native Albania, he walked on, paused, retraced his steps, and walked on once more in a state of utter confusion. It was already ten o'clock and Mahmud would be waiting, but he did not feel like company at present. He was choking with impotent fury.

He had gone to the Sultana's room, as he did every night after dinner, to ask if she had any further need of his services. On the threshold he was brought up short by an acerbic voice which he at once recognized as that of Haïri Bey. He had stopped and listened uneasily, ready to step in if the violence latent in the Damad's tone turned physical.

It could have cost him his job; he was only a servant. What gave him the right to intervene between his mistress and her husband? His mistress, his *maitresse*. . . . A smile hovered on the eunuch's lips. He had got used to calling her that, savouring the delicious ambiguity of the word in French, that admirable language of love. He would never have dreamed of raising his eyes to the Sultana's face, but in his dreams. . . . Who could forbid him to dream?

Tonight, concealed behind the brocade curtains, Zeynel had waited with a pounding heart, but the Damad had robbed him of the chance to prove his devotion by fleeing from the Sultana's mocking glance. "The coward!" he growled, nervously pulling the leaves from a sprig of magnolia. How could the Sultana have fallen in love with such a worthless man? How could she tolerate his insolence when he owed all he was to her?

In the distance, a church clock in Pera began to chime. Mechanically, Zeynel counted the strokes: eleven o'clock. He could picture Mahmud's uneasy face and his slender fingers impatiently tapping the marble tabletop in the café where they usually met. It was a quiet establishment beside the Süleymaniye Mosque. Zeynel had chosen it because its patrons were all locals: there was no risk that anyone would recognize them.

They met there once or twice a week. The eunuch sometimes missed a rendezvous when suffering from one of his fits of depression – the Sultana could bring these on with a curt remark or simply by seeming offhand. But Mahmud never complained. He was always there when his lover needed him.

The lights of Galata twinkled in the distance. He must hurry. The bridge was still thronged with drunken revellers at this hour, and he would have to endure their vulgarity as he passed by before he reached the quiet little streets of Old Istanbul. His resolution waned, or was it his inclination? He felt unmoved by the memory of that young, docile body, those childish eyes and caressing hands. Why did the boy love him so much? He was fond of Mahmud, but as for love, for passion. . . . Between creatures like themselves it struck him as absurd.

He hesitated. If he did not keep their appointment Mahmud would be undeservedly hurt, but if he did. . . . Being as preoccupied with the Sultana as he was tonight, he would feel he was betraying her and take it out on the boy – he knew he would.

Better to go home.

Furious with himself, with Mahmud, with everything and everyone, he turned and headed back to Ortaköy Palace.

The next morning was "narcissus weather," as the inhabitants of Istanbul called the mauvish light that suffused the sky after rain.

Sultana Hatijé had decided to take Selma on a pilgrimage to the Mosque of Eyüp, burial-place of a standard-bearer of the Prophet killed during the first Muslim siege of Constantinople in 670. Also preserved there was the sword of Sultan Osman, founder of the Ottoman dynasty, which each new sultan wore on the day of his coronation. Situated at the end of the Golden Horn, the little mosque thus had two claims to be considered a symbol of Islam's long struggle with Christianity, and many Turks went there in these times of humiliation and adversity to seek fresh hope and courage.

Selma liked this tranquil island in a sea of greenery. Best of all she liked the cemetery enclosing it, which extended as far as the summit of the hills overlooking the sea. It was one of the oldest in the city, and each tombstone was a work of art. Some were carved with ceremonial turbans whose height was relative to their antiquity and the importance of the deceased, others of more recent date displayed plain fezzes. Women's graves were adorned with delicately-carved cornucopias, children's with slender little headstones bearing a diminutive fez or a garland of roses. Selma noticed there were many of these.

The two sultanas roamed the cemetery for nearly an hour, the child daydreaming while her mother told the ninety-nine names of Allah on her alabaster rosary. From time to time they paused before the tomb of a famous person or an old friend of the family. Hatijé would recite the prayer for the dead while Selma, standing beside her holding her breath, strained to hear the message that she was sure the dead were trying to send her. But she heard nothing, which made her feel that she was failing in a sacred duty. Still, she was convinced that one day, if she tried hard enough, she *would* hear what the dead were saying to the living.

Communication between the two worlds seemed quite natural to a child whose wet nurse, a buxom Sudanese, regularly conversed with the trees and flowers she regarded as reincarnations of the souls of the dead. Although the majority of such spirits were benign, others tried to lead people astray, and these she had to frighten away by yelling at the top of her voice.

On their way out of the cemetery Selma and her mother passed the café where Pierre Loti had come to seek inspiration for his novels, a modest building flanked by a jasmine-scented terrace from which customers could contemplate the opalescent waters of the Golden Horn.

"He at least has remained faithful to us," Hatijé murmured. "Our fair-weather friends have turned their backs on us, but he never stops pleading our cause. We poor Turks are so surprised, so unused to being understood by a European, that we return his love a hundredfold. There is not a foreigner more beloved in this country than Pierre Loti."

On their way back to the city, the coachman had great trouble threading his way through the streets, which were unusually crowded. Knots of excited townsfolk had gathered around every newsboy in sight. Alarmed, the Sultana sent Zeynel to find out what the matter was. He returned a few minutes later, so upset he could not talk. He was carrying a black-bordered newspaper, which the Sultana snatched from him impatiently. Splashed across the front page were the peace terms the Allies were imposing on Turkey. She skimmed through them, turning paler by the second, then sank back against the cushions.

"They are mad! They are asking us to sign our own death warrant. . . ."

For the rest of the journey she remained motionless, her head back, her eyes closed. Selma watched her apprehensively, not daring to move.

The days that followed were dark indeed. The people of Istanbul were in a state of shock, unable to understand the extent of their misfortune. Not even the worst pessimists among them had dreamed that the Allies would impose such harsh terms. They amounted, quite simply, to the dismemberment of Turkey.

Eastern Thrace was to go to Greece, together with the prosperous city of Izmir and its environs. Eastern Anatolia would become Armenia and Kurdistan an autonomous state. As for the south of Anatolia, it was designated a French and Italian zone of influence. All that Turkey retained was the Anatolian plateau, with a corridor to the Black Sea, and Istanbul itself, a small enclave surrounded by a few dozen square miles of territory. But not even that enclave was independent, nor were the narrows that constituted its sole access to the sea; the latter were to be placed under international trusteeship and the Ottoman capital would be subject to military and financial control by the Allied powers.

The situation in the city was tense, and demonstrations became more and more frequent. Those who for months had been advocating a policy of flexibility and negotiation no longer dared make themselves heard, whereas the supporters of Mustafa Kemal and armed resistance had ceased to be a sprinkling of radical groups and become the overwhelming majority. Every day, in a wide variety of disguises, hundreds of patriotic Turks set off for the front. Although the censored press made no mention of events in Anatolia, no one spoke of anything else but the fighting there and the Kemalists' successes. The bazaar in the heart of Old Istanbul had once more become the city's principal clearing-house for news. Sitting over glasses of tea outside their premises, shopkeepers guardedly exchanged titbits of information gleaned from peasants come to sell their produce or the volunteers who maintained the lines of communication between the occupied zone and the areas liberated by the nationalists. Everyone harvested his own crop of rumours while out shopping.

At Ortaköy, contact with the outside world was maintained by eunuchs who faithfully relayed all the latest gossip. One day toward the middle of June, Zeynel hurried to his mistress's boudoir beaming with triumph.

"The Kemalists have routed the caliphate army – they have even bypassed a British outpost and reached Tuzla. They are only twenty miles away! It seems they plan to enter Istanbul a week from now, on the last day of Bairam, in time for the Festival of Sweetmeats."

"How do you know?" the Sultana demanded, making an effort to control her excitement.

"I had it from the coachman of the senior editor of the *Alemder*, who had it from his wife, who is the best friend of the grand vizier's nieces. Damad Ferid is frantic, apparently. The British are furious with him for making them look ridiculous with his 'invincible' caliphate army, which has not lasted two months."

Hatijé's eyes sparkled derisively, but her elation soon gave way to anxiety. If the Kemalists advanced any farther the enemy forces would abandon their passive stance. It would mean war all over again, but a more horrible war than before, because it would involve civil war as well. The battles would not be confined to a distant front; they would take place here, inside the city itself. She pictured the street-fighting, the shelling, the thousands of casualties – including women and children. She shuddered. When she had prayed for a nationalist victory she had never imagined that. Suddenly she caught herself hoping that the Kemalists would be thrown back before they reached the outskirts. Then she pulled herself together: what! She was beginning to think like a traitor! Surely it was better to die than to live under the heel of foreign oppressors! Surely. . . .

She shut her eyes, and saw her beloved Istanbul, lying in ruins before her. Destroyed the Topkapi Palace, home of twenty-five sultans; pillaged the marble pavilions, and the fountains of alabaster and porcelain; destroyed Dolmabahçé, a pale dream beside the Bosphorus; in flames the thousand mosques, the caravanseries, and the ancient medreses[1]. All those centuries-old marvels, that harmony, that enchantment, consigned to oblivion. . . . To her astonishment Hatijé realized that she was far more appalled by that prospect than by the loss of human lives.

Selma did not share her mother's forebodings. To her, everything seemed quite straightforward: Mustafa Kemal was going to drive the foreign armies away. The Sultan would regain power and make laws designed to restore the country's prosperity and its people's happiness. He would no doubt appoint Mustata Kemal grand vizier, for he knew how to reward his loyal supporters.

And Halidé Edib? In Selma's eyes, the black-clad woman who had harangued the crowd in Sultan Ahmet Square was the personification of freedom. She was going to champion the rights of women, do away with those awful charshafs and stifling moucharabiés, throw open carriage windows and harem doors, and Selma would help her. Between them they would build a new world in which no one would ever be bored and women could even become Sultan, as they did in England.

Istanbul spent the next few days in a fever of excitement, alternating between dreams and nightmares. People's nerves were on edge. They burst out laughing or lost their temper at the smallest thing. Rosettes in the nationalist colours were surreptitiously sold by women in the street and worn beneath the lapel in anticipation of victory. The whole city was on the alert, but the news remained the same: the Kemalists were mustering at Tuzla.

The Festival of Sweetmeats came, and still they made no move. The inhabitants of Ortaköy Palace were half disappointed, half relieved, with the exception of Selma, who was so frustrated that she gobbled up the entire big sugar doll her mother gave her and had to take to her bed with an upset stomach.

It was her Sudanese nurse who brought her the bad news.

1 Centres of Koranic study.

"Little Sultana, Kemal Pasha won't be coming now. The Greeks have sent six divisions against him. His troops are outnumbered and ill-equipped – they're retreating everywhere. . . ."

Four days in bed, and the world had turned upside down! She had stopped concentrating and neglected her prayers, so Allah had abandoned them, and the invincible Kemalist army was falling back! Selma felt betrayed. By God? By the Kemalists? By the Greeks? She was not sure, but "they" had certainly taken advantage of her inattention. She gripped the nurse's big black hand.

"Get down on your knees beside me, Dadde! We are going to pray to Allah till he simply *has* to listen to us. He, the compassionate, the generous, cannot possibly be so unfair."

Quickly they performed the ablutions that purified the heart and unrolled the little mat that defined the sacred place of prayer, and side by side the buxom black woman and the dainty little auburn-haired girl intoned the ritual words: "There is no God but God, and Mohammed is his prophet. . . . There is no reality but that of God, and nothing is made save by him. . . ."

Could God prefer the money-grubbing, garrulous Greeks and the vapid, conceited British to the honest Turks? Selma could not believe it. Her palms open towards the sky in the gesture indicating submission, but which in this moment was one of impassioned entreaty, she repeated over and over: "O All-Powerful One; you must help us; you must give victory to Mustafa Kemal Pasha!" And she wept till her white lace collar was wet with tears.

One question bothered her especially. It was something the Sheikh had taught her: there was only one god; the god of the Muslims was the same as that of the Christians. But if Christian children prayed just as hard as Muslim children, God would have a very hard time choosing! The only answer was to tip the scales in the "right direction."

The following day Selma assembled the palace slaves' children, some fifteen boys and girls aged between six and twelve, and announced that they were going to pray. Five times a day they gathered in a secluded spot near the rose garden. There, having ceremoniously spread their silk mats on the grass, they bowed toward Mecca and fervently repeated the sacred verses after the little Sultana, who conducted the devotions.

But every passing day, with inexorable regularity, bore another crop of evil tidings. The defeat of the nationalist forces was confirmed. The Greeks were advancing at lightning speed. Towns and cities fell in quick succession: Akhisar, Balikesir, Bandirma, and, finally, Bursa! Bursa, that erstwhile capital of the Ottoman Empire, that sacred city housing the tombs of the first sultans, that purest expression of Islamic art whose mosques and palaces celebrated the strength and daring of the horsemen that had come from the east six centuries ago, was in infidel hands.

To the Turkish people, Bursa's capture was as traumatic as the occupation of Izmir. So they had been wrong to pin their hopes on Mustafa Kemal! All eyes turned once more to the Sultan Caliph. Surely he would react now – surely he would give his children a word of encouragement or an order of some kind? But no, the gates of Dolmabahçé remained shut and silence continued to reign in its marble halls.

Selma was beside herself with indignation. Edirne and the whole of Thrace were occupied, and still the Greek divisions continued their advance. Why didn't the Sultan declare war? She bombarded her mother with questions but got no answers. Disheartened, the little girl lost all interest. She gave up her prayer meetings and took refuge in dreams and books, or else had one of the old kalfas tell her the stories of the great sultans of the past. There was Mehmet the Conqueror, who at eighteen vanquished the Byzantine Empire, and Selim the Terrible, a fierce warrior who, at the side of his beloved, turned into a poet: "Lions tremble at my powerful, destructive claw, but Providence made me the weak slave of a youth with the eyes of a gazelle."

She loved to hear how Sultan Ahmet III, transported by joy as his friend Nedim recited poetry, rewarded him by filling his mouth with fine pearls. She thrilled to the tales of the great deeds of Suleyman the Magnificent who led the Ottoman army to the very gates of Vienna. She begged to hear once again how her great-grandfather, Mahmud the Reformer, an enlightened ruler, had brought Turkey into the modern age. Their martial valour, their splendour and astuteness had honoured the name of the house of Osman. But now all that was over, and the Padishah walled himself in silence. Selma was even more appalled when, passing by the palace kitchen, she overheard the kitchen hands snidely insinuating that the Sultan was afraid. . . .

One morning she reassembled the children of the palace. In addition to the sons and daughters of her parents' stewards and secretaries, they included those of the coachmen, cooks, and porters whose families occupied little houses tucked away on the edge of the grounds not far from the kitchens. (In good Turkish households, and especially in the royal household, the kitchens were located as far away as possible from the rest of the house, so that the cooking smells would not cause any discomfort.) All the children were devoted to Selma, especially Gulnar, a dark-haired, temperamental Tatar girl, and Sekerbuli, or "little piece of sugar," with her pink cheeks, fair hair, and dimples. Last but not least there was Ahmed, the youngest son of Haïri Bey's private secretary. Ahmed was only eleven, but he had been madly in love with the little Sultana for as long as he could remember. He blushed and stammered whenever he saw her, much to Selma's irritation. She bullied him for fun, but the more she teased him in the hope of meeting some resistance, the more submissively he gazed at her and the more he loved her.

This morning, before the full assembly, Selma decreed that the time for prayer was over: from now on they would play war. One side would be the Turks commanded by the Sultan – herself, of course – and the other the Greeks. Everyone applauded this new order of the day and scattered in search of thin, supple branches to serve as swords. When the time came to pick sides, however, an unforeseen problem cropped up: no one wanted to be a Greek. Flattery, promises, threats – nothing worked. Selma could have wept with rage. She was angrily prodding the ground with the tip of her stick when a meek voice made her look up.

"*I'll* be a Greek."

It was Ahmed gazing at her with doglike devotion. Selma glowed with gratitude. He had not only braved opprobrium to please her but restored her authority by undermining the united front against her. She smiled at him with all the charm she could muster.

"Good, you be General Paravescopoulos, but what about your army?"

An army was the little boy's least concern. He was so happy to be in his Sultana's good graces at last, he would have fought the rest single-handed. In any case, there was no question of the Greeks defeating the Turks, still less of him, Ahmed, defeating the one he loved.

Selma, however, did not see it that way. Too easy a victory would not be a victory worthy of the name.

"Who will be a Greek with Ahmed?" she demanded, surveying her followers with an imperious eye. To her surprise, two shy little girls and a chubby-cheeked boy stepped forward.

"If Ahmed's going to be a Greek, we'll be Greeks too," they said.

Selma stared at them in bewilderment. Why, when her own threats and promises had failed to move them, had they volunteered to side with Ahmed? What was the source of his power? His simplicity? His gentleness? She shrugged. Absurd – those were not the qualities of a leader. It annoyed her that the ones who had chosen to support her whipping-boy were the shyest children of all. She felt that, without actually saying anything, they were teaching her a lesson.

Now they were all looking at her awaiting the signal for battle to commence. Not wanting it said that the Turks had defeated the Greeks because they outnumbered them, she reduced her own army to four, though she took care to pick the biggest and strongest children available. At last, when all was in readiness, she drew herself up majestically, her auburn hair gleaming in the sunlight, and brandished her stick in the air.

"*Allah Akbar*!" she trumpeted. "Allah is the greatest!" And, with her troops at her heels, she charged the enemy.

It was clear from the very first moment that the Greeks were outclassed by the Turks. They fought bravely, but the two little girls and the fat boy were no match for Selma's hand-picked troops. They were Greeks, anyway, so their defeat was inevitable. After putting up a show of resistance for form's sake, they surrendered.

Not so Ahmed, who fought on with a tenacity of which no one would have thought him capable. Selma's troops surrounded him but failed to penetrate his guard. His stick whirled like quicksilver, mercilessly connecting with any leg or cheek that ventured too close. Ahmed had by now entirely forgotten that he was General Paravescopoulos: he was a knight doing battle to impress his lady.

But Selma was Selma no longer: she was the all-powerful Sultan, God's shadow on earth, and no soldiers of hers could be held in check by a miserable Greek general. Abandoning her prisoners, she charged to the attack, broke through her own lines, and confronted the enemy. She was drunk with fury. This was the Paravescopoulos who planned to take possession of Turkey and reduce its people to slavery! His army was burning villages and slaughtering women and children, and he thought he could occupy Istanbul and overthrow the sultanate! Well, this dog would soon see what the Padishah and the Turkish army were made of! Enough was enough. The Greeks had gone too far and now they would be sorry! Selma struck out with her stick, struck and struck again as hard as she could, her strength increased tenfold by her anger and indignation. The Turks were finally venting all the frustration and resentment of the past few months in an uncontrollable outburst of violence.

Whether because her weary arm was aching or because she had suddenly become aware that the children's excited shouts had been replaced by a strange hush, Selma stopped short. General Paravescopoulos was lying at her feet, writhing in pain and shielding his head with his bleeding hands. His clothes were torn, and the bare skin showing through the rents was crisscrossed with angry welts.

"Have you gone mad?"

The Sultana loomed up in front of her, white-faced. She looked less angry than stunned, as if her daughter had turned into a monster. Selma abruptly came to her senses. She was not the Sultan and the groaning boy lying unconscious at her feet was not General Paravescopoulos, he was her friend Ahmed, and she had killed him. Tears blinded her as she knelt beside him. She laid her cheek against his smarting face, gently stroked his hair and whispered soothing words, thereby convincing Ahmed that he was already dead and in paradise.

The children looked on in consternation. Their parents were bound to whip them – they might even be locked up in the gloomy palace cellars. They were not consoled by the thought that the arrogant little Sultana would also be punished and that Ahmed would receive a magnificent funeral, complete with the finest hired mourners in the city. Why had the silly boy let himself be killed, anyway? He had fought like a lion to begin with, then instead of defending himself against Selma's onslaught he had simply looked at her and dropped his guard. And she, so carried away that she had not even noticed, had belaboured the unarmed warrior with redoubled ferocity.

The Sultana's icy voice rang out again.

"Enough of this playacting! Go up to your room at once!"

Sobbing, Selma tried to explain that she had meant to kill General Paravescopoulos, not poor Ahmed, but Sultana Hatijé would not listen. She knew only that her daughter had struck a defenceless inferior, and that her disgraceful behaviour merited the harshest punishment. The honour of the family was at stake.

Eunuchs summoned the elderly palace physician, who swiftly examined the "body" and pronounced him in poor shape but still very much alive. Complete rest and a salve made from the fat of a Bengal tiger, specially imported from India, would soon have the boy on his feet again.

Selma spent the next few days confined to her room. All her books were removed with the exception of the Koran. She saw no one but the maidservant who brought her meals, which consisted of stale bread normally reserved for the horses. The woman was forbidden to communicate with her, but she was so touched by Selma's concern for Ahmed that she nodded reassuringly when questioned about him. Two whole weeks went by in this way: the Sultana wanted her daughter's punishment to be examplary.

One morning Selma was roused by an unaccustomed sound of chanting voices. Straining her ears, she recognized the dirge the muezzins sent echoing from minaret to minaret to signify that the nation was in mourning. She ran to the window and saw crowds surging through the distant streets. What had happened? Was the Sultan dead?

There were tears in the eyes of the slave who brought her breakfast of bread and water, and this time she answered without demur. No, the Sultan was not dead – it was worse than that: the Ottoman negotiators in France had failed to sway the Allied powers. They had been compelled to sign the iniquitous Treaty of Sèvres, a document of which everyone had been talking for the last three months without dreaming that it would actually come into force – a treaty that provided for the total dismemberment of Turkey.

This day of mourning turned out to be Selma's day of liberation. Sultana Hatijé considered that her daughter had been punished enough. In any case, she felt the situation was now so grave that all else paled into insignificance.

CHAPTER 13

Spring was gilding the domes of Istanbul after the gloomiest winter Selma had ever known. Following the large-scale demonstrations against the signing of the Treaty of Sèvres on 10 August 1920, the city lapsed into sorrow and humiliation. Even the recent dismissal of the government headed by Damad Ferid, the most universally hated man in Turkey, did little to dispel the general mood of apathy. This plump, pompous little man had fallen prey to his pro-British sentiments: his compatriots could not forgive him for having signed the infamous treaty, still less for having tried to obtain the Sultan's endorsement of it.

Life in the capital was becoming more and more difficult. Unlike the French and Italians, who fraternized with the inhabitants as the occupation dragged on, the British remained inflexibly aloof and continued to institute harassing measures on the pretext of maintaining order. These rained down on a people who could make nothing of them. The latest, proof of the English love of animals, had left the whole city stupefied: anyone callous enough to carry a live chicken by the feet would be fined ten Turkish pounds – a stiff penalty in a city where a workman earned some eighty pounds a month. Should the luckless Turk protest, he would be fined an additional twenty pounds, and so on until he was reduced to penurious silence and confirmed in his belief that the British were either insane or the scum of the earth.

Most of these draconian measures were, in fact, masterminded by the Levantines[1], some of whom had been locally recruited and put into British uniform. Rapidly promoted to the rank of captain or major, they took advantage of their new-found authority to settle old scores and feather their own nests under the aegis of the Union Jack.

Discouragement took hold of the population. Yet early in January hopes of a change in Turkey's fortunes had been kindled when Ismet Pasha, one of Mustafa Kemal's lieutenants, succeeded in rebuffing the Greek advance near the Inönü, a small river in Anatolia. Everyone hailed this first nationalist victory with joy and remained on tenterhooks for days, expecting it to develop into a counteroffensive,

1 In this context: European Catholics, usually of Italian or French stock, whose families had been resident in Istanbul for generations.

but nothing more happened and Istanbul relapsed into its former lethargy.

The Kemalist army was too weak to follow up its advantage. For months now it had been obliged to fight not only against the Greeks but against increasing numbers of armed Turkish peasants as well. The Sheikh ul-Islam's anathema had caused great confusion of mind among the faithful. Mustafa Kemal's claim to be fighting for the Sultan Caliph was only half believed, and many villages refused to cooperate with him.

Hoping to regain the confidence of the population, Kemal decided to send for the Crown Prince, who was known to have nationalist sympathies. Abdul Mejid was a dreamer and an artist, however, not a man of action. He continued to vacillate and confer with his advisers until the British got wind of the scheme and put a stop to his shilly-shallying by cordoning off his residence with a hundred men.

That was when his son, Omer Faruk, decided to join Kemal in Anatolia. The energetic and ambitious young prince burned to distinguish himself in the defence of his country, but being very much in love with his wife Sabiha, who was pregnant at the time, he waited until the baby was born. By the time he left, in the greatest secrecy, spring had come.

Selma was a fervent admirer of "Uncle Thunder," as the children called Prince Faruk, who was as famous for his quick temper as for his good-looks. How she longed to be a man and accompany him to Anatolia! She looked with redoubled scorn on her brother Haïri, who calmly continued to stuff himself with sweets and play the violin.

She was bored. At the palace, the days seemed to crawl by. Social functions were few and far between because upper-class families were beginning to feel the pinch. They no longer received any income from their estates in the Ottoman Empire's newly independent territories, and since the occupation the Christian tenants of their apartment houses in the city had conveniently forgotten to pay rent. Sultana Hatijé managed to keep her household going only by selling more jewellery, and Selma grew accustomed to Memjian Agha's regular comings and goings with his case under his arm.

Fortunately, spring heralded the return of the dressmakers. It was wardrobe-replenishing time, especially for Selma, whose short skirts were eyed with disfavour by the older kalfas. She was nearly eleven now, and the Sultana's elderly retainers argued that it was time for her to don the charshaf. Hatijé protested that Selma was still only a child. Did she really think so, or was she trying to preserve her daughter's freedom for as long as possible? Whatever the reason, she firmly announced that the little Sultana would not take the veil till she was twelve, and that tongues could wag as much as they liked.

The sewing room, whose walls were lined with white cretonne and long mirrors, buzzed with activity. The dressmakers, who were traditionally Greek, came bearing bolts of the finest materials and copies of the latest Paris magazines, which were full of La Ferriere models. For the first time Selma was allowed to choose for herself. She wavered between various models and draped herself in one dress length after another without managing to make up her mind. But that did not matter, there was all the time in the world to discuss styles, feel and compare materials, decide on minor details, and then change one's mind again. The more their clients hesitated, the happier the dressmakers were as it transformed them from mere needlewomen into personal advisers and arbiters of taste. "The Sultana and her daughter trust my judgement implicitly," they could tell their other clients, who would be duly impressed. "You know the gowns they wore at the last reception? I was the one who suggested the design and colour."

Selma, still engaged in deciding which styles were the most becoming, stole surreptitious glances at these women. There were nine of them: two cutters, three seamstresses, and four embroiderers. All had worked for the palace for years, and Selma knew each of them by name, and was familiar with their ailments and the names and ages of their children. The only subject never discussed was the war. Selma itched to ask them why the Greeks of Istanbul had turned against their Turkish compatriots, but she did not dare.

The sun was setting by the time the senior cutter, cocking her head and narrowing her eyes in a professional manner, began to take measurements. She had to do so at a distance, physical contact with members of the imperial family being forbidden. This presented no problem in the case of voluminous traditional robes, but figure-hugging European gowns were another matter, and Sultana Hatijé was obliged to adjust the pins herself during fittings. Although she privately cursed this custom, she accepted the need for it. The maintenance of etiquette was more important than ever in these troubled times. Etiquette was as much a basis of respect as a sign of showing respect, and respect, now that the Sultan had been stripped of his power, was the bedrock on which the sultanate ultimately reposed.

For some time now, Selma had taken to daydreaming by herself. Her favourite haunt was a little rosewood gazebo, enclosed by a delicately carved balustrade, known as "the Nightingale's Pavilion" because it was tucked away in a corner of the grounds where nightingales usually nested. Selma never tired of listening to their song. Legend had it that once upon a time a nightingale had declared its love to a rose but to no avail. In despair the nightingale spent the rest of its life in song, hoping to seduce the rose.

It was a balmy spring day. Stretched out on the kilims[2] covering the Pavilion floor, Selma amused herself by screwing up her eyes and squinting at the sun, a pastime prohibited by Mademoiselle Rose and her nurse, who both claimed that it would ruin her eyesight. Suddenly the sun's rays were blotted out by a fleeting shadow. Opening her eyes, Selma saw a figure heading for the palace. She was still too dazzled to see anything clearly, but it looked like Uncle Thunder. That was impossible, of course – Uncle Thunder was in Anatolia, fighting at the side of Mustafa Kemal, and his wife, who was with Sultana Hatijé at this moment, had only just received a letter from him. Selma rubbed her eyes: it really did look like Prince Omer Faruk! She scrambled to her feet and tiptoed after him.

Just as she reached the blue drawing-room, a man's voice rang out.

"He wants nothing to do with me, and that is that!"

It *was* Prince Faruk! He was pacing to and fro with his hands behind his back, scowling. His wife and Sultana Hatijé ventured a few questions. The result was an explosion of anger.

"How naive of us to imagine that Kemal would accept our help in saving Turkey! He welcomes the help of communists and bandits, yes, but the last thing he wants is assistance from imperial princes! Our family made this country great, and the people know it only too well. We might eclipse Kemal's reputation if he allowed us to fight alongside him. He sent for us when he thought he was done for, but the Inönü victory and his alliance with the Bolsheviks have let him off the hook. He thinks he does not need us any more – in fact a lot of people think he will try to make us look like traitors so that he can abolish the sultanate and seize power himself. Well he is not going to manage that any time soon!"

The Prince brought his fist crashing down on a delicate table, which collapsed under the impact. Paying no attention, on he went.

"The Turkish people love us. If you could have seen the welcome I got from the townsfolk of Inebolu when I landed there. The good people wept with joy as if the Sultan himself had come to fight at their side. During the days I spent there waiting for Kemal's response to my offer to serve with him, peasants from all the neighbouring

2 Turkish carpets.

villages flocked to see me, touch me, reassure themselves that their Padishah had not abandoned them. They never tired of hearing me tell how the boat that had brought me from Istanbul was searched from top to bottom by the British, and how I spent six hours hiding in a locker with a revolver in my hand, ready to blow my brains out rather than be taken alive."

"But in that case, why the devil did you come back?"

General Prince Osman Fuad, who had just arrived, spoke with ill-disguised impatience. He did not like any story of which he was not the hero. Omer Faruk turned and looked his cousin up and down.

"What about you, Prince?" he said coldly. "Why the devil didn't you go?"

The air was thick with tension.

"Please, please!" intervened Sultana Hatijé. She turned to Prince Faruk with her most admiring expression. "What happened then, Highness?"

"After several days I received a letter from Ankara. The general very courteously thanked me for having come and praised my fighting spirit but said he did not want me to run any risks. I must preserve myself for a higher destiny in the supreme interests of the nation. In short, he politely but flatly refused my help and told me to go home."

Sultana Sabiha, the Prince's young wife, shook her head and sighed.

"I am worried. The Pasha is a brilliant soldier, one cannot deny, but he is immensely ambitious as well. Everything you have told us confirms my father's worst fears. His Majesty trusted Kemal when he sent him to Anatolia. Now he would not put anything past him."

Silence descended on the blue drawing-room. Troubled by Faruk's story, Sultana Hatijé began to suspect that Sultan Vahiddedin might be right, and that Mustafa Kemal, whom she had always defended, was preparing to betray them.

CHAPTER 14

The little Sultana had changed a great deal in recent months. She was entering adolescence at last. "Slender as a young cypress and pale as the moon" – such were the comparisons she evoked from the slave women in her entourage. Sultana Hatijé decreed that she should learn to play the harp as well as the piano. It would also show off her arms, which promised to be particularly shapely. Selma revelled in all these compliments. She was becoming aware of her physical charms and tried them out on Ahmed, who, after she had almost killed him, had become her best friend.

Her two weeks in solitary confinement had been a formative experience. Having wept many resentful tears at what she considered an unjust punishment, she ended by deriving a certain satisfaction from it: that of being universally shunned and misunderstood. She had spent hours recalling tales of the Islamic martyrs and sufi ascetics who had been ostracized by an uncomprehending society. Their fate, which bore a resemblance to her own predicament, had given her the courage to endure her ordeal.

She had needed to enlist the help of all these heroes of the past because she had just lost the living heroine she venerated above all others. Her perfect mother, the person beside whom she had always felt so unworthy, had condemned her unfairly and made no attempt to see her point of view. Selma had examined and reexamined the problem from every angle, but in vain: one of them had to be wrong, and she knew it was not herself. Although this conclusion should have satisfied her, it depressed her even more. She was sadder than she had ever been in her life.

And then, one night, she had a dream. She was in a prison cell so dark and cramped that she hit her head on the bars whenever she moved. All at once she heard a voice: "Why not take the bandage off your eyes? Then you will be able to see clearly and stop hurting yourself."

The only trouble was, the bandage formed part of her: it was so firmly glued to her eyes that they might be ripped out if she removed it. She lay there in a state of utter indecision. What should she do: remain in the dark without moving, or remove the bandage and risk blinding herself? Finally she chose the second alternative and with terror raised her hand to the bandage. To her surprise it came away at the first touch, and the world looked brighter and more vivid than ever before.

The morning after this dream Selma felt much better – so much so that she failed to understand how she could have lived with such a nightmare bottled up inside her for days. The world looked as luminous as it had looked in her dream. She no longer needed Annéjim's eyes to see with.

Her all-powerful mother had been wrong, and she, Selma, had not died. It was a discovery that seemed to open up vistas of infinite freedom. . . .

For the second time the Kemalist forces had succeeded in repulsing the Greeks near the Inönü River, and a temporary lull set in. Istanbul felt emboldened by this limited success to celebrate once more. It was the middle of April. The light was clear and the air as silky as the lips of a youth. Mingling with the fragrance of hawthorn and jasmine that drifted over garden walls and scented the streets, the perfume emanating from the luxuriant clusters of wisteria on the walls of the palaces beside the Bosporus was so heady that it made the senses reel.

At this time of year river trips were popular, and caiques upholstered in rather faded, gold-embroidered velvet glided silently along the little river Göksu as they used to in their heyday. The only sign of the times was a dearth of oarsmen, many having left to fight in Anatolia.

The river was so narrow that the caiques often grazed each other in passing. Salutations of various kinds would then be exchanged. Occasionally, a young man would pluck up his courage and try to catch a pretty girl's eye. If she was respectable she would take refuge behind her parasol; if not, she would gaze dreamily into space. Her admirer would then take the flower from his buttonhole and put it to his lips. If the girl smiled – a sign of great emancipation – he might toss the flower into her lap. Before taking such a liberty, however, he had to run through a whole gamut of carefully codified gestures. If he toyed with a piece of sugar it meant: "My heart desires you passionately." With a plum: "I am pining away." With a blue silk handkerchief: "I am desperately in love."

Selma noticed these discreet exchanges for the first time, and a velvety sensation pervaded her innermost being. Sitting upright beside her mother, holding her breath, she dreamed of Aprils to come.

The lull was shortlived. On 13 June 1921, King Constantine of Greece landed at Izmir with eighty-five thousand men. Instead of disembarking in the harbour itself, he symbolically landed at the very spot where the Crusaders had stepped ashore centuries ago. His objective: to crush Ankara, the heart of the resistance movement, and take possession of Istanbul. God, after all, was on his side. According to a celebrated papal prophecy, His Most Christian Majesty would enter the capital, which Westerners still called Constantinople, before October and drive the barbarians from it forever. On the strength of this prediction, on 13 August Constantine launched his major offensive against Ankara.

The Greeks, superior in numbers and better equipped, advanced rapidly. Panic seized Ankara as the Turkish forces retreated before them. Some inhabitants of the Kemalist capital, and even some members of the popular assembly, prepared to flee. Infuriated by their cowardice, Mustafa Kemal demanded full powers and the title of commander-in-chief, hitherto a prerogative of the Sultan. Mobilizing the entire peasantry of Anatolia, he drafted men and women alike into the nationalist army. His plan was to halt the Greeks at the River Sakarya, a last natural line of defence, some eighty miles south-west of Ankara.

The people of Istanbul had abandoned all hope. In the Greek Levantine districts of Pera, where rumour had it that Mustafa Kemal had been taken prisoner, people were already bringing out the champagne. Revellers thronged the restaurants and nightclubs, especially the famous Rose Noire, the city's most luxurious establishment, where beautiful Russian emigrées – royal princesses, so it was whispered – served drinks with an air of supreme distinction and waltzed with customers until dawn.

For twenty-two days and nights, the Kemalist forces fiercely, desperately stood their ground knowing that the survival of their native land was at stake. By 11 September the Greek army was in full retreat: Turkey was saved.

There was jubilation throughout the country. In Istanbul the mosques were overflowing. Everyone celebrated Kemal's victory with a noisy disregard for the occupying powers. People no longer hugged the walls – they strode down the middle of the street with their heads held high, and passing British soldiers were treated to mocking stares, as if to say, "You won't be around much longer!"

Yet the war was not over. In addition to the capital, half of Turkey was still under occupation. But governments abroad were beginning to realize that the wind had changed. Paris wasted no time in sending her most charming ambassador, Franklin Bouillon, nicknamed "the

Prince of the Levantines," to negotiate with Mustafa Kemal. He came bearing several dozen cases of the finest cognac – the great man's weaknesses were by now common knowledge in the chancelleries of Europe – and a promise that French troops would quit the province of Cilicia. To London's fury, he also brought an offer of peace.

Months went by, and Kemal steadily reinforced his army. The Greeks, too, were girding themselves for a renewal of hostilities, but public opinion at Athens was growing more and more averse to continuing the war and morale in the trenches was declining.

At last, on 26 August 1922, after the unofficial cease-fire had lasted almost a year, the Turks attacked. To cries of "Soldiers, forward: your objective is the Mediterranean!" they advanced on Izmir. The Greek forces retreated in disorder.

Although the inhabitants of Istanbul hardly dared believe these preliminary reports, it was soon confirmed that Aydin, Manisa, and Uşak had been liberated. A frenzied outburst of rejoicing ensued.

At the palace of Yildiz, where he lived, having long ago spurned the luxury of Dolmabahçé, Sultan Vahiddedin was devoting his days to prayer, pausing only to send his personal secretary in search of the latest news. How far had the nationalist forces advanced? Were they nearing Izmir? Were we really winning?

Crowds stormed the newspapers' offices. It was impossible to go out to distribute the freshly printed copies, so they were thrown from balconies into the street. Life had come to a stop: the Kemalists' advance was charted minute by minute.

Finally, on 9 September, it was learned that the General's troops had entered Izmir, from which the last Greek soldier had fled. In streets ablaze with lights and bedecked with flags and streamers the inhabitants embraced each other, weeping for joy. After twelve long years of hardship and humiliation, the Turkish people could hold up their heads, at last.

From countless minarets muezzins sang the greatness of Allah and prayers of thanksgiving were offered ceaselessly in every mosque. Most moving of all was the celebration at Aya Sofya, to which Selma and her mother went on the very day Izmir was liberated. There, pressed against each other in the midst of a crowd, they stood motionless for hours, weeping.

Two weeks later the Greek fleet sailed out of Istanbul. On 11 October, this time at the request of the occupying powers, an armistice was signed. Victory was complete: the war was well and truly over.

CHAPTER 15

Selma was in a black mood. Yesterday she had celebrated her twelfth birthday. The unhappiest day of her life.

The big mound of presents in her room included a long, flat box like those in which her mother's Paris gowns were packed. Feverishly, she shut her eyes as she lifted the lid, then opened them to see that the box contained a turquoise silk charshaf with a matching muslin veil.

Her throat tightened and her eyes filled with tears. Heedless of the kalfas who were congratulating her on her promotion to woman's estate, she had turned her back on this "portable prison" and refused point-blank to try it on.

She was furious with her mother for bowing to convention, especially as the charshaf was going out, if not in provincial towns, at least in the capital. Women of fashion had modified the voluminous garment into a matching two-piece of which the veil, coquettishly raised on one side, was just a decorative adjunct.

"They are hussies – women of ill repute," the kalfas protested indignantly. "Either that or, worse still, intellectuals and revolutionaries like that Halidé Edib and her ilk. All their talk of 'emancipation' is just an excuse to walk around with their faces bare, in skirts that expose the ankle – even the calf! A Sultana cannot stoop to such behaviour. She must safeguard morality and the traditions of Islam."

Morality! Where was the morality in that? Why should it be more immoral for a woman to show her face and hair than a man? Selma refused to be appeased.

Now that she knew enough Arabic, she went back to her Koran with all the fervour of a neophyte. She spent days perusing every verse relating to women. Nowhere, absolutely nowhere was it written that a woman should cover her face, or even her hair, yet the sheikhs pronounced it sinful to show either. The Koran merely enjoined women to cultivate a modest manner. Selma was furious. The Prophet himself did not insist that his wife Aysha wear a veil, and had taken her to dinners at which she conversed freely with men. As for Sokaina, Mohammed's great-granddaughter, she had stubbornly refused to wear the veil. "It would be an affront to God," she said. "He did not give me beauty that I should hide it!"

All around Selma, Istanbul was coming alive again. For the first time in years, its inhabitants could breathe freely and face the future with hope. The young girl felt their joyous elation flood through her like a wave breaking against the constraints of convention, like a rushing river held in check by Ortaköy's silk-hung walls, the kalfas' polished courtesy, her mother's indulgent smile. She felt stifled.

As Selma was nursing her grievances in one corner of the little pink boudoir her mother, seated at her desk and pretending not to notice her daughter's ill humour, was putting the finishing touches to a letter.

All at once they heard hurried footsteps and Haïri Bey burst in unannounced.

"It's incredible, quite incredible!" he blurted out, neglecting to greet his wife for the first time in fourteen years of married life. He looked utterly dismayed.

Hatijé regarded him uneasily as he slumped into an armchair.

"You will never believe it, but the Grand Assembly at Ankara has voted to abolish the sultanate!"

She started despite herself. "You mean they have deposed the Sultan?"

"No, they have abolished the sultanate for good." Haïri Bey stressed every syllable. "From now on, Turkey is to have no sultan, merely a caliph – a religious leader devoid of political power. See for yourself."

He handed his wife a bunch of newspapers with glaring headlines. She glanced at them and shrugged.

"Impossible. No one will accept such a decision. In Islam, political power and religious authority are inseparable."

"That is precisely what a majority of the deputies objected to the measure," replied Haïri Bey drily, exasperated by his wife's imperturbable manner. "Kemal's views are far from shared by the conservatives, or even by the moderates. They want a constitutional monarchy under nationalist control."

"If they are in the majority, why didn't they win?"

"Because Kemal bullied them out of it. He mounted the rostrum and – listen, I will read you exactly what he is reported to have said: 'All members of the assembly would be well advised to support this measure. If they did not, nothing would alter the ineluctable reality of the situation, but heads might roll. . . .'[1] His opponents promptly shut up because they knew the Pasha was not joking. Plenty of heads have rolled since the start of the civil war. One deputy actually apologized

1 Cf. Lord Kinross: *Atatürk*.

and said: 'Forgive us for having considered the question from the wrong angle. Now we see it much more clearly.' They were terrified, poor devils! A few hours later the Grand Assembly voted to abolish the monarchy – unanimously."

Selma was dumbfounded. What did no more sultan mean, a masterless country where everyone did as he pleased? Impossible! A country governed by Mustafa Kemal? If so. . . . A vague hope dawned in her mind: if Mustafa Kemal became the new sultan, she might not, after all, be compelled to wear that hateful charshaf. Kemal's wife, Latifé Hanum, never wore one, nor did his friend Halidé Edib, nor any of the women in his entourage. They were free to dress and go around as they chose.

Suddenly, Selma began to hope fervently that her father was right – that Turkey would never have another sultan and Kemal Pasha would become its master. Of course it would be annoying for the princes of the family, who spent their days waiting to inherit the throne and now would not know what to do with themselves. Poor Uncle Fuad and Uncle Thunder would be terribly disappointed. And Sadiyé? Selma had an almost irresistible urge to laugh. The news would simply shatter her cousin, who had been more conceited than ever since her father became Crown Prince.

At that moment, her aunt Fehimé entered the room. The Butterfly Sultana was wearing grey and looking tearful, but Selma noticed that her eyes were bright and her cheeks quite pink, as if she privately relished her role as a bird of ill omen. She had just been visiting His Majesty's first wife at Yildiz Palace.

"The Cadin is very worried. The new governor, Refet Bey, called on the Padishah this afternoon to inform him that he had been deposed, but His Majesty replied that he would never abdicate. Everyone is wondering what will happen. Nobody defies Mustafa Kemal with impunity. What form of pressure will he bring to bear? His Majesty is prepared for the worst. It has even been intimated that his life is in danger."

"They are quite capable of assassinating him and assassinating us all," Haïri Bey said darkly. "Kemal's Bolshevik friends did not balk at murdering the Czar and his family. They did not even spare the children, the brutes!"

Selma could not believe her ears. Would they really be murdered by Golden Rose, the Pasha for whom she and her family had so often prayed? She dismissed the idea. So, to her great relief, did her mother.

"There is no need to exaggerate – the situation is serious enough as it is," she said irritably. "Our Turks are more civilized than those muzhiks."

"But the civil list[2] will be abolished too," moaned her sister. "How are we going to live?"

"You will have to buy less lace, that is all," Hatijé said crisply. "In any case I doubt if you will need any."

And she nipped further comment in the bud by going back to her embroidery.

Two days later Tewfik Pasha, the Ottoman Empire's last grand vizier, left the Sublime Porte to return his seals of office to the Sultan. Refet Bey took over the city's administration, the police force included, and the various government ministries were instructed to cease all activity. From now on, Ankara was to be the seat of government. To please the masses, who would not have understood the term "republic," the new regime was christened a "monarchy of the nation."

Ali Kemal's death occurred some days later. A distinguished journalist who had campaigned against the Kemalists, he was arrested at his barber's, but, before he could be taken to Izmir to stand trial, he was stoned to death by an angry mob.

The Sultan's entourage was incensed by this news, not only because they considered Ali Kemal a good and decent man whose sole crime was to have stood up for his beliefs, but also because his lynching proved that the police were reluctant to risk protecting members of the old regime from popular fury. Inside his palace the sovereign himself no longer felt safe. The Grand Assembly at Ankara had voted to try him for high treason, and some deputies were demanding that the "friend of the British" be put to death.

Many palace servants had already fled, and even the Sultan's personal staff were beginning to desert him. Day after day, Yildiz Palace was being abandoned. But the hardest blow of all was the furtive departure of the Padishah's former grand vizier and injudicious adviser, Damad Ferid. Sultan Vahiddedin greeted the news of his defection with a bitter smile. "So he did not even have the courage to say goodbye," he sighed, and his drooping shoulders sagged a little more.

The following Friday, Sultana Hatijé decided to attend the selamlik ceremony at Hamidie Mosque. The Sultan had let it be known that he

2 Allowance allotted to members of the imperial family by the government for their personal expenses.

would go there as usual, and she was anxious to show him support.

Just as she and Selma, shrouded in her charshaf, were boarding the dark green carriage bearing the imperial coat of arms, Mehmet the coachman, a big, mustachioed Montenegrin, ventured to remark that it might be wiser, in these troubled times, to hire a cab. The Sultana rounded on him, eyes blazing.

"You were proud enough of being an imperial coachman a few weeks ago. Are you frightened now? In that case, go – I will not detain you. The steward will pay you your wages."

"Forgive me, Sultana," Mehmet pleaded. "My children are young – I've no right to make orphans of them."

Hatijé relented. "Very well, Mehmet, you are excused, but send me the other coachman before you go."

Mehmet turned scarlet and became even more flustered.

"The fact is, Highness, he has an old mother to support. He left yesterday."

"Without telling me?"

"He didn't dare. He was ashamed – you've always been so kind. . . ."

This was how such people repaid her kindness, Hatijé thought bitterly. It was almost funny. "I see," she said, "so we do not have a coachman any more. Fortunately, Zeynel is here. He can drive us."

She drew the veil over her hair with a sweeping gesture. Then, looking more majestic than ever, she boarded the carriage.

The Hamidie Mosque was little more than a mile away. As custom prescribed, ladies were to follow the proceedings from their carriages in the courtyard. Selma and her mother got there just as the gates of Yildiz Palace swung open and the Sultan emerged in an open phaeton drawn by two horses. Following him on foot were three aides-de-camp, four secretaries, and several black eunuchs: not a single minister or dignitary in sight. Selma looked on in dismay. Was this a selamlik? She recalled the magnificent processions of former years, when bemedalled princes and damads, viziers and pashas had filed along behind the Sultan's carriage to the rousing strains of the Imperial March. Today's ceremony was as grey and dreary as a funeral. Where was the military band, where were the handsome lancers in their blue dolmans, where were the various regiments lining the route at attention and hailing their sovereign with the traditional cry: "May Allah grant our Padishah long life!"? There were only a handful of soldiers on duty preserving an impassive silence.

Sultan Vahiddedin, wearing his general's uniform with no decorations, descended slowly from his carriage, as if every movement were a supreme effort. He looked so thin and exhausted that Selma wondered if he were ill. She hardly recognized him; in a few months he had become an old man.

Lost in his own thoughts, he headed for the mosque just as the muezzin's voice rang out. Then he paused to listen to the call to prayer: "In the name of the Commander of the Faith, Caliph of the Faithful. . . ."

For the first time in centuries, no reference was made to the title of sovereign of the Ottoman Empire.

Retracting his long neck and hunching his narrow shoulders as if he suddenly felt cold, Sultan Vahiddedin disappeared into the mosque.

On the way home, Selma and her mother, saddened by the deposed Sultan's tragic demeanour and the infinite melancholy of the scene, did not exchange a word. Any conversation would have seemed out of place.

They were only a few hundred yards from the palace when two men darted out from the side of the road. The frightened horses reared, and Zeynel had to control them by hauling on the reins with all his might. The coach came to a screeching halt. While one of the men levelled a revolver at the eunuch, the other, wearing ragged trousers and a faded military tunic, strode up to the screened carriage window.

"Traitresses!" he bellowed at the passsengers inside, whom he could not see. "It won't be long before we kill the likes of you! Long live Mustafa Kemal!"

A crowd of onlookers had started to gather. They were watching the scene, open-mouthed, when a voice rang out.

"Stand back, you scum!"

The speaker was a grizzled giant of a man in the baggy trousers and short jacket of an Anatolian peasant. His face was dark with rage.

"Filthy swine!" he went on. "How dare you threaten women, let alone ladies of the family to whom your country and your pasha owe everything. Beg their pardon at once or I'll brain you!"

The crowd muttered approvingly and began to surround the two men. The latter, nationalist newcomers to the capital by all appearances, wavered. Zeynel took advantage of their hesitation to whip the horses into a gallop.

It was all over so quickly that Selma had no time to be frightened, but the ragged man had used a word that cut her to the quick: traitresses! She had heard that term of hatred and disdain applied to Ottoman citizens who sided with the occupying powers. But Selma and her family? That anyone could possibly spit such an insult in their faces was monstrous. She looked at her mother, who was staring majestically into space.

"Annéjim, why did he call us. . . ." The sound of her own voice surprised her, it was so hoarse, faint, and she could not bring herself to say the word. She pulled herself together. "Why did he call us traitresses?"

The Sultana gave a little start and looked at her so sadly that Selma felt ashamed, as if she had repeated the insult by asking what lay behind it. She lowered her eyes, abashed, but her mother answered gently.

"When you fall, Selma, there will always be weaklings to abuse and kick you. But of one thing you can be sure: whatever the faults and failings of the Ottoman family, it has never betrayed this country. The very notion is absurd. Turkey's greatness is our own – by betraying it we would be betraying ourselves."

They returned to the palace to find Haïri Bey conferring with Prince Osman Fuad. The two men looked worried when told of the latest incident.

"Don't say I didn't warn you," grumbled Haïri Bey. "And this is only the start."

The Prince frowned. "My dear aunt, you really must be more careful. There have been a number of clashes in the city, provoked either by the nationalists, who want the British out at once, or by the British themselves, who are looking for an excuse to impose martial law. They fear disturbances fomented by Kemalist agents – they even believe that the Sultan's life is in danger. His Majesty has asked General Harington to reinforce his bodyguard."

"A British bodyguard?" exclaimed the Sultana. "Are there no loyal Turks left?"

"The police, the army, and the civil service have all submitted to Kemalist authority, as you know, some from political conviction, others because they are afraid."

But the Sultana was not listening. Turning to her husband, she deliberately repeated her question.

"Are there no loyal Turks left, Haïri?"

The Damad was sullenly toying with his amber beads. Sultana Hatijé had seen little of him since the incident of the broken cane. He kept to his apartments and held endless meetings with his friends, senior dignitaries whose links with the imperial family had lost them their jobs and their incomes overnight. Although he had no wish to quarrel with his wife, he could hardly ignore a direct question.

"The situation is such, Sultana," he said, studying his well-tended nails, "that the wisest policy at present is to yield to *force majeure*. Anything else would mean civil war, and the country has seen more than enough bloodshed in the last twelve years. I suspect that even those who have their doubts about Kemal are grateful to him for saving the country. They want no further dramas."

The Sultana eyed her husband with a smile in which Selma thought she detected contempt.

CHAPTER 16

It was raining so hard the following Friday that Selma strongly doubted if she and her mother would be going to this week's selamlik. There was no question of going for a walk in the grounds either. It promised to be a boring day. She gave a huge yawn without putting her hand in front of her mouth; there was no one in the hallway and she took advantage of the situation to break the sacred laws of etiquette.

Just at that moment Zeynel appeared, running towards the Sultana's apartments. Selma, who had never seen the eunuch carry himself with so little dignity, was astonished. The unwonted exercise imparted a rhythmical wobble to his budding paunch and the flabby cheeks that made him look like a middle-aged baby. Torn between wanting to laugh and feeling alarm, she jumped to her feet.

"What's the matter, Agha?" she called.

But he didn't hear. She set off in pursuit and reached the door of her mother's boudoir breathlessly just as the eunuch was performing his third temenna, staggering with exhaustion.

"Most respected Sultana," he gasped, rolling his eyes dramatically, "most respected Princess. . . ."

He opened his mouth, but all that emerged was a gargling sound. Abruptly, he burst into tears.

Hatijé, having gestured to some maidservants to draw up a chair and bathe his face in cool, mint-scented water, calmly waited for him to pull himself together. Some of the senior kalfas, sensing that something momentous was in the wind, sidled discreetly into the boudoir while Selma, biting her lips impatiently, perched on a little satin-covered stool.

It was several minutes before Zeynel recovered his composure. Still trembling in every limb, he faced the Sultana with his hands folded and his eyes respectfully downcast.

"His Majesty the Sultan," he said in a low voice, "has fled!"

Hatijé turned pale and rose to her feet.

"Liar! How dare you?"

The words died in her throat, and for a moment she seemed about to faint. Her slaves and kalfas stood transfixed, unable to come to their mistress's aid. Then a clear voice broke the silence.

"Please go on, Agha."

Selma, undaunted by the half-swooning women around her, wanted to know the worst.

"His Majesty left Istanbul this morning, together with his son Prince Ertogrul and nine members of his retinue. They sailed aboard a British warship, the *Malaya*."

Zeynel bowed his head, and tears spattered the broadcloth of his fine black stanbulin[1].

"How shameful!" Selma was indignant. "How could he do this to us? The kitchen boys were right to call the Sultan a coward. Annéjim was angry when I told her – she said kitchen boys only understand how kitchen boys behave, not sultans. But they were right after all: the Sultan has acted like a kitchen boy!"

Pacing her room furiously, she was kicking at the furniture.

"What do we look like now? What will people think – that we are *all* cowards? I will never leave this room again!"

A quarter of an hour later, her anger having subsided, she tiptoed out into the corridor. Silence reigned, but she seemed to hear whispers in every corner – whispers that ceased at her approach. The kalfas she passed pretended not to see her. *They don't dare look at me, they are ashamed for my sake!*

Look at me, she wanted to call out. Look at me: *I* have not changed, *I* have not run away! I am still the same person, so why blush for me?

But she did not have the courage. She squared her shoulders and forced herself to walk with serene deliberation and head erect, the way a princess should, even though she secretly felt more lost than the latest addition to the haremlik. Without the deference and respect she had always taken so entirely for granted, she felt naked.

The following day, Istanbul's newspapers were filled with detailed "descriptions of the flight." Stretched out on a divan while a slave massaged her neck, Sultana Hatijé was making Zeynel read her every article from beginning to end. He tried to skip the most hostile and insulting comments, but the Sultana was not fooled. She scolded him so sharply that he reluctantly had to obey.

After expressing outrage at the Sultan's "ignominious flight" aboard a "British ship," which proved beyond doubt that he was in league with the enemies of Turkey, almost every commentator

1 Traditional black tunic with Mandarin collar.

alleged that the sovereign had absconded with the crown jewels in his baggage, jewels which belonged to the State Treasury. The governor of Istanbul had sealed the doors of Yildiz Palace prior to making a careful inventory of what had been removed. It was even claimed by some that the Sultan had appropriated the relics of the Prophet Mohammed. Without those relics, they lamented, Turkey would lose the right to enthrone the caliph of Islam and, thus, its centuries-old preeminence in the Muslim world.

Selma stared at her mother in consternation. Surely the Sultan would not have done such a thing . . . or would he? Could *all* the newspapers be wrong? Could they *all* be telling lies? She felt exhausted; her body ached as if she had been beaten. She thought of leaving the boudoir so she would not have to hear any more of it, but she did not even have the strength to move. She closed her eyes and prayed hard that this day would simply cease to exist, that it would all turn out to be a bad dream and when she awoke she would find everything in its place as before. But Zeynel's voice droned on inexorably, cataloguing all the supposed misdeeds of the fugitive, and Selma had to clench her fists and screw her eyes up tightly to stop the dizzying spiral into which she felt herself falling. Why oh why did Annéjim insist on having these awful things read out loud?

There was a sudden silence. Selma turned to see that Nessim Agha, Sultan Vahiddedin's favourite black eunuch, had just entered. She wondered why he had not left with his master. The Sultana sat up, her face brightening a little.

"Blessed be God who sent you, Agha!"

In token of her gratitude to a loyal old retainer in a disintegrating world, she invited him to sit down, but he politely declined. What better moment to demonstrate his respect, when the imperial family was being subjected to scorn and slander? Hatijé did not press him. She was grateful to the eunuch for being so tactful, and also for involuntarily teaching her a lesson: despite her agony of mind, she must behave as she always had in the past.

"My master sent for me the night before he left," the eunuch told her with tears in his eyes. "He confided his intention and told me to pack a few bags. I ventured to look at him and saw that his eyes were red with weeping. 'Be economical,' he said. 'Only take the barest essentials.' I packed only seven suits of clothes and the full-dress uniform he wore at his coronation. He asked Omer Yaver Pasha how much money he had. Then he told me, smiling sadly, 'You may join us in a few days' time, my dear Nessim, but be prepared for some very hard times, for as God is my witness, I do not have sufficient resources to support my entire family. Promise me that no one will learn of this, however, for the people measure our honour by our wealth.'"

How strange, thought Selma. Her mother always denied that wealth had any bearing on a person's reputation. What if the Sultan was right? She shivered, recalling the look of humiliation on the faces of the Russian officer and his little daughter when the kitchen boy spurned their request for bread. Was that what lay in store for her and her family?

"Efendimiz," the eunuch went on, "you remember the gold écritoire and the ruby-encrusted cigarette case our Padishah always used. The day before he left he instructed Yaver Pasha to return them to the treasury and bring him the receipts. Zeki Bey and Colonel Richard Maxwell, who were present, expressed surprise at this and urged His Majesty to take a few valuables with him to help finance his future existence abroad. The Padishah turned pale. 'I am grateful for your concern,' he told the colonel, very coldly, 'but the articles in this palace belong to the state.' Then, turning to Zeki Bey, he lost his temper. 'What right have you to speak to me like this? Do you want to besmirch the good name of the Ottoman dynasty? No member of our family has ever been a thief. And now get out!' All he took with him when he left was thrity-five thousand pounds sterling in banknotes."[2]

"Absolutely correct. I can confirm that."

Everyone turned to look. General Prince Osman Fuad had just appeared in the doorway, accompanied by a tall man in army officer's uniform. It was the officer who had spoken so unceremoniously. The kalfas stared at each other aghast, wondering whether to withdraw, but curiosity proved stronger than convention and they merely drew their veils over their faces.

With a mechanical gesture the Sultana reached for a silk scarf to conceal her luxuriant hair from the stranger's gaze. Not finding one handy, she gave an almost imperceptible shrug. What did it matter, after all? The situation was too serious to take offence. In any case, there was something familiar about the man, who was now standing just inside the door with his head bowed, embarrassed by his own audacity. It was Selma who solved her mother's embarrassment.

"Don't you remember, Annéjim? It is the attic rat!"

It had taken her a few moments to identify him, because the strong, healthy figure at her uncle's side bore little resemblance to the fugitive they had sheltered not so long ago. Selma recognized him by his

2 Memoirs of Nessim Agha.

eyes, which were dark green and fringed with long black lashes – eyes like a girl's, she had thought at the time.

Prince Fuad apologized profusely.

"Please forgive this intrusion, Sultana, but the palace is deserted and we could find no one to announce us. My friend Colonel Karim has some information about His Majesty's departure – information so surprising that I insisted on his conveying it in person."

"You were right to do so, Nephew. The colonel and I are old acquaintances, by the way."

The Sultana smiled, savouring the flabbergasted look on her nephew's face. She loved to shock. It was her discreet revenge on the strict rules of Ottoman society, which she had always thought it necessary to observe but essential to know when to break. She invited the two men to sit down and sent a maid for some sherbets. Even if she were at death's door, thought Selma, Annéjim would serve sherbets to those who came to pay their last respects. She herself found extremely irritating this sacred law of hospitality, which was given prime consideration even in the most urgent circumstances. "Rituals and deliberation are like velvet cushions," her mother had once told her, "necessary for absorbing shocks." The young girl rejected this view of life. What she wanted from life was not softness, but angularity – spurs to stimulate her.

The officer seemed ill at ease. "Although I hold the rank of colonel in the nationalist army" – he nervously cleared his throat a couple of times – "and although I do not disown the cause we fought for, I should like you to know, Sultana, that many of us deplore the abolition of the monarchy. We had long suspected Kemal Pasha's intentions, but we were compelled to choose between the dynasty and the country. It was a difficult choice because, as Ottoman officers, we had sworn allegiance to the Sultan. Some of us resigned. I, despite the bonds existing between myself and your family, decided to serve on. Turkey has need of all her soldiers."

Colonel Karim had obviously rehearsed his speech with care, but he was nonetheless embarrassed. The silence in Hatijé's boudoir became even more oppressive. The kalfas held their breath, the Sultana toyed with her rings. Suddenly she looked up.

"Well, Colonel, I do not suppose you came here to enlighten me on your state of mind?"

Selma started. She had never heard her mother speak so cuttingly to a subordinate. But perhaps she no longer considered the colonel a subordinate, but rather the representative of the new powers. Perhaps it was on these new powers that she was pouring her scorn.

The colonel flushed, and Selma thought he would get up and go. Instead, he smiled sadly and gave a little bow.

"In fact, Sultana, all that emboldened me to come was the memory of your past kindness. I now see that I was mistaken, and that certain things, unfortunately, are irreconcilable."

Hatijé bit her lip. Her sense of injury had made her unjust, and now the harm was done she was certainly not going to apologize.

"I am listening," she said simply. Although she tried to inject a little gentleness into her tone, the words sounded like an imperial decree. Prince Fuad stepped into the breach.

"Speak up, my friend, we are dying to hear what you have to say."

The colonel suppressed his urge to walk out and settled himself in his armchair.

"It so happens that the Sultan's naval attaché is a childhood friend of mine. This morning he called on me in great distress. From what he told me, I can assure you that the Sultan was browbeaten into leaving by Ankara."

A murmur of disbelief greeted this statement, but the colonel ignored it.

"When His Majesty refused to abdicate," he went on, "the Kemalists did all they could to intimidate him. They started a rumour that he might by lynched by the mob. They even instructed Refet Bey – who refused – to organize hostile demonstrations around the palace. The Sultan is an old man exhausted by four years of humiliation, threats, and pressures of all kinds. Their aim was to break his spirit, and they succeeded. Think what a godsend it is from the Kemalists' point of view, the Sultan's sudden flight! No more need to arraign him for high treason, which would have alienated the majority of public opinion. By leaving in this way the Sovereign not only incriminated himself in the eyes of the people but brought disgrace on his entire family. The Kemalists have disposed of the sultanate for good without having to soil their hands."[3]

3 Lord Kinross, Mustafa Kemal's principal biographer, describes in his book *Atatürk* how at 6 A.M. on 17 November 1922, the Sultan's naval attaché, who had been assigned to his entourage to spy on him, saw Vahiddedin leave the grounds of the palace by a secret door and get into a British ambulance. Highly alarmed, the attaché ran a mile in his bedroom slippers before finding a cab. He then drove straight to the palace of the Sublime Porte, two miles away. The whole journey could not have taken more than half an hour.

To his great surprise, the governor told him to go back to bed and said that, as soon as he had telegraphed the information to Mustafa Kemal, he proposed to do likewise. It also transpires, from a telegram dispatched to London by the British

The Sultana's eyes flashed. "Ankara's interest in this affair is obvious," she snapped, "but, pressure or no pressure, the Padishah should never have fled."

"He has dishonoured us all!" Prince Fuad chimed in.

Paradoxically, it was the Sultan's own family who condemned him and the Kemalist officer who came to his defence.

"The Sultan's departure may have prevented a civil war," he said. "Refet Bey warned him that blood would flow again unless he abdicated. Who knows, perhaps he hopes to return some day by forming an Islamic alliance in his capacity as Commander of the Faithful. In any case, he left in the firm belief that no member of the Ottoman family would agree to take his place and be content with the title of caliph alone."

"Really?" Hatijé permitted herself a sceptical smile. "We shall soon see, but I am afraid His Majesty is deluding himself. Not all our princes are heroes."

The very next day, Crown Prince Abdul Mejid accepted the Kemalist government's invitation to become caliph in Vahiddedin's place. He was installed at Topkapi Palace on 24 November 1922, at a ceremony graced by the sacred relics of the Prophet and the presence of a delegation from Ankara.

Embassy, that the *Malaya* did not sail with the Sultan on board until 8.45 A.M.

In view of Lord Kinross's account, it seems clear that the Kemalists facilitated Vahiddedin's escape in collusion with the British. More than two hours elapsed between the time the governor was alerted and the departure of the *Malaya*, yet no attempt was made to track the Sultan down.

CHAPTER 17

The ashes in the big silver brazier had long grown cold, and the servants would not be lighting it again until bedtime. Coal was scarce in January 1923, Turkey's first year of independence. All over Istanbul, teeth were chattering in palace and tenement alike.

Although the Sultana was opposed to asking favours on principle, Haïri Bey had taken it upon himself to seek help from his few remaining friends in the civil service, but to no avail. However honoured people had formerly felt when asked to do the imperial family a favour, today no one would risk lifting a finger for them.

Selma, muffled up in a sable-lined caftan, was sitting motionless in her room. Neatly laid out on the silk carpet were her three charshafs: the pink, the green, and the turquoise. She contemplated them dreamily. She did not even dislike them any more. Now that she had decided to sacrifice them she found them almost pretty – in their own way.

There was a light footstep, and a slim, fair-haired girl slipped into the room. It was Sekerbuli, her best friend now that Gulnar, the fiery Tatar, had left Ortaköy for the imperial harem at Yildiz Palace.

Several months had passed since Gulnar's departure, but Selma trembled with fury whenever she thought of it. The decision to let Gulnar go had been taken at short notice – indeed, she had not learned of it until the next day, when it was too late even to bid her friend goodbye. Her indignant protests had met with a concerted response from the Sultana and her kalfas: Gulnar had been fortunate enough to catch the eye of the first Cadin, who had expressed a wish to employ her as a lady's maid and promised to find her a good husband. Gulnar was nearly fourteen and already a woman. What more could any girl hope for?

"What more can *we* hope for?" Selma sneered. "I will tell you: this!" And she solemnly brandished her gold-plated scissors.

"Must we really?" Sekerbuli murmured apprehensively.

"Yes, really!"

Selma's lingering doubts were banished by her friend's misgivings. Resolutely she bent over the three charshafs and slit them up the middle. "Take that, and that, and that! That will teach you to keep me prisoner!"

Sekerbuli plucked up her courage and lent a hand. Silently and systematically, in the knowledge that they were performing a necessary sacrilege, the two girls savaged the delicate material. What a job it was, though! They would never have believed it would take so long.

"We must be quick," Selma whispered. "Someone may come in and stop us before we have finished."

They abandoned the scissors and used both hands, suddenly convulsed with laughter now that the garments were beyond repair. How sweet it was to tug at the silk and hear it rip, hear the crisp and astringent sound of freedom! The floor at their feet was littered with colourful strips like festival streamers.

"Now to make up the parcels," said Selma. "One for Halidé Edib, the other for Latifé Hanum. I bet they will be delighted."

Selma still preserved a special regard for the young woman who had galvanized the crowd in Sultan Ahmed Square. Her memory of the demonstration was like a blinding light. And although she had been nine at the time, she felt it was then that she had really been born.

More recently, however, the two girls' attention had been monopolized by Latifé, Mustafa Kemal's vivacious wife, whose doings they followed with keen interest through the medium of feminist periodicals smuggled into the palace by Mademoiselle Rose.

Latifé Hanum, whose avowed aim was to "liberate her sisters," set them a conspicuous example. The first woman to attend meetings of the Grand Assembly, she had scandalized everyone by receiving deputies in her husband's office, next door to the chamber itself. When castigated for meddling in politics, she merely laughed and retorted that women now had the right, and even the duty, to assist in shaping their country's destiny.

"But women have always helped to shape this country's destiny," protested Sultana Hatijé, who was irritated by Latifé's more dogmatic pronouncements. "They simply did not find it necessary to shout it from the rooftops. Concealed behind the moucharabié, our great cadins have followed the deliberations of the Divan[1] for centuries, and the direction of the empire's policy was often affected by the advice they gave the sovereign. In the East, any intelligent woman knows how to influence her husband's decisions, but she is wise enough not to flaunt the fact. That creature Latifé Hanum behaves like the Western women who feel they do not exist unless they are constantly seen and heard. That is how children and prim-

1 The Sultan's privy council.

itive tribes behave."

Selma sadly, helplessly shook her head. How could her mother fail to understand? Who cared if Latifé Hanum was vain and conceited? What mattered was that she had broken down barriers and let a little fresh air into the claustrophobic world of the harem. *Don't you feel just as suffocated as I do, Annéjim? Or are you simply resigned? Resigned . . . no, that word does not fit your royal pride. It is more that you have become philosophical over the years. But me – I am young! I want to live!*

She breathed deeply. She felt strong, so obviously destined for great things that the sensation made her tremble with expectancy like a thoroughbred at sunrise quivering at the sight of meadows stretching away to the horizon.

"What should we write?" asked Sekerbuli.

Her friend's voice brought her down to earth. Yes, what should they write and tell their heroines? That they were only twelve but had been longing to join them for years; that they were ready to do anything in their power to help; that they could not remain cooped up in the haremlik when life was seething all around them; that they wanted to escape and take part in the struggle, or die!

"Die?" Sekerbuli looked aghast.

"Of course!" Selma retorted sternly.

She burned with impatience at what she overheard from the tradeswomen who still visited the palace and what she read in the newspapers she filched from Mademoiselle Rose. Her country was in the throes of transformation – Istanbul was undergoing a revolution – and she, Selma, was forced to sit there over her embroidery frame!

The other day, when she had mooted the idea of going to one of the new schools for girls set up by Halidé Edib's educational association, the Sultana had glared at her. When she ventured to persist, arguing that the standard of teaching was said to be very high, Annéjim had not even deigned to reply. She was not disheartened, though; she always got her way in the end. It would not be long before Halidé Edib and Latifé Hanum came to speak to her mother. Meantime, she was preparing herself.

Together with Sekerbuli, she read and reread accounts of the intrepid women who had distinguished themselves in the struggle for independence. The girls were conversant with every detail of the life of Munever Saimé, better known as "Soldier Saimé," decorated for exceptional gallantry. Likewise with the adventures of Makbulé, who had set off for the mountains on her wedding day and joined the guerrillas in company with her bridegroom. Likewise with the prowess of

Rahmiyé, who was killed at the head of a detachment of the Ninth Division while leading a successful attack on a French command post.

The traditional image of the flower of the harem, a shrinking violet, had been superseded by that of the celebrated or unsung heroines without whom, so Mustafa Kemal declared, Turkey could not have won the war. "The war is over, but the struggle continues," had said Latifé Hanum, and it was true that every day brought a new crop of innovations. Selma and Sekerbuli enthusiastically followed their progress: this, even more than the fight against the Greek invader, was *their* fight.

The chief of police had published an ordinance abolishing the curtains and wooden screens that separated women from men in streetcars, trains, and ferry boats. Wives were now entitled to sit beside their husbands without becoming liable to a fine. The same applied in restaurants and theatres, though few families took advantage of this new freedom for fear of being abused or even molested by traditionalists who proclaimed that it was contrary to the spirit of Islam.

But the real scandal had been a decree announcing that classes at Istanbul University would in future be mixed. Classrooms had hitherto been divided by thick curtains to safeguard the modesty of the few Turkish girls who pursued a higher education. From now on, Muslim families were confronted with a thorny problem: they could either put an end to their daughters' education or almost certainly condemn them to die unwed. For even the most progressive young man – the most sincere and ardent champion of women's emancipation – bowed to his mother's wishes when embarking on a step as serious as marriage, and his mother, with loving care, chose him a traditional bride whose face no other man could boast of having seen.

It was five o'clock, and the light was already fading. Sekerbuli had gone home to her mother. Left alone, Selma contemplated the two neat, multicoloured mounds of shredded silk. Shadows were creeping into the room. This afternoon's fine resolutions were becoming tinged with uncertainty. . . .

"What is the matter, Djijim? You look sad."

"Oh, Baba!"

Selma cast etiquette to the winds and rushed into her father's arms. It was at least a week since she had seen him. The Damad's visits to the haremlik were growing steadily rarer. In the old days, when Selma wanted to see him, she had devised a variety of pretexts for sneaking into his quarters, but her fateful twelfth birthday had deprived her of the right to pass the massive door that separated the domain of women from the outside world. In vain had she stormed and pleaded that she wanted to see her Baba. "Come now, Princess," was the kalfas' and eunuchs' disapproving response, "you are not a child any more."

Not a child any more! What did they mean – that she was too grown-up to need a father's love? He had never paid her much attention, admittedly, but the simple fact of sitting beside him while he read or chatted with his friends had always seemed an infinitely precious privilege. She gazed at him in silence. How handsome he was! She loved everything about him, even the hurtful sarcasm and offhand manner that impressed her as a mark of superior intelligence. She needed his presence; it made her happy just to look at him. Impulsively, she seized his hand.

"Baba, couldn't you ask Annéjim – please?"

She broke off. His hand stiffened and the smile left his eyes.

"I am not your errand boy, young lady!" he said icily.

It was as if a slab of marble had hit her full in the chest. She winced and hung her head. Why was he so hard on her – what had she said? All at once she understood: how stupid of her, when she knew perfectly well that her parents had not communicated for weeks except through Zeynel! She had even scolded two young kalfas for commenting on the situation aloud, and now she had been as tactless as those two silly girls. Baba had been in such a good mood, too. He had come specially to see her, and she had gone and spoiled everything. . . .

"However, Selma," he went on more gently, "if you have something to say to me, I am prepared to listen."

She kept silent. If she opened her mouth, she would start to cry and there was nothing he disliked as much as tears. Yet she had to say something or else he would think she had something against him, or that she was taking Annéjim's side. That wasn't it; she wasn't on anyone's side. She loved them both, but loved them in such different ways that sometimes she felt as if there were two different Selmas who loved. She had often thought about this: when her mother smiled at her, she felt as if she could take on the world; when her father smiled at her she forgot the world and instead melted with happiness, sweetly, like a fruit drop on the tongue. She didn't know why, but she knew she didn't want to have to choose between those two smiles.

She looked up – gazed with shining eyes at his long, pale face, his thin lips, and the countless little creases that formed stars at the corner of his eyelids. She gazed at him as if she wanted to keep him within her forever. He produced a cigar and gave her a conspiratorial wink.

"Speak up, Djijim. What is this terrible problem of yours?"

"Baba, I want to go to school!"

"I see. Presumably you have been told that school is an unsuitable place for a princess?"

Selma refrained from commenting on this allusion to the Sultana. "But Baba," she insisted, "everyone's going to school these days. Soreya Ağaoğlu has even enrolled in law school – all the newspapers published her picture and Kemal Pasha congratulated her. Turkey's future depends on the emancipation of women, he says, and a country where half the population remains shut up is a country half paralyzed!"

"Hm. . . ." Haïri Bey stroked his moustache. "That is one of the few points on which that bandit and I agree."

Selma ignored this insult to her hero. Her father agreed, that was the main thing.

"You mean I can go?"

"Go where?"

"To school, of course."

Haïri Bey shrugged. "Since when has a father decided how his daughter should be educated, especially when her mother is a Sultana? Do not belabour the subject, Selma. I cannot help you."

"Yes, you can! You could if only you wanted to!" Her face crimsoned with frustration. "I cannot stand it any more, Baba! Everything is changing in our country – everyone is coming to life! We are the only ones that are still asleep, as if nothing had happened. I want to leave this palace – I want to *leave*!"

A shadow of sadness flitted across the Damad's face.

"Don't worry, dearest Selma," he said with a sigh. "You may leave here sooner than you think, and I am very much afraid you may regret it. . . ."

Neither Latifé Hanum nor Halidé Edib replied to the messages smuggled out of the palace in the basket of an obliging tradeswoman. Selma and Sekerbuli abandoned all hope. As for the charshafs, the Sultana did not even trouble to ask what had happened to them: she simply instructed the dressmakers to make some more – in black.

Life at Ortaköy Palace went on as it always had, discounting enforced economies. The new governor had abolished the civil list, so members of the imperial family received no more than the derisory allowance that had been voted them by the Grand Assembly. They did not mind too much because all their unemployed relatives and friends were in similar straits – in fact they found their situation a source of amusement. As Sultana Hatijé wryly remarked: "It's better to be *nouveaux pauvres* than *nouveaux riches*."

Although the Sultana had been compelled to dismiss several of her maidservants, her establishment still included "the children of the house," the female slaves who had always formed part of the family. The only thing that really distressed her was having to give up "the soup of the poor," not for reasons of economy – she would happily have limited her own meals to a single course rather than know that people outside her walls were close to starvation – but because the government looked with extreme disfavour on such generosity. Members of the Ottoman family could not afford to draw attention to themselves. So she gave orders that those who knocked at her door – and many did – should be fed in secret.

The situation in 1923 was desperate, not only in Istanbul but throughout the country. Ruined by twelve years of war and occupation, the people of Turkey were sick of hardship. A loaf of bread that had cost one piastre before the war now cost nine, and meat was twelve or thirteen times as expensive. At this price it was available only to a few privileged people. Every day hundreds died of cold and starvation.

The country's difficulties were aggravated by the chaos that reigned at Ankara, where the new government had installed itself. All the authority once vested in Istanbul had now been transferred to the overgrown Anatolian market town that Mustafa Kemal had chosen to be Turkey's new capital. He planned to turn his back on the past and build a modern country along the lines of the European great powers. Republican and secular France, which had influenced the Turkish intelligentsia for almost a century, was to be its model.

Republican and secular . . . that was where the shoe pinched, for although the victorious generalissimo and president of the Grand Assembly was currently all-powerful, many of his comrades in arms were worried by what they regarded as his "despotic" tendencies. They had not forgotten how the abolition of the sultanate had been forced on them in defiance of public opinion, which expected the Sultan to be replaced by a constitutional monarch with Mustafa Kemal as his prime minister.

The Ghazi[2] was, in fact, distrusted by the entire Grand Assembly

2 "Victorious," a title conferred on him by the Grand Assembly in recognition of his victory at the Sakarya River.

and his original associates in particular. They had rallied around him during the war because they recognized his military genius. When it came to setting up a legally constituted government, however, they were chary of entrusting its leadership to a man whose violence and lack of scruples they had experienced to their cost.

That spring of 1923, the assassination of Ali Chukru Bey had terrified them. Ali Chukru Bey was the member of parliament for Trebizond, one of the principal leaders of parliamentary opposition, and had often challenged Kemal. In particular, he advocated restoring some of Caliph Abdul Mejid's secular power. One morning, he was found strangled and it soon became clear that the assassin was Osman the Cripple, the Ghazi's chief bodyguard. Before Osman could talk, however, he was killed in a confrontation with the police. This incident caused a great outcry and Mustafa Kemal was accused outright of suppressing a political opponent. The members of parliament, alarmed, considered themselves warned.

Kemal, who sensed that opposition was growing, even among his parliamentary supporters, proceeded to build up a firm popular base. The committees formed in 1919 throughout Turkey to carry on the nationalist struggle were dependent on him as commander-in-chief of the army. He decided to transform this paramilitary organization into a political party, "the People's Party," with a branch in every village, and for that purpose undertook a nationwide tour: "The country is teeming with traitors," he was telling the committees' representatives. "Be vigilant! It is for you, the People's Party, to govern!"

Meanwhile, in Istanbul, some journalists were taking advantage of his absence to criticize the new "dictatorship" and predict that the sultanate would soon be restored. On his return to Ankara, Kemal let it be known that persistent critics were liable to be hanged. He banned all public debate and even tried to abolish parliamentary immunity in an effort to snuff out opposition from deputies whom he considered reactionaries or fools. In the latter instance he failed; the "fools" were not foolish enough to saw off the branch they sat on. . . .

Rauf Pasha, one of Kemal's oldest friends, resigned in disgust. Other longstanding associates such as Rahmi, Adnan, Refet Bey, Ali Fuad, and Karabekir, all of them leading members of the nationalist movement, distanced themselves from him. Kemal's parliamentary majority was melting away before his very eyes, alienated by his brutality and authoritarianism. But the army remained loyal to him and the People's Party was spreading its tentacles throughout the country.

And . . . above all, peace had just been concluded! On 24 July 1923, after eight long months of negotiation, the Lausanne Conference attended by representatives of the Western Powers and Ismet Pasha[3], the Turkish foreign minister, ended in triumph. The Turks had lost their empire but were now a free and independent nation, and that, they knew, was primarily the achievement of Mustafa Kemal.

Forever afterwards, Selma would remember the departure of the last remnants of the forces of occupation. She accompanied her mother to Dolmabahçé where, with her aunts and cousins, she pressed against the tall windows overlooking the square on the banks of the Bosporus where the military ceremonies were to take place. The October sunlight played on the marble fountains and both banks of the river were crowded with onlookers.

At 10.30 A.M., preceded by a naval band, a contingent of Turkish infantry took up its position in the square beneath the national flag, a white crescent and star on a red ground. The French 66th Regiment appeared a few minutes later, proudly bearing its bullet-riddled colours, followed by contingents of British and Italian troops. They formed up facing the Turks while the diplomatic corps, which had turned out to a man, stood stiffly waiting.

Eleven-thirty saw the arrival of the Allied high commissioners, General Pellé, General Harington, the Marchese Garroni, three pale figures in gold-braided uniforms. Briskly but unable to conceal his emotion, the governor of Istanbul stepped forward to greet them.

Then the bands struck up the fanfares. In turn they played the national anthems of Britain, France and Italy. At last the tones of the Turkish anthem rose solemnly, while the large red and white flag unfurled in the wind. Slowly the Allied troops marched past to salute it, then they made a dignified exit from the square and headed for the docks.

One by one, each playing its own national anthem, the foreign warships drew away from the land that had witnessed their victorious arrival five years earlier. Silently the crowds watched them until they dwindled to little grey specks on the blue waters of the Bosphorus.

At the window in Dolmabahçé, a girl squeezed her mother's hand. They looked at each other and smiled through their tears.

A few days later Selma tumbled out of bed to the sound of gunfire. Her worst fears had come true: "they" had only pretended to leave and were now returning in force! She darted to the window in her

3 Subsequently known as Ismet Inönü when the Turkish government required everyone to adopt a surname.

bare feet and scanned the horizon: not a warship to be seen, just a few inoffensive caiques and fishing boats gliding across the Bosporus in the limpid morning light. Yet still the bombardment continued, steady, inexorable. Selma's cheeks burned with indignation. She slipped into her caftan, and two minutes later she was in her mother's room.

"No, Djijim, it isn't the British or the French or the Italians – nor the Greeks, thank God! It is in honour of the Republic."

"The Republic – like in France, you mean?" Selma promptly regretted having paid so little attention to Mademoiselle Rose's history lessons.

The Sultana pursed her lips, looking sceptical.

"To many people in this country a republic signifies liberty, equality, and fraternity. But I am very much afraid it will not turn out to be any of those things. Rauf Bey is furious, I gather. He was not even told of the decision, it was taken at such short notice, nor were a hundred other opposition deputies. He claims it is another strong-arm tactic on the part of Kemal, who has had himself elected president at the same time!"

The Istanbul newspapers shared this sentiment. Their headlines harshly condemned the instigator of what many regarded as a brazen coup d'état: "The Republic has been inaugurated with a gun to the nation's head!" – "A constitution concocted in days by Kemal and a handful of yes-men: is that the new Turkish state?" – "The powers accorded to the Ghazi are greater than any sultan's!" Mustafa Kemal was compared to the Holy Trinity of the Christians: Father, Son and Holy Spirit in a single person. He did, in fact, embody every available form of authority. He was President of the Republic, head of government and parliament, commander-in-chief of the armed forces, and leader of Turkey's only political party. To those who had dreamed of a constitutional monarchy or a democracy in the Western mould this came as a rude shock. They realized that, from now on, nothing and no one could oppose the Ghazi's decisions.

In the streets, by contrast, enthusiasm reigned. Townsfolk acclaimed the news in song, and torchlight processions wound through every district. No one knew what a "republic" was, but it sounded fraught with promise. Even the inmates of the central prison demonstrated with ringing cries of "Long live the Republic! Justice forever!" and demanded to be released on the spot.

It mattered little to Selma whether Turkey was a republic or a monarchy, since Mustafa Kemal was in charge anyway. At the same time, certain aspects of the man she still privately thought of as "Golden

Rose" were beginning to annoy her, notably the whim that had prompted him to make Ankara the capital of Turkey instead of aristocratic Istanbul. Although this step had long been discussed, no one had believed that it would ever be taken. How could a market town in the depths of the barren Anatolian plateau replace the pride of the Ottoman Empire? Poised on the threshold of two continents, Istanbul had been born of an Apollonian oracle thirteen centuries before the Hegira. Permeated by every culture and civilization, it had become a unique crossroads between East and West. To a man like Mustafa Kemal, however, questions were a luxury, he was only interested in answers. On 13 October 1923, Istanbul lost the age-old status that had made it one of the world's focal points.

It was at this period that Ahmed's father decided to quit his job as the Damad's secretary, an unpopular one in the triumphant heyday of Kemalism, and take up a new post at Ankara. It was months since Selma had seen Ahmed – to be precise, since her twelfth birthday – but they had exchanged long letters. These had been reluctantly delivered by Zeynel, who could refuse the little Sultana nothing, but when she asked him to arrange a meeting with the boy, he merely raised his eyebrows.

"You are the light of my eyes, Princess, but you know I cannot do that."

"Agha, you are the only person who can help me! He is leaving, and I simply must see him one last time!"

She wept so bitterly that the eunuch gave in. His love for her was exceeded only by his need to be loved in return. One of her smiles – she had her mother's smile – was compensation enough.

The farewells took place in the Nightingale Pavilion with Zeynel standing guard outside the door. He had granted them a quarter of an hour together. Ahmed, very pale and wearing his best clothes, stared at the ground.

Why on earth did I ask to see him? He does not even look particularly pleased. . . . If only I had known. . . . Still, he did write me all those beautiful letters. . . . Why doesn't he say something? Now he is blushing! The poor boy never was very resolute. No, I am being unfair – he is unhappy. But I am unhappy too! Very unhappy! He is leaving me, after all, not the other way around. God, I never knew a quarter of an hour could last so long. Say something, Ahmed, say something before I explode. . . .

"Ahmed!"

He raised his head, and she saw that he was crying.

"Ahmed, please don't cry, I forbid you to! I am the one who should be crying."

"You? Why you, my Princess?"

"Because you are deserting me."

I should never have said that. How sad he looks. So silent. . . . He does not even try to defend himself. How could he, without condemning his father? Grown-ups are like that – always talking about their principles but forgetting them when it suits them. Annéjim is not like that, thank goodness. Nor is Baba, of course. . . .

"Don't be sad, Ahmed. You will make lots of friends at Ankara – you will soon forget me. . . ."

"Forget you, my Princess? How could I?"

He gazed at her so reproachfully that she felt ashamed – ashamed of the pain she was inflicting but could not manage to share. And yet, when she had learned of his departure her heart had felt like lead and she had thought: so this is love. She had even imagined him asking her to run away with him and toyed with the idea of saying yes. Instead of that, he was sitting there crying – he had not even taken her hand. Her throat contracted, not because Ahmet was leaving, but because she had suddenly grasped the truth: she did not love him.

She removed her blue velvet hair ribbon and held it out. Ahmet's face lit up. He looked so overjoyed that it made her feel bad, as if she had lied to him, but could she tell him that a ribbon was after all only a ribbon? Besides, what did she really know herself?

A few days later Selma lost her beloved Gülfilis as well. The former slave girl turned up in tears one morning, clasping her baby to her breast. Her husband, an official in the Ministry of Finance, had been transferred to Ankara, but Gülfilis refused to go. She had come to beg her "adoptive mother" to take her in, with her little boy.

The Sultana took hours to convince Gülfilis that it was her duty to accompany her husband. Selma, seated at the young woman's side, spent those hours hoping for a miraculous change of heart on her mother's part, but in vain. When the sky became tinged with purple and gold, it was time for Gülfilis to return home.

To dispel the melancholy atmosphere, Selma suggested giving a farewell party for the pretty Circassian and all her old friends from the haremlik: an excursion by ox cart to the hills above Eyüp and a picnic overlooking the Golden Horn.

These were the last days of autumn and coppery light glinted through the amaranth leaves fringing the narrow, stony paths. The oxen, their heads daubed with henna and their horns entwined with strings of blue beads to ward off the evil eye, drew the brightly painted carts, decorated with garlands and bunches of sweet-smelling flowers. They seemed like the rustic carriages of some olden-day yeoman.

Inside them, hidden from view by silk curtains and reclining on plump cushions, the women chattered and laughed as they had in the good old days. Only the guest of honour remained silent and withdrawn in the midst of all this gaiety. Selma nestled against her and took her hand. Gülfilis's mournful expression wrung her heart. She had the same sad eyes as Ahmed, eyes that said "never again" even as her lips murmured, "We will be seeing each other soon!"

The excursion to which Selma had so much looked forward proved to be as cheerful as a visit to a graveyard, and she cursed herself for having insisted on it. She should have clung to her image of Gülfilis as a light-hearted, carefree girl; now that happy picture was gone. In spite of all their pleasantries and promises – Gülfilis would spend some weeks at Ortaköy in a year's time, and Selma would surely visit Ankara when she was older – their tears told them with painful certainty that they would never see one another again.

The new Caliph, Abdul Mejid, led a peaceful existence at Dolmabahçé Palace. An affable man of fifty-five, he divided his time between painting, music, and theology. He made no attempt to meddle in politics. Being very devout, however, he took quite seriously his role as Commander of the Faithful and spiritual leader of 350 million Muslims.

He left the palace once a week only, when he attended the selamlik, and had made a point of restoring its pristine pomp and ceremony. Every Friday he betook himself in state to Aya Sofya or some other of the city's principal mosques. Escorted by a troop of hussars, he would sometimes exchange his carriage for a magnificent white charger and ride through streets lined with cheering crowds, an impressive figure with a long white beard and eyes of an unusual violet shade.

Sometimes the Caliph would cross the Bosporus in the imperial caique of white and gold and go to pray in the great mosque at Üsküdar. On two or three occasions he even donned the coat and tall turban worn by his ancestor Mehmet Fatih, the eighteen-year-old sultan who had captured Constantinople in 1453.

The new master of Turkey was profoundly annoyed by these demonstrations and the Caliph's evident popularity, the more so because Abdul Mejid's visitors included not only foreign ambassadors and dignitaries but Turkish politicians and heroes of the war of independence such as Rauf Pasha and Refet Bey, who continued to address him as "Your Majesty." Refet had even presented him with a superb stallion, a gift to which the newspapers of Istanbul devoted as many column inches as they did to all the Caliph's doings.

Abdul Mejid was involuntarily becoming a focus of resistance to the regime. Like a lodestone, he attracted dissidents of all kinds: impoverished aristocrats, retired generals, dismissed officials, former palace dignitaries, and, last but not least, Muslim clerics.

The fact was that Mustafa Kemal had abandoned all pretence of religion since his victory. Recently he had outraged the faithful by hurling a Koran at the Sheikh ul-Islam. It was said that women at Ankara were compelled to go around unveiled, and that the same rule would soon be applied throughout the country. Most scandalous of all, the Ghazi erected a statue of himself, something no sultan had ever dared to do because representations of the human form were forbidden by the Islamic religion, which regarded them as idolatrous.

Gradually, Kemal's opponents regrouped under the banner of Islam. In mosques and public squares, sheikhs and hojas[4] anathematized his "pagan" government. Pamphlets and caricatures were distributed by the very monasteries that had once assisted Kemal in his struggle for independence. The head of state was accused of immorality as well as despotism. Infuriated by Latifé Hanum's jealousy, he had just divorced her and resumed his bachelor ways. From now on he spent his nights in bars, gambling, drinking, and flaunting his affairs with prostitutes.

His reputation was not enhanced by Fikriyé's suicide in the fall of 1923. A young kinswoman who had always been madly in love with the handsome general, she returned to Ankara as soon as she learned of his divorce, prepared to live with him on any terms. Kemal unceremoniously threw her out. Fikriyé's body was found in a ditch the next day: she had shot herself.

By this time, hopes were being pinned on the Caliph not only by monarchists and clerics but also by numerous democrats sickened by Kemal's excesses. Abdul Mejid would, they felt, make an ideal constitutional monarch: a man of wisdom and integrity, but not sufficiently forceful to clash with his ministers.

Mustafa Kemal saw the danger coming. So far he had not dared to defy public opinion by abolishing the caliphate, which he privately termed "a medieval tumour," but he knew that he would never be the country's absolute master until he had done so.

4 Muslim teachers.

It was Abdul Mejid himself who furnished the pretext he needed by requesting an increase in his civil list allowance on the ground that it was insufficient to enable him to fulfil his official duties in a worthy manner. Kemal bluntly replied that "a caliph should live frugally, and that the caliphate had become a historical relic whose continued existence was totally unjustifiable."

From now on it was open warfare. At the Ghazi's instigation, the official press whipped itself into a fury. "What use is the caliphate?" it demanded. "It is a function that costs the state a great deal of money and threatens to become a springboard for the restoration of the sultanate!" To which the moderate papers replied: "The caliphate is invaluable to our country. If we abolish it, Turkey and its ten million inhabitants will forfeit all importance in the Muslim world and become, from the European perspective, an insignificant little country."

On 5 December a bomb burst in the shape of a letter from the Aga Khan, which was published by three Istanbul newspapers. The head of the Ismaeli community protested at the harassment of the Commander of the Faithful and demanded that he be maintained "in a position that will assure him of the esteem and confidence of all Muslim nations."

Though anodyne enough, the letter had been mailed from London. This was too good an opportunity to miss. Mustafa Kemal cried conspiracy and denounced the Aga Khan as an agent of foreign powers seeking to divide the Turkish people. The editors of the newspapers that had dared to publish the letter were arrested and tried. The Grand Assembly passed a "treason law" under which those who demonstrated against the Republic or in favour of the old regime would be punished by death, and Kemal informed the commissioner for religious affairs, who had been rash enough to speak in the Caliph's defence, that if he continued to talk that way he would risk hanging. Throughout the country army officers, civil servants, and clerics were arrested. Turkey appeared to be on the verge of a putsch.

Abdul Mejid remained silently in his palace until the storm had passed. But the Ghazi was firmly resolved to get rid of him. He ordered the Governor of Istanbul to ban the selamlik ceremony. If the Caliph wanted to pray in the mosque, let him take a cab. The hussar escort was disbanded, the imperial caique confiscated, and the Caliph's income reduced to the point where he could no longer maintain his staff of secretaries and advisers. Any loyal retainers who insisted on standing by him were advised "for their own safety" to leave the palace as quickly as possible.

Two months passed. Mustafa Kemal went off to supervise the annual military manoeuvres near Izmir, and the Caliph's immediate circle took heart: it had only been a false alarm. In reality, the Ghazi had gone to confer with his military commanders. After discussions lasting several days, he succeeded in persuading them that the religious authority of the Ottoman family must be eliminated for good.

The army was behind him; he could strike. As for the Grand Assembly, he knew he held it in the palm of his hand. Although numerous deputies would express their usual reservations, none would dare disobey him. In any case, he had taken certain precautions. Summoning Rauf Pasha, his most prestigious opponent, before the central committee of the People's Party, he had compelled him to swear an oath of allegiance to the Republic and its president on pain of being expelled from parliament and exiled from Turkey. Aware of what was in the wind but conscious that they were powerless to prevent it, Rauf Pasha and Refet Bey left Ankara.

The final assault was launched on 27 February 1924. The Kemalist faction, having denounced the supporters of the old regime for conspiring against the Republic, demanded the abolition of the caliphate. On 3 March, after a week of protests and altercations, the Grand Assembly finally complied: by a show of hands it voted for the immediate expulsion, not only of Abdul Mejid, but of the Ottoman princes and princesses as well.

"We all have to leave within three days!"

It was only nine o'clock in the morning, an unconventional hour at which to call on Sultana Hatijé, but General Prince Osman Fuad was beside himself with indignation. He had just learned that the Caliph, accompanied by his two wives and his children, had boarded the Orient Express at dawn, bound for Switzerland.

"The governor and the chief of police turned up late last night while the Caliph was reading in the library, so his chamberlain told me. They even surrounded the palace for fear that he might escape! The Caliph behaved with great dignity: he merely asked if he might have a few days to put his affairs in order, but the rascals refused point-blank. They have forbidden the press to mention it for another twenty-four hours, afraid of a public outcry. They barely gave him time to pack his bags.

"At 5 A.M. the staff assembled in the great hall. Everyone was weeping. The Caliph was deeply moved. He shook a few hands and said, 'I have never done my country any harm and I never will. On the contrary, I shall always pray to God, to my dying day and beyond, that it will rise again.' Then the head of security hustled him into a car. They did not drive him to the central station for fear of demonstrations. He boarded the train at a little place fifteen miles outside town."

Selma listened stupefied and uncomprehending. For years they had gone in fear of the foreign troops on their soil: nothing the English or the Greeks could have done would have surprised them. Yet now that the war was won it was Turks who were getting rid of the Caliph and all his family. They must be mad – the whole thing had to be a misunderstanding. Uncle Fuad had always been quick tempered, but Annéjim would calm him down as usual – she would explain and put things right. Selma looked at her mother inquiringly, but the Sultana had buried her face in her hands.

"Exile?" she murmured, so softly that Selma could scarcely hear her. "It is not possible."

In the boudoir overflowing with tuberoses, the General Prince paced like a lion ready to pounce.

"We have been stripped of our nationality and forbidden to set foot here ever again. Our property is confiscated – personal effects are all we are allowed to take with us. Oh yes, I had forgotten: the government has generously voted us a thousand gold sovereigns[5] apiece to live on for the next few months! Well, my dear aunt, there you have it: we have been banished like common criminals, even and perhaps especially those of us who have shed our blood for this country!"

Lips trembling, he laid his hand on his chest, which was covered with decorations for gallantry in the field. He looked as if he might burst into tears at any moment. Selma's head was spinning – she simply did not understand. Must they really go away? Why? Where to? For how long? Uncle Fuad had said forever.

"What does 'forever' mean?" she cried out involuntarily.

Her mother turned to look at her. How pale she was. . . .

"Annéjim!" Selma threw herself at the Sultana's feet. "It isn't true – say it isn't true! What did we do to them? Annéjim, Uncle Fuad, answer me! What is happening?"

"Mustafa Kemal. . . ."

"The Pasha?" She got to her feet, feeling reassured. "But in that case, nothing is lost. We must go and see him – we must explain that he has made a mistake, that we have never done anything to harm him. Don't you remember, Annéjim? You used to call him a great patriot and make us pray for his victory every night. . . . There was

5 About £35,000, or $60,000 in today's currencies.

that officer we hid, too. . . . We must go to Ankara and tell the Pasha everything. I am sure he will understand!"

Why did her mother turn away? Why did Uncle Fuad shrug like that? No one ever listened to her.

"Don't forget, Sultana, we only have three days."

Swiftly, Osman Fuad bowed and left the room.

Turmoil . . . that was all her mind retained of what followed: a hazy recollection of tears, panic, grief, pettiness, devotion, unexpected acts of loyalty and betrayal. . . .

For three days she roamed the palace, driven from room to room by maidservants and eunuchs who were folding, wrapping, packing and endlessly squabbling among themselves. For three days she strove to escape the noise, the commotion, the kalfas' lamentations, and – most of all – Mademoiselle Rose, whose tearful attempts to console her were more than she could bear. In this pandemonium, her peaceful, dainty palace was unrecognizable; this was her home no longer: the turmoil and the crying had taken it away from her before the time had come to leave.

Eventually she took refuge in her room, where she looked at all the familiar objects she loved, one by one, to imprint them on her memory. But she could not see them any more: they had become blurred, as if robbed of substance. So when two maidservants came in carrying a big trunk and asked her to choose what she wanted to take with her, she tossed a volume of poetry and her exercise books into it and left the task of selection to them; and, when Haïri complained that his own trunk was too small to take all his clothes and toys, she gave up half of hers to him.

Of the few images that did emerge from the fog around her, like little islands of colour, one was of her mother's dressmakers busily sewing jewels into the hems of her gowns. The Sultana was entitled to take them, they said, but one never knew with customs officers: some of them could be overly zealous. Then there was Zeynel, dear Zeynel, standing on a crate and waving his arms like a conductor as he scolded the servants for inefficiency. Finally, in the midst of the turmoil, there was her mother, the Sultana, smiling again, full of consolation and reassurance. "Never fear, my children," she kept saying, "it is only for a month of two. The people will soon recall us. . . ."

For the moment the people said nothing – the government had seen to that. Extraordinary tribunals empowered to mete out sentences of death had been set up in every large town, and the "law relating to treason" now extended to all who discussed the expulsion of the

Caliph and the princes.

For three days the Sultana received a series of visits from those of her women friends who were undeterred by government surveillance. For three days they debated where she should go. No Ottoman princess had ever left the country before, and few of the older princesses had ever left their palaces.

At first they had talked of France – of Nice, where the climate was almost as mild as that of Istanbul, and where the sky was said to be always blue – but the Sultana had finally settled on Beirut, "because it is so near, and we will be able to return more quickly."

Selma wondered what her father thought of this idea. She had not seen him since the news of their expulsion. Poor Baba, he must be overwhelmed sorting out his innumerable books and papers. . . . She could not stand all those women weeping and kissing her hands; all of a sudden she wanted badly to talk to him.

The door of the haremlik was no longer guarded. She ran through the great hall to the Bey's apartments. The study was deserted, likewise the drawing-room, and the drawers in his bedroom were open and empty.

She raced back across the hall, bumping into some kalfas on the way, and threw herself on her mother.

"Annéjim!" she cried. "Baba! Where is Baba?"

The Sultana stroked her hair with unaccustomed gentleness.

"You must be brave, Selma. The damads were given a choice. Your father will not be accompanying us."

An icy void seemed to yawn within her and expand until it filled her from head to toe, an echoing void in which the words reverberated: "will not be accompanying . . . will not be accompanying. . . ."

She did not understand. . . . Her whole body suddenly felt leaden, but her head seemed to be floating on air. . . . She did not understand.

He had gone without even saying goodbye to her.

It was eight o'clock on that Friday morning of 7 March 1924, and the sky was translucently blue.

Selma, huddled in a corner seat aboard the train that was bearing them away from Istanbul, gazed out at her country drifting away from her. Lofty pine forests glided by, and sparkling rivers, and fields of colza dotted with women in white headscarves.

Before her eyes, the landscape misted over.

PART TWO

LEBANON

CHAPTER 1

She can slap me as hard as she likes, I refuse to look down. One little whimper would be enough – then she could forgive me and would not have to slap me any more – but I will not give her the satisfaction. It would be as good as admitting that she is right. . . .

Down in the playground, a silent crowd had gathered around the woman in black and the teenage girl with the red-gold curls. What had started as a regular treat – they were going to see her cry at last, the stuck-up creature! – was developing into a drama. The girl was such a slip of a thing. Mother Achillée was slapping her too hard – she would kill her if she wasn't careful. It was silly of her not to cry. Didn't she know it was better to cry *before* you were hurt? The nuns were softhearted – they could not bear the sound of crying.

Mother Achillée's arm was tired. She stopped. Selma lifted her chin and looked as contemptuous as she could: a martyr defying her tormentor.

"You will copy out that lesson a hundred times!"

"No, I won't."

The other girls looked aghast. The little Turk certainly had guts.

Mother Achillée had turned pale. "You are the devil incarnate!" she hissed. "We will see what Reverend Mother has to say about this." With a flurry of skirts and angel sleeves, she turned on her heel and headed for the Mother Superior's office.

A dark-haired girl shyly approached Selma. It was Amal, who belonged to one of the great Druze families that had wielded feudal power over the Lebanese highlands for centuries. Her name meant "Hope."

"You will be expelled," she said uneasily. "Whatever will your mother say?"

"She will congratulate me."

Amal raised her eyebrows.

"My mother would never permit anyone to insult our family. That so-called teacher of history is nothing but a liar."

A nun a liar? Selma's fellow pupils could not believe their ears. Some of them hurried off to regale their friends with this sensational piece of blasphemy. They did not dare to think what would happen, but it was bound to be fun.

Closeted in her gloomy, panelled office, Mother Marc gazed at the crucifix and prayed for inspiration. Deliberate disobedience called for drastic action, but could she really compel this little girl to speak ill of her ancestors? She had been faced with a similar problem last year, after a lesson on the Crusades: the fathers of the two Muslims in the class had come to the school, collected their children and left without saying a word.

Institutions such as Les Soeurs de Besançon, the Beirut school directed by Mother Marc, were open to children of all religions. Although they did not aim to convert "lost sheep," they always cherished the hope that the word of the Lord might some day germinate like seed scattered in the wind.

There were three discreet taps on the door and the girl came in. A white lace collar enlivened her austere navy blue uniform. The face beneath the mop of flaming curls was a stubborn mask. She curtsied low with downcast eyes.

"You may rise." Mother Marc's long, ivory fingers drummed on the desk. "I am in something of a quandary, my child. What would you do in my place?"

She was prepared neither for Selma's reproachful look, nor for her bitingly polite reply.

"I do not have the honour of being in your place, Reverend Mother."

"Mother Achillée wishes me to expel you. She tells me you are a threat to the discipline of the entire class."

Selma said nothing. She thought of her mother: Poor Annéjim! Haïri had refused to go to school because his classmates made his life a misery – they called him "Royal Assness" instead of "Royal Highness" – and now she was about to add to her mother's worries. She weakened a little at the thought of distressing her.

"Reverend Mother," she said in a muffled voice, "what would you do if someone forced you to repeat, out loud, in front of the class, that your grandfather was insane, your great-uncle a bloodthirsty monster, your other great-uncle feeble-minded, and the last of your dynasty a coward?"[1]

Mother Marc looked at the crucifix once more. Then she turned to Selma with shining eyes.

"Our Lord Jesus Christ was crucified because his contemporaries thought him an imposter. Human judgements reflect human limita-

1 The last four sultans of Turkey in chronological order: Murad V, Abdul Hamid II, Reshad, and Vahiddedin.

tions, as you see. There is no such thing as History, there are only points of view. The truth is known only to him that has no point of view because he occupies no single viewpoint. He is everywhere: he is God."

Mother Marc, herself descended from an illustrious line of Crusaders who had fought and died for the truth as they saw it, felt troubled, as if she were betraying their memory. Eager to terminate the interview, she delivered the verdict in a rather tremulous voice.

"You are excused from history classes from now on – you may study the subject on your own. I do not consider it necessary to report this incident to the Sultana."

"Oh, thank you, Reverend Mother!"

Selma impulsively kissed the Mother Superior's hand and put it to her forehead in the manner of the Ottoman court.

The nun looked surprised. "Go in peace, my child," she murmured.

Without thinking, Selma replied in the Muslim fashion.

"And peace be with you, Mother."

It seemed to Mother Marc, as she turned to the crucifix again, that the Christ was smiling.

Though provincial by comparison with the Ottoman capital, Beirut was nonetheless a charming city of some one hundred thousand inhabitants: a vista of white, sun-drenched walls and red-tiled roofs interspersed with shady gardens.

The Sultana had taken a house on Rustem Pasha Street in Ras Beirut, a district in the west of the city. The sea, which could be glimpsed from its balcony, looked so preternaturally blue that Selma's first reaction was one of shock, as if the colour was somehow improper. By degrees, however, she came to realize that like the Mediterranean, Beirut brimmed with life and laughter; so different from Istanbul and the Bosporus, whose delicately iridescent colours, permeated with nostalgia and dreams, made you long to weep with tenderness.

The Lebanese lady who had rented them their new abode declared that she "adored Turkey and the Turks" as did everyone else in the neighbourhood, she claimed. She proudly took them on a tour of the little house, which was embellished with fig trees and succulent plants, but refrained from pointing out that the gutters leaked – hence the patches of mildew on the walls – or that the ill-fitting French windows let in draughts.

"Ras Beirut," she announced, "is where all the oldest Sunni families live – the ones that dominated the city for four centuries until the French arrived here. It is home to the Ghandours, the tobacco magnates, and the Baltadjis, who control the port. Over there live the Daouks, and the Beyhums, and the Solhs – all extremely wealthy! They speak Turkish as well as Arabic – in fact they often pride themselves on having inherited Turkish blood from some Circassian or Stambouliot ancestress."

She added that the members of this Sunni *beau monde* were on good terms with the big Greek Orthodox families who formed a powerful minority. They called on each other most days to play cards, the gentlemen poker, the ladies pinochle. Later on, at the end of the afternoon, they would go horseback-riding in the nearby hills, especially in springtime, when the thyme and hawthorn were at their most fragrant.

The Sultana nodded politely. Her prospective landlady, construing this as an invitation to go on, hastened to tell her that the best parties were given by bankers such as the Sursoks, Trads, and Tuenis. "They are attended by everyone who is anyone, Muslims and Christians alike – Christians of the Greek Orthodox persuasion, of course, as there are not many Maronites in the city apart from a handful of families who settled here centuries ago. Most of them still live in the mountains – they are peasants wedded to their land and their church. Unlike the rest of us Lebanese, many Maronites don't regard themselves as Arabs. They claim to be directly descended from the Phoenicians who ruled the seas for centuries until they were crushed by Ptolemy, one of Alexander the Great's lieutenants. As evidence of their different origin they cite the fact that they did not speak a word of Arabic until the seventeenth century, only Aramaic. . . ."

Quite naturally the French, who had acquired this former Turkish possession as a mandate, created Greater Lebanon, and made Beirut a capital city, depended for their support on the Maronite Christians who had been under their protection since 1860; especially as most of them had been educated by French missionaries and spoke the language perfectly. By offering the Maronites government posts and commercial concessions, the mandate authorities lured them to the city and made them their most loyal supporters. The bulk of these new townsfolk installed themselves at Ashrafieh because it was almost uninhabited and less expensive than the seaside neighbourhoods in the west of Beirut, which boasted many fine residences. Ashrafieh's additional advantage was its proximity to the mountains where most of the Maronites still had family and retained small houses and plots of land.

Beirut's development into a patchwork quilt of cultural and religious enclaves was thus motivated by considerations of sentiment as well as expediency. These enclaves were not, however, completely impervious. Over the years, many up-and-coming Maronite families settled in the chic Arts et Metiers district in the heart of Ras Beirut, while "the Sursok quarter," the city's smartest neighbourhood, had been taking shape on the peaceful, wooded hill of Ashrafieh for the past hundred years or so. There, as under Ottoman administration, so under the French mandate, leaders of high society such as lovely Linda Sursok, the dashing Bustros boys, and the handsome brothers Tueni continued to give glittering soirées at their sumptuous nineteenth-century houses of Florentine and Venetian design.

A peaceful oasis between sea and mountains, Beirut was a pleasure-loving city, and the French, no one could deny, had brought to this once provincial town a touch of Parisian sparkle and gaiety.

The tolerant coexistence of the various communities did not, however, preclude social ostracism. It exasperated families of long standing to see Maronite peasants fresh from the mountains transformed within a few years into parvenus devoid of tradition and social graces.

The gap grew between the old and new Beirut. However the French authorities did not confine their support to the Maronites; they needed a firm foothold in the Muslim community as well. They knew they could hardly hope for enthusiastic support from the Sunni upper class: as far as the Sunni were concerned, not only had the French and the British dropped the promise of an Arab kingdom in which Syria, Lebanon, and Palestine would finally be united, but the French presence in Lebanon had necessarily eroded the economic privileges enjoyed by these wealthy Sunni. So the Sunni maintained relations with the French that were good on the surface – the Lebanese having always been born diplomats – but privately they accused France of having impaired the country's economy, notably by linking its currency to the franc. Above all, they were indignant that nearly all the plum jobs in the administration, judiciary, and army were reserved for Christians. On the other hand, there did exist a Sunni Muslim middle class whose members had never been able to aspire to senior posts under Ottoman rule. By favouring some of these families, the French gained their allegiance.

Such was the society – a society in the throes of transformation under the aegis of new masters and "friends" – into which Sultana Hatijé had arrived together with her children, Zeynel, and two kalfas.

The Turkish newcomers were viewed with curiosity, even sympathy. After all, Murad V had never oppressed anyone for the simple reason that his reign had lasted only three months, poor man. As for his unfortunate daughter, thirty years a prisoner, twenty years divided between a husband who doubtless beat her and another who was certainly unfaithful, then war and revolution, and finally exile! Everyone's heart bled for the Sultana, and the lionesses of Beirut society jostled each other in their eagerness to call on her.

However, if they expected dramatic revelations and hitherto unpublished details of the scandalous treatment accorded to the imperial family, or simply a few sighs and tears that would enable them to seize the Princess's hand and swear eternal friendship, they were quite disappointed.

Seated in a drawing-room hung with rather faded yellow silk, the Sultana received them with the gracious smile and dignified reserve of a sovereign accepting her subjects' homage. She answered her visitors' questions, which became steadily less discreet and more forthright as their impatience mounted, with unruffled serenity. No, she really had nothing of interest to tell them. Kemal had only done his duty as he saw it. How did she rate the prospect of a counter-revolution and the restoration of the monarchy? Allah's will would prevail. Who would be the new caliph? Just what she herself had been about to ask them. On the morrow of Abdul Mejid's departure the newspapers had announced the nomination of Hussein, King of the Hejaz, by his own sons. Now there was talk of King Fuad of Egypt, "but we are not in touch, so I know no more than you."

And the visitors went home bewildered, their vague feeling that the Sultana had outwitted them, a feeling only partly dispelled by the exquisite courtesy she had shown them. One or two of the more exalted ladies invited her to their homes "to meet a few friends" on any afternoon that suited her, but the Sultana declined with a regretful air.

"How kind of you, but I never go out. On the other hand, I shall always be delighted to see you here. . . ."

The yellow drawing-room was thronged for several weeks. Then visitors became rarer. The Princess whose intelligence and strength of personality were a byword seemed in the end to have nothing to say. Wearying of her, Beirut's high society sought titillation elsewhere. Her only occasional visitors were snobs of more modest standing who liked to bedazzle their relations by remarking that "their friend the Sultana" had a slight cold today, or that she was wearing a green silk gown that lent her "a truly regal" appearance.

Now that peace was finally restored, the Sultana welcomed its return with quiet amusement.

"I taught a lesson to those bumpkins who wanted to strut around with a sultana in their buttonhole! Invite *me* to their homes? Expect an imperial princess, and of *my* age, to call on *them*? Really, they stop at nothing! Bear this in mind, Selma: just because we have lost our money, we do not have to lose our dignity as well. You are a princess, always remember that."

Selma sighed. What did an impoverished princess amount to? She was the laughing-stock of the entire class, with her darned stockings.

"It would be difficult to forget, Annéjim," she said ruefully.

The Sultana looked at her, astonished.

"Is something the matter? Is it school?"

"Oh, no, Annéjim, school is great fun."

She was anxious to spare her mother's feelings at all costs. Although the Sultana held her head high, a film of melancholy seemed to have dulled the keen and penetrating gaze of former times. She could not understand her people's silence; she refused to accept it.

Morning and evening, she strained to hear news of Turkey on the radio. The suppression of religious schools and institutions and the closing of convents had enraged her. On the other hand, she felt a thrill of triumph when she read that women were being forcibly unveiled and men forbidden to wear the fez, that symbol of allegiance to Islam, on pain of hanging. This time, surely, the Turks would rebel!

But this time, as before, the Turks acquiesced. Day by day the creases at the corners of Hatijé's mouth deepened. She had left her country in the belief that the people would soon tire of Kemal's excesses and recall the imperial family, but almost a year had passed and still they held their peace. The "special courts" were omnipresent, of course, and the press was strictly controlled, but was it really possible to suppress ten million Turks permanently? Her husband's desertion had left a bitter taste, but what rankled with Hatijé more than anything else was the indifference of her people.

Like some valiant knight of old, Selma had vowed to protect her mother. The adoration she had always felt for her had lately become tinged with affectionate concern. It was as if, having found her mother vulnerable, she feared that a new misfortune might break her altogether.

She always came straight home after school – where else would she go, having no friends? – and there, seated on a little cushion at the Sultana's feet, she would spend hours telling stories to amuse her. They had never spent as much time together at Ortaköy, where ceremonial and the constant presence of kalfas rendered intimacy impossible. Exile had at least brought them closer, she sometimes told herself, but she knew that this consoling thought was a delusion: the Sultana had never seemed so remote.

One day when her maths lesson had been cancelled because the teacher was ill, she came home an hour early. She paused on the doorstep, brought up short by the sound of laughter. Tiptoeing to the drawing-room, she saw Annéjim laughing as she had not heard her laugh since they left Istanbul. Zeynel, seated at her feet on Selma's favourite cushion, was happily holding forth.

Her throat tightened: somehow, she felt cheated. When Selma was around, her mother never seemed anything but melancholy. How was it that with Zeynel her former gaiety returned? She walked in, looking very pale. The eunuch rose to his feet, the Sultana stopped laughing.

"What is the matter, Selma, are you ill?"

She pretends to care, but I might just as well be dead as long as Zeynel is there. . . .

Haïri, whom Selma had failed to notice, snickered.

"She is jealous, that is all! Mademoiselle cannot bear you to take an interest in anyone else, Annéjim, me included. She goes as yellow as an old quince if you so much as smile at me."

Selma shot him a venomous glance. Her pudgy brother was more perceptive than she had thought. He would pay for that remark, but not till later. First she had to salvage the situation.

"Jealous? What an idea! I'm not jealous, just surprised and happy. It's nice to hear you laughing, Annéjim."

She sounded insincere, she knew. To cut the moment short she said she had to put her books away and retired to her room. Sultana Hatijé followed her upstairs with an air of concern.

"What is it, Selma?"

"Oh, Annéjim!" Selma's eyes filled with tears. "I love you so much – more than anything or anyone in the world – and I want you to love me too."

"Of course I love you, Selma. I love you just as I love Haïri – more than anything or anyone else." Her mother's tone became icy. "On the other hand, I will not take emotional blackmail from anyone, least of all my children. As for passion, which is what you are talking about, I believe, it has always struck me as undesirable – except when it is passion for one's country."

Selma hung her head. How could her mother, normally so good-hearted, be so hard at times? *Baba used to say that when she was angry she had no idea how cruel she could be. Baba, whom I adored . . . and who deserted me . . . and now SHE is doing the same.* Selma bit her lips, trying desperately to hide her confusion. *If only I could love her less – if only I could be more aloof and less clumsy, less eager to please – then Annéjim would surely love me. Now it seems I get on her nerves. How often has she told me not to be so "clinging."*

Selma took a deep breath, determined not to let her feelings get the better of her.

"But Annéjim, weren't you passionately devoted to your father?"

"My father?" Hatijé's frown dissolved into a gentle smile. She suddenly looked like a young girl. "Yes, I was. . . . He was one of those rare beings whom one can adore without demeaning oneself."

Selma regarded her in silence.

That is it, Annéjim, that is just what I feel for you, so why do you reject me? One day you said it must be hellish to be God, with all the love and hopes of humankind clinging to the hem of your robe. What a terrible burden to bear, you said, and you pictured the Almighty pleading for a little less emotion, a little more room to breathe. I laughed, because I thought you were joking. Now I realize how serious you were.

Whatever we do, we are always to blame: either we love too little or we love too much.

CHAPTER 2

"They are killing our people by the hundred!"

Amal had drawn Selma aside into a corner of the playground. Her face was even paler than usual.

"The French have been burning whole villages up in the Jebel, regardless of the women and children inside. They will regret it, though – the revenge of the Druzes will be terrible!"

Two younger girls laughingly scuffled for possession of a ball that had landed at their feet. It was early in the autumn, and the sunlight had a silky quality.

Selma took Amal's hand. The little Druze was her only friend at Soeurs de Besançon, the only girl to have dared to penetrate the barrier erected around her by the others. She sympathized with Selma's distress because she herself had shared it. "Amal is a nice, pretty, intelligent girl," the nuns used to say of her. "What a pity she is a Muslim, poor little thing!" She had not wanted to stay at first – she had cried every day – but her father was adamant. The best schools in Lebanon were Christian schools, and the highest Muslim families considered it *de rigueur* that their daughters should attend them.

"But, Amal," Selma said softly. "I do not understand, the other Lebanese have accepted the French mandate. Why are the Druze fighting on?"

"It is a question of honour!" Amal's blue eyes flashed. "We were not against the French to begin with, but their high commissioner, General Sarrail, insulted our leaders."

In the spring of that year, 1925, a delegation had come from Syria to discuss the status of the Druze community. It had lodged a protest against the steps taken by Carbillet, the French governor, who was overturning ancestral traditions, and demanded the appointment of a Druze governor in accordance with an agreement signed in 1921.

The high commissioner, who gave them a frosty reception, replied that he fully approved of Carbillet's reforms and that the agreement of 1921 had been superseded. Subsequent delegations to Beirut were not even granted a hearing. To Sarrail, "the left-wing general," the Druze were simply "savages," just like the Blacks of North Africa he was used to dealing with. No need to waste any time on them.

One day, when trying to dodge yet another delegation of Druze notables, who had been escorted by a hundred armed horsemen, he slipped out through a side door and . . . came face to face with them on the stairs. For the Druze it was an intolerable insult. They hurled their keffiyehs[1] to the ground: from now on they were at war with the French. To make matters worse, the high commissioner instructed his representatives in Damascus to convene a meeting of Druze leaders, ostensibly to review their demands, and then arrest them. Three of the most prestigious among them fell into the trap.

This time the French had gone too far. On 17 July the redoubtable Sultan el-Atrash launched a revolt. Several columns of French troops sent to quell it were ambushed and cut to pieces.

"And it isn't over yet," Amal scowled belligerently. "The Druze of Lebanon have joined forces with the Druze of the Syrian highlands. There are over fifty thousand of them now."

"There you are, then," said Selma. "They are bound to win in the end, so why worry?"

Amal sighed. "Because like you, the French government thinks we have a chance of winning. So they have sent General Gamelin against us with Circassian and Tunisian cavalry, not to mention seven battalions of infantry and a lot of modern artillery. They are reducing our villages to rubble. Our men are fighting like tigers, but what use are rifles against field guns?"

Selma put an arm around the girl's shoulders. She remembered: occupation, humiliation, impotence . . . rebellion, and then final victory. She hugged her friend hard.

"You will beat them, Amal, I am sure you will, just the way we beat the foreigners in Turkey."

We? Who were "we"? Even now, years later, Selma found it impossible to reconcile herself to what still seemed a ridiculous paradox: her country's victory and her family's expulsion. Somewhere history had gone astray. . . .

"The worst of it," Amal went on, "is that the French are convinced they are in the right. They are dividing our land and our people, yet they claim that in reality –"

"What reality?" Selma burst out. "The reality that compels them to kill your fellow countrymen? The reality that compelled Mustafa Kemal to drive us out of Turkey? I used to be like you once: I thought it was just a misunderstanding – I was angry with my mother for keeping quiet instead of protesting our innocence. What a fool I was! Too young to understand. Don't laugh. I am only fourteen, it is true, but

1 The Lebanese name for a fez.

that is not what matters. I grew up the day it dawned on me that good intentions are worthless. What matters is not who is right but who is the strongest. That was when I stopped complaining and made up my mind that some day I would be the strongest."

"Plotting, are you?"

The two inseparables, Marie-Laure and Marie-Agnès, came sauntering up. Each as pretty and supercilious as the other, they were the daughters of senior French army officers. Amal turned on them with all her claws out.

"How smart of you! If you really want to know, we happened to be discussing the best way of kicking you out of this country."

"No need to get so worked up." Marie-Laure treated her to a condescending stare. "After all, if it were not for us you would still be an Ottoman province."

"Stop it, both of you," Marie-Agnès broke in. "People are listening. If the nuns hear we have been talking politics we could be expelled."

"That's too easy," Selma said sharply. "You cannot just insult us and walk away."

"I see," sneered Marie-Laure, "so Her Highness demands satisfaction! I suggest we settle things on the sports ground. You can have the choice of weapons: running or jumping."

"Parachute jumping."

Marie-Laure was a good four inches taller than she, and Selma knew she had no chance of beating her in a foot race.

The sports ground was a little way away from the main buildings. On the right was a big sand pit and a climbing frame with an adjustable metal crossbar.

"Shall we start at two metres?" asked Marie-Laure.

"All right."

"You go first, since you think you're the injured party."

The two girls exchanged defiant stares. They had entirely forgotten about Amal, even though she was the cause of the dispute – or the pretext for it. Marie-Laure and Selma had been spoiling for a fight for ages. They both had the same brand of pride and intolerance. Under other circumstances they might have been friends. As it was, they detested each other.

They had collected an attentive audience by now. Two of the girls volunteered to keep watch – there was not much time left before the end of recess – while another pair were to raise the crossbar twenty centimetres at a time.

The first jump was child's play.

"Two metres twenty," announced the self-appointed referee.

Selma landed lightly. Marie-Laure, more muscular, followed suit.

"Two metres forty!"

It was getting serious now. They each jumped in turn, concentrating hard, totally absorbed in what they were doing.

"Two metres sixty!" the referee announced.

Poised on the crossbar, Selma caught sight of Amal's little face in the crowd. She gave a reassuring wave. She felt a trifle nervous, never having jumped from that high before, but with all that sand to break her fall. . . . She flexed her knees a couple of times, then launched herself into space. Made it!

She barely had time to get up before Marie-Laure landed beside her. Their eyes met, locked for a moment, then turned away.

"Two metres eighty!"

Selma felt strangely tremulous as she climbed the ladder. Silence reigned below: twenty pairs of eyes were riveted on her. She could not possibly back out now. A deep breath, and then. . . .

She knew it as soon as she jumped. Like an observer divorced from her own body she registered a snapping sound, a sudden stab of pain, and at the same time, an odd sensation of relief: it was over – she did not have to be scared anymore.

A babble of voices. Everything was spinning, turning black. She must not be sick, she. . . .

Where was she? What had happened? Why was Mother Jeanne bathing her face in cold water? Why was she looking so alarmed?

The pain in her right leg recalled her to reality.

"Do not move, child, the ambulance is coming. How silly of you, though – you might have killed yourself! What ever made you jump from such a height?"

Selma forced a wry little smile.

"I was practising for the Olympic Games."

The apprehensive faces around her cleared. Everyone laughed except Marie-Laure, who could contain herself no longer.

"I am to blame, Mother. I was the one who –"

"It was you that got me interested in sport," Selma said quickly, "but I should have known I could not beat you."

"My poor child," sighed Mother Jeanne. "You see? Pride comes before a fall."

The ambulance finally arrived. The whole class gathered around to see Selma off as the ambulance men carefully lifted her into it on a stretcher. Amal was sobbing, with a white-faced Marie-Laure beside her.

"Goodbye, Selma, come back soon."

The two adversaries looked at each other and smiled timidly. Selma caught herself feeling pleased that she had broken her leg.

The doctor diagnosed a compound fracture and prescribed six weeks' complete inactivity at home. Amal would come to see the patient every day after school. Her friendship for Selma had deepened into devotion.

"I will never forget what you did for me. Everyone in school keeps saying how brave you are, and they admire you most of all for not telling on Marie-Laure. You have taught them a real lesson!"

She gave Selma an affectionate hug, gently straightened a curl on her moist forehead, covered her hands with little kisses. Forgetful of the exercise books spread out on Selma's bed – she was supposed to be keeping up on her schoolwork with Amal's help – they talked endlessly.

Amal, who had lost her mother at the age of two and could not remember her at all, had been brought up by her aunt, a cousin of Sit Nazira, the Druze chieftainess.

"I only saw Sit Nazira once – it was in her palace at Mukhtara, in the heart of the Shuf Mountains – but I shall never forget the sight of her. Sitting on a low divan in a plain black dress and a white headscarf like the ones our peasant women wear she looked like a queen."

The heads of a score of clans were conferring with her, Amal recalled, and as a mark of respect they had left their rifles and bandoliers in a heap outside the door. They were men with rugged, weather-beaten faces – the kind you never saw in towns – but their manner in the presence of that frail old lady was that of timid children.

"Sit Nazira addressed them for a long time. Then to each of them in turn, she asked the same question, examining their loyalty, fixing them with those bright eyes of hers. One by one they nodded. Then they bent down and kissed the hem of her dress. She had not moved or raised her voice once – that was what impressed me most of all."

"She sounds like my mother," Selma murmured dreamily, "– or rather, like my mother in the old days. Poor Annéjim, she has changed a lot since we were exiled. . . ."

"And your father?"

Selma's eyes darkened.

"I don't have a father any more."

"Forgive me," Amal said hurriedly, "I didn't know."
"Nobody knows except me."

Selma was still on crutches when she returned to school two months later. She received a warm welcome, even from the girls who had never spoken to her before. Marie-Laure, who was hovering in the background, strolled casually over.

"It is good to see you again," she said.

A trite remark, but everyone grasped its significance: coming from the leader of the Franco-Maronite camp, it made the reconciliation official.

Her first day back in the school was like one long party – even the nuns fussed over her. That afternoon Marie-Laure offered her a lift home. Like most of the French girls, she always had a chauffeur-driven car waiting for her outside the gates. Selma was tempted to accept until she caught sight of Amal's dejected face.

"It is kind of you, really it is, but I need the exercise. Amal offered to carry my books."

Marie-Laure shrugged. "A pity, I thought we might have had a chat. You are right, though," she added in an offhand tone that failed to conceal her disappointment, "Loyalty comes first."

Selma watched her walk off, hating herself for having spurned the hand of friendship. She felt she had failed. However much she reasoned with herself and strove to justify her refusal – how could she have deserted someone who had stood by her through thick and thin? – all the joy had gone out of the day. Even the sun seemed to have lost its warmth.

"Well, well," sneered Amal, as she walked along beside her, "so the condescending creature is jealous, is she?"

"That's enough!" Selma snapped. "Keep your comments to yourself!" But she promptly regretted her outburst when she saw how hurt Amal looked. Now she had offended her too. What was the matter with her? Why did friendship have to be so exclusive? Why was it essential to take sides?

Some days later, while Mother Teresina was delivering a lecture on French literature, in which she was contrasting Corneille's morality to the amorality of Racine's characters, the classroom door opened to reveal the Mother Superior accompanied by a distinguished-looking gentleman wearing a tarboosh and carrying a silver-knobbed cane.

At the first sound of Mother Teresina's hand bell all the girls rose; at the second they curtsied as well as they could within the cramped confines of their desks, covertly studying the stranger as they did so.

"Forgive us for interrupting your lesson, Mother," Mother Marc purred in her melodious voice, "but His Excellency Damad Ahmed Nami Bey, governor of Syria, has done us the signal honour of visiting our establishment. I should add that his niece is in your class. Selma, come and pay your respects to your uncle."

Selma, blushing furiously, hobbled up on her crutches. The governor greeted her clumsy attempt at a curtsy with a loud guffaw.

"You were not so shy as a little girl! Now, now, not too much formality or you will break the other leg!" He gave her cheek an avuncular pinch. "Well, how did it happen?"

Selma could have sunk into the ground. He *would* have to draw attention to her just when she was beginning to be accepted!

"It is nothing, Excellency," she stammered. "I was jumping and I landed badly, that's all."

"Was it a competition?"

"In a way. . . ."

"Bravo!" cried the governor. "That is Ottoman blood for you," he added maliciously, for the benefit of the nuns.

Selma was crimson. To add to her embarrassment, a brace of photographers who were dogging His Excellency's footsteps proceeded to take her picture just as he assumed a pose and laid a protective hand on her shoulder. She would have almost wept with rage. All her efforts had gone for nothing: tomorrow, no matter what she did, her classmates would again call her a stuck-up outsider.

But the next day, to her great surprise, they seemed more impressed than anything else. The society page of the morning paper, *L'Orient*, carried a picture of Selma and the governor captioned "The gallant little princess." The other girls' parents had questioned them about her, intrigued that she should be the niece of a man on whom so many hopes were now riding. The Damad had just been appointed governor of Syria by the new French high commissioner, who calculated that Ahmed Nami Bey, an Ottoman close to the Druze leaders but also pro-French, was the man most likely to negotiate an end to the disastrous war in the Jebel.

Conversation at the breakfast table was brisk. "Why not invite the girl home sometime?" more than one of Selma's classmates were asked by her father. "She could be a useful person to know." Their mothers also approved of the idea. "She may be a Muslim, but she *is* a princess after all. . . ."

Selma, who for the past year had heard her fellow pupils discussing their excursions and parties without ever being asked to them, received half a dozen invitations within the space of a week. She thanked the girls politely. She felt like being rude to them, but simply told them that she would ask her mother.

Standing in the background Marie-Laure gave her a wink as if to say, "Don't take it to heart too much." She, at least, had refrained from joining the rush, and Selma was duly grateful to her.

What about me, don't I exist? A title, is that all I mean to them? And I thought for a moment they had started to like me. How silly I was!

Pebbles went flying as Selma angrily swiped at the ground with one of her crutches. She was hardly aware that Amal, distressed at seeing tears in her friend's eyes for the first time, had put an arm around her.

"Don't be sad, they aren't worth it."

"I know they aren't, Amal, but I can't help it. I want to be loved."

"*I* love you, Selma," the Druze girl said shyly. "I know my friendship isn't worth much. . . ."

"Of course it is, Amal – it means a lot to me!"

Selma did her best to smile, but all her trembling lips could produce was a pathetic grimace. She squeezed Amal's hand.

Yes, Amal, you love me, but why? Because like you I am a lame duck in a bevy of swans? Because we are Muslims surrounded by Christians who despise us?

Through tears she no longer tried to restrain she had a vision of Ortaköy, the snow-white palace where a mulish and mischievous "little sultana" had commanded the admiration and adoration of a score of other children. How long ago it all seemed. . . . *Do you still remember me, Gülfilis? Do you, Ahmed? You loved me and I took your love for granted. Now I don't have anyone . . . even Baba . . . no, I don't want to think about him ever again!*

She shook her head and wiped her eyes on the back of her hand.

What am I saying? I still have the most important person of all. Annéjim . . . she loves me! Of course she does . . . I am her daughter. . . . But would she love me if I were not? Would she love me for myself?

During the next few weeks invitation cards poured in, but Selma surprised her mother by refusing even to look at them. She said she disliked these parties where every girl was preoccupied only with her own appearance and most of the conversation was devoted to malicious gossip about those who had not been invited.

Sultana Hatijé did not press her. Selma's stubborn expression suggested that she had been hurt in some way, but she knew her daughter would not talk about it until she was ready. *She used to be so open and now she has become so secretive, she thought. Sometimes I blame myself for paying too little attention to both children. But I do not have the courage any more, nor the inclination. Anyway, what would I say to them? However deeply I search within myself, I find nothing but silence. . . .*

Selma, seated between Zeynel and the kalfas, idly traced the arabesques on the carpet. They really looked as if they were dancing. She had heard Marie-Agnès say that at these parties an instructor came to teach the guests how to do the Charleston. She could almost hear the laughter and music now – her legs twitched involuntarily – but what was the use of dreaming? She would not go. Anyway, she did not have a suitable dress, and besides, if she did accept the other girls' hospitality her mother would have to return it, and where would the money come from?

The family was already living on the tightest of budgets. Two or three times a month, through a cousin of Memjian Agha's, a little Armenian jeweller who had spent his youth in Istanbul and was devoted to the family, the Sultana sold some piece which the newly-rich ladies of Maronite society eagerly snapped up, less because of its beauty than to preen themselves in plumes borrowed from the Ottoman dynasty that had ruled their country for four centuries.

But the Sultana's stock of jewels was not inexhaustible, and she sometimes spoke sternly of the need to economize – a source of secret amusement to the members of her household, who knew that the Sultana had no sense of money whatever. She never checked an account – "What do you take me for, a shopkeeper?" – and flatly refused to handle what she called "those disgusting bits of paper."

It was Zeynel who took charge of the domestic finances. Haïri was still a fat, sulky boy of sixteen, so the eunuch was the only man of the family. Delighted to be relieved of this "intolerable" chore, the Sultana left him an entirely free hand. She never remarked on any deficiency and seemed unaware that their meals were sometimes on the meagre side: she was far above such mundane details. On the other hand, she could never bring herself to refuse the poor who knocked at her door, and her generosity had become a byword in the district.

No one, least of all Selma, ventured to point out that times had changed and she ought to be less open-handed. Selma had always seen the members of her family give to friends, servants, slaves, beggars. Giving was part of the natural order of things. Today the money had gone: was this a reason to change? She was no more able than her mother to resist a pair of imploring eyes. It made her so happy to give pleasure.

One day, annoyed to see her empty her purse every time a beggar held out his hand, a fellow pupil lost her temper. "Stop playing the princess!" she snapped.

Selma was taken aback at first. She wondered if the girl was right, and that her only motive in giving was to preserve the illusion of a superior status she no longer possessed. The question tormented her for some time, but she finally came to the conclusion that she had merely obeyed her natural instinct: just as the soldier's instinct was to fight and the doctor's to heal, so it was in the nature of royalty, she reasoned, to be regal.

The letter was delivered by a Nubian. Proud of the handsome red uniform that set off his ebony skin, he stood to attention in the drawing-room doorway while the Sultana opened the envelope, which was adorned with a heavily embossed gold crown.

It is true that, thanks to the British, the "Khedive" now bears the title "King of Egypt," she reflected with a wry smile. *If he continues to be a good boy he might some day be crowned emperor!* She had always viewed the petty vanities of her fellow creatures with amused indulgence, but her attitude today was tinged with disenchantment. She would never forget that in the spring of 1924 the pusillanimous Egyptian monarch refused to offer the exiled Ottoman family a home.

The big, slanting hand denoted that the writer was conscious of her own importance. Princess Zubeyda, a niece of King Fuad's, was visiting Beirut and requested "the pleasure" of calling on the Sultana.

The *pleasure*? When the Ottomans were their sovereigns only twelve years before, this family used to request "the honour" of being received! Very well, she would receive Zubeyda in a fitting manner, but whether the Princess would find it pleasurable was another matter. . . .

With a malicious smile, the Sultana took one of her last sheets of parchment bearing the imperial coat of arms and penned a few lines inviting the Princess to call on her the following day at tea time.

The heavy emerald necklace sparkled, the quail's egg of a diamond at its centre emitted a firework display of every colour in the spectrum.

Princess Zubeyda paused in the doorway, dazzled by the thing around the Sultana's neck and unable to tear her eyes away from it.

"Do come in, my dear."

Immediately Zubeyda recognized the imperial tone of voice, with its unaffected mixture of courtesy and hauteur – the tone that had filled her with admiration and resentment since her girlhood because, try as she might, she had never managed to imitate it.

The figure in the wing chair sat motionless, waiting.

Hurriedly pulling herself together, the Princess performed a graceful temenna, hand on heart, lips, and forehead in turn. She straightened up to find herself the target of a cold, inquiring stare. Her hostess was obviously expecting the three temennas required by etiquette at the Ottoman court. Even in the little drawing-room of her modest Beirut abode, she was more than ever "the Sultana." Zubeyda laboriously complied, purple with shame at having been tacitly but firmly put in her place from the outset.

The Sultana finally favoured her with a smile and waved her into a small armchair beside her. Only when she sat down did Zubeyda discover that it was lower than the wing chair, so she was obliged to arch her neck when addressing Sultana Hatijé, like a duchess seated on a stool at the foot of a throne.

More and more ill at ease, the Princess was just wondering whether to feel insulted and show it when the Sultana, in the gentlest of tones imaginable, thanked her for devoting a little of her precious time to a poor exile. Was she being sarcastic? Even if she was, how could anyone have adopted a surly attitude in the face of those candid eyes and honeyed words?

The hour that followed was one of the longest Zubeyda had ever endured. Having gone there, girded about with wealth and power, to gloat over the downfall of a family she had always envied – having come to condole with the Sultana and tactfully present her with a small gift of money tucked away in the bottom of her purse – she had been greeted with more condescension, more veiled arrogance, than in the days when the Ottomans still reigned.

How could she have been taken in by all those rumours of their poverty – even of their destitution? The house was not large, admittedly, but no one in financial straits could have afforded to wear such jewels or entertain in such style. Three well-trained servants came and went with a succession of sherbets and cakes arrayed on sumptuous silver gilt plates. How did the Sultana manage it – how was she faring these days? Zubeyda itched to ask this nagging but unaskable question.

As soon as she decently could she thanked her hostess profusely and took her leave, not forgetting her temennas this time – three of them performed while backing out of the room. The Sultana, sitting very erect in her wing chair, treated her to a parting smile of majestic benevolence.

What the unfortunate Zubeyda did not hear, and what she would never have dreamt of hearing, was the peal of laughter that burst from Sultana Hatijé once she was safely off the premises.

"The conceited creature could not believe her eyes! That taught her a lesson – I think we will not have any more of these kind of visits! Come, children, these cakes are delicious."

Elated by the success of the Sultana's practical joke and infected by her high spirits, Selma, Haïri, Zeynel, and the two kalfas, who were still disguised as parlour maids, sat down at table. They were joined by a swarthy little man whom Hatijé seated on her right and served with her own fair hands. Her faithful Armenian jeweller left an hour later carrying a big leather bag containing the superb necklace and the silver gilt plates he had lent her for this very special occasion.

CHAPTER 3

"A letter for me?" Selma stared at the stamp in surprise. Who could have written to her from Iraq? She did not know anyone there.

The postman who usually put the mail in a green box to which Zeynel held the key, had stopped her as she was leaving for school.

"There's a surcharge of ten piastres to pay. Please sign here, mademoiselle." And off he cycled in the May morning's golden sunlight, whistling as he went.

Selma curiously weighed the envelope in her hand. The big, elegant handwriting looked very familiar, and yet. . . . She resolutely put it in her pocket. She was already late for her geometry exam.

She quickened her pace. Once she had turned the corner and was out of the sight of the kalfas, who were watching from the upstairs windows, she broke into a run. Hurry up, only ten minutes till the bell rings. . . .

The exam was easy. When it was over, the other girls compared notes, but today Selma had not time for isosceles triangles and parallelograms.

"Sorry, someone is waiting for me," she said, ditching Amal, who wanted to check her answers.

Why had she said that when she hated lying? Her only appointment was with the envelope in her pocket.

Instead of going straight home she made for the coast road, walking slowly and enjoying the sun at her leisure. She smilingly rejected the blandishments of the ice-cream and lemonade vendors who made a fortune at this time of the year. Eventually she reached her destination, a quiet nook not far from the old Hotel Bassoul.

There, seated on a wooden bench, she toyed with the letter. The nicest part of a letter was the time before you opened it. You could pretend it was from a Prince Charming who had seen you from afar and was declaring his love, whereas when you opened it it always turned out to be from some female cousin who bored you with her dreary doings or some aunt mildly reproaching you for having left her without news for so long. Male cousins never wrote letters.

She tore open the envelope.

Baghdad, 1 May 1926

My dear little daughter,

I am sending you these few lines rather like someone throwing a bottle into the sea, because I have written you so often in the past two years and heard nothing. Did my letters go astray, or was it simply that you did not feel like answering them?

Your father is very unhappy to have lost his pretty Selma. It is my own fault, of course. I chose to remain in Turkey because I thought my country needed me. What vanity!

Not a day has gone by since then without my regretting that decision. Can you believe that and forgive me? I feel so lonely and would so much have liked to watch you growing up. You were a delightful-looking child. You must now be a beautiful young girl.

I thought you might possibly care to see your old father again after all this time. At present I am our consul at Baghdad, which is a very pleasant city. Would you care to pay me a visit? Let me know if you would, and I will send you the fare for yourself and your kalfa. You could stay for several months, or longer if you liked. Nothing would make me happier.

I eagerly await your reply.

Your loving father.

P.S. I should also like to see Haïri, of course, but he must complete his studies first. Kindly convey my respects to the Sultana, whom Allah preserve.

My father . . . ! My father? Selma was stunned, overcome with mingled resentment and happiness. *Why are you doing this to me? What did I ever do to you? You abandoned me and now you want me back. You love me, you love me not, then you love me again. . . . What am I to you?*

She hugged the letter to her, sobbing with bittersweet tears. A passing stranger slowed down, his curiosity aroused at the sight of the young girl whose despair was flooding out so violently. Selma did not see him. Nothing existed for her but what she held in her hand.

You miss me? And what about me? Did you ever ask yourself how your darling little daughter was taking your betrayal? Because you did betray me. You had been thinking of walking out for a long time – I sensed it. Your absences had grown more and more frequent, everything about that house seemed burdensome to you. You wanted your freedom back. The order of exile was only an excuse.

My father. . . .

What really hurt me most was you leaving me without a kiss. If you had only talked to me everything would have been easier.

Did you think I would not understand? Did you know me so little? One is not a child any more at thirteen; often one knows things better than the grown-ups who are blinding themselves to the truth for fear of what the truth will do to them.

I did not have any armour. I did not want to shield myself from raw feeling. I want to dig through the lies, the subterfuges, to try to get to . . . what? I don't know. I only know . . . that is what living is. There is no other way.

It is hard. One has to be strong. . . . And I am strong when I feel loved. You took away my strength when you abandoned me without a word. I was so hurt, Baba, if only you knew. . . .

Without realizing it, Selma had cried out loud. Through her tears the sun was whirling. She felt a sudden intense weariness overcome her, a desire to sink into the earth, to bury herself in its depth, in peace.

How long had she been sitting on the bench? The sea was tinged with red by the time she decided to go home.

Her return was greeted with cries of alarm. "Where were you? What happened? Are you all right?" The kalfas scurried around her like a pair of hens reunited with a lost chick. Zeynel, who was in the drawing-room trying to call the police station for the umpteenth time, stared at Selma open-mouthed with the receiver posed in midair, while Haïri gave a scornful laugh.

"What did I tell you! She simply went for a walk, that's all. It wasn't worth making such a fuss!"

But the Sultana could tell from her daughter's odd expression that something had happened.

"What is it, Selma?"

Selma seemed not to have heard. She turned to Zeynel and glared at him accusingly.

"Who's been taking the letters my father has sent me in the last two years?"

There was a shocked silence. It was the first time anyone had mentioned Haïri Rauf Bey in the Sultana's presence since their exile, but Selma was past caring about the proprieties. Furious, she continued hammering away.

"Who took my father's letters? Who was it?"

"Pull yourself together, Princess," Hatijé said coldly. "And stop accusing Zeynel. *I* took those letters and had them destroyed."

"You, Annéjim?" Selma stared at her mother in dismay. "But

why? You knew how hurt I was by his silence."

"It would have hurt you much more to hear from him!" Hatijé's voice softened. She took Selma's hands in hers. "You would have been shattered, my child. You would have asked yourself a thousand questions. Given that the break had occurred, I thought it best to make it a clean one. It was hard at first, I know, but you gradually resigned yourself to the inevitable and began to forget him."

"Forget him? Oh, Annéjim, how could you have thought I would ever forget my father?"

The Sultana hesitated. "I acted for your own good, and I still believe I was right. Look what a state you are in now!"

Yes, thought Selma, thanks to you and your blindness! Her eyes flashed, but she pressed her lips together tightly. Don't say anything irrevocable. Vanish, just vanish. The door seemed infinitely far away. Get to your room. Turn the key. No one, see no one any more. . . . She collapsed on the floor.

"You shall kill your father and your mother." What did Mother Barnabé say, was it the sixth or seventh commandment?

"You really do have a brain like a sieve."

"Yes, Mother Achillée."

But when grandpa comes
He'll hang you upside down
That'll teach you to be bad,
To say all around the town
That the king is mad, that the king is mad.

I am so cold
Cold in the morning
Like an impish little sprite
Warm in the evening
Strangled out of spite.

"What a lot of people! Who are these weeping women in white? And what is this hole that keeps widening all the time, is it . . .? NO! Don't bury me, I am not dead, stop!"

"The poor child does not even know she's dead."

"But I am not dead!"

"Look, she is losing her mind on top of everything else! What anguish she must be causing that wonderful mother of hers. She always was a difficult child."

"Her father died of grief. She was the one who killed him."

"That's a lie! My father loves me! I'm his little darling."

The whole class burst out laughing. You too, Amal? Are you laughing with them? What are they singing now – "God Save the Queen." That's much nicer.

What? It isn't for me? I'm not the queen? But I am the queen – I must be, since my father is the king. My mother? Poor mama, she died when she was a little girl. It wasn't I who killed her.

"Tell me, doctor, will she recover? Please be frank."

The Sultana looked pale. She had watched over Selma for a week, refusing to leave her side for a moment, as if her very presence could prevent her daughter's condition from deteriorating.

"It is hard to say, Sultana. It is a case of a bad shock acting on what was a highly-strung temperament to start with. Are there any precedents in the family?"

"Not exactly, though my father suffered from – well, spells of melancholia."

"Forgive me, Sultana, but I must know the truth. Did your father have similar fits of delirium?"

"I don't know, doctor." Hatijé felt faint. "I was very young. When my father was ill we were kept out of the way. Later on he got better."

The doctor straightened up, puffing out his chest and thrusting his thumbs into his vest pockets.

"So you don't know whether or not your father suffered from attacks of insanity, nor, to the best of your knowledge, does your daughter. That explains a great deal."

"I don't understand. . . ."

"You've never heard of Sigmund Freud, I suppose?" The doctor adjusted his pince-nez with a self-important air. "Freud is an Austrian psychiatrist whose theories have revolutionized the treatment of mental illness. Having compared them with my own observations, I have drawn certain practical inferences with which, though I say it myself, I am not dissatisfied." He raised his voice, carefully enunciating every syllable. "On the basis of Dr Freud's theories and my own, I think I can safely say that your daughter is faced with a problem she finds insoluble. It is a common enough condition, and everyone copes with it in his or her own way. Pleasure, work, drink, what have you. But some people, possibly of a more sensitive disposition, choose to take refuge in madness."

"They *choose* to?"

"Yes, Sultana, it could be called a choice, though not a really conscious one. That is the whole beauty of Dr Freud's theory: various levels of consciousness. An intellectual feast, don't you agree?"

"So my daughter –" Hatijé began, but the doctor did not hear her.

"Why madness, you may ask, and not another, more 'rational' choice? Well, the patient may be motivated by several factors – sometimes by the influence of someone he or she admires and identifies with. That's why I asked if your daughter knows that her grandfather *may* have suffered from attacks of insanity. If she does – as seems likely, servants being notoriously indiscreet - we may hope that her self-identification will not last because it is based on mere hearsay. If the pressures upon her are reduced, I can assure you that this unwholesome condition will disappear by itself." The doctor's tone became grave. "And that, Sultana, is where you have a part to play."

"Tell me how, doctor. I will do anything. . . ."

"Do nothing at all! Take some rest and leave others to look after your daughter. She can sense your anxiety even, or especially, in her present condition, and it aggravates her sense of guilt towards you. She does not know how to please you without betraying her father, and vice versa, so she burrows ever deeper into unreality. You want my professional advice? Leave your daughter in peace."

"Are you implying that my presence at her bedside is harmful?"

"I am not implying it, I am stating it as a fact. My respects, Sultana."

"That doctor is worse than an ass – he is an ill-mannered lout! How can a mother's love possibly harm her child?" Sultana Hatijé paced furiously up and down her drawing-room. "And to think he is supposed to be the best psychiatrist in town! What are we to do now?"

"With your permission, Sultana," Zeynel said cautiously, not daring to look at his mistress, "I should take his advice. I do not for one moment believe in his nonsense, but you certainly need some rest. You seem worn out. Don't worry about the Princess. I will sit with her and let you know at once if there is any change."

"You are going to pay!" The amorphous shadows had emerged from the white walls and were hemming her in.

"But what have I done?"

"She wants to know what she has done!" They laughed uproariously.

How idiotic they sounded! Still, she must not make them angry.

"I swear I don't know," she said in her mildest voice.

"And you never will! That is your punishment: knowing you have committed a terrible crime but not knowing what it is."

"I don't understand. . . ."

"It is simple enough: if you know your crime and are punished for it, your punishment becomes a means of redemption. You carefully weigh the harm you have done against the pain you are suffering, and after a while you think you have wiped the slate clean. That's too easy: punishment salves your conscience and tidies up your little world. Well, we are not going to punish you. Hell is what you deserve, and hell is the absence of punishment."

Selma was terrified. "No," she implored, "not that, I beg you!" She strove to capture a wisp of shadow, but she could not move.

"I want to die," she moaned.

"What did we just tell you?"

The shadows hissed at her irritably.

"In our world – the real world, not your little hole of a room or your little hole of a country – no one ever dies. There is no life or death, no true or false, no beginning or end. What you have done is unimportant, because our world knows neither good nor bad, just nor unjust. It is a limitless world, therefore there are no rules."

"But if what I have done doesn't matter," Selma broke in, "surely you can forgive me?"

"This is really an obsession with you! Forgive you? We could not, even if we wanted to. It is our prerogative, you see, to be entirely free, and our freedom prevents our making even the smallest decision. We are like scales on which nothing weighs."

Selma angrily burrowed down into her pillows. "That's meaningless," she protested.

"Perhaps, but can you quote us any words that are meaningful? How could paltry words coined by limited human intellects ever apprehend reality? Forget about it. Go on amusing yourself and stop trying to escape from your three-dimensional box. We did not even have to intervene when your predecessors tried it in the past: their brothers and sisters put them away behind bars and pronounced them insane, if they did not crucify them or burn them at the stake.

"You would do better to stay quietly in your corner, take it from us. You find it boring, confining? You're right, but infinity is just as monotonous. Boundless space, never a wall to lean on, never a door that closes, furthermore one is dying of cold, for there is never a blanket which tucks in, never an end to anything: it becomes exhausting after a while. . . ."

"She's asleep at last," Zeynel murmured to himself. "How feverish she is, the poor little thing!" He gently drew the sheet over her, not for fear of some nonexistent draught, but to protect her slender form from the evil spirits he sensed were abroad. When she had cried out just now, wrestling with those invisible phantoms, the eunuch had taken his Koran in his right hand, flung the windows wide, and searched every closet in the room. It was no use telling him that ghosts were an old wives' tale. He could well remember that no one in his native village in Albania ever went to bed without leaving some bread and fruit outside the door to dissuade any hungry spirits from entering, and there was seldom anything left in the morning.

He brushed the girl's cheek with a plump forefinger, trembling at his own audacity. How would he have explained such disrespect had someone caught him in the act? A momentary lapse, a senile desire for contact with youthful flesh? Even under torture, he would never divulge the truth, the terrible and delicious secret that plagued and thrilled him, that enabled him to hold his head up, even in times of direst adversity, and feel like a king, like a god, like a man!

"Baba!" Selma sat up with a start, her eyes wide with fear. "Don't kill me! Put that dagger away – I am your little girl, don't you recognize me? Look, I will take this skin off!" She clawed frantically at her cheeks, thrusting Zeynel's hands aside when he tried to stop her. "Look, it is me! Don't you recognize your little baby, your dear little baby?"

She drew up her knees, rested her chin on them, and clasped her shoulders.

"Can you still see me? I am shrinking so fast, I will soon be just a little pink shell you can carry around in your pocket. I won't be a nuisance, I promise, but will you gently stroke me every now and then?"

"Yes, dearest child, I will, never fear. . . ." With infinite tenderness, Zeynel laid his hand on the moaning child's brow.

"They are driving nails into my head to stop me thinking! Don't leave me, Baba!"

"I am here, Djijim. Don't be upset, I will never leave you."

She nestled against him, trembling all over.

"I love you so much. No one but you!"

The eunuch's big eyes were misty with emotion. He clasped her to his chest and rocked her tenderly.

"And I, if you only knew how much I love you, like no father ever loved his child."

A father, the eunuch at whom the maidservants used to laugh behind their hands? . . . Had he dreamed it, that blessed night sixteen years ago, or had it really happened?

*

His Sultana was asleep in a great bed enclosed by curtains of mist. A strong wind had arisen and wafted him irresistibly toward her, his mistress, his queen. An unfamiliar Zeynel, freer and more himself than he had ever been, had bent over her and put his lips to the marble brow. A light had seemed to explode inside his head, and then. . . . He could remember no more.

When Selma was born nine months later, everyone rhapsodized about her resemblance to Haïri Bey. Zeynel had said nothing, but he had felt drawn to the little creature with every fibre of his being – felt his flesh rent by a kind of recognition.

For a long time he had thrust these wild fancies from his mind. But they had obtruded more and more often, especially now that exile had transformed the Sultana's household into a family.

And today it was she, his little girl, who was crying out to him for help. Overwhelmed by the thought, he gently drew away for a better look at her.

"My Selma," he murmured. "You are my miraculous gift from God. You are the tear that Allah shed on my anguished heart. . . ."

She stopped sobbing and smiled up at him. "Go on, Baba. Say some more nice things."

"Poor little flower, one ray of sunlight and you burst into bloom. . . . There, rest your head against your Baba's shoulder. Do you understand now?"

"Yes," she said softly. Her eyelids drooped.

"It was hard, terribly hard, but what could I have told you? You would never have believed me. You had to discover our secret for yourself."

"Our secret. . . ." She nestled closer and sighed with contentment.

"Promise not to tell – they would say we are mad! The infidels! Do they think anything is impossible for the Almighty!"

The eunuch straightened up in indignation. His blood boiled at the thought of such impiety. Selma opened her eyes, astonished. Why was he suddenly so red; why was he talking so loudly?

"They call us lunatics! But you keep your wits about you, you conformist worms!"

He grasped Selma's hand.

"Join me, my child, in blessing madness. It is the royal road to the infinite, the ultimate point where all is merged, all is clear. Let us thank God for helping us to stumble on. Let us give praise for the drop of mercury loose in our prosaic heads. May it multiply! May it burst into a thousand points of light! Thou, All-Merciful One, whose light illuminates all light!"

"What a funny dream I had, Zeynel – if you only knew. . . ."

All pink-cheeked and bright-eyed, Selma stretched and yawned luxuriously.

"What time is it? Is it a nice day? Good morning, Leila Hanum, I am absolutely starving. Can I have some strawberry jam for breakfast?"

"Straw –" The kalfa stared at her open-mouthed. "You recognize me, Princess?"

"Why shouldn't I recognize you?" Selma said anxiously. "Are you feeling all right, Leila Hanum?"

"Allah! Allah be praised!"

The kalfa scuttled out of the room, trembling with joy. "Sultana," they could hear her calling, "the Princess – the Princess has recovered!"

"What's the matter with her? Have I been ill, Zeynel? What was it?"

"Nothing much, just a touch of – well, a kind of influenza, that is all."

"Poor Zeynel, you are an awful liar. That's a shame, in a courtier!"

The Sultana came hurrying in.

"Why are you looking at me like that, Annéjim? What happened? Tell me!"

Why was her mother hugging her so affectionately? It was unlike her.

"You had a sort of fever, Selma."

She said nothing. If the Sultana was hiding the truth too, it must have been serious. She searched her memory but could recall nothing – nothing except that dream in which Zeynel had said. . . . Now what *had* he said?

Two months went by before Selma made up her mind to answer her father's letter. She could not come to Baghdad because of school, she said, but why didn't he come to Beirut to see her? "It would give me so much pleasure," she wrote. Pleasure . . . was that a proper description of those tears, that pounding of the heart? These things she did not want to write. "Pleasure," the stock word found on invitation cards printed by the hundred, struck an appropriately impersonal and ambiguous note. Her father could read whatever he liked into it.

Her letter was returned after several weeks, accompanied by a note from the Turkish ambassador in Iraq. Haïri Bey had resigned his post and left the country. He had not returned to Istanbul and his present whereabouts were unknown.

Selma stared devastated at the black characters on the elegant ivory notepaper. Too late – she had written too late. Baba had gone, believing that she did not want to see him again. She had lost him once more, and this time the fault was hers.

She had no urge to cry. She simply felt cold inside.

CHAPTER 4

There was a good view of Beirut harbour to be had from a low cliff overlooking the sea beside the beach at Minet El Hosn. Every Thursday the big white steamship *Pierre Loti* arrived with its cargo and passengers and a few hours later headed back to Istanbul again laden with merchandise and more passengers: with it went the dreams of a girl who leaned on the stone parapet and watched intently until it disappeared over the horizon.

In the early days Selma had gone down to the harbour and mingled with the jostling, bustling crowd, shutting her eyes in an attempt to rediscover the sounds and scents of her native land. When she was completely steeped in them, but only then, she allowed herself to look. They seemed familiar, all those faces. She scrutinized them avidly one by one, as if a glance could summon up visions of the city she loved or a smile convey the splendour of those sunsets over the Golden Horn. With difficulty she would refrain from asking some stranger: Are the people happy in Istanbul? – or from begging a morsel of sesame-seed bread from the brimming basket on some woman's arm, drinking in the warmth of an accent, the scent of a faded rose. She gazed so pathetically at these travellers who seemed haloed with her dreams, that they hurried past her looking startled and reproving.

Later she withdrew to the rocks overlooking the deserted shore. Far away from the crowd which retained its aura of mystery, and far from the enormous boat, resting in the water like some placid, welcoming sea-monster, she found it easier to recapture her dream. For months on end she went there regularly like a pilgrim. She did not want to forget. She did not have the right. . . .

Little by little, though, the *Pierre Loti* lost its fascination and became a steamship like any other, just as its passengers' faces took on the stereotyped air of satisfaction of those who have safely reached their destination, and became like travellers arriving from anywhere else. For several weeks Selma strove to recreate the nostalgia that identified her with the Selma she used to be, but in vain. Now that even her sorrow had waned, she felt she had lost everything.

It was only later, long after she had forgotten the way down to the port, that she wondered if her purpose had been to nourish her grief or use it up slowly and free herself from its clutches.

No one at home had known of these weekly excursions. There was no school on Thursdays, so she officially spent them with Amal. A kalfa escorted her to her friend's home in the morning and did not return to collect her until the end of the afternoon.

Amal and her brother Marwan, who was three years older, lived in an imposing house in the heart of the Druze quarter. Their mother had been carried off by a heart attack when they were very young, and their father had died in a riding accident some years later, so an aunt had moved into the big house on Mar-Elias Street to look after the two orphans. The aunt, who was very strait-laced, had brought them up in the traditional manner. No one in school knew better than Amal how to make a deep curtsy or blush when addressed by an adult, but the aunt was elderly, and her afternoon siestas, which lasted until early evening, allowed her wards a certain freedom.

Being a solitary child herself, Amal sympathized with Selma's need to be alone at times. She never questioned her about her mysterious walks, but simply took her friend's hand when she returned, eyelids red and swollen with weeping, and silently kissed her cheek. Because Amal was so tactful and undemanding, Selma gradually confided in her. She spoke of her father, who was not dead as she had implied. Every few months since leaving Iraq he had reminded her of his existence with a postcard mailed from the other side of the world.

"The first came from Brazil, the second from Venezuela, and yesterday I got one from Mexico. I cannot reply – I do not have his address. He promises to let me know as soon as he's settled. For the moment he is permanently on the move, on business. Latin America is an extraordinary place, he says: if you are prepared to take risks you can make your fortune out there. He says he will come and fetch me soon – he wants me to live like a princess again. He never asks me what *I* want. . . ."

What did she want – did she know herself? There was such an aura of unreality about those unanswerable missives from an elusive father, those grandiose schemes and promises.

"Sometimes I wish he would stop writing to me, so I wouldn't have to hope against hope all the time, but if he didn't write any more, I think I would. . . ." Almost inaudibly, she added, "You see, Amal, I love him, but I know he could easily desert me again tomorrow, so I catch myself hating him and wishing he were dead." She clasped her head tightly. "I couldn't bear it if he didn't love me! Oh Amal, I don't know where I stand or what I think any more!"

She felt an arm encircle her shoulders and a pair of cool lips brush her forehead. And for the rest of the afternoon they remained curled up together in the depths of a divan. Amal said nothing. Instinctively she knew that words would only chafe the wound: to someone so grief-stricken, any encouragement would have been unseemly, any advice offensive. What her friend needed, and what she freely gave, was her love.

The kalfa who came to fetch Selma early that evening noticed nothing. She was soothed and relaxed. Amal's tenderness had restored her strength.

A cab was waiting outside the gate that led into the little garden. Selma wondered who the caller could be. The Sultana received few visitors now that she had cold-shouldered the snobbish Beirut society ladies. Selma was proud of her for having refused to play their game, but she sometimes wondered if the price she paid was not too high. Annéjim led such a solitary existence.

Ortaköy had always swarmed with visitors. In the old days the Sultana had divided her time between good works, political argument, family councils, friends, parties, and an army of slaves and maidservants whose problems she attended to in person. For the past two years, however, she had been confined to this small house with no one for company but two devoted but dejected kalfas and a eunuch. Zeynel was far more than a servant, of course; he had become her steward, secretary, and adviser on all things to do with everyday life, but a friend, a confidant? Knowing her mother as she did, Selma realized that she would never confide in an inferior. Her reserve was attributable not to condescension – the Sultana respected Zeynel a great deal more than most of the princes in her family – but to a system of values too deep-rooted to be shaken by any cataclysm: you did not ask for help from those whom tradition ordained you to protect. You shared your joys with them, but never your woes.

The majestic, dark-haired woman seated in the drawing-room was Sultana Nailé, daughter of Sultan Abdul Hamid. The two branches of the family had seen little of each other at Istanbul, but exile had brought them closer, especially since so few of them had gone to Beirut. Most of the Ottoman princes and princesses had followed the ex-Sultan to Nice, where a little court had reassembled "in the land of pretty women," as Uncle Fuad flippantly called it to disguise his sorrow. The Butterfly Sultana, who had always longed to visit the Côte d'Azur, was there too. Selma often thought of her gay, elegant aunt who took refinement to the point of upholstering her carriages to match the colour of her gowns. What had become of her? Was she happy in France? Selma had no conception of her life there because the Sultana Fehimé wrote so seldom. Sultana Fatma, on the other hand, was a faithful correspondent. Settled in Sofia with her three children, she led a peaceful life illumined by the proximity of a great dervish teacher whom she visited several times a week with her husband, Refik Bey. "We are progressing along the Way," she wrote. "I realize more and more clearly that everything else matters very little. . . ."

It was "everything else" – exile and the possibility of repatriation – that Sultana Hatijé and her cousin Princess Nailé were now discussing. The news from Istanbul was bad. Mustafa Kemal had had his principal opponents arrested on the pretext of an alleged plot to assassinate him. After a farcical trial during which the judge, "Ali the Bald," announced in advance that the defendants were guilty and the gallows had already been erected, the executions had taken place that very morning, 27 August 1926. The country remained calm, according to the radio report from London; the "independence tribunals" were functioning throughout the country.

"Really!" Hatijé exclaimed indignantly. "What about all the heroes of the war of independence? Aren't there any of them left?"

"There is the premier, Ismet Inönü, but they call him 'the Ghazi's scourge,' so hard he is on anyone who strays from the official line. Most of the others – Rauf Pasha, Rahmi, Dr Adnan, Halidé Edib – went into exile several months ago. As soon as Kemal dissolved the political parties they realized there was nothing more to be done, and that they themselves were in danger."

"Poor Turkey," sighed the Sultana. "To think that the government has actually changed the name of Allah, and that worshippers in mosques are now obliged to pray to 'Tanri' because it is supposedly a more Turkish name! I have been expecting some reaction from our people for a long time, but now I see they are tied hand and foot." Her voice broke. "I am beginning to doubt we will ever be able to go home."

This was the first time Selma had ever heard her mother voice such doubts and it stunned her. She came toward the two sultanas, kissing her aunt's hand and sitting on a cushion next to her mother.

"But of course we will, Annéjim! Everyone in Istanbul is discontented: the students, the intellectuals, the clergy, the shopkeepers – especially the shopkeepers! Don't you remember what Memjian Agha wrote to his cousin? 'When the bazaar becomes restive, the government had better watch out!' We'll soon be back in Turkey, Annéjim, you'll see!"

She gazed at her mother with all the conviction she could muster, willing her not to give up hope. The Sultana gently stroked her flaming curls.

"You are right, my child. I get depressed sometimes, that's all. Pay no attention."

Selma felt her heart constrict. Her mother was only agreeing so as not to depress *her*. They were playacting for each other's benefit when deep down they both knew. . . . Knew? What did they know? Nothing! They were simply accepting defeat. Well, she, Selma, refused to. "Never give up," Annéjim used to say. "Nothing is impossible."

Overcome with excitement, Selma got to her feet. She felt a sudden, violent urge to fight. She would explode if she did not find some outlet for the tension inside her. What if she ran away to join Halidé Edib and Rauf Pasha? What if they slipped back into Turkey under assumed names and led an army of dissidents against the regime? Anything was possible!

Selma worked on her battle plans until the small hours. Seated at her little writing desk, she covered page after page of her diary. How many times had she been told that you could do anything if you really wanted to? Well, she wanted more than anything to go back to Istanbul, and she refused to take no for an answer.

The heady scent of jasmine drifted through her open window. She filled her lungs with it, inhaled the warm night air, yielded to the touch of a tremulous breeze, let the chirping of crickets fill every corner of her being. Her body was growing immense, imperceptibly dissolving into a dark blue void, soaring among the myriads of stars overhead. She was their playmate and plaything, vibrant and happy, bathed in their scintillating light and at one with their beauty. . . . Dawn had broken by the time she fell asleep, tired out but at peace with herself.

The next few days went by in a dream. Everyday problems seemed ridiculous now that she *knew*. Everyone in school and at home was surprised to see her so light-hearted. The Selma who usually bristled at the slightest remark was now all tolerance; normally so impatient of rules and regulations, she now seemed to have all the time in the world. Not even Amal could guess what underlay her uncharacteristically gentle smile; she might have been a different person.

And then, without warning, she woke up one day feeling depressed and drained of energy. She surveyed her shabbily furnished room and thought, "*This* is reality." All at once a tide of despair engulfed her: she sank back on her pillow and began to sob. How she detested

Lebanon, with its immutably blue sea, its obstinate sunshine, its gaiety! How she hated all those who welcomed her to *their* home, who could speak of "our" people and "our" country without wanting to weep – all those who *belonged*. . . . She would never return to Istanbul, never belong there again. She had been lying to herself all the time: you cannot fight unless you have a country to fight for, a land to fall upon, and from which to rise again. When your surroundings strike no chord in you, when your hands have nothing to hold that is yours, when your words are condemned to be so much hot air, how *can* you fight? Against what? Against whom?

She had deluded herself: an exile's pipedreams were not battle plans, they were just another form of escapism. To think that she had prided herself on her courage and despised those who came to terms with reality! Could true courage be acceptance, as they claimed? She did not know, nor did she know what purpose courage served and why you should smile when you felt like weeping. She only knew that even animals had their lairs, their territories, and without those, they died.

"Who has stolen my pretty cousin's smile?"

His Imperial Highness Prince Orhan, grandson of Sultan Abdul Hamid, had just turned up at the wheel of a splendid white Delahaye. He worked as a taxi driver, which meant that he was at everyone's service and no one's. Though short and slight, he was immensely strong and very quick-tempered. If a passenger's manner displeased him, Orhan would not hesitate to grab him by the scruff of the neck and eject him bodily. Some of his fares had found themselves stranded beside the road before they knew what had happened to them. His Highness had simply felt insulted.

Selma adored Orhan. He was so amusing and unconventional – so unlike her brother Haïri, who at eighteen wore dark suits and stiff collars even in high summer. Orhan was two years older but took nothing seriously. He refused to talk about Turkey and laughed at Selma's moods.

"It is your Slavonic blood coming out, our heritage from those beautiful Ukrainian and Circassian girls who adorned our ancestors' harems. Why not make the most of your freedom, little girl? If you were still at Istanbul you would be shut away, you know that perfectly well. Go and make yourself look pretty – I am taking you for a drive."

Sultana Hatijé smiled indulgently as they got into the big white car. Selma needed cheering up, and with Orhan she was in safe hands.

They took the Damascus road, which wound its way upwards,

flanked by jacarandas, flame trees, and junipers. Selma had asked Orhan, in her most cajoling voice, to drive "really fast, really far." She knew he would have preferred to stop at Aleyh, a smart summer resort some twelve miles out of Beirut, but she also knew that he could refuse her nothing if she smiled at him and fluttered her long lashes. Sighing contentedly, she wound her window down and let the breeze fan her face. The air became fresher and the light more limpid as they climbed, and the umbrella pines and cypresses gave way to majestic firs and carob trees with smooth trunks and bronze-green leaves so satiny that you wanted to stroke them.

They passed Bhamdoun. The Lebanon range loomed up before them, bluish and hazy, with the snowy summit of Mount Sannin outlined by a shaft of sunlight.

Selma asked Orhan to pull up beside the road. Jumping out of the car, she started running off along a path flanked by tall grass and clumps of broom, head back and arms wide as though to embrace the splendour around her and make it her own. On and on she ran, wanting never to stop, heedless of Orhan's distant cries, just eager to be alone in this natural world in which she could at last be herself. It was a world more familiar to her than her dearest friend and she abandoned herself to it without fear of abandonment, feeling it enter every pore of her body, giving her new strength and intensity.

She flung herself down in the grass, eagerly breathing in its moist fragrance until her head swam and her limbs seemed to melt into the warm, vibrant soil beneath her. She had ceased to be Selma; she was much more. She was that wisp of grass, those trembling leaves, and those twigs groping like fingers for the clouds overhead. She was that tree whose roots snaked down to the dark and mysterious place where its life had begun. She was the murmur of that nearby stream. She was the sun's caress and the dying breeze. She was herself no longer: she simply *was*.

On the way home she did not utter a word – she was too anxious to keep her frail little flame of joy alight. Orhan thought she was feeling depressed and tried his utmost to entertain her, telling dozens of stories that she scarcely heard. She would have liked him to keep quiet, but how could she have explained that silence can be the warmest, the most attentive, the most generous of companions?

Whenever she looked back on this phase of her adolescence, Selma felt that it was her profound sense of kinship with nature that had kept despair at bay and returned her to her true self. But for her lengthy excursions into that magical realm, she would never have endured separation from all she loved, nor would she have resisted the melancholy that was slowly but surely invading the house on Rustem Pasha Street.

Sadness. The Sultana's health was steadily deteriorating. Mustafa Kemal's reelection to the presidency in November 1927 had dealt her a blow from which she never recovered. It compelled her to acknowledge that the Turkish people would never fight for the restoration of the Ottoman dynasty, and her condition worsened in consequence. She smiled when the doctor diagnosed heart disease. "Yes, my heart. That *is* where my trouble lies." But to reassure Zeynel and her kalfas she obediently took the pills and medicines arrayed in order of battle on her bedside table.

What worried Selma even more than her mother's illness was this uncharacteristic docility. It stemmed from indifference and resignation, she knew, not from any hope of recovery. The compassion she felt was mingled with anger that the Sultana should have given up the struggle. The woman who had been so strong through every adversity, who had been known as "Jehangir" or "Conqueror of the World" simply did not have the right to give up. She could not show weakness like any other mortal – she must continue to be "the Sultana". If the idol begins to crack, then the whole world crumbles around her.

30 June 1928: the end of the school year. Little groups of senior girls – the ones that were leaving Soeurs de Besançon for good – had assembled in the courtyard to bid the nuns farewell. Their eyes shone with excitement at the thought of "going out into the world" at last but they were also bright with tears. They had been happy here: cloistered and cosseted, occasionally reprimanded but always protected. The nuns were kindly creatures at heart, even the strictest of them, and the girls were almost sad to be deserting them. Punishments, injustices, tears – all were forgotten. Those who were leaving expressed their thanks and promised to come back often, feeling a trifle awkward, a trifle ungrateful for being so glad to leave. But the nuns seemed to understand. They eyed their former pupils affectionately, said they were proud of them, told them what accomplished young ladies they had become. The girls had never felt so close to them in all those years of school.

How wonderful to be seventeen and on the threshold of life!

Some of Selma's classmates were leaving Lebanon altogether. Marie-Agnès was returning to France. As for Marie-Laure, she was moving to Buenos Aires, where her father had been appointed military attaché.

"Buenos Aires?"

"Yes, isn't it incredible? They say the city is pure white and great fun!"

"Yes, so I have heard. . . ."

It was from Buenos Aires that Selma's father had mailed his last letter to her over a year ago. It announced that he had finally found the country of his dreams and decided to put an end to his nomadic existence. He was looking for a pretty house for his lovely princess and would write again as soon as he was settled. Since then Selma had heard nothing. Was he ill? Had he had an accident? She fell prey to wild conjecture and even wondered if. . . . No, that was unthinkable! How could she find him again, though? She could not ask her mother's advice, but who else was there?

And now Marie-Laure was off to the place that had haunted her dreams for months. Marie-Laure would be able to help her. The two girls had become friends since their duel. Not really close friends, the way she and Amal were – they never exchanged confidences – but a real bond of mutual respect existed between them. Their attitude was a little like that of comrades-in-arms to whom bravery and loyalty matter more than love and tenderness.

Selma resolved to take Marie-Laure aside as soon as she had finished saying goodbye to Mother Achillée. She hovered in the background, studying the French girl's creamy complexion and blue eyes, smooth brow and haughty mouth, picturing her as the knight errant who would cross the ocean and bring her father back. She would explain the whole situation and tell her. . . .

Tell her what, precisely? That her father had deserted her? That he was somewhere in Buenos Aires but had never sent her his address? That he was not writing to her any more. The words froze in her mind. She could already see the almost imperceptible tightening of the lips that would signify, not pity – Marie-Laure would never subject her to *that* insult – but disbelief in the face of this call for help, disappointment at this frailty and lack of dignity. Was the brave, reticent Selma whom Marie-Laure respected, the Selma as hard as a diamond and in whom Marie-Laure saw herself, was that girl just another helpless victim?

In the end she said nothing, less from pride than because she knew it would be pointless. Marie-Laure possessed the strength of those who have never known misfortune: she could not tolerate weakness.

Later on Selma often wondered if she had been right to keep silent. Marie-Laure might have been her last chance.

She never heard from her father again.

Beirut offered few distractions to an impoverished princess of seventeen. Selma had eagerly awaited the end of school, school with its timetables, uniforms and notebooks. She had entertained a rosy picture of all the things she would do as soon as she was free to embark on real life. Now that time's limitless horizon had opened up before her, she paused to savour this void rich with the promise of possibilities. It surprised her to find that her favourite occupation was doing nothing: doing nothing, to live life more fully, stripped of all the activities that cluttered and disguised its true nature; to be totally alive to the world's vibrations and taste eternity in every passing moment.

The Sultana, observing Selma from the armchair where she now spent most of her days, was worried that such a spirited girl should have become so outwardly apathetic. Could she, like her brother, have inherited her father's natural laziness? It was painful enough for Hatijé to acknowledge, with her customary perception, that Haïri was a born failure. She was determined not to be equally disappointed by the daughter in whom she now placed all her hopes, so she insisted that Selma should occupy her time.

"You must work on your English and Italian – your accent is deplorable. I have also asked Leila Hanum to teach you some new embroidery stitches. You had a definite talent for Arabic calligraphy, too, but it has not escaped me that you have been neglecting it lately. You are a beautiful, intelligent girl, Selma, and you are a princess: you have a brilliant future ahead of you. You must prepare for it, not waste your time."

Selma would have covered her ears if she had dared. She could not stand the constant barrage of *you must* and *you must not*. She felt as though someone were trying to steal her life. When she was little, Mademoiselle Rose would make her say aloud her French lesson: "They call you this," "They call you that." But Selma heard: "They kill you." "They call you" – that's how they define you, limit you, pin you down. No more fluttering, you beautiful butterfly. Your days of freedom are gone. They call you; they kill you. How could her mother possibly be so unsympathetic? Wasn't she ever young once herself?

Life would have been dull indeed but for the frequent visits of Amal and her brother Marwan. The Sultana had taken a great liking to them both – they were so very well-mannered! – and could have wished her daughter no better companions in this foreign city. She had such faith in Marwan, who at twenty possessed the maturity of a grown man, that she no longer insisted on Zeynel's chaperoning the trio when they went out walking in town. Worried by Selma's extreme sensitivity, her silences, her escapist tendencies, she actively encouraged her to go out from time to time. Although she long resisted the idea, Sultana Hatijé had finally admitted to herself that Selma reminded her less of her husband, Haïri Bey, than of her father, Sultan Murad. She looked at her daughter dreamily playing the piano for hours on end, or fluctuating between elation and despair, and with a pang of recognition saw the mixture of strength and fragility which might someday collapse unless she found a field in which to use it, or a cause to which to dedicate it.

That was why the Sultana made no attempt to oppose Selma's budding passion for the cinema, telling herself that the girl's fancies would find more wholesome sustenance in screen romances than at home in a house where everything reminded her of the past. The "seventh art" was just emerging from its infancy: a major Hollywood production company, Warner Brothers, had just scored an extraordinary success with *The Jazz Singer*, in which the characters actually spoke!

Selma and Amal got into the habit of going to the movies every Friday at 3 P.M., when a performance was reserved for women only. Marwan would drive them to the door in his Chenard and Walcker cabriolet and pick them up after the show. But technical hitches were frequent, and the girls, tired of waiting in the dark room for the projectionist to fix the machine, would sometimes sneak out and go for a stroll in the sun.

It was an adventure in itself to walk through the old quarter of Beirut, where all the movie theatres were concentrated. It had spread out around Cannon Square, also known as Martyr Square since 1915 when the Turkish governor, Jemal Pasha, had had eleven nationalist opponents hanged there. The city's liveliest district, it abounded in Arab cafés outside which grave-faced men wearing tarbooshes and smoking nargiles spent all day playing backgammon. It was also the centre for restaurants and nightclubs, those sinks of iniquity where – so said the Muslim matrons of Ras Beirut – women danced naked. Selma and Amal walked along hand in hand, hearts pounding: even to pass such places was to sample forbidden fruit. Certain that all eyes were upon them, they sauntered with assumed nonchalance past the Grand Restaurant Français – "an amusing place," according to Orhan, who had been there once, and very popular with the cosmopolitan socialites of Beirut. After the floor show, which was often provided by artistes from Paris, patrons danced until dawn on a terrace overlooking the sea. Selma cast an envious glance at the poster advertising the latest attraction, on which was written in big red letters in French: "Miss Nini Fantastique in her fantastic dance!" "That would be fun!" she sighed. But she would never be allowed to set foot in such a place. It would be improper for any young woman to do so, especially a Muslim.

One day as they were walking along, they headed for the Little Seraglio, a long building of ochre stone with arched windows and doorways. This was the seat of the Lebanese government, but apart from several dozing bailiffs it was, as usual, completely deserted. After all, who would waste time there when it was common knowledge that everything was decided up at the Grand Seraglio, on the hill overlooking the city, at the offices of Henri Ponsot, the High Commissioner.

A party of French soldiers, tantalized by the sight of two such pretty young girls out walking unescorted, started to follow them. Blushing, Selma and Amal quickened their step and pretended not to understand their rather indelicate compliments. They eventually shook them off only by plunging into the maze of alleyways known as the Souk el-Franj, or foreigners' market, a paradise for those in search of vegetables, flowers, or merchandise imported from Europe. It was much patronized by ladies of the Lebanese middle class, who came to do their shopping accompanied by little boys with baskets on their heads. The girls, however, preferred the jewellery souk where craftsmen sat in little booths, their nimble fingers braiding gold and silver wire. They also liked to stroll through the nearby Tawilé souk, which was noted for tailors, Armenian shoemakers unequalled at copying the latest Paris models, and curio shops selling all manner of "authentic" and useless trinkets.

The sun was going down. It was the hour when women emerged to go shopping or simply to enjoy the cool of the evening. The vendor of orange-blossom water cried his wares, his voice mingling with that of the little pin seller. The city had a festive air, as it always did at this hour. The air was balmy.

Selma, lost in the crowd at Amal's side, savoured her freedom. For the moment Istanbul was forgotten.

The family to which Amal and Marwan belonged was one of the oldest in the country and still dominated a large tract of the Lebanese highlands, so the two orphans were welcomed with open arms in Beirut's most exalted social circles. Amal, who had just turned eighteen, was beginning to be asked out and longed to take Selma with her. Her friend was so beautiful that invitations would be bound to come pouring in from all sides once people set eyes on her. But how was she to convince Sultana Hatijé that there were certain ancient Lebanese families whose hospitality an Ottoman princess could accept without demeaning herself?

Amal's opportunity came when Linda Sursok gave a *thé dansant* at her Ashrafieh mansion. After discussing the matter at length, the girls decided that a *thé dansant* would make an ideal introduction. It sounded less daring than a ball, which the Sultana would have firmly forbidden, and besides, Linda Sursok was almost a relation – she insisted that Marwan and Amal call her "aunt" – so the dance could be represented as a family gathering.

Amal "happened" to be there when Selma's invitation card arrived.

"Who are these Sursoks?" Sultana Hatijé inquired with disdain. "Tradespeople, unless I am much mistaken!"

"Oh no, Highness," Amal politely assured her. "The Sursoks are one of the greatest families in Beirut – they have been established here for centuries. They own banks and big commercial concerns of all kinds."

"Precisely," snapped the Sultana, "– tradespeople!"

As luck would have it, Madame Ghazavi was also present. A Lebanese born at Istanbul and married to a senior government official, she patiently explained that the Sursoks represented "all that was best" in Lebanon.

"They are Greek Orthodox, admittedly, but quite as refined as the Sunni bourgeoisie. They only entertain the *crême de la crême.* If Princess Selma is to go out into society, there could not be a more appropriate place to make her debut than the Sursok Palace. But of course, if Your Highness thinks it better for her to remain at home. . . ."

Although Selma felt like hugging Madame Ghazavi for this effective little speech, she went on casually leafing through a magazine as if the conversation did not concern her.

Sultana Hatijé hesitated. Madame Ghazavi was an expert on Lebanese society and her advice had always proved invaluable, but it was her last remark that really tipped the scales. For some time now, the Sultana had lain awake at nights worrying over Selma's future. The question had not arisen while her daughter was still in school, but now? Now that their exile was dragging on and their return to Turkey seemed a mirage, what was to become of her? A husband had to be found for her – a Muslim, of course, and wealthy, and a prince at the very least: three conditions impossible to fulfil in Beirut, where not even the greatest Sunni families were worthy of an alliance with the Ottoman dynasty. Someone from the Egyptian royal family, perhaps, or the Indian principalities. . . .

Meantime, Madame Ghazavi was right: Selma could not afford to remain shut up at home; she must learn to hold her own in society. For all that the Sultana Hatijé had taught her, secondhand knowledge was no substitute for confrontation with reality. At Ortaköy, which was a little court in itself, Selma would naturally have acquired the *savoir-faire* and experience of human relationships essential to one of her rank, but life in the seclusion of this house in Ras Beirut, cooped up with Zeynel and the kalfas, was no kind of preparation for the world in which she would some day be expected to live.

The Sultana turned to Amal. "Come back tomorrow, my child," she said amiably. "I will give you my answer then."

She had, in fact, already decided that Selma would go, but one problem remained: what was the girl to wear? If the family exchequer would not run to the price of a suitable gown, how could she hold her own in a roomful of Lebanese women smothered in jewels and dressed by the great Parisian couturiers? The ever resourceful Madame Ghasavi had an idea.

"If I may be so bold, Highness, why shouldn't Leila Hanum, who has such a magical way with a needle, alter one of your old court gowns? There are some wonderful brocades going to waste in your closets."

Her ingenious suggestion was approved. Selma, having looked through dozens of gowns, each more splendid than the other, selected an aquamarine silk that brought out the colour of her eyes.

Suren Agha, apprised of the situation by Zeynel, turned up at this point. The Armenian jeweller had endeared himself to the Sultana by persuading her, against his own best interests, to assure herself of a small income by purchasing securities with the proceeds of the jewellery she sold him instead of spending the money little by little. He had even assisted Zeynel in carrying out these transactions, and his loyalty to the family had earned him the trust and affection of the entire household.

This afternoon he seemed preoccupied as he paced up and down watching the kalfas at work on the blue silk gown. At long last, blushing furiously, he disclosed the purpose of his visit.

"I hardly dare to suggest this, Sultana, but Princess Selma's beauty is such that she deserves to outshine all the rest. I have some fine pieces of jewellery in stock. Would she care to pick out the one that suits her best? All that I possess is hers as often as she wishes. I should consider it a great honour."

Touched, the Sultana smiled at the little man and held out her hand, which he awkwardly seized and kissed with fervour.

CHAPTER 5

"Mademoiselle Amal el-Daruzi! Mademoiselle Selma Rauf! Monsieur Marwan el-Daruzi!"

The butler, a stiff figure in a dark suit, glanced curiously at the young woman accompanying the Daruzis. She was a newcomer to Linda Sursok's "Wednesdays." That was not surprising in itself – his mistress kept open house and was always entertaining new friends of friends – but he, who after thirty-two years in the profession prided himself on his unerring ability to spot an upstart masquerading as a duchess or a duchess trying to rejuvenate herself by dressing like a salesgirl, hesitated this time: the girl certainly knew how to walk – she even carried herself with a touch of arrogance that hinted at blue blood – but the preposterously ruched gown might have come straight from some little Babed-Driss dressmaker and clashed with the sapphire necklace, which was quite out of place at an afternoon function.

The hostess had already hurried forward.

"Amal! Marwan! How delightful to see you, my dears! So this is your friend Mademoiselle . . . Rauf? Welcome! Any friend of these dear children is a friend of mine. Their mother and I were very close – she was like a sister to me. . . ."

She sighed and shook the celebrated red curls that peeped from beneath her no less celebrated gold lamé turban. At forty Linda Sursok was still one of the most attractive women in Beirut, less because of her beauty than by virtue of her wit, charm, and *joie de vivre*. Some maliciously claimed that her zest for life had redoubled as soon as she was widowed at the age of twenty-four, but even they conceded that she had a big heart, and her parties were the best patronized in town.

"Forgive me, I must desert you – there is His Eminence the Archbishop!"

She bustled off to be the first to kiss the ring sparkling on the churchman's perfumed hand.

"She took to you," said Marwan. "But then," he added with a chuckle, "she always did love the Turks."

Selma did not understand the murderous look Amal gave her brother. Not until much later, when she herself was well launched in Beirut society, did she learn that the flamboyant Linda had been intimately acquainted with Jemal Pasha, the Ottoman governor sent to keep order in Lebanon during the war.

Elegant men and women crowded the interconnecting reception rooms, which were a mass of pale pink gardenias. At the far end was a delicate drawing-room in the Moorish style, a cool oasis dominated by the melodious sound of water splashing into a marble fountain. The open windows overlooked spacious grounds, and through them drifted mingled scents of orange blossom, Arabian jasmine, and mimosa.

Marwan steered the girls outside and on to the terrace, an ideal spot from which to observe the colourful gathering. As Selma's self-appointed mentor, he pointed out various celebrities.

"The dashing gentleman with the white carnation in his buttonhole is Nicolas Bustros, who belongs to another big Greek Orthodox family and whose hospitality rivals the Sursoks'. Next to him is the Marchioness de Freige, of the pontifical nobility. The snide people in town call her Marchioness Fresh-off-the-Press. You see the little man beyond her, the one with the birthmark on his chin? That is Henri Pharson, president of the Literary Club. He may not look very impressive, but don't be misled, he owns the finest art collection in Lebanon – and Syria too, no doubt. He buys up old mansions in Damascus and Aleppo, has the panelling and fireplaces dismantled, and reassembles them in his own reception rooms. His house near the Great Saray is a real Aladdin's cave. It is a great privilege to be invited there, as he seldom entertains, but he is to be seen at the race track every Thursday. His stud farm houses two hundred horses, and he likes to supervise their training from a belvedere covered with greenery, drinking coffee with his friends. It is the hub of the Lebanese political scene, so they say. . . .

"Look, the Emira Shehab has just arrived – she belongs to the oldest princely family in the mountains. And there is the beautiful Lucile Trad, escorted by Jean Tueni, that very distinguished-looking old gentleman – he was the Ottoman Empire's ambassador to the Czar and a personal friend of Edward VII. You see the red-haired man on the left? That is Nicolas Sursok, one of our most original characters – Kees van Dongen absolutely insisted on painting his portrait. He is rather crusty, and you have nothing to fear – he does not care for the girls!"

They laughed, unaware that two men on the far side of the terrace had been eyeing Selma with interest for several minutes.

"She is French, I tell you. Look at that wasp waist, that creamy complexion . . . absolutely gorgeous!"

"You don't know what you are talking about, Octave. With those dreamy eyes and those soft, full lips, half innocent, half sensual, she can't be anything but an Oriental."

"All right, Alexis, let's have a bet, but not just on her origins. Let's bet on which of us wins her favours first."

"Always on the attack, eh? Trust a French officer! Be careful, though, she isn't wearing a wedding ring, and unmarried girls in our part of the world need careful handling. Still, she might be flattered by the attention of two of the inner circle's most illustrious members. Let's give it a try!"

They approached her nonchalantly.

"Marwan, old boy, how are you?"

They gave Marwan a familiar slap on the back and bowed to his sister, then turned inquiringly to Selma.

"Mademoiselle?"

"Mademoiselle Rauf," Amal said quickly. "Selma, allow me to present our hostess's cousin, Alexis, and Captain Octave de Verprès."

A lively conversation ensued. The newcomers were not only amusing but good-looking, which never hurts. Their admiring glances made Selma feel quite light-headed. To think that she had been reluctant to come, partly out of shyness, partly because she thought she would be bored! Alexis discreetly questioned her.

"You live in Beirut, do you? Your father is a diplomat, no doubt. No? He is dead?" Selma nodded. He looked suitably distressed. "I am so sorry. Your mother must feel very lonely here. I am sure my mother would be delighted to invite her to tea. She never goes out? She is ill? How sad! I see, so you are a lovely, lonely rose. . . ."

Selma blushed. No man had ever said such things to her before – in fact the only males she had ever conversed with were her brother's friends, who treated her like a sister. Her heart beat faster. Was this what they called flirting?

Marwan, unaware of what was afoot, chose this moment to remember that he had not yet paid his repects to Aunt Emilie.

"You see that charming old lady in the corner of the room, Selma – the one with all the people around her? She is the senior member of the Sursok clan – she loves to recall how she danced with Napoleon III as a girl. If Amal and I do not go over and kiss her hand she will consider it a major crime. Will you excuse me for a moment? I leave you in safe hands."

"That Marwan, what a gentleman!" said Alexis, smiling as he watched the other two walk off.

Selma missed the point. "Oh, yes indeed!" she said, much to

Octave's amusement.

"What a boring party," Alexis drawled. "There isn't even any decent music. Are you fond of dancing, mademoiselle?"

"Very," replied Selma, who would have died rather than admit that she had never danced with anyone but her classmates.

"In that case, I suggest we do something much more amusing than stay at this starchy affair. We'll organize a little party at my place – just a few friends and some other charming ladies. I have all the latest records from Paris. You won't be bored, I guarantee."

Selma, cursing her vanity, turned scarlet. Why had she told him she liked dancing? What would her mother say if she found out? There was no question of her going.

"But," she stammered, "I don't know if Marwan and Amal. . . ."

Octave winked. "Oh, they are old-fashioned – you have no need to tell them anything. We'll say we're escorting you home because your house is on our way, and that will be that."

Alexis knew they were moving in a little too fast, but they were running out of time. Marwan might return at any moment. He decided to play his trump card.

"Don't say you don't trust us!" he said, looking hurt.

He was not really annoyed that she should play hard to get – easy conquests did not interest him – but he was not going to stand for any airs and graces either. Alexis had experience of women, and this one, even if she were still a virgin, could not possibly be innocent – not with eyes and lips like hers! To crown it all, her mother was incapacitated and she had no father to be reckoned with. They were on to a good thing.

Octave de Verprès came closer. "Come on, sweetheart. Do you really find us so unattractive?" With a gesture that had more than once proved its worth, he put his arm around her waist.

"Let me go!" Selma broke away from him, trembling with indignation. "You disgust me!"

So that was all their gallantry and civility amounted to! She should have realized it sooner, but how could she have even suspected that they mistook her for . . . for a loose girl? She felt sullied and humiliated – on the verge of tears.

"Good heavens, Princess, what are you doing here?"

Across the terrace a tall, stately woman approached, and, to her astonishment, Selma recognized her aunt, Sultana Nailé. It seemed miraculous that she should be there at all, she went out so seldom. What Selma did not know was that the Sultana had been a friend of

Aunt Emilie's at Istanbul, and that she had decided to make an exception for old time's sake. Terrified at the thought that she might have seen the incident a moment ago, Selma curtsied low and kissed her hand. The two young men, looking dumbfounded, bowed respectfully.

"Highness. . . ."

The Sultana Nailé regarded them with a scaly eye. Then she said crisply, "I propose to deprive you of my niece's company, gentlemen. I have not seen her for a long time. . . ."

She took Selma firmly by the arm and led her off.

"Are you mad, my child? Fancy standing alone on an ill-lit terrace with two young men of dubious reputation! If your own good name means nothing to you, that of our family means a great deal to *me*! You must promise to behave with greater dignity in future. Otherwise I shall feel bound to inform your poor mother and advise her to confine you to your room until a suitable husband has been found for you."

"Honestly, Selma," Amal protested, "it is your own fault for putting us in such a difficult position. Why did you insist on being introduced as Mademoiselle Rauf? Aunt Linda was furious. As for Alexis, he accused me of making him look a fool. Well, why *were* you so set on going incognito?"

Selma, huddled up in the corner of the carriage that was taking them home, stared sullenly into space. She did not feel like talking, but Amal refused to let the matter rest.

"Listen, Amal: have you ever heard of Harun al-Rashid, who was caliph of Baghdad in the eighth century? He liked to dress up as a man of the people and walk the streets at night. They say he did it to gauge the state of public opinion, but I think he was mainly interested in finding out about himself. His relations with the people he met on his jaunts were not distorted by self-interest or fear. He made friends who appreciated his personal qualities and enemies who were not afraid of criticizing him to his face. He also made plenty of casual acquaintances who treated him with indifference because they did not find him a particularly interesting or remarkable person. He learned to see himself through the eyes of strangers; he had finally found the mirror that had always been denied him. Well, Amal, I also learned a lot about myself this evening."

Still smarting from her unpleasant experience, Selma shut herself up at home. She hated the world for not loving her, but she was mistaken: people did not love her, perhaps, but already they adored her! Word of the young, shy, haughty princess with emerald eyes had quickly spread, and every day brought a fresh batch of cards bearing invitations from the illustrious of Beirut. In a closed society where everyone knew everyone else to the point of nausea, a new face was a pearl beyond price.

Although Selma had sworn never to attend another social function, she eventually gave in. She had just turned eighteen: from now on, she decided, she would enjoy herself! During those few weeks of self-imposed seclusion she had sharpened her claws, and an entry in her diary – made more to convince herself than anything else – stated that the time of her childhood was over.

To signify her transition to the adult world she paid a surreptitious visit to the hairdresser's. There, in a tone rendered doubly imperious by the fear that she might change her mind at the last minute, she dismayed the poor man by ordering him to cut off her luxuriant hair and give her a bob, the latest Paris fashion. A few snips of the scissors transformed a romantic-looking damsel into a copper-helmeted Amazon whose disturbing blend of frailty and rebellion displayed that hint of sexual ambivalence extolled by the avant-garde and condemned by champions of femininity.

Cries of horror greeted Selma on her return home, but she paid no heed to her mother's remonstrances or the criticism of girlfriends who envied her daring, still less to the disappointment of her admirers. She had no regrets. Unconsciously, she had exorcised the mythical image, so often favoured by classical painters, of the beautiful slave girl dragged off by her lone tresses to the bed of some potent, dominant male.

She was now ready to face the world.

Selma took only a few months to carve herself a coveted niche in Beirut's high society. It was not that she surpassed all others in beauty. Rivals called her nose a trifle too long and her chin too angular, but the men appeared not to notice such minor shortcomings. They all fell under the spell of her innocently provocative smile, her mixture of coltishness and grace, and the faintly aloof manner that hovered between shyness and arrogance.

She had finally decided to use her title – it was her way of repaying the hospitality she could not afford to return. Everyone was thrilled to entertain a princess. Although she sometimes wondered if it was not demeaning to take advantage of the fact, she quickly dismissed such intrusive ideas – after all, what choice did she have? – and snapped to Amal when she anxiously remarked: "How you have changed, Selma! Are you happy?"

Happy? Of course she was! Her sense of power grew with every passing day. She loved to charm people – she had never known it could be so intoxicating.

The Sultana, having originally urged her to go out, was becoming concerned. No suitable match could possibly be found for her among the gilded youth of Beirut. How shameful it would be if her daughter fell in love with a Christian or some nobody of a Sunni!

"Are you sure," she asked when Selma described yet another ball she had just attended, "are you really sure you have not taken a fancy to some young man or other?"

"Don't worry, Annéjim," Selma assured her with a carefree laugh, "my heart is made of stone."

She forbore to add that she had vowed never to love anyone so as never to be hurt again. Her mask of indifference concealed the tear-stained face of a thirteen-year-old girl deserted by the only man in her life.

The Sultana's neighbours criticized her for allowing her daughter so much freedom. To middle-class Sunni women who still hid their faces behind black veils, the revolutionary mores introduced by the French threatened their daughters' virtue, the stability of family life, and the fabric of society as a whole.

It would not be the first time, said some, that Europeans had corrupted the nations they governed in order to sap their moral fibre and dominate them more easily. If anyone argued that the French merely lived as they thought fit and compelled no one to follow suit, they retorted that, where impressionable young minds were concerned, example was an insidious form of coercion.

The local matrons inveighed against Sultana Hatijé on the ground that her status should have made her the foremost guardian of tradition. "If her state of health prevents her from keeping an eye on her daughter," one of them went so far as to tell Zeynel, "why doesn't she get you to do it for her?" She only just stopped herself from adding, "After all, they didn't make a eunuch of you for nothing."

"The Sultana knows what she is doing," Zeynel replied curtly, and turned his back on the interfering busybody.

In fact, he also felt that Selma was becoming far too independent, even though she was always escorted by Haïri, who took his chaperon's duties very seriously, or by Marwan and Amal, so nothing untoward could happen to her. He himself had accompanied her to a few balls at first. Tightly buttoned up in his severe black stanbulin, he watched the couples disporting themselves from his post beside the footmen in the doorway. He soon realized, however, not only that this situation was humiliating – he was not a domestic servant, after all – but that his presence was superfluous. The girls were closely supervised by their mothers, who sat at the edge of the dance-floor and exchanged the latest rumours without for a moment losing sight of their precious offspring.

But Zeynel disapproved of such functions on principle. He couldn't understand or accept these European dances, these public embraces between men and women. Everything in him rebelled at the thought of strange male hands daring to touch his Princess's arm or waist. She was so pure – she had no inkling of what lurked in the minds of all those men, concealed beneath a veneer of good breeding. He, Zeynel, knew full well what it was.

He wanted Selma to be the loveliest and most feted young woman in Beirut, but also the most honoured and respected; to see so many dandies paying court to her simultaneously pleased and angered him. He liked her to be admired but could not bear anyone to go near her. His mental picture of her resembled one of those statuettes of the Virgin Mary which Christians kept under glass domes and worshipped. His little girl. . . . He must protect her, even against her will. He made up his mind to speak to her.

The eunuch's first few words reduced Selma to stunned silence, but indignation soon got the better of her. What right had he to speak to her in this way? She had never accepted a reprimand from anyone except her mother and occasionally – a very long time ago – from her father. But from Zeynel? His new status as the Sultana's sole adviser and confidant must have gone to his head. He had forgotten what he was and whom he was addressing!

She declined to explain that her emancipated behaviour was a form of self-defence, a way of concealing her excessive sensitivity; she would not demean herself by justifying her conduct to him. Infuriated by the fact that he had presumed to judge her, she construed it as an insult and, more hurtful still, as disloyalty on the part of an old retainer whose duty it was to lavish unstinted admiration and devotion on her.

Defiantly, she pulled on her coat, clapped a green felt cloche hat on her head, and went out, slamming the door behind her.

"What is it, Agha?"

To the Sultana, ensconced in the little sitting-room where she spent her afternoons, the minor commotion outside her sounded unusually loud in this house of muffled footsteps and subdued voices. She could tell from the eunuch's weobegone expression that some drama had occurred, but he said nothing until she ordered him to speak.

Then it all came out with a rush: the neighbours' criticisms, their spiteful innuendos, his own misgivings. Was it fitting for an Ottoman princess to lead the life of an ordinary Lebanese society girl? Shouldn't she remain aloof and refuse to mingle with those who were not of her world? He was bound to admit that it angered him to see the little Sultana laughing and dancing with young people who would never, in the normal course of events, have been privileged even to set eyes on her.

He expected the Sultana to agree, or at least to understand – wasn't pride all that remained to those stripped of everything else? – so he was unprepared for her irate expression and scathing tone of voice.

"You are a fool, Zeynel. I don't care what those women said, and I am surprised at you for lending such a receptive ear to their idle chatter!"

Zeynel turned pale. The Sultana's tone promptly softened.

"My poor Zeynel, you knew me when I was a prisoner at Çerağan. Surely you remember how unhappy I was? Someone who has spent youth confined within four walls knows the value of freedom. At Ortaköy I was free, even if I seldom went out. I want Selma to feel free too, and you must realize that freedom in Beirut and freedom in Istanbul are two different things. If my daughter can enjoy life without overstepping the bounds of propriety – and I trust her in that respect – I am delighted that she has the opportunity to do so."

She refrained from mentioning the other reason for her tolerance – a reason directly related to her illness. She knew she might survive for another few years, but she also knew that a heart attack might carry her off overnight. If her daughter remained naively ignorant of the world, like all girls subjected to too sheltered an upbringing, what would become of her? Many of the Sultana's prejudices had been dispelled by her two divorces, the downfall of the empire, exile, and financial ruin. It did not displease her that Selma was becoming a sophisticated young woman: she might some day have to fend for herself.

CHAPTER 6

"*Veladetin tedrik ederrim!* Blessed be the day of your birth! May the roses in your cheeks bloom for many years to come, may the perfumes of paradise fill your nostrils, may your life be all milk and honey!"

Everyone had gathered to celebrate Selma's twentieth birthday in the yellow drawing-room, which the kalfas had decorated with bunches of hibiscus and datura. Gifts neatly wrapped in glazed paper were arrayed on the gilded table. Nervin and Leila Hanum had embroidered some fine cambric handkerchiefs with Selma's monogram surmounted by a crown. Zeynel's present – dear Zeynel, he had gone without cigarettes for weeks to buy it for her – was a bottle of Millot's *Crepe de Chine*, her favourite perfume. Haïri, ever practical, had given his sister a box of candied fruit that everyone could enjoy. As for the Sultana . . . draped over an armchair was a superb sable coat that Selma could recall her wearing to receptions at Dolmabahçé Palace in the old days.

"But Annéjim," she protested, "why?"

"I have no further use for the thing, my darling – I would be delighted if you wore it." Selma started to thank her, but Sultana Hatijé cut her short with a laugh. "In any case, I have always thought it an insult to fine furs to put them next to a wrinkled old face. Contact with a nice fresh complexion has a rejuvenating effect on them."

Twenty candles were burning on the big chocolate cake. Nervin Hanum, knowing Selma's sweet tooth, had risen at dawn to bake it: no day-old cake would do for the little Sultana's birthday.

As she dreamily contemplated the dancing flames, Selma seemed to see them multiply until they became the hundreds of candles burning in the crystal chandeliers at Ortaköy Palace, all of which were lighted to mark her birthday as a child. She could remember every detail of those lavish celebrations: the orchestra that woke her with music and continued to play for the occasion; the twelve young kalfas who came to fetch her, all dressed in new caftans given them by the Sultana, and escorted her to the Hall of Mirrors, where her father and mother would be waiting with the rest of the haremlik staff. As she entered the orchestra struck up a birthday melody – a new one especially composed each year – and the kalfas showered her with tiny jasmine flowers whose fragrance filled the entire room.

Then would come the distribution of the gifts chosen by Selma and her mother for everyone, from the ladies-in-waiting to the last one of the palace slaves. For in the oriental world, it was considered more blessed to give than receive, so a birthday had to be a festive occasion for everyone around you, not just for yourself. At long last, when these presents had been handed out and opened with exclamations of joy, two slaves ceremoniously drew aside a silk curtain to reveal a multicoloured mountain of packages of every shape and size.

It would take Selma two or three hours to open them all and examine their contents. They included little gifts from the kalfas and maidservants, "joke parcels" from her brother, and magnificent presents from the Sultana and Rauf Bey. She had a particularly vivid recollection of her thirteenth birthday, the last she spent at Ortaköy. Her father had written off to Cartier, the great Paris jeweller, for a little clock of such unusual design that she had not at first known what it was. The crystal dial was surrounded by pearls and diamonds. The hands, too, were stubbed with diamonds, and the gold pendulum, suspended between two little columns of pink quartz, was reflected in a base of rock crystal. Unwilling to keep any memento of a father who had ceased to love her, Selma had given the clock away to Gülfilis before leaving Istanbul. How bitterly she now regretted the loss of that tribute to the refined taste of the man she could not forget. . . . What would he have given her for her twentieth birthday?

The flickering flames conjured up a picture of herself as a girl in a long gown with a train, crowned with a tiara. Fireworks illuminated the grounds of Ortaköy and its lacy architecture while musicians concealed amongst the shrubbery played romantic waltzes. She walked through the gardens once more, her cheeks fanned by a breeze from the Bosphorus, her ears filled with the happy laughter of her female attendants in their gold-embroidered caftans. . . .

The wax was beginning to drip on to the chocolate cake. With one determined puff Selma extinguished all the candles. The kalfas clapped excitedly and hailed this as a good omen – a sign that the Princess would be married within the year.

Married? To whom? Selma knew that her mother had been exchanging letters with a number of princely families, one-time vassals of the Ottoman Empire. She guessed that she was the subject of this correspondence but feigned a total lack of interest. In any case, she felt she was too young to marry. Having discovered how pleasant it was to be courted, she had no wish to forego that pleasure too soon.

And yet, when Prince Umberto of Italy and Princess Marie-José of

Belgium had married a few months before, escorted to the alter by ten reigning monarchs and sixty princesses of the blood, Selma had felt an involuntary pang of envy. She could never hope to make such a prestigious marriage, although she was just as blue-blooded as Marie-José and much more beautiful. But the only dowry she possessed was herself.

In the spring of 1931, Beirut was paralyzed by strikes and demonstrations. While some were for frivolous reasons – like the student protest for cheaper movie theatre seats – there were frequent clashes with police in the streets. A committee of merchants, students, and various prominent public figures organized a boycott of the tramways and the electricity company which lasted until the end of June. Parliament held several sittings by candlelight as a demonstration of solidarity. The government, which was nominated and controlled by the French High Commissioner, had to give in and ask the utility company to lower its prices. The company was Franco-Belgian, one of the many foreign concerns that had controlled the Lebanese economy since the mandate, and it was these foreign monopolies that the Lebanese were determined to do away with. They accused France of being in Lebanon only to impose the heavy taxes that went to support an army of incompetent bureaucrats, of exporting her own inflation by linking the Lebanese currency to the value of the franc, and of failing to respect the constitution which she herself had given Lebanon in 1926. The current High Commissioner, Henri Ponsot, who had succeeded Henri de Jouvenel, had in effect suppressed the Senate, increased executive power at the expense of parliament, and had virtually forced the reelection to the presidency of his protégé, Charles Debbas.

Marwan, who was studying law at the American University, came home every day seething with excitement. Even his Maronite classmates were beginning to grumble about Lebanon's dependent status. After all she had experienced in Turkey Selma could well understand her friends' exasperation. She had seen it all: the cry for independence, and the scandal of foreign occupation, diplomatically termed here a mandate. It seemed as though now everyone was interested in politics: next year, an election year, everything could topple.

Most of the presidential hopefuls were Maronites. Among the most prominent of them was Emile Eddé, a little man of forty-seven, known for his integrity and his pro-French leanings, and Bechara el-Khoury, a brilliant lawyer sympathetic to Arab concerns and an outspoken critic of the mandate. For the first time, the Christians were being opposed by a Muslim, Sheikh Mohammed el-Jisr, the leader of the House. A handsome man with a white beard, he was respected by his Christian as well as his Muslim peers. During the war, this former Ottoman representative and vice-governor of Beirut had given great service to the Maronite community, and had even saved their patriarch from exile. So he was supported not only by the Shiites, the Sunnis and the Druzes, but also by quite a few Greek Orthodox and Maronites. Given the divisions among Christians, he had a good chance of winning the election.

A Muslim head of state? To many Lebanese Christians, this seemed as unthinkable as it did to the French, who counted on retaining Lebanon as a sure ally in the Middle East. With a Muslim in charge there would be a strong risk of Lebanon's moving into the Syrian and Arab sphere of influence. Indeed the idea of a Muslim president was so unthinkable that a year later, in May 1932, when the Assembly showed every sign of electing Sheikh Mohammed – whom even Emile Eddé had decided to support, for reasons of electoral strategy – Henri Ponsot suspended the constitution three days before the election. Kept in office by the French for another twenty months, President Debbas was to govern by means of statutory orders framed in advance at the Grand Seraglio.

In the summer of 1931, however, no one foresaw such a development. On the contrary, the success of the strikes and boycotts encouraged people to challenge the mandate's abuses of power.

Selma spent hours talking politics with Marwan and Amal. She railed against the French and fervently supported Sheikh Mohammed, a friend of the Sultana's who had done his best to help her in exile. He had never forgotten that once, when he was four years old, he had spent a night at Dolmabahçé when his father was visiting Sultan Abdul Hamid. Selma remained one of his most dogged supporters until the day when her cousin Orhan, who had come to collect her from Mar-Elias Street with Haïri, firmly put her in her place.

"Lebanese politics are none of your business, Princess," he told her curtly. "You should not meddle in them." He was even more explicit on the way home. "Are you crazy, Selma? Do you want to get us kicked out again? Where would we go? Please be more discreet. This is not our country, remember."

As if she could forget it! Orhan was right, though: members of the Ottoman family were still regarded as Lebanon's former masters and could not afford to take sides. "You must remain neutral, even among friends," Orhan insisted. "Nothing ever remains a secret for long."

Although Selma realized that this was the only sensible attitude to adopt, it went against the grain. She had inherited her mother's passion for politics and the urge to fight for a cause. That passion, first aroused at the age of nine when she joined the weeping multitude in Sultan Ahmed Square and vowed to save her country, could find no outlet now that she had no country anymore, now that she was merely a guest. . . .

All that remained to her were the social functions – the dinners and balls – at which it amused her to shine. And during the day the cinema was her salvation. She hated playing cards or calling on friends to take tea and swap gossip, and she did not have enough money to while away her time at the dressmaker's or the hairdresser's. Her afternoons would have been long indeed without those visits to the Rialto and the Majestic.

For ten years now Hollywood had been the film capital of the world. In an article in the *Reveil*, one of the two biggest newspapers in Lebanon, Winston Churchill, in a brief interlude from politics during a visit to the US, described the new movie town as "a carnival in fairyland." He wrote: "The studios cover thousands of acres, employing thousands of actors and highly-paid technicians. Armies of workers create streets of China, London or India virtually overnight. Twenty films are made at a time. Youth and beauty reign supreme."

The real queens, actually, were the stars who set the fashion for women all over the world and whose appearances on screen made the crowds swoon. No queen in history was ever as celebrated as "The Blue Angel" or the Divine Garbo.

Selma saw all their films over and over again. Marlene Dietrich both shocked and fascinated her. As Lola, her husky voice and dark sensuality were eye-opening for the young woman. When she sang "I'm full of love from my head to my toes," Selma wondered if you could really drive men wild like that. She found Dietrich even more beautiful in other films: in *Morocco*, for instance, when in a top hat and tails she bewitched Gary Cooper, or as Mata Hari, alternating between a uniformed aviatrix and a *femme fatale*, whose last gesture was to use the sword of the officer who was going to execute her, as a mirror in which to apply her lipstick.

Garbo fascinated her more, however, and she yearned to look like her. She plucked her eyebrows, grew her hair again and wore it in a pageboy, and spent hours in front of the mirror, trying to imitate her slightly abrupt gestures, her casual manner, and the aloof expression that hinted at a flame resembling Selma's own passion. Depending on whether Selma had just seen her heroine in *Love, Anna Karenina, the Courtesan Christie*, or *Mata Hari*, she would be frail and romantic, voluptuous or intrepid by turns, much to the bewilderment of Zeynel and the two kalfas, who found her sudden changes of mood incomprehensible.

One night at the Trads, a leading family of Beirut bankers, Selma noticed that a big man of around fifty had been eyeing her all through dinner. When they retired to the drawing-room for coffee, he came over to her.

"They forgot to introduce me. My name's Richard Murphy, artistic director with Metro-Goldwyn-Mayer. I'm spending a few weeks in this beautiful country of yours. Pardon me for asking, but I've been watching you all evening: are you an actress?"

Selma, rather flattered, gave a little laugh. "Do I look like one?"

"You're lovely to look at, sure, but there's more to it than that. You've got 'presence,' and that's extremely rare. Ever thought of going into movies?"

"I would never be up to it. . . ."

"You're too modest. Anyone can learn how to move in front of a camera – it's an acquired skill like any other. What we need in Hollywood is young women like yourself: vivacious, graceful, classy – classy most of all. I'm going to say something I rarely say: you've got star potential. What's your name?"

"Selma."

"Terrific! Give me a year, and Selma will be a household name worldwide. I'm going to make you a star, Miss Selma. Will you let me?"

Murphy neglected to tell her that he had already done his homework. He knew exactly who she was, and that was precisely why she interested him. Pretty she might be, but she would probably make a mediocre actress. What mattered, though, was that she was a princess. A genuine princess in Hollywood! He could already see the headlines. Americans went crazy for anything with a whiff of real aristocracy. With a sultan's granddaughter under contract, even if her films were trash, MGM would beat Columbia, Warner Brothers, Twentieth Century Fox, and anyone else in the movie business hands down.

It was not going to be easy, though. From what he had heard of the Sultana, she would never permit her daughter to embark on a career she probably equated with prostitution, least of all in Hollywood, that den of vice on the other side of the world. Murphy smiled to himself. What if they invited her to come along as her daughter's chaperon? A veiled sultana in Hollywood? What a publicity coup *that* would be, he reflected before banishing the idea to the realm of impossible dreams. It was the girl he must dazzle with visions of glory to the point where she would, if necessary, dispense with her mother's blessing. She was of age, after all. Opportunity seldom knocked twice in a lifetime: she must seize it with both hands.

Such was Murphy's line of argument in the days to come. The Trads, with whom he was staying, bombarded Selma with invitations to tea at his request. He knew just how to handle ambitious but unsophisticated girls: they must be swept off their feet and given no time to think. It was a surefire tactic. . . .

"You are insane, Selma, utterly and completely insane!"

The Sultana, sitting bolt upright in her armchair, stared at her daughter with knitted brows as if trying to discern what stranger lurked beneath that familiar exterior. Selma repeated her explanation for the third time.

"Annéjim, please try to understand. MGM is the biggest film company in the world, and they're dying to hire me. It is a gold mine of a contract: five films a year and the leading role in each! Do you know how much they are offering me? A hundred thousand dollars a year! Just think, Annéjim, we could buy ourselves another palace – you would never have to worry about money for the rest of your life!"

"You are a mere child. You have no idea how immoral and corrupt the acting profession is. . . ."

"Oh, I know how to command respect," Selma exclaimed, drawing herself up proudly. "I stipulated that I would not take part in any risqué scenes and they agreed."

"They agreed, did they? How magnanimous of them!" Sultana Hatijé shook her head. "I refuse to discuss this crazy scheme a moment longer."

Selma did not even try to hold back the tears that sprang to her eyes. She rose and paced up and down with long, tigerish strides.

"I'm sick of my present existence! Tea dances, dinners, balls, receptions, more balls. . . . It's four years since I left school. I am twenty-one, Annéjim. Time is going by and I still haven't done anything with my life!"

The Sultana was touched by the bitterness and despair she could sense in this outburst of youthful vehemence.

"Come, now," she said in a more affectionate tone, "do not take things so tragically. You have too much personality to go on leading the life you do, I agree. You must marry."

"Oh, yes?" Selma said mockingly, coming to a halt. "And where am I going to find the Prince Charming?"

The Sultana refused to be provoked. "I thought a king might be more appropriate."

Selma stared at her in bewilderment. Her mother was not given to joking. "A king? But – "

"A few kings still walk the earth, Allah be praised. The one I have in mind is King Zog of Albania. I have been putting out feelers for some time – very discreetly, of course. You know that his sister has just married your uncle, Prince Abid, Sultan Abdul Hamid's youngest son. That made it easier to open negotiations. . . . I will not pretend that Zog is a great monarch – his subjects number only a million or so – but he is still young, he is handsome, he has very refined manners, so I am told, and he does not suffer from any known vices that would preclude him from marrying you. He also speaks fluent Turkish, having studied at Istanbul, and professes the greatest respect for our family.

"There are some who claim that Zog is an upstart. His original name was Ahmed Zoglu. He comes of the petty nobility, it is true, and he only got himself crowned by means of a coup d'état. On the other hand, his poor country had been torn apart by warring factions since it became independent in 1913, and he restored order with a firm hand. Whatever else he may not be, he is a brave man. Not overendowed with intelligence, apparently, but that is a point in his favour: you will find it all the easier to dominate him.

"Well, what do you say? Would you like to be a queen?"

What a part! Selma tossed and turned all night long, too excited to sleep. The lights of Hollywood seemed suddenly tawdry and ridiculous: she was going to be a queen, not a celluloid queen! Tomorrow she would tell the MGM man she did not want to sign the contract after all. Why not? Because she had better things to do. She relished the thought of his surprise: he would open his mouth as wide as the roaring lion that introduced his company's movies and ask her endless questions which she naturally would not answer.

During the next few weeks, Selma immersed herself in all the books and magazine articles on Albania she could find. Amal was the only person she took into her confidence. Together they raided every bookshop and library in town, and together, lying stretched out in their slips on Amal's big bed, they enthusiastically read and debated for afternoons on end. The results of their research were not entirely favourable. The little mountain kingdom was a land of great beauty inhabited by tough, honest peasants who had retained their ancestral customs and code of honour. Peace now reigned in place of the strife that had long prevailed between the country's great feudal families, but this, according to certain newspapers, was only because King Zog did not balk at liquidating those who got in his way. Other correspondents praised the King's generosity but stated that, in making gifts to his friends and relatives, he tended to confuse the public exchequer with his privy purse.

Selma dismissed all this. People always liked to blacken the reputation of those in power. Experience of the slurs cast on her own family during their last few years in Turkey had taught her that many newspaper reports were figments of the imagination – had there not been stories that the Sultan had taken with him part of the treasury as well as some of the relics of the Prophet? She did, on the other hand, pay close attention to the facts and figures that conveyed what a backward and impoverished country Albania was. Schools and hospitals would have to be built. She could already picture the trustful smiles of the women and children to whom she had resolved to devote her life. She realized that her task would be a difficult one: there were ingrained habits and vested interests to contend with, but she would triumph in the end, strengthened because she would be loved by an entire people.

Impulsively, she put her arms around Amal's waist. "You won't forget me? You'll come and see me often, won't you?"

Amal gave her an affectionate hug. "Of course I will, I promise."

She shared Selma's happiness, but also shared misgivings. In spite of all their reading and the bits of information they had managed to glean from here and there, neither of them could really imagine what the future held in store. Amal, being a Druze from the mountains, knew how difficult highlanders could be. Selma was a city girl accustomed to the measured rhythms and urbane manners of oriental cities lapped by the sea. How would she react to a rugged and utterly unfamiliar environment? Amal pensively stroked her friend's auburn curls and satiny shoulders. She wondered if Sultana Hatijé had made the wisest choice – if the girl whom she loved like a sister would be happy in her glamorous new existence – but she said nothing. If Selma was destined to be a queen, her destiny must be fulfilled.

Every evening from now on, when Selma came home, she closeted herself with Zeynel. For hours at a time, they discussed "their" country, its vast forests, its foaming waterfalls, its picturesque white villages perched on mountainsides. They spoke of long evenings by the fire, where stories were told of knights of yore whom fairies protected, of the miraculous kid whom the king's son married because beneath her skin and horns hid the most beautiful woman in the world, of the "Penitent Bear" and the "magic pony." Zeynel had been thirteen when the Sultan's soldiers escorted him from his Albanian village to the capital of the Ottoman Empire. He had tried to forget his native land and partly succeeded, but now it all came back to him, as fresh and vivid as if he had left it only yesterday. To the eunuch, Selma's forthcoming marriage was a sign from heaven. It confirmed his strange dream about that night in the palace at Ortaköy. . . .

He fantasized that his little girl was returning to the fountainhead of her blood. Not that she knew it, but everything within her was propelling her towards the unknown and from whence she came. And he, the peasant boy who had run barefoot in the mountains, who had been often cold and always hungry, who would never have dared raise his eyes to the mukhtar, the village headman – he, Zeynel, would become the father-in-law of his king!

He was so overcome with pride and joy, he felt like singing for love of the girl who was to become his queen. Snatches of old Albanian lullabies and folksongs drifted up from depths of his memory, and in his reedy voice, he recited the words he had once heard murmured by his mother.

Would that I might come to you,
O little lamb with the black-rimmed eyes,
Would that I might come to you, my plump one,
And sit myself down, O little lamb,
And drink wine, my plump one,
From a rose-coloured glass, O little lamb,
And make you forever happy, O little lamb,
Now and forever, my plump one.

"Go on, Agha, go on!"

Marvelling that Selma should hang on every word as if enthralled by these disjointed snatches of song, Zeynel told himself that they must have struck some chord of recognition deep inside her.

Two months went by, and still no word came from Albania. The Sultana, having given her consent in principle, declined to reopen the correspondence. Negotiations of this kind were naturally delicate. They took time, and any impression of haste would ruin everything.

At last the long-awaited letter arrived. Sealed with the royal coat of arms, it was signed by the king's private secretary, a distinguished man whom the Sultana had known in the days when he held a diplomatic post in Istanbul. He opened with the customary salutations and good wishes for the health and prosperity of the imperial family. Then:

> You must be aware, Sultana, that in consequence of the marriage between His Majesty's sister and His Highness Prince Abid, President Mustafa Kemal decided to break off diplomatic relations with Albania. His Majesty has a duty, for numerous reasons that will be apparent to you, to restore our country's links with Turkey. By marrying an Ottoman princess, he would undoubtedly jeopardize the chances of such a rapprochement.
>
> It is with profound regret, therefore, that His Majesty feels constrained to abandon a project so dear to his heart, but affairs of state must take precedence over a sovereign's personal desires. . . .
>
> I remain, Sultana. . . .

The Sultana, who had gone very pale, handed the letter to her daughter. Selma read it, burst out laughing, and firmly tore it up.

CHAPTER 7

Battalions of clouds like puffs of luminous ash were gliding westward in serried ranks. It was dusk, and birds wheeled madly in the sky in search of the departed sun. The earth breathed a sigh of relief, delivered at last from the feet that had trampled it all day. Sap and fragrance rose from its depths.

Selma, leaning out over her bedroom balcony, listened to the voice of the muezzin punctuated by the bells of Saint-Louis-des-Français, which were tolling the Angelus. It was time she got dressed. The Tabets, one of the wealthiest Maronite families in Lebanon, were giving a dinner in honour of Count Damien de Martel, the new High Commissioner. Martel was said to be a seasoned diplomat of keen intelligence, sharp-tongued but not without charm, and everyone was counting on him to restore the constitution suspended by his predecessor and proceed with the presidential elections.

The dinner was bound to be attended by the cream of Beirut society, a world in which business and political interests largely coincided. Emile Eddé and his friend and rival Beshara el-Khoury would be present. So would Emir Fuad Arslan, a Druze deputy, and Ryadh el-Solh, a Sunni deputy, both of them harsh critics of the mandate and both madly in love with Yumna el-Khoury, the presidential candidate's beautiful sister. Camille Chamoun, a rising star in the political firmament, would also be there. Reputedly the best-looking man in the Near East, he was said to have broken many a heart when he married Nicolas Tabet's daughter.

To adorn their party the hosts had invited the city's leading belles: Yvonne Bustros, Maud Farjallah, Nejla Hamdam, an intense, dark-eyed Druze, Isabelita, formerly the mistress of Alfonso XIII of Spain and now the vivacious wife of Robert Sabbagh, and a host of others. When Beirut set out to charm a visitor, its generosity knew no bounds. It lavished its loveliest jewels on him, dazzled him with its gaiety, enchanted him with its sparkling and often subtle wit, turned his head by enmeshing him in a thousand friendships as instant as they were eternal – or ephemeral, which amounted to the same thing, for the Lebanese, being true Orientals, were well aware that eternity resides in every fleeting moment.

The visitor around whom Beirut planned to spin its shimmering web tonight was the city's new master, and Selma had been invited to be one of the components of that web, which was designed to envelope and, if possible, absorb him.

The prospect amused her, whereas two years ago she would have refused to play such a subordinate role and insisted on being liked and invited for herself alone! Herself? She no longer knew what that meant, now that so many of her mirrors had broken: the mirror of multicoloured lights that had reflected a glamorous queen of Hollywood; the worn old gilt-framed mirror in which she had glimpsed the grave, gentle features of a youthful queen of Albania; even the mirrors at Ortaköy, in which an intrepid little Sultana had tidied her curls before setting out to conquer the world. . . .

Selma abruptly tossed back her hair. She was a woman of twenty-two now, not the wistful adolescent who had striven to find her true identity, and who, when she thought she had discovered the real Selma behind the Ottoman princess, had begun to wonder what lay beyond that Selma. It was like the game of the Russian doll: you unscrewed it and found another inside, and another, and another, never the original doll. But *was* there an original doll? Who could tell if a real Selma existed independently of the roles she played? In any case, she was incapable of solving that problem, and refused to spend any more time in that pointless quest. She was young, she was one of Beirut's most feted women, and she did not want to think any more – thinking gave you wrinkles according to Nervin Hanum. She simply wanted to have a good time.

"Heavens, Selma, aren't you ready yet? It is nine o'clock!"

Amal had come in, looking delightful in a close-fitted gown modelled on the latest fashion launched by Lucien Lelong, the celebrated Paris couturier.

"I knocked but you didn't answer. What is the matter? Are you feeling all right? You know we have to be at the Tabets' by 9.30, before the High Commissioner arrives."

"Standing at attention, I suppose!" Selma retorted. "Don't worry, Amal, I'm feeling fine. I *want* to turn up late tonight, that's all." Amal gave her a reproving frown. "It's an act of pure kindness," Selma went on sarcastically. "The poor creatures are always short of small talk, so it will give them something to chew on. Why, don't you think they will invite me again?"

There was so much insolence in her face and defiance in her voice that Amal thought it better not to reply. She hardly recognized her friend in this arrogant stranger. Once so sensitive and vulnerable, Selma had grown hard since the failure of her plans for a career in

Hollywood and for her royal Albanian marriage. Far too proud to betray her disappointment, she never alluded to these grandiose projects except in tones of self-mockery. It was as if she reproached herself for dreaming and resented having shared her dreams with Amal – as if she were determined never to let her hair down again, merely to lead people on and then spurn them rather than run the slightest risk of being spurned herself.

The effect of this was to make her all the more popular in a little world where everything – love, money, success – palled because it came too easily. The men who flocked around her watched each other like hawks, wondering which of them would win the favour of this hard-hearted beauty? Her aloofness was legendary. No one could boast of having stolen a kiss, or even of having held her hand. Actually, they were grateful for her indifference because they felt sure it was just a ruse designed to captivate them. The final victory would be all the sweeter.

They were wrong, though, Amal told herself as she studied Selma's uncommunicative face: she was genuinely indifferent these days. Even when enjoying herself, she seemed to do so out of duty.

There was a knock at the door. Haïri and Marwan had come to see what was keeping them. Selma noted with amusement that Haïri was dressed to the nines – cream shantung tuxedo and red carnation in buttonhole – to impress Amal.

"I am in love with her," he had confided a few days ago. "Do you think she would like to become a princess?"

"I think that is the least of her concerns," Selma had answered him, but Haïri had dismissed this as pure spite and opened his assault on Amal by sending her a spray of red roses every day for the past week. Tonight he was hoping to be rewarded with a smile; he would ask her, then, to reserve all the after-dinner waltzes for him. Amal neither smiled nor mentioned his flowers, but Haïri put that down to shyness. Later on, when Marwan took him aside and explained that his sister detested roses because their scent gave her a migraine, Haïri was touched by such delicacy and felt even more enamoured. Meantime, he chided Selma for not being ready.

"You are planning to turn up late on purpose, just to draw attention to yourself!"

"You go on ahead," she retorted impatiently. "Zeynel will hire an arraba[1] and escort me there."

Marwan hesitated. He did not like the look in Selma's eyes, still

1 An open carriage.

less her new laugh, which was forced and brittle. He had meant to speak with her tonight, but perhaps it would be better to pave the way first. He produced a slim package from his pocket.

"I have brought you a book by Fariduddin Attar, the greatest of our Druze poets and mystics. If you decide not to come, it will keep you company."

"The birds of the entire world," Selma read, "gathered to go in search of the Simurgh, their long-lost king. No one knew where he dwelled save one very old bird, but he could not find the King alone beause the route was full of pitfalls, so they all had to go. The Simurgh did, in fact, live in the Qaf, a mountain range encircling the earth, and to reach it one had to penetrate curtains of fire, swim across raging rivers, and do battle with armies of ferocious dragons.

"They set out in their thousands, but most of them perished in the course of the journey, which took years. Only thirty of the wisest birds, after many tribulations, reached the Simurgh's court in the Qaf Mountains. There they were dazzled to discover thousands of suns, moons, and stars, and reflected in each of those heavenly bodies they saw themselves and the Simurgh. They no longer knew if they were themselves or had become the Simurgh, until at length they realized that they were the Simurgh and the Simurgh was themselves, and that they were one and the same being, and that their King, the God whom they had come so far to find, was within them. . . ."

Selma laid the book aside. In a tekké on the outskirts of Istanbul, a little girl kissed an old sheikh's upturned palm. Suddenly blinded by the light, she felt she would dissolve if she kept her eyes open. She was afraid, so she shut them, and everything resumed its normal, reassuring place. . . .

She had never forgotten her longing for the brilliance and her shame at having been afraid – a shame of which she was paradoxically proud. She cherished the sensation, for being ashamed was a proof of a spiritual superiority that constantly strives to surpass itself.

Selma had long been preoccupied with the search for unity but had always stopped short on the threshold. She was afraid of reaching for it – afraid of being wholly possessed by it for she sensed that no bounds could be set on this quest for the absolute, and that there was a danger of losing oneself in it, like the Simurgh's mŷriâd birds that had died before attaining the light.

To take refuge in strict religious observance, on the other hand, might destroy one's fruitful sense of insecurity. Marwan, who was an akkal, or initiate in the Druze hierarchy, had told her one day that religion and morality were the surest means of never finding God. "Commandments and prohibitions are walls erected to help one reach the heavens," he said, "but the higher they rise the more the sky shrinks, until all one sees is a wretched little square of blue bearing no resemblance to the sky at all. They speak to us of marble staircases and a golden throne, a world as dead as their moral code. They fail to understand that the heaven is life in its infinite variety. How can the route to infinity be hemmed in by walls?"

Selma felt giddy. Why had Marwan brought her this book? She had been content to revel in the attention and adulation she aroused, so why had he spoiled everything? Why couldn't he let her live and be happy like everyone else?

Happy . . . the word seemed to ring in her ears, vulgar and almost obscene. She was constantly surprised at her ability to convince herself of anything she chose. She had not sunk so low, even now, that she could be content with that kind of happiness!

She recalled those women in the palaces of Istanbul with eyes free of turmoil: they were identical with the smart society women of Beirut. Was *that* what she was in process of becoming? She shivered. The words of Jelaleddin Rumi, the Sufi poet and scholar, came back to her: "May I never lose thee, blessed sorrow more precious than water, searing of the soul without which we should be dead wood, nothing more. . . ."

She went down the stairs, out into the garden. The night sky looked down on her benevolently, the stars were strangers to her no longer. She felt like someone returning home after a lengthy absence.

Clicking his tongue and cracking his whip, the coachman urged his horse along and the arraba went merrily down the avenue. He was proud to have in his carriage two such pretty young ladies garnering the admiring gaze of all the passers-by. This was Amal's idea. Several weeks ago she had heard of this woman with amazing powers, a new oracle, it was rumoured, sent by God – or perhaps the devil. They had decided to go see her without telling Marwan, who would only get angry.

A thin youth had let them into the shuttered house and had silently guided them to a dark room where incense burners did futile battle with the bittersweet odours of mingled breath and sweat. There on a high bed sat a corpulent old woman surrounded by a throng of devotees. For these she was distilling drop by drop a redeeming and chastening potion of words and silence. A few words, like honey after vinegar, fell from her thin lips as her burning eyes pierced the gaze of the onlookers, boring through their breasts to their hearts.

The two girls stopped in the shadows near the door, but not before the old woman spotted them. Instinct told her they were choice prey. A fat hand beckoned to them to approach and enter the circle of the elect near the bed. They refused. Rebels, were they? The old woman smiled. That was how she liked them – impudent and presumptuous, like children naked beneath the sun. She had a particular taste for these unselfconscious children who thought themselves beloved of God. These were the kind from whom she drew life. She had no time for the prostrate slaves around her, she had already devoured them. They had become her tentacles, going to the towns to spread her word and bring back new prey thirsty to hear her, the inspired prophetess.

At the sides of the bed some hesitated. What kinds of spirits ruled this magnificent, terrifying crone enthroned there? Were they from heaven or hell? Little by little the idea took hold in them that these spirits were the same, after all, that God was light purified of all the fetid slag which gave birth to the devil, and the bravest, the rashest among them, set out on this journey from which there could be no turning back, where the only certainty was that of being consumed forever – whether in the fire of hell or the flames of divine love.

There were those who would always be dallying, who would never rid themselves of the vaguely sickening feeling that they were incapable of attaining the Ultimate, whether it be of happiness or misery. But to all, both those who had cleared the first fearsome hurdle and those who had not yet dared, the old woman offered the same royal gift: eternal restlessness.

The auburn-haired young woman in the doorway turned her eyes away. "Let's go," she whispered to her companion. "The light in here is dark." Had the old woman heard? She drew herself up on the bed and from her lips thundered the ominous curse: "You – the proud one – you will lower your head! In two nights I shall come to you. Remember – in two nights!"

Selma had not had so much fun in a long time. The theme of Jean Tueni's costume ball was "Les Indes galantes," after the opera by Rameau. Selma had gone as a maharajah in white satin jodhpurs and a plumed turban – the plume plucked from Nervin Hanum's feather duster – with six strands of fine pearls around her neck, courtesy of Souren Agha. Under the black mask worn by all the guests, no one recognized her. At the end of the evening when all the masks were raised, she had surprised everyone yet again.

Still, she had almost begged off from the ball at the last minute. She was tormented by the witch's threats. She had vainly tried to banish them from her mind but they returned relentlessly. All day long Amal had drawn on her wealth of persuasive powers in an attempt to convince Selma that the old hag's power extended no further than her submissive throng of followers. When she had sensed a rebel in Selma she had simply said whatever she thought would frighten the girl.

"Be reasonable, Selma. How do you think she could take defiance in front of that bleating herd of hers! And besides, how could she possibly come here? She is too fat to go anywhere!"

Selma was not convinced and countered by telling her friends stories of Turkish women with evil powers. This was too much even for the usually good-natured Amal.

"You really surprise me! Honestly, you are just as gullible as the peasants in our villages."

In the end Marwan, let into the secret of the pair's adventure, managed to persuade Selma that under the circumstances it would be better not to be at home that evening. And he stressed that Zeynel and the kalfas should be given strict instructions not to open the door to anyone for any reason.

The band struck up a final tango. It was four in the morning, and most of the guests had already left. The candles in the silver candelabra, which were burning low, cast dancing shadows that seemed to bring the tapestries on the walls to life. Selma, in the arms of handsome Ibrahim Sursok, allowed him to lead her as he chose. This was the best time of all – the time when only a small circle of friends remained and a second, more intimate party began.

Moussa de Freige got out his violin to accompany Henri Pharaon, who had a fine baritone voice and sang popular ballads. Gabriel Tabet told funny stories, and Isabelita, who had brought her castanets and her flounced red dress, performed flamenco dances. It was not until the sky began to pale and cups of piping hot coffee had been served that the revellers reluctantly decided to disperse. Selma had never stayed out so late before. Haïri usually insisted on leaving by two o'clock, but this time, at Selma's instigation, Amal had danced with him often enough to make him forget his principles.

A big black Citroën was parked outside the gate and the front door was wide open. Selma ran up the steps and into the house. All the lights were on, but there was no one to be seen. She took the stairs two at a time and paused outside her mother's room, listening. Something terrible had happened, she could tell. The sorceress. . . .

She pushed the door open with a trembling hand. The room was in semidarkness, and all she saw at first was a broad back swathed in a grey frock coat. Gradually she made out the two kalfas and Zeynel, who put a finger to his lips. As she slowly came towards them, scanning the gloom for her mother, the grey frock coat swung around and a monocled eye glanced disapprovingly at the strange turbaned form. Selma walked past, unaware of him, then all at once caught sight of a figure stretched out on the floor, utterly inert . . . dead!

"Annéjim!" she cried but before she could reach her mother's side a hand grasped her roughly by the arm.

"Quiet! This is no time for hysterics!"

Thrusting her unceremoniously into Zeynel's arms, the doctor knelt down and resumed his examination. Hours or minutes later – her sense of time had deserted her – he straightened up and called for some blankets.

"She can't be moved at present, but we must keep her warm."

Keep her warm? So she isn't . . .?

Haïri had followed Selma into the room. He calmly stepped forward, and for the first time in her life she felt a stirring of admiration for him.

"I am her son, doctor. Tell me the truth," he said in a measured tone.

The doctor looked at him and nodded.

"Your mother has suffered a very severe stroke, young man. Luckily her heart withstood it. She will live, but. . . ."

"But what?"

"I am afraid she will be permanently paralyzed."

Selma sat at the piano, silent and motionless. She had just played the Schubert impromptus her mother liked best, the second and fourth, followed by Liszt's variations on a theme by Haydn. The Sultana, confined to the wheelchair she never left except when Zeynel carried her to her bed, had listened with half-closed eyes and a look of supreme contentment.

Her legs had now been paralyzed for six months, but Selma had never once heard her complain, never once seen her impatient or depressed. On the contrary, her mother seemed at peace for the first time in the eleven years since their exile.

And yet . . . Selma could not help drawing poignant comparisons between this ageing, helpless woman and the Sultana of old. She pictured her as she used to be, a resplendent figure in her long robe trimmed with sable, the broad imperial sash across her breast; the glacial and majestic princess who had refused to admit the police to her palace and risked her life for a stranger; the goddess, compassionate in the face of human frailty but adamant in her conception of honour. Gentle she may not have been, but how admirable!

During these six months Selma had seldom left the house, nor had she even wanted to. At first she had convinced herself that she was keeping her mother company, but then she suspected it was to redeem herself: she knew that her mother's heart condition could lead to a stroke, but deep in her heart she believed that it was the sorceress taking her revenge. She was worried. The doctor had warned them that a second stroke might prove fatal. Repugnant and unthinkable as it seemed, the idea had gradually grown in Selma's mind until she realized, to her utter dismay, that her mother was mortal, and that the rock that had supported her and formed the one immutable element in her life might give way and leave her teetering on the brink of an abyss. Until now, the thought had never occurred to her. Death was always for someone else – but if her mother died? . . . it would be as if the best part of herself would die along with her.

When word of the Sultana's illness first spread, many of Selma's friends had written or called on her to express their sympathy. The flood of invitations resumed after a month's respite, only to dry up when she left them unanswered. She had withrawn into her shell and spent whole afternoons composing melancholy ballads and sonatinas. Marwan and Amal, now the only regular visitors to the house in Rustem Pasha Street, were as concerned by this development as the Sultana herself, who took Marwan aside one day.

"Selma really must go out. Please find some way of persuading her, or her health will suffer – and two invalids in this house would be too much." The Sultana gave a little laugh. "After all, being ill is *my* prerogative!"

It was springtime, and the season of outdoor balls had just begun. The handsome gardens in the Sursok district were alive with armies of gardeners busy tending clumps of hydrangeas imported from Europe and trimming hedges of oleander and hawthorn.

The most original and amusing social function of all was the Admiralty Ball held annually aboard the *Jeanne d'Arc*, the French training ship in Beirut harbour. Those invited to attend it were selected with the utmost care, and the guest list included Marwan and Amal. They were Druze, of course, but the Franco-Druze war was a fast-fading memory. The Jebel had been granted self-government in

1930, and the French authorities in Lebanon and Syria were at pains not to offend the mountain lords.

Marwan, who had managed to wangle Selma an invitation to the Admiralty Ball, countered her predictable refusal with a show of annoyance.

"You just can not do this to me!" he protested. "There is a sit-down dinner first – the seating plan has been all mapped out for the past month."

"The atmosphere is completely different from all the other balls," Amal chimed in. "It is like a pleasure cruise on an ocean liner. Besides, I want you to meet my cousin Wahid. He has agreed to leave his mountain lair for once. You will see, he is a bit eccentric but very charming."

Under their combined onslaught, Selma eventually yielded.

CHAPTER 8

The *Jeanne d'Arc* stood out against the gloomy waterfront like a Christmas tree festooned with coloured lights. The admiral and his officers, all in full-dress uniform, received their guests on deck while in the background a naval band played the overture to Offenbach's *La Vie Parisienne*.

Uttering little cries of alarm and delight, women in high heels and long evening gowns ventured timidly up the narrow gangway with their escorts in close attendance. The admiral, a suave and sophisticated man, said a few words of welcome to each. He was feeling pleased with himself. The evening promised to be a resounding success: his few hundred square yards of deck space had attracted everyone in Beirut who mattered.

Marwan and his two companions were late. A pair of young naval cadets hurriedly conducted them to their table, which was some distance from the orchestra. The other members of the party were already seated around its damask-covered surface, which was almost buried beneath a profusion of roses, silverware, and Limoges china. The latecomers got a noisy reception.

"We had given you up for lost!"

"Congratulations, Amal," drawled a lanky young man. "Only an hour late – you're improving."

"Wahid, I'm sure you will forgive me when you see whom I have brought you. Selma, allow me to present my cousin Wahid. Don't worry, his bark is worse than his bite."

The long, lean figure rose with studied nonchalance and bowed.

"Ah, Princess!" he exclaimed in a histrionic tone that caused heads at neighbouring tables to turn. "Had my ancestors only dreamed of your existence, our families would have been spared centuries of bloodshed. Proud warriors though they were, they would have surrendered to the Ottomans on the spot."

Half captivated, half mocking, his blue-eyed gaze enveloped Selma from head to foot. Imperiously, he rearranged the table plan so as to seat her on his right. Ignoring the other guests, he plied her with questions about her life, her activities, her tastes. He seemed wholly entranced and quite unaware of her embarrassment at being courted with such singleminded enthusiasm.

Selma's ordeal lasted only a quarter of an hour. Abruptly, as if his curiosity were satisfied and his interest had waned, Wahid Bey turned his back on her and joined his friends in a heated political discussion. Selma's neighbour, a small, slender, distinguished-looking man, hastened to take advantage of this unlooked-for piece of luck. He did not know the name of this charming young woman, but that did not matter – he would find it out later.

"Allow me to introduce myself: Charles Corm, poet. Do you like poetry, mademoiselle?"

"Oh, very much," smiled Selma, relieved to hear the mild, well-bred tones of a Beiruti after the Druze storm she had just endured.

"They call me 'the Phoenician Bard.' Have you read my latest collection, *The Inspired Mountain*? It has just won the Edgar Allan Poe prize."

"I have heard of it," said Selma politely.

"Would you like me to recite a few verses from it?"

"Certainly," said Selma, inwardly marvelling at the boundless vanity of writers.

The bard cleared his throat, and then, staring absently into the faraway horizon of tablecloths, began to declaim:

Tell, oh tell the story dear
How through the ages without fear
Alone in this our Lebanon
Our people bore the cross on high,
Upheld it midst the turbanned throng
That dwelt beneath the Asian skies

Indeed, my Muslim friend so dear,
Frank I speak now, without fear,
And trust your sympathetic part
To grant supremacy is due
To him whose faith is mirror true
Of Pelican's self-giving heart.

Selma started. Could this nice man possibly intend to be so provocative? As she met his earnest, myopic gaze, she managed to restrain her laughter. The poor man obviously had no idea who she was. Now she understood his pride in claiming his title of "Phoenician Bard": she remembered several of her Maronite classmates at school adamantly refusing to be called Arabs. They called themselves Phoenicians, discendants of the ancient race who had once ruled all the

Mediterranean, whose civilization had flowered and then died over two thousand years ago. She suddenly felt an urge to amuse herself, and avenge the "Turbanned throng" at the same time.

"But, Monsieur, surely the Phoenicians were neither Christian nor Muslim?"

The poet flushed crimson as he tried to explain to this emtpy-headed young socialite that "the Christians remained faithful to their origins. And while Lebanon had, alas been Arabized, they, the true Lebanese, had. . . ." Selma turned and happened to catch Wahid's eye as he gave her a conspiratorial glance. So he had been listening! He was only pretending to ignore her! Selma felt her heart beating absurdly. The man was behaving like a complete cad and here she was, forgiving him after one glance. Just what was so appealing about this romantic Pierrot? His elusiveness? Or was it the way he seemed to mock everyone and everything?

Dinner drew to a close and stewards circulated with coffee and liqueurs. Having played softly until now, the naval band launched into a spirited tango. The first couples took the floor. Selma watched them with a mixture of curiosity and envy. She would have liked to join in, but her mother had denounced the tango as a series of primitive contortions and would only allow her to waltz.

Minutes later, when the orchestra struck up a Strauss waltz, she beat time with her foot and glanced swiftly at Wahid, wondering if he would ask her to dance, but no, he was deep in conversation with his friends.

"May I have the honour, Princess?"

A French officer had appeared at her elbow. Very slim and elegant in the tropical whites that effectively set off his tan, he bowed respectfully.

"You may not remember," he said with a disarming smile, "but we were introduced at Bustros': George Buis, captain of cavalry."

It was not customary to accept an invitation from someone in another party, but Selma did not care. She was too eager to dance – too eager to show Wahid that his capricious behaviour left her cold. She gladly succumbed to the lilting rhythm of the music. The orchestra played three waltzes in succession. People would gossip, she knew, but she danced them all with the handsome young officer.

No sooner had she returned to her table, rather dizzy and out of breath, than Wahid turned to her abruptly.

"It amazes me that any Muslim girl, let alone an Ottoman princess, should dance with a French officer. How broad-minded, how noble of you to forgive and forget!"

Selma flushed. The others stared at Wahid open-mouthed. Marwan, looking thoroughly disconcerted, tried to salvage the situation.

"Ah! Wahid Bey the moralist!" he said. "Is this your latest foible? I always knew you had a sense of humour, but aren't you overdoing it a bit?"

"I was not being humorous," Wahid retorted coldly.

Marwan clenched his teeth. Clan solidarity forbade him to insult his friend and relative but he could not allow him to humiliate a guest.

"Selma, my dear, would you grant me the inestimable pleasure of this dance?"

Selma rose like an automaton. Wahid balefully watched them take the floor. Conversation at the table resumed, twice as volubly as before to cover everyone's embarrassment. Without a word, Wahid started drinking. He must have been on his fourth or fifth cognac when he brought his glass down on the table with such force that the stem snapped off.

"Waiter, this cognac is undrinkable! Bring me something better!"

The steward hurried over. "But Monsieur," he said helplessly, "this is a very old cognac – it's the only one we have."

"The only one you deign to offer us, you mean! I suppose our French masters consider us too uncivilized to know the difference!"

His voice grew louder. By now, all eyes had turned in his direction.

"Rotten cognac, a puppet government, a sham constitution – that's good enough for primitive Lebanese! Surely they wouldn't aspire to self-government! Well, gentlemen we have had enough of it. We want you out of our country, and fast! We won't always ask you so nicely!"

Silence fell. By an unfortunate coincidence, the orchestra had just stopped playing. No one dared move. Sitting back in his chair with a bellow of laughter, the young Druze chieftain raised his stemless glass.

"I drink to Lebanon's freedom and independence!"

"My God," Selma muttered to Marwan, who was escorting her back to the table. "He is completely drunk."

"Oh no, he never gets drunk. I don't know anyone who can hold his liquor better than Wahid. The more he drinks the more clear-headed and cynical he becomes. What he just said is what we all think, discounting a few families who owe their rise in the world to the mandate. Before the war the French had promised us independence, and what did they do? They imposed an artificial frontier between Lebanon and Syria, two areas that have formed a single economic and financial unit for centuries, and turned us into a satellite. We have been negotiating for fifteen years now without success. Even the Maronites are growing restive."

"All the same, imagine saying such things aboard a French ship!"

"That's Wahid all over – he loves being provocative. The French will pretend to think he is drunk to avoid having to throw him out, and that will amuse him even more. As long as he sticks to verbal escapades they will leave him alone – they lost too many men in the Jebel to dare lay hands on a Druze leader. Still, I did think he might restrain himself tonight." Marwan gave Selma a mischievous grin. "I believe we owe that little outburst to you."

"You are joking!"

"Far from it. Wahid was furious because you danced with that French officer. His modern, easygoing manner is a veneer. He is really an out-and-out feudalist, and far more hidebound than he thinks. He still abides by tradition and a code of honour centuries old. His sophisticated education and his wide reading did not change a thing."

The next morning, when Zeynel answered the door, he was confronted by a bearded man with a rifle slung across his shoulders, half-obscured by an enormous bunch of gladioli.

"The Chief told me to deliver these to the Princess," he announced.

Zeynel stared at him in bewilderment. "The Chief?" he repeated.

"The Chief, Wahid Bey, who else?" growled the man, and thrust his burden into the eunuch's arms. Then, readjusting his rifle and bandolier, he clicked his heels and made a dignified departure.

Amal and Selma had finished shopping and were relaxing over a sherbet at the Patisserie Suisse, the only tearoom in Beirut where a lady could afford to be seen.

"What a strange man your cousin is," said Selma, who had been itching to bring up the subject of Wahid all afternoon.

Amal smiled. "It takes all kinds to make a family. Some people say he is crazy. Personally I think he is the most intelligent of the lot. His branch of the family was deposed a century and a half ago, after a series of plots and assassinations, but it claims to be the legitimate line. Wahid has a small but devoted band of supporters. They revered his father, Hamza Bey, a hero of the Arab cause who was killed just before Wahid's tenth birthday. When Fuad Bey, Sit Nazira's husband, was assassinated in his turn, they hoped the title would revert to Wahid, but the majority of the clan was loyal to Sit Nazira and her son Kamal, who was then a baby. They were also strongly supported by the French, as they still are. Who knows, though? If anything happened to Kamal, Wahid might become the zaim, the clan chief, so everyone handles him with kid gloves, especially the French. . . ."

In the weeks that followed Selma went out often. She did not admit it to herself, but she wanted to see Wahid again – and she did. There was scarcely a dinner or reception at which she failed to come across the young Bey. Although he greeted her each time with rather exaggerated courtesy, he never tried to pick up the threads of their original conversation.

In any case, he was much in demand with the ladies, who found his indifference irresistibly attractive. Some of them pronounced him rather ugly, with his beaky nose, strangely piercing blue eyes, and high, prematurely balding forehead, but they all acknowledged his devastating charm. He had a boyish smile and a way of looking surprised and delighted at the least sign of friendship, as though amazed that anyone could feel well-disposed toward him, but if any of his conquests became overly familiar, the smile turned sardonic and a scathing remark would put her in her place.

Selma, who sometimes sensed that he was looking at her, behaved like any young woman eager to attract a man: she flirted openly with her band of regular admirers, who could not believe their good fortune.

At long last, Wahid came over to her one night.

"Princess," he asked in a studiously mournful voice, "why are you avoiding me? Are you still angry with me? Haven't you guessed the reason for my boorish behaviour at the Admiralty Ball? Overpowering jealousy, that's all it was."

His earnest tone was belied by an ironical smile, but Selma detected an anxious look in his eyes. It dawned on her that he was fundamentally shy, and that his sarcasm was merely a form of self-defence. Even so, she could not resist giving him a little taste of his own medicine.

"Angry with you? Why? Because of that scene on the ship? I had forgotten all about it."

"So you won't refuse me this waltz?"

Was he joking? They looked at each other and burst out laughing. He led her on to the floor. God, how badly he danced!

CHAPTER 9

Summer had come, and with it the annual mass exodus from the stifling heat of the city. Everyone who could afford it went off to spend four months in the mountains at Sofar, Alley, and Bikfaya, either in the big hotels, or in luxurious private houses enclosed by terraced gardens. Even the government moved out.

Amal had invited Selma to Ras el-Metn, her former family seat in the mountains. Abandoned in the last century when her grandfather, the first Daruzi to go to university, had moved to Beirut, the austere old mansion that had witnessed so many decisive events in the history of the Druze nation was now no more than a summer residence.

Though rustic in flavour, social life in the mountains was even livelier than in the capital, as the summer refugees had nothing to do but enjoy themselves. Neighbours exchanged informal hospitality. Family parties boarded arrabas and drove along narrow mountain roads to picnic at the foot of some crystalline cascade or congregate at some country inn, which would be rented *in toto* to assure them of privacy. Those of a sporting or adventurous disposition went trekking through the highlands on horseback, returning only at dusk.

But the nights were devoted to large gatherings. There were parties all over the place, and people would drive for miles along winding mountain roads to attend them rather than offend their hosts by declining an invitation. Dancing went on until dawn, when the servants laid out cotton mattresses in every room. In the mountains no one stood on ceremony and the houses were big enough to accommodate everyone. Guests would finally depart late in the day, well rested, after an ample breakfast of grilled ortolans, beans, and hummus.

Wahid's house was near Ras el-Metn, but few Lebanese had ever set foot in it. His mother, who lived there all year round, led a very secluded existence. The only people ever admitted to the premises, so it was said, were the local Druze peasants and a few sheikhs loyal to the family. Although the young Bey spent nearly every day at Ras el-Metn with Amal and Marwan, he never invited them home.

"It is because we don't wear the veil," Amal said dryly, when Selma expressed surprise at this. "He's afraid we'll shock his orthodox household."

Her tone was jocular, but Selma got the impression that she meant it. In any case, Wahid had never before spent so much time at Ras el-Metn. Did he come for her sake, as Marwan claimed? If he did, he had a strange way of showing it. He seldom addressed a word to her, devoted most of the time to shooting contests or endless political arguments, and seemed greatly to prefer male company. However if a man lingered with Selma for more than a few moments Wahid would appear from nowhere and, ignoring her admirer's furious glances, butt into the conversation.

"Excuse me, my dear fellow," he would say, looking preoccupied. "Selma, I want a word with you." And he would take her firmly by the arm and bear her off.

She bristled the first time he abducted her in this way.

"Really, Wahid, who do you think you are? You are acting as if I were your personal property!"

He looked at her. "Would you dislike it so much if you were?"

When she said nothing, at a loss for words, he gently took her hand and kissed the hollow of her palm. A shiver ran through her – a sensation unlike any she had ever experienced. She closed her eyes and thought: "Yes, I will be yours."

"Selma," he went on in a low voice, "you must know how much you mean to me. Don't flirt with those idiots!"

And then, abruptly turning on his heel, he went off to rejoin his friends.

Amal was concerned to see Selma becoming dreamier every day. "Watch out," she advised her. "Wahid has never known his own mind. I would not want you to be hurt."

But every woman in love believes she is an exception, and Selma, for the first time ever, was in love. The shell she had built up in recent years, looking on with a mixture of pity and contempt at the havoc wrought by love in others, had cracked overnight.

Wahid, for his part, seemed to be mellowing. When he looked at her these days he forgot his sardonic smile and his eyes overflowed with tenderness. Often they went together for long walks, heedless of the inevitable gossip. He told her of his childhood and of the father who continued to cramp his existence from the grave.

"Being the son of a hero is not a fate I would wish on anyone. Hardly a day goes by without some well-meaning person saying, 'Ah, what a man your father was!', implying that I am unworthy of him." He ran his bony fingers through his hair in a characteristic gesture. "It took me years to shake off his ghost. Sometimes I wonder if I have really succeeded."

He seemed so lost in such moments that Selma's heart ached for him. She took his hand and gazed into his eyes.

"Wahid, I *know* you will do great things. Having faith in yourself, that is what matters."

He smiled at her gratefully. "You are so different from the other women I've known. You look so vulnerable, yet you are so strong. . . ." Selma started to protest, but he cut her short. "I know you are strong, which is why I love you."

He wanted his own decisive, dauntless image of her, whereas she would have liked to show herself at last as she really was, divested of her role as a haughty, self-assured princess. But whenever she tried to confide all that was most gentle and genuine in herself, he shied away as if he were afraid – as if he wanted her to be a rock without a flaw because, if such a rock existed, he could dream of becoming one himself some day.

So she listened and said nothing, surprised to find herself capable of such feminine forbearance – was it strength or weakness?

Meantime, Amal kept plying her with annoying questions.

"Has he at least raised the subject of marriage?"

"Not in so many words, if you really want to know, but everything he says and does points in that direction."

"Listen Selma, the Druze hardly ever marry outsiders. Wahid's mother is very conservative – she would never accept a foreign daughter-in-law, especially as she is anxious to consolidate Wahid's position in case her clan gets a chance of regaining power one day."

"Wahid is the most independent-minded man I have ever met, Amal. Do you honestly think he would let his mother dictate to him?"

Amal shook her head despondently. "Either you are blinded by love, or you don't know anything about our men. . . ."

This exchange made an unpleasant impression on Selma. Why should her best friend keep warning her off instead of rejoicing in her happiness? Why should she cast doubt on Wahid's love? Could she be jealous? Amal had known the young Bey since childhood – he was only four years older than her – so naturally she would feel, consciously or unconsciously, possessive toward him.

Selma could not resist mentioning their talk to Wahid. She jokingly reported Amal's words and confided her doubts.

"Jealous?" he exclaimed sarcastically. "Of course she is jealous, but you are wrong about the object of her jealousy. It isn't me she is in love with, my dear, it's you."

Selma could not have been more shocked if he had slapped her in the face.

She stared at him, dumbfounded. The blood rushed into her cheeks. How could he make such an appalling insinuation? She loved Amal and Amal loved her. She was not going to let him defile such a pure and innocent emotion. Filled with resentment she drew away from him.

"It seems you just like spoiling everything!"

"Oh, no!" he protested angrily. "Surely *you* aren't going to reproach me for being frank – not you too! It is what I love best about you, your ability to face facts, your – "

"My strength? Yes, I know. Well I am sick of being strong. I need gentle handling too. I don't like people trampling on everything that is dear to me, even in the name of honesty!"

She turned her back on him. She did not want to spend one more second with the man. She did not want to see Amal – she did not want to see anyone. She wanted to be alone.

Selma left Ras el-Metn the next day without seeing Wahid again. She owed at least that much to Amal, whom she had almost betrayed, if only for a moment. She wanted to forget his disgusting remark, which had been far less of an aspersion on Amal than an insight into his own character. She had always known he was self-centred, but she had not thought him capable of such a vile slander. All night long she cried, angry with him and angry with herself for being taken in by him. Then she decided never to see him again.

And yet, when she kissed Amal goodbye, she felt strangely inhibited. It was intolerable, this feeling that she was hiding something from her friend, and when Amal gazed at her with concern she had to bite her lip to prevent herself from crying out: "Please stop loving me so much!"

Wahid . . . now Amal. . . . Had she lost them both because of a few words that should never have been uttered?

Only three days after she returned to Beirut, the bearded man with the rifle and bandolier turned up with a note. It read: "I cannot endure being apart from you. I spoke without thinking. Can you forgive me? I shall be in the tearoom of the Hotel Saint-Georges at four this afternoon. Please come, I beg you! Yours as ever, Wahid."

What nerve! Did he think he had only to say sorry and she would come running? Well, he could think again! It was all over between them – over and done with. Besides, she felt nothing for him any more. She could not understand why she had ever found him attractive in the first place.

Selma busied herself around the house all day, humming merrily. It was a long time since anyone had seen her so bright and cheerful. With a smile on her lips she pictured Wahid waiting for her in vain. He would be miserable to the point of despair. He would bombard her with letters and flowers, but she would not reply. Now that she knew him for what he was she would not be taken in again!

At five past four, wearing a green silk suit that set off her complexion, she walked into the Hotel Saint-Georges.

No lovers are closer than those that have nearly lost one another. Selma, pretending to her mother that she was with Amal, saw Wahid every day. He no longer rambled on in long monologues of his own; for the first time he really listened to Selma and she for her part was happy to talk. They would walk for hours along the red, sandy shore, then relax in one of the little cafés on piles that served mezzes and grilled green peppers, or drive up to the Grand Saray to admire the view, and from there, abandoning the car, ride the streetcar that rattled and clanked downhill to the Place des Canons. They loved to stroll through the narrow streets of the old city, where they could be sure of meeting no one they knew, exchanging a thousand confidences and forging a thousand plans.

One day, when they were returning by way of the Avenue Weygand, they were forced to the side of the road by a galloping troop of black-cloaked cavalrymen: the spahis that escorted the High Commissioner's car wherever it went. Wahid swore under his breath.

"Poor fools! If they only knew how soon we'll be rid of them!"

He spoke as if it were a certainty. Surprised, Selma looked at him inquiringly. He gave her a long, searching stare.

"If you promise not to talk I will take you to the Aeroclub tomorrow night. Then you will understand."

The Aeroclub was the favourite haunt of Beirut's anti-French conspirators, who had avoided the Hotel Saint-Georges ever since word had got around that Pierre, the capital's finest barman, was in the pay of every secret service in the Near East.

The arrival of Selma and Wahid caused an immediate sensation. For this evening meeting was unusual: the representatives of various groups opposed to the mandate were gathering to discuss joint action. Questioning looks were exchanged as they wondered if it were really prudent to trust a stranger. On the other hand no one wanted to send away such a charming young lady. The Lebanese were gallant to the core: after all, if Wahid Bey had seen fit to bring her, it would be an insult to him to distrust her. So space was made for Selma at the head of the table and the discussion begain in earnest over some old brandy.

In a low voice, Wahid began pointing out the people present to Selma.

"The man with curly hair is a freemason sent by his lodge, which has just come out against the mandate. Next to him is Gebran Tueni, the head of the '*Al Nahar*,' the most important paper to speak out against the mandate. He is just here to observe but he knows the French political scene inside and out, so his opinion could be really valuable to us. Opposite him, the man with the lively facial expressions is the notorious Antoun Saadeh, founder of the Syrian People's Party, which is advocating a Great Syria including Lebanon and Palestine. His theory that this entire region is actually a single nation going back to Canaanite antiquity is based on the work of a Belgian Jesuit, Pére Lammens – sort of ironic, isn't it? To his right are two champions of Pan-Arabism, who see Great Syria as just a stage along the way to the unity of the whole Arab world."

All of this made quite an impression on Selma, as she scrutinized the faces of these heroes who tomorrow would perhaps give their lives "to free their country from the clutches of the enemy." Somehow she had imagined them less urbane. Their shirts, with starched white collars and pastel shirtfronts, must have come straight from Sulka in Paris and she was a little taken aback by the restrained elegance of their three-piece suits. She would have preferred them to look more revolutionary. But that was childish! After all, a conspirator was not supposed to look like one. Still Selma found the club's atmosphere of muted elegance and the men's fat cigars at odds with the radical positions that were being taken. Only one of them had the haunted look of a man ready to sacrifice everything for his ideas: Antoun Saadeh. He inspired confidence. Wahid, too, of course. He had begun to outline the Druze position:

"We are in constant contact with our Syrian brothers. We have arms. But a lot of our people at the grassroots level are hesitant. They are afraid that if Syria becomes a reality, they will be no more than a minority with no voice and no rights, drowning in a sea of Sunni Muslims. They have not forgotten that it was the French mandate that gave the Druze religion official status in the first place. Sit Nazira takes care that they don't forget it, either! Nonetheless, they still want independence. The important thing, then, is to unite all our forces against the French. The people are totally fed up. Now is the time to act."

That spring of 1935 the strikes had been very serious. The depression and inflation which had come from Europe had emptied pockets and given platforms to politicians. At Zahle, the butchers' strike which had started as a protest against the imposition of a new meat tax had ended with rioting. Demonstrators had stormed the government offices, the police had arrived and fired on the crowd, leaving many wounded. In Beirut the taxi strike dragged on for weeks – at the instigation of the communists, rumour had it. Immediately after that strike followed the lawyers' strike, protesting against the opening of the Lebanese bar to French attorneys.

But the real cause of discontent among both the Christian and Muslim middle classes was the business of the Tobacco Board. The concession had been confiscated by France in 1920 but was due to expire this year and the Lebanese business community was demanding its return. A tobacco boycott had even been organized. The High Commissioner had nevertheless coolly gone ahead and granted the concession to a French group – and for twenty-five years at that!

Beneath the bar's dim lights, the conspirators were rubbing their hands. Irritation with the mandate was turning to bitterness. All that was needed now was a little organization. Selma only half-listened to the rest of the discussion, which concerned who could call meetings, where they would be held, and what new action should be launched. She looked admiringly at Wahid, who, together with Antoun Saadeh, had taken charge. She knew now why she loved him.

And when he said to her in a serious voice as they were walking to the car: "It will be a hard struggle. Are you willing to fight with me?" she put her hand in his and squeezed it fervently.

It was nearly midnight when Selma tiptoed into the house, only to find that her mother was waiting up for her in the living room. Coldly, Sultana Hatijé inquired after Amal's health but gave her no time to reply.

"Spare me your lies. This is the second time you have been seen alone with that Druze. What is going on between you? Tell me the truth."

Now that it was out in the open at last, Selma felt relieved. "The truth, Annéjim, is that we love each other."

The Sultana frowned impatiently and tapped the arm of her wheelchair. "That is not the quesion. Does he want to marry you?"

"Of course. . . ." The words were preceded by a momentary hesitation. Wahid had never formally proposed, but his intentions were plain.

"In that case, why hasn't his mother come to talk to me?"

"She lives in a faraway mountain village called Ain Zalta and I think her health makes it hard for her to travel."

"All right, you will bring this young man to see me at teatime tomorrow."

"But Annéjim. . . ."

"No buts. Either you do as I say or you never set foot outside this house unless Zeynel or one of the kalfas goes with you. And think yourself lucky that I am willing to receive this boy at all. It is only because you have already compromised yourself with him. As Allah is my witness, I had visions of a different marriage for my only daughter! When I think of it . . . Druze – not even a Muslim!"

"But Annéjim, the Druze *are* Muslims!"

"That is what they claim, but they do not acknowledge the five pillars of Islam and they believe in reincarnation, like the Hindus. Now leave me alone before I get angry!"

The interview was a disaster. Wahid genuinely meant to marry Selma but he could not bear to be forced into any commitment. When the Sultana questioned him about his life and future plans, his replies were evasive and monosyllabic to the point of rudeness. Selma's name was never mentioned. He mechanically stroked the purring Persian cat that was rubbing itself against his legs.

The Sultana bit her lip, almost unable to contain her irritation. She had summed him up at first glance as an irresponsible young dreamer. As for Wahid, who detested dictatorial women, he wondered if Selma's strength of character, as he now saw it, was really an ominous sign. Besides, he felt ill at ease in this house. He had not expected it to be luxurious – he knew that Selma and her family had lost everything – but it might at least have contained a few precious relics of their former grandeur: some old family portraits or a few pieces of fine silver. Never having pictured his Princess in such mediocre, middle-class surroundings, he felt vaguely cheated. As soon as etiquette permitted, he took his leave.

While Selma was showing him out, he announced that he would be leaving for the Jebel the next day. There were important decisions that needed to be made, and his presence was essential. Surprised, she asked why he had not told her before.

"I didn't know myself. The message only came this morning. Don't be sad – the mountains are not the other end of the world!"

"How long will you be gone?"

"I can't say, exactly. Three or four weeks at most. I will get in touch as soon as I'm back."

She sensed that he was lying.

"Wahid, I beg you, tell me the truth. Don't you love me any more?"

"You have a rich imagination, my dear." He chuckled teasingly, all boyish charm again. "Don't you know how much you mean to me?"

He took her hand in that now familiar way and lightly kissed the hollow of her palm.

"I will see you again very soon, my little princess."

She stood watching in the doorway until he disappeared from view.

He did not look back.

A month went by without news of him. Although Selma knew he hated writing letters, she began to get worried. Was he ill? Had he been wounded? Mountain people were quick on the trigger, and Wahid had many enemies.

Unless . . . unless his mother had taken him in hand again, convinced him that his first duty was to the clan, and found him a Druze fiancée. . . .

One night at a dinner party Selma was delighted to find Marwan and Amal whom she had rather neglected of late. Conversation at table consisted largely of rumours and she was listening with amusement to the latest gossip when the sound of Wahid's name made her start. A blond whom she had never seen before was holding forth in a shrill voice.

"Have you heard the news? He's getting married!"

The speaker paused for a moment, savouring the effect of her revelation. Everyone stopped talking.

"And guess who to? A young American millionairess, the daughter of the president of Am Air, a major airline. For someone who needed money to finance his political career, you have to admit he has done pretty well!"

Wahid engaged to an American? Selma's heart sank. Marwan, who was sitting across the table from her, fixed her with a look that implored, commanded her to stay in control. *Don't worry, Marwan. I know everyone is watching me. I am not going to make a spectacle of myself. Besides, it's impossible. The woman must be mistaken. It's just another of Wahid's little practical jokes. He loves starting false rumours to tease. But . . . she said she saw him. He's in Beirut and he didn't call. . . . Wahid, my Wahid!* Her head was spinning. Suddenly she knew that the woman was telling the truth.

Marwan and Amal took her home in silence. What could they say? There was nothing *to* say.

Selma spent the whole of the next day sitting near the telephone. He would call her – it was impossible that he would not call her, if only to explain. But the only call she got was from Amal, who sadly confirmed the news. "Thank you," she replied, without any real idea of what she was thanking her friend for. She climbed the stairs like a sleepwalker and took refuge in her room.

Stretched out on the bed with her eyes wide open, she had the impression that she was floating. She felt no pain; she just kept wondering why Wahid had behaved this way. She could have understood his marrying a Druze for political reasons. But an American millionairess? Was he just a common fortune-hunter? If so, why had he bothered with her? She recalled all he had said, even more, his silences, in the months they had spent together. Every detail of every day came back to her. He had been sincere at the time, she knew. Was it possible that he had forgotten her almost as soon as they were apart or had he sacrificed their love because he needed money to carry on his struggle?

If he had come to her and told her that, she would have believed him and resigned herself to the inevitable. She could have understood anything except this silence, this cowardly and unexplained betrayal.

A pain began to overcome her, a pain that seemed familiar, like that of an old wound destined to reopen one day. Knowing that sooner or later it would, you waited for the moment with morbid curiosity and calm resignation.

Wahid's face became blurred, and Selma saw Haïri Bey regarding her with dispassionate amusement.

"Why do you always blame others?" her father seemed to say. "If they desert you, it must be your own fault."

Probably. . . . Try as she would, however, she failed to understand what had prompted Wahid to desert her just as, before him, her father had. What had she done? What law had she broken? She struck her head with her clenched fist. There had to be a reason – there always was. If not, it meant that the world was a crazy place devoid of laws and landmarks. She could not face that. She preferred to draw the bewildering but reassuring conclusion: she was the one who was wrong.

From her armchair, the Sultana observed her daughter with mounting anxiety. Selma had not eaten for days. She remained closeted in her room or roamed around the house with blank, staring eyes. Something had to be done soon, or she would make herself genuinely ill.

"Selma," her mother said one morning when the girl seemed a little less withdrawn than usual, "you must not think that the young man lied to you. He was obviously in love with you – that is why I admire him for having been wise enough to give you up."

Selma looked at her reproachfully. "Annéjim, I am not in a joking mood."

"He loved you, believe me, but he was not self-assured enough to take on a woman of your calibre. He needs a docile, complaisant wife – one that will welcome him back and ask no questions if he disappears for a week on some secret mission, or goes hunting with friends, or visits a mistress. You would not have tolerated such a role, even for a month. The women of our family have always been spirited mares."

Selma was studying her fingertips with an expressionless face. Sultana Hatijé had been watching her while she spoke. She had to restore her daughter's self-confidence, even at the expense of a white lie.

"The young man was frightened," she went on. "If he 'deserted' you, as you choose to put it, it was not because he had ceased to love you. On the contrary it is because he loved you too much."

CHAPTER 10

Spring 1936. The Popular Front had just won the elections in France and formed a government under the presidency of Léon Blum. In Beirut these events were followed with interest: people wondered whether this new "socialist" team would at last grant Lebanon independence.

A first step had been made: on 20 January Emile Eddé had become president, the first elected head of the state in ten years. The High Commissioner, Damien de Martel, who in 1934 had re-established the constitution in his own way, himself naming the head of state and reducing Parliament to a rubber-stamp, had been compelled by the mounting dissatisfaction to authorize elections.

But the Lebanese were not inclined to settle for half measures. They felt ready and able to manage their own affairs and chafed under the restrictions of the Mandate. In February 1936, the Maronite patriarch, Monseigneur Arida, decided to convoke a congress of prelates, which drafted a manifesto addressed to the High Commissioner. It demanded real independence for Lebanon and during the transition period, the establishment of a new constitution guaranteeing freedom of the press, freedom of assembly and the right to form political parties.

Even the President, who was a supporter of the Mandate – he judged that the country, divided as it was between Lebanese nationalists, and Arab nationalists calling for unification with Syria, was not sufficiently stable to do without the presence of the French – ran up against Count Martel's authoritarian stance.

"Actually," Amal would scoff, "if they hate each other so, it is all Raiska's fault.

Raiska de Kerchova, the wife of the Belgian consul, was a stunning White Russian with whom the Count had fallen madly in love. The social and political inner circle of Beirut, which had learned of this passionate affair, avidly followed its many and varied gyrations. Raiska was both whimsical and unpredictable, and often slammed her door in the Count's face, to his great despair. The only people who seemed to be totally unaware of the affair were her husband, the good and decent "Robertito," and the most worthy – and extremely ugly – Countess de Martel.

Now Emile Eddé had seriously offended Raiska! It was said that she had put considerable effort into backing his candidacy, especially with the Count de Martel. And, would you believe it! – the ungrateful wretch had not even invited her to the luncheon he had hosted the day after his election for all the important personages of the city. An unpardonable oversight! It was rumoured that the High Commissioner felt as insulted as did his lovely mistress.

Selma knew Raiska well: it was in fact at a dinner Raiska gave recently that she had seen Wahid again for the first time. Not that she had dealt with her disappointment in love by shunning the outside world; on the contrary, she had made it a point of honour to attend every ball. And her women friends, who were preparing to offer their condolences, might just as well have saved themselves the effort: never had Selma looked more radiant.

That evening at Raiska's when Selma made her entrance, late as usual, she saw her hostess in conversation with a tall, familiar figure. Her heart missed a beat.

"I believe you know each other. . . ." said Raiska.

Everyone around them stopped talking. With an immense effort, Selma smiled and held out her hand.

"My hearty congratulations," she said, mastering the tremor in her voice. "You are married, I hear."

Wahid, who had turned pale, stammered his thanks without even meeting her eye. All of a sudden he seemed spineless and lacking in stature. And Selma laughingly rejoined her escort and took his arm on the way to the dining room, with a new-found happiness as light as swansdown. Life, she told herself, was sweet after all.

Amal arrived one afternoon with some momentous news: she was to marry one of her el-Atrash cousins, a member of the most powerful Druze family in Syria. They had met only twice, years before, but she preserved a recollection of a tall, smiling, broad-shouldered young man eighteen years her senior. "Brave as a lion and honest as the day," was the verdict of her aunt, who was anxious to arrange the marriage before she died – not that she was ill, "but at my age one must be prepared," she said firmly. Amal's new home would be in Damascus, jewel of the Middle East, heart of the Arab world, and living testimony to the splendour of the Ummayad caliphs.

"After all," she concluded with a faint smile, "every girl has to get married and settle down sometime." Then, realizing what she had just said, she frowned. "What about you, Selma?"

"Me? The world's my oyster, Amal. Sometimes I think I ought to become a racing driver or go off to Africa and nurse lepers. The only trouble is, fast cars frighten me and sick people give me the shivers. What should I do? Marry a king? I tried that and failed. Become a film star? That did not work out either. Fall in love? Even less of a success. If you can come up with another idea, I am ready to give it a try."

She was saying anything just to disguise her distress. She resented Amal's imminent departure. Her friend's forthcoming marriage had brought her face to face with a reality she had always avoided until now: she was twenty-five years old and the only unmarried member of her set. It was not that she wanted to get married. Having already burned her fingers twice, she had no wish to risk a third rebuff that would hurt her pride or cause her emotional suffering. As for renouncing her freedom just to "settle down," as Amal put it, she was not prepared to do that.

On the other hand, she could not sustain her present way of life indefinitely. Looking back over the past few years, she felt as if she had been going in circles, anaesthetizing herself with an endless, futile round of social functions for want of anything better. She had a growing urge to leave Beirut. Beneath its metropolitan veneer, the city was a village whose possibilities she had exhausted long ago.

If only she had money. . . . She could travel, visit Paris, New York, Hollywood – not alone, of course, Zeynel would accompany her – but their financial position was more than precarious; it was becoming disastrous. The cost of living had risen steadily, and their real income had just as steadily dwindled in spite of Suren Agha's judicious investments.

Selma sometimes caught herself wondering if she could get a job of some kind. A few middle-class women worked, so she had heard, but she dreaded to think of how her mother would react to such a suggestion. Besides, what qualifications did she have?

"Do you think someone would employ me as a lady's maid?" she asked defiantly. "I am good with a needle – I arrange flowers beautifully. . . ."

Amal rose and put her arms around her.

"Don't be bitter, sweetheart. There are a dozen men here who would like nothing better than to marry you. Is there no one that appeals to you?"

"No, not one," Selma said flatly. "The truth is," she added, to mitigate any impression of conceit, "this place is suffocating me. I would like to escape to the other side of the world – America, for instance – since I cannot go back to Istanbul." Her eyes flashed. "I need a change, Amal. Life here is too sweet, too easy. Don't you remember how idealistic and ambitious I used to be? These days I am just a socialite, and I am beginning to hate myself. . . ."

"Forgive me for asking," said Amal, feigning an interest in the hem of her dress, "but, well – do you feel this way because of Wahid?"

Selma burst out laughing. "Of course not – what an idea! Wahid has fallen from me like an old garment, so much so that I wonder if it was he I loved or the thought of fighting at his side. I am no sentimentalist, believe me . . . but I would follow a man anywhere if he offered me a chance to take part in some great crusade. For the sake of the crusade, not the man."

Amal smiled. "That is just what I adore about you – you are such a romantic."

And, without giving Selma time to think up a retort, she kissed her lightly on the cheek and slipped away.

Marwan had come to take Selma shopping in his red convertible. She had lost her regular chauffeur several weeks ago: Orhan had gone off to Albania, of all places! Now that Mustafa Kemal's hostility had burned itself out and relations with Turkey were restored, Prince Abid, the king's brother-in-law, had remembered his nephew and thought that rather than drive a taxi in Beirut, he would make an ideal aide-de-camp to King Zog.

It made Selma nostalgic to see her favourite cousin depart for the country of her former dreams. She dug out all the books and magazines she had studied so earnestly four years ago, and which she had never had the heart to throw away.

"Take them," she told Orhan, trying hard to sound detached, "they have been cluttering up my cupboards long enough." Zeynel, who had never got over the thwarting of her projected marriage, was less philosophical. With renewed venom, he secretly called down the wrath of Allah on the Turkish tyrant who had prevented his little girl from fulfilling her royal destiny.

But Albania seemed very far away this lovely autumn afternoon. As soon as they turned the corner, Selma removed her hat and rested her head on the back of the seat. How she loved to feel the wind ruffling her curls, and how much at ease she felt in Marwan's company. He, at least, was no stickler for social convention. If ever Haïri caught her going out hatless he made a scene and promptly reported her to their mother.

"I always dreamed of having a brother like you," she sighed. "Haïri is always so unsympathetic."

"You are being unfair," Marwan protested. "I don't think you realize how much you bully him."

"Me, bully him?" Selma said indignantly. "Is it my fault he is slower than a snail?"

Marwan, who recognized the impossibility of convincing the hare that the tortoise possessed a few good qualities, smiled and said no more. He was not overly fond of Selma's brother himself, but the other night, when he had seen Haïri greet the news of Amal's betrothal with a dignity that failed to conceal his hurt and disappointment, he could not help feeling sorry for him.

They did their shopping at Bab-e-Driss in the centre of town and afterwards Marwan suggested going to Ajami, which had the best sherberts in Beirut. As they passed Cannon Square they were stopped by a demonstration: fifty or so young men in shorts and dark blue shirts were marching around the square like a detachment of soldiers.

"Let's watch!" said Selma.

They got out of the car and joined the crowd of curious onlookers, where sarcastic commentary was flowing freely.

"More of Gemayel's militia. He's really become unbearable since he went off to Berlin for the Olympics."

"You know what he calls them? The Phalange! His hero is Mussolini. He claims this is just a sports and social association, but what he really wants is a Lebanese organization along the lines of the fascist youth – hard, pure, ultranationalist."

"What's that supposed to mean? We're all nationalists!"

"That's what you think! According to these kids, anyone who wants union with Syria – which is half the population – isn't a loyal Lebanese. That's why they recruit almost exclusively from among Maronites, though they've attracted a few Muslims here and there."

"This is ridiculous. He'd be better off helping his father at the drugstore."

"The drugstore?"

"The one across the street, at the entrance to the red-light district. It's because of his . . . advantageous location that they call him the Condom King." This was greeted with howls of laughter.

"What are they talking about?" Selma asked Marwan.

"Never mind. Come on, let's go." And he hustled her away, frowning.

The Sultana was eagerly awaiting them on their return to Rustem Pasha Street. Selma, who sometimes felt that her mother's devotion to the rites of hospitality verged on mania, was surprised when she did not invite Marwan to stay for tea. After a few minutes' polite conversation, he took his leave.

The door had only just closed behind him when Sultana Hatijé happily announced that she had an important matter to discuss. This type of preamble usually put Selma on her guard, but today her mother seemed to be in excellent spirits.

"You must be thinking me a very neglectful mother not to have secured your future before now, Selma. No, do not interrupt! Nearly all your friends are married, and Amal herself is on the point of leaving you. I have, in fact, received a number of requests for your hand in recent years, but I did not even trouble to inform you as I refused to throw you away on some nonentity of a minor aristrocrat. I wanted you to have a husband worthy of your blood and your beauty. I have spent a long time looking for such a man, and now, perhaps. . . ."

She left the sentence suspended in mid-air like an actor with a keen sense of timing. Then, as Selma remained silent, she went on.

"Now, perhaps," she repeated with a touch of dramatic emphasis, "I may have found him!"

She was expecting a question, or at least some sign of curiosity, but Selma still said nothing. Her daughter never ceased to surprise her: fire one day, ice the next – totally unpredictable. She felt a trifle disappointed.

"Well what do you say?"

Selma sighed. "Do I really have to get married, Annéjim?"

"What a question! Of course you must, unless you want to die an old maid! And don't pretend you're still pining for that young Druze. Come, Selma, be serious for once. You're not an impressionable young girl anymore. It's time you built yourself a life of your own, and to do that, as you're well aware, a woman must marry."

Hatijé produced a long blue envelope from her reticule.

"Here is a letter that will interest you, I think. It's from His Excellency the Maulana Shaukat Ali, founder of the Indian movement in favour of the caliphate. It was he, you will recall, who helped to negotiate the marriages of your cousins Nilufer and Durushevar to the sons of the Nizam of Hyderabad, the greatest princely state in India. The Maulana is not only discreet but deeply devoted to our family, so I got in touch with him a year ago – I even sent him a photograph of you. Having heard nothing in the interim, I'd almost forgotten the matter until this morning, when I received his reply. Would you like to hear the gist of it?"

"Of course, Annéjim." Selma sounded thoroughly unenthusiastic.

The Sultana glanced at her indignantly but refrained from saying anything that might antagonize her. What mattered was that the girl should listen. After that she would have to be persuaded to meet the young man – no easy task in her present state of mind. . . .

"His Excellency writes of a rajah, age thirty, handsome and wealthy – that goes without saying – but also cultured and modern in outlook. Half his life has been spent in England, first at Eton, then at Cambridge University. His name is Amir. He rules the state of Badalpur, not far from the Nepalese frontier, but spends most of the year at his palace in Lucknow, one of the largest cities in India. His Excellency states that he comes of an illustrious family directly descended from Hazrat Hussein, the Prophet's grandson. His ancestors were among the first Arab conquerors to reach India in the eleventh century.

"What more can I tell you, except that he saw your photograph and fell in love with it? Accompanying this letter is a formal request for your hand in marriage. Naturally, I shall reply that he must make your acquaintance first. He is engaged in an election campaign at present – the British have authorized elections in India for the first time, which are due to be held at the end of this year. He will come to Beirut as soon as possible thereafter."

"There is no point," Selma said firmly.

"Be reasonable, I beg of you! At least consent to see the man. We will not tell anyone so that you can feel free to decline his offer if you do not like him. But who knows, perhaps you will. It is not often one comes across a man with so many points in his favour. Most of the Indian princes are extremely old-fashioned and unsophisticated, whereas this one, with his European education –"

"You misunderstand me, Annéjim. I mean it is pointless for him to come here. I will marry him."

Nothing would induce Selma to reconsider, neither the remonstrances of the Sultana, who was worried by her lightning decision, nor Zeynel's prayers, nor the kalfas' tears. She remained adamant, all the more surprised by their anxiety: the women of the family had nearly always made arranged marriages, she told her mother pointedly, and the rare exceptions had not proved an unqualified success, had they?

Sultana Hatijé ignored this gibe because she sensed that Selma was on the verge of breaking down: provoking her would be the last way of getting her to change her mind. She, who had never in her life had to ask for anything more than once, displayed boundless patience.

"Think carefully, Selma. I mentioned the Rajah only to cheer you up – to prove that men worthy of interest do exist. I would not want you to plunge blindly into marriage on the other side of the world, in a country of which you know nothing."

"I have thought carefully, Annéjim. I will go mad if I stay in Beirut. I need a complete change. 'Don't confuse marriage with love,' that is what you said when I became involved with Wahid. Well, what you tell me of this Rajah sounds convincing enough. Why hesitate?"

The Sultana was dismayed. Knowing her daughter's passionate, sensitive nature and her regrettable tendency to hurl herself from one extreme to the other, regardless of the consequences, she was afraid that Selma would ruin her life for the sake of a whim. On the other hand, how could she rebut a chain of reasoning that coldly and logically cited arguments she herself had used in the past?

"Very well," she said at last, "so be it. The choice is yours. At twenty-five you ought to know what you are doing, but at least exchange letters and get to know each other a little during the next few months. We will not tell anyone of your plans, Selma, but remember this: once you are married, there will be no turning back. You will have given your word freely and you will have to keep it, even if you discover you have made a mistake."

The Rajah wrote every two weeks without fail. Selma found this clockwork regularity unnatural, but the Sultana pronounced it a good omen. His letters took the form of a journal dominated by references to the political convulsions of his country thirsting for independence. He seemed mainly concerned to convey the immensity of the problem confronting India, the joys and cares of a head of state, and, last but not least, the hope he and a few of his friends cherished: that it would be possible to defeat the forces of prejudice and obscurantism and gradually build a modern Indian nation.

He seldom wrote of his personal tastes or habits, as though these were secondary to the struggle in which his country was engaged. Selma, whose initial reaction to his letters had been a mixture of curiosity and scepticism, began to develop an interest in the strange world he described with such fervour and caught herself dreaming of the part she might play at his side.

She was grateful to him for eschewing sentimentality, which would have been out of place in a marriage of convenience. She had no illusions about the "love at first sight" that was said to have smitten him on seeing her picture. What had most attracted him, no doubt, was the prospect of marrying an Ottoman princess. Even in exile, the imperial family was still regarded by the Muslims of India as the family of the caliph, Allah's earthly representative, and an alliance with that family was no mean asset to someone with political ambitions. As far as Selma was concerned, it must have been obvious to the Rajah that his wealth and status had predisposed him in her favour.

With a touch of cynicism, Selma recalled the principle dinned into her at home and in school alike: "Losing your wealth and social standing are nothing so long as you hold on to your integrity." Until the last few months she had wanted to believe that. She owed this much to Wahid: he had brought her face to face with reality.

The winter passed quietly. In spite of her mother's advice, Selma had let it be known that she was betrothed to a rajah. The few friends she told were quick to spread the word, enthralled by romantic visions of the life that awaited her amid the fabled treasures of India. Once an object of pity, she was now envied. She even received a congratulatory letter from Wahid. "I hope you have forgiven me," he concluded. "My decision was dictated by necessity – you cannot imagine how hard I found it. You are the only woman I have ever loved. I shall never get over the pain of having lost you."

He had not changed: as usual, he talked only of himself. . . . Selma deliberately burned his letter with a touch of regret and a great deal of contempt.

The Rajah's public position required that the wedding should take place in India. The Sultana had expected him at least to come to Beirut to fetch his bride, but he explained in a series of long and apologetic letters that the political situation was too delicate to permit him to leave the country for several more months. The wedding had been fixed for April. Should he postpone it?

Sultana Hatijé was apprehensive about letting her daughter embark on such a venture without even having seen the man whose life she was to share, but Selma, determined to give herself no opportunity to reconsider, stubbornly insisted. If the Rajah could not come to her she would go to him, accompanied by Zeynel and Madame Ghazavi, who had volunteered to act as her lady-in-waiting. The Sultana sensed that her little girl shared her fears about the far-off world in which she had chosen to live, but she knew that nothing and no one would now make her change her mind.

The few remaining days were taken up with feverish last-minute preparations that left no time for emotions. When the moment of departure came, however, and Selma went to the drawing-room to kiss her mother for the last time, the Sultana could restrain her tears no longer. She was old and ill. Would she ever see her daughter again?

"Dearest child," she said, holding Selma very tight, "are you absolutely sure?"

"Oh, Annéjim!" Selma buried her face in her mother's shoulder, inhaling the faint scent of tuberoses that had been so familiar to her since childhood. "Annéjim, you know I must go – you know I have no choice."

She raised her head. They gazed at each other for one long moment, so intently that the years seemed to melt away and mother and daughter became one flesh once again.

"My little girl. . . ."

Selma shut her eyes. She must not weaken now, of all times. Gently she released herself; tenderly she kissed her mother's beautiful hands.

"I will come back, Annéjim, never fear. Wait for me!"

And she left swiftly, as though she were running away.

PART THREE

INDIA

CHAPTER 1

"But where is the Rajah's train?"

Selma felt she had been walking for hours through this sun-drenched miasma, this medley of cries and colours, this seething throng that might well have swept her away but for the tall, mustachioed bodyguards who formed a rampart around her and forged a path through the crowd with liberal applications of their whips and lathis. It was a sweltering day in March, and Bombay station resembled a merry-go-round gone mad rather than British India's most important railroad terminus. A clamorous tide of humanity flowed beneath the lofty neo-Gothic arches and between the sandstone columns whose capitals were adorned with carved flowers, deaf to the strident solicitations of youthful chickpea vendors, indifferent to the sickly scent of jasmine garlands mingled with whiffs of stale sweat and urine.

Selma felt stifled, but she would not have wished herself elsewhere for anything in the world: so this was her new homeland! Only now, far from the white marble halls and fountains of the Taj Mahal Hotel, where she had been taken for a night's rest after coming ashore, was she really setting foot on Indian soil. Wide-eyed, she tried to take in the stream of jostling images that created such a violent cacophony of colours: the big scarlet turbans of porters wheeling precarious pyramids of luggage, the rich saffron robes of Buddhist monks, the red and gold saris of young married women, the drab grey rags of beggars clustering like flies around the splashes of white provided by first-class passengers in immaculate kurtahs[1].

Her head throbbed, bursting with this superabundance of beauty and ugliness. She was bewildered by the sight of so much poverty borne with haughtiness, by this multitude that seemed at once cruel and good-natured. Had she not just seen an old man fall, unheeded and unaided, as the crowd pressed on, indifferent? What lay behind those swarthy faces, those dark, intense eyes? Troubled, she turned to Rashid Ḳhan, the Rajah's private secretary, who had met her at the ship. His response to her unspoken query – she did not have words enough to formulate such a vast question – was a reassuring smile.

1 Kurtah: long muslin shirt.

"Do not worry, Highness. India comes as a shock to every new arrival. You will get used to it." He paused, then added as though to himself, "Insofar as one *can* get used to the inexplicable. . . ."

Awaiting them at the very end of the platform, guarded by armed men wearing dark blue uniforms emblazoned with the Badalpur cypher and vainly besieged by hordes of less privileged travellers, was a private railroad car.

Selma suppressed a start of surprise: she had been expecting an entire private train like that of her cousins Nilufer and Durushevar, the wives of the princes of Hyderabad. She now knew why Rashid Khan had told her that it would take them three days and two nights to cover the eighteen hundred miles from Bombay to Lucknow. This self-styled express must stop at every last little village en route!

She felt vaguely offended, as she had the day before, on finding that the Rajah had not come to meet her in person. Her escort, far from suspecting that a storm was brewing, smiled at her blandly. His placid attitude worried her even more: from the look on his face, the Rajah's secretary found the situation perfectly normal.

Had she been mistaken? She had expected to be greeted like a queen – after all, wasn't her fiancé the ruler of a state almost as big as Lebanon? The Maulana Shaukat Ali's representative at Beirut had discoursed at length on the fabulous wealth of the Indian princes, their numerous palaces, their coffers overflowing with precious stones. These descriptions, which recalled the splendours of her own childhood, had kindled her imagination and reinforced her decision to marry. And now all her dreams had been dispelled by the sight of this dusty station, this rattletrap of a railroad car, this ridiculous carriage that was supposed to whisk her away to glory.

Inside, there was movement. Turbanned servants craned their necks, eager to catch a glimpse of the new Rani. From within, muffled by the thick black veils covering their faces, came the sound of women's shrill voices.

"Your attendants, Highness," Rashid Khan explained. "The Rajah insisted on their coming to keep you company, but they do not have the right to leave the train. Shall we get in? It is almost time."

Selma breathed a sigh of relief as the train pulled out. The interior of the car was gloomy but comfortable, all brass, mahogany, and lamps with cut glass shades. The plush seats and heavy curtains seemed more appropriate to foggy England than to this torrid climate, which was hardly surprising: all the rolling stock came from the mother country, whose colonies and dominions were generously presented with anything it considered obsolete.

Half a dozen women were seated cross-legged on the floor, staring at Selma and commenting on her appearance in a rather guttural tongue. They were a colourful sight now that they had removed their burkahs, the black, tentlike garments that made them look like crows, and their throats, ears, and arms were laden with gold. They pointed with surprise and disapproval at their mistress's unadorned hands and the single strand of pearls around her neck. Selma smiled to disguise her faint irritation, wondering how to convey to these tactless creatures that, by her standards, their mass of jewellery was the height of bad taste. They gave her no time to do so. Before she knew what was happening, they divested themselves of their bracelets and rings and decked her out like a heathen idol. Then they delightedly clapped their hands.

"Khubsurat, bahut Khubsurat!"

Khubsurat, "beautiful," was the only word of Urdu Selma knew, having heard it repeated a hundred times since her arrival. This compliment failed to mitigate her annoyance at being played with like a doll, but the women's pleasure was so naively wholehearted that she ended by joining in their laughter.

If the Sultana and her kalfas could see her now! How different her new companions were from the dignified ladies-in-waiting of the Ottoman court, who would never have dared to take such liberties, even with a princess whom they had known since childhood. But the women were still dissatisfied: Selma's white silk suit, a Paris model in the height of fashion, struck them as inauspicious: white was the colour worn by widows. The youngest attendant, a girl with plump cheeks, went over to a trunk and took out a long fuchsia gown embroidered with silver. Her initiative was greeted with a murmur of approval: *there* was a garment worthy of a bride-to-be! They were preparing to undress Selma despite her protests, which they put down to modesty, when someone knocked at the door. Instantly, the gaily coloured buterflies fled for their burkahs and turned back into crows.

Rashid Khan paused on the threshold, swiftly suppressing the glint of admiration in his eyes. "Is there anything you need, Highness?" he asked respectfully. "Zeynel Agha and your companion, Madame Ghazavi, are in the adjoining compartment. They wish to know if you require them."

"Thank you, Khan Sahib." The secretary's manner bespoke his aristocratic origins, and Selma, reared in court etiquette from birth, was careful not to treat him like a servant. "What I should like, if possible, is a little peace and quiet."

Her female attendants' whims had tired her out. She wanted to be alone, but how could she convey as much without offending them?

Rashid Khan smiled. "I will tell them you wish to sleep." The women were indignant – it was unthinkable that their future Rani should be left to her own devices like any ordinary mortal; even if she slept, they should be there to watch over her slumbers – but he politely ushered them out.

Selma stretched out at full length. Having removed the heavy earrings and the necklace that was weighing her down like a yoke, she shook out her hair and let the draught from the decrepit old ceiling fan play over her perspiring forehead.

Gliding past the window were sun-scorched fields in which half-naked peasants trudged along behind emaciated oxen hauling ploughs of prehistoric design. Lean, dark-skinned women squatted outside thatched huts, busily moulding some glutinous substance into flat cakes which they stuck on walls to dry and then transported in baskets balanced on their heads. Swathed in brilliant saris, the women walked with such an erect and stately tread that Selma, watching them, wondered how many queens would have envied their deportment. Farther on, huge black water buffaloes were wading in a pool alongside white cows with rouged horns – almost, thought Selma, like the black-clad eunuchs at Dolmabahçé Palace mounting guard over the lily-blossoms of the Sultan's harem.

Ah, Istanbul . . . will I ever see you again? In Beirut I was near you, and at night I dreamt of returning to you. Now I have gone to a strange world, far away, as if I had lost all hope of ever coming back to you.

The fields and rice paddies outside the window faded, to be replaced by that other landscape at which an auburn-haired girl had gazed from her window seat in another train, the one that thirteen years ago had carried her across Turkey and into exile. . . .

Selma sat up abruptly. She refused to mourn and moan forever like her old aunts. She was young, seductive and stronger-willed than any of her cousins, who devoted their time to drinking and daydreaming about an unlikely revolution. She would win out. Win out to what, she did not exactly know. Her one certainty was that she must regain her proper place in the world. No one had compelled her to leave the sweet, soft atmosphere of Lebanon. It was she who had resolved to put down new roots and create a new country for herself, a kingdom where she would be queen – where she would be loved.

Having ceased to believe in the love of men – she had never forgotten her father's betrayal, and Wahid's desertion had only reopened the wound – she wanted to be loved by an entire people. That was what being a queen meant: being surrounded, not by pomp and riches, as some naively imagined, but by love.

"Pomp and display," the Sultana used to say, "serve no other purpose than to bring beauty into the lives of the poor, as if their wretchedness was being contemplated by a good fairy, not some dour civil servant or some lady bountiful with a face so long that those she is supposed to be helping feel the urge to comfort her. The poor do not realize the inestimable value of what they give their rulers: they *need* us! They make us feel necessary!"

Selma shivered despite the heat, wondering how the people of Badalpur would receive her.

The train had reached the Ghats, the range of hills that traverses India from west to east. The grass was becoming greener. Flocks of sheep and goats were grazing under the eye of a shepherd in a purple turban. Floating mirage-like in the distance was a little white stone temple surrounded by prayer flags fluttering at the whim of the wind.

It was the hour before dusk, a time for relaxation and meditation. Selma put her face close to the iron grille over the window and avidly inhaled her first few breaths of cool evening air. She savoured every moment, every new impression, forbidding herself to think of the face that awaited her at the end of her journey.

The disappointment she had felt on arrival, when she found that Amir had failed to turn up, still rankled. Wasn't he as eager to meet her as she to meet him – was it enough for him that she was a Sultana? Was their marriage merely a bargain?

Then again, what am I complaining about, when I myself am marrying him for his money? Close to tears, she nervously chewed a strand of hair. *I am being absurd: we have never even met, why should we pretend to be in love?* But it was no use reasoning with herself – she could not contain her sobs any longer. She felt so alone. What was the point of lying to herself and putting on a show of cynicism? She was an incorrigible romantic at heart. . . .

She had dreamed of this dashing, dazzling Rajah. It had inspired her to read of his plans for reform and the ambitions he cherished for his country. But over and above all that – why not admit it? – she had been entranced by his beautiful face.

She removed the locket from its velvet case and studied it intently: the dark eyes were almond-shaped, the thin nose was slightly hooked, the full lips above that funny little dimple looked soft and gentle. Two months ago, when a messenger from Badalpur had brought her the Rajah's portrait, she had felt an involuntary thrill of anticipation. Cold and calculating as she strove to be, she knew that her misgivings had actually been dispelled by the charm of that handsome face, so like the face of an Oriental god.

But why had he only sent his secretary?

Poor Rashid Khan! He was so well-meaning. Weighed down by an enormous bunch of flowers, he had reeled off a speech of welcome in Turkish, which he had obviously memorized, because instead of presenting "his humble respects" he had laid "his burning heart" at Selma's feet. Seeing her stupefied expression, he had immediately realized that some Turkish friend had played a trick on him, and had blushed so that she had burst out laughing. That had broken the ice: from then on they had become friends.

Selma's spirits revived at this recollection. The marriage was bound to be a success: all the makings of happiness were there in abundance.

Sixty long hours . . . sweltering days and chilly nights, dozens of stations identical in their motley crowds, their vendors of tea and sweetmeats, and, above all, the beggars who thrust their hands through the grille and caught Selma by the sleeve, gazing at her earnestly. Her throat tightened as she looked into those burning, delirious eyes from a world of which she knew nothing. Were these the eyes of madmen or of sages, who could say? To shake off the spell they cast, she slipped a few coins into their owners' outstretched hands. But they went on staring at this gilded white goddess sprung from some exalted nirvana and continued to stand there, motionless, until long after she had disappeared over the horizon. . . .

"We'll reach Lucknow in two hours' time."

Rashid Khan's tall figure stood framed in the doorway. Selma gave a start. Her sense of time had deserted her after so long a journey. Lucknow already? Her heart began to pound. The Rajah's secretary, moved by the sudden look of apprehension on her face, did his best to reassure her.

"Believe me, Highness, all will be well."

How kind he was! She rewarded him with one of her most seductive smiles, not only in gratitude but to kindle the little flame in his eyes that told her she was beautiful and capable of charming anyone.

"Would you be kind enough to send Madame Ghazavi to me?"

Outside, fields of grain were trembling in the sun's first rays. There was no time to daydream – she had only two hours in which to get ready. Selma was determined to dazzle her Prince Charming. Seldom had she spent so long arranging her hair and making up her face, and yet, for all Madame Ghazavi's efforts, she found the result dissatisfying in the extreme. Seldom, too, had she hesitated for so long over her array of dresses.

"But what am I thinking of!" she exclaimed at length. "I must wear a sari."

A sari, of course: the national costume of her adoptive country, worn in honour of the fiancé who would be waiting at the station with his retinue. It would show the journalists and crowds of curious onlookers that, from now on, she was an Indian. . . .

The train pulled into the station. The usual hubbub could be heard outside. Selma strained her ears impatiently. It was all she could do to remain seated in her compartment, which was in semi-darkness as Rashid Khan had inexplicably lowered all the blinds. A sudden commotion. Amir? Her heart missed a beat: it was only Rashid.

"Not long now, Highness. They are getting the purdah[2] ready."

"The what?"

He looked embarrassed and said nothing. Beside her, Madame Ghazavi muttered that something was wrong. Selma irritably told her to be quiet. The Lebanese lady had never stopped complaining since their arrival in India, probably offended that so little notice was being taken of her.

Selma's Indian attendants reappeared, eager to reclaim the rights of which they had been so shamefully deprived during the journey. With the formidable benevolence of nuns welcoming a novice to their fold, they held out a long black cloak like the ones that enshrouded them from head to foot. In response to their mistress's look of astonished inquiry, they resolutely surrounded her.

"No!" Her reaction was shrill and loud.

Hearing it, Rashid Khan came dashing along the corridor. Selma was standing in a corner, trembling with anger and trying to tear the burkah to shreds while the flabbergasted women conferred together, uncertain what to do. The Rajah's secretary struggled to retain his composure. The journey had gone off well, and now these idiotic women were spoiling everything. What would they think at the palace if the bride-to-be arrived in tears!

He abandoned his usual courteous tone and brusquely ordered them out of the compartment. After a show of resistance, they obeyed, but not without loudly complaining that they had once more been prevented from doing their duty.

"It is nothing, Highness," Rashid said consolingly once they were alone. "Do not be upset, I beg you. There is no need to wear that burkah. Do you feel sufficiently recovered to get out? Everything is

2 Drapery that separates women from men.

ready for you."

Two long screens of coloured cloth had been erected outside the door of the railroad car, forming a corridor that would enable her to leave the station unobserved. A car stood waiting at the far end.

Rashid Khan bowed, but Selma was too dumbfounded to notice.

"Farewell, Highness, and may Allah preserve you."

By the time she turned around he had gone. In his place was a stout little woman who introduced herself as Begum Nusrat and covered Selma's hands with kisses.

"Welcome, Huzoor, Your Excellency," she gushed, "this is the happiest day of my life." From what she could understand of her fluent but quaintly-accented English, Selma gathered that this corpulent personage was the wife of the diwan or prime minister of Badalpur State. She knew she should not ask the question on the tip of her tongue, but she could not stop herself.

"Where is the Rajah?"

"But, Huzoor!" The little woman looked thoroughly shocked. "You cannot see His Highness before the wedding. Do not worry," she added quickly, seeing the look on Selma's face, "the ceremony will take place very soon – a week from now, to be precise. Meanwhile you will live at the palace with His Highness's elder sister, Rani Aziza."

Ensconced in the back of the huge Isotta Fraschini, Selma could no longer control her dismay and disappointment. What she mainly noticed about the luxurious white limousine, with its gold-plated bumpers and headlights, were the blinds over the windows. They reminded her of the carriages of her Istanbul childhood. Anger welled up inside her: must she now, after all these years of freedom, accept what she had rebelled against at the age of twelve? Never! But this was surely a false alarm! She had seen press photographs of her cousins Nilufer and Durushevar opening exhibitions and presiding over banquets. She had not dreamt all that! She tried to reassure herself and stem the rising tide of panic that threatened to overcome her, but she felt stifled. She recalled Rashid Khan's pitying glances and the embarrassed silence with which he had greeted some of her questions. For the first time since her arrival in India, she genuinely suspected that a terrible misunderstanding had occurred. . . .

The car slowed. Through the curtains, which she drew aside despite her companion's protests, Selma caught sight of Kaisarbagh, "the King's Garden," an immense rectangle of lawns and flower beds. Bigger, so it was said, than the Louvre and the Tuileries combined, it formed the centrepiece around which the princes' palaces were grouped.

Kaisarbagh was the brainchild of Wajid Ali Shah, the last king of Oudh, a royal musician and poet whom the British had deposed in 1856 without explanation. Far more interested in arts than in politics, he had wanted to make his capital the eighth wonder of the world. Kaisarbagh was to be his Versailles, and it was for himself and his four hundred wives that he constructed this series of big, ochre stone palaces punctuated by balconies and festooned arches whose profusion of decorative motifs in white, straw-coloured, or sienna stucco-work were of the purest rococo.

It should have been the height of bad taste, thought Selma, but it was not. It was quite delightful: as dainty and refined as the society which, instead of resisting, had allowed itself to be dominated by the men in red coats, the barbarians from the West.

Selma's destination, the palace of Badalpur, was one of these baroque mansions.

"It is the Rajah's town house," Begum Nusrat explained, "his pied-à-terre in Lucknow, which is now the British administrative centre for some fifty princely states. The Nawab of Dalior, who owns the finest stable in the city, resides next door; farther on is the house of the Rajah of Dilwani, a celebrated organizer of quail fights; opposite, the Maharajah of Mahdabad, a great connoisseur of classical poetry. . . ."

Begum Nusrat recited the names of these exalted persons with undisguised relish, as if breathing the same air and knowing their habits made her a member of the family.

To Selma's relief, the car pulled up at last. She could not have stood much more of the Begum's incessant chatter and, on the threshold of her new life, yearned to collect her thoughts. The cloth screens had been re-erected, and right at the end, in front of a massive door, two black eunuchs were bowing so low that their turbans brushed the ground.

The eunuchs of her childhood! The sight took her back fifteen years. Were it not for the fact that these eunuchs wore baggy shalvars[3] and dark blue kurtahs instead of austere black stanbulins, she could have imagined herself at Dolmabahçé. As soon as she climbed the imposing stone steps, however, the sense of familiarity faded. India reasserted itself in its lacework balconies, verandas opening on to interior courtyards where fountains played, bevies of women who clustered around and kissed her hand or humbly touched the hem of her

3 Loose trousers caught in at the ankles, worn by women and men.

sari while their half-naked children gazed at her with huge, dark, kohl-rimmed eyes. Begum Nusrat impatiently brushed them aside. They must hurry, she said: Rani Aziza was expecting them.

Rani Aziza . . . Selma was curious about her future sister-in-law, and Begum Nusrat was only too happy to enlighten her.

"The Rani[4] is the Rajah's half-sister by a different mother," she explained. "He was only a boy when he lost his parents in a mysterious accident, and so, being fifteen years older, she took his mother's place. She is a very great lady, and quite as intelligent as a man. When our Prince nearly died at the age of fourteen, probably poisoned by his uncle the regent, Rani Aziza decided to send him to school in England and took over the running of the palace. The stewards fear her far more than they ever feared the old Rajah, who never asked to see their accounts because he considered it beneath his dignity."

The Begum lowered her voice.

"They are hoping that the young Rajah will be less strict than the daughter. The unfortunate young man has only just returned from his twelve years abroad, and already the rogues are planning to swindle him. Luckily the Rani is there!"

Selma frowned. *She* did not count, of course! Even before meeting Rani Aziza, she instinctively felt that she was not going to like her.

At last, after several minutes' walk, they entered a lofty chamber. A dozen women, seated on the ground, were chattering as they cut up betel nuts with little silver shears. Selma's arrival unleashed a torrent of delighted exclamations; the women surrounded her, clasped her in their arms, rhapsodized about her beauty. Half dazed, half reassured by the warmth of their welcome, she allowed herself to be led off by the laughing band. They drew aside a last silk curtain and propelled her into a huge room lined with mother-of-pearl mosaics and mirrors shaped like birds or flowers. More women seated on charpoys[5] with silver legs were talking and chewing pan[6] or dreamily inhaling perfumed tobacco smoke through the long tubes of crystal hookahs. At the back of the room on a raised bed whose gold legs gleamed in the subdued light, a woman was reclining against cushions while attendants, stationed behind her, wielded broad fans made of peacock feathers.

4 A Rani is either the wife of a Rajah or a woman who is a ruler in her own right. Aziza was actually a Rajkumari, the daughter of a Rajah. She was called 'Rani' by the family and servants to accord her extra respect.

5 Charpoy: bed made of rope.

6 The national habit: a preparation of betel nut rolled in betel leaf.

One look at her imperious expression told Selma that this was the Rani: a middle-aged but still beautiful woman with sharp features, deep-set eyes, and a mouth whose arrogance no smile could disguise.

"Come and sit beside me, my child."

The voice was melodious but the welcoming embrace as cold as ice. In singsong English the Rani questioned Selma about her journey, all the while inspecting her from head to toe.

"You are very pretty," she said at length, "but" – she raised her voice so as to be heard by all present – "you must learn to wear the gharara[7]. The sari is a Hindu garment. This is a Muslim household."

Selma turned scarlet. That the woman should have reminded her, the granddaughter of a caliph, that she was a Muslim! A slap in the face would have been less humiliating. Their eyes met. From now on, they knew they were enemies.

Almond and honey cakes were brought, together with some syrupy tea – "to sweeten the sour reception, no doubt," thought Selma, moistening her lips with it. She absently answered a few polite inquiries about her mother's state of health and her life in Beirut.

"Excuse me," she said at length, when the conversation had limped along for a while, "but I am very tired after my journey. May I retire to my room?"

Her request was greeted with raised eyebrows.

"But this *is* your room, my child. You will be living here with me for the next few days. Is there a problem? Is the room too small?"

Selma was spared the need to reply by the arrival of a maidservant carrying a green gharara.

"There, change into that. The colour will suit you admirably. What is more, it is the colour of Islam."

"I am quite aware of that," Selma said sharply.

"Then you will also be aware, no doubt, that our family is directly descended from the Prophet through his grandson Hussein. We are Shiites. You, of course, are a Sunni." Rani Aziza emitted a sigh of studied regret. "Never mind. After all, we are all Muslims. . . ."

The viper! What is she trying to prove? That I am a mere outsider and she is still the mistress here?

But Selma's ill temper was soon dispelled by the pleasure she derived from her bath: silver ewers of hot, perfumed water, pastel-coloured lather, crystal flasks of oil scented with ambergris – all the luxury and ceremony of her childhood. What a delight it was after the

7 Long, voluminous skirt worn by the Muslims of India.

functional bathroom in the house at Beirut! Shutting her eyes and almost forgetting where she was, she surrendered herself to the maid-servants' expert hands. Depilated, massaged, and made up, she surveyed her reflection in the mirror with some satisfaction. The only problem was those curls! She wondered where Madame Ghazavi was.

"Do not worry," the Rani said reassuringly, when Selma inquired after her companion. "I sent her off to rest. Her quarters are on the other side of the hall, beyond the second women's courtyard."

"But she is my lady-in-waiting! She should be here with me!"

"Don't you have enough maidservants? You may have ten, twenty – as many as you wish. If they fail to meet your requirements we will dismiss them and engage others."

Selma was on the verge of tears. Madame Ghazavi and Zeynel were her only links with the past – she felt lost without them, but she would have died rather than admit it. The Rani gave a thin smile.

"Do you not feel at home with us? We are your family now. You must forget the past."

Selma said no more. Her enemy had scored a point. Would she be able to endure a whole week at close quarters with this woman, under her malignly observant eye? Well, only another week, and Amir would be there. She would explain the situation and he would help her. Meantime, perhaps Rashid Khan. . . . Of course, that was the answer! Why hadn't she thought of it before? She injected as much self-assurance into her voice as she could.

"Would someone kindly tell Rashid Khan that I would like a word with him?"

"Rashid Khan?" Rani Aziza raised her eyebrows. "There is something you should know, Princess. My brother's secretary went to fetch you from Bombay because you needed a man to escort you here, but from now on there is no question of your seeing him again. Men never enter the zenana[8], just as women never leave it."

Pleading a headache, Selma went out into the garden. Suffocating, she removed the scarf that modestly veiled her throat. Prisoner – she was a prisoner! She had stumbled blindly into a trap, but there was still time to escape. She would retract her promise. They could not keep her here by force, after all. She was still struggling to regain her composure when she felt a hand on hers.

"Never fear, Huzoor, the Rani is not such a bad woman. She simply wants to maintain the traditions. Society itself would collapse

8 Women's quarters.

without them."

Begum Nusrat had joined her, a sympathetic smile on her pudgy face.

"Be patient, it is only for a week. Your future husband is a man of modern outlook – almost an Englishman. With him you will lead a life of freedom. You will be mistress here, and Rani Aziza will lose her authority. She knows it, that is why she feels bitter. Only a week, Huzoor. Surely you can make the effort?"

She was right, Selma thought. *I should not let that woman drive me away*. She valiantly produced the semblance of a smile, but the strain of the day proved too much for her. The smile trembled on her lips. Forgetful of the dignity proper to an imperial princess, she broke down in tears.

CHAPTER 2

A hundred times during the week that preceded the wedding, Selma had been on the verge of giving up. What dissuaded her – even more, perhaps, than the thought of Amir – was the feeling that the Rani was playing with her, pushing her to the limit, to induce her to leave. All the signs were that Rani Aziza hated her.

She decided to confide in Begum Nusrat. The Begum was the only person in the zenana who spoke English, discounting the Rani herself, and Selma had discovered that her rather vain, frivolous exterior concealed a discerning mind and a fund of sound common sense.

The governor's wife hesitated. To speak would be to take sides. She regarded Selma as her protegée, having been the first to welcome her, but the Rani was powerful and unforgiving. Her own future and that of her husband would depend on the decision she took in the next few seconds. Would the Princess be astute enough to supplant the Rani? Wasn't a wife more influential than a sister? Begum Nusrat hated taking risks, but Selma was so insistent that she could not equivocate any longer.

"I am sure it is on account of Parvin," she said with a sigh.

"Parvin?"

"Rani Aziza's niece on her mother's side. The Rani brought her up at the palace like her own daughter. I have often wondered if her motives were truly motherly – after all, she renounced marriage in order to devote herself to her brother and run the palace – or if Parvin was just a willing tool to be sharpened and polished for future use."

Selma looked intrigued.

"Yes, that is the fact of the matter. Everyone here knew that Parvin had been elected as the Rajah's future bride, and most people thought her a wise choice. She is pretty, well-educated, and of princely blood. Having been reared in this palace, she knows its ways. There would have been none of the problems that inevitably arise with a wife from another house or another part of India. Above all, the Rani knew that a niece who owed her everything would help her to retain power. But then. . . ."

Begum Nusrat hesitated. She was reluctant to hurt Selma, but since she had insisted on knowing the truth. . . .

"Then Maulana Shaukat Ali appeared on the scene. The Maulana is a remarkable man, certainly, but his intervention upset all the Rani's plans. Because he dreamed of reinforcing the links between the Muslim community in India and the Ottoman caliphs, he had the idea of marrying you to our Rajah, whose political prospects he rates very highly. It was a great honour for the house of Badalpur, of course, but a disaster from Rani Aziza's point of view. Not only had her niece been ousted, but the new Rani of Badalpur would be a foreigner whom she could neither control nor crush. If the Rajah had lost his heart to some nobody of an English girl, she would easily have dealt with her. But she knows that you, with your title and exalted ancestry, and your commanding personality that no amount of courtesy can disguise, – you could very quickly rob her of her place here."

Selma felt her throat tighten. Having expected to be welcomed with open arms, she suddenly realized what an intrusion she was, not only to the Rani but to this entire little society whose existence had been governed for centuries by the same unchanging laws. The familiar sense of rejection overcame her. Would she always be an outsider wherever she went?

Fortunately, Zeynel and Madame Ghazavi were there to distract her. They reappeared the day after her arrival, seemingly through the good offices of Rashid Khan. How had he known that she had asked for them? How did things come to be known in this vast palace?

Much to the annoyance of the Rani, who suspected that they were scoffing at her, the three of them spent most of their time in Selma's corner of the big room, laughing and talking in Turkish. Rashid Khan had tried to reason with Selma, using Zeynel as a spokesman.

"In India, patience and tolerance are everything. Rebelling does not get you anywhere: you have to outwit your opponent."

"Why should I pretend?" Selma retorted. "I am used to fighting openly, the way the Turks always have."

The eunuch started.

"You mean like the powerful – like all who can impose their will because they are stronger! The weak have to be subtle and flexible, even dishonest at times. It is less glorious, but they have no choice, and I am not sure that you, Princess, still have that choice."

For a moment Selma thought she detected a hint of satisfaction in his tone, but she dismissed the idea. Dear old Zeynel was simply reacting, as she had, to the hostile atmosphere created by Rani Aziza.

The Rani did things on a grand scale, however, and Selma's resentment was temporarily dispelled when she summoned Lucknow's leading jewellers and invited her to make a selection from their magnificent wares. After witnessing the gradual disappearance of the jewels she had admired on her mother in the great days of the empire, sold one by one to cover their expenses in Beirut, Selma had never dreamed that she herself would own any equally fine pieces. But now, as in a fairy tale come true, she was being offered jewel cases overflowing with long necklaces of blue diamonds, pearls, and the purest emeralds.

She tried on one necklace and pendant after the other, unable to make up her mind. Madame Ghazavi, who was advising her, showed no such indecision. Ever practical, she discarded the simpler pieces Selma would have been tempted to choose on grounds of taste and avidly selected all that was most elaborate and expensive.

"Don't be childish, Princess," she whispered sternly. "Jewels are a woman's only form of security, you should know that by now."

With a sigh, Selma resigned herself to wearing a fortune around her neck and wrists rather than the little miracles of craftsmanship that appealed to her so much more.

"Are you sure there is nothing else you would like?" purred Rani Aziza as the stack of jewel cases mounted.

The Rani's sarcasm was lost on Madame Ghazavi, who construed this as an invitation, but Selma exploded.

"I don't need any of these things," she snapped. "You can send them all back!"

"Come, my child. Whether or not you think you need them, you will wear them. I will not have my brother's wife looking like a pauper."

"In that case, tell your brother to find himself another wife. I have had enough of your venomous remarks." She turned to Zeynel. "Go straight to Rashid Khan and tell him I want a berth on the next boat for Beirut. Meantime, he is to find me a room in a hotel!"

The Rani's ill-disguised air of satisfaction conveyed that nothing could have delighted her more. Selma had lost their war of nerves, but she did not care. Her one desire was to return to Beirut and the dignified simplicity of her maternal home. She was not equal to this power game.

The next day it became known that Rani Aziza was ill: she had moved to the other end of the zenana and wished to see no one. Selma never discovered exactly what had happened, except that the Rajah had lost his temper and that his sister had given way for the first time ever.

Selma's rebellion did more for her prestige than all her previous efforts to endear herself. The women of the palace had always taken their cue from the Rani and blindly adopted her prejudices. Now, contrary to the tradition that a young wife's opinions carried no weight, they started to look on Selma as their new mistress.

After the jewellers came dealers in brocades, silks, and lace. The inmates of the zenana set to work with a will. They had only five days in which to complete the bride's trousseau, which was usually prepared years in advance: five days in which to cut, sew, and embroider the long ghararas, the chikan kurtahs – lawn tunics so fine that you could thread them through a ring – and the dopattas, figure-concealing stoles adorned with gold thread and pearls.

Never had these normally indolent women exerted themselves so hard. Relatives and neighbours were called in to help and the zenana was transformed into one big sewing room. Any trousseau had to comprise at least a hundred outfits, but would three hundred suffice for this fairy-tale Princess whose beauty the women never tired of extolling? The oldest of them disdainfully recalled that the present Rajah's great-grandmother had never worn the same clothes twice, yet dozens of trunks containing her trousseau were still unopened when she died after twenty years of married life. Three hundred ghararas were a mere nothing!

Much discussion was devoted to this topic. Should the wedding have been postponed to enable their future Rani to receive the treatment she deserved? A sultana's daughter, a caliph's granddaughter, had honoured them by consenting to enter the family, yet she was being offered a pauper's trousseau! What was to be done? The Rajah refused to wait a day longer – he had grown as impatient as an Ingrez, an Englishman. They grumbled, but they also glowed with pride: this marriage would put the house of Badalpur on a par with that of the Nizam of Hyderabad, India's richest and most powerful ruler. His daughters-in-law, Princesses Nilufer and Durushevar, were household names; Princess Selma would soon be just as celebrated.

In the two centuries since the Mogul dynasty had been run out of Delhi by the British army, Indian Muslims had considered the Ottoman royal family as their own. The Mogul sultanate was also of Turkish origin and the grandeur of the Ottoman Empire consoled them through the long years of humiliation at home. When the caliphate was threatened in Turkey in 1921, the Muslim masses in India revolted against the British Raj in an uprising more violent than any before it. Supported by Gandhi, the Muslim movement was joined by Hindus, and thus began the first big wave of demonstrations for independence.

One young girl alone remained aloof from all this bustle and commotion. Plump and pale-complexioned, with a braid of dark, well-oiled hair falling to her waist, she was a beauty by local standards despite her rather snub nose and heavy chin. Selma had taken some time to grasp that the main aesthetic criterion here was whiteness of skin, and that a woman was considered ugly, however fine her features, if her skin was dark. Great importance was attached to colour, it had been explained to her, because pigmentation was a far surer guide to a person's noble or humble ancestry than any family tree. The conquerors of India – Aryans, Arabs, Mongols – had all been pale, whereas the aboriginal peoples they subjugated were dark-skinned. Hence the ingrained equation of white skin with the race of masters and black skin with the race of slaves.

The girl ostentatiously turned her head away whenever Selma looked at her.

Could she be . . . yes, of course, she must be Parvin. Unlike the others, she has not addressed a single word to me. Poor thing! Reared in the belief that she would marry the handsome Rajah, she was no doubt in love with him – until this newcomer came along to ruin her dream, a foreigner whose only advantage was the unfair one of superior birth! What will become of her? Who will want a girl once promised to a man and then repudiated? How many respectable families will request her hand in marriage now that she had been "soiled," as they say, by another man's desire? In their narrow-minded view, her virginity is no longer absolute!

Selma smiled at the girl and tried to engage her in conversation, but it was no use. Parvin did not want her sympathy. She finally gave up with the clear conscience of those who feel irked when their charitable impulses are spurned by people less fortunate than themselves.

In any case, she had other things on her mind. While exploring the palace one morning she was appalled to find that her bridal chamber was being made ready in the middle of the zenana, immediately next door to Rani Aziza's bedroom. Thus the Rani would be able to observe the movements of the newlyweds to her heart's content! Begum Nusrat received the full force of her fury.

"Who am I marrying," she burst out, "the Rajah or the Rani? Is there no privacy in this country? In Turkey, when a sultana got married, she had her own palace, her own servants. She was independent!"

"Those things are mere details, Huzoor, be thankful you only have a sister-in-law. If you had a mother-in-law, even the most adoring husband would be powerless to oppose her." She smiled. "In any case, why do you wish to be alone? Solitude is the saddest thing in the world. Here, when a problem arises, our whole family is there to help us – to solve it for us."

"No, no!" Selma cried angrily. "I *have* little enough I can call my own. At least let me keep my problems!"

The Begum thought it wiser to tiptoe away.

Massage, as Selma was reminded yet again, is a sovereign remedy for mental as well as physical ills. Her cares melted away under the pressure of her maidservant's soft, supple hands. Smeared with a thick yellow paste compounded of mustard seeds steeped in milk, powdered sandalwood, rare perfumes, and seven finely ground spices including turmeric, she submitted to the girl's ministrations with delight. She was vigorously kneaded from the roots of her hair to the tips of her toes so that every square inch of her skin would become pure satin and every pore would exude a delicious fragrance. For five days she would be forbidden to wash. Her protests were unavailing. It was explained to her that the miraculous yellow ointment, exclusively reserved for brides-to-be, must be left to penetrate the flesh and purify the blood. On the morning of her wedding, when she was finally permitted to take a bath, she would emerge from it as resplendent as a butterfly emerging from the chrysalis.

Selma took refuge in her thoughts as she sat cross-legged beside Rani Aziza, who had made a smiling reappearance that morning, greeting her with: "What a joy it is to see my beautiful Princess again!". How else was she to endure the long days that still remained before her wedding, and, above all, the flow of commentary and curious glances of her women visitors? Every female of importance in Lucknow came to inspect the young Sultana who sat there with downcast eyes for hours on end. At first she thought she would go mad. Then, just as she had during the interminable ceremonies at Dolmabahçé Palace, she began to tell herself stories – or rather, her story, because in comparison to what she was living through now, anything else seemed dull. She never tired of picturing the moment when Amir and she would meet for the first time. He would take her in his arms and kiss her until her senses reeled. She would look into those dark, liquid eyes and hear his melodious, rather husky voice telling her that he loved her. . . .

"Rani Bitia[1] has arrived!"

The room rang with delighted, excited cries. What was it this time?

1 Bitia: the daughter of the house.

Lost in her daydream, with her head on Amir's shoulder and his fingers gently stroking her hair, Selma shut her eyes and obstinately refused to come down to earth. She scarcely felt the light touch on her arm or heard the voice that addressed her in perfect English.

"Won't you look at me, Apa[2]? I am Zahra, your little sister."

A slender young girl was kneeling in front of her, smiling. Selma came to with a start. Of course, this must be the Rajah's teenage sister, Zahra, who had been left behind in Badalpur with an ailing grandmother. She surveyed the fine-boned face, the dark and pensive eyes. How pretty she was, so much like Amir's portrait! Zahra, for her part, made no secret of her admiration.

"You are so beautiful!"

She covered Selma's hands with rapturous kisses. Still a trifle taken aback, Selma felt a kind of warmth flooding into her. The tension of recent days gave way to a sense of well-being, and it dawned on her that in this alien world, she had at last found a friend.

In the next few days Zahra's charm and gaiety smoothed Selma's path a great deal. Brought up by an English governess – Amir had insisted on this, though tradition had it that girls were harmed by excessive education – she was passionately addicted to European literature. She had read Keats, Byron, Stendhal and all of Balzac and, although she had never left the zenana, except to be conveyed to another zenana in a closed carriage, she seemed to know something of life.

Instantly perceiving Selma's irritation at being confined in this stifling environment, she won a hard-fought battle for permission to accompany her on walks in the inner garden without the chattering bevy of attendants. A single eunuch followed them at a respectful distance. There, divested of the muslin veil that was meant to conceal her hair, even in that secluded spot, Selma felt her spirits revive.

In her confusion, she longed to confide in Zahra – to speak of Amir and voice her hopes and fears – but she quickly saw that the girl's apparent maturity and sophistication were acquired solely from books and disguised her total innocence. Zahra worshipped her brother and was convinced that anyone who married him ought to be the happiest woman in the world. She would have found the slightest reservation not only incomprehensible but hurtful. Selma was not so selfish as to want to disturb the girl's peaceful state of mind, so she kept her misgivings to herself.

2 Elder sister.

Selma was roused at dawn by the laughter of young girls. The air was still cool and fragrant with the scent of the jasmine on the veranda. Why should she be feeling sad on such a beautiful day?

"Wake up, Apa!" called Zahra. "We have to draw the signs of happiness on your hands and feet with henna. Open your eyes on this, the happiest day of your life!"

The women cheerfully busied themselves around the bed, singing the love songs that traditionally accompanied a bride's toilette. Selma watched them as they carefully adorned her palms with intricate arabesques – watched them as if the proceedings did not concern her at all. The more she strove to take an interest in the festivities of which she was the heroine, the more she was overcome by a sense of unreality.

As if in a dream, she saw Rani Aziza walk up to her, place a thin bracelet of cloth around her wrist and slowly recite the time-honoured formula.

"I give you this bracelet. It contains rice to bring you prosperity, green grass to assure you of fertility, and an iron ring, the token of your fidelity."

The women had fallen silent, lost in their own memories.

There came a sudden loud hammering on the bronze door that separated the zenana from the men's quarters. The younger girls, each carrying a rose, darted forward with joyful cries: the bridegroom had come to make a symbolic attempt to carry off the bride, and their task was to drive him away, lashing him unmercifully with their flowers. After a few fruitless attempts he withdrew, amid jeers, and rejoined his relations and friends in the family imambara, the marble and mosaic-adorned Shia shrine adjoining the palace, where the religious ceremony would take place.

Selma was left alone in a chamber above the women's quarters. This was where the bride, surrounded by her closest friends, would normally indulge in childhood reminiscences and shed a few tears for the life she was about to leave, but Selma's friends were far away and she had no desire to weep any more.

Downstairs the guests were arriving. She could hear them exclaiming at the magnificence of the gifts set out in each of the five reception rooms. Custom prescribed that all should have a chance to gauge the in-laws' generosity toward the young bride. Jewellery, silverware, glass, and silks were piled up, a heaping monument to vanity. The women scrutinized them out of the corner of their eye: weddings provided conversational fuel for years, if not decades, and reputations could be made or ruined on such occasions.

How long had Selma been waiting upstairs? She had no idea. Madame Ghazavi, seated beside her, was growing impatient, the more so because a clatter of crockery denoted that refreshments were in prospect.

"It is a disgrace!" she grumbled. "All of them are having a good time while you are left up here on your own, the barbarians! Princess, I beg you, abandon this insane marriage while there is still time."

"Be silent!"

Selma was not in the mood to tolerate her companion's jeremiads, even if the local customs struck her, too, as decidedly odd. She could not understand why no one had come to help her get ready. The nikkah or wedding ceremony must be imminent. When would they come to bathe and dress her? The women downstairs were enjoying each other's company so much, they seemed to have forgotten all about the bride.

"Listen, Apa," Zahra announced, "the maulvi[3] will be here in a minute."

Selma's female attendants were holding up a length of fabric to shield her from the maulvi's gaze. Where, she wondered, was the bridegroom? Zahra began to laugh at her puzzled, anxious expression.

"Come now, Apa! You will not see him till tomorrow."

Tomorrow? She did not understand, but there was no time to ask questions. From the other side of the screen came the sound of whispers, shuffling feet, throats being cleared. Then silence fell, and a solemn voice began to intone some verses from the Koran. Suddenly it broke off and addressed her with ritual emphasis.

"Selma, daughter of Haïri Rauf and Hatijé Murad, will you take Amir, son of Amir Ali of Badalpur and Aysha Salimabad, to be your husband?"

No, I will not!

It seemed to Selma that she had shouted the words at the top of her voice, but the faces of the women beside her were impassive. She looked around for Zahra, panic-stricken, only to meet the stern and unbending gaze of Rani Aziza: everyone was waiting for her to reply. It dawned on her that up to now she had only been playing the fiancée – that she had meant to defer her decision until this final moment when, in the maulvi's presence, she could at last see Amir and look into his eyes. . . .

They had deceived her – or did the fault lie with her? She searched

3 Muslim cleric who officiates at various ceremonies.

her memory. Yes, it was true: according to Islamic tradition, bride and bridegroom did not meet until after the nikkah. They made their vows to the maulvi before either of them had seen the other. It was different in the last days of the Ottoman court – that was why she had thought. . . .

The voice reiterated its original question. Wasn't she to be allowed a moment's pause for thought? The women around her seemed to be all bared teeth and mocking smiles. Did they think she was afraid?

"Yes, I will."

Was that voice hers? Three times the maulvi repeated his question, and three times she heard herself reply "Yes!" so resolutely that the women glanced at one another in surprise. The whole ceremony had lasted five minutes at most. Now the maulvi hurried off to the imambara, where the bridegroom and his family and friends were waiting in ceremonial attire. Filled with curiosity, the women followed by way of a secret staircase leading to the circular gallery overlooking the shrine. From there, they could see everything without being seen.

Only Zahra stayed behind. She sat down beside Selma in the upstairs chamber and silently held her hand as if she understood everything. They remained together motionless for several hours, dreaming. Much later on, when shadows came creeping into the room, Zahra lit a copper lamp and softly began to recite some mystical verses by Jelaleddin Rumi. Although Selma had not heard them since leaving Istanbul, she recalled every line with deep emotion.

Your love makes me resound like a lute
And my secrets stand revealed at your touch.
My whole, weary being resembles a harp.
At each touch of your hand to its strings, I sigh.

Our love-laden caravan has left emptiness behind.
The wine of union forever illumines our night.
Our lips shall be moistened until the dawn of the void
With that wine unforbidden by the religion of love.

We are in truth one soul, you and I.
We reveal and conceal ourselves, you in me and I in you.

Therein lies the deeper meaning of my bond with you,
For there is nothing between us, not you, not I.

The flame of the oil lamp had started to flicker. An astonishing calm fell, and the air was light as thistledown. Her spirit appeased, Selma drifted off to sleep.

Water at last! Selma could not have enough of the cool liquid streaming over her whole body. She had dreamt of this moment for days and now, feeling completely refreshed, she shivered with pleasure. Was it the water, or the prospect of seeing Amir?

Once more the women anointed her with perfumes and dressed her in her bridal gharara of red and gold. Diamonds sparkled at her throat and in her ears, dozens of gold bangles encircled her slender arms from wrist to elbow. Even her ankles were laden with gold and her big toes adorned with precious stones. The only thing missing was the solitaire diamond that should have been inserted in her left nostril. No bride could account herself truly beautiful without this, but Selma had objected so fiercely when the women proposed to pierce her nose some days before that they had finally given up.

The sun was already high in the sky. Selma waited, roughed and arrayed like the idol of a goddess, her movements hampered by the stiffly-embroidered gharara. She was ready. When would her handsome Rajah finally appear?

One last thing remained to be done. A woman approached, solemnly bearing a red muslin veil covered with a curtain of roses, jasmine and garlands of gold thread. This was the bridal veil that would conceal her face throughout the ceremony. Selma almost suffocated beneath its three layers, but she knew that on her wedding day no bride could refuse to wear this symbol of virginity.

The girls began to sing, while strong hands lifted her and delicately conveyed her, like a parcel done up in crimson and gold, towards what she guessed to be the zenana's central courtyard. Peering through her veil, she made out the ceremonial bed on a dais. She was carefully assisted on to it. From this moment on, tradition forbade her to make the smallest gesture or emit the faintest sigh: she was supposed to be all meekness and feminine frailty, resignation and anticipation.

Women and children clustered around her. Rani Aziza, in her role as mistress of ceremonies, raised a corner of the veil from time to time to permit them glimpses of her beauty. They jostled each other, stared at her appraisingly, uttered cries of admiration. Flushed with embarrassment, Selma felt like a slave being put up for auction. What reinforced this impression was that each woman, having looked her over, deposited some gold coins at her feet – an odd number, as custom prescribed, to ward off bad luck. Fighting off the dizziness that threatened to overcome her she smiled faintly.

"Lower your eyes! It is unbecoming for a bride to smile!"

Rani Aziza was outraged. The little fool would disgrace them all. Did she not realize that, although it was insulting to a bride's new family to look sad, it was equally improper to seem happy when exchanging a girl's life for that of a woman? That was not so hard to grasp, after all!

It was becoming steadily hotter. Selma could scarcely breathe. Birdlike cries of wonder, figures crowding around, heavy perfumes mingled with the odour of perspiration – they were all too much for her. She felt her senses slipping away. . . .

How long had she been unconscious? Her head was throbbing; it felt about to burst from the din. The sun seemed suddenly dark. Struggling with a sensation of nausea, she opened her eyes. A few yards away, the entrance to the courtyard was blocked by something huge and bulky surmounted by a glimmering spot. As she watched, the grey mass slowly wavered and lowered. Taking advantage of the fact that nobody was looking, she lifted one corner of her veil. The royal elephant, richly caparisoned in brocade and daubed with paint for the occasion, its ankles weighed down with gold bracelets, was ponderously kneeling. A tall man, his face concealed beneath a veil of tulle adorned with jasmine and roses, stepped down from the howdah.

Amir. . . .

The women emptied the bride's bath water at the Rajah's feet, then respectfully withdrew. He walked lithely over to the ceremonial bed and sat down beside Selma, taking care not to touch her. Although she still could not see his face, she could hear his hurried breathing and wondered if he shared her emotions.

A voluminous scarlet shawl, that hid them from the onlookers' gaze, was lowered over their heads. One woman held a Koran above it while another placed a mirror at their feet. It was in this mirror that they would see each other for the first time.

Lift the veil; he is waiting to lift his, too, Selma thought. *At last I am going to see him. What am I afraid of?*

Suddenly she was assailed by horrific visions: her husband's veil concealed a simian face pitted with smallpox and sprinkled with pustules – the face of a monster. She knew it – she could sense it! Why had she not guessed the truth sooner? *That* was why he had refused to meet her before the wedding! The portrait? A forgery, sent to persuade her. . . .

Never had her hand felt heavier than when she mustered all her energy and raised it to the veil. As if that were the signal he had been waiting for, Amir briskly removed his own. Through the mirror, his beautiful, burning gaze drank in the reflection of two emerald-green eyes filled with tears. . . .

Selma did not hear the concluding prayers. She realized that the ceremony was over only when two women guided her to the howdah[4] and installed her in it beside her husband.

Through the curtains that hid them both from view she now caught sight of the wedding procession. Nawabs[5] and rajahs aglitter with precious stones rode their own caparisoned elephants, followed by standard-bearers, lancers, and retainers in ceremonial livery, and behind them, proudly mounted on Arab thoroughbreds, came the petty aristocracy of the entire province. Bringing up the rear was an Indian band dressed as if for hunting in red coats and white breeches. At a signal from the bandmaster, who was wearing a powdered wig, drums, cymbals, flutes, long silver trumpets, and bagpipes launched into a wild combination of native melodies and rhythms borrowed from the far-off depths of the Scottish highlands. Galvanized, the procession moved off to the cheers of the crowd that had gathered to watch the gorgeous spectacle. It was usually an emotional moment when a bride left her home forever and set off for that of her husband, but Selma possessed no family home, so the procession contented itself with five symbolic circuits of the palace grounds and returned to its point of departure.

In the privacy of the howdah, where there was no one to see or criticize, Selma lifted her veil and gazed with surprise and delight at her husband, who had taken advantage of this respite to do likewise. He gave her a conspiratorial smile, and her heart overflowed with happiness: he understood – he realized how difficult she found it all!

The elephant came to a halt and slowly knelt down. A little gold ladder was propped against its flank. Below, a party of female attendants waited to carry Selma to her apartments. She shook her head, preferring to walk, but Amir intervened.

"You must observe our customs," he said firmly.

They were the first words they had exchanged. She would never forget them.

The bridal chamber was a mass of flowers. Pyramids of fruit and

4 The covered divan on the back of an elephant.

5 The Muslim princes of India were generally entitled nawabs. In the province of Oudh, however, many were known as Rajahs like their Hindu counterparts.

sweetmeats were arrayed on silver dishes, and incense burners standing in all four corners of the room gave off a scent of musk and sandalwood. In the centre was the bed, a huge expanse of white satin and lace. Selma was involuntarily reminded of a courtesan's bed in a Hollywood costume drama.

The women had set to work on her again. They exchanged her wedding attire for a silk caftan and indefatigably brushed her light auburn hair, which never ceased to amaze them – "a sunset encircling the moon," they called it.

At last the bride was ready. She waited, reclining against a lacy mound of pillows. What could be keeping Amir?

Seated on the floor around the bed, her attendants continued to chatter and chew pan, periodically squirting long jets of reddish saliva into the spittoons that stood here and there. Selma, who could not get used to this habit and never would, winced every time.

Minutes dragged by. Selma felt ridiculous, all alone in such a gargantuan bed – ridiculous and humiliated. She gritted her teeth, determined not to show how dismayed she was.

It was an hour before Amir appeared. He had been with his sister, he explained: an urgent problem requiring his immediate attention. Selma was cut to the quick. An urgent problem – yes, specially fabricated by Rani Aziza so as to detain her brother and publicly reassert her authority vis-à-vis his new wife! As soon as the women had left the room, blithely speculating on the night ahead, she burst into tears.

"What is it, my dear?" Amir paused beside the bed with an air of concern. "Are you feeling unwell?"

Selma buried her face in the pillows, sobbing.

"Shall I call a doctor?"

"No!" She sat up, flushed and indignant. So he did not understand!

Amir hesitated, uncertain what to do. She looked angry. Had he said something to offend her? She had seemed so happy just now, during the ceremony. What was wrong? He longed to take her in his arms and console her, but he did not dare: she would have spurned his advances without a doubt.

Why is he simply standing there looking at me? I am cold. If only he would take me in his arms, kiss me, warm me in his embrace. . . .

What a fool I am, he thought. *The poor little thing is obviously terrified – she thinks I am going to throw myself upon her and claim my conjugal rights. She does not realize I respect her feelings. I will wait till she gets used to me – there is plenty of time*. He perched on the edge of the bed.

"It has been a tiring day," he said. "You need rest – I shall leave you in peace."

She stared at him, dumbfounded. Was he being sarcastic – was she really so undesirable? What a fool she had been to dream of this moment! Theirs was just a marriage of convenience, after all: he was merely conveying that she did not appeal to him. She squared her shoulders and looked as aloof as she could.

"You are right," she replied. "I am exhausted. Good night."

She turned over and curled up as far away from him as possible. Amir heaved a sigh. He had hoped at least for a smile, a few kind words that would convey her appreciation of his tact and delicacy. Carefully, so as not to disturb her, he stretched out on his own side of the bed. For months he had gazed at her photograph and dreamed of having her here beside him, and now. . . . This was not the way he had imagined their wedding night.

CHAPTER 3

Sunlight was streaming through the bedroom curtains; shadowy figures moved silently around the bed.

"Annéjim?" Selma murmured, still half asleep. "Leila Hanum?"

Whispers and smothered laughter were the only response. Slowly it dawned on her: she was not in her little pink bedroom in Beirut, she was in India, and since the day before . . . a married woman. What were these women doing here? Why could they not leave her alone with her husband?

She put out a languid arm and felt the bed beside her.

"Amir?"

Fully awake now, she sat up in bed.

"Where is Amir?"

Exchanging sly glances and amused comments, the women came closer. Selma felt herself blush: how could she ever have let herself go like that? Back in Istanbul the kalfas were forever scolding her for being too impulsive. "In happiness or in misfortune," they used to say, "a noble soul remains serene," and they would cite Sultana Hatijé as a prime example. But no matter how much she admired her mother the little girl could not help thinking that a noble soul may well have more nobility than soul.

Amir's absence made her uneasy. Could he be angry? Last night, when the room was in darkness, he had moved over and gently stroked her hair. That one gesture was enough to dispel all her accumulated tension: she gave a deep sigh and laid her head on his shoulder. They stayed like that for a long time, listening to the faint, rhythmical squeak of the ceiling fan, and then. . . . Then she must have fallen asleep.

But he . . . had he continued to caress her . . . had he. . . ? A sudden thought took her breath away: was it possible that while she was asleep he had. . . ? Surreptitiously she slid her hand beneath the sheet to feel if . . . ; worried, she questioned her body. She could not detect anything unusual, but. . . . *"Good Lord, will these women ever stop moving? I cannot even see whether. . . ."*

Her attendants were less prudish. They unceremoniously thrust her aside and stripped off the nuptial sheet. It was spotless!

Exclamations of disappointment and sidelong glances greeted this revelation. Crimson-cheeked, Selma took refuge at her dressing table and pretended to ignore the chattering women, who swiftly bore their damning evidence off to Rani Aziza's apartments.

Half ashamed, half furious, Selma fidgeted feverishly with the array of brushes, powder boxes, perfume bottles. What would everyone think? That she had failed to please her husband? Or, worse still, that she was not a virgin? She was so upset that she took it out on the lace cloth that covered the table and mechanically tore it to shreds.

"Apa! What on earth are you doing?" Zahra had appeared in the doorway. She hurried over to Selma. "What is wrong?"

"Where is Amir?" Selma demanded.

Reassured, Zahra suppressed a smile. That's all! How she loves him already!

"He has gone riding as usual. He always rides between six and eight, to avoid the heat."

"As *usual*?" Selma's eyes flashed. "On the first day of our marriage?"

"A man has the right, if he wishes . . . " Zahra said. She was astonished, but also filled with admiration. *How beautiful she looks in the role of an angry empress*, she thought. "Why don't you let me show you around the zenana?" she suggested, to calm the storm. "You have not seen half of it yet."

Selma hesitated. Any distraction would have been welcome, but she was sure everyone would be talking about that cursed sheet. . . . No, she did not have the courage to run the gauntlet of all those mocking, pitying, accusing faces.

"Our guests would be so happy to meet you," Zahra insisted. "Their quarters are miles away from Rani Aziza's suite," she added with a touch of malice. "Do come!"

And, taking Selma by the hand, she led her through the endless corridors to a totally unfamiliar part of the palace, a labyrinthine series of galleries separated by courtyards and terraces with spiral staircases leading up to them. They came at last to a huge, vaulted rotunda flanked by numerous rooms, in each of which a family was encamped. How long had they lived here? Who were these grandmothers with hennaed hair and these young women with hordes of children?

Her visit caused a considerable stir. They clustered around her, vied for her attention. Messengers bloated with their own importance, the children ran off to spread the word. From neighbouring galleries other women flocked to the scene in joyous confusion, arguing over who would have the honour of inviting the Rani to their quarters for tea. If Zahra, the consummate diplomat, had not been there to fend off their tyrannical hospitality, Selma would have been compelled to drink at least a hundred cups.

Zahra led the way, pausing awhile outside each room, adjusting the length of their stay to the importance of its occupants, and refrained from entering unless the motionless figure enthroned on the bed inside was that of a kinswoman or a representative of some noble family.

A number of the women had arrived only days before, to attend the wedding, but many had been there for months, if not years. Having come to the palace on the occasion of some festivity or other, they had stayed on, not only because they liked it there, but on the oriental principle that a person who visited you honoured you, and the longer the visit the greater the honour. A few old women or widows had settled down there for life. During the early stages of their stay they would raise the possibility of an early departure in their daily conversation with their hostess. At which point the Rani would wax indignant: were they unhappy? Were they not being cared for properly? To please her they would consent to stay on a bit longer. After a few months they had become part of the household: it would have seemed improper and insulting for them to leave.

Impoverished female relations and their children resided in the zenana as of right. In princely families, where estates were never divided and the eldest son inherited everything, distant cousins were sometimes completely destitute. It was the Rajah's duty to take care of their needs: to pay for their sons' education, provide their daughters with dowries, and, if they wished, accommodate them in the palace that would, had Allah willed it so, have been theirs.

Selma's polite and unassuming manner immediately endeared her to these women, who treated her more like a daughter than a new Rani. They hugged her to their hearts, placed their hands on her temples and pressed her to come inside and sit down. But Zahra was adamant: the order of precedence must be respected. They accepted tea only from the old Rani of Karimpur, whose son ruled one of the largest states in the United Provinces, and from Amir's wet nurse, a motherly woman whose radiant good humour immediately won Selma's heart.

The tour lasted nearly four hours. Thanks to Zahra, who constantly plied her with whispered instructions on how to behave in every case, Selma made very few blunders. How else, confronted by such a plethora of names, titles, and ties of kinship or friendship, would she have known who to greet with greater respect, who to grace with an affectionate smile, and who with just a benevolent inclination of the head?

When she finally got back to her own quarters, she flopped down in a chair, exhausted but exhilarated by the spontaneous warmth of her reception. How she loved to be loved! She had not felt such an outpouring of love since she had gone into exile! . . .

Amir had not yet returned.

"Government business," Zahra explained. "He has been having a few problems lately." She was anxious to allay Selma's disappointment without alarming her. There was no point in telling her the truth: that the peasants of northern India, incited by the Congress Party, were beginning to rebel against the big landowners, most of whom were hostile to Gandhi's economic policy and considered him a communist.

But today Selma was not interested in affairs of state. Her joy quickly vanished: the day after their wedding Amir was neglecting her!

She waited for him all afternoon. Convinced that he would return for a siesta, she carefully bathed and perfumed herself, but by teatime he still had not reappeared. Mortified, she pretended to read. She had absolutely no intention of asking where he was.

A slight breeze had come up.

"Let's go for a drive, Zahra," she said. "I would like to see some of the mosques and imambaras."

Surprised and pleased by her sister-in-law's unsuspected interest in religious matters, Zahra wasted no time. "Salim," she said to the eunuch, "go and ask Rani Aziza which carriage we may use," without understanding why Selma was giving her such an angry look.

The Rani found Selma's request unusual. "But who am I," she exclaimed, "to quarrel with a young bride's whims?" Although the palace owned a dozen carriages – the cars could only be used with the Rajah's express permission – she saw to it that the stables took nearly an hour to produce one.

The light was fading by the time they set off, accompanied by two attendants. The palaces and mosques were tinged with gold, and the lawns, freshly watered by an army of gardeners, scented the air. Against a background of luxuriant flower beds and shrubs trimmed to resemble mythical beasts, the marble fountains and delicately colonnaded pavilions seemed to be awaiting improbable visitors.

The carriage made its way slowly past the elegant mausoleums of Nawab Tikka Khan and his wife, and Lal Baraderi, the red sandstone palace where the kings of Oudh had once received princes and ambassadors, and the little imambara surmounted by its graceful domes, and a succession of palaces that seemed to float above their silent gardens like the notes of a romantic sonata. Dominating the city on a hill surrounded by fields of golden colza stood the Friday Mosque. Attracted by the peace and beauty of the place, Selma suggested stopping there to pray.

Zahra raised her eyebrows. "But that is impossible, Apa. We are not allowed to."

"Not allowed to pray?"

"Not allowed to go inside. Only men can enter a mosque. Women pray at home."

"What nonsense!"

Selma got out of the carriage, adjusted her veil, and, like a martyr bent on defending her faith against heresy, brushed past the attendants who tried to bar her path. No one was going to prevent the granddaughter of a caliph from entering a mosque!

The spacious courtyard was deserted. Now that the sun had set, the balmy air felt like silk. Birds twittered in tribute to the cool of the evening. A single star twinkled overhead.

La Illah Illallah. . . . There is no god but Thou, O God, for Thou art the Infinite, the Eternal. Nothing exists apart from Thee. . . .

Selma had knelt down. In this silence, this beauty, the oft-repeated words burst, bathed her in their light. Quietly, simply, she opened her heart.

She neither saw nor heard the shadowy figure fidgeting beside her until she felt a tug at her sleeve. There, looming over her a big black fly was gesticulating wildly. She shut her eyes and tried to recover her composure. But the maulvi launched into an angry tirade. She rose to her feet. How dare this creature interrupt her meditations!

"Silence, you demon! Women are admitted to mosques in all Muslim countries! Don't you know that Fatima, our Prophet's daughter, used to pray at the Kaaba[1] in company with men? Would you dare, you wretch, to refuse what Mohammed the magnanimous permitted?"

The maulvi stared at her open-mouthed. What was she saying, this white she-devil, this infidel whose mere presence has defiled this holy place?

"Translate for me, Zahra! Translate every last word!"

1 Kaaba: principal sanctuary of Mecca, protecting the "black stone." This "black stone" is, according to the Muslims, the remains of the first temple raised by Adam to honour God. The sins of men turned it black.

Utterly exasperated, Selma tugged at the young woman's arm. "Tell him that he and his kind debase our religion with their petty-mindedness, their foolishness, their hypocrisy. In fact, what right do they have to exist? Islam admits of no intermediary between God and his creatures – no clergy. The only recognized guides are the Koran and the words of the Prophet. These maulvis, mullahs, and imams are impostors who prey upon the ignorance of the people!"

The maulvi turned pale and beat a hasty retreat, leaving her to indulge her fury to the full.

Back at the palace, Selma went straight to her apartments without looking in on Rani Aziza, whom the chaperons had been quick to inform of her scandalous behaviour. She found Amir pacing up and down.

"Where were you?" he asked, sounding irritable despite himself. "I have been waiting for you."

"And I waited for you all day long. I only went out for an hour."

Amir said nothing, hurt that she should not have displayed the patience proper to a young bride. He refrained from telling her about his problems; one did not discuss such things with a woman. Besides, he was not in the habit of accounting for the way he spent his time. Selma's impatience offended him, as though she did not trust him.

". . . Why did I say that? All of a sudden he looks like a little boy who has just been scolded. . . . All day long I have dreamed of him and when he is there all I can do is insult him. Oh, if only I could apologize, tell him how much I missed him!" She stared fixedly at the top of her shoes. *"How can I make him understand? Isn't my impatience proof enough of my love?"*

How lovely she had looked in her sleep last night, thought Amir. *A childlike beauty, different from that of the women here, with their dark, sensual looks.* He had lain awake for a long time, savouring that innocence, that gentleness. Now she was furious with him and he did not even know why. . . . He had been warned that Turkish women were volatile by nature, unlike their docile Indian sisters. . . . But why such thoughts? She was simply nervous. Everything was so new to her. He must give her time to get used to their way of life.

He had hastened to finish his day's duties with one thought in mind, happy and excited at the prospect of a long evening with his young wife, of a night, perhaps, in each other's arms. . . .

Reluctantly, he walked to the door.

"You are tired, I will leave you to rest. Would you like your dinner served in here, or would you prefer to dine with my sister?"

Where are you off to now? Selma was on the verge of shouting the question aloud, but she restrained herself.

"I will dine here, thank you."

He left. Motionless, she sat staring at the white wall opposite, the thick wall between her and Amir. A feeling of blunders, of pointless suffering. Why was it so hard for two people to meet?

"My princess, my beloved nightingale," Madame Ghazavi moaned. "How they neglect you, these barbarians!"

Hadn't she always said this marriage would prove a disaster? She had known it all along. What did a Sultan's granddaughter have in common with a family that could not even afford a private train?

Selma realized that Madame Ghazavi was being histrionic, that she loathed India and above all the Indians, who failed to treat her with the respect to which her white skin entitled her. She usually told her to keep quiet, but tonight she felt like being consoled.

Zeynel, standing in the corner with his hands respectfully folded on his paunch, looked on: *what a mistake to have brought this madwoman! She poisons everything she touches; she could even get the sun fighting with the moon. I had warned the Sultana, but Selma had insisted. She is fond of the scheming creature who had spotted her weakness in a flash: she likes to be flattered and fawned on as if she were still an imperial princess at the Ottoman court. If someone does not put a stop to her, Madame Ghazavi is going to get what she wants: to break up the marriage and take Selma back to Beirut with her. Well, I am not going to let it happen: my Sultana would be heartbroken.*

"Let us all have dinner in my boudoir, the three of us."

Selma had decided to forget about Amir and enjoy herself. This was their first time alone together, out of range of Rani Aziza's mocking glances and sarcastic comments – the first time she had felt genuinely free since her arrival.

"Tonight we are going to celebrate. I forbid you both to be sad or serious about anything!"

"Bravo! That's my brave princess!" cried Madame Ghazavi. "Poor little thing," she added, imitating Rani Aziza's voice, "she is only a Sunni, whereas *we* are Shiites!"

They all rocked with laughter, even Zeynel. The woman was a born mimic. Dinner was a thoroughly cheerful occasion. They indulged in happy reminiscences and made plans to travel, first to Beirut to see the Sultana, then to Paris. Now that money was no obstacle, Selma felt as if a world of pleasure were opening before her. Amir? She would win him over – no one could resist her when she turned on the charm.

She felt young and carefree again. Why on earth had she been so unhappy just now? She wanted to dance, to sing.

"I am going to install a piano here – we'll organize some musical evenings. Meantime, Zeynel, fetch my guitar, quick!"

It was a fine, thoroughbred instrument that had been presented to her by an Andalusian guitarist appearing at the Cristal, Beirut's smartest nightspot. Dreamily, Selma remembered the time when men could still pay homage to her beauty. How long ago it seemed. . . .

"Let's sing! And no more feeling sad or sorry!" Standing with one foot propped on a chair, she struck a few chords and began to sing in her warm, resonant voice. "Two loves are mine: my country and Paris. . . ." She had only seen Josephine Baker and Tino Rossi at the movies, but so often that she knew every one of their songs, every single intonation, by heart. *"Ah, Catarinetta bella, chi, chi,"* she sang cajolingly, *"écoute, l'amour t'appelle, chi, chi, pourquoi refuser maintenant, aha, ah, ah, ma belle Catarinetta!"* Her two companions delightedly beat time.

"Ssh!"

Two dumbfounded faces were peering into the room: two of Rani Aziza's attendants. Their eyes widened in disbelief at the spectacle of the princess singing. Terrified, they gestured to her to stop, but Selma only sang on, louder still: *"Si j'avais su en ce temps-là, ah, ah, ah, ma belle Catarinetta!"*

They fled. Another two maidservants came, and another two, but they only made Selma sing with even greater gusto. Tonight she felt like exploding – tonight she would have defied the entire world.

"What is going on?"

The voice was like a whiplash. Selma fell silent. Rani Aziza had walked in and was staring at her.

"I am enjoying myself, sister. I often play the guitar and sing. I presume you don't mind."

"Not I personally, but you must think of the ignorant creatures around us. To them, music and singing are symptoms of a dissolute life. That professionals, women of no account, should act this way is acceptable – Lucknow is a city devoted to the arts – but that their mistress the Rani should do so they consider scandalous."

"Let them be scandalized. I am doing nothing wrong."

"Right and wrong are relative notions that vary from place to place. I repeat: it is unacceptable for you to play music here. You will shock people – you will forfeit their respect, and their lack of respect will impinge on Amir. And that I shall never permit."

The implication was obvious: your music or your marriage.

"Come, be reasonable." Rani Aziza's tone became honeyed. "You are beginning a new life, my dear. You must learn to reap its advantages, which are considerable, and accept its few drawbacks."

She walked out before Selma could reply, not that she would have known what to say. Much as she detested the Rani, she had to concede that she might be right on this one point. But what had she meant by "considerable advantages"? Was she alluding to money? Was that the weapon they were going to use against her, again and again?

The little party had lost its momentum – all the fun had gone out of it. Selma sent the other two away. Her one remaining desire was to sleep.

She dreamed that her handsome husband had slipped into bed beside her and furtively kissed her forehead, and that she had impulsively opened her arms and nestled against him. How smooth his skin was, and how good it smelled! And now he was caressing her: planting kisses on her cheeks, her throat, her shoulders, murmuring that he loved her. There was something awkward and touching about him, she thought – almost like a puppy. She felt like laughing. Could one laugh in one's sleep? But then. . . .

She opened her eyes. Amir was bending over her, his face taut and strained in the gloom. He resembled a swarthy archangel.

"Amir!"

She held out her hands. Could he see her? His eyes looked so strange and blurred, like the reflection of a mirror in a mirror. Why didn't he put his arms around her? Why did he remain so motionless?

"Amir, love me," she murmured plaintively.

She did not know exactly what she meant by that. She knew only that she needed reassurance, needed to exorcise the violence she felt lurking everywhere.

His long, slender fingers seized her neck and lingered there, toying with it, then slowly his hands glided beneath the lace of her nightgown and cupped her breasts, fondled them, and then. . . .

"No!"

She sat up with a jerk. There were five red weals on her right breast. She stared at them, then at him. He was insane – she had married a madman!

Amir had shut his eyes. When he opened them again their metallic glint had gone. His smile was warm and disarming.

"Forgive me, my love," he said haltingly. "You are so beautiful, I lost my head. I have dreamed of you for so long. . . ."

He cradled her in his arms and gently, almost shyly, brushed the scratches with his lips.

"Don't be angry with me. Those marks are a tribute to your beauty and its effect on me. Not many women can boast of having unleashed such storms. I am ashamed and happy at the same time. I have never experienced anything like this."

Selma studied him through her long lashes. He seemed genuinely abashed. Little by little she yielded to his caresses and relaxed. He looked at her so lovingly she felt ashamed of having doubted him.

"I love you," she smiled at him.

Amir clasped her to him very tightly, as if afraid of losing her. She had always thirsted for affection. Her kalfas had scolded her as a child for flinging herself at them and smothering them with kisses. Such familiarities were frowned on at the Ottoman court. At most, her father patted her on the cheek. As for her mother, kissing her children on the forehead was as much sentimentality as she ever permitted herself.

Slowly, Selma was sliding into the river and allowing its gentle eddies to carry her along. A warm breeze had sprung up. It ruffled her hair, lifted her nightgown, caressed her belly. Stars danced in the darkness behind her eyelids. . . .

Suddenly, a sharp pain jolted her out of her dream. She looked at Amir; his face was tense, his eyes shut. Was he in pain too? She tried to release herself. What was he doing? Why didn't he stop? He was hurting her!

"Stop!" she cried, but he didn't hear. Panic seized her. She lashed out and rent him with her nails, striving to break his hold, but he did not seem to notice. She flopped back on the pillow, exhausted. Tears blinded her – tears less of pain than of surprise and anger: for the first time in her life she had to yield to superior strength.

Amir moaned and went limp. Frantically she tried to extricate herself from the heavy body that was crushing her. She had to escape, to go and wash herself to sluice away the blood and sweat and vileness.

She pushed him off, ran to the bathroom, and turned the taps full on. Then she washed herself furiously, as if trying to scour the shame from her skin. Would she ever be clean again? Was that what people called love? No, it could not be. A man who loved a woman gazed at her, spoke to her tenderly, was considerate of her feelings, forever close to her. Selma had read forbidden French novels and overheard married women exchanging confidences: she knew what love meant.

She was feeling sick, but not in the least like crying. And still the blood continued to seep from her. It seemed that she would never stop washing this body of hers, which suddenly disgusted her; she had a wild desire to chastise and mutilate it for provoking so much horror.

What if she died? What if she were bleeding to death – what if Amir had killed her? For a moment she savoured the delicious thought. What sweet revenge, what a beautiful picture: the Sultana in tears, and she, Selma, pale as wax in a spotless shroud, heartbroken to see her mother weeping. "Forgive me, Annéjim, I did not do it on purpose. . . ." How they would grieve for her, poor things. . . .

A worried voice from behind the curtain: "Are you feeling ill, my dearest?"

"No, I will be with you in a minute."

Quick, a bit of cotton, a clean nightgown, most of all conceal the hurt. She had no intention of begging for love.

Amir was lying sprawled across the bed. He smiled at her voluptuously, totally unaware of the drama he had provoked.

"Happy?"

She nodded, averting her eyes. Her seeming shyness enchanted him.

"Come here."

He drew her unresisting body gently toward his. Docile and inert, she felt as if her nerves and muscles had deserted her. He ran his hand over her belly and laughed contentedly when she gave an involuntary shiver, convinced that he had rekindled her desire for him.

"Give me a few minutes to recover," he said.

She flushed. "But I did not mean. . . ."

He laughed all the louder. How she hated his complacency!

"This pretty little belly of yours is going to make us some fine sons, eh?"

Selma felt infinitely weary. She did not even have the energy to feel sick any more, only to take note of what she was destined to be from now on: a belly to produce heirs for the state of Badalpur. She did not balk at the idea; she simply failed to understand how she, Selma, could have come to such a pass. As though in a dream she heard her old self retaliate.

"Fine sons – or pretty daughters!"

The man beside her laughed again.

"Daughters too, if you want, but sons first."

She had the distinct impression that he was not joking, that it was an order.

Fascinated, she stared into his eyes, which seemed to be stretching and stretching, more and more, while his face narrowed into an almost triangular shape. . . . She uttered a sudden cry: the menacing face so close to hers was that of the Cobra God!

Utterly incapable of moving, she felt his gaze slowly suck her in. Resist. Take refuge in her innermost self. With all her force she clenched her fists, trembling with the effort, and managed to lower her eyelids. Safe!

From far away an ironic voice reached her ears. "You seem exhausted, my dear. With your permission, I will bid you good night."

With a graceful nod, the Rajah disappeared.

But the cobra? Had she dreamed it? Was she going mad?

CHAPTER 4

A foretaste of eternity, a foretaste of hell . . .

For two whole weeks, seated on the Rani's gold bed, Selma had to endure visits from all the countless relatives, friends, neighbours, and gossiping women who came to observe her marital bliss at first hand. Those who had met her before the wedding could not refrain from remarking how much lovelier she looked. "She was so pale. Look at those pink cheeks and shining eyes, those rosebud lips. Even her figure is fuller! Truly, love works wonders, and our handsome Rajah is a magician!"

They laughed, joked, envied her. Endlessly chewing pan coated with a thin film of silver, they commented on her jewels and garments one by one. A bride was expected to show off the finest items in her trousseau, albeit with modesty: Selma had to change her clothes several times a day to satisfy the women's voracious curiosity.

Beaming as if her own personal triumph were being celebrated, Rani Aziza played hostess. Artistically arranged on silver-gilt trays, pyramids of balaiki gilorian – cones of thick, fresh cream whipped up with nuts and flavoured with cardamom – were accompanied by various halvas compounded of flour, dried fruit, and honey, and mutanjan, a confection of venison, all of them sweet things traditionally served at wedding feasts.

After being invited to do so seven times – Lucknow prided itself on the strictest etiquette in all India – the women feasted on the food, their delighted expressions conveying that the palace cooks had lived up to their high reputation.

Selma was condemned to watch this succession of culinary marvels with a wistful eye but leave them untouched: a young bride was supposed to be too sated with happiness to have an appetite.

Fortunately for her, these celebrations were soon to be cut short by Muharram. The period of mourning was dedicated to the memory of Hussein, the Prophet's grandson, whom the soldiers of the tyrant Yazid had killed in 680 with all his family. For sixty-seven days, Shia Muslims would be mourning the man they regarded as Mohammed's spiritual heir, the first three caliphs revered by the Sunnis being, in their view, usurpers.

Muharram brought sixty-seven days devoid of festivities,

jewellery, and finery, just funeral processions and majlis or prayer meetings at which cantors skilled in lamentation moved all present to tears by recalling the massacre at Kerbela and chanting the virtues of the martyred Hussein and his family. Lucknow was renowned throughout India for the poignant beauty of its religious ceremonies.

That year Sir Harry Waig, governor of the United Provinces of Agra and Oudh, was feeling apprehensive. The ninth and tenth days of Muharram, when the mourning reached its climax, would this year coincide with Holi, the great Hindu spring festival, and there were fears that the two communities might come to blows.

The inhabitants of Lucknow were tolerant people, however. Pleasure-loving by nature, they took an extremely sceptical view of anything with pretensions to seriousness, notably politics, and the riots that had disrupted other parts of India for several years had not spilled over into their city. In fact, many Muslims deplored the unfortunate coincidence that would prevent them from taking part in the Hindu festival, as they did every year, and spraying each other with red and pink dye to bring good luck. This coincidence was equally regretted by many Hindus, who made a habit of joining the Muharram procession, partly for the sake of the spectacle and partly in devotion to a great religious martyr. That the religion was not theirs did not matter: they believed that all religions were merely "different paths to the same Reality."

But in the spring of 1937, when the whole country was still in a ferment after the first provincial government elections, and when Jahawarlal Nehru's Congress Party and Mohammed Ali Jinnah's Muslim League were squabbling over the composition of those governments, the smallest incident might trigger an explosion.

Sir Harry had accordingly decided to implement Ordinance 144, which prohibited the carrying of weapons, called up police reinforcements, and banned public meetings and demonstrations. Since there could be no question of banning religious processions as well, it had occurred to him to purchase several tons of barbed wire from the army with a view to keeping the two communities' processions apart. His Indian subordinates, whom he took care to consult, confirmed the brilliance of this idea.

Sir Harry had served in India for twenty years and knew it well. Unlike most of his compatriots, who were irked by its heat, humidity, and, above all, its teeming masses of dark-eyed, dark-skinned inhabitants, he loved this strange country, which he had once described, when feeling poetic one evening, as "a black diamond in the heart of the Empire."

Although his appointment to Lucknow was an honour and a mark of trust – the United Provinces, which embraced Allahabad, Nehru's birthplace, and the great Muslim university of Aligarh, were central to India's political life – it meant social oblivion. Sir Harry, and, more particularly, his wife Violet would have preferred Bombay, Delhi, or even Calcutta. In those metropolitan cities the British community had managed to re-create a home of its own with just the right dash of exoticism, and even the Indians – those with whom one mixed socially, of course – having largely been educated at British universities were less . . . well, less Indian.

Lucknow, by contrast, had remained terribly "native" and seemed, for some strange reason, to glory in the fact. Sir Harry deplored this all the more because it had once been the cultural beacon of northern India in succession to Delhi, whose sovereign, the Grand Mogul, had been deposed by the British army. Renowned for magnificent festivals attended by leading artists, and celebrated as the pearl of the "Ganga-Jumni" civilization, so called after the two rivers that traversed it, the Ganges and the Jumna, the river of gold and the river of silver, Lucknow symbolized the fusion of Hindu and Muslim traditions encouraged by the Shia ruling class.

Today it was just the capital of a province, even if its rajahs and nawabs, enthusiastic sponsors of poetic contests and concerts, helped to preserve some of its former decadent splendour.

His Excellency the Governor did not attend these functions, at which exclusively male audiences listened enthralled to interminable pieces of music or improvised poems sung with one monotonous voice.

During his early years in India Sir Harry had tried to initiate himself into such things, partly from curiosity and partly because of a well-meaning disposition that made his compatriots smile. Although he had a sound knowledge of Urdu, however, this type of poetry remained a closed book to him, either because the words employed were too abstruse, or because the imagery struck him as meaningless, if not ridiculous. As for the music, he found it irresistibly soporific.

In any case, he had very soon grasped that attempting to understand the Indians' tastes, interests, and customs was no way for a Briton to gain their friendship, still less their respect. Was it the result of a hundred and fifty years of colonization that had taught them to admire and envy Western values and manners, even if they sometimes rebelled in an unpredictable way against this mental servitude? Or was it their pride which convinced them, maybe rightly, that no foreigner could ever fathom what lay in the depths of their souls, nurtured on an entirely different set of age-old traditions and modes of thought? To each his proper place: such was the principle that had governed Indian society since time immemorial.

The most perfect illustration of this was the caste system from which no Hindu could ever escape. Sir Harry had given up trying to understand this "fatalistic attitude." According to the Vedic scriptures, actions performed in a previous life determined whether one was born into a noble priestly or warrior caste or born an untouchable. To rebel against this just arrangement would be sacrilege and could only entail a worse fate, such as being reincarnated as an earthworm or a cockroach. Conversely, an untouchable who lived in strict accordance with his status, accepting its humiliation and degradation with serenity, was assured of a more favourable caste in a future life.

This attitude was so deeply ingrained in the Indian mentality that the Muslims – whose religion was based, like that of the Christians, on equality – had been influenced by it over the centuries and had developed a kind of caste system of their own. An Indian Muslim was either ashraf, noble, or ajlaf, of no consequence, depending on whether he was descended from the Muslim conquerors or from Hindu converts of inferior caste.

The young Harry Waig's idealism and democratic notions were definitely unappreciated in India, and His Excellency Sir Harry Waig had come to the conclusion that it was just as well. The caste system at least guaranteed stability to a social structure that would otherwise have had every reason to explode.

To each his proper place. . . . It was as futile for one of His Majesty's representatives to try to comprehend an Indian as in former times it had been for a master to try to comprehend a slave – futile and dangerous. This did not, however, preclude the existence of relations between them which were all the more "amicable" because each knew the rules of the game and its limits – and there were, thank heaven, a lot of upper-class Indians who had assimilated those rules.

Sir Harry prided himself on having built up a substantial network of personal connections in Lucknow, unlike many of his colleagues, who avoided mixing with the natives except at work and official functions. A broad-minded man, he detested racial prejudice, the more so because, where certain Indians were concerned, "if it were not for the colour of their skin you could even forget they were Indians!" Most of the latter were aristocrats brought up in England like the Rajah of Jehanabad, president of the National Agricultural Party which represented the great landowners, a perfect gentleman who organized splendid tiger hunts; or the Nawab of Sarpur, who served nothing but French champagne at dinner; or the Rajah of Badalpur, a brilliant young man who had just succeeded on two fronts: getting himself elected to the legislative assembly and marrying an Ottoman princess.

His Excellency took a long pull at his favourite briar pipe. "Young Amir's quite a chap," he remarked to his wife. "We must have him to dinner. I'm curious to meet that Sultana of his. . . ."

The palanquin threaded its way through the dark streets, gently swaying to the rhythm of the porters' swift, supple strides. Selma peered through the black curtains embroidered with silver teardrops. Tonight was the ninth of the month of Muharram, the night when Hussein and the last defenders of Kerbela had died, and half the city's inhabitants were heading for the Great Imambara to weep and pray in remembrance of them. Thousands of devotees had also poured in from neighbouring towns and villages. For nowhere was Muharram observed with greater pomp and fervour than in Lucknow, India's Shia centre ever since the kings of Oudh, who were of Iranian origin, had made it their capital in 1724.

Several hundred yards short of the Great Imambara, the crowd was so dense that the porters slowed to a halt. They tried to make further progress by shouting, kicking, and using their elbows, but tonight these time-honoured claims to precedence were invalid: no longer a prince or a pauper, you were simply one believer among many. The Rani and her companion, the noble Begum, would have to walk.

Selma, only too delighted to do so, was just about to get out when an anxious voice recalled her to reality.

"Your burkah, Princess!"

Begum Yasmin had reminded her just in time. How scandalous it would have been to go unveiled in the presence of all these men!

"I forgot," she said, half annoyed, half disconcerted. "I'm not used to it yet."

"You'll soon learn, especially when you discover that our burkah is really an aid to freedom."

An aid to freedom, this black silk prison whose only access to the outside world was a mesh-covered rectangle at eye level – what did this amazing woman mean? The Begum took Selma's hand.

"Trust me. I know how difficult you are finding your new way of life, but I am here to help you. Shall we be friends?"

She gazed at Selma fixedly, her eyes unexpectedly blue-grey in her dark face. If she were not beautiful, she was certainly impressive.

About thirty-five years old, she was tall and slender – unlike most of the women here, who doubled in size almost as soon as they got married. Begum Yasmin made such a forceful impression that Selma could not decide whether she found her fascinating or alarming. Amir seemed to hold her in high esteem; she was the wife of his best friend.

The porters carved a way through the crowd to the edge of the huge courtyard, the holy place from which men and women, like two diverging black rivers, set off to pray apart. In the background loomed the imambara, its hundreds of arches ablaze with gold chandeliers and crystal candelabra. Once a year the giant mausoleum emerged from its torpor, dusting itself off and dressing up like a king on his coronation day to celebrate the triumph of self-sacrifice and death.

"Hussein! – Hussein!"

The incantation rose from the black-robed crowd, as raw as a sob, as fervent as a call to arms. As if one, the mourners rhythmically beat their breasts, slowly at first, then faster and faster. With mounting abandon, on and on they went, gasping for breath, their faces ecstatic until finally the full force of their passion was suddenly unleashed.

"Hussein! – Hussein!"

Swift and staccato, the chorus swelled, soared skywards to the minarets' corbelled balconies, rose to the stars, permeated the depths of the heart. As calmly as if they were treading a silken carpet, penitents made their unhurried way on a path of glowing embers. The spectators watched with bated breath, enthralled by this miracle of faith.

High above the crowd in his minbar[1], the maulana called for silence. With his sonorous voice, he had the crowd in the palm of his hand as he recalled the last moments of the Prophet's grandson, the final, heroic battle, the blood spurting from a thousand wounds, the spear-thrust, the supreme sacrilege, the horror. His listeners hung on every word, sobbing and groaning. He soothed them, lulled them, then galvanized them once more, whipping them into an extremity of grief.

Several camels with black trappings were led forward. "Behold," cried the maulana, "behold the camels of the martyred caravan! Yazid's soldiers have killed all the menfolk, not even sparing a baby six months old, and the women, the women of the Prophet's family, have been taken captive."

1 Pulpit in a mosque.

"Ya Hussein!" The chanting began again, a muffled, fierce sound. Fists belaboured breasts, nails lacerated flesh. The drama was reaching its climax. No suffering could ever equal that of the martyrs of Kerbela. . . .

Selma had been resisting the atmosphere with all her might, scornfully at first – *Typical of the Shias, this delirium; working themselves up into an absurd, hysterical frenzy! Thank goodness Sunnis do not have anything like this!* – and then with self-mockery: *If my French friends could only see me now!* She enlisted happy memories of Beirut, drew on her reserves of cynicism, carried disrespect to the lengths of blasphemy – resorted to anything that might combat the insidious thrill of the moment, but in vain. Unbidden tears streamed down her cheeks, blinding her. Why? What did Hussein's fate matter to her? She had never regarded him with any special veneration. If the crowd had been mourning the death of Jesus or Buddha with the same fervour, she would have wept just as bitterly. She gave up trying to control herself, stopped trying to think. Emotion engulfed her, sweeping reason away like a tidal wave. She no longer felt an outsider; she was at one with this multitude, absorbed into this great, palpitating body, carried away from herself, at peace.

Dawn had broken, illuminating the pale, exhausted faces around her. The ceremony was over. It was time to go to sleep, but only for a few hours. Then the festivities would start again.

"My dear, there is no question of your going out. Last night was a different matter – no one could have recognized you in the darkness. To be honest, I only agreed because Begum Yasmin went with you. She is a sensible woman – I knew you would be safe in her company. But today neither she nor any reputable woman would venture out into the streets."

"But the procession, Amir – I am told it is a splendid sight."

"It is. The contingents from the princely states look magnificent, ours especially. What spoils everything are the hordes of primitive wretches that follow behind, making an exhibition of themselves. If you really must watch, why not do so in comfort from the main veranda? You will be able to see everything perfectly from behind the moucharabié. My elder sister will keep you company, I am sure. For some obscure reason, women seem to love the sight of blood. . . ."

He was gone before Selma could ask what he meant. She shrugged. If he had seen her weeping last night, he would surely have thought her mad. What a disconcerting man he was! Could he really be so indifferent to what stirred the emotions of his people – was he really as insensitive as he wanted to appear?

The veranda was already occupied by Rani Aziza's attendants, who had staked their places early that morning and were waiting expectantly. Although Selma would have preferred to sit elsewhere, the place of honour beside the Rani was hers by right, and when she appeared, dressed all in black, Selma could hardly spurn her gesture of invitation.

Distant at first, the sound of funeral drums was drawing nearer. Clouds of dust went up as a file of elephants lumbered into view, caparisoned in black. Standard-bearers, seated on their backs, brandished the colours of the princely states, together with flags captured on the field of battle and devoutly handed down from generation to generation.

Then, swaying leisurely along on camelback, came riders bearing sacred banners embroidered with verses from the Koran and surmounted by a big bronze hand. Was it the hand of Abbas, Hussein's half-brother, whose hands had been cut off for having fetched water to slake the thirst of his beleaguered kinfolk, or was it five fingers of one hand, a symbol of the Shia pentarchy: the Prophet Mohammed, his daughter Fatima, his son-in-law Ali, and their two sons, Hassan and Hussein? Who could tell, and what did it matter to the fervent crowd of onlookers?

The bandsmen's red coats provided the one splash of colour, though turbans were of black muslin. Playing an insistent, mournful, monotonous lament, they paved the way for the solitary figure of Zuljinah, Hussein's horse, a picture of exhaustion and despair with its drooping head and bloodstained saddlecloth.

The crowd surged forward to touch this beast, the imam's last surviving companion; and to caress the tazzias, replicas in coloured wax or gold and silver paper of Hussein's tomb at Kerbela; to stroke the red-stained cradle of the murdered baby, and the banners steeped in the blood of martyrs. Eager to share their agony and partake of their self-sacrifice, the crowd wailed and beat their breasts while singers mimed and narrated the heroic end of Hussein's family.

Last of all came the penitents: men, youths, even children. Stripped to the waist and carrying lengths of chain with five fresh-sharpened steel blades attached, they halted below the veranda.

"Hussein!" the crowd shouted.

"Ya Hussein!" the penitents replied.

As one man, they brought the chains down on their bare backs, gashing the flesh. Blood spurted everywhere.

"Ya Hussein!" They whipped themselves in time to the chant, ever harder. The gashes became wounds, blood streamed down their legs and formed black puddles in the roadway.

"Ya Hussein!"

One man collapsed, then a youth who was little more than a child. They were quickly borne off on makeshift stretchers. The hail of blows redoubled. The penitents were now lashing themselves in a frenzy, chests heaving, unconscious of anything other than their pain and their demented, desperate attempt to escape the body and attain the ultimate state of unity with the One.

Would they never stop? Selma had shrunk back in horror, but she could not tear her eyes away. There was a taste of blood in her mouth, and she felt sick and faint. Beside her, the Rani was impassively sipping a cup of tea while her ladies in waiting commented on the spectacle through mouthfuls of crystallized fruit. Selma stood up, anxious to leave, but the Rani, without so much as turning her head, caught her by the arm and firmly forced her to sit down again.

"It is not over yet. You must see it all, right to the end."

She said this as if giving an order, with narrowed eyes, her lips set in a peculiar smile.

The crowd had fallen silent. The flagellants staggered off to catch their breath and sponge their wounds before resuming the macabre ceremony below another veranda, where other women would look on curiously, nibbling sweetmeats.

"Hussein! Hussein!"

No triumphant battle cry this time, it was a long-drawn-out murmur tinged with respect and fear. A small group of men had appeared carrying drawn swords. The hushed crowd looked on as they took up their positions.

"Morituri te salutant. . . ." Selma shook her head, irritated. Why did the phrase obsess her so?

And then, with absolute precision, the swords came down on the penitents' heads, slicing through the scalp. Blood streamed into their eyes and mouths, blinding and choking them. In silence they raised their swords and struck again. Their faces were already so thick with blood that only their staring eyes could be distinguished. One man's sword slipped and sliced off an ear, leaving a black hole with blood spurting out. The crowd gasped, transfixed by the sight. At the third swordstroke a man collapsed face down and lay there inert with his skull split open.

Whistles shrilled as men in khaki uniforms forged their way through the crowd, batons flailing. Having disarmed and handcuffed the stunned, unresisting swordsmen, they hustled them into army trucks and drove off before the startled spectators had time to react.

"It was only to be expected," said the Rani. "The government had forbidden it. Too many of them die every year, but how do you prevent a man determined to kill himself?"

Her philosophizing was lost on Selma, who was vomiting into one of the damascened spittoons.

"How odd of Sir Harry to invite us to dinner tonight of all nights. Doesn't he know we are supposed to be in deep mourning?"

Selma, seated at the dressing table, checked her mascara, retouched her powder, and dabbed some perfume at the base of her throat. She was as happy as a lark: this was to be her first night out since their wedding!

"Perhaps it is his English sense of humour," Amir said dryly, adjusting his tie for the umpteenth time.

He had decided to wear European dress tonight. It was an informal dinner, not an official function, and he felt more comfortable in it. Selma, on the other hand, was wearing a sari of heavy blue Benares silk. A gharara, however gorgeous, would have been inappropriate and overly traditional, if not dowdy. The more urbane Muslim ladies had abandoned it in favour of the Hindu dress, displaying a broad-minded attitude of which Amir, being a man of modern and secular outlook, approved.

Lining the steps of the governor's residence, a brilliantly illuminated building enclosed by spacious grounds, were turbaned soldiers with faces like dark brown marble. These Indian Army sepoys were the successors of those who had mutinied and massacred Lucknow's British garrison in 1857, thereby setting the whole of northern India ablaze. Studying their expressionless faces, Selma wondered what they were thinking and where their allegiance lay. It puzzled her that they should continue to serve the British now, in 1937, when all India was demanding independence.

Sir Harry Waig had absolutely no misgivings on the subject. "Those men are devoted to us," he declared, adding with a sly smile, "Anyway Indians are pacific by nature, and when they fight, they prefer to fight among themselves."

To Selma's surprise, none of the men present disputed this statement. They merely laughed. She felt ashamed for them.

Nonetheless the evening had begun well: foie gras and Sauternes followed by pheasant washed down with a heady Burgundy. His Excellency was an impeccable host and very attentive to the ladies. Selma had almost forgotten how much she enjoyed the company of men, especially when she kindled that little spark in their eyes. She felt like a woman again.

But why had they started talking politics? Sir Harry, whom she had found an intelligent and charming companion only minutes before, now struck her as smug and pompous. Not content with discoursing on Muharram to these Muslim princes and describing the Shiites as "fanatics," he had the gall to apply that term to Islam as a whole.

The Rajah of Jehanabad, who prided himself on being a better judge of Scotch than any Scot, would never have contradicted him, but what of the Rajah of Dilwani and the Nawab of Sharpur? Those perfect gentlemen, who had assimilated all the British mannerisms but kept their wives in the strictest purdah, preserved an embarrassed silence.

"What about you, Amir? I always think of you as a rationalist *par excellence*. What do you think?"

"Our people are illiterate, sir, that is why they are so attached to their religion. They don't have anything else to cling to – or rather, they didn't until recently."

Amir said nothing more. His meaning was plain enough. The two men exchanged a challenging stare. After a moment's hesitation the governor decided to laugh.

"My dear fellow, if the people who are demanding independence were all like you, we would leave here tomorrow, satisfied that our two countries would remain friends because they would share the same interests and ideas. But given the type of hotheads in charge of the so-called nationalist movement these days, it is our duty to protect your people from themselves."

Amir gave a frigid little bow. "Very good of you, Your Excellency."

A young man at the end of the table, the only guest wearing a shirwani[2], intervened.

"Sir, we all approve of the measures you have taken to prevent clashes between Hindus and Muslims, but had it occurred to you that Easter falls in two days' time? May we take it that the Catholics' processional route will also be fenced off with barbed wire?"

His tone was courteous and guileless in the extreme, but the governor flushed.

"I don't see that that should be necessary," he said curtly.

Selma bit her lip. She flashed a smile at the young Indian and in a soft, sweet voice entered the fray.

2 Long coat with mandarin collar, similar to a stanbulin.

"Your Excellency," she inquired mildly, "is it true that in Spain penitents go out into the streets every year and whip themselves till the blood flows to commemorate the death of Christ, just as the flagellants do here in memory of Hussein?"

Sir Harry glowered at her. "There is a fine distinction there, Princess," he spluttered, "and I fear you have not quite grasped it."

That effectively put an end to the discussion. Here was the old root of the British sang-froid: that unshakable sense of their own superiority, a superiority so evident there was no need even to discuss anything. A Frenchman – Selma thought of those she had known in Beirut – would have exploded at such provocation. Less sure of himself, he would have made strenuous efforts to convince, in the process making himself look ridiculous, but at the same time so much more likeable.

"What did you think of the last polo match?" someone interjected. Yes, polo – that was a suitably harmless subject to divert the course of conversation. Suddenly everyone was interested in polo and the governor forgot his ill-humour.

When dinner ended the gentlemen retired to the smoking-room and the ladies to the small drawing-room, where Lady Violet served camomile tea. Aside from the hostess, none of the ladies present had understood who this beautiful young woman with the French accent was, but His Excellency had been most attentive to her and addressed her as "Princess," which was enough to make her charming. One little fair-haired woman, bolder or more inquisitive than the rest, took the plunge.

"Tell me, Princess," she said, pleasurably rolling the title around her tongue, "is it long since you left France?"

"I have never been to France," Selma replied, puzzled for a moment. "Oh, I suppose it is my French accent," she added, seeing the look of surprise on the others' faces. "The fact is, I was brought up in Beirut."

"Ah, Beirut," sighed another lady, "the Paris of the Middle East! The French have certainly succeeded in civilizing those people. I suppose your father was a diplomat or an army officer?"

"I do not think my father ever did much except take an interest in his horses," Selma said. She could not quite grasp the point of the conversation.

The ladies nodded. "Naturally," said one, "being a prince. . . ."

"He was only a damad. My mother is a Sultana, you see."

Damad, Sultana? Something was wrong: was she making fun of them?

"So you aren't French at all?"

"Oh no. I am Turkish."

Turkish! A dozen lips curled disdainfully. So she *had* been tricking them! But how had she acquired that pale, porcelain skin? The Turks were a swarthy race, everyone knew that. Her mother must have had an affair with a British soldier during the occupation of Istanbul. . . .

One charitable soul tried to rescue Selma from her embarrassing predicament.

"You mean," she said, "you are a Turk of Greek descent – a Christian, in other words?"

"Not at all," Selma said indignantly. "I am a hundred percent Muslim Turkish. My grandfather was Sultan Murad."

That made no impression at all. In the view of these middle-class ladies, a Muslim Turk, Sultan or not, was scarcely fit to polish a Briton's boots.

"So what are you doing here all by yourself?" the charitable lady inquired compassionately.

"I am not all by myself, I am married."

To a Frenchman, no doubt. Perhaps she was socially acceptable after all. . . .

"My husband is the Rajah of Badalpur."

Married to a native? But of course! Being a Turk and a Muslim into the bargain, what more could she expect? They all turned their backs, suddenly remembering that they had a whole host of personal matters to discuss. The charitable lady engrossed herself in her embroidery, not daring to address another word to Selma for fear of being ostracized by her friends.

Not even at the French school in Beirut had Selma found herself the victim of such blatant racial prejudice. Astonished at first, she could not help smiling: to think that in Istanbul these civil servants' wives would never even have dreamed of approaching her! It was really quite funny. . . .

Or was it? Suddenly she was not so sure. She was fortunate, she had been brought up to be proud of her race and social status. But what of those into whom a sense of inferiority had been instilled for generation after generation – those who had become convinced that the colour of their skin, their religious beliefs, and their different way of life rendered them subhuman?

Her desire to laugh deserted her. Till now she had looked upon the European as an adversary whom her countrymen had fought on equal terms, or almost, so that their defeat had stemmed from concrete, quantifiable factors such as inferior equipment, a ruined economy, and political and strategic blunders – all regrettable but acceptable matters. In the course of this evening, however, she had discovered something far more shameful and unacceptable: a people who submitted because they were fundamentally convinced of their own inferiority, even if they proclaimed the opposite; a people who demanded independence but had lost their soul, and whose only real ambition was to resemble the masters of whom they claimed they want to be rid.

She hated them all: Amir and his ultra-English friends, Sir Harry, who honoured them with his friendship, and Lady Waig, who had just now been gracious enough to come over and talk to her. Never had she felt such hatred.

"Be careful, my dear," Amir told her in the car as they were driving back to the palace. "You smiled at that young Indian – quite innocently, of course, but you do not know those people. They may get the wrong idea."

Those people. . . .

Although no riots occurred in Lucknow itself during Holi[3], disturbances were rife in the surrounding towns and villages. At Patna, Bareilly, and Ratnagiri, the two religious communities clashed, most of the time for trivial reasons: in one case because Hindu musicians had "deliberately" played their flutes and drums outside a mosque while the mourners were at prayer, in another because some Hindu youngsters, carried away by the excitement of the spring festival, had sprayed the tazzias with coloured water. The most serious incident occurred near Aurangabad, where eight hundred Hindus armed with cudgels and pitchforks surrounded a Muslim village whose inhabitants had slaughtered an ox to mark the end of Muharram. The villagers were rescued by the police, but not before a score of men had been killed or wounded. Muslim public opinion accused Nehru of supporting the violence by declaring that he could not pass an abbatoir without sympathizing with those who were horrified by such things. It also bitterly reproached Gandhi for keeping silent and preaching nonviolence toward the British alone.

On both sides, resentment was steadily mounting; mutual intolerance becoming more entrenched.

3 A Hindu festival in which red-coloured water is freely thrown.

CHAPTER 5

The setting sun had turned the water in the fountains to molten gold. Selma, reclining on the white marble beside it, was enjoying her first few breaths of cool evening air. No maidservants ever came to disturb her here in this walled garden on the edge of the zenana, which had become her private retreat. This was where she daydreamed, wept, and wrote her mother letters saying how happy she was.

It was two months to the day since her wedding. Two months only, yet it seemed an eternity. She sat up in sudden torment, wondering what she was doing here – what she was doing with her life. Tea parties and yet more tea parties with multitudes of women, pleasant women to whom she could find nothing to say, Zahra's innocent chatter, endless contention with Rani Aziza. . . . And Amir . . . Amir by day, Amir by night, the handsome Rajah and perfect gentleman preoccupied with politics and the administration of his state, and the big, swarthy body, silent, greedy, insensitive. After the shock of that first night she had become inured. Inured . . . a horrible word, but how could she help it if her husband was blind, deaf, and dumb?

Footsteps on the flagstones. Who would dare to intrude on her?

"Ah, Zeynel! Dear Zeynel, why such a long face?"

"Your pardon, Princess, but I cannot stop thinking of the Sultana all alone in Beirut. Her state of health. . . ."

Poor Zeynel, what a worrier he was! Annéjim's two kalfas tended her day and night, but it was true that her stroke had left her almost as helpless as a baby. Selma could not resist teasing the eunuch gently.

"You mean you are planning to desert me? Don't you love your Selma any more?" Seeing him flush and bite his lip, she promptly regretted her flippancy. "Come now, I was only joking. I agree – it's time you went back to Beirut. I'll feel easier in my mind, knowing you are with my mother."

He looked at her, as if in despair.

"But what about you, Princess?"

"Me? You presumptuous old man! You do not imagine you are indispensable, do you?" She laughed deep in her throat. "Can't you see how pampered I am here? You must tell Annéjim that no wife could ask for more."

Zeynel had tears in his eyes. "At least promise to let me know if anything goes wrong," he said, "and I'll come back right away."

"I promise, but now stop fretting or I'll lose my temper, and when I lose my temper. . . . Oh Zeynel, do you remember my tantrums when I was little? You used to tell me my nose was growing longer – you used to say I was beginning to look like Sultan Abdul Hamid! That did the trick. . . . Come, sit down here beside me. Tell me something: do you think we will ever see Istanbul again?"

He made no reply, knowing that she did not expect one. She merely wanted to share her memories. He was her only link with the past; that was why she would miss him, and that, perhaps, was why it would be better if he went.

"I almost forgot, Princess: Madame Ghazavi wants to talk to you."

"Does she want to go too? She's right, there is nothing for her to do here."

Selma was sick of Madame Ghazavi's eternal complaints and criticisms, and the woman had been sulkier than ever since Zahra had told her off for being a troublemaker. In any case, total solitude would be easier to bear. Her life was here from now on. Nostalgia was for weaklings and imbeciles, not for her. There was so much to be done in this country, so much to be done for its people. What did Rani Aziza matter? *She* was the Rani now.

Zeynel and Madame Ghazavi almost missed the train. A suitcase lost then rediscovered at the last moment had allowed everybody to avoid emotional farewells. Now they were safely on board. Down on the platform, in the sweltering heat of a May morning, Selma smiled at them. Amir had found it incomprehensible that his wife should feel it necessary to accompany her "domestics" to the station. Poor Amir!

"Goodbye, my Princess. . . ."

Zeynel, puffy-eyed with weeping, stood at the window waving his handkerchief. The train got under way, gathered speed. "Goodbye!" he called, again and again. "Goodbye!" Selma had a lump in her throat. Because they were leaving, or because she was not leaving with them?

"Don't be sad, you have friends here too."

Begum Yasmin took her hand and gave it a gentle squeeze. Selma turned. She had forgotten all about her, though it was thanks to her that she had been able to go to the station in the first place. Amir would never have agreed if Begum Yasmin had not prevailed on her husband to talk him into it.

"I understand your distress – everything is so new to you. Amir is a fine man, but he is not the easiest person. Come and see me any time you are feeling lonely. I would be only too happy to see you."

"She is so devoted!" thought Selma. "Strange – at the beginning I did not trust her at all."

During the next few days she visited Begum Yasmin often, at first for want of anything better to do, then because she began to enjoy her company. The atmosphere at her home was so much more relaxed than that of the palace. More interesting, too. An intelligent person with an inquiring mind, Begum Yasmin had collected a little coterie of educated women whose intellect counted far more with her than their social status. She was no aristocrat herself, having come from a family of university teachers and writers, and her husband, indisputably the finest lawyer in Lucknow, was a self-made man. They were now very wealthy. Every feature of their luxurious home bore witness to this, but without ostentation. It was modern, comfortable, and unencumbered by relics of the past. Had it not been for the Begum's strict observance of purdah – her salons were restricted to women – Selma might almost have thought herself back in Beirut.

Amir welcomed his young wife's new-found friendship as a sign that she was beginning to adapt – to take on the rhythms and customs of local society. He himself was too preoccupied with affairs of state to devote much time to her.

In order to win the peasants' votes, the Congress Party had incited them against their princes, whom it branded as enemies of the independence movement. Congress propagandists were particularly active in provinces where the largely Muslim ruling class opposed a policy it considered dangerously pro-Hindu and had reacted by turning to Ali Jinnah's Muslim League. Many peasants had rebelled against their administrators and refused to pay taxes. Grain stores had even been looted in the state adjoining Badalpur. Things in Badalpur itself seemed quiet for the moment, but the Rajah's secret police reported that outside agitators had begun to hold secret meetings in the villages.

Selma, to whom he at last confided his misgivings, expressed surprise. "Why don't you go there yourself?" she asked. "You could assess the situation and talk to the peasants in person."

"Talk to the peasants?" he chuckled at her naiveté. "What would I tell them – that they are being manipulated? They wouldn't believe me. Besides, it would disturb the existing equilibrium and show them that I'm worried. They would be bound to take advantage of the fact. The weakest man will rage against a master who seems weak – I thought the history of the Ottoman Empire would have taught you that."

"What it taught me was that if the Sultan had been less remote from his subjects they would not have allowed Kemal to overthrow him. I am afraid you are making the same mistake."

He leaned toward her, gently laying his hand on her arm. "You think I am a despot, don't you? I was even more of an idealist than you are, once upon a time. . . ."

It would have taken more than a few religious riots and peasant revolts – incidents that one could not even imagine – for Lucknow's high society to forgo its amusements. The kite-fighting season had come around again. For two weeks now, the entire city had been spellbound by these hard-fought aerial contests, in which every princely family and aristocratic household took part. Lucknow was noted for such duels, which could go on for months, and people came from far and wide to watch them.

On Begum Yasmin's terrace the women were gazing up at the sky and eagerly discussing the course of the latest dogfight. Selma had never seen them so animated. One of them pointed out the Rajah of Mehrar's kite, which was fringed with gold thread and adorned with ten-rupee bills. Whoever caught it, kept it: that was the rule. The Rajah had already lost some fifty kites this season – not surprisingly, since they were heavy and unmanoeuvrable – but he did not care. His kites were not meant to win; they were meant to surpass all others in beauty and publicly display his wealth and generosity.

"They say he is almost bankrupt," remarked someone. "They say he will end up like Yussuf Ali Khan."

Nawab Yussuf Ali Khan was a legendary figure who, fifteen years earlier, had sold forty-eight villages to defray the upkeep of his stables. He had owned a hundred thousand kites and used to challenge all Lucknow to single combat every year. The most famous contest had lasted six months. He had even had the idea of attaching little lamps to his kite tails rather than break off for the night. His son, who had inherited his passion as well as his debts, was taking part in every contest and had earned himself a considerable reputation, though friends claimed he did so only out of filial respect. He had married a wealthy cousin and was now busy squandering her fortune.

Many people had ruined themselves at this game. It cost a great deal to build such elaborate kites and enormous sums were wagered in spite of the Islamic ban on gambling. But those who ruined themselves accepted the fact philosophically because the popularity and respect they gained would guarantee them a lifelong place of honour in Lucknow's smartest set.

"This really borders on the ridiculous," thought Selma, but she could not help being fascinated by the spectacle of these huge coloured birds hovering gracefully in the sky, then swooping on an opponent and skilfully severing the string that anchored it to the ground. Techniques had steadily developed in the course of time, she was told. Not only were kites lighter and stronger every year, but their strings became ever more murderous: dipped in egg white and studded with small, razor-sharp fragments of glass, they were formidably effective.

"In the old days people were content just to fly them," said Begum Yasmin. "Their beauty was an end in itself. Some of them represented mythical figures. The Hindus, in particular, used to make effigies of their gods. Then the vogue for kite-fighting spread here from Delhi and we adopted it, probably because it was the only kind of warfare we were capable of waging. . . ."

The Begum's present guests were unlike those whom Selma usually met at her house. These were the wives and daughters of Oudh's highest nobility. When Selma had remarked to Amir on Yasmin's wide range of social contacts, he had laughed and said she was an astute diplomat and a valuable asset to her husband. How did he know? He had laughed again.

"The telephone, my dear, that devilish device condemned by our maulvis. Truly devout Muslim women refuse to use it, and they are right: a voice can sometimes reveal much more than a face and encourage improper thoughts. . . . Don't be annoyed, though, my relations with the Begum's voice are purely professional. I am in regular touch with her husband, as you know. He is not just my best friend. He is my legal adviser as well."

Selma already knew this, of course, but she felt a trifle jealous all the same. Some of these women in purdah wielded an influence that many of their European sisters might have envied them. Their husbands led an active public life and made important decisions, but it was they who really held the reins of power. The anonymity of the veil made them all the more redoubtable and effective. Their thirst for power was unbounded as they lived in a dream untrammeled by reality, and their husbands were the instruments that enabled them to manipulate the outside world.

The Begum sent for a silver box inlaid with gold – her pan box, the most indispensable item in any Indian household. Divided into a number of compartments, it contained the various ingredients necessary to the preparation of this national delicacy. The Indians could not do without their pan, and it was claimed that, if the British really wanted to paralyze the independence movement, destroying the betel fields would bring the entire population to its knees within twenty-four hours.

Selma had never understood the appeal of this bitter, fibrous plant. She watched the Begum carefully select the greenest leaves and coat them with a little shell lime and some katha, the bark extract that gave the pan its red colour and extreme bitterness. Then, having added several small fragments of betel nut, a pinch of tobacco, two cardamom seeds, and – for the benefit of some – a little opium, Begum Yasmin folded the leaves into a perfect cone and presented her handiwork to some specially favoured guest.

Chewing pan was a custom that went back to Indian antiquity, but it was undoubtedly in the Moghul court that it first acquired its aristocratic pedigree. When the Sultan wanted to show his appreciation for loyal service, he would give, in addition to the usual sumptuous gifts, betel leaves.

Selma, who preferred the hookah, savoured the Begum's delicious tobacco as she reclined against a nest of cushions. Nowhere save here in Lucknow had she ever encountered such a divine preparation. The tobacco was blended not only with molasses, which imparted a faint flavour of honey but with various spices and perfumes whose exact recipe was a carefully guarded secret.

Through half-closed eyes Selma surveyed the women reclining in her vicinity. All of them had partly undressed because of the heat, and some were delightful to look at. They combed their long, sleek hair, massaged each other's legs, arms, and shoulders with the freedom permitted them by the absence of male company, joked together, exchanged confidences, radiated contentment.

A woman with white skin and blue eyes was sitting a little apart from the rest and watching them with a trace of amusement. Selma had been told that she was the new wife of the Rajah of Nampur, who had married her for her beauty, even though she was not of royal blood. Her mother, Selma's informant had added with a disdainful pout, was English. Catching Selma's eye, she got up and came over.

"I have been longing to meet you," she said, sitting down beside her. "How do you find it here? Not too strange, I hope?"

Selma took to the young Rani at once, partly because of her charming, open face, but also because the others ignored her. She longed to ask her if it was difficult being half English, and if she did not suffer from divided loyalties, but experience had taught her that race was a delicate subject in India and she was afraid to offend her.

"You simply must pay me a visit and meet my mother-in-law. She is an extraordinary woman with a passion for politics and a great admirer of Jinnah and the Muslim League. She does not waste her time on affairs like this – she says we women have a part to play in the future of this country."

"You mean she does not observe purdah?"

"Of course she does. What difference does it make?"

Selma was puzzled. Begum Yasmin had said much the same thing the other day. Just at that moment she came over.

"You naughty girl," she told the Rani, "you are monopolizing my guest of honour! Come and sit with me, Princess."

Selma detected a note of irritation in her friendly tone. Could she be jealous?

Night was falling. Maidservants brought oil lamps and big copper trays laden with food. Outside, kites soared and swooped in the sky like balls of fire.

"Look how beautiful it is!" the Begum said eagerly, sitting down beside Selma and putting one arm around her waist. "See how fast that little kite travels – it is bound to catch the big one. See, I told you so!"

She was trembling. Selma, a trifle surprised, discreetly tried to release herself, but the Begum was holding her tight and she did not want to seem unfriendly. Privately, she chided herself for feeling embarrassed. Had the nuns brought her up to be so prudish that all physical contact struck her as indecent? It was so natural here, this lack of inhibition, this innocent display of affection between women – so natural and so much more wholesome. Christianity had spoiled everything. Islam was not ashamed of the body; that would be an affront to the Creator.

The Begum had jumped up and was circulating among her other guests. Selma felt remorseful. How could she have doubted the purity of her friendship, even for a moment?

Trot, my beauties! Faster, faster!

The carriage made its way along the peaceful avenues of Kaisarbagh past flower-filled gardens and palaces slumbering in the afternoon heat. Quickly, though there was nowhere to go, nothing to do but enjoy the breeze filtering through the blinds. It was only four o'clock, and the afternoon would be a long one. Selma was on her way to Aminabad Market to choose some rose garlands. They were always at their freshest there.

They passed through the West Gate and entered the narrow streets of the old city. Here the horses slowed to a walk to avoid fruit sellers squatting amid their baskets, cows majestically taking their ease in the middle of the roadway, and half-naked children daring each other to run between the wheels.

Aminabad Market was a huge square flanked by ochre buildings with ornate balconies and arcades sheltering hundreds of booths and stalls. It was the city's largest and busiest commercial centre, discounting Hazratganj, which boasted smart stores selling imported goods and was patronized almost exclusively by the British colony. Selma liked to stroll from one establishment to another, having a look at the shopkeepers' wares, making them unpack everything, sometimes without buying. Nobody minded – it was an accepted custom: lady customers were entitled to be choosy, and fat shopkeepers enjoyed trying out their sales technique on a woman with skin as white as Selma's.

She had eventually resigned herself to wearing a burkah, but as soon as she was out of sight of the palace she undid the strings, removed the veil, and the horrid black tent became a long, extremely elegant cloak. The maidservant accompanying her would never have given her away for fear of instant dismissal. Selma had chosen the girl as her personal attendant because she was new and not yet under Rani Aziza's thumb. Although no word of complicity had ever passed between them, Selma showered her with little presents.

The market was comparatively empty, half the shops being shut. Selma wondered if this was a holiday. But how could it be? Muharram did not end until the following day. In a small park not far from the mosque, a man was addressing an attentive audience seated on the ground at his feet.

Suddenly, without warning, the other end of the square was invaded by a yelling mob. A hundred or more strong and armed with an assortment of clubs and cudgels, the rioters overturned stalls and struck out indiscriminately at old men, women, children – anyone in their path. The people in the little garden had risen and were calmly preparing to defend themselves.

"Huzoor! Come quick!"

The frightened coachman tugged at Selma's sleeve. Looking around her, she saw that they were alone: the square had emptied in a matter of seconds, the shopkeepers had closed their shutters. She dived into the carriage just in time. Stones had begun to fly and shots could be heard. The horses reared in terror, the coachman bellowed and lashed them with his whip. Through the blinds Selma could see buildings on fire and people running madly in every direction. In a few minutes, the square had become a battleground.

The horses bolted, foaming at the mouth. Terrified pedestrians flattened themselves against the walls as they galloped past. Selma shut her eyes and braced herself for the worst. Finally the carriage jolted to a halt and the coachman's face appeared at the window, deathly pale and streaming with sweat. The maidservant was sobbing in a corner. It would be better not to return to the palace in this state if they wanted to avoid awkward questions.

"We'll go to Begum Yasmin's house," Selma decided. "It is not far. But first, Ahmed Ali, tell me who those rioters were, Muslims or Hindus?"

The coachman hung his head in disgust.

"Well?"

"They were Muslims, Huzoor, all Muslims. There were no Hindus."

Selma irritably repeated her question. The man had been so frightened, he obviously did not know what he was saying.

"They were Muslims, I assure you, Huzoor, but not good believers. They have been fighting in the old quarter for two days now, but I never thought they would come to Aminabad, so near the palaces."

"What are they fighting about?"

"The Sunnis started it. They atacked a Shia religious procession, claiming that it was an affront to Hazrat Omer, the second caliph. A score were killed and hundreds wounded, including women and children. Part of the old quarter was burned down. Of course the Shiites were not just going to accept this without retaliating. The old quarter is under curfew now, but no one can understand why the police took so long to step in. . . ."

Selma sank back against the cushions, utterly appalled. As if there were not enough hostility already between Indians and British, Hindus and Muslims. . . . Now it was Muslim against Muslim! That was all this country needed!

Begum Yasmin's drawing-room was more than usually animated this afternoon. The newspapers had just announced the happy culmination of a love story, which for months had dominated conversation, alienated friends, divided families, provoked tears, stirred the imagination, and aroused enthusiasm or indignation from one end of the British Empire to the other. Some called it courage and an example of all that was noblest in man, others condemned it as cowardice and a betrayal of the country and duty: Edward VIII, the King Emperor, having already abdicated for love of a twice-divorced

American, was about to seal that love by marrying her on 3 June at the Chateau de Candé in France.

As Selma walked in, a plump little woman was holding forth: "Ah love, love. . . ." Love! What did she know about love, Selma wondered irritably. What did she herself know about it, for that matter? Sitting a little apart from the rest, she was surprised to see these Indian women so enthralled by the private life of a royal family whose country had dominated their own for a century and a half and still maintained an army that arrested, imprisoned, and sometimes killed those who resisted that domination.

In recent days, despite the bloody clashes taking place between Hindus and Muslims throughout the province, the royal love affair had remained the principal topic of conversation. Disgusted by it all, Selma had preserved a polite silence, but today she had had enough.

"What does it matter, all that nonsense?" she burst out. "Look around you – look at what is happening in your city, outside your very windows: people are killing each other. *Muslims* are killing each other! I have just come from Aminabad – I was nearly lynched there!" Her composure suddenly left her. She could hardly breathe. The women scurried to her side, calling for cold water and smelling salts. When she had calmed down sufficiently, she continued. Her audience was stunned, disbelieving. "Between *Muslims*?" Nothing like that had happened since the 1908 prohibition of public recitation of the Mad-e-Sahabah, a Sunni text praising the first caliphs and regarded by the Shiites as insulting to their martyrs. They countered by reciting the Tabarah, a work in which the caliphs were depicted as usurpers. What would happen now? Was it all going to start all over again?

Begum Yasmin shot an unpleasant look at Shahina, the young Rani of Nampur.

"It's another manoeuvre on the part of the British, no doubt. They foster internal division simply to be able to reply, when we demand independence, that they would like to oblige us but they cannot till we settle our differences."

"In my opinion," Rani Shahina retorted calmly, "it's a ruse on the part of Congress, who want the Muslims to be divided and incapable of defending their interests against Hindu supremacy."

Rani Shahina's husband was a leading member of the Muslim League, whereas Begum Yasmin's was one of the few Muslims to have sided with the Congress Party in the belief that India should get rid of the British first and settle their internal problems later. The women's political arguments were the reflection of the personal rivalry between their husbands.

To defuse the atmosphere, someone wondered aloud which princes would be going to London for the coronation of the new king. Politics was instantly forgotten as the ladies, with shining eyes, compiled a list. It included the great Maharajahs of Gwalior, Patiala, Jaipur, Indore, and Kapurthala, the Nizam of Hyderabad, of course, and a whole prestigious delegation led by the old Maharajah of Baroda. Nilufer and Durushevar were bound to be going, thought Selma. She wished the British would invite her so she could snub them by refusing, but she knew she would not have that satisfaction. She suddenly resented the fact that Amir was not the prince of a more important state.

On 12 May, George VI's coronation day, Lucknow was gaily decorated with flowers and coloured lights. Tonight's reception at the governor's residence promised to be a splendid affair, and every aristocrat and dignitary in the city would be attending to express best wishes for the health and prosperity of the new king Emperor.

Amir, wearing a ceremonial shirwani, knocked at Selma's door.

"Aren't you ready yet? Hurry up, or we will be late."

Selma looked him in the eye.

"You can leave as soon as you like. I am not going."

His jaw dropped. "You don't understand. You cannot offend the governor like that. What on earth is the matter with you?"

"You don't understand?" she said. "Well, *I* don't understand how you and your friends can bring yourselves to attend this thing. What about all your speeches attacking British colonialism and supporting the struggle for independence? It's just hot air, isn't it? As soon as the governor snaps his fingers you all come running. You are prepared to celebrate the coronation of a foreign ruler you claim you want to get rid of with just as much enthusiasm as if you had chosen him yourselves!"

Amir's face reddened. No husband could tolerate such an insult from his wife. He took a step toward her, then restrained himself and clenched his fists.

"You are mistaken, Princess. India is not Turkey. The British have done a great deal for this country. We simply think we are capable of governing ourselves from now on. We are not at war with the British, but negotiating an orderly transfer of power."

"You call it negotiating when British soldiers are carting the negotiators off to prison and firing on their supporters?"

"That's the fault of that madman Gandhi, who persists in stirring up trouble when everything could be settled amicably." Amir paused. "So you won't come? Very well, don't!"

And he strode out, feeling furious and vaguely ill at ease.

CHAPTER 6

The journey from Lucknow to Badalpur had once been a major undertaking. For three whole days, elephants wearing the colours of Badalpur State would cover the hundred or so miles at a slow, lumbering walk, followed by palanquins borne by eight sturdy porters and camels laden down with heavy packs.

The caravan would set off at dawn and call a halt at midday, when the heat became unbearable. Once the servants had erected some huge tents in open country and covered the grass with carpets, everyone slept till sunset. Then, when the air cooled, the caravan resumed its journey, swaying along beneath the stars with a protective screen of armed guards on either flank.

Today the trip took four hours in Amir's white Isotta Fraschini, which was as spacious as a small drawing-room with its bar and mahogany drop-leaf tables, its tea service and cut glass decanters filled with rose water. A few old princes still clung to the majestic, romantic travelling habits of yore, but Amir, somewhat to Selma's regret, was a modern man who liked to get places fast and in comfort.

He did, however, make one concession to tradition and public entertainment: the car pulled up a mile short of the state border to enable the royal elephants, which had set out at dawn from the palace of Badalpur, to escort it the rest of the way.

Amir proudly explained to his young wife that although Badalpur no longer counted for much, with its capital of thirty thousand inhabitants and its two-hundred-odd villages, it had once been among the greatest states in India.

"Our resources were drained by all the wars my ancestors fought against the powerful Mahrattas of Deccan, and later against the British. After the mutiny of 1857 my great-grandfather lost two thousand six hundred villages, an area the size of Switzerland. A British general wrote in his memoirs of the time that the Rajahs of Badalpur should never be trusted: 'They pretend to accept our authority, but they will always rebel.'" Amir gave a rather wistful laugh. "That is our greatest claim to fame. But a few years later we became subject to the Crown[1]."

1 Between the Indian Mutiny in 1857 and the granting of independence in 1947, the

The car was now gliding majestically along beneath arches of foliage and flowers, preceded by six elephants with gold trappings and the Rajah's band playing the state anthem. The crowds of Hindus and Muslims lining both sides of the route bowed silently as the procession passed by. There was no clapping or cheering. In this country of noisy multitudes, silence was the supreme form of homage.

Amir sat motionless and aloof in the front seat. It mattered little that the British had been the true masters of the country for nearly a century; to his subjects he remained the all-powerful sovereign, the source of all grace and favour. In the back, concealed by brocade curtains too heavy for the breeze to disturb, Selma peered out at her people, who were not entitled to set eyes on her, their Rani.

The crowds became even thicker on the outskirts of the capital. Beneath the red stone arch at the entrance to the town, an old man touched his forehead repeatedly as a mark of respect. Then, plunging his hand into a bag, he provoked a near riot by showering the spectators with rupee coins. Amir, with a face like stone, affected not to notice, but Selma heard him mutter. "What the devil does that old fool Hamidullah want out of me, demonstrating his generosity like that?"

The cortege entered the main street, which was flanked by shops decorated with streamers in the state colours. There were portraits of the Rajah everywhere. Women on balconies sprinkled the car with rice, a symbol of prosperity and fertility, crying, "Rajah Sahib *zindabad*! Long live our Rajah!" Some young girls were so carried away that they broke into cries of "Rani Sahiba *zindabad*!" Long live our Rani! But their elders hurriedly silenced them, outraged by this public and highly improper allusion to the sovereign's wife: "May he not hold it against us!"

The car emerged from the town and headed for the palace some ten miles beyond it. Until the last century the Rajahs of Badalpur had lived in the old fort in the centre of the town, but one summer night, whether by accident or criminal design, the fort and part of the old quarter surrounding it were gutted by fire. For the sake of peace and quiet as well as safety, the Rajah of the day had proceeded to build a new palace in the country, in front of a lake covered with water-lillies.

This palace, shielded from the gaze of outsiders by high walls,

majority of the princely states had come under British control. They had to pay taxes and were subject to restrictions on the levying of troops for internal use. Although the Rajahs remained sovereigns in name, they were really answerable to the British governors or residents for the smooth running of their states.

stood in the midst of a Mogul garden. Its white arches and openwork balconies were surmounted by a green and gold ceramic frieze incorporating horns of plenty, spears pointing at the sky, and a wealth of creatures such as peacocks, tigers, and fish. The terraces surrounding it on all four sides looked out over fields and villages, and, in the north, afforded a distant view of the bluish foothills of the Himalayas. Some way from the main palace stood three smaller palaces which seemed to have been abandoned. The old Rajah had built them for his wives and the wives of his heirs, but today they served as guest-houses.

Selma loved her new estate immediately; its tranquil whiteness, its flower beds traversed by streams of limpid water flowing along miniature canals lined with mosaic, its shady walks bordered by evergreen shrubs, its palm trees standing out against the sky like birds with ruffled feathers. . . .

Drawn up in force outside were the members of the palace guard, some fifty men with dark blue tunics and turbans, well-waxed moustaches, and long Mauser rifles dating from the last century. A small army of servants, their white robes set off by dark blue sashes and turbans, stood bowing at the foot of the steps, flanked on one side by grooms and mahouts, cooks and kitchen boys, gardeners, barbers, butlers, and footmen. Also present, though in the background, were the more lowly servants, who performed the menial tasks. To Selma's considerable surprise, the women drawn up on the other side of the steps were unveiled. There were only about twenty of them – laundresses and ladies' maids, all exclusively at the Rani's service.

"Huzoor, what a pleasure, what an honour!"

A little ball of red silk had bustled up to Selma and was smothering her hands with kisses. It was Begum Nusrat, wife of Amir's prime minister, who had met her at the station the day she arrived. Her husband the diwan, a dignified-looking gentleman in a black shirwani, was talking with Amir. Selma wondered why he had not greeted her.

She might have been invisible. None of the men present, whether dignitaries or servants, seemed to notice her at all. Although their attitude was evidently a mark of respect, it gave her the unpleasant impression that she did not exist. She would simply have to get used to it. At least it was preferable to wearing a burkah. The black prison was not *de rigueur* at Badalpur, as it was in towns where fathers and husbands insisted on shielding their women from indiscreet glances. No one here would have dared to take such a liberty. Here she was not a woman: she was the Rani.

"Come, Huzoor," Begum Nusrat said eagerly, "Rani Saida is

anxious to meet you, and I must make the introductions. It would not be proper for the Rajah to do so. A husband and wife must never appear together – it is unseemly. If the wife is with her mother-in-law, and her husband is announced, she must cover her face and leave before he enters."

Rani Saida . . . Amir's grandmother had governed the state from the seclusion of purdah during his years in England while Rani Aziza ran the palace at Lucknow. Selma was curious to meet this masterful old lady.

Begum Nusrat escorted her up a marble staircase, through a little reception room stuffed with armchairs and gilt console tables, across a council chamber furnished in the oriental manner with low divans, Persian carpets, and Kashmir tables, and into the former throne room, where Selma was proudly invited to admire the massive ivory throne carved with hunting and battle scenes and surrounded by cabled columns supporting a canopy of indigo velvet. Never had she seen anything more hideous; she made no comment, and transferred her attention to the ancestral portraits covering the walls. All the rajahs of Badalpur were there, from the earliest, who had ascended the throne in 1230, to Amir's father, who had died in 1912. The family resemblance was remarkable. Examining them more closely, Selma had to suppress a sudden, almost irresistible urge to laugh: all these monarchs, spanning seven centuries of human history, had been painted by the same man, a certain Aziz Khan. Either he must have been exceptionally long-lived, or Amir's father, having felt the need to provide himself with this flamboyant gallery of ancestors, had forgotten to obliterate the artist's signature. Pride and disarming naiveté mixed . . . was that also Amir? Selma dismissed the thought. She had never thought of Amir in such terms before, and it made her uneasy.

"Come here, my child."

Selma warmed to the old lady at once. She was dressed in white, as befitted a widow, and wore no jewellery. Her sole adornment was a comb set with turquoises, the Shias' favourite stone, which gathered her snow-white hair into a knot on her neck.

"Come and give me a kiss."

Blue eyes sparkled in a pale face whose contours were softened by a fine mesh of little wrinkles. She could only be a Kashmiri, Selma guessed, for nowhere else in India were women so fair. She wondered why the old Rajah had imported a bride from so far afield when it was considered customary and diplomatic in his day to form alliances with neighbouring states.

She bowed respectfully but was clasped to the old woman's ample bosom. A delicious scent of wistaria blossom enveloped her. Selam felt she had come back home. The Rani took her by the chin and looked her over carefully.

"I was afraid you would be merely pretty, but I can see you are far more than that. Amir is a lucky man. He needs a wife like you. You will help him, won't you – you will give him the reassurance he needs when I am no longer here to do so?"

Selma must have looked surprised.

"I know what I am talking about," Rani Saïda said. "From the age of six, when his parents died, he was surrounded by courtiers who flattered him to his face and laughed at him behind his back. Being a perceptive and precocious boy, he instinctively sensed this. I was the only one who expected nothing from him. Even Aziza took care never to cross him, for fear that he would hold it against her later on."

The old woman paused for a moment, lost in thought.

"And then, when he was fifteen, he suffered a terrible emotional shock. His paternal uncle, whom he adored, tried to poison him and take over the state. For weeks he shut himself up in his room and refused to see anyone but me. 'I do not want to be a Rajah,' he kept saying. 'I want to go far away where no one will know me – where someone may love me for my own sake.'"

Selma shivered. How often had she had the same thought: of wanting to be an orphan, with no noble name and no ancestry, but sure of being loved for herself alone.

"That was when we decided to send him to England," Rani Saida went on. "We did it to guarantee his personal safety, but also to restore his mental balance. The death of his parents, which unconsciously he took as an abandonment, the duplicity of his courtiers, his uncle's treason, and, to crown everything, an unhappy infatuation for a cousin who was making eyes at him but secretly seeing someone else – all that had sapped his self-confidence, and broken his will to fight on against the odds – in short, his manhood. When he left us he was a nervous, suspicious adolescent. He came back a man, spirited and energetic but level-headed and rational at the same time – perhaps a little too rational. I always feel he is frightened of his emotions, and so he holds them in check. Has the wound really healed, or has he simply learned to hide it? Poor Amir, how I wish he would allow himself to be happy!"

The old woman looked at Selma with tears in her eyes.

"Promise me you will help him!"

The heat at the end of June was overpowering. Both humans and animals scrutinized the sky, always so hopelessly blue. They knew that it would remain that colour for weeks to come; it would be unreasonable to expect that the monsoon would break so early in the year, not unless God took pity on those parched fields, that cracked soil, those exhausted creatures dragging themselves around in that furnace.

Twenty times a day Selma immersed herself in a big copper tub of cold water – a delicious few moments of relief that made her feel human again – but as soon as she got out the moisture on her skin evaporated and the wall of heat closed in once more.

Stretched out on her bed and careful to move as little as possible, she greedily turned her face to catch the faint puffs of air dispensed by the punkah, an archaic swinging fan operated by a boy squatting outside on the veranda. The palace did have electricity – Amir had installed the latest model of huge steel fans on his return from England – but the generator had been out of commission since their arrival, and Selma had given up all hope of ever seeing those big, shiny blades revolve instead of glaring balefully down at her from the ceiling.

In spite of the scorching heat, however, Badalpur appealed to her far more than Lucknow. Life was simple here, out of range of Rani Aziza's machinations and the intrigues and gossip of a big city. Amir, too, seemed more relaxed, despite his official duties. Early in the morning, when it was still relatively cool, they would both go riding through the nearby fields and forests, sometimes accompanied by Zahra, her clear laughter ringing through the dawn. Intoxicated with freedom, the Rani and her young sister-in-law galloped along while astonished peasants turned to watch them pass.

This was the first summer the Rajah had ever spent at Badalpur. Normally, all those who could escape the heat of the Indo-Gangetic Plain fled to the luxurious Himalayan hill stations. Even the Viceroy and his civil servants moved out and took up their summer quarters at Simla.

But this year the countryside was in ferment, because of the Congress Party, and Amir had thought it wiser to remain on the spot. The peasants of Badalpur had no particular cause for complaint. Their Rajah was a just man, and more generous than most of the neighbouring rulers. If the harvest had been poor he refrained from demanding taxes in full, and if a man had run up debts because of illness or the cost of a daughter's wedding the Rajah would often pay off the village money-lender himself. For the past few months, however, men who knew how to read and write had come from the cities and claimed that no taxes should be paid at all, and that the peasants were entitled to keep their crops, down to the last ear of maize and grain of wheat. The peasants did not believe it, of course, and would never have dared to mention it to the Rajah, but it made them think all the same.

Meantime they confined themselves to pleading that rain, cold, heat, or drought had rendered them incapable of paying their taxes this year. Accordingly, having convened his advisers and talked things over with the diwan, the secretary of the treasury, and the chief of police, Amir held open court every morning. There was no need to request an audience: anyone, whether landowner, the village headman, or humble peasant, could air his problems and request the Rajah's assistance or his mediation in a dispute.

Selma liked watching Amir receive his subjects. She would slip out on to the terrace and watch. Amir would sit just below the main veranda dressed in a white muslin kurtah embroidered with seed pearls. Two turbaned servants fanned him while half a dozen armed guards stood motionless at his back – more for appearance's sake than from any real necessity, Amir admitted. After all, the people were coming to see their Rajah; they should not be disappointed!

One morning Selma was surprised to see a woman among the petitioners – what was she doing there? Disputes were invariably settled between men. The lower part of her face was concealed by a piece of black cloth, which lent it a curiously flat appearance. This was also unusual: peasant women habitually went unveiled because they had to toil in the fields beside the men. The veil and seclusion were actually status symbols proving that a woman had no need to work.

The woman in the black veil was surrounded by gesticulating men, who seemed to be abusing each other. Other men joined the group and gave evidence in turn. The Rajah listened gravely and asked a few questions. At length he passed judgement: the woman's husband was to pay her family damages of three rupees. The men walked off with the woman trailing silently along in their wake.

"What was that all about?" Selma asked Amir when he finally joined her for breakfast.

"Oh, nothing much," he replied. "The husband accused his wife of being unfaithful and punished her by cutting off her nose. She swore she was innocent, and her family lodged a complaint."

Selma was horrified. "What!" she exclaimed. "Only three rupees for cutting off her nose?"

"She got off lightly. If she were guilty, he could have killed her without my having the right to punish him. That is the custom."

"But what if she were innocent?"

"She was still guilty of behaving in a way that aroused suspicion and dishonoured her husband's name."

Selma stared at him in dismay. It just was not possible that her husband, with his public school education and progressive outlook, could approve of behaviour more suited to the Middle Ages. Amir noticed how upset she was.

"It was the only ruling I could have given. If I had been harder on the husband, no one, not even the woman and her family, would have understood."

"But that's just it! They have to be made to understand, and you are the only person who can do that."

"Change their mentality, you mean? You're joking! It would take centuries. In any case, who am I to pass judgement on their moral code, still less try to change it? The most I can do is ensure that it is observed."

"But you cannot approve of it, surely?" Selma's voice shook.

"Don't worry, my dear," he said, giving her a sidelong glance. "I would sooner see you dead than mutilated. These people have no aesthetic sense, but on many other matters" – he dreamily toyed with his amber beads – "I am no longer so sure they are wrong. . . ."

The village of Oujpal was less than a mile from the palace. From the terrace Selma could make out the cluster of mud walls and thatched roofs enclosing the inner courtyards where women squatted over fires and prepared chapatis, those flat disks of unleavened bread which, together with onions, formed the basis of a peasant meal, if not the meal itself.

Discounting her rides with Amir, Selma had not once left the palace precincts in the week since their arrival. She was beginning to feel like an exile from real life – the sort of life that went on in that village, where women busied themselves among children at play and men talked endlessly over glasses of tea while graceful girls with copper pots balanced on their heads fetched water from the well, followed at a distance by groups of young men trying to look indifferent.

For the first few days Selma had been content to bask in the novelty of it all: the beautiful landscape, the picturesque white palace, the feeling that she was at last "the" Rani, and not just a foreigner whose whims were tolerated. Now, especially since Zahra's return to Lucknow to continue her studies, time began to drag. She wanted to fill it, but how?

She confided in Rani Saida, who suggested that she might care to receive some of the local women in audience – in the afternoons, as their mornings were devoted to housework or helping in the fields.

"Let it be known that any who want to come may do so, and that you will try to help them." She laughed. "I warn you, there will be so many of them you will not know which way to turn. But you are right, my child – it's your duty as their Rani. I used to do the same, but now I am too old."

Her blue eyes clouded for a moment.

"They are our children, you see – they expect everything of us. I should have liked to do more for them, but in my husband's day it was impossible, and by the time he died my enthusiasm had waned. You are young, but you have seen something of the world. You can change many things here for the better, and I shall die happy knowing that the women and children of Badalpur will not be abandoned."

Selma had a ground-floor room prepared for her audiences. As Rani Saïda had foreseen, it never emptied. Peasant women accompanied by swarms of children arrived all through the afternoon, sat down at the Rani's feet, and gave vent to torrents of words she could not understand. Begum Nusrat's eldest daughter had been to school at a convent, the best girls' school in Lucknow, so she translated the women's words into English for Selma. Two maids had also been detailed to serve tea, which they did with a very bad grace. Proud of having been chosen as the Rani's personal servants, they thought it demeaning to have to wait on dirty, primitive peasant women. Selma was adamant, however: the law of hospitality demanded that these women, who had walked a considerable way to see her, should at least be offered a cup of the milky, syrupy tea they liked so much.

Some came from distant villages. For them, white sheets were spread on the floor of a large room where they could spend the night before returning home. They liked it so much, they had no desire to leave, especially the older women who had no husbands or children to look after; so they settled in. After all, wasn't the Rani their mother and protectress? Selma was perturbed by this growing invasion. Amir would be bound to notice in the end, lose his temper, and send them all packing. What was she to do? She consulted Rani Saida, who laughed heartily.

"They cannot leave before you give them a little present, my child! Have some cardboard boxes of kebabs and burfis[2] made up and put in five rupees as well – and above all, make it clear that they are farewell gifts."

2 Little cakes made of sugar and cream.

"But . . . won't they be hurt?"

"Hurt? Of course not! On the contrary, they will be honoured. They will treasure those cardboard boxes like precious relics and show them off to their neighbours. Make sure you tie them up with nice red ribbon. Red is a lucky colour – it brings happiness."

Happiness. . . . Did any of the women who came to the palace know the meaning of the word? One after another they recounted their pitiful tales of woe: an only son who had caught cold and died despite the brahmins' prayers; a daughter repudiated by her husband because she had failed to conceive – there were said to be lady doctors in the city, but they cost money; an unemployed husband, starving children, a usurer already owed fifty rupees and threatening to seize the family home. . . . They gazed at their Rani with hope-filled eyes: she seemed so kind – surely she would help them.

For the first few days Selma granted every request. Twenty rupees here, thirty there – it took so little to alleviate such abject misery. Then she realized that the flood of unhappy petitioners was growing, that their poverty was like a bottomless pit, and that not even the state exchequer – if it were hers to distribute – would suffice to fill it. She was powerless to solve the innumerable problems piling up on top of her. How could she make these women understand that she could not help them all? They would not believe her. They would merely assume, without saying so, that their Rani was like all rich people, and that their hopes had been unfounded. They would stare at her with their sad, submissive gaze – the gaze of paupers resigned to their poverty.

"I know," Amir said sombrely one evening, when Selma confessed her dilemma, "but you will come to terms with it like everyone else. That is the sad part – the best of us end by becoming hardened. What else can we do? Live abroad, commit suicide, drink ourselves into a stupor rather than face up to a situation that would otherwise drive us mad? For nothing can justify this eternal suffering of an entire people. When I was at Cambridge I thought the answer was socialism. My friends used to laugh and call me 'the Red Rajah.' It didn't take me long to realize, when I came back, that no one here wants a revolution, the peasants least of all. Centuries of servitude have convinced them that nothing they do will ever change things."

Selma shook her head. "If that were the case, they would not be following the Mahatma."

"That's true, but they are making a big mistake. Gandhi's doctrine of nonviolence is the finest defence against social revolution the middle class could possibly find, that's why they are financing him and his followers so generously. Of course, they also want his help in ridding them of the British, who control the economy and prevent them, the baniyas[3], from filling their pockets as full as they would like. Don't delude yourself: the peasants will be just as wretched after the British leave, the sole difference being that they will be exploited by people of their own colour."

"They are already being exploited by people of their own colour – big landowners, princes."

"In other words," Amir said cuttingly, "you and me. Well, what are you waiting for? Why not put on a cotton sari and go around preaching equality and revolution? The peasants will either think you are insane or lynch you. Believe me, things are not that simple. Self-sacrifice is just another form of self-indulgence – it only makes matters worse. If you don't believe me, try it. You will see."

Among Selma's regular visitors were two beautiful girls. The elder, who looked sixteen or so, was identifiable as a married woman by the red tikka[4] on her forehead. The other, little more than a child, wore a plain white sari and no jewellery at all, not even the traditional glass bangles without which any Indian woman feels undressed. Selma was so intrigued to see them sitting side by side for hours, watching her, that she eventually asked if she could do something for them.

"No, Huzoor. We simply want to look at you. You are so beautiful, it makes us happy."

They explained that the elder of the two, Parvati, was married to a man forty years her senior. He was kind to her, he did not make her work in the fields and gave her a new silk sari each year for Diwali, the Hindu festival of lights. The younger, Sita, was a widow. Married at eleven, she had lost her husband after barely six months. She lived with her in-laws, performing household chores – though not working in the kitchen, of course. . . . Selma's heart bled for the poor little thing. She had not been long in India, but long enough to know the fate reserved by Hindus for a widow. If she was lucky enough to escape cremation on her husband's funeral pyre – suttee had been banned by the British in 1829 but was still common a century later – she led the life of an outcast for the rest of her days. Widows were held responsible for their husbands' death in consequence of sexual

3 Wealthy Hindu businessmen.

4 A mark on the forehead worn by married Hindu women. It symbolizes happiness and the age of wisdom.

offences committed in a previous existence. Their in-laws employed them as drudges and fed them on leftovers. Being impure, they were not entitled to go near the kitchen, still less share the family's meals or look after their own children.

"I'm lucky," Sita said with a smile. "I don't have any children and my mother-in-law isn't so bad. She doesn't keep me locked up or shave my head according to custom. What I really miss, though, are the festivals – I love the music and colour – but I'll never be allowed to take part in another. They say I'd bring everyone bad luck."

Selma was indignant. "What nonsense!" she told her. "Come and sit here beside me."

Sita cast an apprehensive glance at the others. She wished she were a million miles away, but she could not disobey the Rani.

"Poor child," said a woman in a gharara, very loftily. "We Muslims don't mistreat our widows. On the contrary, we think it better for them to remarry. Our Prophet set an example in that respect: his first wife, Khadija, was a widow." This elicited some murmuring among the women but no one dared say anything. After all, wasn't the Rani a Muslim?

Sita's friend Parvati stepped forward.

"Huzoor," she said, "why don't you visit our village. Many of the women would like to see you, but they don't dare come to the palace. There are the others, too, the untouchables whom the headman has forbidden to trouble you."

"The untouchables?"

"Yes, the ones we have to avoid because their very shadow would defile us. You couldn't enter their homes, of course, but at least they could see you from a distance. It would make them so happy."

Selma was at a loss. How could she tell this child that her Rani was as much a prisoner of custom as anyone in the room?

"I will come, Parvati," she told her. "I promise.

"I forbid you to go! What good do you think it would do those people to mingle with them? You would only shock them."

"I am going."

Amir was white with rage, but this time Selma refused to yield. She had given her word. She could not disappoint those village women now, making them think she really did not care about them at all.

"Nilufer and Durushevar are always visiting hospitals and orphanages."

"Not villages, though."

"You're wrong, I have seen pictures of them!"

It was a lie, but no matter, she had scored a point. The Nizam's daughters-in-law were widely admired and respected in India. Anything they did was acceptable.

Amir hesitated. "Very well, we will ask Rani Saida what she thinks."

His faith in the old lady's judgement was absolute. Having governed the state for fifteen years, she could gauge the peasants' reactions better than anyone. To him, torn between his Indian sensibilities and his European education, they often seemed an enigma.

"Let her go," the old lady told him. "Times have changed. I myself might have made fewer mistakes if I had been able to make certain that what my advisers told me was true."

The Rajah frowned. His grandmother's unconventional views never failed to surprise him, the more so because she never set foot outside the palace; but he had promised to abide by her decision.

"All right," he said curtly to Selma, "you may go, but only with an armed escort."

CHAPTER 7

"You cannot imagine what an Indian village is like," Selma wrote to her mother. "Seen from the palace terraces, the mud walls and thatched roofs look quite romantic. But when you get near them this bitter stench seizes you by the throat – the smell of human excrement you are likely to tread on if you are not careful. The peasants relieve themselves anywhere, preferably as close to the village as possible. They do not bother to be discreet about it either, on the principle that it is the most natural thing in the world – which it is, after all – so you can see them as you pass in your palanquin, squatting by the roadside with an air of profound meditation. The men, that is. I have never seen any women doing this.

"The houses have no windows, just a small door opening into the inner courtyard where everyone lives. This combines the functions of a kitchen, dining-room, and reception room, and serves in the summer as a bedroom. The house itself consists of one room, or two in the case of the better-off, where men, women, and children huddle together in cold weather. The room is quite spacious, however, because the furniture is limited to one or two charpoys[1] and a chest containing clothes worn on special occasions.

"I was intrigued to see the women kneading a kind of mud into flat cakes and sticking them to the walls of their houses. When the sun has dried these cakes, they stack them in artistic pyramids. Guess what it is that they knead so carefully with their bare hands? Cow dung! It is an excellent fuel, apparently, and used for heating and cooking. You will laugh, but perhaps it is we that are laughable, with our distaste for bodily secretions of all kinds.

"You will have read newspaper reports of riots between Hindus and Muslims, but do not worry, the villages around here are models of religious tolerance. Oujpal's population is sixty per cent Hindu and forty per cent Muslim, and the villagers get on perfectly well together. Their houses and wells are separate, being grouped around the mosque or the temple, but they visit each other's homes. Not for meals, though. The Hindus consider Muslims impure, a stigma that

1 Bed with a base of tightly strung criss-crossed string, stretched on a four-legged wooden frame.

doubtless extends to me, their Rani. They themselves are divided into several castes, all of which consider the others to be 'impure,' except for the highest caste, or brahmins, who partake of the divine essence and call themselves 'pandit' – meaning 'learned' – even if they are illiterate.

"The lowest rung of the ladder is occupied by some luckless creatures who are despised and considered barely human by everyone else. These are the 'untouchables,' who, as their name implies, have no place in society. Anyone who comes into contact with them, even accidentally, has to undergo ritual purification. They live in some wretched huts on the very outskirts of the village and perform menial tasks regarded as degrading by the others, such as cleaning out latrines or mending shoes. They are not permitted to pray in the temple or draw water from the communal well. If their own well dries up, as it did recently, the women have to walk for miles to find another.

"The first time I visited Oujpal I created a positive uproar by insisting on seeing the untouchables. I hoped it would please the poor things, but I think they were more frightened than anything else. Not of me, but of the possibility that the others would resent my breaking the rules and make them pay afterwards. Now they are used to me. If you only knew how grateful they are, less for what I give them than for the mere fact of my presence. They are so tactful too, they would never dream of offering me a glass of tea!

"So as not to defile the others' houses, I have made a habit of visiting them last. That, I think, has solved the problem. I am really happy for the first time since my arrival in India. At last, I feel useful and loved. . . ."

From then on, Selma visited Oujpal several times a week, bringing medicines, clothes, and pencils and exercise books for the children. Having prevailed on the guards to go and drink tea with the village elders, she was free to spend hours sitting with the women. They all vied with one another for the honour of entertaining her, so she had to be very careful not to hurt anyone's feelings. She did, however, have her favourites. In addition to the two young Hindus who had first invited her to the village, particularly Sita, the little widow, whom she had taken under her wing, they included Kaniz Fatma, a robust and intelligent Muslim matron whose forthright manner had earned her a number of enemies. A fine figure of a woman with an unlined face, she was the mother of eleven children, and her eldest daughter, a girl of fourteen, had just given birth to a son. Selma could not resist asking her one day how old she was. Kaniz Fatma thought for a moment.

"Let's see. I remember crying when my father went off to fight for the British at the beginning of the Great War. I must have been nearly three at the time."

Three in 1914! Selma stared at her in amazement. They were both twenty-six. . . .

One day, with a conspiratorial air, Kaniz Fatma and a dozen other women took Selma aside.

"You know so many things, Rani Sahiba, whereas we are just poor, ignorant peasants. . . ."

Selma smiled at this preamble. It had long been apparent to her that these women were wiser and more perceptive than many an intellectual, but she could not tell them so. Their admiration for anyone who could read and write was so great that they would have thought she was just making fun of them.

"We'd like our daughters to have a better life than ours," they went on, "but how can they, if they only know how to weed the fields and make chapatis? The old Rajah built a school for the boys of the village. As a result, the men despise us still more, even if they can only sign their names. Rani Sahiba, we want a school for our daughters."

They gazed at Selma, radiant with hope. In their eyes a school seemed the answer to all their ills, the gate to paradise.

"What do your husbands think of the idea?"

"We haven't told them – they would beat us. They must not know we've mentioned it to you."

"Are all the other women in favour?"

"Nearly all, but they say their husbands would never allow it. Still, if the Rajah approved, what could they do?"

Selma promised to speak to him about it, and the women enthusiastically kissed her hands. Feeling that the battle was already won, they got down to details: where the school would be built, how many pupils it would accommodate, where they would find the teachers. Their enthusiasm was infectious. The more Selma thought about it, the more convinced she became that a school was the best way of helping them.

Selma was so caught up in her new activities that when she came home in the evening to find Amir worried about the events that were shaking the world, she had difficulty keeping her mind on what he was telling her. Hitler's successes and the threat he posed for the rest of Europe, the Spanish Civil War, the British plan to divide Palestine between Jews and Arabs – it all seemed part of a completely different universe, a universe to which she no longer had any ties. Besides, she had never understood why people worried about events over which they had no control. She looked at Amir with a touch of pity, while he irritatedly thought to himself that women were like little animals, concerned about nothing beyond their own burrows.

Selma's burrow now was Badalpur, and India; so she emerged from her cocoon of indifference when Amir began telling her of his worries about the positions the Congress Party had been taking recently.

"The Muslim League is furious because the Congress Party has just decided to form local governments made up exclusively of its members. This past winter the two parties had agreed to join forces against the reactionary movements the British are supporting. It was understood that the higher-ups in the League would have a place in the government – in Lucknow there were supposed to be two League members among the seven ministers.

"But now Nehru, who is president of the Congress Party, claims it is impossible, as it is against party rules. He says that if there are going to be any Muslims in the government they should resign from the League and join the Congress Party. He even had the nerve to repeat his old line about how there are only two parties in India, the Congress Party and the government (that is, the English). Everyone else should follow. He just will not admit that the Muslim minority is worried.

"What status would that minority have in an India governed by Hindus? Jinnah insisted that this should be clearly stated from the beginning. To which Nehru disdainfully replies that there are no problems between the two communities and that the Muslim League is a mediaeval organization with no real reason to exist."

"And what does Gandhi say?" asked Selma.

"These details are of no concern to Gandhi. He's looking for *Truth*. Every morning he reads the Bhagavad-Gita, the Bible and the Koran. He thinks all men are brothers – if they do what he says and try to attain moral purity, all the problems will just melt away.

"More and more Muslims, including Jinnah, say that the Mahatma is an imposter who is using religion for his own political ends. I don't believe that. I think Gandhi is a lunatic who is chasing after a completely unrealistic utopia. But it is an extremely attractive utopia and his power over crowds is enormous. Gandhi is the spark that starts the fire and the Congress Party carefully maps out the path this fire should take. I don't think Gandhi is really aware of the way he is being used."

That evening the village elders called a meeting of all the heads of family, Hindu and Muslim alike, with the natural exception of the untouchables. Something momentous was afoot, but the women could not discover what.

The men sat there on sacks of jute, gravely passing the hookah from hand to hand. Nobody should speak without careful thought. The matter was a momentous one, and fraught with consequences for the future of the community.

"Times have changed completely," sighed one old man. "I never thought I'd live to see the day."

"See what, baba[2]? Nothing's decided yet."

"I knew it would end badly," said someone else. "No Rani ever set foot in this village before. Visiting respectable families is one thing, but sitting down with untouchables. . . . She's disgraced us – we've become the laughingstock of the whole district."

They all nodded darkly.

"She isn't a bad woman, for all that," another voice put in. "No Rani has ever been so kind to our women and children."

"You call it kind, putting ideas into their heads? She's trouble. What else would you expect from an Englishwoman?"

"She isn't English, she's a Muslim."

"Perhaps, but she's still English!"

The village headman got to his feet.

"I think the wisest of you should come with me to see the Rajah. We have to act soon, before he makes up his mind, or we won't have any choice but to obey."

Everyone nodded approvingly: the headman was noted for his ability to solve the most delicate of problems. Several elders were delegated to accompany him – without argument, for everyone knew who the wisest of their number were – and they all dispersed with an easy mind. The Rajah was, after all, one of them, in spite of his "Ingrez" education. He was bound to see their point of view.

"You should have warned me! They came to talk about 'the plan' and I did not even know what it was."

Amir was fuming. He had been made to look like a fool in front of his peasants, and all because of a woman.

"I had already mentioned it to Rani Saida – I was going to discuss it

2 Father. In India, a familiar form of address used to old men.

with you tonight."

The Rajah refrained from asking what his grandmother thought of the scheme. The old lady seemed completely under Selma's spell.

"Obviously, I had to tell them that it was only a vague idea, and that they were not to worry – there was no question of putting it into effect."

Selma jumped up, her cheeks burning. "Why?"

"Because India is not Europe, that's why. Girls do not go to school here."

"But it was not my suggestion. The village women asked me first."

Amir raised his eyebrows. "In that case our politicians are nearer the mark than I thought: India really must be changing after all." He sighed. "I would have liked to approve this school of yours, but it is just not in my power. The men were courteous enough, but I could sense they were totally opposed to the whole idea. They believe the education of women spells anarchy, immorality, broken homes, unhappy children, disrespect for tradition, in other words social ruin. I may be their Rajah, but nothing I could say would ever convince them otherwise. You'll just have to leave it at charity – which does not solve anything in the long run, I know, but I did warn you that you cannot just override them. I have enough problems to deal with without creating any more."

He went on to explain that the Congress-dominated government had just passed a law forbidding princes and big landowners to evict peasants for nonpayment of taxes.

"That means we don't have any hold over them now and since I refuse to resort to force, Badalpur will be bankrupt in a month if they decide not to pay." He stroked his moustache. "It's funny, I have always been in favour of land reform and a fairer division of wealth, but I dislike being bullied into it by those Congress bigwigs. Many of them are businessmen and industrialists far wealthier than the princes of small states like mine, but we are the ones they brand as vile exploiters of the poor. . . ."

In the ensuing weeks, the villages of Badalpur received a succession of unusual visitors. They would turn up at nightfall in twos or threes, ask to see the headman, whom they always seemed to know by name, and introduce themselves as representatives of Congress, the party that was going to drive the British out of India. They delved in their leather briefcases and brought out closely-printed documents bearing impressive seals. These, they said, were the new laws enacted for the people's benefit. At Oujpal, having gathered the men together, they announced that the hour of justice had struck: the villagers must rise against their Rajah, who was shamefully exploiting them, and refuse to pay their taxes. Under the new law, they could not be evicted or even prosecuted; they need not fear any unpleasant consequences. If the Rajah tried to intimidate them, Congress would come to their aid.

The peasants listened open-mouthed. Some were tempted but sceptical – how could they trust a bunch of city strangers whom they had never seen before? – others were openly hostile: these agitators would only get them into trouble; their Rajah was more powerful than any so-called Congress Party. Besides, they had no quarrel with him. He had always been fair and understanding in his dealings with them.

"Your Rajah, fair?" the strangers' spokesman retorted. "Justice demands that the land should belong to you. That is what Congress has promised. That is why your Rajah hates us and supports the British. He does not want India to be independent because he would lose all his property and you would be the ones to get it. Be honest, wouldn't you like to live in his palace?"

Although the peasants laughed at this preposterous idea, the strangers' arguments were beginning to take effect.

"Your Rajah married an Englishwoman, that proves he is against the independence movement. How could the husband of an Englishwoman want to drive the British out of India?"

This evoked a general murmur and one or two cries of approval.

"Those who pay their taxes," the stranger went on, "are traitors, not patriots. They are destroying their own future and that of their children and grandchildren. Come on, start acting like men! The Congress Party will back you up. But you have to do exactly what we tell you. We only have your best interests at heart."

"After your own!" cried someone at the back.

Three sarcastic words were enough to break the spell and disconcert the stranger. Sensing that their mood had once again become suspicious, he adopted a less rhetorical tone.

"It's up to you, of course. Think it over. I'll be back."

And so it went on for weeks. The peasants listened and argued among themselves, sometimes heatedly. They dispatched emissaries to other villages to find out what they thought, but they could not reach a decision. They were almost tempted to consult the Rajah, whose advice had always proved sound in the past. . . .

Amir knew more or less what was going on. He had spies – he preferred to call them informants – in every village, but were they telling him the whole truth? They might be minimizing the threat to ingratiate themselves or exaggerating it to inflate their own importance. He took to consulting Selma, whose contacts gave her access to more reliable and objective information. Most of the women condemned their husbands for flirting with the Congress Party, which meant as little to them as the British, whom they had never seen, and whose rule seemed totally abstract. The Rajah's authority and the Rani's charity – those were the realities that governed their daily life, and they resolved to remain loyal to them like their mothers and grandmothers before them. How could their idiotic husbands forget those age-old ties of allegiance and allow strangers to turn their heads with pretty speeches? They would make them see reason in the end.

The monsoon broke at last, the sky delivering itself from the heat that had prostrated man and beast for the last two months. Torrents of rain came down on the villages, poured through the peasants' thatched roofs and flooded their homes. They stacked their chests and sacks of grain on makeshift platforms, but in vain: food went mouldy and clothes became covered with mildew.

The countryside looked dark and desolate. Sometimes, however, a huge rainbow of mauve, gold, and pink would light up the sky between two cloudbursts. Children clapped their hands with joy at the sun's benign reappearance, and their parents sallied forth to enjoy the fresh scent of rain-soaked soil. Every leaf glistened, washed clean of dust, and the landscape took on colour again. The world was reborn.

Selma would take advantage of these lulls to tour the villages and distribute blankets and dry clothes, which were more than ever welcome. There was no question of going by carriage, the roads were such a quagmire, so she had to travel in a dandi, a kind of litter carried by four men who sank into the mud up to their knees. It still distressed her to see human beings acting as beasts of burden, even after six months in India, but everyone, including the porters themselves, seemed to regard it as a job like any other. Besides, Amir had pointed out that her scruples would only cost them their livelihood. Half convinced, she resigned herself to being carried around and tried to salve her conscience with grateful smiles and gifts of money.

The monsoon brought an invasion of snakes and big, black rats. The villagers drove them away with sticks and stones, but not a day passed without a child being bitten, and the hakim's herbal poultices and potions sometimes failed to save him.

One afternoon while Selma was resting, Kaniz Fatma asked to see her.

"Rani Sahiba," she said, looking quite distraught, "two of the village women are dead. They had been vomiting bile for several days. Allah preserve us, but I think it's the sickness."

"What sickness?"

"The one that cannot be cured."

Alarmed, Selma sent someone to inform Amir, who came at once and questioned the peasant woman closely. The more she told him, the graver his face became.

"We must summon a doctor from the city without delay," he said. "I'm afraid it's the plague."

Selma's blood ran cold. The plague? She had thought it was a thing of the past. The very word conjured up visions of depopulated cities and streets littered with thousands of rotting corpses. She stared at Kaniz Fatma in horror: they would have to flee, flee as quickly as possible. Amir, seeing her expression, tried to reassure her.

"It's serious, but we are not living in the Middle Ages. The plague is a scourge we have learned to control. Drugs and hygiene are the answer. Would you prefer to go back to Lucknow?"

"What about you?"

"First I have to take care of everything here. I cannot abandon my people now without help, since if I did so they would have no chance of escape."

Selma shut her eyes. She was ashamed, but her fear was stronger.

"I think that . . . I'll stay."

What made her utter these words? It was the opposite of what she wanted to say. Her confounded pride had played another trick on her! Was it the note of condescension in Amir's voice, or the look on Kaniz Fatma's face?

Selma would remember the days that followed as one long nightmare. The doctor from Lucknow turned out to be a young man. His older colleagues were loath to leave their comfortable city practices for the country and saw no reason to risk their lives fighting such a dangerous epidemic, but Doctor Rezza was an unconventional type. Two days a week he closed his office, loaded his little cart with medicines, and toured the outlying villages. It was his reputation that had encouraged Amir to send for him.

Having given Selma an injection – "ninety-five per cent effective" – Dr Rezza asked her, as if it were the most natural thing in the world, if she would be prepared to assist him.

"I'll never get in to see the women if you don't. Most of those peasant women would die rather than let a man examine them, and I could not find a female colleague to come with me." Selma must have looked dismayed, because he smiled and said gently, "You are their Rani, after all – 'in sickness and in health,' as the Christians say when they get married. . . ."

Although her whole being rebelled at the idea, she said yes. For days she followed the doctor around like an automaton, going into house after house clad in gloves and a muslin mask. The most vulnerable of the peasants – women, children and old people – had already been smitten with the disease. Purple in the face, they retched and vomited incessantly, bringing up a foul, black liquid. The stench was so unbearable that Selma tried not to inhale. Calmly, the young doctor felt pulses, examined throats, armpits, and groins, lanced pus-filled boils, sponged off sweat, and dispensed encouragement and reassurance. Kaniz Fatma and another two women had volunteered to help him. Selma watched them hold basins, heat water, mop up pus and excrement. She recalled her fear and disgust at the wounded soldiers in Haseki Hospital in Istanbul, where her mother used to take her, and felt incapable of doing a thing. But Doctor Rezza did not spare her.

"I need your help," he said one day. "Bring me those dressings."

He waited. Reluctantly she approached the bed, and handed him the swabs and squares of gauze.

"Please stay here. I'll tell you what to pass me when I need it."

Meekly, she did as she was told. He carefully attended to the patient for several interminable minutes. When he straightened up at last, his eyes smiled at her for the first time.

"Thank you," he said.

She shook her head, suddenly overwhelmed by his kindness and intelligence.

"No, I am the one who should thank you."

From then on she remained at his side. He never asked her to touch the patients, simply to be there – to talk to them and smile at them.

It took two weeks to control the epidemic. Miraculously, only fifty villagers died out of a population of two thousand. Amir decided that it was time to return to Lucknow. Doctor Rezza would stay another few days for safety's sake.

On the morning of her departure he came to say goodbye to Selma.

"You wouldn't believe it," she said, "but I'm almost sad to be going."

"That makes two of us. I am losing my best nurse."

Their laughter was forced. It was rare for two people to be as close as they had been, but now they were returning to their own separate worlds. They would probably never see each other again, and perhaps it was better so. What, after all, could a Rani and a humble doctor have in common?

Rain was teeming down as the car drove out of the palace yard. With a tightening of the heart, Selma caught a last glimpse of the doctor's slight figure standing motionless in the downpour, watching them depart.

CHAPTER 8

"You are looking very pale, my dear."

Rani Aziza surveyed Selma, who had come to pay her respects on returning from Badalpur, with eagle-eyed intensity.

"I hope you have not caught the sickness! Or perhaps. . . ." She ran her eyes over Selma's slim figure. "Could you by any chance be in an interesting condition?" She sighed when she saw her sister-in-law's dumbfounded expression. "So you are not? How tiresome, after six whole months of marriage. I warn you, people are beginning to talk. . . ."

What business was it of hers? Furious, Selma retired to her room. After the relative freedom of Badalpur she found the atmosphere in the palace at Lucknow oppressive and her sister-in-law's malice intolerable. As for her doorless apartment, separated from the Rani's only by a curtain, it was time to put a stop to *that*! She called the eunuch who was dozing on the threshold.

"Fetch me a carpenter, quick!"

The eunuch was gone for a long time. He returned with the information that the carpenter was waiting outside the palace; being a man, he was not entitled to enter the zenana. In her fury, Selma had forgotten this detail. Who could help her? Amir was closeted with his advisers. Then she thought of Rashid Khan – dear Rashid, always so happy to be of service. The Rani must not hear about the door until it was in place. She hurriedly scribbled a note.

"Here, take this to Rashid Khan."

The eunuch bowed. Not a muscle of his impassive face betrayed his amazement at this unspeakable misdemeanour. That his Rani should have written to a man! No such outrage could have occurred in his late master's day, if only because, to preclude liberties of this kind, women had wisely been forbidden to learn to write.

"My dear," Amir told Selma when he joined her for dinner that evening, "you have stirred up a regular hornets' nest. There have never been any doors here. Curtains have always been considered sufficient – besides, they allow the air to circulate. My sister is furious. She says she will not let anyone turn this palace into an English house."

"And shall I have my door?"

"If you really insist, but is it worth antagonizing everyone for the sake of something so trivial?"

"You call our privacy trivial?"

"Of course not, but. . . ." Amir seemed touched but unconvinced. "Privacy does not exist here, you should know by now – we are one big family. Still, we will see. . . ."

Selma got her door a few days later. She heard from Begum Yasmin, who came to call on her, that she owed it to Rashid Khan's good offices. Apparently, he had persuaded Amir that a minor concession now would enable him to stand firm later, when something more important cropped up.

The new-found peace and quiet of Selma's boudoir overjoyed her, but it was weeks before she taught her maids to knock. More often than not, their goodwill led them to knock conscientiously – but only after they had already entered. As for Rani Aziza, who regarded the door as a personal insult, it was a long time before she deigned to address a word to Selma, who could not have been more delighted.

Selma resumed her visits to Begum Yasmin. She was beginning to find her a little too possessive and preferred Zahra's company, but the girl would be taking her finals in a few weeks' time and was studying all day long. Having completed her course at the palace with the aid of private tutors, she would take the examination at college, but chaperoned and wearing a burkah. Amir was determined that his sister should have a sound education – educated women, though still frowned on in traditional circles, were highly thought of by the more progressive aristocratic families – but it never occurred to anyone that a girl student's store of knowledge should be put to practical use. The very notion of utility seemed vulgar in the extreme.

These days Amir was busy helping to organize a conference between the Rajahs, nawabs, and big landowners affected by the recent laws concerning the rights of the peasantry. As a member of the legislative assembly, he was further confronted by a number of new problems.

In the euphoria of victory, the Congress government had enacted various measures unacceptable to a substantial section of the population. Schools, whose pupils included Muslims as well as Hindus, were compelled to fly the Congress flag and adopt the *Bande Mataram* as a national anthem. This infuriated the Muslims, who regarded the song as an affront to Islam and their entire community. The words of the *Bande Mataram* had, in fact, been taken from an eighteenth-century Bengali novel in which Muslim landlords were described as Hindu-exploiting tyrants. The song itself was a hymn to the soil of India, the "mother goddess," and that, from an Islamic point of view, was pure idolatry.

Demonstrations against these abuses of power were taking place throughout India. Fighting had broken out in schools and universities, and in Madras Muslim members of parliament had even walked out of the chamber.

"Should we do the same?"

Amir and a few of his fellow deputies were heatedly discussing this question at an informal meeting in his drawing-room. Some objected that the Congress deputies would be only too happy to be left on their own and enabled to pass laws unopposed, to which others retorted that the Congress deputies, with their commanding majority, could do as they pleased in any case, and that the only pressure the others could exert was moral. If they boycotted the assembly and made their reasons public, the Congress deputies, wanting to preserve their image as a great national party representing all communities, would have to give way.

Selma, seated in a small adjoining room, listened intently. She blessed the moucharabié, which allowed her to see and hear everything without being observed. If she had been present, the men would have felt obliged to engage in small talk suitable for a woman's ears. She was beginning to understand Begum Yasmin's allusion to the advantages of purdah: they were the same as those enjoyed by the wives of the Ottoman sultans, who never left the harem but influenced national policy, sometimes decisively. Selma's Catholic education at Beirut had almost made a European of her, but here in India, in this traditional Muslim society, she found her old cultural instincts reasserting themselves.

She jumped at a sudden commotion in the gathering, quite surprised, for even in the thick of a political argument Lucknowis never abandoned the courtesy which the middle classes of Bombay or Delhi dismissed as languid. Leaning forward and straining her ears, she caught a few snatches of conversation.

"Faster but less stamina. . . . Not at all, it has far more staying power! A magnificent pedigree. . . . It won first prize for looks last year. . . . You don't know what you are talking about, my dear fellow. . . . Those long-haired Afghans are stayers, certainly, but Russian greyhounds are faster!"

What did Russian greyhounds have to do with Congress policy? Leaning forward a little more, Selma made out three new faces, the Rajah of Jehanabad and a couple of his friends, also nawabs. One of the wealthiest princes in the province, the Rajah was a great dog fancier and joint organizer of the thirty-eighth annual dog show, which was due to be held at Lucknow in a few days' time. One reference to canine pedigrees had been enough to banish all thought of politics. A minute later, everyone was enthusiastically debating the relative merits of spaniels and labradors as gun dogs.

Selma flopped back in her chair. *They are mad,* she thought. *Just as frivolous and unconscious as Ottoman high society on the eve of its downfall. They could still avert disaster, but will they? Have they any idea of the forces at work in India? Even if they have, are they capable of changing their way of life to challenge them? Are they willing to?* She could have wept with frustration.

"It's no use," Amir told her when she broached the subject that evening. "It doesn't matter what one says, they won't listen."

He had no illusions about their unthinking attitude, but he was young and wielded little influence over his elders.

"They will lose everything," sighed Selma, haunted by visions of insurrection, "just as we did. . . ."

Late in August 1937, Jawaharlal Nehru, president of the Indian National Congress, officially proclaimed his party's intention to do away with big landed estates and distribute them among the peasants.

Three weeks later, three thousand delegates met in the red palace of Lal Baraderi. Ranging from great maharajahs to lowly members of the petty nobility, they represented the landed aristocracy of the entire province, not an acre of which belonged to anyone but them.

If a fire were to break out, thought Selma, surveying the conference from a gallery reserved for women, all the peasants' problems would be solved: the land will all be theirs, if Congress really means what it says.

The proceedings were opened by the host and president of the Indo-British Association, the Rajah of Jehanabad, a stout, pale-skinned gentleman with a nose so aristocratically hooked that it almost met his chin.

"My friends," he began, "never in this historic hall have we had to address a problem as grave as the one that now confronts us. We did not realize that the advent of democracy and provincial autonomy would spell the extinction of our class. We are the natural leaders of millions of peasants, but that they now dispute, inflamed by the false promises of those who claim to have their best interests at heart. We must put aside our differences and unite against this threat. We must regain the peasants' allegiance, the backbone of our authority, by introducing reforms that will satisfy them."

A woman in a black burkah rose to her feet. A widowed Rani, she was representing her state as of right.

"Socialism, communism, and revolution are at the gate," she cried. "They threaten our very existence. The only way to preserve our identity is to organize ourselves as a class."

This drew murmurs of approval. Someone proposed the formation of a militia of young landowners: carried unanimously. Someone else proposed the adoption of a flag symbolizing the new union, namely, a cart drawn by two buffaloes: loud applause. A flag. . . . Just what was needed!

But who was this young troublemaker who claimed that they were talking nonsense, and that definite steps must be taken without delay? The Rajah of where? Ah yes, Badalpur, that little state up north. What was he saying? Unless the peasants were given plots of land at once, the landowners would lose everything? The man was a fool, a dangerous fool! A communist? No, educated in England. Ah, that explained it! Socialism was all the rage among the young over there, but that did not excuse his unwholesome ideas. He was a Rajah – he had no right to betray his class.

The rest of Amir's speech was drowned by angry booing. Disheartened, he sat down again. He had done his best to inject some commonsense into this charade, but his worst fears had proved well-founded: he had merely incurred universal opprobrium. At least he had tried. . . .

Selma, looking on from the gallery, felt thoroughly depressed. It dawned on her that Amir had become an outsider in his own country. His sincerity, his passionate desire to build a more modern and equitable society, the ideas he had evolved in conversation with the upper-class liberals he had met at Eton and Cambridge – all these things were unacceptable to the society from which he sprang and to which, in spite of everything, he still belonged.

When he came home that evening, tired out, she gently urged him not to give up. He was right, she said, and she shared his beliefs. Amir grinned at her sardonically.

"So the two of us are going to change the world all by ourselves? Unfortunately, my dear, being right but out of step with everyone else is the same as being wrong. That is one of the bitter rules of social existence. I tried to convince them but I failed. Unluckily for me, and for all of us. However," he added with sudden exasperation, "the one thing I can dispense with is your pity."

And he strode out, making her regret that she had spoken at all. "Why am I so tactless with him? It's as though he is being skinned alive. He is as vulnerable as an unhappy child. He never relaxes for an instant – it's as if he mistrusted me."

The next day Rani Shahina came to take Selma to the movies, one of Lucknow's few forms of entertainment. British and American films were shown there only a few months after they opened in the West. Greta Garbo and Marlene Dietrich were at the height of their fame. Tyrone Power and Clark Gable haunted every woman's dreams. Selma recalled the days when she had been offered a Hollywood contract. Was she sorry that it had come to nothing? She preferred not to ask herself that question.

When she suggested that Zahra should take a rest from her books and come too, the girl was overjoyed. She had never been to the movies before. The carriage dropped them at the rear entrance, which was reserved for women. From there they climbed some stairs to the balcony and took their seats in a curtained box. The curtains would remain drawn until the lights went down and the film started, so no one could see them.

The film was *Queen Christina*. Captivated by Garbo's acting, Zahra pronounced her almost as beautiful as Selma.

The atmosphere when they got back to the palace was electric. On learning that Selma had invited Zahra to accompany her, Rani Aziza had gone to Amir and complained that his wife was corrupting the girl.

"But we were in a box," Selma protested. "No men could see her!"

"But she could see men," the Rani hissed venomously, "and I dread to think how they behaved!"

"What men where?"

"What do you mean, where?" exclaimed the Rani, outraged. "On the screen, of course!"

Amir, caught in the crossfire, preserved an embarrassed silence. For weeks now his sister had been nagging him for allowing Selma so much freedom. He had no more authority over his wife than an Englishman, she said, and people were beginning to laugh at him.

"She walks the streets with her face unveiled, an impropriety of which no member of our family has ever been guilty! She is a foreigner, granted, but she must observe our customs. For the sake of our good name, my brother, do something quickly!"

But when Amir made a halfhearted attempt to convince Selma of the need to wear a burkah, she jibbed like an unbroken mare at the first touch of the bit.

"Never! I observe purdah. I never leave the palace except in a closed carriage, and I spend my days in the company of women who bore me to death. Don't expect me to imprison myself in one of those humiliating cages, because I warn you, I will not stand for it!"

Shaken by her vehemence, Amir consulted Rashid Khan.

"It is not my personal wish that she should wear the veil. After all, many women of good family go around unveiled these days – it is the mark of a modern upbringing – but people at Luknow are so ignorant and hidebound. . . ."

"Highness," said the secretary, "in my opinion, Rani Aziza is alarming herself unnecessarily. Everyone here is aware of your wife's illustrious background. Her cousins, the princesses of Hyderabad, show their faces everywhere, and no one would dream of criticizing them. If you compel the Rani to wear the burkah, I am afraid she may. . . ."

He broke off. Amir glared at him, but they both knew what he meant: if the Rajah were too strict with his wife she would leave him, at least as long as she remained childless. To be deserted by his wife was a disgrace Amir refused even to contemplate. He overrode his sister's protests and gave way.

In any case, he had plenty of other worries. The situation had deteriorated badly in the last three months, especially in a Congress-governed area like the United Provinces, where Muslims represented only fourteen per cent of the population but were regarded as the living heart of Islam in India.

Particular resentment was aroused by the decision to compel schools and government departments to use Hindi in parallel with Urdu[1], which had been the official language for centuries. The recruitment of Muslims into various administrative agencies, notably the police, from which many were dismissed on spurious grounds, was suspended. The new government felt justified in manning them in conformity with the demographic ratio of Hindus to Muslims, heedless of the latter's traditions and advantages acquired over the centuries.

What really added fuel to the flames, especially in rural areas, was the zeal with which Hindu extremists strove to convert Muslims to Hinduism. According to the Mahasabha, a militant cultural and religious organization, India's eighty million Muslims were really Hindus converted under duress and must therefore be returned to the fold. The Muslims of today were, it claimed, simply a historical

1 Spoken Urdu is closely related to Hindi. But written Urdu employs Arabic characters, whereas Hindi is written in Devnägiri, an Indic script of great antiquity.

digression. The future of India lay in a national Hindu state founded on Hindu institutions.

Although these organizations did not reflect the views of Congress, which proclaimed itself a secular party, Muslim fears were intensified by its failure to condemn them and by the fact that Gandhi, in his fervent desire for a return to Hindu values, had described certain Hindu fanatics (like Malaviya) as patriots.

Recent events seemed to prove that the Muslims had already waited too long, and that it was time to get organized.

On Friday 13 October 1937, the quiet city of Lucknow bustled with activity as it prepared for an extraordinary session of the Muslim League to be opened by Mohammed Ali Jinnah. Five thousand delegates had arrived, the most illustrious of them staying in the various royal palaces and the others in gaily-coloured tents erected in the Kaisarbagh gardens.

All of it was organized and financed by the Rajah of Mahdabad. Selma had often caught a glimpse of him. He was a friend of Amir's although they differed on a number of issues. The Rajah was a devout, idealistic man. He lived an ascetic life, confining himself to a single room of his enormous palace. Spread over the floor of this room were countless stacks of books: copies of the Koran and the Bible, the novels of Dickens, which he said brought tears to his eyes with their descriptions of the misery of the poor in nineteenth-century England, and the works of Tolstoy, for whom he felt a special affinity, since Tolstoy had also revolted against the feudalistic society in which he was born to a noble place. The Rajah ate only barley bread baked by his wife, like the Prophet, and when he was in his home state he sometimes laboured in the fields alongside the peasants. He had even decided to devote himself to raising sheep, his ideal being to return to a life close to the land. Jinnah had been one of the Rajah's tutors after the death of his father, the greatly respected Maharajah of Mahdabad, and it was Jinnah who had dissuaded the Rajah from burying himself in a purely pastoral life. "You must work with me," he had said. "Your duty is to struggle for Muslim emancipation." And so the young man who dreamed of nature, art, and philosophy had become one of the pillars of the League.

That October Friday, the Rajah of Mahdabad met Jinnah at the train station. When the League's leader made his appearance, the honour guard of volunteers in green shirts was totally trampled by the enthusiastic crowd. The station rang with cries of "Jinnah *Zindabad*! Muslim League *Zindabad*! Long live Jinnah! Long live the Muslim

League!" Jinnah's car was literally carried to the gigantic pandal[2] which had been erected in Lal Bagh square, where the conference was taking place.

The pandal was bursting with delegates who had come from all over India. Particularly notable were the Bengali and Punjabi Chief Ministers, leaders of states with a Muslim majority, who had come to lend their support to the League. In the stands, hidden behind the moucharabiés, the wives of prominent men jostled to get a look at this lawyer from Bombay who in just two years had become the champion of the Muslim cause.

Tall, slender, with white hair and a piercing gaze, Mohammed Ali Jinnah was an impressive figure. He walked stiffly towards the platform and, standing there motionless, began to speak in his vibrant, authoritative voice. The audience was captivated. Without wasting any time on preambles, he went straight to the heart of the matter.

"Brothers, in pursuing an exclusively Hindu politics the Congress Party has alienated the Muslim masses. They have broken their election promises and have refused to recognize the existence of the Muslim community or to cooperate with us. Hindu governors are not making any attempt to protect threatened minorities. Their actions are only worsening the friction between the two communities, and by doing so they are also reinforcing British power. We Muslims must start trusting ourselves. We must stop looking to the British or the Congress Party for help. In fact, anyone who joins the Congress should be considered a traitor."

The break which had been brewing for months had now erupted. Outside the crowd was chanting opposing slogans.

"*Jai Hind*! Long live India!" shouted some.

"*Taqsim Hind*! Divide India!" shouted others in response.

This was the first time Selma heard the slogan which several years later would become the order of the day. For now the notion of a Muslim state was still far off. This idea was the brainchild of Mohammed Iqbal, a poet and philosopher who advocated the regrouping of the Muslims scattered over the Indian subcontinent into an independent Muslim state. Jinnah himself did not take this idea seriously, although he thought it a useful tool in pressurizing the intransigent Congress Party.

Fazl ul Haq, Chief Minister of Bengal, a state containing one third of the Muslims in India, approached the platform and announced that his party had decided, in view of the present threat, to merge with the

2 A large, multicoloured tent erected for conferences and weddings.

Muslim League. Amid scenes of wild jubilation, it was decided that the League's emblem should be a green flag adorned with a white crescent, and that the anthem composed for the conference should become the party's anthem and a rallying cry for all Muslims.

Finally, it was unanimously resolved that the ultimate objective of the League should no longer be to obtain just a responsible government; it should be nothing less than the independence of India. To attain this end, Jinnah declared that the party should be reformed along more democratic lines. Up until now, it had represented a mostly élite urban constituency. From now on a branch of the League would be opened in every village where anyone could join for the nominal sum of two annas. The Rajah of Mahdabad would take charge of this organization at grassroots level. Women were also to play an important part and a women's branch would be created, headed by the old Rani of Nampur.

When the conference was over two days later, everyone had the feeling they had taken part in a historic event: the transformation of the League into a popular party which could further the dream of all the Muslims of India. The new programme actually galvanized the people. In three months in the United Provinces alone, ninety branches would be created with more than 100,000 members. However, this did not prevent Nehru from claiming that the League was only defending reactionary interests, and from dubbing it hysterical.

Although life in Lucknow resumed its tranquil course once the conference fever subsided, in the neighbouring towns and villages, unpleasant incidents multiplied. The most serious of these was the massacre by Hindus of some forty Muslim butchers at the annual cattle market in Ballia.

This "barbarous act" made headlines in the capital of the United Provinces, but the indignation it provoked was soon forgotten in the excitement of the polo season, which turned out to be a vintage occasion. The upper classes being passionately devoted to polo, the government took advantage of their preoccupation to cancel the peasants' arrears of debt. Certain landowners demanded immediate action but were ignored. After all, what true Indian gentleman would worry about a sordid subject like money when engrossed in a sport as noble as polo?

At the same time, moviegoers clapped and wept over *Lives of a Bengal Lancer*, a film based on events of a century ago, while magazines fiercely debated whether Shirley Temple was really a little girl or a female dwarf of forty-five. . . .

CHAPTER 9

"The singular honour done us by Your Excellency and Your Ladyship. . . ."

The great banqueting hall at Jehanabad Palace was brilliantly illuminated. Emeralds and diamonds sparkled in the light of hundreds of candles burning in massive silver chandeliers and flaming torches held aloft by servants in brocade turbans.

The full flower of Oudh had gathered to honour the British governor, Sir Harry Waig, and his wife. Rajahs and nawabs, sovereign lords of states large and small, they held themselves proudly erect with an air of casual hauteur conferred by centuries of power and boredom. Except that their power was no more: these royal tigers' teeth had been filed. All that remained was boredom coupled with utter conceit.

"Our family, which has always served the British Crown loyally. . . ."

The Rajah of Jehanabad, having deluged the governor with flowery compliments and protestations of loyalty, had begun to invoke the history of his illustrious ancestors. Sir Harry only just suppressed a yawn. He wondered what the Rajah was leading up to. They could never ask for anything straight out, these people. It got on one's nerves! Judging by the scale of his welcome – fifty-odd princes mounted on elephants, four bands, and a detachment of lancers – the Rajah intended to ask a substantial favour. Sir Harry hoped he could grant it. He had no wish to lose one of his country's staunchest allies.

Lady Waig could sense her husband's impatience. Personally, she was having a good time. She liked being the only woman in a roomful of men and enjoyed the frisson of excitement she detected beneath their respectful glances. Harry always said she should not bare her shoulders, but she was not going to dress like Queen Victoria just because the Indians kept their wives shut up. She had beautiful shoulders and liked them to be noticed. It made her feel like a gazelle among tame jungle beasts. But had the Raj really tamed them, she wondered, or simply put them on a leash?

"And that is why we request Your Excellency to authorize and facilitate the construction of this road. Only ten miles long, it would provide a direct link between this palace and the main Lucknow-Delhi highway. Our peasants would find it invaluable."

Sir Harry remained impassive. *Your peasants, forsooth! Your peasants have handcarts – dirt roads are good enough for them! This new road is intended to keep your stable of Rolls Royces, Lincolns and Bentleys free from dust and mud. I know it, and you know I do. But that is not the point: if the old scoundrel does not get his road he is quite capable of making overtures to the Congress Party.*

Lady Waig surveyed the "jungle beasts" and observed: *This young Rajah of Badalpur has splendid eyes – a pity he has married that little fool who has the nerve to cold-shoulder Harry and myself. As if we were the savages! It is like turning the world upside down. Talking of savages, I simply must pay an after-dinner visit to those poor women. They must be dying of boredom, cooped up in the zenana, and the Rani will feel honoured that I have not forgotten her.*

She leaned towards the Rajah of Jehanabad and said a few words. His immediate reaction, a worried frown, was quickly erased by a broad smile.

"But of course, Your Excellency. What a charming thought! I shall warn the Rani to expect you."

Sir Harry Waig had risen, his well-cut tails looking supremely elegant in the midst of all the brocades. He raised his champagne glass in a silent toast as his affable gaze swept the room with that touch of condescension proper to a distinguished servant of the Crown, as manifest a token of superiority as the hallmark that denotes pure gold to those incapable of recognizing it any other way.

"Your Highness, Your Highnesses, it gives me the greatest pleasure . . . the honour is mine . . . the Empire . . . His Majesty . . . our mission . . . your loyalty. . . ."

Lady Waig listened distractedly. *Harry is overdoing it,* she thought. *He always makes the same speech. Suppose they notice. These coloured people are so touchy . . . though the Rajah of Jehanabad is perfectly civilized. . . . If it were not for his skin one could almost mistake him for an Englishman . . . almost, but not quite. Even among these members of the élite, with their public school education, something is always amiss: an exaggerated Oxford accent, an excessive devotion to cricket . . . and most of all, they are either too obsequious or too haughty with us. Strange, but they can never succeed in being natural!*

The chief eunuch whispered something in her host's ear. Whatever it was, it prompted a gesture of exasperation. As soon as Sir Harry had concluded his speech, which was greeted with polite applause, the Rajah rose to signal that dinner was at an end.

"Could Your Excellency possibly wait a moment? The Rani is so delighted by your forthcoming visit, she begs a few minutes' grace. She wishes to receive you in a fitting manner."

In a vaulted chamber at the other end of the palace, the Rani of Jehanabad was reclining on a divan and chatting with her lady guests. In contrast to the rigid etiquette prevailing at the Rajah's dinner table, the atmosphere here was quite informal. All the women were friends or relatives of princely stock, as centuries of aristocratic intermarriage had built up a network of relationships as close knit and complex as a spider's web. Some families were wealthier or more illustrious than others, but it would have been in poor taste to show it. Only the baniyas, the merchants who dared to rival the princes in wealth, behaved in such a vulgar fashion – and, of course, the Ingrez. . . .

A eunuch announced the Rajah, and the women fled to the adjoining rooms like startled birds. Only the Rani and her two daughters remained. The Rajah, perspiring beneath his turban, looked highly agitated.

"What is this I hear, Rani Sahiba? You are feeling too ill to receive Lady Waig?"

"I am feeling perfectly well, Rajah Sahib, but the sight of that . . . that *lady*" – she stressed the word with contempt – "is bound to make me feel sick."

The Rajah was used to his wife's whims. Very beautiful and still in her early forties, she took advantage of their difference in age to behave like a spoiled child. Most of the time he could refuse her nothing, but tonight she had overstepped the mark.

"You cannot offend the governor's wife. He would never forgive us."

"Forgive?" the Rani burst out. She had been nursing her anger for months, but this was too much. "Why should we need their forgiveness, those pork-eating bandits who have stripped us of power, extort taxes from us every year and to crown it all despise us!"

She wanted to say, "Who despise *you*, the Rajah of Jehanabad, who prides himself on being their best friend among all the princes of Oudh!" but she restrained herself just in time. She hated the British, but not so much because they were occupying her country – the independence movement struck her as futile; India had seldom been independent, and the Grand Moguls had ruled the country no more gently than the British crown. No, she hated them most of all because of the transformation they wrought in her husband. Proud of his origins and his ancestors' feats of valour, respected by his subjects and his peers, the Rajah would become a docile, submissive little boy in the presence of these arrogant white overlords.

Why? She could never fathom it, any more than her friends could. All of them, the wives of Hindu or Muslim princes, watched their lord and master court thc favour of the outsiders with bitter disbelief. The husbands whom they had been taught to revere both as men and as sovereigns even before they had met them, the men whose honour was what assured their honour and their families', would become fawning sycophants in the presence of the British. Oh, they probably had their reasons, their wives told themselves – for they would never let themselves doubt their husbands. Indeed they could not. No, the ones to blame were these British!

"I refuse to receive that woman!"

"Come, Rani Sahiba, be reasonable! The new road-"

"Ah, why did you not say so before?" She took his point at once. "If it is to hoodwink her husband then our honour is safe. I was afraid it was only to give her pleasure."

Somewhat taken aback by his wife's reasoning but happy to have won the day, the Rajah was careful not to contradict her. If he had explained that he had no intention of hoodwinking the governor, and that their relations were based not only on mutual interest but on a genuine feeling of friendship and esteem which he believed Sir Harry reciprocated, she might well have changed her mind.

Lady Waig was surprised, on entering the Rani's presence, to find her surrounded by elderly women only. She construed this singular fact as a mark of respect, never dreaming that the Rani had told her younger guests to withdraw. The mere shadow of this immoral, half-naked creature would bring them bad luck.

The one exception was the Rani of Badalpur, who had not only "seen the world" but could act as an interpreter. Selma, who already spoke passable Urdu, welcomed this opportunity to amuse herself at Lady Waig's expense.

"How kind of Your Excellency to visit me in my humble abode," purred the Rani. "Please excuse me, but my poor leg prevents me from rising to greet you."

Lady Waig, noticing that the other women had also remained seated, wondered vaguely if they all had bad legs. But the Rani gave her an apologetic smile, and graciously the governor's wife bent down to kiss her on the cheek. The Rani promptly recoiled. *How shy these poor women are*, Lady Waig reflected as her lips brushed the Rani's veil. *They are so unused to displays of friendship from British women.*

I have always made a point of showing them I regard them as equals. Harry thinks I overdo it – he says you have to command their respect – but I feel so sorry for them, cut off from everything, slaves in a man's world!

They conversed rather lamely over mango sorbets: the weather, past and future, the beauty of court dress, the health of children. Lady Waig racked her brains: what *did* one talk about to these uneducated women?

"I am very fond of your poets," said the Rani, "Lord Byron in particular."

Lady Waig looked startled. "You know English?"

"I read it, I do not speak it. But tell me, what exactly is Milton trying to say in *Paradise Lost*?"

"Oh," Lady Waig said haltingly, "it is a rather woolly theory about life and death." She had never read a line of Milton, but she would have died rather than admit it. "In any case, it is completely out of date."

"Is that so?"

The governor's wife detected a hint of mockery in the Rani's expression. *The little bluestocking*, she thought – *I'll take her down a peg or two*!

"Your husband the Rajah is a *fascinating* man," she gushed. "We spend hours together discussing books. The governor is not interested in literature, I'm afraid. He abandons us for the golf course."

"I know. The Rajah spends almost more time with you than with me. It makes me quite jealous to hear him describe his visits. All he talks about is the beautiful –"

Lady Waig bridled. "Oh, come now!"

"No, really. He is always talking about the beautiful Sarah – that is your niece's name, is it not?"

"Sarah?" The governor's wife had turned pale. Selma found it hard to keep a straight face, but the Rani continued in an absolutely natural tone.

"The Rajah has marriage in mind, did he tell you?"

"My niece . . . marriage?" The shock had rendered Lady Waig almost inarticulate. She pulled herself together. "Would you consent to it?"

"Oh, I am broad-minded. I think it would be a good idea."

Lady Waig found the idea so absurd, she laughed lightly. Her blonde Sarah married to a native? These Indians had some nerve! Fortunately, she had a ready-made objection.

"I am extremely flattered that the Rajah should have taken to my niece, but she is only twenty-two. The difference in age would be too great."

"Too great? My son is only twenty-five!"

"Your son? But –"

"What am I thinking of? You cannot bc cxpected to decide without seeing him, of course! Please let me know when you have a free afternoon and we will arrange a meeting. I am sure you will take to him. What a handsome couple they would make, and what a charming seal to set on the ties of friendship between our two families. It will prove that persons of quality can always surmount the ridiculous prejudices of the common herd, and –"

The Rani broke off. Selma's warning glance conveyed that she was going too far, and that Lady Waig would soon catch on. But Lady Waig was too upset for that. Her one desire was to escape. Collecting her bag and gloves she rose, thanked the Rani effusively, promised to come again soon to meet the Crown Prince, kissed the Rani three times, in her confusion kissed Selma too, and hurried out.

The Rani's drawing-room rang with laughter. "At least we can be sure we will never see her again!" she said. Then, with a sudden grimace of distaste, "A cloth and some rosewater, quickly! What a mania those Englishwomen have for kissing people!"

Seeing her scrub her face vigorously to remove the impurity, Selma was reminded of her great-grand-aunt, the wife of Sultan Abdul Aziz, who had scraped her cheek with a knifepoint to cleanse herself from the kiss of an infidel. The "infidel" in question, then on an official visit to Istanbul, was Empress Eugenie of France.

The Isotta Fraschini sped along the dusty road, swerving abruptly – for who would have deigned to slow? – around water buffaloes and supercilious camels, sacred cows and funeral processions, water carriers and a bridegroom on a white horse riding to the house of his betrothed with a party of exuberant wedding guests. Selma was continually surprised that the powerful car should manage, at fifty miles an hour, to avoid the peaceful hazards that turned every Indian highway into an obstacle course.

"Jehanabad will have to organize a tiger hunt for the governor if he wants his road," Amir said with a laugh. "That is the least he can do. The British think they are all such fine shots. If they knew how we drug those poor tigers! On the eve of the great day we force-feed some young water buffaloes with opium and let them loose near the streams where the tigers come to drink. Just in case that does not do the trick, we post a guard behind a bush with orders to fire at the same time as the illustrious guest. That way, everyone is happy: the great white hunter photographed with one triumphant foot on the corpse whose head will later adorn his drawing-room and make the ladies shudder; and the princely host whose delighted guest will not dream of refusing him some little favour or other."

"Do you despise them?"

Amir was taken aback. He stared at her for a moment.

"The British, you mean? I do not like them, but I admire them. If we had a fraction of their energy, their stamina, their devotion –"

"Their devotion?"

"Yes, to the Empire. There is nothing they would not stoop to for the Empire's sake. The favours they do us never conflict with the interests of the Crown. And where so-called Oriental cunning is concerned, we cannot teach them a thing. That is what makes our relations so – " Amir shrugged. "So stimulating, I suppose."

As stimulating as it is for a mouse to be played with by a cat, thought Selma. Do the Indians not realize how the British deride and use them? Veiled or not, their wives are more perceptive.

"The Rani of Jehanabad detests the British her husband thinks so much of. She and her friends claim they are too white to be human – they say the British Isles are dotted with huge, egg-bearing trees, and it is from these eggs that they are born."

Amir cast his eyes up to heaven. Women! Their foolishness was beyond belief.

"By the way, my dear, we'll be having some visitors soon. An old Cambridge friend of mine, Lord Cuddesdon, is spending his honeymoon in India. He and his wife are coming to Lucknow in a few days' time, so I have invited them to stay at the palace. I hope your nationalist sentiments will not prevent you from making them welcome."

What a handsome couple, and how much in love they seemed. . . . Selma had been wistfully observing them all evening like a child gazing at a shop window filled with forbidden delights. She was smitten with despairing envy of their gilded, carefree youth, their happy laughter and sidelong glances.

Dinner had been a cheerful affair nonetheless. Conversation centred on London and Paris, the latest stage shows, the restaurants currently in vogue, the season's balls, the latest scandals. Amir inquired after various mutual friends, uttered exclamations of surprise, roared with laughter. Selma, who had never seen him so relaxed, was surprised to find that he seemed to know everyone.

Edward Cuddesdon leaned over and addressed her in a confidential undertone. "Your husband was the livewire of our set," he said. "We were a pretty lively bunch, but Amir had a knack of setting the dullest party alight. Everyone competed for his attention, especially the ladies. They were crazy about him!"

Amir a livewire? Selma could not believe her ears. Would things have been different if they had met in London? Could they have loved one another? What was the emotion that linked them now? If only he would lower his guard, just once, but he claimed that love was a mental disorder. The only time she had ventured to ask him what he felt for her, he had replied: "I admire and respect you." She had never repeated the question.

She made her way slowly to the piano, that blessed refuge where she could seek solitude without seeming to run away. She owed its presence to Rashid Khan, who, much to Rani Aziza's fury, had persuaded Amir to acquire it for her.

Dear Rashid Khan! She had been agreeably surprised to see him this evening for the first time since her return to Lucknow. Amir did not have the courage to explain to his old friend from England that a rational, modern-minded, unprejudiced Indian like himself kept his wife in purdah. Hence Rashid Khan's and her combined presence at dinner[1].

Pensively caressing the keys with her fingertips, she played the opening bars of a Chopin nocturne. It conjured up melancholy and hope, love and despair. Tremulous as a leaf stirred by the wind, delicate as a rose petal bathed in dew, it scaled the heights of passion and finally expired.

She could almost feel the warmth and tenderness of Rashid's gaze on her hand, on the back of her neck. They had avoided each other's eye all evening, and now, only now, when he thought her immersed in her music, had he dared to look at her. She held her breath so as to capture every particle of that emotion, that adoration which, like a ray of sunlight falling on a flower of the field, made her blossom and revive.

She was not in love with Rashid, she knew, but all she wanted to do at that moment was nestle in his arms. His look of love and understanding had sufficed for her to become again the Selma she had been eight months ago, the radiant and expectant young woman whom he had met off the boat at Bombay.

1 European-educated Indians often insisted on their wives' keeping purdah in the presence of Indian men but not foreigners.

Edward Cuddesdon's voice broke in on her reverie.

"Amir, what say you we round off the evening with a nightcap at the Chatter Manzil Club? It's a magnificent place, I'm told. Used to be the palace of the kings of Oudh, didn't it?"

Amir had turned pale. "I am not a member, I'm afraid."

"Never mind, you can be my guest. The governor was kind enough to arrange temporary membership for me when I called on him this morning."

"You are new to this country, Edward," Amir said with a faint smile, "but you must have visited the Yacht Club while you were in Calcutta."

"Of course, and very pleasant it was too."

"Do you know the difference between the Yacht Club and the Chatter Manzil?" Amir spoke slowly, rotating his brandy glass as if fascinated by its amber contents. "No? I'll tell you: the Calcutta Yacht Club is out of bounds to Indians and dogs. At Lucknow they are more tolerant: they admit dogs."

There was a stony silence. All eyes turned to Lord Cuddesdon, whose jaw had dropped. He had never been so embarrassed in his life.

"You must be joking," he said. "That must only apply to natives – I mean, ordinary folk, not people like you."

"What do you mean? Do you not regard me as an Indian?"

"Come on, Amir, you know exactly what I mean. You belong to one of the oldest families in India. In London, duchesses called you 'Highness' and vied with each other for the pleasure of entertaining you."

"That was London. Things are different here."

Cuddesdon shook his head uncomprehendingly. "And people are surprised at the Indians for demanding independence. All those minor British civil servants, those sanitary engineers and tax inspectors – how dare they look down on you! Come with me, we'll barge straight in. They won't say a thing, or if they do they won't know what's hit them!"

Amir hesitated. He had not the least desire to provoke a scene. On second thoughts, though, this might be an ideal way to embarrass the authorities. Cuddesdon was a rising star at the Foreign Office and had already made his mark in the House of Lords. It was worth a try. He could not lose: either his friend would get him in and create a precedent injurious to the doctrine of British superiority, or they would be ejected. With the struggle for independence in its present stage, a scandal of this kind might pay off.

*

The moon was full. The Rolls purred up the main drive, an avenue flanked by palm trees with silvery trunks and banyans three centuries old. Floodlights illuminated Chatter Manzil's broad frontage and struck sparks from its three small domes of gilded bronze. Lady Grace, Cuddesdon's bride, was ecstatic.

"What a beautiful sight!" she said rapturously.

Amir restrained himself from telling her that the original domes had been made of solid gold, but that her compatriots had – how could you say this politely? – well, stolen them.

The Rolls pulled up outside the imposing entrance, where a score of cars were already parked. Preceded by the ladies, Cuddesdon had taken Amir's arm and was steering him resolutely up the steps past a fragrant curtain of flowers and foliage when a turbanned figure stepped forward.

"Excuse me, sahib, but it's forbidden to-"

Cuddesdon's stride never faltered.

"Whom do you think you're addressing?" he demanded haughtiy. "Nothing is forbidden to me!" And with one wave of his hand he brushed aside both the rules and the pipsqueak who was supposed to be enforcing them.

That's a good start!" thought Selma, and she turned to smile at him. It was the first time she had warmed to an Englishman. She relished his defiant attitude. Beside her, she felt Lady Grace stiffen: they were nearing the reception rooms, which were bound to harbour adversaries more formidable than a solitary doorman.

Chatter Manzil's huge lounge was a mass of roses tonight, and a string orchestra was playing softly on a platform in the corner. Turbanned waiters padded silently around bearing silver salvers laden with multi-coloured bottles. Nearly all the tables were occupied, and the presence of an unusual number of women suggested that tonight must be a special occasion of some kind. Selma was delighted: by tomorrow this incident would be the talk of the town. She felt a slight tremor: she had the feeling she was entering an arena.

The low hum of voices, already muted by thick carpets and panelled walls, ceased abruptly, and the music seemed to increase in volume. All eyes swivelled in their direction. Cuddesdon, perfectly at ease, asked for the table he had booked. The head waiter, an Englishman resembling a ducal butler, looked aghast. He opened and shut his mouth several times like a stranded carp, unable to get a word out. Finally he spoke.

"Your table is over there near the orchestra, your lordship, but. . . ."

"But what?" Cuddesdon demanded curtly. "Well, what are you waiting for? Take us to it. Really, the manners of people here are extraordinary!"

"I cannot, your lordship . . . the gentleman with you – club rules do not permit it, I am afraid. . . ."

"You are beginning to annoy me, young man! The Rajah of Badalpur is my guest. If you fail to show him respect, you are also failing to show me respect. Or are you being deliberately offensive?"

The head waiter's cheeks were ashen. He retired without more ado.

Cuddesdon surveyed the room with a mocking smile. Everyone avoided his eye and conversation hurriedly resumed.

"Well, Amir, let's sit down, shall we? The ladies must be tired of standing around like this."

The youngest of the Indian waiters had been delegated to take their order. His hands trembled as he wielded his pencil, careful to avoid looking at the Rajah. The occupants of the neighbouring tables had begun to drift away, some in icy silence, others loudly voicing their disapproval, but none of them ventured to tackle this arrogant young pup who had the gall to smile at his own audacity while his wife, pink with embarrassment, stared fixedly at the tablecloth.

They had not been seated for more than five minutes when a distinguished-looking man in a dinner jacket approached the table.

"Lord Cuddesdon, isn't it? Welcome to Chatter Manzil, sir. I am James Bailey, club secretary.

"How do you do, Mr Bailey. Allow me to present my wife, Lady Grace, and my friends the Rajah and Rani of Badalpur."

The club secretary bowed to the ladies and studiously ignored Amir.

"It is a pleasure to see you here, Lord Cuddesdon – the ladies, too – but I'm afraid I can't extend the same welcome to this gentleman. Club rules strictly exclude . . . natives."

The last word was uttered in a tone so scathing that Selma's blood boiled.

"Natives? The Rajah is my husband, so I am a native by marriage. Do you intend to throw me out too?"

The secretary pursed his lips.

"No, Madam, you may stay if you wish."

"My dear Mr Bailey," said Cuddesdon, "we are all staying. Unless, of course, you care to eject us by force and risk a scandal."

"I am sorry, your lordship, but the members make the rules and I have to abide by them."

The two men glared at each other, neither of them prepared to give an inch. It had become a matter of honour. Amir sipped his brandy as if the argument had no connection with him. A dozen waiters had mustered in the corner of the room, awaiting orders. At that moment Lady Grace chose to intervene.

"Edward," she moaned, "my head is absolutely splitting – it must be the heat. Let's go, please, or I may disgrace myself and pass out."

Cuddesdon glanced at her with barely suppressed annoyance. She really did look faint. He was momentarily tempted to ask Selma to escort her to the ladies' rest-room, but he restrained himself. The poor little darling was not used to such confrontations – it would not be fair to involve her in a scene on their honeymoon.

"Can I help any way?" the secretary inquired briskly.

"No – or rather, yes," replied Cuddesdon, not looking at him. "Kindly call our car."

"What a coward!"

Now that they were home and alone together, Selma gave vent to her anger. She did not know which emotion was uppermost in her, resentment or disgust. An embarrassed silence had reigned during the drive back to the palace, broken only by Cuddesdon's furious avowals that he intended to raise the matter in London. Nobody commented. They all knew the incident would seem remote and trivial when he got back to London, if he had not already forgotten it by then. They had wished each other good night, knowing full well what a bad one it would be.

Amir was pacing up and down with his teeth clenched. He had not said a word since they entered the club. Selma could sense that he hated everyone at this moment: the friend who had embroiled him in a humiliating scene and betrayed him at the first excuse, and herself, who had likewise betrayed him, albeit involuntarily, because of the white skin that was her passport to the other side of the racial barrier.

She wanted to speak to him, tell him that the only answer to contempt was contempt of even greater intensity. She could not understand why, after so many rebuffs, Amir and his fellow aristocrats continued to mingle with the British and court their friendship. How could such proud men behave with such singular humility? Did they not realize that they would never regain their self-respect until they not only evicted the British but rejected the entire system of values which the latter had the effrontery to impose as a code of universal application?

She said nothing, knowing that her silence was all he would tolerate in his present mood. But might he think she was indifferent? He was so wounded. . . . She went over to him and laid a hand on his arm. He brusquely shook it off.

"Leave me alone!"

There was hatred in his eyes, as if she were an enemy – as if she were his rival in some absurd contest that required them both to demonstrate their superiority or be trampled underfoot. She, too, was guilty of perpetuating the comedy they had enacted since the start of their marriage – their "bargain": an imperial pedigree in exchange for wealth – because they both believed themselves incapable of being loved for their own sake. Had he, like her, hoped for something more? Had he wished that they would somehow, by some miracle, recover their innocence? But he had immured her in her role as a princess and a pretty woman, the future mother of his children. He wanted nothing else from her, least of all a sympathy that might crack the shell he had built up – a shell he still needed to reinforce, as tonight's incident proved, for only his naive faith in friendship had exposed him to such a humiliation.

Selma curled up in the big bed and tried to sleep. She was just dozing off when Amir lay down beside her. His breath reeked of whisky. He started to caress her without a word. Clumsily, he slid his hand up between her thighs. She stiffened – he was hurting her – and tried to push him away.

This was all that was needed to revive his anger! Was she rejecting him too? He would show her!

Roughly he seized her by the shoulders, pinned her on her back and entered her with a kind of vengeful ferocity. Then he turned over and instantly fell asleep.

Selma, lying there with her eyes wide open, was surprised not to find herself weeping. Only a few months ago she would have cried all night long. Was she so hardened or was it that tonight she could sympathize with the anger he felt?

Tonight. . . . Never before had Amir been so aggressive, never had he deliberately tried to hurt her. She had grown accustomed to his inept, abrupt lovemaking – accustomed but not resigned. There were still times when the sight of his handsome face and lean, muscular body made her tremble and conjured up dreams of sweet, endless embraces. He did not know how to satisfy her – no, but he quickened her sensuality. Every night she was torn between hope and despair. Her desire was so intense that it gnawed at her legs, her knees, her belly.

Alone in the darkness, she bit back the cry that rose unbidden to her lips.

CHAPTER 10

When Selma awoke the sun was already high in the sky. Amir must have gone out long ago, but she felt no inclination to get up. Her body ached all over.

There was a discreet knock at the door.

"Am I disturbing you?"

It was Zahra, coming to have breakfast with her as she did every morning. Selma, who was touched and amused by the girl's innocent charm, had grown genuinely fond of her. Breakfasting together had become a ritual without which neither of them could conceive of starting the day.

Zahra unceremoniously installed herself on the bed just as a maidservant came in bearing a huge tray laden with silver coffee pots and fine china.

"You cannot imagine what an odd dream I had last night!" Zahra said. "We were walking along hand in hand, and all at once you underwent a transformation. Your dress became studded with precious stones, and you looked so radiantly beautiful that I was dazzled and had to look away. I clung to your hand, but it was icy cold. I felt rejected; I broke down and sobbed. When I woke up I really was crying!"

Selma smiled at her and stretched luxuriously. "Did I look so beautiful?"

Zahra seized her hands and covered them with little kisses.

"Much less beautiful than you are in real life. The other you shone like a dead star; this one here is all warm and golden. Anyway," Zahra added, sinking her teeth into a slice of toast and marmalade, "you know you are beautiful, I have told you so a hundred times."

They both burst out laughing. The girl's unqualified admiration for her sister-in-law had become a standing joke, even with Amir, who claimed that he could not get Zahra to do a thing unless he approached her through Selma.

"I am so happy," she sighed. "My life has changed completely since you have been here. I felt so lonely before, with no one to confide in. My brother was either away or far too busy for me to bother him with my problems."

The girl had removed her sandals and stretched out across the bed with her head resting against Selma's hip. Selma idly stroked the dark hair and rounded forehead that reminded her so much of Amir's. Zahra shut her eyes and gave a little cry of pleasure. Then, raising her head a little, she moved it into the warm hollow of Selma's hip. The young woman shivered, seized by a wild urge to take the silky head and press it hard against her. Instead she quickly pushed the girl away.

"Don't be babyish, Zahra! Anyway, it is time you went. I have to get dressed – Rani Shahina is expecting me."

Zahra sat up, looking disconcerted. Selma had never snapped at her before. Wondering what she had said or done to annoy her, she silently left the room.

Alone at the dressing table, Selma put her head in her hands. She was still breathless, still bemused by the surge of desire that had almost overwhelmed her. She had had to summon up all her will power to resist it, but now her body exacted its revenge. She was assailed by stomach cramps so severe that they brought tears to her eyes. She took little gulps of air, trying to get her breath back and control the pain.

The iron grip relaxed by degrees, leaving her drained and exhausted. When she raised her head, the mirror showed her the face of a stranger with dark shadows under the eyes and a wry, bitter mouth.

At the entrance at the entrance to Nampur Palace Selma was greeted by a brace of tigers whose glass eyes and rather moth-eaten fur did not detract from their air of hauteur. The Rani's lady-in-waiting apologized profusely: Rani Shahina was not quite ready, so might she show Her Highness into the drawing-room, where refreshments would be served? Selma assented, glad of these few minutes alone.

The hush that reigned in the spacious, heavily curtained room was soothing compared to the aviary-like twitter and turmoil at Badalpur Palace. Its calm, melancholy atmosphere restored her serenity. Two maidservants brought refreshments sufficient for a dozen starving people, then discreetly withdrew. Selma was surprised. This was the first time anyone in India had made her the gift of a little solitude. Being half English, Rani Shahina had evidently contrived to enforce a respect for privacy inconceivable in a wholly Indian household.

She was sipping a cup of perfumed tea when she thought she heard a rustle from behind a lacquer screen at the back of the room. She strained her ears: nothing. She must have been mistaken, and yet . . . she could have sworn there was someone there, furtively watching her. "Well, after all," she thought, mocking her own naiveté, "it may look like an English drawing-room but we *are* still in India!"

She had only to call "Who is there?" to send the intrusive creature scuttling off, but in a friend's home that would have been discourteous. Anyway, what difference did it make, whether someone peered at her from behind a screen or gaped at her from a range of six feet? In this country, curiosity was inescapable.

The rustling sound became louder, as if its author had abandoned any attempt at concealment. Selma identified it as the rustle of a gharara, but a gharara made of heavy silk, not the light taffeta worn by maidservants. She waited, intrigued by the sound. All at once four thin, bony fingers crept around the edge of the screen and gripped it, very white against the black lacquer. Selma stared in fascination at the motionless hand, that no arm seemed to support.

"Go away!"

The voice sounded thin and plaintive, a woman's voice. Selma gave a start. She did not believe in ghosts, but this unseen, unwelcoming presence and the drawing-room's curiously dreamlike atmosphere were beginning to unnerve her. She gripped the arms of her chair and peered at the dark corner from which the voice and the bony hand had come.

"Go, go quickly!"

A figure emerged from behind the screen, an emaciated old woman with snow-white hair falling to her shoulders. She walked with difficulty, as if the thick brocade gown were too heavy for her frail body. Her blue eyes gazed at Selma intently, her lips trembled.

"Save yourself, child," she said, "before it is too late."

Her eyes became clouded, her head rocked slowly from side to side.

"Too late," she repeated, "too late. . . ."

"Ah, I see you have met my mother"

Rani Shahina's cheerful voice and smiling face dispelled the morbid fascination that had taken hold of Selma. The room seemed to brighten.

"Come on, Mummy." Shahina put her arm affectionately around the old woman's waist. "You are tired, you must go and rest."

She rang, and a maidservant hurried in.

"Take Begum Sahiba back to her room and don't leave her unattended. How many more times must I tell you?" She escorted the old woman to the door before rejoining Selma. "I am sorry about that. You are looking quite pale, my dear. Was it something Mummy said? She is not right in the head, you know."

"Are you so sure?" Selma looked pensive. "She advised me to

leave this country before it was too late."

"Poor Mummy, you must have reminded her of her own early days here. She was trying to warn you – she does not want you to suffer the same fate as she did, but things have changed a lot in forty years. Besides, you are half Oriental – you understand our culture."

Rani Shahina seemed to be forcing herself to go on.

"She was just a young English girl from a middle-class London home. She fell madly in love with my father while he was at the university. He was handsome, wealthy, and full of charm. They married. A year later he brought her back to Lucknow, but his family never accepted her because, being the eldest son, he was expected to marry an Indian.

"To begin with, I suppose she thought she could overcome their hostility by being nice to everyone. She soon realized that it was impossible, and that she would always be an outsider. Why did she stay – why did she resign herself to leading an even more cloistered life than we do today? Because she loved my father? That was her original incentive, no doubt, but he soon began to neglect her. She stayed because of us, her children. My father scarcely saw her, but made her pregnant every year, as if he realized that it was the only way of keeping her. She gave birth seventeen times, but most of her babies were still-born. I am the youngest of the six that survived."

Rani Shahina's voice cracked.

"The saddest part was, her babies were taken away from her at birth. My grandmother refused to let her grandchildren be brought up by an Englishwoman, even if she was their mother, so we were handed over to the women of the house to be nursed. We were not allowed to see Mummy more than once a month, and then only for an hour or two. I used to cry every time I had to say goodbye to her, I remember. I yelled and kicked and sobbed, and she, her eyes full of tears, would beg me to be good. . . ."

The two women stared at each other, deeply moved. Had things really changed so much? Selma did not think so, but she wouldn't argue; she knew how to win respect.

Rani Shahina quickly changed the subject. Why not pay a visit to Hazratganj, Lucknow's smartest shopping centre, to admire the Christmas decorations?

"It is a pretty sight. The English do their utmost to pretend they are back home. All that is missing is the snow."

Hazratganj's main street was festooned with a multicoloured cobweb of lights spanning the roadway from one sidewalk to the other, and dwarf palms in wooden tubs glittered like Christmas trees.

Like the Indian women of Lucknow, Selma rarely visited this part of town, which was patronized almost exclusively by the British. The majority of the shops, restaurants, and movie theatres were British-owned, and the staff, if not English, were Anglo-Indian.

Hazratganj on Christmas Eve was a hive of activity. The sidewalks outside the stores were lined with sleek limousines and a sprinkling of horse-drawn carriages, but there was not a palanquin in sight, let alone a doli, the more modest litter carried by two men, or one of the small painted wagons known as tonkas. These humbler or more traditional types of conveyance, which were perfectly suited to the narrow streets of the old quarter, would have seemed out of place here.

"Let us go to Whiteway's," Rani Shahina suggested. "I want to buy some ribbon and lace. I hear they have just received a consignment from London."

Whiteway's, the biggest store in Hazratganj, sold every kind of imported merchandise, from the pert little hats that were all the rage this year to the ingredients needed for a Christmas pudding.

The carriage dropped them just outside the main entrance. Selma removed her burkah, only worn to pass the portals of Nampur Palace. To her this was Europe, and she meant to enjoy her brief taste of freedom. Her friend, by contrast, had carefully lowered her veil.

All eyes converged on them as they entered the store. Although wealthy Indian men often visited this temple of elegance to buy themselves Harrods shirts, Pope & Bradley suits, or Loeb shoes, their wives seldom ventured inside. This morning's customers included two or three Hindu ladies in colourful saris, but Selma and Rani Shahina were the only Muslims. Selma would have liked to browse through the tailored suits, evening gowns, and furs – the latter striking her as unwearable here, though some of the Europeans present were sporting otter or sable stoles – but the Rani seemed ill at ease. Taking Selma's hand, she steered her towards the lingerie department at the back of the store.

Three salesgirls were busy behind the counter, trim young things in black silk dresses with white bows at the neck. They might have passed for English, with their pale skin and impeccable accents, but their doe eyes and raven hair betrayed that they were of mixed parentage. Having served their customers, they ignored the newcomers and stood there chatting.

"Excuse me?" Rani Shahina said quietly.

The youngest of them grudgingly turned her head. "Yes," she drawled haughtily, in an exaggerated public school accent. "What do you want?"

"Who does she think she is?" thought Selma in amazement. But she refrained from interfering. It was up to the Rani to put her in her place, but she seemed unaware of the girl's insolence.

"I would like to see your latest consignment of ribbon and lace."

"What colour?"

"Something in a pastel shade. Could you show me what you have?"

The girl cast her eyes up to heaven. "I don't have all day. You'll have to tell me the exact colour. You aren't the only customer in the store, you know."

Selma's patience snapped. "That's enough! Apologize to the Rani at once!"

"But. . . ."

"At once, or I will report you to the manager and have you dismissed on the spot!"

"I am sorry," the girl mumbled.

"And now," Selma went on, her cheeks burning with anger, "get out every bit of lace and ribbon you have in every shade, and smile while you are at it. How dare you speak to a woman of your own country like that! You *are* Anglo-Indian, aren't you?"

The girl turned pale. Selma's remark was deliberately malicious. Persons of mixed blood, often the product of fleeting affairs between prostitutes and British soldiers, were looked down on in India. Obsequious toward the British and condescending toward the Indians, they were used by the former and hated by the latter, whom they scornfully referred to as "darkies."

"You should not have been so hard on the poor little thing," Rani Shahina said reproachfully when they emerged from the store. "Those Anglo-Indians are in an impossible position. They talk about England as 'home,' though they have not the slightest hope of ever going there. They call themselves 'the English of India' and despise the Indians proper. They do not seem to realize the British will never accept them, will even make fun of their pretensions to being white. They are more to be pitied than condemned."

Selma shook her head. It had been wrong of her, perhaps, but she had no sympathy for people who denied their origins. She wondered if Rani Shahina's tolerant attitude did not stem from the fact that she herself was half English – not "Anglo-Indian," of course, a term that was exclusively used for a class that was scorned. Actually, the few marriages between Indian aristocrats and Englishwomen of good family were well regarded. The Rani was living proof of this, since as the offspring of such a union, she had been chosen to become the wife of the Rajah of Nampur. Even so, Selma wondered how in her heart of hearts she managed to live with her mixed heritage.

"Forgive me if I am being indiscreet, but you always say, 'The English this, the English that. . . .' Don't you feel a bit English yourself?"

The Rani paused and looked at her with a sad little smile.

"Neither of us will ever feel we really belong anywhere," she said. "It is a constant suffering we have to try to turn into a strength!"

The coachman opened the carriage door. Rani Shahina started to get in but Selma caught her by the sleeve.

"Let us walk a little. I need some fresh air."

"Wouldn't you prefer to go to the Residency[1] Gardens? It is so much less crowded there."

How could Selma explain that crowds – different faces, noise, dust, ugliness – were precisely what she yearned for. Even if she were jostled, what did it matter? She was suffocating in the confines of the zenana and needed to reimmerse herself in reality. With a pang of nostalgia she recalled Beirut and the freedom she enjoyed there. She had never dreamed that the simple act of walking along a street would become such an adventure.

They strolled a little way despite the protests of their two attendants who sternly readjusted Selma's veil whenever it threatened to slip. Harassed at every step by vendors of sweetmeats, powdered incense, and garlands of scented jasmine, they were also accosted by swarms of half-starved beggars, mostly women with children. Selma was surprised that they looked so clean, with a dignity about them which was unusual in people who make a living off public charity.

"The women are peasants from the surrounding countryside," Rani Shahina explained. "There is a terrible famine this year. First, there was a long drought, and then there was too much rain. The crops that did not get shrivelled up have rotted in the fields. These people are too poor to keep any food in reserve. In good years they just about manage to survive. When the harvest fails, as it often does, their only hope of survival is to come to the city and beg."

Rani Shahina gestured to her maid to distribute the money left over from shopping. Selma, feeling ashamed of her fine clothes, hurriedly followed suit. The women obviously sensed her compassion; they clustered around this beautiful white lady and thrust their children toward her. One of them actually refused to take money. She was

1 The Residency was an old British Army fort which was destroyed in 1857 in the Chipoy rebellion. Its grounds became a recreational area.

young and would have been pretty, but exhaustion and hardship had taken their toll. With a look of utter despair, she put her little girl's hand in Selma's.

"Why won't she take any money?" Selma asked. "What does she want?"

"She wants you to take her daughter so she will be fed and cared for and have a roof over her head. In the old days, wealthy families used to buy children from famine-stricken parents for a small sum of money and train them as servants. They were quite well treated on the whole, but they were not free to leave. Few of them would have dreamed of running off anyway, they were part of the household.

"The British outlawed the practice decades ago," she went on. "They called it slavery, and perhaps it was, but these women are desperate. They cannot understand our rejection of what they still regard as a tradition – even, from their point of view, a right."

Gently, but firmly, she tried to make the woman understand. Selma, listening to her mixture of local dialect and Urdu, heard her say the word "Ingrez" several times and saw the faces around her harden.

"And now let us go before they attach themselves to you for good. You are soft as butter, Selma, they can tell."

They got back in the carriage and drove off. The women stared sadly after them. For one moment they had believed that the rich begums would save their children from a slow death. . . .

When she came home, Selma shut herself up in her room. She needed to be alone, could not endure the idle chatter of the palace women who stuffed themselves with halva all day long. She not only hated them, she hated herself. *But how am I any better than they? I am unhappy – so what? When women and children are dying of hunger at my door. . . .*

"You will get used to it," Amir had told her.

Never! God forbid that she should ever feel less distressed, ever forget the look on those women's faces, the look of hope that turned to reproach when the carriage doors slammed. Reproach? Not even that. The resignation in their eyes was a far more terrible indictment than abuse or rebellion. They had neither the strength nor the inclination to rebel. Did they even realize that they had as much right to exist as everyone else?

The poverty she had seen as a child at Istanbul was just as terrible, but it stemmed from long years of war. It was an exceptional situation – one that could be fought and overcome. Here in India, thousands of children every day died of starvation. It was an accepted, even expected fact. It is the contrary that would have been surprising. *Do the wealthy eat with added appetite*, Selma wondered, *because they know that eating is a privilege and obesity a status symbol? Would they derive the same pleasure from their wealth if there were no poor to remind them daily of their good fortune*?

There was a knock at the door.

"Rani Sahiba, there is a beggar woman outside with three children. She insists on seeing you. We told her it was impossible, but she says she knows you and refuses to go away."

"Show her in."

It was the peasant who had thrust her daughter into Selma's arms only a little while before. She hovered timidly in the doorway. Selma smiled at her, glad of this opportunity to atone for what must, to the woman, have seemed like callous indifference. She would take the pretty little girl and have her trained as a personal servant. Amir could not possibly object.

The woman had understood. She threw herself at the Rani's feet and kissed the hem of her gown, weeping with joy. Her daughter was saved!

The eunuchs had informed Amir, who came at once. Selma briefly explained the situation.

"I know we cannot do much to remedy such a disaster, but we can at least give this child a home. One addition to the household will not make any difference."

Amir shook his head, upset.

"I am sorry, it cannot be done – it is against the law. I don't trust all the palace staff: one of them would be sure to report it. It is not the law itself that worries me, of course, it is the possibility of a political scandal at a time when everyone is trying to catch the princes out. Think what a meal Congress would make of a Rajah who employed a peasant's child as a slave! The British would have to take a serious view of the case or stand accused of favouring the aristocracy at the expense of the people, and certain circles in England would call it yet another proof of our unfitness for independence. No, honestly, I would like to oblige you, but the present situation is far too delicate. . . ."

He gestured to the woman and produced a gold coin from his pocket. Selma bowed her head. She did not watch them leave.

Some weeks later, while Selma was shopping in Aminabad Market with her maidservant, she was accosted by an old beggar woman leading a little girl dressed in a jute sack. The arms protruding from the sack ended in a pair of stumps. Selma shuddered and turned to the maid, intending to tell her to be more generous than usual, but the child gave her no time. She rushed at Selma with a series of inarticulate little cries, her open mouth disclosing the remains of a mutilated tongue. Selma shrank back, appalled by the sorrow and hatred in the girl's dark eyes, then pulled herself together. What a coward she was! The poor little thing seemed to be trying to tell her something. Overcoming her repugnance, she looked more closely at the child's thin face. She felt she had seen it somewhere before, but where?

With a smothered exclamation she brushed aside the matted hair and looked again. Her blood ran cold: it was the little girl she had wanted to harbour. "What happened to you?" she cried. "Where is your mother?" She turned to the old crone and shook her. "Who are you? What have you done to this child?"

The beggar pushed her roughly away, grabbed the struggling child, and scuttled off. Selma tried to follow, but the crowd had already swallowed them up. There was no point in pursuing them further. Her only hope was the police.

Aminabad police station was next door to the market. The Indian desk sergeant was intrigued to see a white woman dressed like an Indian, but he could not fathom the reason for her agitation.

"This child, Memsahib – am I right in thinking that she is a member of your family?"

"No, but –"

"In that case, why upset yourself? What's the problem? Life would be impossible if we had to worry about all the poor wretches in this country."

"I did not ask for your opinion," Selma said curtly. "I am asking you to do your duty as a policeman. Take some men and search the market at once. I will make it worth your while."

The sergeant nodded. "Very well, Memsahib, we'll try."

No trace of the little girl was ever found.

"It was only to be expected," said Amir, when Selma told him of her encounter. "Those beggars are professionals – they have a well-organized network. The police are paid a retainer to leave them alone, so they don't want to make trouble for themselves."

"But . . ." Selma hardly dared ask the question, yet she had to know. "What could have happened to the poor child? An accident?"

"Why ask me? You must have guessed. . . . There are too many beggars in India. Holding out a hand does not work any more, so people buy children from destitute parents and mutilate them to arouse pity. The practice has become much more common since they abolished slavery."

Livid, Selma seized his arm. "But Amir, one must do something!"

"What, for instance? Reintroduce slavery?" Amir's dark eyes darkened still more. He gave a weary shrug. "Imagine the outcry in the so-called civilized West. People live on ready-made ideas; they do not want to see things as they really are. From the government's point of view, what matters is that India should look respectable to the outside world.

"The dice are loaded, believe me. There is nothing to be done."

CHAPTER 11

"Did the English people have a fever last night?"

Selma greeted her maidservant's anxious inquiry with a blank stare. *What English people? And anyway, how should I know if they had a fever? That lunatic would do better to enquire after my own state of health.*

She had been confined to bed since yesterday, her nerves frayed by the emotional turmoil of recent weeks. She was bathed in perspiration, and her head felt as if it would explode any moment.

"The English have flushed cheeks – I heard them coughing," the woman persisted.

"That's enough about your precious English!" Selma snapped. "Why should I care about them?"

Zahra, who was sitting beside the bed, burst out laughing.

"Do not be angry with the poor thing, Apa; she is only following tradition. Associating people you like with something unpleasant brings them bad luck, so you never say, 'Are you ill?' You say, 'Are your enemies ill?' Because the local women dislike the English, they have taken to saying 'English' instead of 'enemy.' She was really asking if *you* had a bad night."

Someone knocked at the door and announced that Hakim Sahib, the family physician, had arrived. Hakim Sahib was at least eighty years old, according to Zahra. They had sent for him last night, but he was too busy resting, so he had dispatched one of his assistants with three pills wrapped up in a piece of newspaper and promised to call at the palace the following morning.

The maidservants fussed around the bed. They carefully cut two holes of different sizes in a blanket and held it between them, entirely concealing Selma, Zahra, and themselves from the rest of the room. Selma looked mystified and asked what they were doing.

"I should have thought that was obvious, Apa," said Zahra. "We have to keep purdah, of course."

"Purdah, for a doctor of his age!"

"He is still a man." The girl seemed puzzled by Selma's surprise.

"But how is he going to examine me?"

"Simple. You put your arm through the big hole so that he can take your pulse and check your reflexes. The little one is for your tongue and throat."

Selma flopped back against her pillows. "If that is how he examines his patients, I hope it is nothing serious."

She peeked through the hole when the hakim entered. He walked with difficulty, assisted by two youths carrying large baskets filled with flasks of different sizes and colours. Hakim Sahib practised an ancient system of treatment based on the ingestion of decocted or macerated herbs, barks, and leaves.

He delicately felt Selma's arm, palpating it with each finger in turn, and laid his forefinger on the artery in her elbow joint. All these operations were punctuated by grunts and brief instructions to his assistants, who respectfully noted down their master's observations. Then, from one of his innumerable pockets, he produced a silver scraper.

"Would Rani Sahiba consent to open her mouth?"

Taking the scraper, he deftly removed a little of the whitish matter coating her tongue and sniffed it with a look of deep concentration. He narrowed his eyes and deliberated for a moment. Then he delivered his diagnosis in a solemn monotone.

"The liver has become congested by reason of an irritation of the nerves. By inhibiting the circulation of the blood and the elimination of waste matter, this congestion is causing fever and headaches. Rani Sahiba must take a dose of this yellow liquid every odd hour, and a dose of this pink liquid every even hour. She must be sure to follow the instructions exactly. She must also take a pinch of blue powder mixed with two pinches of white powder, night and morning. This is a simple remedy for a minor ailment – one from which Rani Sahiba will be fully recovered by the time the moon begins to wane."

"The old witch doctor!" Selma exclaimed indignantly as soon as the hakim had hobbled out. "I will certainly not take all these potions of his!"

"You are wrong, Apa. Herbal remedies have often proved more effective than European medicines. Last year I was cured of jaundice in two weeks, whereas friends who were treated by British doctors could hardly get out of bed after two months."

"And that stuff about the moon?"

"Body fluids subside when the moon wanes, it is a well-known fact," Zahra said gravely. "Relax, Apa. We are lucky, you know – in my mother's day a hakim was not even permitted to *see* a woman patient's arm or tongue, let alone touch them. He had to gauge the severity of her fever and make his diagnosis sitting outside the door holding a piece of string attached to her wrist. All he had to go by were the vibrations."

"I don't suppose he made many cures."

"You are right, a lot of women died," Zahra said, failing to note Selma's sarcasm. "Luckily, we have come a long way since then."

The women of the palace took advantage of their Rani's illness to invade her bedroom. The door that was usually kept shut, much to their annoyance, had become a useless appendage swinging in the breeze, and they revenged themselves by surreptitiously kicking it as they came and went. They crowded solicitously around the patient's bed. To these idle women their mistress's smallest indisposition was a godsend, an opportunity to display their devotion and make themselves important. They competed for the privilege of dosing her with medicine, plumping her pillows, bathing her forehead with rosewater, or massaging her feet while they entertained her by reciting poetry, like bees fussing over a queen too weak to resist their attentions.

Begum Yasmin's arrival rescued Selma from their excessive zeal. It was a good two months since Selma had seen her, preferring the company of Zahra or Rani Shahina, and she was afraid the Begum might have been hurt by her silence. Her fears were groundless, however: Begum Yasmin behaved as if they had seen each other only yesterday.

The vigorous woman soon got rid of the crowd around the bed.

"A sick person needs peace and quiet!" she told the women sternly. "Do you want to kill the Rani with your incessant chatter?" Unceremoniously hustling them out of the bedroom, she restored the door to its former dignity.

"Poor child, you must be exhausted. There, now rest. . . ."

She sat down beside the bed, a silent, soothing presence. Selma closed her eyes. Her head and neck were encircled by iron bands.

"Let me massage you. They say I have the hands of a magician."

They were indeed magician's hands, simultaneously firm and gentle, cool and warm. Selma's headache slowly subsided, to be replaced by a pleasant glow. She began to float. Her neck, her back, her shoulders – her entire body, so racked with pain only minutes before – relaxed.

The soothing hands were removed all too soon.

"Now you will sleep. I will leave you and come again tomorrow."

A light kiss on the forehead, and the magician disappeared.

She returned the next day and every day after that. Selma's pains vanished at her touch, and the fever itself fought no more than a rearguard action. With her eyes closed, Selma surrendered to the imperious gentleness that took possession of her body limb by limb, kneading it in a way that electrified and soothed by turns. She felt as if honey were trickling into her veins and permeating them. Hardly conscious of where she was or who was with her, she had a delicious sense of well-being.

The deft hands glided down her spinal column and lingered on her hips as though taking possession of those too, then swiftly raised one thigh and gave it a series of brisk little taps. Finally, they concentrated on the solar plexus and the nerve centre above the navel.

"That is where the pain accumulates," Begum Yasmin explained. "You feel it when your stomach tenses in response to some emotional disturbance and you find it difficult to breathe."

Now, with a rhythmical, circular motion, she began to massage Selma's abdomen. Almost imperceptibly, the hands slowed and increased their pressure. The young woman felt a shudder run through her. She shot an uneasy glance at the Begum, who seemed not to have noticed and was gravely, methodically continuing her treatment.

Selma felt ashamed. Why should a simple massage make her respond in such a way? She caught herself imagining that it was Amir who was caressing her, that the hands were those of a lover – strong, sensitive hands that slowly, very slowly, descended from her stomach toward the forest where flowed the river of musk.

"Look at me, my love."

Selma sat bolt upright, sobered by the words that had shattered her dream. What was she doing half-naked in the arms of this woman, who was covering her body with kisses? She forcibly released herself.

"Stop it! Are you mad?"

She pulled her nightgown down and stared aghast at the Begum's twitching, imploring face.

"Don't toy with me, please. You know I love you."

Selma could scarcely recognize the proud, self-possessed Begum in the creature who was holding out her arms to her with such an incongruous, unbecoming look of despair.

"Selma, have you any idea at all what passion is?"

The Begum's hands were trembling, but she would not admit defeat. She had kept silent for too long. Now she was going to speak out, and this beautiful, golden-haired girl who was gazing at her with such distaste would listen whether she liked it or not.

"I spent nights dreaming about you and days despairing because my dreams seemed hopeless. Now do you understand why I came running every time you called? Yet I am not submissive by nature. And you . . . how casually you accepted my friendship!

"You remember the kite-flying festival? I playfully put my arm around your waist and you recoiled. It was worse than a slap in the face. From that moment on I resolved to forget you – as if one ever can forget by an effort of the will! Anyone who thinks so has never loved. . . .

"And then, this last few days, my hopes revived. You seemed glad to see me again, and your body told me what your mind refused to admit. No, please don't deny it – don't demean yourself by lying! You are entitled to reject my love, but not to degrade its object to the level of a prudish, plebeian housewife! You think I did not feel your breasts and belly thrill at my touch, then gently submit? It was not long before your entire body cried out, reached out, starving for my caresses."

It was true, Selma told herself, but why did the Begum have to speak – why had she dispelled the nebulous, sensual haze in which she, Selma, had wallowed? Was it pride, this urge to possess more than just a body or was it simply passion that refused to limit itself? But was passion's demand for totality not a sign of inordinate pride? If only the Begum had remained silent and left things as they were, vague and ill-defined as a dream. . . . Selma had not been surprised by her caresses. She had probably been expecting them for some time and maybe had even encouraged them. Had she done so out of curiosity, impelled by an urge to break down barriers and explore unknown territory, or simply because she knew how good they would feel? Whatever the reason, now the spell was broken.

"You are insane," Selma said curtly. "I love my husband."

"Really? And does he love you?" The Begum's voice had lost its note of entreaty and turned to ice. "Have you seen yourself in the mirror? You look like a wilting flower. Is that the face, is that the radiant body of a woman fulfilled? No one knows better than I that Amir neglects you. He married you for dynastic reasons, but his love goes elsewhere."

She is lying out of pure spitefulness, thought Selma. *I am not going to give her the satisfaction of asking the question.*

"Well, aren't you curious?"

The Begum's eyes narrowed. She stared at Selma fixedly, like a snake about to strike. She knew how to take her revenge on this proud young woman. She would sow a seed of doubt in her mind that nothing could eradicate.

"Hasn't it ever occurred to you that the intimate friendship between your husband and mine might be more than mere friendship? Don't look shocked – these tendencies are common in a society like ours, which thrives on the ambiguous, the useless, the outlandish. We women are brood mares, nothing more. Lovers or mistresses would just shock everyone. We belong to our husbands, but are not foolish enough to believe that they belong to us. They protect us, give us sons and tolerate our daughters. As a bride I, too, experienced endless nights of frustration. I adored my husband – I would not have hesitated to poison the man whose embraces he preferred to mine, had there been only one, but there were many, a constant parade of new ones. I became used to it. Nowadays I observe his goings-on with a certain amusement." Watching Selma closely, the Begum noted with satisfaction that she was listening with bated breath. "Just lately, I have noticed he has become faithful to one of his lovers."

"You are lying!"

Selma shouted the words at the top of her voice, unable to restrain herself. Amir in the arms of another man? The very notion disgusted her. This woman had invented it in a frenzy of unrequited love, out of pure spite.

"Not so loud, my dear, the servants will hear you. The golden rule here is that anything is permitted as long as it remains a secret. That is what I meant when I told you that the burkah is our aid to freedom. Having declined to wear it, you may come to appreciate its advantages after all." The Begum's tone became grave again. "You are unhappy, Selma, and it hurts me to see you so because I know how much joy we could give each other. This is not a passing fancy of mine: I love you. Remember that."

She rose, perfectly self-possessed once more. Her eyes held Selma's for a moment. Then, with great dignity, she left the room.

Zahra's face came nearer and nearer. Selma saw herself reflected in the girl's gold-flecked eyes, which seemed to widen infinitely. She held out her hand, and the face receded. Youthful breasts, soft and cool, brushed against her lips. She tried to caress an insolent, dainty nipple with her tongue, but Zahra laughingly eluded her and ran to Amir, sat on his lap and embraced him with passion.

"Come back, Zahra!" Why did the girl enjoy hurting her? "Come to me. It is you I love, now I know."

Amir eyed her sardonically, but she did not care. She was not afraid anymore – she was past being deterred by his sarcasm or threats. Never had she experienced such desire. It rendered her invulnerable. All she wanted was to take the girl in her arms for a moment, to melt into her and die of happiness. All she wanted was paradise, nothing more.

Zahra hesitated. Loving them both as she did, how could she choose? She looked at them in turn, wild-eyed with indecision. Slowly, her hand left the broad chest and moved towards the young woman's, but, strain as she might, she could not move. The tension was unbearable, the air had become treacly, suffocating. Selma was struggling in a welter of sticky moisture, her throat on fire. . . .

She awoke to find her nightgown soaked with sweat. Thank God it had only been a dream! What with her fever and yesterday's distressing scene with the Begum, her mind was playing tricks. Or was it? She could still feel the velvety softness of Zahra's breasts against her lips. Suddenly she recalled the turmoil that had engulfed her like a hot wind when, a few days before, the girl's silky head came to rest on her hip.

"*I love you, Zahra, I know that now. . . .*"

The words rang in her ears as if she had just spoken them aloud.

This is ridiculous – the girl is like a sister to me.

A sister . . . of course . . . but would she have resisted yesterday had the hands and lips on her body been Zahra's?

She gave a furious tug at the bell-pull and tongue-lashed the startled maidservants when they hurried in.

"My bath, quickly, and send word to His Highness that I wish to see him before he goes out." She did not quite know why, but she felt she had to see Amir.

"Congratulations, my dear, you are looking much better today. Our hakim's medicines and your friends' visits have obviously done you good."

Had she imagined it, or was there a mocking glint in his eye when he referred to her "friends"? Who cared? She had something of importance to tell him. The idea had occurred to her in the bath, and the more she thought about it the more it seemed the only way to avert disaster.

"Amir, I had a dream last night – that is why I was so anxious to see you. It has to do with Zahra."

"Zahra? Why, what was the dream about?"

Selma shook her head mysteriously. "When I was a child they used to say you should not tell bad dreams or they will come true. Zahra was in danger, that is all you need to know. Luckily, there was a man at hand to save her."

"A man? Me, you mean?"

"No, an older man. I could not see his face."

Amir was growing restive. Dreams and premonitions and old wives' tales got on his nerves. He was surprised at Selma – he had thought her more sophisticated.

"You are imagining things, my dear. Zahra is in no danger, believe me."

"You may be right, but you know how fond I am of the girl." If he really knew. . . . "I am worried about her. She is so sensitive, so vulnerable – and she is lonely. We surround her with love, I know, but there is no substitute for the love of a mother and father. Or a husband."

"A husband?" Amir had started at the word. "What an idea! She is far too young!"

"She is sixteen. Most of your Indian girls are married at that age."

Amir rose and started pacing nervously up and down the room. Although he knew he would have to part with his delightful young sister some day, he hated the idea. She was the only person he really loved, the only person to whom he was attached by ties of both affection and blood – the two rarely went together, as had been amply proved by all the family dramas that troubled his life. There was an element of selfishness in his love for Zahra, he had to admit: she was the one person in the world who loved him unreservedly. In her eyes he was a god – the supreme embodiment of beauty, intelligence, and kindness – and her adoration was his greatest solace in times of adversity. His wife? He loved her, of course, but he could not share with her the kind of intimacy and deep trust that one could have with a woman of one's own blood.

"You are rushing things. Marry her off? To whom? I know all my fellow princes' eldest sons: they are spoiled, conceited brats who have never set foot outside their province and think the world revolves around them. There is not one that is fit to be mentioned in the same breath as Zahra."

"Who is talking about a youngster? Zahra needs cosseting – she would be far happier with a mature man."

"But the rajahs are nearly all married. I would not dream of allowing her to become a second or third wife." Amir knit his brow. "There is the Rajah of Larabad, of course, but he is too fond of the bottle. The Rajah of Kotra is charming but he is almost senile, and the Nawab of Dalior seems to be as bird-brained as his father. Who else is there? Oh yes, the Rajah of Bilinir, but he has been living so extravagantly he is almost bankrupt. No, there is no one suitable. In any case, I really do not see why we have to part with Zahra for a couple of years yet."

"Who is talking about parting with her?"

"I do not understand, Princess. You know the custom here: a wife has to move into her husband's home."

"What if the husband's home were here, in this palace?"

Amir scrutinized his wife closely, wondering if the fever had unhinged her. "I still do not understand," he said.

"I was thinking of Rashid Khan. Yes, I know he is not a prince, but he is the nephew of the Maharajah of Bipal, one of the biggest states in India. No one could find fault with his ancestry. Above all, he is an intelligent, modern-minded, kind-hearted man of great integrity. You know that perfectly well, or you would not have appointed him your private secretary. A marriage between Zahra and Rashid would be ideal from every point of view. We would not lose her, and you would not risk losing him."

That was Selma's secret weapon, carefully held in reserve until now. She knew that Rashid Khan had received tempting offers of employment from states far more powerful than Badalpur. In the present situation, an efficient and incorruptible man was worth his weight in gold. Rashid had so far refused out of loyalty to Amir, but for how much longer? Amir, whose reliance on Rashid was total, dreaded the prospect of losing him.

Her point was well taken. Amir sat down again, looking thoughtful.

Selma, of course, refrained from adding that she, too, was anxious not to lose Rashid; after all, he was her only ally in the palace. He often interceded for her with Amir and though she seldom saw him, she knew he was looking after her interests. Their only meeting since her marriage had, in fact, been that night at dinner with the Cuddesdons. She had sensed his emotion on seeing her and had been surprised by her own response. She had then realized how thirsty she was for love, how vulnerable she had become – just as she had been vulnerable towards Zahra's innocent sensuality.

Frightened by her own emotions, she had formed the idea of uniting these two people who loved her – to keep them near and far at the same time. Was it monstrously self-centred of her to play with the lives of others for the sake of her own peace of mind? No, that was too far-fetched. . . . The more she thought about it, the more the success of the marriage seemed assured. Zahra's generous nature would blossom, and Rashid, she felt certain, would fall madly in love with his child bride. As for herself, once he was a member of the family she would be able to see him as often as she wished, she would at last have a friend to confide in.

"What does Zahra think of the idea?"

Amir had regained his composure and Selma sensed that the game was almost won.

"Would I have mentioned it to her without consulting you first?" she protested, every inch the model wife.

Amir had to admit he was tempted.

"Well, it is not such a bad idea. Of course, I will be criticized for not having chosen her a prince, but the political situation is so unstable, who knows if tomorrow a prince would not be a liability? I will have a word with Rashid. Would you mind doing the same with Zahra?" Amir unexpectedly leaned forward and stroked Selma's hair. "Thank you. I am touched that you should take such an interest in family matters. You are becoming a real Indian woman!"

She was almost annoyed by his confidence in her.

"Say no more, I quite understand. You want to be rid of me!"

The girl was making a valiant effort to control her voice and hold her tears in check, but her knees had begun to tremble. She stiffened, determined not to break down.

"Zahra, my dearest child!"

Zahra raised her head. Her eyes were filled with pain and incomprehension. What had she done to deserve this act of betrayal – to be rejected by the woman she had adopted as a sister and mother combined? She felt as if she were being ripped apart. It was like being orphaned all over again.

"Nobody is forcing you into anything, Zahra. The choice is yours." Selma was appalled by the look of despair on the girl's face. She had not foreseen, or had not wanted to foresee, such a reaction. "We just thought. . . ."

But Zahra was not listening. She was staring at Selma's face, that face which once had been so full of tenderness. . . .

"Tell me," she said. "Did you ever love me, or was it all an act?"

Dear child, if you only knew how much I love you, that it is because I love you too much. . . . But you would not understand. How it hurts me to make you suffer like this. . . .

"Zahra, do not be childish. You know how fond of you I am."

The words sounded laboured and insincere. Zahra's only response was a bitter smile. At that moment Selma would have given anything to take the girl in her arms and kiss her – tell her it was all a bad dream, that she really loved her. Instead, she heard herself say, "I have a photograph of him. Would you like to see it?"

"What is the point? You have already made up your mind and persuaded my brother. What is left for me to say?"

Selma's sorrow became tinged with irritation. Zahra was playing the martyr and casting her, who liked to think of herself as a champion of freedom, in the role of a cruel stepmother.

"Nothing is settled and you know it! You are free to do as you wish."

She had raised her voice and exaggerated her annoyance, clinging to her anger because she knew it was her best defence against the emotions that threatened to sap her willpower. Zahra said no more, but her look of bitterness gave way to contempt.

Gradually Selma's anger subsided in the face of her silence. The damage was done and nothing could undo it. Whatever Selma said now, Zahra would feel unwanted.

CHAPTER 12

The wedding had gone off well. Amir, stretched out on the divan in his sitting-room heaved a sigh of relief. After the last two tiring weeks, with their endless round of ceremonies and receptions, the return of peace and quiet was a boon. He was happy. Beside him, the perfect wife, Selma, was making him a pan. He watched her contentedly with half-closed eyes: her behaviour throughout the wedding festivities had been irreproachable, even though things had begun badly.

As Amir had foreseen, tongues had wagged at the news that his younger sister was to marry his private secretary, even though everyone conceded that the bridegroom had "good bones," or an aristocratic pedigree. However, disapproval of the match waned considerably when it became known that the wedding would be attended by the entire royal family of Bipal – even, an unprecedented honour, by the Maharajah himself – and when it was seen what sumptuous gifts they brought the bride. After all, the bridegroom was the eldest son of the junior branch of the family and the Maharajah's two sons looked rather sickly; an ill wind might some day blow the couple some good!

Amir was not unaware of this gossip, nor of the rumour that he had consulted a soothsayer before deciding on the match, but he simply smiled and said nothing. His hardest battle, though, had been waged inside the palace itself, where Rani Aziza refused to be appeased. Selma had not thought it necessary to tell him that the Rani had accused her directly of trying to oust Zahra because she was jealous of her. When Selma had enumerated Rashid Khan's good qualities and argued that he would make Zahra happy, she had thought the Rani was going to choke.

"What has happiness to do with it? As if a woman marries to be happy! She marries to perpetuate her husband's line – to give the state an heir! Poor Zahra will not have to worry about that!" She glared at Selma venomously. "To think that some women have a name they are supposed to pass on and are incapable of doing so. . . ."

She stalked out before the younger woman could reply, but the shaft had gone home. Selma knew that people were beginning to wonder why she was not pregnant after a whole year of marriage. Amir himself had sometimes seemed worried. She knew that Rani Aziza had advised him to take a second wife, and that he had bluntly told her to mind her own business. Selma was grateful to him, for she could imagine that the silences and innuendos around her husband were more hurtful than any words.

What she herself had found most hurtful in the last two months was Zahra's polite but frigid indifference. Without the girl's laughter, trust, and affection, the world, and the palace in particular, seemed bleak indeed. Yesterday, however, Rashid had taken Zahra off to Europe for a three-month honeymoon, and Selma felt strangely relieved by their absence. As long as Zahra was not there, Selma could imagine that she would one day come back to her.

Her reverie was interrupted by the appearance of a eunuch who announced that the perfume dealer had arrived.

Perfumes, which loomed large in Amir's life, were a genuine passion with him, not a fleeting craze. His interest in the subject was scientific as well as aesthetic, and there was no mistaking the warmth of his welcome when the old dealer walked in followed by an assistant carrying two leather cases.

"I have known him for as long as I can remember," Amir told Selma, who was faintly surprised by what seemed to her a rather effeminate hobby. "He used to supply my father before me, so you see, love of perfume runs in my blood. My grandfather, the Maharajah, a rough, tough hunter who could scarcely read, was mad about perfumes and owned one of the finest collections in India. People came from far and wide to sample these divine fragrances, some of which were as much as two centuries old. Unfortunately, the collection disappeared during a fire started by someone who took advantage of the commotion to steal it. My grandfather was so upset, I think it shortened his life – this same man who had behaved stoically when his wife died."

On a square of black velvet the dealer set out a score of small flasks and phials, miniature works of art one and all. Some were of cut glass embellished with gold, others of finely carved jade or coral.

"A flask must be worthy of its contents," said Amir. "The interior and exterior must harmonize, so the sages have taught us. They, of course, were speaking of the body and the soul, the essence of man. These perfumes are the essence of nature – they cannot be kept in crude receptacles."

With the ritual gestures of a high priest the dealer picked up each flask in turn and, with the aid of thin slivers of ivory, deposited minute drops of perfume on the Rajah's hand. Amir shut his eyes and inhaled the various fragrances with a look of ecstasy. His beringed fingers caressed the precious phials for minutes on end while the dealer respectfully awaited his pleasure. He would have waited all day long, so delighted was he to see his treasures appreciated by a connoisseur as discriminating as the Rajah of Badalpur.

Reluctantly coming down to earth, Amir picked out half a dozen of the flasks. The old man bowed and smiled.

"Your Highness is never wrong. You always deprive me of my favourite children."

"You old rogue," Amir said jocularly, "I suspect you hide your choicest perfumes away. I can understand your keeping them to yourself because I share your passion, but I warn you: sell them to someone else and I will never forgive you!"

No one had shown any interest in the second leather case, which was bigger than the first. Selma's curiosity got the better of her.

"Aren't we going to see your other marvels?" she ventured to ask.

"Those, Huzoor, are perfumes unworthy of Your Highnesses' attention. They're much younger – I offer them only to clients less demanding than the Rajah Sahib."

"I had no idea that the value of a perfume depended on its age."

"To a certain extent, yes." The dealer was obviously delighted by this opportunity to lecture a novice. "It does, of course, derive its specific fragrance from various essences: vegetable essences such as iris, jasmine, myrrh, and patchouli; animal essences such as ambergris, civet, and musk. Perfumes are seldom one or the other – they are usually a subtle blend of several ingredients, but their fragrance soon evaporates unless it is fixed, and fixed without distortion.

"It was Nur Jehan, the adored wife of Emperor Jahangir, who invented a means of conserving the fragrances she loved so much. She steeped them for weeks in a highly refined oil. Alas, Huzoor, the exact method has been lost, though one or two experts have partly succeeded in imitating it.

"In fact, the great tradition of perfume-making came to an end in the eighteenth century, when perfumers began to adopt the Western habit of adding alcohol to their products. Alcohol is an aggressive liquid: it heightens a fragrance at first but distorts it within months and destroys it within a few years. The perfumers persisted in its use, however, because it was good for business: it enabled them to manufacture perfumes in much larger quantities."

Selma looked puzzled. "But if the scent is almost identical at first, how can you tell the difference?"

"Very simply, Huzoor. Look. . . ." The old dealer anointed her hands with a drop of perfume from each of two different flasks. "Both those perfumes are tuberose. They smell identical? Good. Now blow on the perfume on your right hand. It's cold, isn't it? That's because the essence is mixed with alcohol. Blow on the other hand and the temperature remains the same. That essence is pure: it will perfume your skin for days and retain its fragrance in the bottle for decades, even centuries."

Selma laughingly protested that she did not expect any perfume to last that long, but the size of the purse her husband handed the dealer indicated that the transaction was no laughing matter: it must have contained at least fifty gold sovereigns.

Amir surprised her even more, when they were alone again, by opening a wall safe and carefully adding his purchases to a collection of several hundred bottles.

"Some of these essences are worth their weight in diamonds," he explained to her, "but I value them far more highly than that. They have magical properties, you see. One drop can be enough to brighten a day that promises to be depressing or just boring. I think I acquired my taste for them as a child, when perfumes were one of the essential ingredients of a happy and peaceful life."

"Happy? But you lost your parents when you were six!"

"I hardly knew them. I was brought up by my grandmother and my sister Aziza, both of whom doted on me. My mother had lost her first two sons, so everyone thought she had the evil eye. As for my father, he was much too preoccupied with affairs of state to bother about a child. Besides, a prince's son used to remain in the zenana until he was seven. His education was not entrusted to men until then."

Amir had stretched out on the cushions beside Selma. He puffed thoughtfully at his hookah as he watched the last rays of the sun gilding the tops of the cypresses.

"I was very fond of my wet nurse, who used to take me to visit my parents once a week. I remember those visits as being very brief and formal. I had to call my father 'Abba Huzoor' and my mother 'Ama Huzoor' – in other words, 'Your Excellencies.' They called me 'Wali Ahed,' or 'Crown Prince,' never Amir, and addressed each other as 'Sarkar,' or 'Highness.' I hated all this etiquette and could not wait to go back to my games.

"Later, when my parents were killed in an accident, the women in the palace continued to take care of me. Until I was fifteen my playmates were the servants' daughters. We used to make up all kinds of stories. Usually I was the king and they were dancing girls. I loved them in all innocence.

"Since I was the only male heir I was very spoiled. I refused to eat, I remember, so they employed a courtesan to sing for me during my meals. That is how at the age of five I came to like music so much.

"There was no question of my taking a bath alone, either. Four or five young women were appointed to soap, massage, and perfume me. I found that very nice. I continued to enjoy their attentions throughout my childhood and into my adolescence, until I left for England."

He caught sight of Selma's raised eyebrows and smiled.

"Come, my dear, it was all completely chaste, I assure you."

"I see. So you spent your time being pampered by all those women. What about your education?"

"At seven I was given a tutor to teach me the rudiments. He could not enter the zenana, of course, so I went to the mardan khana, the men's part of the palace, for several hours each day. Even then I could not wait to get back to the zenana and my female playmates. Theirs was the only company I enjoyed. Although I started feeling romantic towards them as I grew older, I did not even know what a kiss was. When I turned eight my grandmother thought it time for me to learn something other than English and mathematics, and so, like all youngsters of good family until very recent times, I was schooled in the social graces by courtesans. I used to visit them in the mardan khana, but I was never left alone with them. My nurse or a manservant always came too.

"These courtesans were middle-aged women, very beautiful and highly cultivated. It was their intelligent conversation and exquisite manners that taught me how to speak and how to behave – in other words, how to become a man of the world. Some were musicians and I learned from them how to judge the quality of a ghazal[1], a thumri[2], or even a raga[3] but there was no question of my singing or playing an instrument myself. A prince is supposed to know how to appreciate entertainment, not how to entertain.

"Some of the courtesans were distinguished poets who trained me in the composition of poetry – Lucknow is famous for this art, as you know. It is one pastime that the nobility can engage in without demeaning themselves. My life was a dream. . . .

"When I was twelve my grandmother decided to send me to the

1 Lyric poem.
2 Piece of light classical music.
3 Traditional melodic theme in Indian music.

Princes' College so I could start studying seriously. I used to be accompanied to and from school every day by my tutor, my English teacher, my Urdu teacher, the manservant who carried my books, and, of course, the chauffeur. I had no opportunity to make friends with the other boys, nor did I want to. I was not used to male company, I felt uncomfortable. I wanted my old playmates back but unfortunately those days were over. I was nearly fourteen and my grandmother thought that it was time my tutor introduced me to the so-called facts of life. From then on, I was not allowed to see my girlfriends.

"Anyhow, a few months later my uncle tried to poison me to claim the throne, and it was judged safer that I complete my education in England. . . ."

"English boarding schools are supposed to be very Spartan!" Selma looked at Amir with sudden compassion. "It must have been a terrible shock, after the life you were used to leading!"

"No, not really – everything was so strange and exciting. But the fact is that I did not know who I was any more, what I was supposed to be, an Indian prince or an English lord."

Poor darling – you still don't, thought Selma, but she did not say so aloud, and just kissed his hand lightly. And he, not realizing that this was the first time he had dropped his guard and confided in her, was moved by her unwonted gesture of affection. A wave of desire surged over him. He longed to take her in his arms but did not dare: he had no wish to spoil a rare moment of happiness.

It had long seemed clear to him that Selma endured his lovemaking merely to please him. His disappointment was all the keener as everything about his young wife – her supple body, her full lips and breasts, her lustrous eyes – appealed to the senses. But whenever he clasped her to him and his caresses became more urgent, he felt her stiffen. He had tried to awaken her sensuality to enforce pleasure on her, only to find himself lonelier than ever. In the end he had bowed to the obvious conclusion: his beautiful young wife was as cold as a marble statue.

Wistfully he ran his hand over her auburn curls and twined them around his fingers. Selma rested her head on his shoulder; the luminosity of the sky made her shiver; she waited. . . . Trembling, she turned. . . . His hand glided down her neck, toyed with her earlobe, brushed her cheek, lingered at the corner of her mouth. She turned and sought his eyes in the gloom. Did he think she was shying away? Suddenly he removed his hand.

"What a beautiful night," he said stretching.

"Beautiful but chilly," she replied curtly and drew her silk dopatta around her shoulders.

Looking resentfully at his ring-laden hand, which sparkled in the light of the rising moon, she had a sudden recollection of Begum Yasmin's spiteful innuendoes. What if they were true? What if her handsome husband preferred a man's embraces and shared her bed only in the line of duty – in the hope of begetting an heir? That would explain his alternations of indifference and hurried, violent lovemaking. No, it was not possible! She shook her head to banish the visions that crowded in on her, feeling ashamed of herself, but the more she tried to dispel them the more insistent they became. She rose abruptly.

"I am suffocating in here. I need a breath of fresh air."

From terrace to terrace she walked, through the luminous darkness to the so-called Sunset Pavilion, which overlooked the city at the westernmost end of the palace. There, leaning against a marble column, she surveyed the shadowy, moon-gilded panorama spread out before her. In the distance, looming above the festooned arches and graceful pillars of the city's mosques, rose the white silhouette of the Hussainabad Imambara. Beside it, like the figment of some demented architect's imagination, the Turkish Gate assailed the sky with its countless lotus blossoms, emblems of peace that looked in the night like the banners of war and victories.

Baroque in its elaborate ornamentation, Lucknow was a dazzling blend of Mogul pomp and Hindu effervescence, French refinement and a Victorian solidity which seemed surprised to find itself in such frivolous company. By day, beneath the merciless sun, it resembled an elderly courtesan whose gorgeous attire fails to disguise her decrepitude, but at night it found its splendour again, its subtle perfumes, its magic, the languorous charm of a woman secure in her incomparable beauty.

She was the mistress of whom all men dream, Lucknow the Muslim, shy, secretive, and passionate, Lucknow the Hindu, graceful and erotic, Lucknow whose sensuality sublimated itself into mysticism, and whose mysticism harboured untold pleasures, Lucknow the enigmatic. . . .

As Selma leaned on the stone balustrade, her thoughts took wing and went soaring over the fabulous, extravagant city toward another, gentler city bathed in azure and gold: Istanbul. . . .

CHAPTER 13

"They slaughtered the women and children, and those who were only wounded they threw down the wells. Then they set fire to the houses. We were among the few that escaped – we managed to hide in a field. At nightfall we crawled into the forest and set off on foot. We walked and walked for days before we got here."

The man was reeling with exhaustion. His wife and two young children stood beside him, weeping silently.

"What's to become of us, Huzoor? There is no peace for us, anywhere."

The Rajah had them seated and sent for some food. Then he patiently questioned them.

It was one more tragic example of the riots that were alienating communities whose relations had till then been relatively amicable – riots sparked off by trivial incidents which, in the climate of tension fostered by extremists, degenerated into massacres.

At Lakhpur, the refugees' villages, the Muslim minority had been terrorized by the local, and very active, Mahasabha cell. Resentful of attempts to convert them to Hinduism, the Muslims had complained to the regional headquarters of the Congress Party, but their complaints were ignored.

The trouble had come to a head during a funeral service in the mosque. A Hindu wedding procession halted just outside the entrance and vented its collective high spirits with the aid of cymbals, drums, and trumpets. Some Muslim peasants emerged and asked the musicians to play elsewhere. Their request was greeted with abusive yells and blasphemies on the Prophet's name, whereupon stones flew, knives flashed, and both sides ran off to arm themselves with cudgels, scythes, and pitchforks. The entire village took part in the battle, which lasted several hours. The police arrived when it was all over.

"We can't go on living this way, Huzoor," groaned the man, wringing his hands. "We're only poor peasants. All we want is to work, so why won't they leave us in peace? The Hindus call us traitors and say that our Rajahs are friends of the British. They tell us we should join the Congress Party and fight for independence. But Huzoor, politics isn't any of our business. Politics is for the rich, educated city people.

We aren't against independence – but anyone can see we were safer under British rule. The Hindus never dared to attack us like this before they won the elections a year ago. Now they think they're our masters. We're outnumbered, Huzoor. What's going to happen to us?"

In a few halting words, the peasant had said more about the current situation than a dozen political speeches.

Amir was under no illusion: if the Muslims had been in the majority, they would doubtless have treated the Hindu minority in much the same way. However, it was not his business to pronounce on the relative merits of two religions that in the course of history had each produced philosophers, mystics, and dictators. This was 1938, and riots and massacres were multiplying throughout northern India. The village of Lakhpur did not belong to Badalpur State – the unfortunate peasant had sought refuge at the palace only because his brother was a cook there – it was situated in the adjoining state of Kalabagh. But news of this kind, peddled from village to village and embroidered on the way, threatened to set the neighbouring states ablaze at any moment.

Amir was so worried that, for once, he confided in Selma.

"Steps must be taken to prevent the fire from spreading before it gets out of control. Perhaps we'll be able to discuss them tonight, at Mahdabad's reception. The Rajah will have invited all the landowning arisocrats of the region, Hindu as well as Muslim. I know it is bad form to talk politics at a mushaira[1], but I don't care. It is time someone woke them all up."

Attended by all the nobility of Oudh, the moushairas were the sole concession the Rajah of Mahdabad made to luxury. He held them not only because he regarded hospitality as a sacred duty, but because these poetic contests, to which he invited the country's finest artists, provided an opportunity for Hindus and Muslims to sit side by side, to dream, to weep, to share the same emotions, and, finally, simply to be men in communion with beauty.

For two centuries Lucknow had prided itself on being the centre of an Indo-Muslim civilization that illumined the whole of northern India, a cultural syncretism achieved against all the odds. This extraordinary venture had been initiated three centuries earlier by Akbar, the greatest of the Mogul emperors, who assembled philosophers, scholars, and mystics at his court in Delhi with a view to making the

1 Poetry recital.

ultimate conquest: having delved deep into various religious beliefs – Hindu, Parsee, Islamic, Christian – Akbar's sages were to isolate the pure crystal nucleus where all converged and from it found the *Din Ilahi*, or "Divine Religion."

This grandiose undertaking was brought to nothing fifty years later by Emperor Aurangzeb, who considered religious tolerance dangerous and restored Islam in all its rigour. That was when the intellectuals and artists deserted Delhi, now the home of bleak religious orthodoxy, and took refuge in Lucknow, capital of the Shia kings of Oudh, who were noted for their splendour, extravagance, and generosity.

But if the kings of Oudh were as tolerant as Akbar had been, it was less from any concern for a mystical quest for the truth than for an eclectic passion for novelties and pleasures of every kind, sensuous as well as intellectual. Lucknow thus became a melting pot in which Hindu and Muslim elements combined to produce the most delicate examples of court music, dance, and poetry. It was there that Urdu, the language of northern India, attained its most refined form, and there, too, that the ghazal, a type of lyric poetry imported from Persia in the thirteenth century, acquired such an exquisite polish that some acerbic souls said its function was the concealment of intellectual hollowness.

The ghazal, or conversation with the beloved, was the king of the mushairas. Selma had learned to appreciate these poems in which the beloved could be the Creator, a dream of glory, the tinkle of a woman's bracelets, or the iridescent gleam of an unattainable universe. Tonight, however, it struck her as senseless and irresponsible for these Indian aristocrats to get drunk on words when the towns and villages around them were awash with blood. When she confided her misgivings to the Rani of Mahdabad, she was treated to an indulgent smile like an excitable child in need of quietening.

"What are we to do? My child, precisely what we are doing at this moment: setting an example of harmony and tolerance, not engaging in sterile argument. Lucknow is the only city in the area where there have not been any incidents; that proves it is an effective policy."

Peering through the pierced marble moucharabié, the Rani pointed out a tall man with a group of people around him.

"Look, there is the Rajah of Kalabagh, where the riots you mention have been taking place. He has chosen to be among his Hindu and Muslim friends tonight. Believe me, familiarity with other people's views breeds respect for their values – it is the only effective road to peace. If our princes did not appreciate the merits of the different religions, and if they did not prove it daily by treating their subjects impartially, we would not be complaining about a few isolated riots. The whole country would be ablaze."

Selma was not persuaded of the power of the example. This aristocratic notion might have been of some value in an age when the social order was undisputed, but was it still valid these days? Was it more an illusion cherished by an aristocracy that had not the inclination, still less the energy, to modify its beliefs and way of life?

Her eyes followed Amir as he approached the Rajah of Kalabagh and tried to speak to him, but the Rajah only shook his head with amused impatience. As Amir persisted, the Rajah led him towards their host, apparently asking him to intervene.

Her face pressed against the moucharabié, Selma vainly tried to read their lips. She gathered from the Rajah's gestures that he was doing his best to calm this young prince recently back from England who was taking things much too seriously. After a few more futile protestations, Amir gave up. He bowed and then vanished into the crowd, a slender figure in a white silk shirwani, the same as all the others and yet nevertheless a stranger.

Selma shuddered. She had a feeling she was witnessing the end of a world. Their blindness angered her, as did their cowardice and refined decadence, which cut them off from reality, paralyzed them.

All around them the struggle against British rule fostered by the Congress Party had turned into a popular revolt against the great landowners and the princes, whom the people regarded as friends of the British. Where the aristocracy was mostly Muslim, as in Oudh, the nationalist battle had become a social battle, a religious war which stirred the crowds to violence.

A sudden silence fell; the mushaira was about to begin. Reclining against cushions scattered over the thick silk carpets, the guests eagerly watched the master of ceremonies approach the dais. He was an old man with sparkling eyes, known throughout the area as the greatest master of his art.

For presiding at a mushaira was no easy task. Throughout an entire night the master of ceremonies had to pay close attention and maintain the enthusiasm of an audience composed of very exacting connoisseurs. There would be about thirty poets reciting in an unbroken stream from sunset to the following sunrise, and it was his task to intersperse the weaker ones between the better so as to keep the audience's attention at precisely the right pitch. He had to be able to greet a mediocre poem with a smile of relish so that the audience would be captivated by its rhythm and not notice its lack of content, for if they became bored or disgruntled the atmosphere of the evening would be spoiled. One must slowly distil the honey, gather the audience into the palm of one's hand, and when it had been won over suddenly stake straight at its heart.

The voluptuous, languorous strains of the first ghazal began, discreetly accompanied by a minuscule harmonium and the beat of the tabla. At Delhi the ghazal was usually recited; the connoisseurs of Lucknow preferred to hear it sung, unwilling to forgo the delights of a subtle interplay between words and music.

Selma had intended to slip away, pleading that she felt unwell, but the Rani's observant gaze deterred her.

"Stay, my dear. The poetry will relax you."

She sat down again, embarrassed that her lame excuse had been so transparent. And little by little she surrendered to the beauty of the verses. Their meaning largely eluded her, but the music was balm to her soul. Below her, the shirwanis swayed to the rhythm of the poems like a serpent of white and silver. The atmosphere attained a culminating pitch of ecstasy when a woman in a black burkah mounted the platform and began to sing a melody so poignantly beautiful that it rent the heart. This, the Rani whispered to Selma, was Shanaz Begum, one of the greatst exponents of the ghazal. She always appeared in public veiled, being a woman of good family. The veil seemed to enhance the vibrancy of her husky voice, imbuing it with a mysterious, forbidden quality that stirred the imagination and the senses to their very depths.

The night wore on. In the women's gallery, one or two old begums had fallen asleep. Selma's soul seemed to be drifting away. She heard the melodious murmur of a stream running along its stony bed, rustling through the leaves, washing into mossy clearings and jumping into crystalline cascades.

All at once, a voice broke in on her dreamlike state.

"I am the I that resides in the heart of all creatures. I am the beginning, and the middle, and the end of all being. . . ."

The music had ceased and the master of the mushaira was nowhere to be seen. Facing one another on the platform were two youths dressed in plain white shirwanis. Selma sat up. She recognized the words as those of a Sufi mystic, but which one? She asked the woman beside her, who stared at her in surprise.

"They come from the Bhagavad-Gita, Princess – the sacred book of the Hindu religion."

Hindu? Selma was amazed – she had known these words for as long as she could remember. She peered more closely through the moucharabié. The youth, lost in contemplation, went on reciting the sacred text.

"I am sovereignty, the power of all who rule, subdue and vanquish. I am the sustaining principle of those who succeed and conquer. I am the silencer of secret things and the knowledge of those who know."

Sitting up very straight, his hands on his knees, his companion responded:

"Glory to Allah, whose unity is preceded by nothing but Himself, being the first, and whose singularity is succeeded by nothing but Himself, being the last. About him there is no before nor after, no high nor low, no near nor far, no how, no what, no where, no state, no succession of moments, no time nor space, no mutable being."

"He is the One and Only, the Subduer."

"He is the first and last, the within and without."

"He discloses Himself in His unity and disguises Himself in His singularity."

Selma gave a start. It was a passage from Ibn-Arabi's *Treatise on Unity*, one of Islam's greatest mystical texts.

Slowly, the two youths repeated the sacred words which, like an echo spanning centuries and continents, conveyed the same deep intuitions, the same eternal truth.

"Some worship Me in My unity, and in each separate being and in My countless universal faces. All that is glorious and beautiful in the world, all power and might – know that this is My own splendor, light and energy, born of a mighty particle, and of the intense power of My existence."

"All that we think is other than Him is not Him. For to claim that anything exists by itself is to believe that this thing created itself, that it does not owe its existence to Allah - which is meaningless, since Allah is all. Beware of equating any thing with Allah, for thus will you debase yourself with the shame of idolatry."

"Through Me this universe has been extended throughout the ineffable mystery of My Being. The man who lives and acts so that he sees the Me in all beings, and all beings in Me, who depends utterly on the Unity and loves Me in all his dreams, that man lives and acts constantly in Me."

"For that which you think is other than Allah is not other than Allah, but you do not know it. You see, and do not know what you see.

When you come really to know what your soul is, you will relinquish dualism and you will know you are nothing more than Allah. The Prophet said: 'He who knows himself knows the Lord.'"

"The Yogis who strive see the Lord in themselves."

"From the moment when this mystery will be revealed before your eyes, that you are no more than Allah – you will know that you are your own end, that there is no need to annihilate yourself, for you have always existed. All the attributes of Allah are your attributes. That is why he who has attained reality may say: 'I am truly divine' and 'Glory be to me, for my faith has no limit!'"

"When through devotion a man comes to know Me, to know who I am and how great I am, and having thus known Me in all reality and in all the principles of My being, then he enters into the Supreme I. And if in his every act he remains in Me, through My grace he will attain the eternal and imperishable state."

Tears ran down Selma's cheeks, but she did not care who saw them. She was more at peace than she had been for a long time. All day long she had been assailed by nightmare visions of hatred and violence. The slaughter of innocent peasants had filled her, not only with disgust and incomprehension, but with an unprecedented craving for revenge: if terror was the only means of enforcing justice, it behoved one to be the stronger – to kill so as not to be killed. She realized that this desperate solution could only bring more misfortune in its wake, but what other answer was there?

She had come to the mushaira hoping that it would be postponed in view of the current crisis, and that the men present would evolve a plan of campaign, or at least of self-defence. Her hopes had been dashed: the host had refused to allow any discussion whatsoever.

And now, at the very end of the recital, he had supplied an answer to the problem: these religions whose faithful were tearing each other apart subscribed to the same Reality. Above and beyond the superfluous rites and customs that obscure religions and set men at each other's throats, they all lead to the Supreme Being, the Absolute of which every man is composed. They urge him not to forget, in his destructive frenzy, that the Infinite resides within him; that he is infinite beauty and knowledge, only a speck of dust but one that contains the universe because he is a particle of God. A particle? No, he *is* God: the Infinite cannot be divided.

Knowing that, how can one despair of mankind and see in the other an enemy to be crushed, when the other is none other than Myself, as I am also He?

"Poor old Mahdabad must be going senile," Amir remarked during the drive home. "Ridiculous of him to round off a mushaira with a lot of religious mumbo jumbo!"

Selma stared at him. "You did not understand?"

"Understand? What was there to understand?"

"Nothing. It does not matter."

He turned away, exasperated by her reticence and the air of queenly umbrage she sometimes assumed.

Selma sank back against the seat. Amir's incomprehension neither saddened nor angered her; she just felt infinitely weary. She tried to recall the words of the Bhagavad-Gita: "Perceive and love God in every creature." She closed her eyes, wondering if she would ever manage to do so.

CHAPTER 14

"Where is Aysha?"

It was over a week since Selma had seen the litle girl who usually brought flowers for her hair every morning. A pretty child of seven, she was the daughter of the couple who had fled from Lakhpur a month ago and taken refuge at the palace. The husband helped his brother in the kitchens, the wife worked as a seamstress.

Selma had heard a rumour that the wife, a proud woman, disliked living on charity and was urging her husband to return to their village now that peace had been restored. The Rajah of Kalabagh had gone in person to see the Congress authorities and obtained certain assurances, so the surviving Muslims had started to drift back and rebuild their gutted homes. In any case, they had nowhere else to go. For generations, their forefathers had tilled the lands that belonged to the Rajah, and they had the hereditary right to cultivate them: Lakhpur was their home.

Besides, would anywhere else be safer? Riots might break out at any moment in town or country. If they did not have a master to depend on, who else would defend them? A vagabond's life was no life at all. Nothing was worse than belonging to no one, and thus having no right to claim protection.

"They are right," an old maidservant told Selma. "It's as if I myself were thinking of leaving the palace. My family has eaten the Rajah's salt for five generations, how could I ever leave here? . . . Aysha's mother is worried about her, though. When men lose their heads, terrible things can happen. . . ."

Selma had listened with only half an ear. She could not see why the family should want to return. They were well off here, even if their quarters were a little cramped; they were sharing the brother's home in the servants' wing, near the provision store: had the woman's sister-in-law made her feel an intruder?

I will have to look into it, Selma had thought, and reimmersed herself in the Bhagavad-Gita and the writings of Sri Aurobindo, copies of which she had sent for the day after the mushaira. For several days she had been absorbed in them, striving to understand their abstruse language and rediscover the intuition of unity that had overwhelmed her years ago on witnessing the ritual dance of the dervishes in Istanbul.

Today, however, she had promised to call on the Maharani of Karimpur. Many social functions were held in April, before the heat of the summer set in, and she had to attend a succession of them. Which gharara should she wear? Whichever one she chose, she would need a jasmine garland for her hair. She had a reputation for dressing with startling but stylish simplicity.

"Well," she repeated, "where is Aysha? Is she ill?"

"Oh no, Huzoor, on the contrary." The maid who was helping her to dress smiled, clearly delighted to be the first to give her the good news. "She's married."

"Aysha married?" Selma looked at her, appalled.

"It's an excellent match, too. A widower of forty, a wealthy businessman from Ahmedabad. He'll take good care of her."

"Take care of her?" Selma almost choked. "But that is criminal – the girl is only seven!"

"Don't worry, Huzoor," the maid said reassuringly. "He'll let her play with her dolls awhile yet. The wives of such marriages seldom produce a baby before they're ten or eleven."

Selma stared at her in horror. Aysha was just a frail little child, not one of those nubile, sun-ripened adolescents that populated the Oriental fantasies of the European male.

"Send her mother to me at once."

The peasant woman did not hang her head under Selma's torrent of reproaches. She stubbornly returned her gaze with a look of resentment verging on defiance. Selma was taken aback.

"But why didn't you consult me first?" she asked eventually.

"The Rani Sahiba is far too preoccupied with matters of importance for the likes of us to dare disturb her."

The accusation was clear: engrossed in her mystical research, Selma had failed in her duty to protect the women and children who depended on her. Aysha's fate had been sealed by her selfishness and indifference.

"He that remains unmoved in any respect, even when good or ill befalls him, and he that neither hates nor rejoices, that man is a sage. . . ." How did the wisdom of the Brahmins appeal to little Aysha and the millions of other unfortunates who inhabited this country? Selma glared at the sacred texts that littered her desk and turned to the maidservant.

"Those books," she said, "put them away in the closet."

She could have wept with rage. No, she had not attained the supreme detachment that enables a person to become one with the

Divine, nor had she acquired "the serene and spacious lucidity of mind that leaves no room for passion or sorrow," and she congratulated herself on her failure. What right had she to stand aloof from all this suffering and seek her personal salvation? What right, Lord, what right?

Restlessly, she paced up and down. "A sage would say that I fail to understand, that I have not yet attained the necessary level of spirituality. It is possible to understand everything, I know, but one has also the right to *refuse* to understand!"

"Go on, Sikander my son, don't spare him!"

"Go on, my beauty, my precious pearl, let him feel your beak! Harder, harder!"

The trainers urged their charges on with cries and gestures while pandemonium reigned around them and bets were laid. Selma had never before seen Lucknowi high society, usually so blasé, yield to such a frenzy. Exclamations rang out around the white cloth on which the two quails were menacing each other with feathers ruffled and claws at the ready. Eyes gleamed, beringed fingers twitched, lips tightened expectantly, then parted to emit cries of jubilation or disappointment. The sums wagered were so enormous that some of the men would be unable to settle their debts on the spot. They would have to pledge their wives' jewellery, but no matter! This was no time to worry about trifles.

All that counted now was the fight in progress. Tamed by the British and enfeebled by generations of self-indulgence, no member of these aristocratic and princely families had waged war for a century. But now, as they watched the birds rear up on their spurs and attack each other with insensate fury, these descendants of the Moguls felt the blood of their heroic forefathers boil in their veins. Dauntlessly they squared their shoulders, hurled themselves at the foe, charged without thought of danger, dealt out lethal sword-strokes. Their desire to conquer or die was irrevocable, their courage illimitable, their thirst for glory unquenchable. . . .

Blood spurted on to the white sheet. The wounded bird was labouring under a hail of furious blows from its adversary who was trying to finish it off with its beak filed to a stiletto point.

Agonized whimpers, spreading crimson stains. . . . Aysha, little Aysha! Selma bit her lips to stifle a cry. There on that white sheet she could see the child bleeding, struggling to resist the monstrous assault, a child doomed to die. . . .

Around her on the platform reserved for women, excitement was at fever pitch. These gentle ladies derived at least as much pleasure from quail fights as their husbands and, instead of money, wagered their gold bangles on the outcome.

"Are you enjoying yourself, Princess?" inquired the Maharani of Karimpur. "Lucknow is famed for its quail fights – they are much rarer than cock fights. Quails are peaceable birds, you see. It takes a great deal of skill and training to make them aggressive. You have to starve them and tease them until the plump little things turn into brawny, belligerent beasts."

"But why?" Selma protested. "Aren't there enough creatures with an instinctive urge to fight each other?"

The Maharani frowned at the incongruous question.

"Really, Princess! All art consists in rearranging the natural order of things. The elephant fights in which our ancestors delighted were merely trials of brute strength, and so were the highly-prized contests between tigers and rhinoceroses. What is the point of pitting natural enemies against each other? Our society has developed more refined tastes: to goad friends and allies into fighting each other is far harder and more exciting!"

The Maharani's smile had become derisive. Selma had a distinct feeling that her hostess was no longer talking about quails but human beings. She wondered if it was a warning, or simply the admission of the everyday pastimes of a bored and indolent society.

"The Lucknowis take nothing seriously except their amusements," the Maharani went on. "That is because we are such an ancient civilization. We have done everything and ceased to believe in much of anything. A pity, you think? I disagree. For a start, it prevents us from looking ridiculous and from having the bad taste to fight for ideas that we will end up abandoning later anyway. We appreciate the beauty of a contest without trying to justify it: it is a game like any other. The decadence of an effete aristocracy? Not at all. You will find the same mentality among ordinary folk, even the poorest of them. The only difference is that, being unable to afford gamecocks, they have invented the egg-fight."

Selma looked mystified.

"Two eggs are produced and bets laid. Then they are thrown at each other. The one that breaks loses, of course, and the money that was riding on it goes to the backers of the egg that remains intact. The British think the egg-fighters are mad – they think they would do better to eat their eggs than 'waste' them. They will never understand our people, these Ingrez. It is insulting to want to reduce them to digestive tracts, just because they are poor! Let them amuse themselves

– let them dream to their heart's content!"

The quail fights were followed by a pigeon show. The women crowded around, eager to see this year's batch of curiosities. Intelligent birds of a gentle and affectionate disposition, pigeons enjoyed an enthusiastic following throughout the East. Although Selma could recall seeing huge aviaries at Yildiz and Dolmabahçé filled with many rare varieties bred for the Sultan's delectation, never before had she set eyes on pigeons as extraordinary as these. Some had one green wing and one bright pink, while others proudly sported on their throats floral motifs in delicate colours.

"You must not think they have been painted," the Maharani explained. "Painting them would be a banal thing to do – and anyway, the paint would wear off. To produce these marvels, specialists pluck out the pigeon's feathers one by one and replace them with coloured feathers taken from other birds, or feathers steeped in vegetable dye for several days. Pigeons that have undergone such treatment keep their gorgeous plumage for years and fetch high prices."

Two servants had stepped forward carrying a big gilded cage between them. With extreme care they reached inside and brought out a strange-looking creature. It was hailed with cries of admiration. The bird – or was it birds? – flew over to the old Rajah of Dirghpur and perched on his shoulder, cooing contentedly. Only then did Selma realize that the phenomenon had two heads.

"Isn't it miraculous?" exclaimed the Maharani. "Did you ever see a double-headed pigeon at the Ottoman court?"

Another half-dozen of these rare monstrosities were produced from the cage. The spectators passed them from hand to hand, gingerly feeling their plumage and uttering rapturous comments.

"What ingenuity! No one has ever produced such marvels since the time of King Nasir ed-Din Haidar. Only Lucknow has experts capable of such skilful work."

Selma, who had thought herself confronted by a freak of nature, realized to her horror that these two-headed pigeons were man-made. The Maharani obligingly explained that the operation was, in theory, quite straightforward.

"They simply take two young pigeons, cut the right wing off one and the left wing off the other, and sew them firmly together. Later, it becomes a delicate matter, because not many survive. You have to look after them with the utmost care. When the wound has healed and the birds are fully grown, they are taught to fly. That requires an immense amount of skill and patience."

"How cruel!" Selma exclaimed indignantly.

The other women stared at her. One of them, a Hindu, leaned forward.

"More cruel than butchering animals for the table, Highness?"

Selma was at a loss for an answer. What *was* the difference between killing a creature to tickle the palate and mutilating one to delight the eye? Unable to define it, she remained silent.

As though in a dream, she heard the women around her discussing the prices fetched by these prodigies. The Nawab of Dalior had vainly offered ten thousand rupees. Ten thousand rupees! How many girls like Aysha could be saved from servitude for the price of a single bird? The Maharani of Karimpur noticed Selma's melancholy expression and tried to distract her.

"Did you know that Bahadur Shah, the last Mogul ruler, owned thousands of pigeons, and that they flew above his head in close formation whenever he went out, to shield him from the heat of the sun? As for Wajid Ali Shah, the last king of Oudh, he owned twenty-four thousand of a very rare variety with silken plumage. He had to part with them when the British deposed him and he lost his entire fortune. His present descendants are destitute. You see that old gentleman in the pleated brocade robe? That is his eccentric but indomitable grandson, Prince Shaad. He refused to let his sons learn English, just in case financial necessity prompted them to work for the British some day. That is why, instead of holding down comfortable jobs in the administration, they wear out their eyes embroidering saris for a miserable three rupees a day – hardly enough to feed their children, and certainly not enough to afford proper treatment for their mother, the Princess, who is dying of tuberculosis."

"He might at least sell his turquoise," said Selma, who had noticed the huge blue stone that almost completely obscured the old prince's ring finger.

"Never! That turquoise is his one remaining source of income. He lives on it."

Selma momentarily pictured the prince swallowing powdered turquoise in the same way as men anxious to enhance their virility used to dose themselves with seed pearls dissolved in vinegar.

"Like the Tibetans," the Maharani went on, "Shias regard the turquoise as a lucky stone. Our princes – who are inveterate gamblers, as I was telling you just now – engage in turquoise contests at which the wearer of the finest turquoise wins all the others. To assist Prince Shaad without offending him, his friends sometimes visit him wearing mediocre stones which they can lose with good grace. That enables him to pay off his most pressing debts."

What a strange code of honour, Selma reflected: rather than come to terms with reality, the old Prince chose to let his wife die of neglect and deprive his sons of a decent living. She could not make up her mind which was preferable, this intransigence or the rajahs' compliant and sometimes subservient attitude toward the British. Was there not a middle way? Those who tried it got lost . . . lost in the maze of compromises entailed by any contact with the colonial power and ended by incurring the mistrust of Indians and British alike.

Wasn't that the risk Amir ran by systematically probing his opponents' defences and patiently appropriating their weapons in the hope of an ultimate victory? Outwardly more English than the English, Amir was convinced that they should be fought on their own ground. That was why, in company with the other princes of Oudh, he would be present at the grand durbar tomorrow morning, when the governor, Sir Harry Waig, made his annual distribution of titles and honours to loyal servants of the British Crown.

A big, bright-coloured tent had been erected in the grounds of the governor's residence. Inside, conversing in hushed voices while awaiting His Excellency's arrival, sat a distinguished assembly of men in uniforms and brocade shirvanis.

Suddenly, with a head-jerking roll of drums and crash of cymbals, the scarlet and gold bandsmen launched into *God Save the King*. It was precisely 9.30 A.M.

With the punctuality befitting a representative of His Majesty, the governor made his entrance, a white-uniformed figure glittering with orders and decorations. Beside him walked Lady Waig in hat and long gloves, and following behind came a bevy of grave-faced aides and officials.

Everyone rose while Sir Harry and his wife took their seats beneath the gilded canopy that had surmounted the throne of the kings of Oudh at a time – less than a century ago but so remote as to seem legendary – when India was not yet under the administration of the British Crown.

The durbar was declared open.

"Khan Bahadur . . . Rai Bahadur . . . Sardar Sahib . . . ." In a sonorous voice, the governor's aide-de-camp read out the titles to be bestowed for services rendered. Swelling with pride, the recipients made their way along the red carpet and bowed respectfully before the King Emperor's representative, who graciously conferred the scrolls or decorations that set the seal on a life devoted to that most noble of causes, the indestructible alliance between the Indian

Empire and the British Crown.

This year a score of titles was bestowed, ranging from the humblest – "Khan Sahib" – to the most prestigious of all: "Knight Commander of the Most Exalted Order of the Star of India." Certain rajahs were invested with the title "mahararajah," which signified "great prince." Discreet applause punctuated the proceedings. Smiles and congratulations were exchanged.

It was hard to imagine that, while this ritual show of allegiance was in progress, vast crowds inspired by Mahatma Gandhi were rebelling against the occupying power, that British troops were firing on demonstrators, and that tens of millions of Muslims led by Mohammed Ali Jinnah were joining the Hindus in a concerted demand for independence.

Independence? For years now the entire country had been throbbing with the word; neither mass arrests nor bullets were sufficient to silence it and indeed, day by day the cry grew louder. Independence! It was a magical word for an oppressed people whose promising future lay just over the horizon.

And here on this immaculate expanse of lawn, amid clumps of begonias, sat the docile, grateful, respectful élite of the country. Unbelievable! Were they spineless or simply heedless? Selma wondered. She had a sudden fierce desire to insult these well-dressed monkeys whose one ambition was to imitate their masters. How the British must despise them! Why had she agreed to take part in this charade? Why had Amir insisted on it?

Her eyes sought him out on the other side of the lawn. He was deep in conversation with a small group of friends, fellow princes who, like him, were supporting and financing the independence movement. Why were they playing this double game? Although they themselves had never accepted any honours from the British, they remained on the best of terms with them. Why? To lull them into a false sense of security before stabbing them in the back? So said Amir, who argued that the British were far too well-entrenched to be driven out by force.

"But is it really essential to attend these degrading ceremonies?" she had asked him again, as they were setting out for the durbar that morning.

He had merely smiled.

"The demonstration of the servility of some of us in the face of British arrogance is useful, believe me: it fans the flames of hatred."

And she had seen his knuckles whiten on the emerald-studded hilt of his ceremonial sword.

Every durbar culminated in a gala ball at the governor's residence, attended by the most illustrious figures in the United Provinces. The guests, Indian and British, numbered some two thousand.

Selma, as excited as a girl about to make her social debut, spent the whole afternoon getting ready. This would be her first ball since arriving in India, and she was determined to outshine everyone there – determined to make the Englishwomen, who pretended to ignore her, green with envy.

She carefully chose a midnight blue sari embroidered with tiny diamonds, knowing that it would emphasize the whiteness of her skin. The emeralds that gleamed at her throat and wrists were echoed by others in her hair.

Amir paused in the doorway: he had never seen his wife look more beautiful. Her grace and nobility, her incomparable radiance, filled him with pride. All Lucknow would envy him tonight. No other prince, and certainly no Englishman, could boast of owning such a jewel.

The governor's palace, a majestic white silhouette, loomed above the palm trees that flanked the interminable drive. Drawn up outside was a guard of honour, dark faces impassive beneath red and black turbans bearing the royal cipher. Guests were greeted at the top of the brilliantly illuminated steps by His Excellency's two secretaries, attired in tails and stand-up collars despite the warmth of the April night. Only when everyone else had arrived would Sir Harry and Lady Waig make their appearance. Dozens of servants ushered the guests across the lobby, with its marble columns and pale pink Corinthian capitals, to the ballroom, a fantasy of turquoise and gold. Soaring thirty feet or more above it on delicate arches accentuated by stucco festoons, a circular gallery ran between small loges with finely carved domes surmounting them.

The room seemed enormous in spite of the people crowding into it. Black tail suits mingled with shirvanis and the colourful uniforms of the Indian Army: short scarlet jackets for the infantry officers, royal blue trimmed with silver for the cavalry. Few Indian men cared to expose their wives to the gaze of strangers, so the few saris in evidence were heavily outnumbered by long evening gowns, some of them in startling shades. Selma thought how strange it was of Englishwomen to borrow India's most strident colours: acid yellows, shrill pinks, dazzling mauves. Were they trying to compensate for their natural insipidity, or was she just imagining it? After all, everything English was the last word in chic by definition, and what we, ordinary mortals, considered insipid must seem to them the height of stylishness. That was the English people's secret of success: they had no doubts, and whatever happened, their belief in their own superiority remained undimmed.

"Princess!"

Amir discreetly nudged her. She had been too wrapped up in her thoughts to notice the arrival of the governor and his lady, who were now standing under the canopy while the band played the national anthem. The formal presentations – the most important part of the evening – were about to begin.

One after another, as the major-domo called out their names and titles in a commanding monotone, couples made their way toward the dais between two rows of inquisitive guests. Some were rewarded with a few words and a smile, coveted marks of favour that were promptly observed and later discussed at great length by all present. Very similar to an audience at the Ottoman court, though more provincial, of course, thought Selma pulling a little face.

"Their Highnesses the Rajah and Rani of Badalpur!"

Silence fell while Amir and Selma progressed across the vast room. They were an impressive sight – so impressive that, when they halted in front of the dais and treated the governor to a gracious smile, the onlookers suddenly felt that this majestic, haughty pair were the royal hosts and Sir Harry and his wife their subjects. No man could have held himself more proudly than Amir, who sensed the significance of the murmur that ran around the room. For one brief moment, he was an Emperor and the sultana beside him a jewel in his crown.

The governor, a trifle disconcerted at first, quickly recovered his poise.

"My dear Amir, what a striking couple you make! I was just saying to Lady Waig that you and your wife are not just handsome – you are elegance personified."

Amir paled. Sir Harry must be well aware that any allusion to the physical charm of an Indian wife was a grave insult, so he was obviously getting his own back for the sensation they had caused. He glanced round quickly: no one seemed to have heard the remark except the governor's aide-de-camp. Amir felt reassured but he had learnt the lesson: never again would he parade his wife before these barbarians!

He felt, now, that every man in the room was mentally undressing her. He clenched his fists; he wanted her to be admired but could not bear her to be stared at. Her graceful walk and shapely figure, set off by the folds of her sari, suddenly infuriated him. Where did she think she was? He must tell her to adopt a more modest bearing. For the first time he caught himself wishing she were ugly.

The presentations came to an end and the band struck up a Strauss waltz. Sir Harry bowed to his wife and opened the ball. Other couples followed them on to the floor. Amir went off to join his friends, leaving Selma helpless among the dowagers. She had hoped he would ask her to dance, but the possibility had not even crossed his mind. He had not indulged in that form of exercise since since his salad days at Oxford, and anyway, he would not have dreamed of making such a spectacle of himself and his wife. To Indians, dancing was an activity restricted to courtesans and transvestites.

Wistfully, Selma watched the couples whirling around the floor and heard the women laugh, intoxicated by the rhythm, as they relaxed in their partners' arms. The fat, the skinny, the ugly – creatures who would have stood no chance of being asked to dance in their own country – were all rare and sought-after objects of attention in India.

Selma was following them with her eyes. How unfair! Here she was, condemned to the company of the old and decrepit. What was the use of being the most attractive woman present? Everyone was having fun – no one paid any attention to her except a few vixens who eyed her with a mixture of pity and derision as they clung to their partners or flopped into a chair, breathless with exhilaration, and feigned surprise at the sight of her sitting there.

"What, not dancing? Why ever not?"

She tried to look as if she did not care, but they were not taken in. It angered her that Amir should have abandoned her to their spite. He was probably busy talking in the smoking-room. He was quite capable of spending the whole night in there, leaving her in the corner waiting for him, and suffering the sarcastic comments. What if she left without him? Would it create a scandal? If so, what of it? Wasn't his casual treatment of her scandalous enough in itself? She knew it accorded with custom in India, where husbands and wives were not supposed to appear in public together, but Amir could not always have it both ways: if he took her to an English establishment, he might at least have the decency to behave like an English gentleman. To these foreigners, his neglect of her must seem rude and offhand.

"May I have the pleasure of this dance?"

She gave a start. A young man with very fair hair was smiling down at her. Her obvious surprise flustered him.

"Forgive me – we have not been introduced, I know. My name is Roy Lindon. I have only just arrived in India – I take up my duties with His Excellency tomorrow. I don't know a soul here, so I wondered. . . ."

Selma was on the point of putting him in his place, but he seemed so shy and awkward. She could not help smiling.

"I do not dance, Mr. Lindon."

"Really?"

The young man blushed like a reprimanded child. He forbore to say that he had been watching her for a long time and could tell that she was longing to dance. What an idiot he had been to imagine that this gorgeous creature would. . . . He was just backing away with another stammered apology when a gesture stopped him in his tracks.

"Why don't you sit down for a moment?"

The women around could hardly believe their ears. What a shameless little creature the Rani was! Scenting a scandal, they glanced at each other delightedly.

Selma surveyed the young man. How would Amir react if she danced with him after all? He would make a scene, naturally. She recalled her days in Lebanon . . . the party aboard the *Jeanne d'Arc*, Wahid's fury when she danced with that French officer. Still, the prospect of a scene did not displease her. It would inject a little life into this conventional existence to which she was slowly but steadily becoming accustomed. She rose.

"Let us dance!"

Roy Lindon waltzed exceptionally well, or was it the exceptional nature of these few stolen minutes that so enchanted her? With her eyes half-closed, Selma surrendered to the whirlwind that carried her away, faster and ever faster, dazed by the music and dazzled by the suns and stars that seemed to revolve above her in the turquoise sky.

Why had the band stopped playing? The sudden immobility made her sway and clutch her partner's arm, but he, instead of supporting her, withdrew it. Surprised, she opened her eyes. Amir was confronting them, livid.

He thrust her aside without so much as glancing at her. This was a matter to be settled between men.

"You will pay for this insult, sir, by tomorrow morning. I will leave the choice of weapons to you."

The Englishman stared at Amir open-mouthed, wondering if he were insane. A little knot of curious onlookers had gathered around, but no one dared to intervene. The Indians among them appreciated the gravity of the situation and sympathized with the Rajah. The rules had to be obeyed. It was a matter of honour for all of them.

"My dear Rajah. . . ."

All heads turned at the sound of the governor's voice. Alerted by one of his aides, Sir Harry had deemed it wise to step in without delay. There could be no question of allowing this ridiculous scene – over a woman, as usual – to end in a death. He did not relish the thought of informing young Lindon's father that his son and heir had perished in a duel for having dared to ask a married woman to dance. There was no doubt in Sir Harry's mind that the Rajah would emerge victorious from such an encounter: he was a redoubtable shot and fencer.

Besides, in the unlikely event that Amir himself got killed, matters would be more serious still. In the current political climate, his death would have an explosive effect. The independence movement would be quick to proclaim him a martyr, murdered by the colonial power for having tried to defend his wife's reputation. The couple would be held up as a symbol of the virtue of all Indian wives and the honour of all Indian husbands. Revolutions had been triggered by less!

The governor devoted nearly an hour to pacifying Amir. To demonstrate the young man's good faith without incriminating the Rani was a task requiring boundless diplomacy and skill of the highest order. Roy Lindon was quite plainly innocent. He frankly confessed to having noticed a young woman sitting by herself and looking bored. He had never dreamed. . . . Far from appeasing Amir, however, his profuse apologies only made matters worse. There had to be a guilty party. If the young man was telling the truth, Amir would be forced to admit that the Rani alone was responsible, and that she had deliberately made him look a fool in public. He had no choice: he had to kill this Englishman.

Sir Harry was growing annoyed. If the Rajah were so insistent on having someone's blood, it would be more logical and effective to kill his wife. He did not say so, of course, but confined himself to remarking that, fortunately, civilized people could settle minor misunderstandings without resorting to bloodshed. It was not the Rani's fault, naturally; her Western upbringing had not prepared her for life in India. However, if certain conventions could be explained to her. . . .

Amir, cut to the quick, drew himself up to his full height.

"That, Your Excellency, is my concern alone. There will be no more problems of this kind. I shall put a stop to them once and for all."

Sir Harry gave a little start. Was the Rajah capable of killing her? Ah well, that was not his concern. Nothing mattered to him provided peace was restored.

"You will remain in your room until further notice. Your meals will be brought to you. You are also forbidden to walk in the palace grounds and receive visits from your friends. From now on, you will observe the strictest purdah."

Rani Aziza, standing at her brother's side like a living embodiment of womanly virtue, was jubilant: she had always known, always predicted that this marriage would turn out badly.

"I treated you too well," Amir pursued in a weary voice. "I trusted you and you betrayed my trust – you humiliated me. Since you are incapable of behaving decently of your own accord, you oblige me to compel you to do so. I do not intend to allow my wife to dishonour me."

They left the room and closed the door behind them. Selma heard the key turn in the lock.

She was a prisoner! How dare they? She would appeal to the courts, to the Viceroy himself. If that was not enough she would manage to send a message to Beirut: surely her mother would know who to contact, what to do. . . .

Suddenly she remembered the terrifying vision of Rani Shahina's English mother crying, "Go, go quickly, before it is too late!" Panic assailed her. She rushed to the door and hammered on it – in vain.

For the first time, Selma felt genuinely frightened. Who could she turn to? Nobody suspected that she was a prisoner. Amir and Rani Aziza would devise innumerable explanations for her nonappearance at public functions. No one would be surprised – women in India went out so seldom – and even if people did wonder a little at first, who would dare to conduct an investigation into what went on in the depths of a princely palace? She would soon be forgotten like Rani Shahina's poor old mother. She shivered at the thought. Never! She would rather die than let them bury her alive.

CHAPTER 15

"I can't. Huzoor, the Rajah Sahib would kill me!"

The maidservant shook her head and retreated with her hands behind her back. No, she would not take the gold necklace – no, she would not smuggle the letter out. The master would guess – he was so powerful, he knew everything.

"No, Huzoor, it's impossible. . . ."

Wearily, Selma dropped the necklace. After three days' confinement she was beginning to lose hope. She had detected compassion in the eyes of the maid, a newcomer to the palace, but fear had overridden it. With what terrible punishment could the servants have been threatened by Amir if even the lure of gold proved ineffective?

Threatened by Amir or by Rani Aziza? Surely it was she who had taken everything in hand on the strength of her brother's anger, delighted at long last to take her revenge and resume her place as the mistress of the house. It would never have occurred to Amir to deprive Selma of her usual servants. And he would certainly not have been so ridiculous as to station that big black eunuch outside her door armed with a huge sword, like a stage ogre intended to frighten a little girl.

She had not seen her husband since the night of that fateful ball. He had emptied their bedroom of his personal effects and moved back into his bachelor quarters. If only she could speak to him, she felt sure she could sway him for, in spite of everything, he loved her. But Rani Aziza supervised all contacts between the zenana and the outside world. There lay the danger: Selma could starve herself to death, Amir would not know until too late.

Never dreaming that they would keep her shut up like a vicious animal, she had spent most of the first day yelling and hammering on her hard-won door. She only made herself hoarse and bruised her knuckles on the thick wooden panels that had been meant to guarantee her privacy and now muffled her cries. The windows afforded no means of escape: they were not only too high up but guarded by another eunuch who paced her balcony day and night.

Selma refused to lose hope. She must conserve her energy for the battle ahead. Yet the longer time went on the more a situation she had at first thought temporary began to take on the relentless quality of routine.

"You will remain in your room until further notice," Amir had said. How long was "further notice"? How many days or weeks would her imprisonment last? She refused, even for a moment, to imagine that it could be permanent, or give way to the panic that had gripped her that first night when the key turned in the lock. She must . . . she must . . . she did not know . . . she just did not know any more what she should do.

As the days went by, she began to leave her meals untouched. It was not an attempt to exert pressure – that would have been wasted on the Rani – it was simply that the very sight of food made her sick.

Meanwhile Rani Aziza's response to the Rajah's inquiries about his wife was that her enforced seclusion was proving beneficial: Selma was thinking things over and beginning to see sense. Should they let her out? Most unwise! Just as wild horses deprived too soon of the bit became more unmanageable still, she would only be twice as rebellious. Unless she was made to realize the full enormity of her behaviour and repent of it, her punishment would have served no purpose.

"What if I spoke to her?" Amir pleaded. "What if I told her that I forgive her this once, but that I would divorce her if she misbehaves again?"

He did not suspect how Selma would have laughed at this suggestion. In the Ottoman family it was for a Princess to divorce her husband, if the Sultan allowed it. A damad was never permitted to repudiate a wife of the royal blood, because that would have been an insult to the sovereign himself. Selma was not an Indian wife for whom a broken marriage spelled a living death because her family would never take her back. The repudiation of an Indian wife was in fact a slur on all her kinfolk: it proved that she had transgressed the rules that governed the life of the community. There was no longer a place for her anywhere. So, rather than be a pariah, she would accept becoming the slave not only of her husband but of his entire household.

Rani Aziza was more perceptive: she realized that her hated sister-in-law was proud beyond measure. She longed to be rid of this insolent foreigner who was not even capable of giving her brother an heir, but she knew that he, for all this threats, would never send her away. The only solution would be for Selma to fall sick – incurably so. That should not be too hard to arrange. . . .

She gazed affectionately, soothingly, into her brother's tormented face.

"Do not worry, I am doing what is best for her. If you interfere now, all my good work will be undone. Be patient: only another two weeks, and you will have the most loving, obedient wife you could ever have dreamed of."

Selma was growing weaker day by day. She tried to force herself to eat, but she could keep nothing down. Even tea gave her nausea. Her neck ached terribly and she felt dizzy whenever she stood up, so she spent most of the time lying down. Usually such a voracious reader, she had even lost any wish to read. She did not feel like doing anything; she simply waited. Having tried at first to fight off her languor and faintness, which she put down to lack of fresh air, she now allowed herself to drift, happy just to be rid of the exhausting vomiting attacks.

It was Rassulan, the young maidservant, who suggested, one day when Selma was racked by a particularly severe fit of nausea, that something in her food might be disagreeing with her. She had said no more, and Selma had dismissed her own suspicions as foolish. But after sending back her meal trays untouched for two days, she found that the bouts of vomiting had ceased.

From then on she restricted her diet to tap water and a few handfuls of almonds smuggled in by Rassulan. Although she felt better, she did not have the strength to get up, even to wash. It was three weeks since she had left her room, but she did not care any more. She felt as if she were floating. All her fear and anger had gone. Pastel-coloured visions of her mother, of Istanbul and her childhood, unfolded before her eyes like a happy dream. Serenity and peace were hers, at last.

"This is criminal! Who gave the order?"

Selma was dimly aware of a commotion around her bed, of voices boring into her eardrums. Why didn't they let her sleep? She moaned, stirred a little, and retreated once more into her warm, comforting cocoon of darkness and silence.

Zahra, timid little Zahra, confronted Rani Aziza like an avenging angel.

"If we had not come back earlier than planned, we would have found her dead! How could you have let her get into this state?"

The young doctor urgently summoned by Rashid Khan had confirmed that Selma's condition was serious. Another few days without food, and her heart could have failed.

Rani Aziza's only response to Zahra's questions was a disdainful silence. Amir, very pale, tried to read his elder sister's expression.

Which of them bore the greater responsibility? He knew she detested his wife, yet he had left Selma in her sole charge and taken her re-assuring reports on trust. Why? For fear of being swayed by his wife's tears? Because she had made him look ridiculous – because he had wanted revenge?

Uneasily, he looked down at the wasted body, the waxen face. He tried to imagine how grief-stricken he would be if Selma died, but in vain: his only emotion was indifference.

It shocked him: he might not have "loved" his wife, whatever that meant, but he had at least been fond of her. Usually so much in command of his thoughts, he could control them no longer. He pictured Selma's magnificent funeral, pictured himself an inconsolable widower, for several months. Then, for dynastic reasons, he would allow his family and friends to talk him into remarrying – an Indian girl this time, a pretty young creature prepared to worship him like a god and bear him many sons. They would live happily ever after. . . .

"Amir Bhai[1]!"

Zahra was looking at him with an air of reproach. He hastily wiped the beatific smile off his face.

"The doctor says Apa needs a nurse who will stay with her day and night and persuade her to take food again. With proper care, he says, she could be back on her feet in a couple of weeks, but she will need a complete change of scene and something to occupy her mind. He thinks she has lost the will to live."

"He *thinks*?" Amir snapped. "What entitles him to *think*, the young whippersnapper? My wife is perfectly happy. Still, a little country air may do her some good. We shall leave for Badalpur as soon as possible."

That was the answer: Badalpur. By the time they returned to Lucknow the scandal at the governor's ball might be forgotten.

Each moment one step nearer death.
Leave each unfilled if you would make it last.
Stir not; do nothing to efface, to destroy
The time that still remains.
By living life, we kill it, so refrain.

Selma laid her pen aside and looked out of the window. Dawn was breaking, and a pall of mist quivered above the distant horizon.

1 Elder brother.

Beyond it lay the foothills of the Himalayas, the sacred mountain retreat of those in quest of the ultimate truth. Such people were willing to put their lives in the balance and risk all in return for nothing – willing even to risk losing hope. She lacked their courage, or perhaps she would acquire it if only she could be sure. . . .

She cursed her recurrent desire for security. It was a bookkeeper's emotion, unworthy of one who prided herself on six centuries of imperial blood. She had not been afraid, though, but blissfully calm, when she had felt the nearness of death. She would have liked to identify that feeling with courage, but she wondered if it had not actually been a craven sense of relief at having completed a tiring journey and attained the point beyond which no more questions need be asked. Death . . . the word had a delicious finality about it, to her who had spent a lifetime searching for a definite goal, a firm objective. What wouldn't she give to be like those fictional heroines who always knew what they wanted and fought to obtain it! As one to whom everything so often seemed absurd, she marvelled at the strength of their aspirations, the violence of their desires.

Was her indifference real wisdom, that detachment from the world of appearances which the mystics advocated? Though tempted to think so, she was too lucid to be complacent. Her capacity for faith and enthusiasm had deserted her years ago, on that spring day when she had lost both her country and her father. Only the love for her of others, and their need for her could keep her alive. That was why Badalpur provided her with an incentive to go on living. The poor peasant women who clustered around their Rani had no idea how much greater was her need of them than theirs of her. All she gave them was a little money, whereas they, with their trusting looks and expectations, gave her life itself.

Last night it had warmed her heart to find them waiting to welcome her. Sita, the young widow, was smiling at her through the gate. The other women had tried to drive her away – a widow brings bad luck and must not be allowed to approach the Rani – but for once Sita had stood her ground. She clung to the bars, shouting at them to let her be, and they had done so for fear of the evil eye. For a moment Selma had not recognized her. The fourteen-year-old girl, so young and fresh the year before, resembled a little old woman with a crumpled face. What she must have suffered to have changed so! Selma had considered taking her back to Lucknow, but she knew that in Lucknow, as elsewhere, Sita would still be a widow and an object of universal revulsion.

"Where is Parvati?" she had asked, a little disappointed that Sita's friend was not there to greet her too.

"I have a message from her, Rani Sahiba. Parvati begs your forgiveness, but she can't leave her husband for a single moment. He's very sick – he's been spitting blood since the last full moon, and the hakim's potions haven't cured him."

"How sad!" Selma had said, secretly rejoicing at the thought of Parvati's relief if her elderly husband died. She decided not to leave her behind in Badalpur, at the mercy of her malevolent in-laws and neighbours. She would find a way of extricating her from this nightmare existence – Sita too, on second thoughts. Life could not stop at the age of fourteen.

She had spent the rest of the evening distributing the trunkloads of gifts she had brought from Lucknow. The resulting commotion might have developed into a thorough-going brawl but for the arrival of some palace servants, who, with the aid of a lot of shouting and beating, had marshalled the women and children into line and convinced them that no one would be sent away empty-handed. They all went home with their gifts clasped tightly to their chests, leaving Selma exhausted but finally at peace with herself.

It was already dark when she had heard a pebble strike the bamboo curtain over her bedroom window. She paid no attention at first. Then, when the sound was repeated, she went out on to the balcony.

"Rani Sahiba?"

Startled, she leaned over the parapet and tried to locate the source of the voice in the darkness below.

"Rani Sahiba, it's me, Parvati."

Selma made out her protégée's slender form in the lee of the column just below her window.

"Parvati! What are you doing here at this time of night? It is silly of you, the guards might have opened fire. Come up, I will tell the servants to let you in."

"Oh no, Rani Sahiba, no one must know I came. I wanted to see you, though, I'm frightened. . . ."

"There is no need, Parvati. If anything happens to your husband, I promise I will take care of you."

"But Rani Sahiba, they want me to. . . ."

Selma never learned what "they" wanted, because Parvati fled at the approach of a sentry.

This morning, recalling their conversation, she could not shake off a sense of foreboding. Parvati's terror was such that not even her Rani's promise had reassured her. Selma was surprised that such a sensible, level-headed girl could be so emotional. She would have to ask Sita if she knew what the matter was.

Selma spent the afternoon with Amir's grandmother. Rani Saida's strength was failing, and she no longer took an active interest in public affairs.

"It is up to Amir now," she said, smiling at Selma. "Amir and you, my child."

The light in her blue eyes was very soft. She had the pale, tranquil beauty of the old who know that the end is near and await it peacefully. Sitting at the foot of the bed Selma eyed her fondly. Rani Saida emitted an aura of serenity that made the problems of everyday life seem trifling and unreal.

Selma continued to sit there until twilight, when she saw that the old lady had fallen asleep. She lingered a few minutes longer, breathing in the faint scent of wisteria that filled the room and absorbing the silence that seemed so much more eloquent than any words. Then she tiptoed out.

Under the sun's dying rays the countryside was becoming tinged with red. From the little village mosque the muezzin's call to prayer rang out, and shadowy figures came hurrying along the lanes and alleyways to give thanks to God for the day that had passed.

Selma, sitting beside Amir on the highest of the palace terraces, savoured the cool, peaceful evening air. It was their first time alone together since the governor's ball. Neither of them had broached the subject of recent events, nor did they intend to. Explanations and apologies would have been idle and intolerable – unworthy of them. They simply sat there, drinking in the beauty of this peaceful summer evening.

In the distance, a little way from the village, Selma caught sight of a reddish glow and a thick column of black smoke. The evening breeze wafted an acrid smell of burning in their direction. She peered more closely.

"What is that, Amir? Are they burning weeds, or has a house caught fire?"

"Neither one nor the other, my dear. That is a funeral pyre. Someone must have died – can't you hear them wailing?"

He was right, she could just hear snatches of the mourners' lamentations. Had Parvati's husband released her from servitude at last?

Suddenly, shouts rang out in the grounds below, followed by the sound of running feet and a piercing cry. Amir jumped up and called to the guards. They appeared a moment later, four turbanned giants with a small, white-clad figure struggling and cursing in their clutches.

"Sita!" Selma exclaimed, seeing the girl's torn sari and tear-stained face. "What is the matter?"

"It's Parvati, Rani Sahiba, Parvati . . ." sobbed Sita, horror in her eyes. Selma took her by the arm and plied her with questions, but the girl was crying too uncontrollably to speak. A maidservant sat her down and bathed her face with iced water while Selma gently held her hands.

"Now Sita, what is all this about Parvati? Where is she?"

The girl gave a moan, and the significance of her broken words dawned on Selma.

"Over there on the fire, with her husband . . . burned alive. . . ."

"Suttee!" Amir's face darkened. "How dare they, the barbarians! Guards, hurry – try to save her!"

The guards arrived too late. All they found when they reached the scene was a circle of mourners praying over the remains of a pyre on which lay two charred black figures.

Selma rose at dawn the next day, her face swollen with weeping. Haunted by visions of Parvati struggling in the grip of her executioners as they thrust her inexorably toward the pyre, she had not closed her eyes all night.

"I am sure they forced her to do it," she told Amir. "She would not have committed suicide, she loved life too much. The death of that old man would have been a relief to her."

"Perhaps," said Amir, "but how do we prove it?" As a Muslim prince, he was loath to interfere with the customs of his Hindu subjects.

"She came to ask my help and I did not understand. I never thought. . . ." Selma stiffened. "Amir, we must avenge her, make an example of whoever was responsible, prevent any repetition of such a terrible crime. Send for the two families and question them – someone will talk in the end. Please, I beg of you!"

"You're deluding yourself, I'm afraid, but . . ." Amir shrugged, "for your sake I will try."

One by one they prostrated themselves, brushing the ground at Amir's feet with their foreheads. Then, eyes lowered for it would have been disrespectful to meet the Rajah's gaze, they awaited his pleasure.

The Rani was seated beside him. Her presence, an unusual breach of custom, was a disquieting sign that the business on which they had been summoned was no routine matter.

Selma scrutinized the members of the dead man's family. Parvati had spoken of them so often that she had no need to hear their names to identify them. There was the mother-in-law, a skinny old woman with more wrinkles than a centenarian and a toothless mouth stained with betel juice. There, too, were the husband's two brothers, oafish men with big, clumsy hands. They had not brought their wives with them – after all, what could the women say that the men would not say better? And there, beaming idiotically, was the dead man's only son, a hulking, simple-minded lout about whom Parvati had complained: he had made more than one attempt to rape her in his father's absence.

Parvati's parents, brothers and sisters were standing by themselves in a compact little group. Why did they look so terrified, Selma wondered? After all, they were the ones for whom justice was being done!

Amir began by reminding all present that they were under his protection and could speak freely. Then he questioned them for over an hour. The old woman, sobbing energetically, swore that she had done her utmost to dissuade her daughter-in-law, but Parvati had been so distressed by the death of her beloved husband that she had taken advantage of a moment's inattention to throw herself into the fire. The men had risked their lives trying to pull her out, but in vain: Parvati was burning like a torch. At this horrible evocation the old crone proceeded to wail, tear her hair, and call the gods to witness until Amir curtly told her to keep silent.

Selma was repelled, but admired her performance. She did not expect the guilty parties to incriminate themselves: only the victim's family could be counted on to tell the truth. To her amazement, however, they preserved a stubborn silence. Under close questioning, one of Parvati's sisters finally stated that the girl had told her what she intended to do. The others tearfully confirmed her story.

They were lying, Selma felt sure. Worse still, they were lying and they knew she knew it. She saw a conspiratorial glance pass between the dead man's brothers. They were laughing up their sleeve at her, and their mockery extended to Amir. She leaned toward him, white with rage.

"How can they be made to talk?"

"Only with the whip, but I will not use it. My fellow princes claim that humane treatment and the exercise of power are incompatible. I rejected their crude ideas long ago, but I am beginning to wonder if they do not have a point after all. For today, by refusing to extract a confession from these peasants by force, I am losing face in their eyes."

The case was dismissed. Having showered their Rajah with salutations and protestations of loyalty, the villagers set off for home. Amir paced angrily up and down, thrashing the air with his fly whisk.

"I knew that is how it would end but you did not believe me, so I gave in to you. I was wrong."

"Why did her own family lie – even her parents?"

"What good would it have done them to tell the truth? Would words have brought their daughter back to life? Her memory will be sacred from now on, and her heroism will purify the family for seven generations past and seven to come. To deny that she sacrificed herself of her own free will would destroy that myth and imply that she was a bad wife. It would tarnish the family's reputation and ruin her younger sisters' marriage prospects. If they had spoken out, the others would have taken their revenge as soon as I turned my back. No one breaks the laws of the village community and gets away with it, even if he is in the right."

"You mean . . . ." Selma was appalled. "You mean you are powerless to prevent other women from suffering the same fate?"

Amir turned on her furiously.

"These are Hindu customs – who am I to change them? What do you want me to do, torture my peasants into abandoning their age-old traditions and force them to adopt a 'modern' moral code? By what right?"

"But Amir, it is so obvious!"

"Nothing in this country is obvious. Do you think I have not agonized over these things? I was like you at first: I thought it was enough to mean well – I thought there was an equitable solution to every problem, but there is not. Life would be too easy if the choice lay between good and evil." Amir put his head in his hands. "Only fools and God know which is which. . . . But we, princes and kings, who are supposed to lead the people, do we have this knowledge? . . . We are just imposters: the fact is, we know no more than anyone else."

For days after Parvati's suttee and the charade of the trial that followed it Amir withdrew into a cloud of anger and depression. He was further enraged when the village elders came to tell him that they were being harassed by a team of agitators from Hindu Mahasabha, the extremist organization dedicated to converting Muslims to Hinduism.

"Political activists?" he said furiously. "Criminals, yes! who try to stir up hatred between the religious communities. I will not allow any religious wars on my territory!"

And he ordered his guards to arrest the men and march them to the state border, chained together like common criminals. Selma had never seen him in such a towering rage.

"Congress disclaims all religious affiliations, yet it gives these people a free hand. And without knowing it, even Gandhi is encouraging them by advocating a revival of Hindu religious values as the best way of ending British rule. He ignores the fears of our eighty-five million Muslims, who regard this trend as a growing threat to their identity." Amir sighed. "What a mess! In the early 'twenties most Muslims admired and supported the Mahatma. Now they have come to regard him as a hypocrite who preaches unity but is really paving the way for the subjugation of the Muslim minority by the Hindu majority."

"That's ridiculous!" Selma protested. "The Mahatma is a living saint – anyone who knows him will tell you so!"

"Calm down, my dear, I am not passing any moral judgements. It does not matter to me whether Gandhi is deceiving himself or other people, the consequences will be equally disastrous. He bases his movement on tolerance and brotherly love. all well and good, but can *you* see much tolerance or brotherly love in this country? Every day brings a fresh crop of riots, rapes, and murders. The Muslims fear and despise the Hindus; the Hindus dream of exacting their revenge for six centuries of Muslim domination. Even the Christians are growing uneasy. They're complaining about forced conversions and now they have decided to demand separate electoral representation, just like the Muslims, so that their voice won't be drowned by the crowd. Meantime Nehru and Gandhi continue to claim that there is no problem between the communities. Are they ill-intentioned or just blind? Only that is not the question, because what difference will good intentions make if there are hundreds of thousands of deaths instead of hundreds?"

"Why put all the blame on them?" Selma protested. "Jinnah and the League are just as uncompromising. They have even threatened to demand an independent Muslim homeland if they don't obtain sufficient guarantees. Isn't that going a bit far?"

Amir waved this airily aside. "To gain an inch you have to ask for a mile. Jinnah does not regard partition as a serious prospect, not for one moment – he said so again in private only the other day. It is simply a threat designed to frighten Congress into guaranteeing that, after independance, the Muslims will not be second-class citizens. It is only fair."

They continued to argue until the small hours. When Amir spoke of the Mahatma, Selma recognized the tones of a betrayed lover. He was not the first in whom she detected this bitterness and disenchantment. Had he and his friends supported Gandhi just because they believed that religion was a means to a political end? Had they not grasped that the Mahatma was aiming at something higher – at an essential truth?

CHAPTER 16

It was early morning, and Selma was sitting by herself on the terrace that led off her bedroom. Amir had left two days ago on a tour of the outlying villages, a decision greeted with shocked disapproval by his advisers and the local dignitaries, who objected that it was unworthy of a Rajah and would expose him to disrespect. No prince had ever been known to visit his subjects; it was for the peasants, if they had a request to make, to call on him. The doors of the palace were open to them every morning.

But how were the poorest peasants, the ones in most need of help, to find the few rupees it cost to make such a trip? How, for that matter, were they to spare the time, when every day was another struggle to keep the money-lender at bay? In any case, what money-lender or village headman would be foolish enough to let them air their grievances?

The result was that the Rajah's public audiences were attended mainly by local notables: schoolmasters, shopkeepers, and representatives of the panchayats or village councils. Ordinary peasants turned up seldom, agricultural labourers never. "They don't like to leave their homes," the notables explained, "so they've asked us to speak on their behalf." Well and good . . . only the Rajah had finally decided to make the journey himself.

Still drowsy, Selma recalled Amir's departure on horseback at crack of dawn. It had been raining, and the soil, like today, was fragrant. Amir was proud of himself and pleased that she had talked him into making the trip. He expected to be gone a week and had made her promise not to leave the palace.

"I am afraid the Mahasabha people may try to get revenge. I have doubled the guard," he told her, "but please do not venture outside the grounds."

She promised, and he left reassured after giving his final instructions to the diwan, old Rajiv Mitra.

The morning air was deliciously cool. Selma, reclining on her chaise longue, stretched voluptuously. The eastern sky was slowly turning mauve. These few minutes, when the countryside emerged, purified, from the womb of the night, were her favourite time of day.

The muezzin's distant call to prayer was answered from the other end of the village by the bells and gong of the temple sacred to Durga, the goddess of fertility. Threads of smoke began to rise from the mud huts as the women prepared sweet tea and chapatis for the men, who were setting off for the fields. If the harvest had been good, they would add an onion and a couple of the little red peppers that burned the throat and warded off disease.

A maidservant brought Selma a cup of translucent china. She sipped its golden contents and reflected that, if the British had any right at all to regard themselves as benefactors of mankind, it was for having popularized this magical plant called *ch'a* by the Chinese.

She had no desire to move – she even breathed quietly, reluctant to disturb the silence. And then, abruptly, that silence was broken by a cry followed by guttural exclamations. Some men had gathered outside the mosque and were gesticulating wildly. From the other end of the village, like an echo, came more cries, shrill and frenzied, accompanied by the persistent booming of the temple gong.

"What is going on? Has someone died – has someone been murdered? We must send some men to find out, quickly!"

Followed by the diwan, who had been hurriedly roused from his bed, Selma made her way to the highest terrace, which overlooked the entire village. Whatever the cause of the disturbance, word of it had spread like wildfire. Within minutes the slumbering village took on the appearance of an armed camp. Men milled around in the courtyards with women clinging to their arms, seeming to entreat them to be calm, while frightened children sobbed and hid themselves in their mothers' skirts.

The guards the diwan had sent to investigate came running back, grim-faced.

"The mosque has been desecrated – they found a sow and four piglets in the mihrab. The Hindus must have been put up to it by those Mahasabha agitators. The men are arming themselves. They're wild with anger and thirsting for revenge."

Just at that moment, some more guards ran up.

"The Hindus are getting ready to fight," they reported breathlessly. "They found a slaughtered cow in their temple – they've sworn to kill every Muslim in the village!"

Selma could see groups of men gathering in every lane and alleyway. They had begun to concentrate around the temple and the mosque, their numbers swelling by the minute. Young and old, all who were capable of wielding a cudgel or pitchfork had answered the call to battle. Selma turned to the diwan, old Rajiv Mitra. In the Rajah's absence, he was responsible for maintaining order.

"We must do something quickly, Diwan, or there will be a bloodbath!"

The old man bowed his head. "Do what, Huzoor? They must be at least five hundred and all we have here are fifty guards who must remain to defend the palace in case of an emergency."

"The palace?" Selma retorted indignantly. "Who is threatening the palace? Send them to the village at once – there is not a moment to lose."

The diwan stared at the gilded tips of his Turkish slippers.

"There are too few of them, Huzoor. It would mean certain death. Only His Highness could make such a decision."

"And the deaths of hundreds of peasants – women and children as well as men – does that mean nothing to you? Are you going to stand here and watch them slaughter each other? Think carefully, Diwan. I would not like to be in your place when the Rajah learns what has happened. . . ."

The diwan winced. "I will send for a detachment of police from Larimpur," he said lamely. "It is only twenty-five miles away."

"By the time they reach here it will be too late, you know that perfectly well. Listen!"

The hubbub was growing ever louder. Two mobs had formed up, one at either end of the village, and were preparing to move off. They would be face to face within minutes.

"It is the only hope," mumbled the diwan.

"Very well," Selma said firmly, "I will go myself. I will try to make them see reason. They like me – perhaps they'll listen to me."

"Don't even dream of it, Huzoor! Those people are out of control – they are quite capable of killing you!"

"Allow me to accompany you, Highness."

A man had stepped forward, a tall, mustachioed figure in officer's uniform. It was Said Ahmad, the colonel of the guard.

"Thank you, colonel, and bring one of your men along, with a drum."

"As you wish, Highness." He hesitated for a moment. "I wanted to tell you that I have taken the liberty of sending a messenger to the Rajah Sahib. He should be here with reinforcements in a few hours' time."

Selma's green eyes glowed: "I will remember you, colonel. And you also, Diwan!"

"Faster, Bagheera, faster!"

The three horses sped across the dusty plain. Selma's black

thoroughbred whinnied madly, unused to such a liberal use of the riding crop.

They passed the mosque without seeing a soul. The alleyways, usually alive with children, were deserted except for a few yellow dogs. Every door was shut and bolted. But for the swelling roar of voices in the distance, Oujpal might have been a ghost town.

"We'll have to cut across the fields, Highness, or we'll get stuck in the crowd. They won't make way for us."

Selma and her two companions galloped across some wasteland to a long ribbon of hard-packed mud, the main thoroughfare linking the Muslim and Hindu quarters of Oujpal.

They were just in time: the mobs were already confronting each other. Brandishing mattocks and pitchforks, cudgels and scythes in their calloused hands, the two ragged, barefoot armies exchanged yells of hatred and contempt. These lifelong slaves of the soil, these toiling rustics, had become soldiers of God, defenders of the faith and dispensers of divine justice.

They were within feet of each other. Any moment now stones would fly, skulls would be smashed and chests pierced by stakes. Yes they were going to die, but it did not matter! They were ragged beggars no longer: they were princes!

But what was this sound of a drum interrupting their orgy of revenge? Into the gap that still separated them galloped a big black horse with a white-robed figue astride it. Transfixed, they recognized their Rani. A few stunned moments passed. Selma knew she had only seconds to win them over, to take advantage of their astonishment, of the silence which had suddenly fallen, leaving them petrified.

"Stop this!" she cried. "You have been tricked, my friends. The politicians are trying to set you against each other. They have paid criminals to desecrate your holy places. Don't fall into their trap!" Then, as persuasively as she could: "Haven't you always lived in peace together like your fathers and your fathers' fathers? There is no reason to fight. If you are killed, what will become of your wives and children? What will become of your sons?"

They stared uncertainly at the figure on the black horse. They did not understand. What was she talking about? What politicians, what criminals? As for their sons, that was their own business!

"It's for our sons we're fighting, so that they can live in dignity, without fear!"

Whoever had said that, Hindu or Muslim, both sides murmured their agreement. Hesitation was giving way to mistrust. Selma tried to speak again, but the spell was broken. The faces around her had turned hostile and menacing.

"My friends –"

Her words were drowned by a babble of cries, and suddenly one voice rose above the rest.

"Go away, foreigner! Let us settle our own affairs!"

Foreigner. . . ?

She felt dazed as if she had received a stab in the heart. An old man seized her bridle.

"It's no use, Highness. Go quickly before you get hurt."

Get hurt . . . she wanted to laugh, but her eyes were filling with tears.

She had no clear recollection of how she extricated herself from the mob and got back to the palace. She could only recall that someone had punctured the regimental drum and this had frightened the colonel.

The battle raged for hours. All Selma heard of it, lying prostrate in her room, was a distant pandemonium punctuated by screams and the howling of dogs. Every now and then, even more sinister than the din of battle, a sudden hush would fall.

At first she had hoped these lulls meant that the two sides, tired of bloodshed, had called a truce, but the fighting only resumed with greater ferocity. In the end she came to dread them: they conjured up pictures of women pleading, wounded men groaning, corpses being borne away by weeping relatives and survivors stubbornly regrouping for an even fiercer onslaught.

She had lost all track of time and stopped trying to count the minutes and the miles Amir had to cover at a gallop. He would be too late in any case. She even ceased to indulge in the macabre arithmetic of hope, the obsessive computation of how many might have died and how many still survived at the end of every hour that passed.

Everything was in ruins, she knew: her village, her India, her hopes – everything. She had been rejected by those whom she loved and whose love she had thought she enjoyed. She felt cold, like a heap of stones. A foreigner . . . again, always a foreigner.

Shots rang out. The diwan hurried in, beaming.

"His Highness has returned, Huzoor!"

"Where is he? What is that shooting?"

The old man's smile broadened.

"It is the Rajah Sahib. He rode to the village with a hundred men. They won't be long."

Selma turned pale. She sprang to her feet.

"What? But why, why use guns? He need only have talked to them – they would have listened to him!"

"He tried, Huzoor, but they have gone crazy – they are deaf to reason. The only way to restore order is to shoot a few."

Volley after volley rang out, crisp as a whiplash. Selma huddled on the bed with her hands over her ears, but it was no use. Every volley made her flinch, every bullet pierced her heart. Amir, whom she had counted on to save the villagers' lives, was slaughtering them. He could have pacified them, she felt sure, but he had chosen the easy way out – the violent way. He, who had always criticized the inhumanity of his peers, was no better than the rest, in spite of all his fine speeches. She hated him. He had betrayed the trust of those whose "father" he claimed to be. So much for their joint intention – hers as well as his – to lead Badalpur State out of the Middle Ages and give its people a new and better way of life!

She would never forgive him.

This morning, in mournful silence, the villagers were burying their dead. The narrow streets were deserted. Every now and then shadowy figures would slink from house to house to inquire after the wounded or pay their last respects to the dead.

Selma stood motionless on her balcony, gazing across at the place she had come to love so dearly. Something told her she would never see it again.

She was leaving this afternoon. Rashid Khan had driven up from Lucknow to fetch her. His arrival was an unexpected consolation, and she clung to his kindly smile as if it were a beacon of hope in a dark pit of despair.

She had not seen Amir. She had shut herself up in her room last night. But her anger had subsided; all she felt now was an infinite sense of weariness and a throbbing pain in her head, as insistent as a drumbeat: *Go away, foreigner. . . .*

In Beirut, too, the other girls at Soeurs de Besançon had kept their distance because she was "the Turk." Ever since her exile, she had been a "foreigner."

But here at Badalpur it was different. Here, she believed, she had found a new homeland. The peasants had taken her to their hearts, or so she thought, and now. . . .

She felt a hand on her shoulder.

"Do not be sad, Princess. Everything will turn out all right, you will see."

"Thank you, Rashid Bhai," she said without moving. "Things always seem better when you are around."

"Look, we have visitors."

Several old men in spotless white dhotis were crossing the grounds on their way to the palace.

"Hindus and Muslims! It looks like a delegation. I wonder what they want?"

Amir, alerted by the guards, came out on the steps. The men kneeled down and kissed the dust at his feet. He took them in his arms and raised them up. Then the oldest of them began to speak, solemnly, to an accompaniment of nods and murmurs from his companions. He spoke at considerable length, and Selma could see that Amir seemed moved by what he heard. He thanked the men gravely, then sent for some tea, which they drank in silence. Selma turned to rashid.

"They seem to have sealed a new alliance," she said.

Rashid nodded. He seemed overwhelmed. "They came to thank their Rajah for having quelled the riot and taken the action they expected of him. They say they now feel satisfied that they have a master capable of protecting both communities in a just and equitable manner. They asked him to forgive them for having doubted him – for having suspected that his ideas were too English. Now they know that Badalpur State has a master who will care for their children and grandchildren. They say they are happy – they can die in peace."

"What!" Selma was thunderstruck. "They came to thank him for having shot at them?"

"Don't be so hard on him, Princess," Rashid said reproachfully. "I know how much that decision must have cost him. It conflicted with all his beliefs, all his principles. But shooting the ringleaders was the only way to stop the slaughter and save the lives of innocent women and children. Poor Amir! There is nothing worse than having to act against one's principles. I admire him for making that choice. I doubt if I would have had the courage."

CHAPTER 17

She is alone in front of the sphinx, who asks her the ultimate riddle in a dispassionate voice: "Which is better, to be dead in a living world or alive in a dead one?" She cannot tear her eyes away from the stone face. All alone in an unearthly void, she struggles with her mounting sense of panic.

Selma woke up bathed in sweat. The sphinx's question still rang in her ears, so loud and clear that it could not have been a dream – unless it was a dream as understood by the ancients: a message from the gods.

Rani Saida's parting words came back to her: "Happiness consists far more in loving than in being loved." As one who had known the pain of unrequited love when very young, Selma found this hard to accept. She could survive her husband's indifference but her rejection by the peasants of Badalpur was another matter. She had hoped to change their lives for the better only to be spurned.

"What do you expect?" Rani Saida had chided her affectionately. "Amir and I are also outsiders to those people. We would still be outsiders even if we left our palaces and adopted their way of life in the hope of understanding them better. That would strike them as ridiculous and offensive. Even if we lost our fortunes, nothing could obliterate our past: they would continue to mistrust us, and rightly so!

"For changing one's skin is a luxury, my child. An impoverished princess remains a princess, just as a peasant who becomes wealthy is still a peasant. Deep down, they know that – it is the reason for the unbridgeable gap between us, and that is why they resent us. They could abolish that gap only if they killed us all – a most radical way of eliminating social differences. The French knew that when they kept that guillotine of theirs going night and day. It was not the aristocrats and the rich they were trying to get rid of – it was the contempt in their eyes, that spoke of their distance. Too bad for the French they were not smart enough to get rid of the middle class while they were at it. It put them to sleep with fine speeches about equality and brotherhood, and the next thing they knew they woke up under the Empire!"

Selma raised her eyebrows. "I never knew you were a revolutionary, Rani Sahiba."

"I am not – I am a staunch conservative. I believe that the Almighty has put us in a certain place to fulfil a certain function, and that half-hearted attempts to alter the divine scheme of things are doomed to fail. All I am saying is, if the masses want to take our place, they must do more than make speeches and riot occasionally. If they develop the qualities needed to gain power and retain it, that power will be theirs by right. And the Almighty, who is also the Most-just, will have to register that slight change on the universe's ladder of infinite variations."

"But how can they ever gain it, starting from nothing?"

The old Rani burst out laughing.

"From nothing? There speaks the voice of charitable condescension! Those peasants are men and women like us – isn't that what you are always saying? How did *we* get where we are today? Centuries ago we were ragged peasants like them. It may take them a long time, but if they succeed it will prove that they are entitled to supremacy, and that we have lost the qualities that enabled us to conquer and rule."

And she concluded the conversation by hoping not to live to see the day when her class, whose decline was already self-evident, would reach the end of the road.

"For Allah is just," she said. "The only fruit that falls to the ground is rotten fruit."

This afternoon, the cloth merchants were to bring their choicest fabrics. Selma had just received the latest fashion magazines from Paris and she had decided to update her wardrobe. Since coming to India she had enjoyed wearing traditional saris and ghararas and regarded with amusement the attempts of her Indian friends to add a "Parisian" touch to their dress by draping a shawl in a slightly different way or adding an ornament here or there. But now she felt tired, she wanted to be herself again. In the beginning, she would wear European dress when she wanted to stage a show of independence against Amir – that is, until the day she overheard him laughingly tell Rashid Khan that his wife's clothes were the best barometer of her mood. She had felt silly, and that same evening emptied her closets of every trace of her childish rebelliousness.

As in Beirut, when her father's abandonment finally became clear to her, and later on, after Wahid's betrayal, Selma sought comfort in trivia. Everything she had tried to do in Lucknow, and even more in Badalpur, had failed. She had only succeeded in disrupting some ancient customs. She had aroused hopes she could not fulfil and had in the end provoked violence, inter-caste tension and quarrels within the families where women had begun to think they could hold up their heads. Wasn't she even, in a way, responsible for the Hindu-Muslim riot? She was the one who talked Amir into a tour of distant villages. If he had been home he would have been able to prevent the whole catastrophe. She had wanted to help them, but all she had succeeded in doing was sowing trouble, and then she had departed, leaving them more unhappy than ever. But she had to leave. Even the women, who were so fond of her, even they had understood – not one of them had tried to hold her back. . . .

In the adjacent room she heard Amir talking to his brother-in-law. She could have joined them – for there were no longer any restrictions on her meeting Rashid – but she did not feel like it. They were talking politics and although she had once taken a passionate interest in them, such discussions now left her strangely bored. Nevertheless, when she heard the name Gandhi, she strained her ears. The old man still fascinated her. Despite the failures, the daily outbursts and bloodshed that were a denial of his philosophy, he continued to preach non-violence; he fasted, and miraculously the crowds calmed down.

"This time Gandhi has lost his mind!" said Rashid Khan. "Do you know what he wrote in the last issue of *Harijan*[1] about the persecution of Jews in Germany? He is telling them non-violence is the only way to win against the Nazis!"

"Poor Jews! I hope they will fight back. Imagine countering Hitler with a Gandhian attitude. It would be sheer slaughter."

"What is worrying is that we have our own Nazis here." Rashid Khan's tone was troubled. "Have you heard the Mahasabha's statement at their congress in Nagpur? They say the Muslims in India are like the Jews in Germany, a minority that does not have any rights. Gandhi has not denounced them and he has not spoken out against those demonstrators shouting 'India for Hindus' either. I do not know what he is thinking of – I only know the Muslims are getting more and more frightened, that there are 85 million of us, too many to ignore, and this might all turn out very badly."

"*Might!*" From her position in her room, Selma heard Rashid's word and shook her head. "It is not a question of might – it is *going* to turn out badly!" She was not about to forget the violence and hatred she had discovered among the villagers of Badalpur who had been living together peacefully for centuries up till now. It had taken only

1 Harijan: literally "children of God." This was the term used by Gandhi for the untouchables and it became the name of the Gandhi movement's journal.

one crude provocation to plunge them into a bloodbath.

As for the provocations, their number grew daily, either to hasten a political decision or to hinder it. It was so easy to tip the scales when dealing with these naive crowds – so easy and so tempting.

But why was she worrying about all that? She could not change anything. If only she had been Indian herself, she could have done something but – as she had been told in no uncertain terms – she was not. She was a foreigner . . . and in the current explosive situation in India a foreigner had no right to meddle in politics. Even less to try and change the ancient customs which were the foundations of social stability. Charity was acceptable; anything else was dynamite.

She had refused to admit it, but now she had to face the facts: it was not just a few peasants who had rejected her. They had only given crude expression to what everyone else had been thinking for a long time. She remembered the frowns and pursed lips which had greeted her when she ever so carefully voiced some of her reservations about Indian society. She had even once overheard someone say that if she did not like it here she should go back where she came from. She had dismissed that as nothing more than a jealous woman's reaction. But now as she pieced together isolated incidents and remembered Amir's constant counsels of moderation, which she had taken to be mere lack of nerve on his part, she saw that he had been trying to protect her from her own enthusiasm and overly frank nature. Those qualities, in India, were intolerable; for they threatened the divinely-ordained social structure.

"Here they are, Rani Sahiba."

"Who?" Selma took a few moments to collect her thoughts. "Oh yes, the dressmakers. Send them in."

The woman's domain! She had almost forgotten it. . . . But now, as everything else was forbidden, she might as well develop a liking for ruffles and bows.

Within minutes the floor was littered with organdie, satin, and brocaded velvet from Europe, where the finest fabrics were made. Many of the once celebrated Indian weaving mills had been shut down by the English who wanted no competition.

The Rani of Nampur, just back from a trip abroad, had come to help Selma make a selection. What selection? With sparkling eyes Selma pointed to bolt after bolt of cloth – enough to have clothed every woman in the palace. To the dressmakers' delight, mounds of silks and satins piled up on every divan in the room. Rani Shahina was surprised by Selma's air of feverish excitement, almost of greed.

"What are you going to do with all those materials?"

"Renew my wardrobe, of course. What else is there to do in this country?"

Rani Shahina was about to comment when a maid announced that the jewellers had arrived. They were the three biggest jewellers in Lucknow, so widely renowned for the quality of their stones and craftsmanship that society women came all the way from Delhi to patronize them.

Selma had let it be known that she was interested only in stones of the first water. The dressmakers crowded around the array of velvet jewel cases, dazzled by the sight of so many superb pieces concentrated in one place. Selma casually inspected them and picked out several matching sets. Rani Shahina had the impression that her friend did not even see them. She leaned over and whispered in her ear.

"Selma, are you feeling all right?"

Selma stared at her sadly without answering.

The jewellers were profuse in their thanks. They bowed their way out, followed by the scandalized dressmakers. Purchasing jewels was a serious transaction, and not to be completed in a few short minutes! Even the Maharani of Jehanabad, the wealthiest princess in Lucknow, devoted several hours to choosing a new set of jewellery.

Gossip-mongers ensured that by nightfall Selma's extravagance was the talk of the town. What was not public knowledge was the Rajah's stupefaction when the three jewellers came to pay their respects – and present their accounts. The state's coffers were almost empty now that the laws passed by Congress had encouraged the peasants to default on their dues. Certain princes bribed the police to bully them into paying, but Amir had always refused to do this.

Although he recovered his composure quickly, the jewellers were observant men.

"There's no hurry. Your Highness can have all the time in the world to settle these trifling matters – we know you have far more important concerns. But if you would deign, perhaps, to. . . . We're only humble businessmen, you understand, and to forgo a return on even such a small capital sum would involve us in a loss. . . ."

"How much do you want?" Amir said curtly.

"Nothing, Highness, nothing!" they protested. "You have unlimited credit – it is an honour for us. Just a nominal sum by way of compensation – ten per cent, let's say. Ten per cent a month, of course."

"Very well," said Amir, mentally consigning them to the devil for doubling their prices in under a year. "And now, gentlemen, I must bid you good day. I have some important business to attend to. . . ."

His gracious gesture of dismissal deceived no one. For the first time in his life, the Rajah of Badalpur was at the mercy of money-lenders.

Selma sat in front of the mirror, humming. She was feeling cheerful and in no mood to wonder if the half-empty bottle of champagne on her dressing table had something to do with it. Her life had changed completely in the past few weeks, ever since Amir. . . .

It had happened on the evening of the day when she ordered all that jewellery. Amir had burst into her room, raving like a madman, and that was when she blew up. She wanted a divorce, she told him. She wanted to return to Beirut at once and would kill herself if he tried to stop her. She could not endure the kind of life he made her lead. He stared at her transfixed.

"What! You have everything a woman could want, but those jewels, honestly! Please be reasonable."

At that moment Selma had hated him.

"You never understand! I could not care less about jewellery and clothes and palaces. I want to *live, live*! I resigned myself to never going out except to stupid tea parties with ranis who do nothing but gorge themselves and gossip. I resigned myself to spending my days buying trinkets and waiting for you. The only place where I could breathe freely, where I felt useful was Badalpur, and now I cannot go there either."

She had burst into tears; she could not stop. Amir had vainly tried to console her, but he did not know what to say. He realized that her grief went too deep to be dispelled by a few soothing words. Selma had grown as fond of Badalpur as he was himself. He had admired her devotion and perseverance, but she had tried to go too fast. Too fast. . . ? The peasants would have rejected her, anyway, sooner or later.

"You have to take her mind off things," Rashid Khan advised, when Amir told him of Selma's despairing outburst. "Enjoy yourselves, see people, take her out more."

"Take her out where?" Amir frowned. "It is not done, you know that perfectly well. Only courtesans. . . ."

"I am not talking about our compatriots, since we unfortunately are only able to regard women as sexual playthings. I mean your English friends. Some of them are charming – if they have any prejudices, they certainly don't show them. They will be delighted to entertain you both. The Rani misses the social life she enjoyed in Beirut. A little of the same kind of atmosphere will do her good."

Since then they had gone out most nights, not to grand social functions, but to dinners attended by congenial people. Selma overcame her own prejudices sufficiently to concede that the English could be pleasant and interesting company, even amusing at times. Some of her husband's friends had been born in India and passionately loved the country, which they regarded as their own and knew a good deal better than many Indians.

One such was Major Rawsthorne, their host this evening. His grandfather, Amir explained, had arrived in Calcutta in 1850 as a young administrator in the service of the all-powerful East India Company. The tenacity and presence of mind instilled in him at Eton and Cambridge had ensured his rapid rise through the company ranks. In 1858 he married the daughter of a colonel who one year before had distinguished himself in suppressing the sepoy mutiny in Lucknow. His father, born in Bombay but educated at Eton and Cambridge, had followed in his grandfather's footsteps and had joined the Indian Army. It was a time of relative calm. Muslim power had been broken during the suppression of the Indian Mutiny, and the bulk of the great Muslim families, dispossessed in favour of those who had remained loyal to the Crown, had withdrawn into sullen and uncooperative isolation. The more adaptable Hindus, on the other hand, had made it their business to learn English and carve themselves a niche in the new society.

Rawsthorne's father never had to use his martial skills. The army, though, made use of his knowledge of Urdu, the language spoken by his aya and the servants who had surrounded him in his childhood. As an intelligence officer with numerous Hindu and Muslim contacts, he acquired an unrivalled knowledge of India's underlying currents of opinion. He did not have time to transmit that knowledge to his son Edward, for he died when the boy was only eight, but he did communicate his love of India and his belief that the British bore a moral responsibility toward his country so fascinatingly diverse and rich in possibilities. That responsibility, as he saw it, entailed that its inhabitants should be pacified and schooled for admission to the modern, civilized world.

Amir suspected that Edward too was something of an intelligence agent, but it did not trouble him overmuch: after all, all the British were to some degree. They called it serving their country and even felt that it was in the Indians' own best interests to forestall any impulsive acts that might compel them to take violent countermeasures.

The Major and the Rajah, who were aware of each other's opinions and found them only natural, given their respective points of view, got on well together.

Tonight's conversation centred on the news that, for the first time ever, a branch of the Muslim League – the one based in Sind Province – had formally demanded that India be divided into two federations: in other words, that the Muslims be granted an independent homeland of their own.

"They could not have done it without Jinnah's approval," said Rawsthorne. "What do you think it is, a genuine threat or a bargaining counter?"

Amir shrugged. "I think it's simply a symptom of popular unrest, and Jinnah has been forced to acknowledge it. The Muslims have lost faith in their Hindu brothers. When the poet Iqbal came up with his 'Pakistan' scheme ten or twelve years ago, it struck them as far-fetched. Now, more and more of them are coming to believe that it may be the only solution."

"And you ask us for independence? My dear Amir, there would be civil war the day we pulled out. Be honest: your people are not ready yet. Settle your differences first, then we can discuss it."

Amir refrained from pointing out that those differences, if not actually created by the British, had been exacerbated by them as a means of undermining the independence movement. He shrugged.

"Why don't you leave and let us settle them by ourselves, or is that too much to ask?"

Selma privately applauded. These Europeans were always convinced that they knew better than the Indians themselves what was good for them. Not content with imposing their political, economic, and social standards, they wanted to impose their mode of thought. The most dangerous of all were those who, like Rawsthorne, genuinely loved India. Realists gave up when a situation had ceased to favour them, whereas they would fight to the bitter end to enforce their beneficence on a people that did not want it.

But wasn't that exactly what I did at Badalpur? I too was convinced that I was right, that certain universal values exist. Now I am not so sure any more. Is there some indisputable foundation you can build everything on? If there is, what is it? Even respect for human life can have terrible consequences. . . .

"The poor thing suffers from bouts of depression. They say she has even contemplated suicide. . . ."

Selma gave a start and glanced at the woman opposite, but no, she was not talking about her. Suicide . . . she had thought of it quite often in recent months, picturing her last few hours and minutes with painful intensity, but had she ever had any real intention of killing herself? What she really liked was to savour the idea of death, lose herself in it, even though she knew she was cheating.

"I suggest we retire to the drawing-room and leave the gentlemen to talk politics."

The women followed their hostess happily: now they would be able to have some interesting conversation. Selma had taken a liking to their hostess, Lucie, a vivacious little Frenchwoman with an outspoken manner. No dinner party could be boring with Lucie around. She slipped an arm through Selma's in her characteristically informal way.

"*Chérie*," she said, "I have a confession to make: I am jealous of you!"

Selma looked puzzled.

"And I am not the only one," Lucie went on. "Your husband is one of the most attractive men I have ever met. You are a lucky girl – he must be a miracle between the sheets."

The other women giggled delightedly at the daring suggestion. After all the champagne that had flowed at dinner they were in the mood for confidences. Lucie, who knew better than anyone how to draw people out, made no secret of the fact that she had had several lovers. Not to make the most of one's amorous oportunities, she said, was to spurn a gift from God.

"Didn't Christ himself have a soft spot for Mary Magdalene?"

They smiled at Selma's embarrassment. The lovely little Rani was so charming, so girlishly shy. They never imagined that what they took for shyness was simply ignorance. After all, Orientals were known to be extremely virile – Muslims especially. Hadn't their Prophet set them a shining example in that respect?

"Is it true that among Muslims, husband and wife are permitted anything, absolutely anything?"

Selma stared at the pretty, dark-haired woman who was asking the question and wondered what exactly she meant.

"Now, now, Armande," said their hostess, "stop pestering Selma and tell us about that handsome young cousin of yours. I have noticed the way he looks at you. . . ."

More giggles. Lucie told the Indian butler to put another two bottles of champagne in the ice bucket and leave them to help themselves.

They were all slightly tipsy and enjoying the sensation. Their ribald remarks made them feel strong and self-assertive, a sisterhood in league against the husbands who boasted of their conquests as soon as they were out of earshot, quite unaware that their wives, too. . . . Well, why shouldn't they take their revenge? They would never have dreamed of leaving their husbands, but to deceive them, in word if not in deed, was a point of honour, and doubly satisfying because the poor dears were so unsuspecting.

To hide her embarrassment Selma did justice to the champagne without missing a word of the others' conversation. She had no idea that women could be so coarse. In the old days her curiosity had been whetted by laughter and suggestive remarks overheard in the hammam at Ortaköy, but no one had ever been as explicit as these European women in their corsets and long gloves. She suddenly felt resentful: was she destined to grow old without ever experiencing the pleasure they spoke of with such misty-eyed fervour, as if no sensation in the world could be compared with it? That would be too unfair. She was beautiful, she knew she was desirable, and she desired Amir, her handsome husband, coveted by every woman here. Should she tell him so? She would never find the words. . . .

She helped herself to some more champagne.

Selma had no need of words. That night, an unknown woman guided Amir beyond their wildest dreams, an avid and generous woman, now a submissive slave, now a priestess skilled in arcane rites, in patient fantasies. She devised a thousand different caresses, not knowing where her hands and lips were straying, not recognizing the source of the strange, plaintive moans that issued from the depths of her throat. Together they deliquesced, vibrated, plunged headlong into subterranean billows far, far away in the earth's core, were swept blindly along by a river that killed or gave life according to whether one resisted the current or yielded. Trembling, they journeyed through a turbulent tempest towards the sun, which suddenly burst and shattered them into a myriad meteorites, an innumerable shower of stars.

"My lover, you, my lover hidden by the ugly name of husband, why didn't I recognize you earlier? My hands guessed but I never dared. It all would have been so simple without this respect, this contempt of our bodies."

Light was streaming into the bedroom. With her eyes still closed Selma put out her arm in the expectation of finding Amir beside her – surely he would be there this very different, very first morning of all? – but her hand encountered nothing, just a cool expanse of sheet. She withdrew it and slid it beneath her pillow. Back to dreams again.

She dreamed of the shadowy figure she had fallen in love with last night, the master whose desires she had anticipated responding to every tremor, every lull as if they were her own. A warm glow pervaded her at the recollection of certain caresses, given and received, and her belly gave a kind of inward shudder. Her whole body seemed to blossom . . . sleep claimed her once more.

She awoke a little before noon, summoned her maids, bade them run her bath, do her hair, perfume her – quickly! Amir would come soon, she felt sure. Wanting to be alone with her thoughts of him, of them both, she sent her excuses to the Rani of Jodbar, who had been expecting her for lunch. She waited for Amir all afternoon, but for the first time ever she found the waiting pleasurable: it was like a foretaste of his presence. She relished her novel sense of submission, the joy of belonging to someone, at last.

When Amir still had not reappeared by dinner time, she became apprehensive. He always warned her when he was going to be out. To calm her nerves she sat down at the piano and played a few bars of *Miroirs*. Ravel's melancholy charm exerted its usual spell. It was not just her hands or her dreams that brought the music to life; it was her whole body, where every note seemed to respond like a caress.

"So, beauty!"

Amir had paused in the doorway and was staring at her oddly, with an expression Selma, to her amazement, realised was one of hatred.

"Well, aren't you going to kiss your lord and master?"

He took her by the shoulders and kissed her savagely, drunkenly. She could smell Scotch on his breath. Disgusted, she struggled in his grasp, but he held her tight.

"Enough of that!" he snarled. "Save your airs and graces for other people, they won't work with me!"

She froze, stupefied: had he gone mad?

"Far be it from me to condemn your expertise," he went on. "I like women who let themselves go the way you did last night. I must have been pretty drunk, because I thought I had come home with someone else – one of those whores who make it their profession to give men pleasure. Imagine my surprise this morning, princess, when I found that the whore in question was my wife. . . ."

He gave a sarcastic little bow.

"I congratulate you on having hidden your light under a bushel for so long. When I think how I have held myself in check these past two years, for fear of offending your innocent sensibilities! What a fool I was!"

She stared at him, stunned, speechless. In a matter of seconds, the rivers had run dry, the desert wind had withered the green fields. And when he took her in a frenzy, doing his utmost to humiliate her, she let him have his way. A kind of stupor descended on her. He had no need to use force: she yielded to his every whim with frightening submissiveness.

CHAPTER 18

"Huzoor, Huzoor, please wake up!"

Rassulan had vainly opened the shutters, coughed, banged closet doors, clattered bowls and ewers together on the marble floor of the bathroom. She had even bent over her mistress's bed and sung in her rather shrill voice, but the Rani's only response was to moan and burrow still deeper into her pillows. Rassulan was beginning to panic. It was past noon and over an hour since the Rajah had ordered her to call the Princess. She did not know which alarmed her more, the prospect of his wrath or hers.

She was kneeling at the foot of the bed, gazing at her mistress's light auburn curls with mingled exasperation and desperation, when she had a sudden idea.

"Listen, Huzoor, terrible news," Rassulan enunciated the words slowly and distinctly. "The King of Turkey is dead!"

A pillow came flying past her head and two green eyes bored into hers.

"What are you talking about? What king?"

"The King of Turkey, Huzoor. Can't you hear the muezzin? Since dawn all the mosques in the city have been calling the faithful to prayer."

Selma sat up, fully awake now. Abdul Mejid dead? She had a vision of the snow-white beard and the violet eyes that terrified her as a child. It was fourteen years since she has last seen him, as the caliph had set up his court-in-exile at Nice. The news of his death did not sadden her – she had not been close to him – but it made her feel a trifle nostalgic, as if the last caliph's demise were the final nail in the coffin of the Ottoman Empire. She pictured the white shape of Dolmabahçé mirrored in the Bosphorus. A little girl, dwarfed by the tinkling crystal chandeliers that overhung its marble halls, was making her way through a sea of gorgeous uniforms and sparkling jewels toward the golden throne on which sat the Commander of the Faithful, God's Shadow on Earth. . . .

"Daydreaming?" Amir had just come in, wearing a formal black shirwani. "I suppose you have heard the news. The ceremony begins in the great mosque an hour from now. Do you plan to go?"

"Need you ask? Of course I will go. Why look so surprised?"

"It is simply that – well, I knew you were a patriot, but I did not think you had so much respect for the General."

"The General?"

"Well, the President, Mustafa Kemal."

"You mean it is Kemal who is dead?" Selma burst out laughing and flopped back against her pillows. "And I thought. . . . It is too funny! No, of course I do not intend to pray for Kemal." She glanced at the black shirwani. "I trust you do not, either."

Amir's expression hardened. "You are forgetting something, Princess. To us Indians Mustafa Kemal is a hero. He did what we dream of doing: he drove the British out of his country. At this very moment, mosques all over India are crowded with Muslims weeping and praying for his soul's repose."

"Really?" Selma eyed him scornfully. "What about you, Amir? How do you reconcile your Kemalist sympathies and your alliance with the Ottoman family?"

Her implication could not have been clearer: she was accusing him of double standards. Amir ached to slap her face, but he possessed a more effective weapon.

"I thought that you, being an Ottoman, would at least be grateful to the general for saving your country. But for him, Turkey would have ceased to exist."

"That is not true! It was the Sultan who ordered him to –"

She broke off. What was the use? How could she convince him that the Sultan had instructed Kemal to organize resistance in Anatolia while he himself had to remain in Istanbul at the mercy of the British, who had threatened to hand the city over to the Greeks unless he "behaved reasonably?" How could she explain that Kemal, having begun by rousing the masses in the Sultan's name, had claimed victory for himself as soon as it was within his grasp? It had been only too easy for him to conceal the existence of their secret pact and accuse the Sultan of capitulating to the enemy. Selma's efforts to reestablish the truth of this episode in her country's history were always greeted with pitying looks and embarrassed smiles. People simply did not believe her – they thought she was trying to defend her family's reputation. She had realized bitterly that only the victor had the power to impose his version of the truth.

But Amir? She would never have imagined that her husband thought the Sultan had betrayed his country, or that he regarded her and her family as cowards. She felt physically sick – unable to endure the sardonic, contemptuous look in his eyes. He had finally found the way to subdue her rebellious spirit! The walls of the zenana were nothing beside that imprisoning gaze, that chill and unshakable certainty.

What if . . . if she rejected his right to sit in judgement on her? What if, from his cell, the criminal and the madman rejected the reassuring chains of assumed guilt and penance, what if they dared accuse their virtuous accusers? . . . The eyes of Medusa can petrify only those who believe in her power.

Selma slowly raised her head and looked at Amir with a thrill of triumph.

"Very well," she smiled calmly. "While you go and pray, I shall invite a few friends to toast the happy event in champagne."

Amir clenched his fists and turned away without a word. Perhaps he thought she was joking.

Servants were dispatched with invitations for Lucie Rawsthorne and her husband, Rani Shahina, Rashid Khan and Zahra. One of the tables in Selma's drawing-room had been decorated with flowers, and on it, ensconced in silver ice buckets, were half a dozen bottles of her favourite Roederer *rosé*, the champagne that reminded her of her Beirut evenings. If they were going to celebrate, they might as well do so in style. It was a sort of tribute to the man who had betrayed her family – betrayed them, yes, but how astutely! Although she hated Kemal, this "Golden Rose" she had dreamed of as an adolescent, she could not help admiring his audacity and lack of scruple, both qualities indispensable for a winner.

"One cannot have a child and preserve one's virginity as well. . . ." Sultana Hatije's words seemed to ring in her ears. She visualized her mother at Ortaköy on the day of Sultan Abdul Hamid's death, paying tribute to the man who had kept her family under house arrest for thirty years and advising her nephews to model themselves on him, not on their grandfather, Sultan Murad V, whose sensitivity and integrity had unfitted him for the power game.

"Princess?"

Rashid Khan was standing just inside the room – she had been too engrossed in her memories to hear him enter. Surprised to see that he, too, was wearing a black shirwani, she gave him an encouraging smile.

"Why so formal, Rashid Bhai? After all, we are brother and sister now. Where is Zahra?"

"I left her at the mosque. I only came to tell you that we cannot accept your invitation."

"Why not?"

"Selma, I beg you, stop this playacting. It does not suit you." He sat down beside her and eyed her with affectionate concern. "You have been looking so unhappy lately. What is the matter?"

Oh, to nestle in his arms, to be a child again, to be consoled. . . . She smiled at him with redoubled charm.

"You are imagining things. Don't you know I am the most pampered, cossetted wife in the world?"

He took her hands and gripped them tightly. She looked at him, surprised: he had never dared to do such a thing before, but this time he seemed quite carried away.

"How you have changed. . . . What happened to that lively, spirited young woman I met at Bombay less than two years ago? You have to fight back, Selma. You are destroying yourself."

"What a loss to the world!"

"I beg you, if you love me a little. . . ."

He broke off. She stared at him in silence. Did he really believe he loved her like a brother? With one little gesture she could disabuse him of the idea and revenge herself on Amir and Zahra at the same time. On Zahra? Yes, an insidious little voice whispered in her ear, on Zahra most of all. Amir was just a man, and no man could disappoint her any more, whereas Zahra. . . . The sudden pang she felt was yet another proof of how much she had loved the girl's eagerness and innocence, and how much she now resented her placidity, the idiotic self-assurance she derived from her married state and the blissful awareness of her swelling belly.

She rested her head on Rashid's shoulder.

"Take me away from here, Rashid Bhai. I cannot stand it any longer."

Had she said that or only thought it? A soothing hand caressed her hair, a hand that reminded her of that other hand, so long ago. . . . Sobbing, she put her arms around him and held him close.

"Don't ever leave me again!"

She pillowed her tear-stained face against his neck. Her one desire was that he should ask no questions, just take her away.

"I love you," she said, only to regret the words as soon as they escaped her lips. He took her by the chin and clumsily wiped away her tears with his handkerchief. He was very pale.

"I love you too, Selma – I have loved you ever since I saw you come down the gangway, looking so lost and vulnerable, but it was impossible: you had come to this country to marry my friend. And now –"

"Now?"

"I love you more than ever, but –"

"But not enough!" She smiled bitterly. "That is the story of my life: everyone loves me, but not enough to keep me in spite of everything – in spite of myself."

"What about Amir?"

Selma drew away from him a little. All of a sudden she felt very weary.

"Amir married my ancestry, not me, you know that very well."

Rashid left, distraught. Selma felt angry with herself for having caused him unhappiness, when he was the one person here who had never done her any harm.

She caught sight of herself in a mirror and took a closer look. Her cheeks were hollow, her eyes black-ringed. It was true that she had changed, but had she aged? Perhaps. Gone was the plumpness of which she had despaired at Beirut when she dreamed of becoming an actress. Her features were finer and more chiselled, and her lips, which she had once thought too thin, seemed to have ripened. She liked her new air, with its suggestion of the *femme fatale* – "the look of a beautiful animal" as Amir chose to call it.

It was already six o'clock and none of her guests had arrived. They would not be coming now, she knew. They probably considered this to be a provocation, a tasteless form of revenge, and a cowardly one at that, to defy a man after his death! They had not understood: is a man ever more alive than when he has just died? Is he ever as great as on the day of his funeral, when tears are exalting the least of his victories, the slightest of humanitarian gestures, and wiping out his failures, his pettiness and his lies? It is a strange blindness on the part of the living that anyone who dies seems exceptional for the few hours or days it takes for the tears to dry.

It was precisely now that Mustafa Kemal was making his presence felt larger than life, that she wanted to flout him – and do so in front of witnesses who could judge the victor in this duel of, yes, shamefully mismatched opponents. They did not come because it all seemed sacrilegious. They must have really had very little respect for the late departed if they were afraid of being flippant about his death. Selma showed more respect for him by not ruling out the possibility of defeat. Yet even entering into battle with him was a kind of victory. . . .

She wanted to confront the man who had shattered her fate and scattered it throughout the world, who had, like a demiurge, changed her life down to the last detail, including her very thoughts and feelings, without even knowing she existed. Sometimes she thought she should be grateful to him; after all, he had destroyed her nest and forced her to learn to fly. Yet at the same time by taking her part of the sky away from her, he had clipped her wings.

Exile. . . . Had he been so afraid of her family that he had had to exile them? He was strong though, strong with that strength characteristic of those who have nothing to lose, who have no past and so need to create a present for themselves, no matter what the cost. She envied him his thirst for power, for that, even more than courage and intelligence, is what enables one to quell one's enemies. This was the undoing of the last of the Ottoman rulers, so was it the undoing of the Indian princes around her who were refusing to fight and just letting themselves be supplanted: over the centuries, their thirst for power had been quenched.

Thus societies renew themselves and power changes hands. Power is not so much taken as it is abandoned by those who have grown tired and have stopped believing in what they stand for.

Kemal had wanted to rule more than the Sultan did. But did he really need to drive the Sultan and his family out of the country, forbidding them ever to return to their native land? Did he need to banish even the dead, whose remains were no longer allowed to rest on the peaceful banks of the Bosphorus?

Those clear mornings in Istanbul, with its narrow streets, its little wooden houses enclosed by quiet, walled gardens, its white mosques whose reflection flickered in the waters of the Golden Horn – what right did Kemal have to take all that away from them?

The Crown Prince had renounced his and his descendants' right to ascend the throne. He had become no more than the shadow of a caliph, confined to his palace under constant surveillance, his every move watched and reported. The whole country, the government, the civil service and the army was Kemalist – or at least, so they said. So what was the great man afraid of? Did he, who called himself "Ataturk" – father of the Turks – fear that the people would reject his paternity? That was all Selma wanted to ask him. She had only wanted to summon the dead general before witnesses the way Don Juan had once invited the dead commander to his table. She would have wrested the truth from him once and for all. The dead have no need to lie.

She opened the second bottle of champagne and refilled her glass, which frothed and sparkled as she held it up to the light. She observed the rosy liquid with a kind of affection, grateful to it for helping her to forget her failure at Badalpur and endure the disgust that sometimes overcame her when Amir. . . .

They hardly spoke now. She had the impression that he wanted to break her, crush her. Every night, when they came home after one of the smart dinner parties at which she sought oblivion in the knowledge that she was a beautiful, desirable woman, he proceeded to punish her. Silently, relentlessly, he would possess her.

Little by little, she had developed a taste for this servitude. She was stunned to find that she enjoyed submitting to his will. An unresisting object of desire, she abandoned herself to unfamiliar delights that left her drained and exhausted. She had been appalled at first, unwilling to admit that her body could betray her so. Where had she sprung from, this woman of the night who enjoyed a slavery, the recollection of which made her shudder with distaste and self-contempt in the morning? How profoundly she had despised the women of the harem whose sole concern was the pleasure they could give their master. . . . Surely she had nothing in common with those creatures! She was proud and ambitious – as unlike them as it was possible to be. . . .

Selma stood in front of the mirror and raised her glass with a theatrical flourish. "To my glorious destiny!" she said. Then she began to laugh and laugh. . . . How prettily champagne sparkled! and how light it made her head! Champagne was the perfect gentleman, a faithful ally. It gave no trouble, derided the dramatic and ridiculed the serious, cocooned her in velvet and taught her that nothing really mattered – nothing, not even the death of her worst enemy. What a fool she had been to want to challenge Mustafa Kemal! It was just another instance of her urge to justify herself and prove to other people. . . . Well, now she had ceased to care what they thought, those idiots who imagined they understood her when not even she could understand herself.

She scrutinized the mirror closely. What was she, princess, courtesan? Discounting her mother, a sultan's daughter, had all her female forebears not been slaves, the harem's most beautiful inmates, those most expert in giving pleasure? How else could they have won the sultan's heart and become his wives? Many tales were told of their intelligence, guile, and spirit of intrigue, all of them qualities indispensable to reach the first place in the harem and above all maintain it. First, however, they had to charm their imperial master. At the Ottoman court, eroticism was the principal art in which they had to excel. Flowing in Selma's veins was the blood of thirty-six sultans, but also of the courtesans who had shared their beds for six long centuries. She was in equal measure the fruit of those two lines: both queen and slave.

With one hand she slipped the dress off her shoulders, revealing two pure-white breasts. The hand descended to her hips, which trembled at its touch. Shiny drops of champagne trickled down her belly, while her trembling hands encircled her slim waist, then glided upward to her throat and shoulders, delighting in the coolness, the warmth, the intoxicating smoothness of her skin, hands that knew how to cajole, and to which she finally surrendered.

But whose were those emerald-green eyes gazing so sadly into hers? She wanted to blot them out and see nothing in the mirror save her own desirable body, but they lingered like uninvited guests at a banquet. Only the golden potion would make them go away.

She picked up her glass and drank in long draughts, glancing furtively at the mirror as she did so. The eyes were still there. They would not go away. All that would efface them was more champagne.

"Selma, you are destroying yourself. . . ."

"No, Rashid Bhai, I am very much alive! See how I am laughing! I am not afraid or ashamed, I am a woman, look!"

The eyes in the mirror became blurred, the lips shaped the beginnings of a kiss, the naked body sank to the floor.

How good I feel. Am I dead? It is dark, perhaps they have already buried me? Amir seemed at his wits' end when he found me. There was blood everywhere – I must have smashed the champagne glass when I fell and cut myself. I cannot remember anything after that. Amir must have cried. Maybe he loved me after all. What a pity. . . .

"Take that thing off, I think she is coming to."

Someone gently raised her head and carefully removed the bandage that had been wound around it. Light suffused her leaden eyelids. She opened them with an effort and saw Rani Shahina smiling down at her from the foot of the bed.

"You look as fresh as a daisy – an absolute miracle, after such a night! You really alarmed us, you know – Amir was panic-stricken. Fancy locking the door like that! They had to climb over the balcony. You were lying on the floor, out like a light. Your poor husband thought you had a heart attack until someone pointed out the three empty champagne bottles. They gave you an emetic and put you to bed with an iced herb poultice on your head. It is just the thing for your kind of – well, indisposition. How are you feeling now?"

"Light and airy, clean, as good as new. . . . Oh, Shahina, if you only knew how alive everything around me seems!"

She got up and took two or three experimental steps before slumping back on the bed. The Rani came and sat down beside her.

"Selma, you need a change of scene. They are doing you no good, all these late nights and days spent lazing in bed. You are terribly thin. Amir says you hardly eat a thing, you just drink all the time. If you carry on this way –"

"I will destroy myself. I know, I have been told already."

"Why not get away from Lucknow for a few weeks? Visit your mother in Beirut, try to pull yourself together and decide what you really want."

"What I want? Do I have a choice?"

Rani Shahina took her gently by the shoulders.

"There is always a choice. The question is, do you have the courage to make one and stick to it? In any case, you cannot go on like this. Last night was a sort of turning point. Take advantage of it and get away for a while."

Selma inspected her pale face in the mirror and sighed.

"I could never appear in Beirut looking like this. My mother would guess the truth at once."

"Yes, and she would help you."

"You don't know my mother. Nothing has ever dented *her* armour – she despises weakness. I dread to think of the look on her face if she saw me in this state."

"But she is your mother, Selma. Surely she loves you?"

"I am afraid that what she loves is mostly her own image of her daughter."

"One for all, all for one!" Inscribed in red letters on a white background, the imposing banner spanned Kaisarbagh's central avenue. Trumpets blared on every side, liveried servants jostled pedestrians out of the way and forced humble street vendors to dismantle their stalls: the procession was coming! Cows alone continued to ruminate in the middle of the roadway, heedless of pleas and entreaties.

Selma, intrigued by all the noise, had slipped out on to the terrace. The skyline bristled with banners and pennants. Horses whinnied and elephants trumpeted in the distance, gold and silver parasols caught the sunlight as they swayed along above the slowly advancing column. At last royal elephants came into view, caparisoned in brocade and led by the white elephant of the Rajah of Bampur, who sat enthroned in a howdah encrusted with amethysts. Around him more banners proclaimed "Down with the Bolsheviks" and "Rajahs and Maharajahs united to protect the people."

Following him were princes and zamindars who had converged from all over the United Provinces to parade in splendour and demonstrate against the iniquitous laws enacted by the Congress Party, those communists who were seeking to foment rebellion among their loyal subjects. It was the so-called Rajahs' Union that had devised this spectacular way of kindling the popular imagination and countering the subversive effects of political propaganda.

Founded at Lucknow some months earlier, in the course of a conference attended by several hundred princes, the Rajahs' Union had decided to fight back. Its president, the Rajah of Bampur, delivered a much-applauded speech in which he stressed the need to close ranks against the new government: "We must forget our differences and be prepared for any sacrifice in order to preserve our honoured and traditional status as leaders." The slogan "One for all, all for one!," whose boldly revolutionary ring amused and shocked the assembled princes, was unanimously adopted. None of them believed in it, but what, after all, did a slogan amount to? The main thing was that it should sound good.

"The fools!"

Amir had followed Selma on to the terrace. With a strained face, he was watching his fellow princes troop past.

"Don't they realize how ridiculous it is to parade their wealth and simultaneously claim that the government is ruining them? It is asking for trouble. I tried to point that out but they would not listen. 'Our people are children,' they said. 'Pomp and power are all they respect. If we look weak they will trample us underfoot. If we show our strength they will be afraid to disobey us – and will think twice about taking orders from Congress.' I told them things were changing – people were becoming aware of their rights – but I only got insulted for my pains. They called me Englishman!"

There was such bitterness in Amir's voice that Selma felt touched. It was the first time for months that he had confided in her. She wanted to tell him that she sympathized with his feelings, but she did not dare. A sort of truce had been in force since her solitary orgy. They lived together, treating each other with distant courtesy. Amir had not reproached her or asked any questions, he had simply moved back into his old quarters. Nor, to her relief, had he ever tried to touch her again. It was as if their sensual frenzy had subsided like some strange and only half-remembered delirium.

Their social life had also ceased by tacit agreement. Selma, feeling like a convalescent, was disinclined to see anyone. As for Amir, who always took such a pride in his appearance, she had lately been surprised to see him strolling around the palace in a pyjama suit or smoking a hookah and playing interminable games of chess with nawabs of his acquaintance. She was now beginning to understand.

"Some of the princes will not speak to me," he went on as if his cup of bitterness were overflowing. "They think I have betrayed them – that I am playing the Congress game because I favour making concessions to the peasants. I cannot even discuss the subject with old friends. Am I really so wrong to believe that democracy is the only way forward for India?"

Amir paced the terrace with his fists clenched.

"I sometimes wonder if my years in England were not a curse. At first I wanted to assimilate the ideas of the British so I could fight them more effectively, but they changed me without my realizing it. I ended up convinced that their values were universal – that the only valid moral code was the white one. Now I don't know where I stand any more. . . . I hate them, but at the same time I feel they are right. That is their real victory. They will leave the country before long, I know, but they will still be here" – he tapped his forehead – "in our minds, our Europeanized brains. Those of us with a Western education are going to take over the running of this country, but who *are* we? Are we Indians capable of understanding and fulfilling the aspirations of our people, or second-class imitations of the British who pride ourselves on gaining independence, but will really be perpetuating slavery?"

. . . *So you too feel like an outsider* . . .?

That night, Amir and Selma slept together and they made love very gently, as if they were trying to comfort each other.

CHAPTER 19

"No, my dear, you cannot go out. The Aminabad district is swarming with demonstrators."

It was over a month since the government had proclaimed a state of semi-emergency under "Article 144," to prevent Hindus and Muslims from coming to blows. Although Lucknow had remained comparatively quiet until now, tension had been dangerously heightened by massacres in the neighbouring towns and villages. Everyone was demonstrating in defiance of police regulations. Muslim students were furious because the authorities had hoisted the Congress flag over their colleges and banned the flag of the Muslim League; peasants urged the government to compel the princes to observe the new laws in their favour; princes signified their refusal to cooperate; untouchables agitated for permission to pray in the temples, a right denied them by high-caste Hindus; Muslims protested at the imposition of a "Hindu-style" education on their children and Hindus at the Muslim insistence on slaughtering and eating cows.

Clashes had been avoided so far, but for how much longer? Protesters temporarily confined themselves to marching through the streets and giving Congress a dose of its own medicine, the strategy of nonviolence that had proved so effective against the British. The prisons grew fuller day by day and police resources were stretched to the limit.

"But Amir, I must go out," Selma said impatiently. "I am leaving for Beirut in a week's time. Don't forget I have to find some presents for my mother."

It would be her first visit to Lebanon since her marriage and the first time she would see the Sultana. Happiness made her restless. The nightmares of recent months were forgotten. She had given up champagne and begun to eat normally. As the days went by her face took on colour and lost its pinched, tormented look.

Her relationship with Amir, too, had changed. It was now devoid of passion and drama. "We are like an old married couple," she told herself wryly, surprised to note that she greeted this development with a certain relief. Though she relished the prevailing atmosphere of comfortable indifference she was faintly disappointed that her husband should accept it so readily.

She had no wish to analyze her emotions, however. All her thoughts were of Beirut, of her mother's smile and the kalfas' little attentions, of Zeynel's adoration, of friendships renewed and youthful memories revived.

"Huzoor," the eunuch said in his reedy voice, "a message for you."

A small blue envelope lay on the silver tray: a telegram from Beirut. She glanced at Amir and hesitated.

"Well, Princess, open it. It is bound to be from the Sultana, confirming that someone will be there to meet you when the boat arrives."

Why should her mother have bothered? Of course she would be met off the boat. Her friends would even organize a welcome-home party. In Beirut hospitality was sacred: they would drop everything and flock to the harbour laden with bunches of flowers.

She turned the envelope over and over in her hands. According to the date stamps, the telegram had taken eleven days to get to Lucknow, and it was only two weeks since she had written to say she was coming, so . . . she drew a deep breath and tore it open. She read:

SULTANA DIED THIS MORNING STOP ALL HERE HEARTBROKEN STOP THINKING OF YOU STOP DEVOTEDLY ZEYNEL.

Zahra, who heard her cries, came running in. Much later she told Selma that, to her amazement, she saw her clawing at her face and banging her head against the wall. Amir and a maidservant tried to restrain her, but she fought them off. Zahra thought she had gone mad. Her cheeks were streaked with blood, her eyes glazed and staring.

That was when Zahra saw her brother pick up a camera lying on a table and start taking photographs. In an instant the woman, who had seemed impervious to anything but her own agony of mind, froze. Then like a lioness, she sprang at Amir, only to stumble before she could reach him and slump to the floor in a dead faint.

For a week they feared that the shock had unhinged her. The finest hakims in the city took turns at her bedside and kept her sedated night and day with esoteric preparations of opium and herbs. "Excessive sorrow cannot be cured by a frontal assault," they said, "or the mind will rebel and take flight." The way to remedy a mental disorder, they explained, was to induce temporary oblivion, maintain the body in a dormant condition, and even weaken it so that, when the patient awoke, her grief would be starved of energy.

"How could he! I will never forgive him."

When Selma slowly struggled clear of the fog that had shrouded her senses for days, her first emotion was one of anger. Amir had behaved atrociously – she never wanted to call him her husband again. How could he have been so heartless, so flippant, instead of helping her in her hour of need? He knew, though, the strength of her feelings for her mother.

Now that Annéjim was dead, she felt as if her childhood and youth had died too – as if the whole of her past life were threatened with extinction. There was no one left to remember with her, to remember within her. The same flesh, a single memory; eyes that were just as her eyes, a breath that took in the world and restored it to her, no longer threatening or alien. She choked on her own sobs, unable to accept such abandonment. She had not seen the Sultana for two years, but that was irrelevant: the mere knowledge of her existence had been a comfort. "What would she think of me?" she used to ask herself. "What would she do in my place?" Her mother had been her constant companion except in the last few months, when she had tried to forget her, unable to endure the thought of her disapproval. Or had it been her own disapproval she could not endure? It made no difference: even though she had rebelled at times, between her mother and herself there had always been this osmosis, this complete understanding on all the things that mattered.

She had killed her. . . . Yes, she, Selma, had killed her. During those crazed months when she had steadfastly tried to destroy herself it was the Sultana she was really destroying. The bond that linked her to her mother, a powerful, living bond, stronger than physical separation, but weak in the face of indifference, had broken. This is what her mother had died of. . . .

But much earlier she had killed her – or rather, like someone pruning a tree branch by branch because it cast too much shade, she had dismantled the image of her mother bit by bit. She remembered being aware of the process already in Istanbul the day she battered Ahmed while they were playing "Sultan against the Greeks." The Sultana had been so outraged she had locked Selma in her room, refusing to listen to any explanation. That was small punishment compared to the child's despair at the injustice of a mother she had thought perfect.

And in Lebanon . . . when the Sultana had hidden her father's letters, and when later she had insisted that she marry a prince at all costs – and all "for her own good. . . ." Selma had always obeyed, but despite her obedience – or was it *because* of her obedience – underneath she had rebelled.

Had Amir understood, before her, these feelings she refused to acknowledge? Was that the reason for his extraordinary behaviour? Had he detected, behind all her tears, a sense of relief which she concealed from herself by carrying her grief to extremes? Had he, with an insight born of long dissimulation, or emotional ambivalence, grasped that her frenzied assault on her own flesh disguised a need to punish herself for not suffering enough?

"Apa?" Zahra's voice was tremulous. "Apa, my brother wants to visit you. You refused to see him yesterday, so I told him you were still too tired, but today. . . . He will not believe me, Apa. He looks so unhappy – he never stops blaming himself for making you ill. Please, Apa, he loves you so much!"

"Does he? In that case he will wait till *I* feel like seeing *him*."

She lay back and closed her eyes, determined not to weaken. If she had to go on living here – and where else could she go, now? – she must impose her own set of rules. She had spent her life trying to please people; trying to be the adored little girl, the beloved wife, the respected rani. No more! The Sultana had been the one person in the world whose word was her law. Her death had revoked all laws.

Selma breathed a deep sigh: she was free, completely free for the first time in her life.

Another week went by, but the bouts of nausea that kept her confined to bed persisted. There was an epidemic of jaundice in the city, and Hakim Sahib, suspecting that this might be the trouble, had prescribed a strict diet.

"Jaundice? What nonsense, you have never looked more in the pink!"

Lucie Rawsthorne, who was paying her a visit, looked arch when she described her symptoms.

"Are you sure you are not expecting?"

"Expecting?" Selma gave a start. "Certainly not!"

Lucie raised her eyebrows at this categorical negative, and Selma could have bitten her tongue off. She could hardly tell her that for months in fact since the night she got drunk celebrating Kemal's death Amir and she had not . . . though, yes, there had been one other night, the night of the Rajahs' parade, when Amir seemed so sad. They had found each other like two lost children. That night of all nights . . . could it be possible?

Lucie, seeing her puzzled expression, decided to take matters in hand.

"I will send my lady doctor to see you this afternoon – and please do not look so tragic – getting pregnant is not the end of the world!"

She hugged Selma and left the room, laughing as she went.

The doctor had hardly gone when the women of the palace swarmed in like bees and clustered around their Rani's bed to congratulate her. After two long years of watching and waiting, alert to the slightest sign of pallor or lassitude, they had almost given up hope. It was sad, they used to say, that so noble and beautiful a lady should be incapable of doing her womanly duty – the master would have no other choice but to divorce her in the end. Many potential replacements for the princess had already been selected, all of them young, healthy, and high-born, and all of them irreproachably Indian. Rani Aziza wanted no more foreigners.

But now he was there, the Rajah's heir, their future master . . . or almost there. . . ! They smothered their princess's hands with kisses of joy and gratitude and told their beads, muttering benedictions and ritual incantations.

Selma, sitting up in bed, neither saw nor heard them. Her eyes were fixed on the flicker of a dying candle at the far end of the room. That was the moment she liked best, when the flame battled bravely against the darkness. As a child she used to hold her breath and stare at candle flames intently, willing them the strength to resist, and when at last they died she sometimes wept.

The candle went out. Her cheeks felt cool and moist. *Annéjim is dead . . . dead the very day when a new life awakens within me, as if she wished to make way for me, or as if I had waited for my mother to depart before taking her place.*

Selma had counted and re-counted the days: there was no doubt about it – she had conceived on the eve of her mother's death. The body had a prescience of its own: it had known long before she knew. . . . It suddenly became obvious to her that as long as her mother was still alive she, Selma, could never have been anything but a daughter. "The mother" was the Sultana; during her lifetime she would never have dared to usurp that title.

Was she delirious again? Could it really be that her body had refused to conceive until the day it sensed, at a range of several thousand miles, that it was finally at liberty to do so? Could that be the reality?

Diffidently, hesitantly, she laid her hand on her belly. That was reality now, and this time she could not, would not shirk it. She kept watch for a tremor beneath her palm. A new world seemed to be awakening within her. She closed her eyes and revelled in the novel sensation.

"My dear, this is wonderful news!"

Amir had walked over to the bed, beaming. He seemed genuinely moved. Selma stared at him in surprise. She had misjudged him; she would not have believed him capable of sharing so wholeheartedly in her happiness.

"You must take good care of yourself – I want my son. . . ."

His son? She froze, deaf to the rest of what he was saying. He was mad! The child was hers and nobody else's! Just because this man had shared her bed, he did not have the right to. . . . She eyed him with revived hostility. At the most he had been a tolerable husband and an indifferent lover, but should she accept him as a father? The father of her child? Instinctively she clasped her arms around her stomach, the fortress that protected the precious thing this stranger coveted.

For suddenly she had the feeling *she* was no longer the stranger, no longer did she feel superfluous, she was there, fixed to this land she now seemed to be a part of, linked to it by a thousand roots. She was the rich red soil and the grass swaying in the breeze; she was the majestic forest and the peaceful warmth of this late afternoon.

By degrees she recovered her composure, surprised at the intensity of her recent fear. Who could possibly deprive her of the life deep within her? They could say what they liked, she would not listen – indeed, she could no longer understand why she had credited them with so much importance. As if her existence depended on what they said and decided – as if she were merely an empty shell!

She looked up at the man beside her and gave him an indifferent smile.

"Eat no fish whatever you do – it ruins a baby's complexion. You mustn't wear perfume or rouge or khol or flowers in your hair, either, or you'll arouse the envy of the jinns: they might put a curse on the child. . . ."

Begum Nimet authoritatively reeled off recommendations and prohibitions – what every pregnant woman should know. The women around her nodded approvingly. Who better to advise the Rani than the old lady whose grandchildren's countless grandchildren were all strong, healthy, and fair of face? Their mothers had strictly conformed to the Begum's precepts; that proved their efficacy.

There was, the old lady declared, a special regimen to be followed at every hour of the day and under all circumstances. Its virtues were obvious to anyone who gave the matter two minutes' thought, but alas, the young women of today put their faith in Ingrez medicine and considered the traditional remedies obsolete. The disastrous consequences were all too apparent: more and more miscarriages and imperfections – why, look at Nishat's child with that purplish birthmark covering half its face, yet she had been warned not to eat beets after the eleventh week!

Selma, listening idly, gratified Begum Ninet by asking her a question or two. She was touched by the solicitude of these women. Ever since word of her pregnancy spread she had been the centre of attention and principal topic of conversation. Life at the palace took its rhythm from her. Everyone waited on her hand and foot, even Rani Aziza, who ordained that every dish she ate, and not only the desserts, should be covered in gold leaf; for gold, as everyone knew, fortified an expectant mother and strengthened her baby's bones.

Although she would ordinarily have been irritated by all this fuss, Selma now found it reassuring. Without it, she might have doubted she was pregnant at all. Nothing was discernible in the mirror where she inspected her breasts and belly every night. Even her spells of nausea had become less frequent. She wondered if the doctor had made a mistake. She grew so worried that the least twinge of discomfort delighted her.

From now on she spent most of the day lounging on a hammock bed in her sitting-room which had been converted into a boudoir. From there she could see only treetops and patches of sky framed by foliage. She did not feel like going out or meeting anyone; she simply daydreamed.

If the child was a boy she would call him Suleyman after his ancestor, Suleyman the Magnificent, and bring him up to be a great ruler. He would introduce bold reforms, and the people, realizing these were for their own good, would applaud them. He would liberate women because she would raise him to be sensitive to their plight. He would accomplish all that his parents had failed to achieve, Amir because he was torn between his feudal reflexes and his liberal beliefs, she because she was a foreigner. With her at his side to advise him, he would transform Badalpur into a modern state to be envied and emulated by the whole of India. They would be pioneers: they would demonstrate that India was capable of becoming a great country without losing its soul or forcing itself into a British mold.

But what if the child was a girl? Selma was assailed by visions of black burkahs and child marriages. A girl . . . veiled, married off. . . . She shuddered at the idea, which returned again and again to torment her in the days that followed. Why had it not occurred to her before?

Everyone in the palace was so certain the baby must be a boy that she herself had become convinced of it. What would Amir do if it were a girl?

One evening, when he seemed to be in a particularly good mood, she plucked up her courage and asked him. He frowned as if the very thought of a girl were offensive.

"If it is a girl," he said, recovering himself quickly, "I will find her the richest, most blue-blooded husband in the whole of India."

"What if she does not want to marry?"

He raised his eyebrows, then laughed. "What a strange idea! Marriage is every woman's aim in life and the key to her happiness. Women are made to bear children. You yourself are the living proof of that, my dear. I have never seen you look so radiant."

Selma hesitated for a moment. She did not want to provoke a scene, but she had to know.

"If it is a girl," she insisted, "will she have to wear the veil and keep purdah?"

Amir shook his head and looked pained. "Why ask? You know she will have to, for the sake of my reputation and her own. She would be socially unacceptable if she failed to observe our customs. Do not worry, though. Never having known any other way of life, she will be perfectly happy."

Far from being reassured by his last remark, Selma was terrified. To think that her daughter would be incapable even of imagining what freedom was like! It was impossible! She refused to give birth to a prisoner, a hidebound creature whose horizons would be limited to her family's well-being. Her daughter must be a leader who would help her fellow women to throw off the constraints that for centuries had fettered their intelligence and willpower. Her daughter would struggle. No one would be able to call *her* a foreigner. At least *she* would be entitled to fight!

But would she want to? Would she, Selma, be capable of transmitting the spirit of rebellion that inhabited her own breast? Could one convey the meaning of injustice to someone who had never known justice?

The inertia of India frightened her. Slowly but steadily, it blunted enthusiasms and indignations, ambitions and initiatives. How would her daughter summon up the strength to combat that inertia? Even she, herself no stranger to freedom, had recently felt that she was beginning to "adapt." She hated the word, but there it was. Volatile and rebellious by nature, she had come to appreciate her cosy, sheltered existence and had gradually allowed herself to slip into a life of ease while nursing the illusion that she was still the same person. Nothing could have brought this home to her more clearly than a remark she had overheard the other day. "Our Rani has changed so much," one of her maids had confided loudly to a friend, hoping to please her. "She has become a truly Indian woman."

The words had conjured up a vision of Rani Shahina's mother. Once a young and adventurous girl, that haggard, haunted old woman had renounced herself rather than lose her children. Finally, unable to live with that self betrayal, she had sought refuge in madness.

"Go, go quickly. . . . Leave here while there is still time!" The cracked old voice rang in her ears. She had not taken the warning seriously then, convinced that she was capable of withstanding any amount of pressure.

Pressure, yes, but gentleness? Selma felt a sudden pang of fear. Nothing, she knew, could be more insidious than the pleasant glow of contentment that people call happiness. Whether from fatigue, cowardice, or despair, she was falling prey to that feeling. She must leave – escape before it was too late. For the child's sake, of course, but also and above all, perhaps, for her own. She must escape, not because she was unhappy but because this kind of happiness was the last thing she wanted.

CHAPTER 20

"Well, what have you decided, Paris or Lausanne?"

Selma's fingers froze on the piano keys. She turned to stare at Lucie. How on earth had she guessed? To conceal her surprise, she fiddled with the ruby ring Amir had just given her.

"I could not possibly travel in my condition."

"In your condition?" Lucie laughed. "Anyone would think you were the first person in the world to have a baby. This is the ideal time to go – the sooner the better. For once, the doctors all agree: before the third month is best. Surely you don't intend to have it here?"

"Of course, why ever not?"

"You are very sweet, *chérie*, but completely out of your mind. *Nobody* has a baby in this godforsaken place. What if there are complications? You think that old hakim of yours, who mistook a pregnancy for jaundice, would know what to do? The only places to have a child these days are Paris and Lausanne."

Selma suppressed a smile at the thought of all the ill-informed women who had had the temerity to give birth elsewhere. Still, Lucie's snobbish notion could be useful. Without meaning to, the Frenchwoman might have provided an answer to her problem.

She had not slept for nights, debating whether to stay or go. If the child were a boy she had no right to deprive him of his legacy, but if it were a girl? Escaping from the palace and Lucknow would not be too difficult – she could bribe a few maidservants – but getting out of India was another matter. She had concocted all manner of scenarios involving disguises and false papers, but she knew that Amir would move heaven and earth to track her down and prevent her from leaving the country.

If she went off to France with his blessing, on the other hand, who could compel her to return once the baby was born? France was a land of liberty, an asylum. The Rajah would be powerless against her there.

"The Ranis of Badalpur have always given birth in the zenana. What was good enough for generations of your predecessors should, I imagine, be good enough for you . . . Princess!"

Rani Aziza enunciated the last word as though spitting out filth.

Was there no limit to this foreign interloper's presumption? If one of her maids had not warned her in time of what was afoot, her fool of a brother might have given in.

Amir would have rather been anywhere else on earth. It did not matter whose side he took, he could look forward to months of recrimination. On the other hand, he was not fundamentally displeased that his sister had intervened. This was women's business, after all. He was against the trip, but he might in the end have been swayed by Selma's arguments in its favour. Suddenly he had a brilliant idea – one that seemed certain to appeal to everyone.

"We will send for an English doctor," he told Selma. "If there is not a suitable one in Lucknow we will get one from Bombay or Calcutta. That will guard against all eventualities and ensure that the traditions are observed. My sister thinks it wrong for the heir of Badalpur to be born abroad, and I am bound to say I agree with her. In these troubled times, certain people might make it an excuse to question his legitimacy."

Amir was so delighted with this solution that he refused to discuss it further. He hurried out, heedless of his wife's crestfallen expression and his sister's outrage at the idea that a Muslim prince should be ushered into the world by an infidel.

Events had to take a serious turn before Amir changed his mind. In that month, March 1939, Hitler had annexed Czechoslovakia and the European nations were wondering how to respond. While Gandhi counselled unilateral disarmament, Lucknow was in turmoil, with a dramatic heightening of the centuries-old hostility between its Sunni and Shia Muslim communities.

The bone of contention was the Mad e Sahabah, an apologia for the first three caliphs, which the Sunnis proposed to recite in public. The Shias, who regarded these caliphs as usurpers and acknowledged the Prophet's son-in-law, Ali, as his only legitimate successor, considered this a provocative act.

The recitation of the Mad e Sahabah had been banned by the British governor of Lucknow in 1905, after riots in which dozens of people had lost their lives. Ever since the Congress Party came to power, however, the Sunnis had been agitating for the repeal of this measure on the ground that the Shias recited the Tabarrah, which they themselves considered an affront to the memory of their caliphs. Being three times as numerous as the Shias, the Sunnis were backed by certain Hindu politicians who hoped to recruit them as Congress voters. Far from fearing the prospect of disturbances, these politicians welcomed any split in the Muslim ranks. Wasn't it the best way of undermining the League and its hated leader, Jinnah? The Sunnis, who sensed that the government was wavering, stepped up their demonstrations. Hundreds were arrested, and the police, overwhelmed by yet another set of warring factions, could no longer keep the peace.

On 31 March, finally much to everyone's surprise, the government gave in: the Mad e Sahabah could be recited anywhere and at any time provided the authorities were notified in advance. This led to immediate chaos. In the streets of Lucknow Shias assailed Sunnis with prayers and showers of stones. Rioting was especially violent in front of the Great Imambara, where the police opened fire killing and wounding many. The government imposed a curfew, but it was not obeyed. Shopkeepers lowered their steel shutters, most people went to ground, and the city divided itself into armed camps. Within a few days thousands of Muslims were arrested, but their detention only provoked fresh disturbances. One group managed to storm the cabinet office and seize the chief minister, whom they intimidated but eventually released. Then the women decided that it was time to support their men and demonstrate in the street, veiled in their black burkahs. By now, seven thousand Shias and several hundred Sunnis were in custody. If the Hindus joined in – and any pretext would have served in such a supercharged atmosphere – even the army would be incapable of preventing the consequent arson and slaughter.

Kaisarbagh was quite close to Aminabad Market, one of the main trouble spots. Although Amir had reinforced the palace guard, his handful of men could never have held off a determined mob. There was no way of knowing how bad the rioting might become. In view of the uncertain situation, the Rajah decided not to take any risks: he would stay, but his young wife must leave. She had delicate nerves and her pregnancy might be disturbed. If even peaceful Lucknow had ceased to be safe, no place in India was. Sending Selma to France might not be such a bad idea after all, he told himself. Zeynel, the eunuch, who had nothing left to do in Beirut after the Sultana's death, could escort her.

Mid-April, dust and heat. An ordinary day at Lucknow station with its half-starved porters and beggars swarming around the garlanded travellers in the huge red sandstone concourse.

Outside the imposing Victorian portico, flanked by Mogul pavilions, guards in the livery of Badalpur State shielded the white and gold Isotta Fraschini from the gaze of inquisitive onlookers striving to catch a glimpse of the auburn-haired Princess through the car's damask curtains.

News of her departure had been going the rounds since dawn, when palace servants had come to erect the long brocade corridor that would enable her to board the royal railroad car without being seen. Her beauty was legendary. Few had ever seen her, but the crowd's imagination had been kindled by her maidservants' descriptions. Her generosity, too, was a byword: would her departure be the occasion for a distribution of alms? The jostling bystanders gave vent to cheers and benedictions.

Inside the car, Amir fidgeted impatiently while Selma struggled with her emotions. She no longer knew why she had been so eager to go. Having yearned to escape for so long, she had found her departure from the palace an unexpected ordeal. All her self-evident reasons for leaving now seemed absurd. There was no mistaking the warmth and affection that had surrounded her in the last few days or the genuine sorrow with which women and children had converged on her from all over the palace, clinging to her sari with tears in their eyes, imploring her not to go. The older women called her "mother" and pressed her hand; the younger ones gazed at her sadly as though reproaching her for abandoning them.

When they finally grasped that nothing would dissuade her, when the Rajah sternly explained that the Princess had to leave "for reasons of health," they all insisted on giving her a little present. If they could not be there in person to protect their Rani in the unimaginable outside world, she must at least go armed with some memento of themselves. Amir had impatiently urged his wife to leave these pathetic little gifts behind, but she had refused, feeling that she would be betraying the givers' trust and courting bad luck. Embroidered handkerchiefs, pretty pebbles, oddments of carved wood – all had been carefully stowed away in one of the trunks she was taking to Paris. If she ever felt lonely there, she need only open it to console herself with these hundred tokens of affection.

"It is ready. We can get out now."

Amir jumped out first. Selma was surprised by his impatience. *He seems to be eager to see me go,* she thought. Although she knew he was simply at a loss and doing his best to hide it, she resented his refusal to unbend and the unemotional facade he presented to her and outsiders alike. On the few occasions when his mask had slipped, he had punished her for days by treating her more coldly than ever.

He preceded her briskly along the same silken corridor that had concealed her two years before, when she walked it in the opposite direction, a radiant bride-to-be advancing confidently to claim her handsome husband and her new homeland.

And now . . . now she was about to board the train that would bear her far away from all who knew and, in their own way, loved her. Behind her came Zahra, whom she had adored as a slender, vivacious girl and could not forgive for turning into a plump, placid married woman – or should she be grateful to her for demonstrating what marriage did to the women of India? Behind Zahra came Rashid Khan – faithful Rashid, who had known and understood all that had happened since her arrival. Did he guess that she might be leaving for good?

She was recalled to the present by the strong scent of jasmine. They had reached the private car in the indigo livery of Badalpur State. Heaped at the foot of the steps was a mass of fragrant white blossom. Jasmine, her favourite flower. . . . She wondered whose idea it had been.

"Amir," Zahra said smilingly in response to her unspoken question. Pent-up tears sprang to her eyes. Amir. . . ? Why so late? Was it only because she was leaving that he had finally brought himself to express a little love?

With a pounding heart she entered the compartment and went over to him. At that moment, if he had asked her to stay she would have fallen into his arms. But he merely looked at her and retreated an inch or two.

He was often to recall that moment. Much as he had longed to respond to Selma's look of mute entreaty, an ingrained reflex prevented him from breaking the iron rule that forbade Muslim husbands and wives to display the least sign of intimacy in public.

And yet no one was present except the immediate family, Zeynel, who had just arrived from Beirut, a few maidservants . . . and his young wife silently imploring a gesture from him.

Every inch the attentive husband, he put a glass of champagne in Selma's trembling hand and proposed a toast to her health, a comfortable trip, and a pleasant stay in France. Not once did he let her feel that he would miss her or count the days to their reunion. His face was impassive.

The guard's preliminary whistle put an end to these strange, strained farewells. Everyone except Zeynel filed out on to the platform. Amir was the last to leave. Would he kiss her? He only gave a gallant bow, as if they would be meeting in a few days.

"Farewell, my princess."

"Amir!"

At her call he turned once more. For a long moment they looked into each other's eyes. Suddenly she knew that they would never meet again; she was leaving India forever.

Standing at the window as the train pulled out in a flurry of smoke, she gazed intently at the slim white figure standing motionless on the platform until it dwindled and disappeared from view.

PART FOUR

FRANCE

CHAPTER 1

2 April 1939

I am writing to you, dear Mahmud, from Paris, where Princess Selma and I have now been staying for two weeks. No, you are not dreaming: your old friend Zeynel has decided to send some news after fifteen years silence!

Do not hold it against me that I did not answer those affectionate letters you wrote me after I left for Lebanon. It was not that I did not care. I simply felt it was pointless – especially for someone as young as you – to rake over memories of past happiness. I wanted you to forget me and make a new life for yourself.

As for me, I was preoccupied. I was devoting all my time and energies to the ill-starred family for which fate had made me responsible. Above all, I was devoting myself to the service of Sultana Hatijé, who, for all her courage, was finding it hard to cope with the shock of exile.

My Sultana . . . my eyes mist over with tears whenever I think of her. It is several months now since she left us, passing away without a word of complaint like the great lady she had always been. I almost went mad with grief. We had grown even closer since her illness. I was privileged to enjoy not only her trust but also that most precious gift of all, her affection.

I can tell you this now, though you probably guessed it years ago – for me her passing meant the end of a long dream of love. I lost my heart to her the moment I entered her service at Ceragan Palace, where she and her father were imprisoned. Although I was only fifteen – she could have been my mother – I felt it my duty to protect her. She was so unhappy! After years spent yearning for freedom, she had finally abandoned hope. Her thirst for life was such that I knew she would some day end by killing herself. . . .

I confided my fears to the doctor who visited the palace once a week on orders from Sultan Abdul Hamid. My audacity surprised him, but he must have said something to His Majesty, for some months later it was decided to marry her off.

The news caused me great agony of mind, for I feared that I would be parted from her. By chance, however, I was included among her wedding presents. From then on I never left her side.

But did this make me happy? No, I was consumed with jealousy. I was jealous of her husband until I realized that she hated him even more than I did. I was equally jealous of Sultana Naimé's handsome husband, whom she encouraged, until I discovered that she did so only to take revenge on Sultan Abdul Hamid. As soon as I realized that, believe me, I helped her with a will. Her revenge was mine, for we were both victims of the sovereign whom the Christians used to call "the red Sultan."

The only person I could never tolerate was Haïri Bey, the consummate charmer who became her second husband. It escaped me how a woman as refined and intelligent as the Sultana could have fallen for that conceited fop who loved no one but himself.

I suffered the tortures of the damned, even though she was nicer to me than ever before. Happiness mellowed her, but I hated the kindness and greater familiarity she showed me, thinking it a mark of trust, when it was really a sign of indifference. When her husband was away she took to keeping me in the boudoir with her women. She would stretch out, loosen her clothing, get a maid to brush her beautiful hair and encourage me to retail all the latest palace gossip. She would throw back her head and laugh, laugh with utter abandon as if I were not a man, despite everything – as if I were incapable of experiencing desire. My pulse raced at the sight of her and her lady's maids half naked in the heat, yet everything about their attitude toward me cried, "Eunuch! You're just a eunuch!"

I grew to hate her unashamed contentment and prayed to Allah to punish her for it. He answered my prayer more fully than I could have dreamed. How cruel of him! Like a fool, I had called down a curse on the one I loved more than life itself, and there was no going back.

And yet I have been happy in Beirut. Exile had made a family of us, and the Sultana came to depend on me more and more, for I was the only man of the house.

The man . . . I can picture you smiling at that word, you poor innocent. Do you imagine that manhood consists in the ridiculous emission of a few drops of cloudy fluid? Anyway, what makes you think I am incapable of such a thing? There have been many instances where compassion has made the hakim's hand tremble while performing its baneful task. . . .

After all, I was a handsome boy of thirteen that fateful spring. I can recall mooning around after our neighbours' fair-haired daughter – recall my daydreams of her and the delicious sensation that pervaded my body as I was clumsily becoming aware of that part of me which was springing to life.

My parents were impoverished countryfolk with seven children of whom I was the eldest. When the Sultana's emissaries arrived that year, as every year, my father – may Allah never forgive him - decided that I should go with them. He dreamed that his eldest son might become the grand vizier, or at least a senior official of the Sublime Porte, so that the family would never want for anything again. Oh, he was not the only man to act in that way. It was a centuries-old tradition that the empire should take the best-looking and most intelligent boys and educate them in the various palace schools, each according to his abilities.

Did it occur to my father that, among the distinguished positions he craved for me, there was one that might carry more power than most? He who controlled the imperial harem controlled the heart and mind of the Sultan. But at what price! My father must have known this, and I can still hear my mother crying when I left, as if already mourning the mutilation of her own flesh and blood.

Why am I telling you all this now, when in the past, laying beside me, you so often urged me to talk about myself and felt hurt because my reluctance to do so seemed to you a lack of trust? Perhaps because I am growing old, and because I have no one to talk with in this big, unfamiliar city. My Princess is much in demand socially and goes out every day. I am happy for her, as I found her alarmingly depressed on my arrival in India. But I myself feel really lonely, for the first time since leaving Istanbul.

I can also confide in you now, because I know that we'll never meet again, and that my weakness for you can no longer give you a hold over me. Yes, I was afraid of you in my way – afraid because your extreme youth and beauty reminded me of what I used to be. I dreaded becoming enthralled by the image of my rediscovered self. Softening towards you would have meant softening towards myself, and that was a luxury I could not afford. How do you imagine I survived the inherent cruelty of a eunuch's existence? Only by mercilessly suppressing my regrets and dreams. For, like many of our kind, when I first realized what they had made of me – an object of derision, scorn, and, worst of all, pity – I longed for death.

Pity . . . it was like being flayed alive each time, as if those who looked with compassion on my emasculated state were castrating me over again. I enjoyed making others unhappy in order to return the insult and pity them myself. I hated happy, self-assured people with a lifetime of opportunities ahead of them. This is why I hated the young. My sympathies were reserved for those who were nearing death and were conscious of its chill creeping through their bones. . . .

Did I love you because you, too, were unhappy? Of course. How could I have loved a radiant, triumphant youth? Having been castrated in early childhood, you were ignorant of physical desire. At your insistence I tried to describe it, and the more I said the more your face darkened at the realization that you had lost something unimaginably wonderful. You listened to me with a mixture of envy and regret, much as a person blind from birth might listen to someone blinded by accident, who, having once overcome his initial despair, can visualize a world incomparably more beautiful than the one he used to know.

I painted a vivid, alluring picture of the irresistible upsurge of desire, the thrill of anticipation, the throbbing temples, the flushed cheeks, the shining eyes, the mysterious fluid that moistens one's lips and turns one's skin to velvet, the languor that pervades one's limbs, the dizziness, the sensation of oneness with the world in all its beauty, the feeling that one is life itself, creature and creator in one and the same person, God himself . . . for a moment.

God? You thought I was exaggerating, and perhaps I was. I had not experienced all those things, I had merely sensed them in the course of adolescent play. Being reduced to imagining them, however, I conceived the ultimate climax – the one in which I would become fused and confused with infinity. As a result, I may have suffered all the more. Given the opportunity to experience the sensation at first hand, I should doubtless have done so in a banal, mundane manner, like a man devouring his daily bread – like all who take their sexuality for granted.

They do not know I do. It is because that ultimate climax has been denied me that I know it so well, just as the man who desires a woman may often know her more intimately than he who possesses her.

Those who claim that desire blinds one are talking nonsense. They are referring to a fleeting impulse, not to the profound desire that can be a more complete form of possession than possession itself.

If you think I am fantasizing to console myself for my inability to possess a woman, you are mistaken. I *have* – in a way – possessed the loveliest, most noble and virtuous woman that ever walked, a queen by nature as well as birth.

I possessed her more fully than anyone. I was alert to her every little tremor and attuned to her resonances. My moods were as much governed by hers as if I were a part of her, not a separate individual – but as if I inhabited her body.

Her death rent my heart. But never fear. I have not let myself go to pieces. I still have my Selma to care for.

If you only knew how beautiful my Princess has become. I sometimes feel I am looking at a reincarnation of the Sultana in all her glory, but she is really very different. There is a touching vulnerability about her – a quality of incompleteness that seems to waver between tears and laughter. Even when she puts on a show of independence, I sense how profoundly she needs her old Zeynel. I am her one remaining link with the past. She knows that I shall remain faithful to her until my dying day.

As for you, dear Mahmud, I have one favour to ask: if this letter reaches you, please do not answer it. Above all, please do not send me a photo of yourself. I want to keep in my heart forever the youthfulness of your body and your adolescent spirit. This may strike you as monstrously selfish of me. It may on the other hand convince you that, in my own way, I love you still.

Affectionately,

Your Zeynel.

CHAPTER 2

"The Maharani's *vendeuse*, please!"

In Nina Ricci's white and gold salon where ladies exchanged the latest gossip while awaiting the opening of the spring collection, everyone turned to stare: a pale young woman in a turquoise sari had just entered, escorted by an elderly man in a high-buttoned black tunic. The Maharani? They had expected to see a dark-skinned beauty like the wives of the rulers of Jodhpur or Kapurthala, but this Maharani – in France all Indian princesses were called maharanis – might have been French but for her high cheekbones and almond eyes. Russian, perhaps?

"No, no, *ma chérie*," a distinguished-looking dowager whispered to her next-door neighbour, "she is Turkish, believe it or not. We met her at the Noailles' last dinner. Her husband is the Maharajah of Badalpur, a state in northern India."

"A little old for her, isn't he?"

"Not at all. That man – I mean, that person with her – isn't her husband. . . ." The woman lowered her voice, and her neighbours strained their ears to catch what followed. "He's her eunuch!"

Murmurs of disbelief and horrified shudders greeted this revelation. "How barbarous!" someone exclaimed. Throwing decorum to the winds, they all turned and eyed the outrageous pair with disapproval.

"But she looks so sweet and gentle! As for him, he does not seem unhappy. He probably doesn't realize how demeaning his situation is – Orientals are used to that sort of humiliation. All the same, pretty brazen of her to flaunt herself in public with a eunuch in tow!"

Their criticism was nonetheless tinged with envious admiration. It was not every day that one encountered such an extraordinary phenomenon, even in cosmopolitan Paris, and several of the socialites present reflected what a stir it would create if they could show off this pretty maharani at one of their parties – followed by her eunuch, of course.

Selma, sitting a little apart from the rest, seemed unconcerned by their curiosity. In fact, it amused her immensely. After less than a month in Paris she had grown accustomed to being the centre of attention and had to admit that she loved it. She felt as if she were back in Beirut, except that Lebanese high society, which she had once found so dazzling, now seemed provincial by comparison. The sophistication and diversity of the Parisian social scene were such that she did not know which way to turn. She wanted to sample everything on offer, and if people cultivated her for the sake of her saris and her eunuch, what did it matter? She had ceased to be a touchy young girl who yearned to be liked for herself alone; she was a woman now, and a wealthy one! After two years of cloistered existence in India, she was determined to live life to the full.

Her first step on arriving in Paris had been to take a suite at the Plaza Athenée, a useful calling card but not enough – as she quickly realized – for one who planned to conquer Parisian society.

Heure bleue, Zephyr, Rose des sables. . . . The show was under way. As she watched the mannequins gliding, wheeling, and posturing with feline grace, Selma's thoughts turned to Marie-Laure, her former "close enemy" from the Soeurs de Besançon convent. It was thanks to Marie-Laure that the hostesses of Paris had begun to invite her to their parties.

In Beirut though, the two girls had not seen very much of each other outside of school. After their first bitter confrontation, they had come to respect each other, each one recognizing the other's pride and courage. Nevertheless they had no social contact. There were too many factors which came between them in Lebanon where the French were, after all, the masters.

Marie-Laure had been the first to leave Beirut. After a brief stay in Argentina she had returned to France and, not long after, she married the Comte de Sierres, an aristocrat whose family fortune derived from alliances judiciously contracted between his forebears and the daughters of bankers and northern mill owners. But Marie-Laure had never forgotten her little Turkish friend and had made a point of sending Selma a birthday card from Paris every year. So it was only natural that, not knowing anyone else in the French capital, Selma should have telephoned her on arrival. Although they had not met for ten years, they greeted each other like the old friends they had never been.

With the pride of a Parisienne born and bred, Marie-Laure not only showed Selma around "her" city but, more importantly, tutored her in all the little niceties without which the doors of high society remained inexorably closed. For it was not enough to be rich or famous. One had to know which night and at which table to dine at Maxim's if one wanted to avoid bores and bump into friends such as the Rothschilds or the Windsors, who were "simplicity itself." The place to go for an informal supper after the show was Weber's, a brasserie much patronized by the romantic and introverted Charles Boyer. As for the races at Chantilly, the last and most elegant meeting of the season, they were an absolute *must*: even if one were at death's door, one had to show oneself there sporting the most outré hat to be found at Rose Valois or Suzy Reboux. Where shopping was concerned, the only two acceptable areas were the Rue de la Paix and the Place Vendôme. At night, however, it was not considered bad form to "slum it" with a party at the Boule Blanche and dance the beguine to the strains of a Negro band, though even there – especially there! – one had to preserve one's dignity. But not even the observance of all these rules would save one from ostracism unless one could precisely gauge what time to arrive at a party, given the importance of the other guests, nor must one congratulate one's hostess on her dinner, which could not be other than perfect; but three dozen roses from Lachaume should be sent the next day. These countless unwritten conventions formed a strict code of etiquette which it was impossible to violate without being branded a provincial or, worse still, "new money." And no one ever shook off that label however hard he tried.

Many people would have paid a fortune for Marie-Laure's few weeks of tuition. But to learn such things one had to be worthy of them – in fact one really had to know them already. Marie-Laure was a willing teacher only because she felt sure her pupil would do her credit, for Selma already possessed what no one could teach. Affable but faintly aloof, infinitely polite but ever so slightly offhand, she had the inimitable detachment of the born aristocrat. So Marie-Laure took her "pearl of the Orient" – her "maharani," as she called her – everywhere she went. It would have been irrelevant to introduce her as an Ottoman princess – the splendours of the sultanate were long forgotten – but India, with its fabled treasures and extravagant princes, was the stuff of dreams. Nothing could detract from its glamour, and certainly not that odd half-naked little man who was making such fools of the English, whom every good Frenchman loathed, in spite of the so-called entente cordiale.

Herbe sauvage, Rêve de lune . . . the mannequins showed off one graceful gown after another. How pretty they looked in those full skirts with lacy petticoats peeping below the hemline! Selma quickly jotted down some models in her notebook. She was going to find it hard to choose. Should she take them all? It would be sheer madness, but she felt like acting mad! During her last few months in India she had been suffocating. Now she wanted to forget, to drown her sorrows in the vernal gaiety of Paris, whose inhabitants, heedless of the alarming news from the East, were solely intent on amusing themselves.

Albania's annexation by the Italians, and King Zog and Queen Geraldine's flight to Greece, had elicited from Selma no more than a sardonic smile. To think that she might have been exiled a second time. . . . As for the war, there were pessimists who proclaimed that it was imminent, but nobody heeded them. Their fears might, of course, have been justified if Premier Daladier and that umbrella-toting Englishman, Chamberlain, had not had the good sense to sign a pact with Hitler at Munich, but now all was well and the Parisians could reapply themselves with wholehearted enthusiasm to the celebrated attractions that made their city the world's most glamorous capital.

Marie-Laure took her friend everywhere. Selma set foot in a music-hall for the first time. There she admired Josephine Baker and Maurice Chevalier, stars who had been part of her world in Lebanon and whose songs she knew by heart. But now her taste inclined more to Edith Piaf, that little wisp of a woman, dressed in black, whose dramatic voice brought tears to her eyes, and the young poet with a crop of blond hair, whose latest hit "Y a d'la joie" was on everyone's lips.

While she went out every night, Selma devoted her afternoons to her old passion, the cinema. She had been so frustrated in that respect at Lucknow that her visits, escorted by Zeynel, to palatial plush and gilt movie theatres such as the Biarritz or the Colisée were almost a daily ritual. Only yesterday she had seen *Quai des brumes* and fallen under the spell of Jean Gabin's husky voice as he laid siege to that new actress with the disconcerting gaze, murmuring: "You know, you have beautiful eyes."

To please her, Parisian friends had claimed she resembled this Michèle Morgan. Little did they know what memories they evoked and how much she sometimes regretted that the prospect of a royal marriage had deterred her from signing a Hollywood contract. But had she had any choice? At the time, becoming a queen had seemed an obligation she could not evade without insulting the memory of her ancestors who had sacrificed everything in the line of duty. Duty or personal inclination? Where did the boundary lie? She did not know. . . . Didn't all human beings pick their way through life, their "duty", in accordance with their ruling impulses? For a long time Selma had felt duty-bound to suppress those impulses. But little by little, she had come to realize that it was better to give them free rein in order to disentangle herself from them.

"Well, Highness, what do you think of our collection?"

Nina Ricci's *première*, Mademoiselle Armande, had sidled up. Her illustrious client seemed to have been daydreaming for a while, and it was time to recall her to the business at hand. Volubly, she extolled the beauty of the inset panels, the fineness of the embroidery, and, above all, the boldness of the new line, which gloried in its femininity.

"Unlike some designers, Highness, Madame Nina Ricci *likes* women. She refuses to caricature them for the sake of originality."

Selma was not listening: she was looking at a model in a bridal gown emerging in a snowstorm of lace and tulle while everyone applauded enthusiastically. As she watched the radiant white figure, spellbound, Selma secretly mourned another young bride in a red and gold gharara, her face veiled, hidden behind a curtain of roses, a betrothed trembling amidst the laughter and clashing of cymbals, awaiting the unknown man who was about to become her master.

That afternoon Selma had arranged to meet Marie-Laure at Madame Cadolle's, the finest corsetiere in Paris, whose establishment on Rue Cambon was much frequented by society women anxious to reduce their waists or give their bosoms a lift. Madame Cadolle was the creator of the first underwired brassiere, the *corbeille Recamier* or Recamier "basket," which was guaranteed to make your breasts look firm and rounded.

Though she was three months pregnant Selma's figure was unaltered. She had no need of Madame Cadolle's ingenious contraptions but accompanied her friend out of curiosity. And because she planned to return to the shop, on her own, in a few weeks' time. Nobody in Paris knew she was expecting – for some reason she couldn't explain, she had not even told Marie-Laure. She had almost forgotten the fact herself, she was feeling so well now that her attacks of nausea had ceased.

India and Amir seemed very far away. She sometimes felt that the past two years had been a bad dream – that she was twenty again and on the threshold of life.

Having finished their shopping, Selma and Marie-Laure repaired to the Ritz for tea. The place was crowded as usual, but Antoine, the maître d'hôtel, could always find a table for his regulars. Over tea and *tartes aux fraises* Marie-Laure eagerly inquired what sari Selma planned to wear tonight. It must be the height of elegance, she insisted. Lady Fellows was a discriminating hostess and the owner of one of the grandest town houses in Paris. There would be a band and dancing after dinner.

"I was thinking of christening my new evening gown from Lanvin," Selma said. "It falls so beautifully."

"An evening gown!" Marie-Laure was appalled. "You're mad, *chérie*. By all means wear your Lanvin in Lucknow, but here you must dress as a maharani or everyone will be most disappointed! Besides, you'd make me look a complete fool. A red-haired maharani in an evening gown? Lady Fellows would think I was playing a practical joke on her."

Selma looked crestfallen. "In Paris at least, I was hoping I could be like everyone else."

"You don't understand, do you? All these women envy you precisely because you are different. They would sell their souls *not* to be 'like everyone else.' You have not been in Paris a month, and already you are the talk of the town. Do you think any European woman, however beautiful, could make her mark so easily? Parisian society is cruel. To hold your own you have to be born into it, or amuse people, or – like you – give them something to dream about." Marie-Laure rose and kissed Selma lightly on the forehead. "I must rush – the hairdresser is waiting. See you tonight, and don't forget to bring that eunuch of yours. You'll have to leave him outside in the hall, but everyone must see him."

Selma did not reply. She settled back in her chair, brooding. Poor Zeynel! Luckily his French was too poor for him to grasp the role in which these Parisians had cast him. They really were incredible – she would never have believed that they could be so titillated by the sight of a eunuch. The situation irritated her and made her feel ashamed, but what could she do? Zeynel at sixty was an imposing figure, and her initial attempts to introduce him as her private secretary had been greeted with knowing smiles. To save her protégée's reputation, Marie-Laure had hastened to set everyone straight.

Marie-Laure. . . . Selma was beginning to weary of her friend's authoritarian concern for her social acceptability. She had not left India and the claustrophobic atmosphere of the zenana to be ruled by the quirks and conventions of *le Tout-Paris*. If Marie-Laure and Lady Fellows were disappointed, too bad: tonight she would not take Zeynel with her.

What a boor. . . .

The man opposite was still staring at her. Selma ostentatiously averted her head and feigned an intense interest in the conversation of her right-hand neighbour, the young Marquis de Belard, who was describing how his thoroughbred, Rakkam, had just failed to win the last race at Longchamp. On her left sat the Prince de Faucigny-Lucinge, a Grand Knight of the Maltese Order, recalling the battles between his forebears and the infidel Turks. He never suspected that the ravishing Maharani at his elbow was a princess of the Ottoman Empire whose warriors had fought to the death against his ancestors. Had Selma enlightened him he would never have forgiven himself, he was such a gentleman!

The same could certainly not be said of the man who had been eyeing her since the beginning of dinner without so much as addressing a word to her. She would have liked to attribute his bad manners to shyness, but he did not seem the type to be transfixed with admiration for a beautiful woman. In this refined company he appeared entirely out of place. Broad-shouldered and square-jawed, he would have looked more at home at a regatta or a boar hunt than here amid the subtle verbal skirmishing of a Parisian dinner party.

He was an American – that much Selma had gathered while the brief introductions were being made. She wrinkled her nose disdainfully. A cowboy: the type of man with whom she had nothing in common. All that conflicted with this reassuring belief were his slender, surprisingly shapely hands and the keen grey eyes, the eyes of a man used to dominating. The other women at the table seemed to find him very much to their taste. Selma had never seen the scraggy Comtesse de Neuville make such a fuss of anyone. As for that little fool Emilie Vianney, she laughed uproariously at everything he said, emitting little screams like a seagull agitated by the ocean air.

Selma was overwhelmed by a sudden sense of loneliness and alienation. She felt an outsider and longed for the dinner party to end. Dreamily, she pictured herself at Badalpur in the light of early morning, sitting over a glass of tea surrounded by peasant women. They always had so much to tell her, so many hopes and fears to impart, so much affection to give and receive. . . . Badalpur . . . There she was never bored.

"But how can I miss that place. . . ?" She drew a hand across her eyes. Badalpur . . . it had nearly been the death of her.

"A million francs! That's official, her legs are insured for a million!"

"And her bosom?"

"Ten francs the pair!"

The ladies snickered maliciously. Mistinguett had just scored a resounding success at the Moulin-Rouge. None of them bore the star any particular grudge, but what mattered was to raise a laugh. They would have betrayed their best friend for the sake of a laugh.

Selma did not even smile. She could not get used to the conversational licence that characterized these Parisian soirées, nor to the alacrity with which these social butterflies tore their fellow women to pieces.

She looked down at her plate, conscious that the American's grey eyes were still on her. The band – in tails and bow ties – had taken its place on a makeshift platform in the big circular ballroom. Lady Fellows had announced that this would be an "intimate gathering": there were only a hundred guests, most of whom had known each other since childhood. So everyone could relax, secure in the knowledge they were among friends.

The band set the tone by striking up a "Chamberlain," an excuse-me dance devised by Ray Ventura and named after the British premier. You performed it with an umbrella, the "chamberlain," which you hooked over the arm of the man whose partner you coveted. But most popular of all was that latest import from across the channel, the Lambeth Walk. In that spring of 1939 the French had evolved a Germanic variety of it: imitating the goose step, they cavorted around chanting, *"Ein Volk, ein Reich, ein Führer, ein Weg!"*[1]

Selma and her currrent partner, the Marquis de Belard, had a good time. Laughing and out of breath they sank into the arm chairs disposed around the small, orchid-bedecked tables beside the floor. Life was sweet and light, and where better to enjoy it than in Paris, a city blessed by the gods?

"Shall we, Madame?"

Selma knew, without even looking, who was addressing her so casually. She felt like refusing but did not want to offend her hostess by turning down one of her guests. Besides, the man intrigued her. She wanted to find out what lay behind that level gaze.

He was even taller than she had imagined. She felt absurdly vulnerable in his arms, and the sensation made her stiffen. If only he would not hold her so tight. It was positively indecent the way he enveloped her – almost as if he were intent on absorbing her. She tried in vain to draw away from the body clamped against hers, the broad chest whose contours she could distinctly feel through her chiffon sari. He piloted her around the floor in silence. Annoyed by the involuntary glow flooding through her, she could sense that everyone's eyes were on them. The man was mad – he might as well be

1 One people, one country, one leader, one way.

making love to her in public!

With an abrupt movement, she unglued her face from his shoulder. She had to say something – anything, as long as it compelled him to look at her and relax his grip.

"Will you be staying in Paris long?"

The grey eyes regarded her teasingly.

"Why, fair lady, would you like me to?"

Furious, she attempted to push him away, but his arm tightened around her once more. Feeling suffocated, but with anger this time, she surreptitiously dug her heel into his foot. He released her so suddenly that she almost fell. She looked at him apprehensively, wondering how he would react, but all he did was smile ironically.

"Some temper!" he said. Then, with the puzzled air of a seeker after truth, he added, "Tell me, Madame, if you don't mind an ordinary mortal asking you a question that's been bothering him for hours. I watched you all through dinner, putting on airs for the benefit of those dummies on either side of you. Does it really give you a kick to act like royalty?"

Selma was on the point of making the obvious retort. "But I am. . . ." She stopped just in time, deterred by his unashamedly mocking expression. Blushing, she cast around for some withering remark that would put him in his place.

"Monsieur, you are a . . . a . . ."

Words failed her. She felt utterly ridiculous. With all the hauteur she could muster she turned and walked off, but his silent laughter seemed to ring in her ears as she went.

She danced until the small hours making a point of being especially seductive with her various partners, but watching the stranger's tall figure out of the corner of her eye. Although he seemed to have lost interest in her, she was sure he was observing her. Sooner or later he would ask her to dance again, and then it would be her turn to humiliate him.

He did not come back towards her. Without so much as a glance in her direction, he left the party accompanied by a gorgeous brunette.

"By the way," Selma said casually, "who was that cowboy?"

For the past hour, she and Marie-Laure had been curled up on the sofa amusing themselves by dissecting the party in every detail, criticizing this woman's dress, that man's affectations. Marie-Laure had an unrivalled knack of spotting absurdities – even the best-concealed flaws did not escape her eagle eye – and although she was longing to ask, Selma had carefully refrained from bringing up the subject of the

American too soon.

"The cowboy? Oh, you mean Dr Kerman, the one who clasped you to his manly breast with such ardour? You looked so angry I couldn't help laughing. Surely it wasn't as disagreeable as all that? He's a most attractive man."

Selma breathed again. Marie-Laure's sensitive antennae had detected nothing.

"He's over here for an international congress," Marie-Laure went on. "He was one of the most brilliant surgeons in New York, but two years ago he chucked it all up and went off to the wilds of Mexico to look after the Indians there. Apparently, his wife was furious. She's the daughter of some eminent consultant, and she married him against her family's wishes. His background could not be more humble: his mother was a waitress in a little Midwest town."

Selma looked puzzled. "But if Lady Fellows is so particular about people's pedigrees, why did she invite him?"

"She met him in New York – Kerman is a celebrity over there. She must have thought he would add a touch of spice to her party, and she was right: the women buzzed around him like flies. The world has changed, *ma chérie*. So many nasty things are going on, people are anxious to have fun while they can. Some say the unions are going to start a revolution, others predict there'll be a war. It's probably all exaggerated, of course, but it gives you the feeling things are getting hot. Everyone wants to live for the moment, and who cares if this means upsetting certain preconceptions. Personally, I'm all for it. We should always live on the brink of disaster."

Marie-Laure's blend of enthusiasm and cynicism had long appealed to Selma. In another time, she might have been a great adventurer instead of just a social butterfly. She stretched luxuriously and raised her glass of lemonade.

"Let's drink to war, as it seems the only thing that can save us from being bored to death."

And, laughing, they raised their glasses.

CHAPTER 3

The bellboy proffered a silver salver bearing an envelope adorned with the arms of Badalpur. Zeynel took it eagerly and gave him five francs. A letter from the Rajah at last! After three weeks without news he had been growing anxious. His Highness had promised to join them early in June; this message would probably confirm his date of arrival. The sooner the better, thought Zeynel. He, at least, would be able to make Selma see sense. A woman in her condition ought to rest, but she was forever going out. At first Zeynel had not said anything, he was so relieved to see her happy again, but she had no sense of proportion. She danced the night away and returned at dawn, and her only response to his worried admonitions was to tease him gently.

"My dear Zeynel, you don't know what you are talking about. The most important thing for a baby's health is its mother's happiness.

And just to convince him, she would give him a little kiss on the cheek. Instantly, he would forget all the arguments he had rehearsed for hours while awaiting her return. Only when he was alone again did he realize to his annoyance that, once more, she had twisted him around her little finger. It had been so for as long as he could remember. Even as a little girl in Istanbul she could wheedle anything out of him.

With letter in hand he knocked at her door.

"Come in!"

Zeynel paused in the doorway, aghast. Selma, wearing striped pants and a matching top, was flexing her arms and legs in front of the open window.

"Shut the door, Zeynel, can't you see I'm doing my exercises?"

"Another American fad!" he grumbled. "The Sultana and her sisters never indulged in such stupidities, and they were beautiful women, as Allah is my witness. Do you really want muscles like a man?"

She laughed and took the letter from him. He did not move, hoping that she would ask him to stay while she read it, but she looked at him and raised her eyebrows exactly as the Sultana used to. He made a grudging exit.

Selma tore the envelope open. For a moment she let her gaze wander over Amir's bold handwriting.

2 May 1939

Dearest,

Contrary to all my hopes, I have some bad news for you: I cannot join you next month as arranged. You must have read in the papers that India is in a ferment as the British have decided to mobilize the Indian Army without consulting the various provincial governments. Everyone is heatedly debating whether, in the event of war, we should back Britain or take advantage of the situation to snatch the independence we have been demanding without success for so many years. Congress is divided on the issue, whereas the Muslim League holds that the democracies should be supported against the Nazi threat, at all costs. As for us, the princes, we have been requested by the Viceroy, Lord Linlithgow, to recruit a certain number of men and hold them in readiness to report for military training at a moment's notice. It is an awkward decision, and I have not yet made up my mind, but in Badalpur nearly three thousand have already vounteered. Surprising that our peasants should be so eager to get themselves killed; or are they simply attracted by the uniform and the pay, which to those poor wretches represents a fortune?

What about you, my dear? I am worried. They say that Herr Hitler aims to rectify "the unjust frontiers imposed by the Treaty of Versailles." If so, France will be first in the firing line. I strongly advise you to leave for Switzerland at once. Lausanne is a delightful town, where you will be safe.

In your latest letter you ask me to send you another banker's draft. I must confess I do not understand how you managed to spend more in a month than it costs me to maintain this place and its two hundred inmates for half a year. I will take the necessary steps, but please be reasonable. I am not the Nizam of Hyderabad, who, as my friend the Aga Khan says, could fill his swimming pool with precious stones. If my ancestors had been allies of the British like his, we would not have lost three quarters of the state and you could buy up every dress house in Paris.

However I am proud they fought and I trust you are too.

Selma broke off. "Why must he always moralize?" she muttered to herself. "God, how tiresome responsible men are!" She did not mean a word of it, naturally. She was far too attached to her own concept of honour and courage not to understand her husband's pride; in fact, it was one of the qualities she most admired in him. As for Switzerland, she would not dream of burying herself there!

In any case, here there was no danger. The experts claimed that Germany was too weak economically to take on the might of the French Army, and that any attempt to do so would be crushed within the first twenty-four hours.

You tell me little about your doings except to say that you see a lot of films and go to the races with your friend Marie-Laure. Do not tire yourself out whatever you do – the doctors say a woman in your condition should spend at least half the day lying down. Begum Nimet urges you to avoid eating melon. Apparently, it is bad for a baby's lungs.

You must be feeling very lonely, my dearest. I hope life is not too dreary for you there. The palace seems empty without you. Everyone misses you.

I kiss your hands.

Amir

Selma put the letter down. "Poor Amir, he didn't even dare to say outright that *he* misses me. He worries about me, yes, but I am afraid he would worry a lot more if he knew how much fun I am having. Even so, I am not doing anything wrong. . . . I keep my admirers at arm's length; not that I deserve much credit for that. They are – what did this American call them? – yes, that is it: 'dummies!'"

She had not met the 'cowboy' since Lady Fellows' party. He must have gone home, which was just as well. After making such a fool of herself the other night she had no wish to see him again.

Applause rang out as the heavy curtain of the Madeleine Theatre descended on the last act of *Une paire de gifles*, Sacha Guitry's new play. Everyone who was anyone in Paris was there.

The crystal chandeliers blazed into life, illuminating the elegant first-night audience. Gentlemen raised their opera glasses for a final look at the boxes offering a view of the prettiest women in Paris. One young man-about-town turned to his male companion and smiled.

"Sacha really pulled off a *tour de force* tonight," he said.

"Oh, sure, the play's amusing enough."

"Who's talking about the play? Look, he's managed to reassemble all his former wives including Yvonne Printemps, escorted by her new husband, Pierre Fresnay, and the beautiful Jacqueline De Tulubac, whom he's just divorced in order to marry Genevieve de Sereville. Guess how he told her he was leaving her? It was during the third act of a play they were appearing in together. 'Madame,' he ad-libbed, 'I am going to present you with a priceless gift: I am giving you . . . your freedom!' "

"Very ingenious. The women adore him, I take it?"

"They are crazy about him, but he irritates a lot of men. I have a friend who claims that Sacha only has to see a dog trot past while he's taking the air on his balcony and he'll strike a pose."

The ladies were beginning to leave their boxes. The young man pointed out the Begum Aga Khan, a one-time Miss France who was now the respected consort of the Ismailis' spiritual leader, and Marcelle Margot Noblemaire, the enchanting wife of the head of Wagons-Lits.

"And here is the little Maharani with the green eyes! Maharani of where? Who cares! Doesn't she look exquisite in that black lace sari with the gold trimming?" The young man was a mine of information. "They say she's quite unapproachable – a paragon of virtue. She even blushes at risqué jokes. Delightful, isn't she? I've booked a table at Maxim's because I happen to know she'll be dining there tonight with the Prince and Princesse de Broglie. They're old friends of mine, and Albert, the maître d'hôtel, has promised me a table right next to theirs. I'm dying to meet her. Do you want to come with me?"

His companion screwed up his eyes, lost in thought.

"We already met," he said. "I'm afraid she didn't take to me."

"All the better. Then I needn't fear any competition from you!"

They headed for the exit, laughing as they went.

Selma's memory of the night's events was a blur. All she could recall was that as soon as she saw him the room came alive. . . .

Now I can take my revenge, she had thought with pleasure, unable to resist a malicious glance in his direction. He must have mistaken it for encouragement, for he came over at once.

And then. . . . She could not understand what happened next: without meaning to, she found herself back in his arms, and they had danced long into the night. He did not enfold her in a possessive embrace; he held her gently, as if afraid of breaking her, and the eyes that smiled down at here were infinitely tender. She sensed that people were watching and whispering but she did not care, she could not help herself. If he had kissed her right there in the middle of the dance floor she knew she would not have shied away from him. All her willpower, all her principles had deserted her. Nothing mattered but the warmth of his gaze and the arm around her waist.

Suddenly, it was very late. He had offered to drive her back to her hotel and she had accepted, heedless of the disapproving frown from the Princesse de Broglie, whose guest she was, and of the fact that this one act would ruin a reputation earned by weeks of irreproachable behaviour. If people wanted to gossip, let them! She marvelled at her total indifference to what others might think.

They had traversed the glittering heart of Paris from Rue Royale to the Avenue Montaigne. The Place de la Concorde was deserted. He was driving slowly past the fountains, so slowly that they could hear the spray as it came down into the stone basins like fine rain. They rode up the Champs-Elysées, as if they were going up the nave of a cathedral. He remained silent, and sitting beside him she was conscious of his sharp profile in the mottled light of the passing street lamps, and she imagined that they were setting off on a long journey together. In front of the Plaza Athenée he had pulled up and turned to her. Once more she was overwhelmed by the strength and gentleness that emanated from him. All the wiles she knew so well were of no use to her now, nor would she have wanted to use them. He had taken her face in his hands and gazed at it intently, then kissed her lightly on the forehead.

"I'll call you tomorrow," he had murmured, and drove off.

She stood there swaying a little, her eyes half-closed, afraid that if she opened them too wide her dream would escape.

H . . . Two arms embracing the sky, two legs planted firmly on the ground: a symbol reassuring in its perfect balance and symmetry, the lines that formed it clean and sober, powerful in their rejection of artifice, their tranquil simplicity, their austere inflexibility. . . . H for Harvey.

Her fingers tightened on the card the bellboy had just delivered, together with a spray of beautiful, exotic-looking flowers. It read simply: "Harvey Kerman." Harvey. . . . She repeated the name silently. Although she had never heard it before, it seemed familiar – as familiar as these unknown flowers whose indigo-flecked, purple corollas proudly guarded long pistils of an even darker purple.

The telephone rang. She made a dash for it.

"Am I disturbing you?"

It was only Marie-Laure, avid for news.

"Not at all, I was just getting up."

"Well?" Marie-Laure's voice was vibrant with anticipation.

"Well what?"

"Come on, don't play the innocent! Did your handsome cowboy live up to his looks?"

"Really, Marie-Laure! We said good night outside the hotel. It was all perfectly respectable."

The little laugh at the other end of the line sounded hurt and incredulous. Obviously, Marie-Laure felt her friend was not entitled to keep any secrets from her. After all, Selma owed every one of her social contacts, including the American, to her.

"If you don't want to talk about it, that's your business," she said primly, "but be a bit more discreet in future. You behaved outrageously last night – I've already had phone calls about you from four different people."

"Really? Don't they have anything better to do?"

"Anything goes in Paris as long as you keep up appearances. Very well, when the love of your life goes off to rejoin his wife – he leaves in a week's time, apparently – call me. But I warn you, mine isn't the best of shoulders to cry on."

She hung up. Selma's joy had evaporated, less because she minded upsetting her friend than because of her realization that Marie-Laure might well be right. She was falling in love with a married man who lived on the other side of the world – a man she would almost certainly never see again.

Unthinkingly, she lit a cigarette – she detested smoking – and was surprised to note that her hands were trembling. Why should she get into such a state over a man she had only just met? Was it because he seemed so different from the others who paid court to her? They proceeded cautiously, whereas his headlong charge had bewildered her. Her imagination had credited him with a whole host of qualities, doubtless in order to justify the spell he had cast over her, but now that she had recovered her poise, thanks to Marie-Laure, she realized that the whole thing was an aberration. The American was attractive, to be sure, but not her type at all: after twenty-four hours together they would have nothing left to say to each other. She straightened up: I must put a stop to this adventure.

The telephone rang again. This time it was him, she knew. She grabbed the receiver.

"Hello, Goddess," he said briskly. "I'll pick you up at twelve. We're going to have lunch at a real Parisian bistro, the kind of place you've never set foot in before."

"But I –"

"You mean you aren't up yet? Okay, make it twelve-thirty. See you then."

La Fontaine de Mars, on the corner of Rue Saint-Dominique, was a little restaurant with red-and-white check tablecloths and menus handwritten by the son of the house, who was twelve years old and the only member of the family who could spell, so Harvey explained on the way there. He gave a spirited imitation of the *patron* refusing to serve any but Cahors wine and bragging that his *cassoulet* was the best you ever tasted!

Selma's arrival in a sari caused a sensation. No one in the neighbourhood had ever seen anyone turn up for lunch wearing an evening gown – in fact a woman had to silence her little boy for asking why the lady was in fancy dress. The *patron*, a strapping fellow with ruddy cheeks, bustled forward to greet "*l'Americain*," who was one of his best customers. Having demonstrated his knowledge of etiquette by seizing Selma's hand and giving it a smacking kiss, he led the way, nimble-footed as a ballerina despite his paunch, to a table at the back of the restaurant reserved for distinguished customers. *You rub shoulders with the best at Père Boulac's*, his beaming smile seemed to tell the rest of the room, *so don't go complaining if your bill seems a little on the high side*.

Selma felt as if she had stepped into the middle of a Marcel Carné movie. She would never have believed that the French could so closely resemble their own stereotype: fat men with napkins tied around their necks, savouring their food with almost religious single-mindedness; pallid children in their Sunday best; lovers kissing between every mouthful under the disapproving eye of Père Boulac, who resented seeing his wife's succulent dishes get cold and had no hesitation in telling them, in a stentorian voice, that "Eating time is for eating!". Selma longed to join in their conversation, but she knew she would only embarrass them. She resolved to wear a dress the next time.

Except that . . . there would not be a next time. She had to make that clear to Harvey, but he had not given her a chance so far, with his incessant flow of good humour. She had to dispel the misunderstanding at once – the longer she left it the harder it would be. She hesitated nonetheless. He seemed so happy. . . .

"Harvey, there's something I have to tell you."

She was startled by the tone of her voice and its breathless quality, but most of all by the fact that she had addressed this near stranger by his first name. Had she done so to soften the blow, or simply because she wanted to utter the name that had haunted her all morning?

He looked at her intently and gave a little wink as if to say, "I know, but don't worry, everything will work out," but instead he only said: "Of course, Goddess but wouldn't you like to order first? This place may not look much, but don't be misled, it's one of the best restaurants in Paris. It hasn't been 'discovered,' thank God, so promise me you won't bring any of your friends here. Let them make do with their Tour d'Argent and their beloved Maxim's. I don't want them butting in on these good people, who regard eating as a serious business, not an excuse for seeing and being seen."

Selma applied herself seriously to the menu, but it was no use, she could not concentrate. The *confits d'oie, poulardes truffées*, and *terrines de foie aux cèpes* kept getting mixed up with what she planned to say. "The truth is, Harvey . . ." – no, too familiar. "Look, Dr Kerman, don't misunderstand me, but. . . ." No, perhaps it would be better to disappear without a word: wasn't any explanation actually a way of avoiding a break-up? What did she mean, a break-up? How could they break up when there was nothing between them!

"Nothing!" she heard herself say.

"I'm sorry?"

She blushed and said, falteringly that she had been thinking about something else. To relieve her embarrassment, he ordered for them both without consulting her further.

"And now, tell me: what's this 'nothing' you're so certain about?"

She did not answer. How could she tell him she was not interested in him when he had not suggested she should be?

"You're right," he went on. "We don't seem to have anything in common. 'What am I, Princess Selma, doing here with this uncouth American' – isn't that what you're thinking?" He silenced her by taking her hands in his. "No, it isn't what *you're* thinking, it's what other people are thinking for you. Isn't it time you started thinking for yourself?"

"How dare you!" Thoroughly offended, she tried to pull her hands out of his, but he held them firmly.

"Actually, I'm being unfair: you *have* started thinking, or last night wouldn't have happened and we wouldn't be here now. It's just that you're so unused to doing what you really want to do that all you can think of is running away." He released her hands. "You can go any time, Selma. Think carefully, though: running away from me may not matter, but are you going to spend the rest of your life running away from yourself?"

Selma felt stunned. This man was actually dangerous. She hardly knew him, yet here he was, intruding in the inner recesses of her mind. She could have stood up and walked out, but she did not.

"You are wrong," she heard herself saying, sounding like a scolded child. "I'm not running away. Quite the opposite, in fact. I spent a long time trying to discover what I was and what I wanted, but the more I searched the less certain I became. In the end I gave up and started living instead."

"You call it living, bobbing up and down on that stupid social merry-go-round like a mechanical doll?" He leaned toward her, looking at her intently: "Selma, what are you so afraid of?"

Why was she letting him question her like this? She wanted to go, but could not move.

"I often feel I am nothing and everything at the same time," she said in a low voice, "and I don't know which scares me more, because my real self disappears either way."

Why on earth was she confiding in this stranger when she would not trust her best friends in Paris? Perhaps it was the sense of calm he radiated, a calm that reminded her of a clear sky after a storm.

"Nothing and everything," he repeated, looking at her gravely. "It may scare our little egos, but that's exactly what we are." He took her by the shoulders. "Stop dreaming, Selma. You're a woman, don't you know what that means? It's the noblest title of all – the rest are just stupid superficialities that stop the flow of life. That's why I refuse to call you 'princess,' because that title is too limiting. You're far more than a princess – you're a human being with all a human being's infinite possibilities.

"But don't let it spoil your appetite," he concluded with a laugh, putting half a spring chicken on her plate.

He was staying at a rented apartment on Rue Montpensier, immediately opposite the fountain in the garden of the Palais-Royal. He took her there after lunch without asking, as if the bond that already existed between them made it only natural, and they spent all afternoon together on his big bed. He kissed and fondled her gently, but he did not make love to her even though every taut fibre of her body begged him to.

At last, when the room became tinged with purple by the setting sun and the scent of evening drifted up from below, where an old gardener was watering the grass, they got up and went out. At a little bar under the arcade they stopped and shared a bottle of crisp white Sancerre and threw pistachios to the pigeons.

The night sky was still clear when he drove her back to the Plaza Athenée. She was trembling so much that her legs threatened to give way, and when he bent to kiss her, she shut her eyes not wanting him to see that they were filled with tears.

"Look at me, Selma."

"I love you," she said softly.

He thrust her back and gave her a long, hard stare. Then, seeing her look of dismay, he softened.

"Selma, try to get this straight: you're a free woman – you don't have to find some grand emotional excuse for everything you do. I can accept everything from you except you lying to yourself."

"But I'm not lying!"

"You are lying to *yourself*, and you are the only person you should be truthful with. I know you long to love someone – maybe to love me – but the moment you think you're letting go you look at yourself to assess the effect. I'm not blaming you – from childhood you've been trained to please. They filed you down and remoulded everything that was spontaneous to fit you for your role as a princess. Until you get rid of this role you'll be incapable of loving anyone." He drew her towards him again and cradled her tenderly in his arms. "It's hard, I know, but don't be afraid, I'll help you all I can." He laughed. "My motives are purely selfish. I love you, so I hope someday it'll be me you love, not the image of a Selma in love. . . ."

The very next evening she was back in Rue Montpensier. She had not called him – she wouldn't have known what to say. In a kind of dream she climbed the stairs. The rags and tatters of her old self seemed to fall away at every step, and the higher she climbed the lighter she felt. Momentary panic seized her as she rang the bell – what would he think of a woman coming to offer herself – but when he opened the door he greeted her with a smile of such tenderness and wonder that she knew that this was their truth, that nothing else mattered. And as he almost shyly began to undress her she felt that no man had ever looked at her body before; and when he brushed her breasts with his lips and kneeled down before her, cupped his strong hands around her hips and moved them around to the small of her back, it came to her, like a dazzling revelation, that never before had she truly belonged to anyone.

With silent, almost reverent passion for hours they caressed each other, trembling not with the joy of mutual discovery, but of mutual recognition, as if they had loved each other once, in some forgotten world. And when their bodies fused there was no more space or time, only eternity in every instant.

Awakened at dawn by birdsong, she lay there motionless, filtering through her lashes the pale rays of sunlight, careful not to disturb the bare arm draped across her belly. She relished her sense of belonging; she was grateful to him and whispered her love softly.

For a long time she studied his sleeping face: the full, firm lips and the little wrinkles at the corners of his eyes. Could it really be that this man loved her, Selma? He had said he wanted her bare, he had said he wanted her a woman, he had said: have faith. He had made her a gift she had long ceased to hope for and dismissed as a childish illusion: he had resurrected the girl who thirsted for understanding, the Selma to whom the world had seemed an inexhaustible source of experience, of boundless possibilities.

From then on, they became inseparable. She cancelled all her engagements, pleading an unexpected trip to the south of France. If anyone phoned, Zeynel was to say that the date of her return was still uncertain. The eunuch did his best to make her see sense – her relationship with this American alarmed him intensely – but she silenced him with a severity he had never observed in her before. Nothing and no one could be allowed to intrude on her new-found happiness.

They spent days walking the streets hand in hand. Harvey introduced her to a Paris she did not know. They strolled beneath the chestnut trees on the Ile de la Jatte, a sliver of land enclosed by the Seine at Neuilly, and sat musing by lamplight on a bench in the Place Furstemberg.

One morning just after dawn Harvey took her to the Quai aux Fleurs, where flower trucks unloaded their fragrant and delicate sheafs in the shadow of Notre-Dame. Then they strolled to the bird market, where he bought her a blue-tit in a white cage.

In the evenings, at sunset, they would often pay a visit to the little cemetery of Montmartre, and Selma wistfully recalled the bright, sunlit cemetery at Eyüp, overlooking the Bosphorus, where she used to walk as a child. Then, to quell her nostalgia Harvey would take her to the famous Lapin Agile, where they crowded around a table among thin, bright-eyed, young people she imagined to be poets or musicians. Selma had abandoned her saris in favour of some dresses they had chosen together. At long last, nobody was looking at her.

One day, while they were sitting on a bench beside the Seine, Harvey told her about his childhood in a little town in Ohio and the truck stop where his mother had worked as a waitress to keep the family alive. His father was an artist. When the mood took him, he would throw splashes of paint at the canvas which was meant, he said, to shatter your eyes and your heart. "That's all that counts," he would proclaim. "They need waking up, the cud-chewing zombies! I'm going to shake them up, jolt them so hard they won't be able to sleep nights!" His paintings were, in fact, enough to give a person nightmares, which was probably why no one bought them.

Harvey had an unbounded admiration for his father and had often fought bigger boys for calling the painter a "good for nothing." He shared this admiration with his mother, who worshipped her husband and would have been amazed to know how many people pitied her for having married him.

Harvey's father always got him ready for school because his mother had to leave for work at dawn. One morning he had put his arms around the boy and hugged him tight. Harvey could recall every detail: he could still feel the rough tweed jacket scratching his cheek, smell the persistent odour of turpentine that he liked and always associated in his mind with artistic genius, and hear, as if it were yesterday, the husky voice saying, "Promise you'll make me proud of you."

His father had left and never come back. His mother moved heaven and earth to find him, convinced that he had had an accident of some kind, but no trace of him was ever found. Even now, thirty years later, Harvey had no idea if his father were alive or dead.

"I started studying like crazy to honour my promise. I was hell-bent on being top in everything. I felt sure my father would turn up one day and pat me on the shoulder, the way he always did when he was pleased with me. I used to spend every evening at the municipal library. I'd go there after school and hide behind a bookcase when it closed so they'd lock me in for the night. You have no idea what a thrill it was to be all alone in that den of learning. At first I devoured anything that came to hand, but it wasn't long before I developed a special interest in books on philosophy and medicine – I thought they contained the meaning of life, I guess. My father's painting was a deliberate attempt to stimulate the eye and stir the soul. He refused to be content with outward appearances. He had a passion for getting to the bottom of things, and that I had inherited."

Harvy meditated awhile in silence.

"When I got my surgeon's diploma and he still did not show up, I knew I would never see him again. A few years ago I organized an exhibition of his work at New York. The critics hailed him as a genius. 'The unknown master of American Expressionism' – that kind of thing. My mother wept, and I was pretty moved myself. I thought the publicity might encourage him to come back to us if he were still alive. You never lose hope of finding your father again. . . ."

Selma looked away to hide her distress. A vivid picture of Haïri Rauf Bey, so handsome in his pearl-grey morning coat, had surfaced in her mind. She had never forgiven him for abandoning her, she had nursed her sorrow and this had affected her life, as a woman; whereas young Harvey, confronted by a similar loss, had turned it into a source of strength. Why? Could it be that happiness and unhappiness were a matter of personal choice? She tried to banish the idea, but in vain, and it tainted her present bliss with nostalgia. She almost resented the happiness Harvey had brought her, for it made her aware of all the time she had wasted. But after all, he too had wasted a part of his life by marrying the daughter of a famous specialist straight out of internship. The next day, after some hesitation, she decided to broach the subject. He stared at her in surprise.

"What can I tell you? We were very young and very much in love. Everyone told me what a catch she was, but I, in my innocence, didn't grasp the insinuation. It may seem incredible, but I was so proud, so confident – I was a self-made man, remember – it never dawned on me that, in the eyes of society, there was a gulf between us. Ursula was beautiful, energetic and intelligent. That was enough to make me believe that she was generous and idealistic as well. Unfortunately. . . ." He broke off. "I don't know why I'm telling you all this."

Selma threw discretion to the winds.

"I've heard she objects to your spending so much time with the Indians in the wilds of Mexico and the Amazon. People say she asked you for a divorce but you won't give her one."

His eyes flashed. "People say all kinds of things. If it were true, why should I refuse her? You disappoint me, Princess – you are demeaning yourself if that's what you believe. Would you really be interested in a pathetic creature who remained with his wife for financial reasons? Don't you think you are worth more than that? You deserve the best, Goddess, and you're right to have chosen me, because I *am* the best!"

His sardonic smile had returned, but Selma felt sure he was thinking over what he had just said, word for word. She looked puzzled.

"But in that case –"

"All right, if you really want to know, *I* myself started divorce proceedings a year ago, but Ursula blocked them. I let things hang fire because I had no intention of remarrying. I wonder. . . ." He eyed her curiously. "I sometimes wonder if one day you could bring yourself to drop those exalted titles of yours and become simply Mrs Harvey Kerman. . . ."

She tried to conceal a faint shudder, but it didn't escape him. An ironic look came over his face, mingled with sadness.

"Just as I thought," he said. "You still have some growing up to do."

She bit her lip. Why had she recoiled like that when her dearest wish was to say yes, to drop everything and go away with him? This was her chance to live, she knew. Harvey was right to poke fun at "that crown" on her head and claim that it prevented her from thinking. But no matter how much she struggled against it, "that crown" had weighed her down for twenty-eight years and encumbered her ancestors for centuries before that; she felt as if it were glued to her head.

The memory flashed before her of Amir exclaiming one day: "What use is independence? It is not just the British we need to get rid of – it is their whole mentality, the mentality of the white man! They have moulded our brains. These white brains of ours we have to tear out of our heads!" Now she knew exactly what he meant. She also was a prisoner of ideas she had ceased to believe in, and every day she spent with Harvey reinforced her conviction that they had prevented her from living.

He took her in his arms and gently stroked her hair. It was as if he had read her mind.

"Yes, my love," he murmured, "start living – start living right away. A lot of people realize too late that they chose the wrong life. That way lies despair." He nodded. "I've seen too many poor wretches who dreaded to die because they said they hadn't lived. But for us, Goddess, there's a whole world waiting, if you want it!"

Three weeks had gone by, every instant of which was engraved on her mind. She would never have believed that happiness could be so intense and, at the same time, so serene.

Tonight Harvey had suggested another visit to La Fontaine de Mars. It was Monday, so the restaurant was almost deserted. The *patron* showed them to "their" table and Selma held out her hand to him as if he was an old friend. Then, looking radiant, she turned to Harvey and laughed.

"Père Boulac has been a sort of good fairy to us, hasn't he?"

Harvey nodded. "You must come and eat here with Zeynel now and then."

"With Zeynel?"

"After I've gone, I mean." His encouraging smile was a failure. "Look, Selma, I've got to go back to New York to settle my affairs. Then I have to take a medical team to Mexico – I contracted to do it over six months ago. I promise I'll be back by the beginning of September. You'll wait for me, won't you?"

Her blood turned to ice. She knew he had to go – he had already delayed his departure for several weeks on her account; she knew he loved her, but she could not suppress a sense of mounting panic.

"Harvey, take me with you!"

She almost shouted the words. He stared at her, taken aback by the note of childish terror in her voice.

"My darling, it's impossible. Besides, you need some time alone to think things over. The life I'm offering you is very different from the one you're used to. It is a vagabond existence – you won't always find it easy. . . ." When she did not reply, he added, "It's lucky we don't have any children, either of us. Our decisions affect no one but ourselves."

Selma had turned pale. She had meant to tell him from the start, but day after day she shied away from the prospect. Harvey was different from other men, yes, but was he *that* different? Would he come to terms with the fact that the woman he loved was carrying another man's child? She was afraid – she could not bear the thought of losing him. If only she could make him understand that the child was hers, and that Amir had nothing – or virtually nothing – to do with it. . . .

It was different certainly for a couple in love. The baby grew under its father's eye, the warmth of his hand caressing the mother's belly, hearing the sound of his voice; it grew and developed because of the love its mother was bathed in. Then one could say that the child really was the fruit of two people. Oh how she would have loved the child to be Harvey's!

She started to cry. Harvey looked at her, disconcerted. He would never have thought she would react so emotionally at the mention of a child.

"Selma, would you like a baby?" he asked tenderly.

She raised her head and looked at him through her tears. Now was the time to tell him, but she did not have the courage.

"Would you, Harvey?" was all she said.

"Given the life I've led, I've never seriously considered it, my time has always been so taken up with other things. Come to think of it, though, a child of yours and mine would be a little miracle!"

His expression was radiant; Selma started sobbing again. Puzzled, he plied her with questions; she said it was nothing, just sadness at the thought of losing him so soon. She would not tell him after all, she decided. There was no point in spoiling their last few days together. Later on, when he was in America, she would write to him. She had always been better at explaining things on paper.

CHAPTER 4

With a thunderous roar, a formation of French fighter planes zoomed over the flag-bedecked length of the Champs Elysées followed by a squadron of British Spitfires. Ploughing through the sky in their wake came scores of Breguet 690's, Marcel Bloch 151's, and Liore-Olivier 45's. The crowds who had been waiting since early morning thrilled with pride as they watched the armada pass overhead. They had been told about it often enough, but till now they had not realized how truly formidable the French Air Force was.

President Lebrun was seated in the official reviewing stand flanked by government ministers in sombre morning coats. Behind them, wearing gold-embroidered jellabas or long, colourful robes, sat the representatives of France's innumerable colonies and protectorates. The parade in honour of 14 July 1939, the hundred and fiftieth anniversary of the storming of the Bastille, was about to commence.

Thousands of periscopes rose from the close-packed crowd. Selma had arrived late, but Zeynel had managed to rent her a soapbox for twenty francs. Standing on tiptoe, she made out the gleaming helmets of the Gardes Republicains who led the parade, followed by the snowy plumes of the Saint-Cyr cadets and the black cocked hats of their counterparts from the Ecole Polytechnique, the military academy of artillery and engineering. How dashing they looked! She had always been enthralled by military parades. The thunder of drums and the strains of a national anthem – any national anthem – brought tears to her eyes and gave her a curious sensation in the pit of her stomach.

Next came the British. Like animated figures from an old military print, straight-backed grenadiers in tall black bearskins advanced with rhythmical tread followed by kilted Scotsmen marching to the skirl of the pipes. *"Vive l'Angleterre!"* cried the spectators, fired with enthusiasm by the sight of the soldiers of their new-found ally. Their interest waned a little as the columns of infantry filed past, but the naval contingents were loudly applauded. It was considered good luck to touch the pompom on a French sailor's cap, so the *marins* would be much in demand later on, when the parade broke up.

At last, detachments of French troops from the four corners of the world appeared: Indochinese and Malagasy machine gunners,

Algerian riflemen, statuesque Senegalese. Then marching majestically along at the rear of this exotic procession were the men of the Foreign Legion, radiating the glamour of those who had defied the desert and looked death in the face. Selma eyed them with curiosity. She had heard it rumoured that Marlene Dietrich, who had sailed in from America the day before to contribute to the festivities by singing *Auprès de ma blonde*, had fallen in love with a handsome Legionnaire.

The crowds were still dazzled by this spectacle when the cavalry, the stamping, snorting, jingling aristocracy of the military world, dashed by: hussars, dragoons, and spahis rode past with a panache that filled the watching men in the crowd, most of whom would not have dared to mount a donkey, with conscious pride. Behind them came the "mechanized cavalry," the invincible French Army's pride and joy. Tanks rumbled menacingly along the Champs-Elysées as if nothing, but nothing, could ever stop them. "They're the tanks from the Maginot Line," Selma heard someone whisper. "There are thousands of them." Everyone seemed faintly awestruck by the steel monsters, and one dignified-looking gentleman gave vent to what everyone was privately thinking. "With those up our sleeve," he said, "we can tell the Boches to jump into the Rhine!"

The parade was nearly over, and the crowds had already broken through the police barriers for a closer look at the splendid soldiers who had warmed their hearts. Still perched on her soapbox, Selma peered at the stand reserved for the diplomatic corps, some of whom she counted as friends. Yes, there was Luka. How happy he looked, and no wonder: he must be feeling thoroughly reassured. Jules Lukasiewicz, "Luka" to his friends, was the Polish ambassador. He had given one of the last great balls of the season at his palatial residence, the Hotel de Sagan, only a few days earlier. Paris rarely saw such spirited dancing. All the most elegant women in town had danced a wild polonaise directed by Serge Lifar tapping out the beat. How dearly they loved Poland and its charming ambassador, and how ridiculous that little German ogre with the toothbrush moustache seemed! Selma, who had been wholeheartedly enjoying herself that evening, has been irritated to overhear a remark made by some diehard pessimist to the man beside him. "How blind can you get!" he muttered. "What foolish gaiety! This is really the blindman's ball!"

It was three weeks since Harvey had left. Although she dreaded his departure, Selma felt surprisingly cheerful. She missed him, of course, and often caught herself looking for his tall figure among the people around her, but she savoured her sense of loss because it was a measure of how much she loved him. For the first time love did not frighten her. She had confidence in Harvey because he had given her confidence in herself: hers was the certainty of one who knew at last where she belonged. She lived for the moment with a new-found serenity, marvelling that it was both so intense and so simple.

During these early summer days, Paris had surpassed itself at holding dazzling social functions. It was as if the City of Light wished its devotees to miss it more than usual when they set off on the annual summer exodus. Selma was much in demand. Far from being cold-shouldered after her three weeks' absence, she was welcomed back all the more warmly for having deprived everyone of her company.

One of the main events in June had been the Eiffel Tower's "Golden Wedding." The grand old lady's fiftieth anniversary happened to fall on the Duke of Windsor's forty-fifth birthday, and all the social lights of Paris had celebrated that happy coincidence on the first floor of the tower. Ladies wearing bustles in the style of 1889 danced lively quadrilles while the sky blazed with fireworks set off in the grounds of the Palais de Chaillot.

But the undisputed highlight of the season had been a fancy dress ball given by Comte Etienne de Beaumont to mark the tricentenary of Racine's birth. Frivolous and affected, the count himself impersonated Lully while his friend Maurice de Rothschild made a magnificent Bajazet in a turban adorned with diamonds. Jean Marais, the latest discovery of Jean Cocteau, who was madly in love with him, appeared as Hyppolite, naked beneath a tiger skin. Schiaparelli came as the Prince de Condé while Coco Chanel chose simply to come as a "bel indifférent."[1] The Maharajah and Maharani of Kapurthala, attired in sumptuous robes of crimson velvet, went as the Duke and Duchess of Lorraine. Also in evidence were a Comtesse de Sevigné, some young ladies from the Saint-Cyr convent school, and a whole embassy from Siam among which Eve Curie and Princess Poniatowska hid their faces behind long, curving fingernails. Selma, dressed as Berenice, a touching, black-veiled figure with a barbaric diadem encircling her brow, was particularly admired. It was not until much later that she wondered why she had chosen to play the role of a queen abandoned by the man she loved.

Now that it was mid-July, however, and all the social butterflies had flown off to seaside resorts or fashionable watering places, she

1 Term used for "les précieux" in eighteenth-century France.

revelled in her leisure as if she were a tourist at large in a city where she knew no one and could dispose of her days as the mood took her. She had declined an invitation from Marie-Laure to spend the summer on her Eden Rock estate. She wanted to be alone – alone with the strange, warm burden whose presence had now been making itself felt in her for several weeks. She needed to relax, listen to her body, collect her thoughts. So far, her only response to the gradual changes within her had been to have her skirt fasteners adjusted when she found that her waist was beginning to thicken. Harvey had suspected nothing. He had simply teased her for being a little plump and blamed it on the French cuisine.

Harvey . . . she had promised herself to tell him. But she had been so busy . . . so busy distracting her thoughts from that promise she now hesitated to keep.

Would he understand her silence? She found it ever harder to justify it as time went by. She had been wrong to recoil when she had the opportunity to speak. A man in love was more easily swayed in a woman's arms. How much power could she wield with a few sentences in a letter written from thousands of miles away? Harvey might think her reticence a sign that she had been divided between Amir and himself. He would be hurt, break off the relationship without further thought and do everything to forget her. No, it was better not to write. If he really loved her, he would understand when she told him on his return in September.

Now that her mind was made up Selma felt calmer and had no difficulty in silencing the little voice that whispered, *What if it is a boy? What will you do then? Does love entitle you to deprive your son of his right to accede to the throne of Badalpur*?

There was no point in burdening her mind with "ifs." Life, as Harvey always said, must be lived in the present.

The early weeks of August passed like a dream. The French capital was almost deserted. Nearly a hundred and twenty thousand Parisians had left on vacation. Everyone had been reassured by a broadcast from Radio-Cité, whose astrological consultants predicted that there would be no war that year.

Concierges had moved their chairs out into the street and eyed with benevolence the rare passersby, as if welcoming them into the community of true Parisians, those who stay! On the bandstands in the public parks, municipal orchestras played pieces by Gounod and Bizet, but nothing of German origin. Even Beethoven was blacklisted.

At Zeynel's insistence – he was worried about their dwindling resources as the banker's drafts from India were slow in coming – Selma gave up her suite at the Plaza Athenée. She told the concierge that she was leaving Paris for a while and asked him to hold her mail.

They had only to cross the Seine to find themselves a rather provincial but quite comfortable hotel on the Avenue Rapp. The deciding factor from Selma's point of view was its proximity to the Champ-de-Mars: she resolved to take daily walks there for the baby's sake. From now on the baby would be her chief concern. She reproached herself for having neglected it – even for having possibly prevented its little lungs from developing by pulling in her waist so tightly. But did it already have lungs? She had no idea what this baby inside her looked like at five and a half months.

As for Zeynel, he was in seventh heaven. For the first time he had Selma all to himself. He had strongly disapproved of her escapade with the American, whom he loathed on sight. Harvey, sensing his hostility, had gone out of his way to be pleasant, but familiarity from a stranger was just what the eunuch liked least. "He is not of our world, Princess," he kept saying. "One can tell he is not used to being waited on." When it dawned on him that the affair was becoming serious, he even threatened to write to the Rajah, who had, after all, entrusted him with his wife's welfare. But the words were no sooner out of his mouth than Selma glared at him and held out a pen.

"Write to him and you'll have my death on your conscience. He'll kill me, you know that perfectly well, and he'll probably kill you too for taking such bad care of me!"

Zeynel bowed his head; he had not really expected to succeed in influencing Selma. No one except the Sultana had ever been able to quell her, even as a child, but at least he had tried. His anger redirected itself at the Rajah. How could he have been unwise enough to leave his young wife alone in Paris after keeping her cloistered for two years? Selma must have read his thoughts, for her parting shot was uttered in a voice so cold it struck him with dismay for the bitterness he heard in it.

"What matters to my beloved husband is his reputation, not my fidelity. That is what he asked you to protect. So it is your duty to help me to keep things hidden. I credited you with more perception, Zeynel."

He nodded as if convinced by her line of reasoning. He could endure anything except the icy attitude she adopted when someone tried to thwart her. Besides, it was not so much her escapade that disturbed him. She was not a young girl any more, after all, and if the

Rajah made her unhappy. . . . No, what worried him was the fact that she seemed genuinely in love, because with her headstrong character he knew her to be capable of giving everything up.

Now that the American had gone, however, things were looking better. He would be alone with his princess, his little girl. He would be able to cosset and care for her. She was so vulnerable, so much in need of love and protection, and he, Zeynel, was all she had. He was her father and mother, brother and husband, all rolled into one. He almost prayed for some disaster to strike so that he could save her – so that she would at last realize the extent of her need for him, the one faithful soul who had accompanied her throughout her life and would always, no matter what happened, remain at her side.

The chambermaid brought Selma a copy of *Le Figaro* every morning with her breakfast, and she used to read the news while nibbling her croissants. For some days now, attention had been focused on the Anglo-French military mission sent to Moscow, and the newspaper, which was always very well-informed, reported that Stalin was absolutely determined to sign a pact with Great Britain and France.

On this day, 22 August 1939, optimism reigned. Paul Claudel, the eminent poet and diplomat, declared on page one that "Croquemitaine" – the legendary ogre of French nursery lore – was about to be "deflated." Croquemitaine, of course, was Hitler, who was being mercilessly mimicked by everyone in France, from schoolchildren to the cabaret artists who brought houses down by imitating him on stage. Only a week ago, the Maginot Line Rosegrowers' Association had sent President Lebrun a magnificent bunch of roses. Initially puzzled by this report, Selma had laughed on discovering that thousands of rose bushes had been planted all along the Maginot Line, and that its garrison had no intention of allowing them to be trampled by German jackboots.

In the paper's daily social column she lingered over a description of "the ball of the little white beds" which had taken place the night before at Cannes' Palm Beach. It was attended by the cream of the aristocracy and the very rich, and was sponsored by none other than Madame Marechale Pétain whose dignified bearing reminded the guests that it was a charity gala.

The news was good and the weather glorious. Selma listened to the radio while she was getting dressed: the popular song of the moment, *Tout va très bien, madame la marquise,* seemed to sum up her mood. *Tout allait très bien* – everything was going fine, and things would be even better when Harvey joined her in a few days' time. She had received only two brief postcards since he left, but he had warned her that he would not be able to write much from the back of the Mexican beyond. Anyway, he would definitely be there by the beginning of September, as he had promised to take her to Cannes for the first international film festival. All the biggest Hollywood stars were expected – in fact the Americans were reported to have chartered a transatlantic liner to accommodate "a whole boatload" of them.

Six years were to pass before that glamorous boatload turned up. . . .

The next day, on going downstairs to the hotel lobby, Selma heard the alarming news that was to change the face of things: Stalin had ended by signing a pact, not with Britain and France, but with Hitler. It was a hard blow; could war still be avoided now?

Even as Premier Daladier was proclaiming France's peaceful intentions over the airwaves, the walls of Paris broke out in a rash of posters recalling reservists to the colours. Distribution centres for gas masks were set up within twenty-four hours. Every Parisian had to provide himself with one and carry it at all times. Memories of the large-scale gas attacks of World War One still lingered. Broadcasters and journalists gave advice on how to equip cellars, block windows, and shield entrances with moist blankets or sheets – unnecessary precautions, no doubt, because the government would manage to negotiate the war away, but it was better to be prepared.

It was a strange week for Selma. She could not decide if the danger were real, for around her the fear and agitation were mingled with disbelief. Long lines of cars brought vacationers back to Paris earlier than planned but equally long lines left the capital in the other direction. Workmen had begun to crate up the Louvre's masterpieces and dismantle the stained glass windows of the Sainte-Chapelle were to be stored in the vaults of the Banque de France. The inmates of Vincennes Zoo were evacuated, to be followed a few days later by thirty thousand children. The railroad stations were thronged with travellers. Schoolchildren outward bound for the country were departing while parties of terrified Jewish refugees from Poland and Germany were arriving.

At last, on 2 September, came the incredible news that Hitler had invaded Poland. Would the French go to war? Many thought they should. Wladimir d'Ormesson, writing in *Le Figaro*, declared: "Our conscience is clear and so is our duty: we shall win."

Like millions of people in France that Saturday night, Selma could not sleep. She tossed and turned for hours, wondering whether to go or stay. For a week Zeynel had been urging her to leave for Lausanne without delay – even if her own safety meant nothing to her, he said, she should at least think of the baby – but she would not make up her mind. She wanted to wait for Harvey, who was due any day now. If things went wrong they would leave together.

That Sunday morning, at dawn, the news-stands were besieged: Britain had presented Germany with an ultimatum. What would France do? The Parisians were almost relieved to learn, around noon, that their country had entered the war at Britain's side. After days of doubt and apprehension, the situation was clear at last.

The sun had dispersed the morning mist, and the people of Paris, with gas masks slung over their shoulders, came out into the streets. Accompanied by Zeynel, who was stunned by the news, Selma walked to the Champs-Elysées. She wanted to gauge the atmosphere, hear what was being said, try to understand what was happening. The pavement cafés were crowded with voluble Parisians, all offering opinions and predictions of their own. The attitude of the United States was debated with particular vehemence: would the Americans remain neutral or come in on the Allied side? Selma, watching the long line outside the special recruiting office for foreigners, thought of Harvey. He should have been there beside her on that sunny afternoon. Would he arrive soon? Would he be in uniform when she saw him next? She shivered. No, the others could go and be killed, but not Harvey. She prayed with all her might that America would stay out of the war.

Within a few days the face of Paris changed. Public monuments were sandbagged and windows painted blue. Women wearing braided caps and armbands replaced the men who had left for the front. Employed by the thousands, they deputized for traffic policemen, mailmen, bus conductors, railroad conductors, truck drivers.

But it was at night that the City of Lights seemed most unrecognizable. Darkness was total from nine o'clock onwards, the street lights having been turned off for fear of air raids. Even cars were forbidden to use their headlights and had to drive with the aid of their parking lights alone. Selma, who, since Harvey's departure, had occasionally dined out with Zeynel, seldom went out any more. Restaurants shut at eleven, and theatres and music halls had closed down. Men in yellow armbands made their appearance in every neighbourhood. Too old for military service, these civil defence wardens combed the streets all night, blowing their whistles at householders who broke the blackout regulations. They were also responsible for maintaining order by day, and hustled people indoors when the air raid sirens sounded.

Selma never forgot the first alert. Rudely awakened by the siren at 1.00 A.M., the hotel guests had pulled on their bathrobes and dressing gowns and dashed downstairs with a great deal of shouting and jostling. Once in the cellar, the apprehensive adults and tearful children huddled in the alcoves that had been furnished with a few old armchairs. One authoritative-looking woman decreed that prayers should be said, and, listening anxiously for the thunder of bombs, everyone recited the Our Father and the Hail Mary with long-forgotten fervour. When the all-clear finally sounded, they all returned to their rooms feeling as if they had barely escaped death.

Selma spent the rest of the night playing cards with Zeynel, as she often did these days when unable to sleep. Even when she woke him, he was always grateful for these moments spent in her company, as if she had given him a gift. That night they talked for hours, and Selma, having finally conceded that it might, after all, be wiser to leave for Switzerland, asked him to buy rail tickets as soon as possible.

But the next morning's papers announced that the alert had merely been a false alarm designed to test people's reactions. The population of Paris had passed that test with flying colours, but – thank God! – no German bombers had entered French airspace. Zeynel pleaded and grumbled, but in vain: Selma changed her mind and decided to stay on. Her obstinacy mystified him. She saw none of her Parisian friends any more, claiming that they bored her. She had not even contacted Marie-Laure, who must have been back in Paris for at least two weeks. Why should she refuse to leave? For a moment he thought she might be waiting for someone – the American, perhaps – but he quickly dismissed that idea as absurd. Their affair was well and truly over. He had been watching the mail, and there had not been a letter from America for nearly two months. He knew Selma well enough, to be sure that she could not still be in love with a man who neglected her so completely.

In the days that followed the sirens went off at all hours. Although the streets emptied at first and everyone hurried home, people eventually got used to the din and ignored it. Their indiscipline drove the block wardens to despair, but the Parisians could not see why they should spoil their lives when press and radio confirmed that everything was quiet.

All the real fighting was going on in the East, where the battle for Warsaw had begun on 9 September. Besieged and bombarded into submission, the city finally surrendered after eighteen days of resistance. Poland was partitioned for the fifth time in her history, in this instance between Germany and the Soviet Union.

The French shed a few tears for the luckless country that had been crushed between "the jackal and the pig," as *Le Matin* phrased it, but congratulated themselves on having nothing to fear, thanks to their hundred miles of Maginot Line. The armies of the Third Reich were inferior to the German army of 1914, and their soldiers, as everyone knew, were undernourished and ill-equipped.

Parisians who had fled the capital at the outbreak of war came drifting back. The October sun shone down on a city where life had largely returned to normal. Most theatres reopened and the fashion houses launched their winter collections, though with fewer frills, out of deference to the soldiers on leave. The watchword now was elegance with simplicity: tailored RAF blue, "camouflage" coats with leopard-skin spots, cotton prints with titles such as "Tanks," "False Alert," and "Offensive," and the occasional chevron or fourragère. As *Le Jardin des Modes* put it: "You must remain beautiful, the way the men at the front wish you to be. Besides, spending money is a patriotic duty. It is up to you to perform this essential task, which you alone can carry out successfully: keep the luxury goods industry going!"

Selma was unable to support this handsome contribution to the war effort; her money had almost run out. She had received nothing for a month. The mails were disrupted but would soon be restored – that was what she told Zeynel when he expressed concern, but she secretly wondered if her husband had somehow heard of her affair with Harvey. Whatever the truth, it went against the grain to beg money from a man she had deceived and was bent on leaving. Amir had always been loyal to her: she did owe him that respect, at least.

She would simply have to get by on her own. If her mother had sold her jewellery, so could she. She saw herself back in Beirut, in the yellow drawing-room with Sultana Hatijé and Suren Agha – saw the marvellous pieces disappearing one by one into the little Armenian's leather pouch. She had vowed then that it would never happen to her – that she would never want for money – but history was now repeating itself. . . .

The next morning she and Zeynel set off for the secondhand jewellery market on Rue Cadet. They visited a number of gloomy little shops where men in well-worn suits screwed magnifying glasses into their eyes and examined her jewellery with an air of suspicion. Gone were the days when kind old Suren Agha used to visit the Sultana's house. These sour-faced dealers made her feel like a thief attempting to dispose of her haul. Two or three of them went so far as to claim that most of the stones were fakes or of poor quality. Selma was grateful for Zeynel's presence. He lost his temper, thumped the counter with his fist, and threatened to call the police. At that the men became slightly less surly, and one of them, "to help the lady out," offered to take everything off her hands for fifty thousand francs. At first Selma thought he was joking.

"But they are worth twenty times that!"

"Take it or leave it," he replied curtly, and disappeared into his back room.

She started to walk out, but then she realized that she had no choice. Her child would be born in the next few weeks and she desperately needed money. She did some rapid mental arithmetic: the sum the bandit was offering would keep them for eight months - possibly ten, if they were careful – and Harvey would have returned by then. She gestured to the dealer to take the lot. The only pieces she kept were her mother's string of pearls and an emerald ring that Harvey liked because it was the colour of her eyes.

Harvey. . . . She had never given up hope. Her letters had remained unanswered, but she was not alarmed. She wrote mainly as a way of being with him for a while, suspecting that it would be a miracle if any letter from Paris reached the remote Mexican Indian village. While she waited she spoke of her lover to the blue-tit, whose cage stood beside the window of her hotel room, and went to sleep each night clutching a tortoiseshell lighter he had given her. He would come soon, she felt sure, especially as America had just reaffirmed its neutrality. It was taking him time to find a ship bound for France, that was all, because sailings had been few and far between since 5 September, when a German U-boat had sunk the *Athenia*, a British ship laden with civilians. Selma had been pursued by doubts all her life, but this time she refused to countenance them. Harvey had urged her to be confident. To question his love would be a betrayal.

Till now she had always sent Zeynel to the Plaza Athenée to pick up her mail. However, it crossed her mind that the eunuch might be capable of destroying any letters from America he found there, so she decided to go herself in the future. This meant braving the concierge's courteous smile, which was growing more and more sardonic each time. Especially since the day he had suggested it might be more convenient to leave a forwarding address. Taken aback, she had blushed and stammered that she was always on the move. He had pursed his lips at this, and she sensed that he had grasped the whole situation, no longer impressed by the pearls and furs she made it a point of honour to wear when going to see him.

No snobs are more snobbish than those who wait on the wealthy, but for Harvey's sake Selma was even prepared to endure a concierge's disdain. In retaliation she slipped him a tip so princely that he could not bring himself to refuse it. It was all the money Zeynel had given her to cover the purchase of baby clothes.

With nothing left but a centime or two, she had to return to the hotel on foot. She crossed the Pont de l'Alma slowly, walking with care to avoid disturbing the baby she could now feel stirring within her. Its first kick – delivered on the day after the 14 July parade – had given her such a fright that she had hurried to the doctor, who smilingly assured her that all mothers experienced the same phenomenon. She thanked him for his advice without believing a word of it. *Her* baby was preternaturally vigorous. She had only to remain still for a while and it called her to order with an imperious kick, as if bored by her immobility and determined to prod her into action. Accordingly, she had taken to walking for hours around public parks and museums, convinced that the emotions their beauty aroused in her were as necessary to the child as the oxygen and nourishment she transmitted to it by means of a process she had no wish to understand.

That day, as she made her way back to the hotel, she told herself that her gesture of pride, which Zeynel would be bound to consider insane, was more important to the child curled up inside her than all the baby clothes in the world. Being as intimately dependent on her as it was, it could not fail to become imbued with her own spirit of pride and rebellion.

"Monsieur, you are the father of a pretty little girl!"

The midwife emerged, beaming, from the room outside which Zeynel had been pacing up and down since morning, endlessly invoking the ninety-nine names of Allah. It was well after dark, and the woman heaved a sigh of relief as she mopped her brow, almost as exhausted as the young mother. It had been a difficult birth – her patient was so frail and the baby so big – and there had been several occasions when the risk of heart failure loomed.

"Three and a half kilos, monsieur. Congratulations!"

Zeynel tiptoed into the room where Selma lay, pale as a marble statue on a tomb. Through a mist of tears, he looked at her: he was back in Istanbul – the motionless form on the bed was the Sultana and the red, squalling bundle beside her little Selma, her child. . . .

"Well, Zeynel, aren't you going to congratulate me?"

Her weary, faintly mocking voice recalled him to reality. What an old fool he was to mull over the past when his little girl had been through such an ordeal! Smitten with remorse, he rushed to the bed, seized her hands, and kissed them again and again, mumbling unintelligible words of gratitude. The midwife discreetly announced that she was going but would return tomorrow morning.

"In the meantime, decide what you want to call the baby. I shall have to register its birth at the *mairie*."

"No need," Selma answered with an enigmatic smile. "My . . . my husband will attend to that."

The night light cast a reddish glow. Zeynel, worn out by so many hours of emotional strain, had gone to bed a long time ago. Selma was alone with the child asleep at her side.

A little girl. . . . God had willed it so and was showing her the path. Everything was simple and straightforward now: her child would live in freedom. Even if she had to hide herself away, she would never return to India – she vowed it on her baby's cradle.

CHAPTER 5

1 December 1939

Highness,

We are just emerging from a long nightmare. That is why you have received no word from us for some time. The princess has been very ill – so ill that we feared we would lose her – but now, Allah be praised, she is better, though still weak.

It grieves me, Highness, to be the bearer of such evil tidings, but you will probably have already guessed their nature. On 14 November the princess was delivered of . . .

Zeynel stopped short. The hand that held the pen was trembling. It was impossible! He could not write that terrible word: it would bring the baby bad luck – Allah would punish them both! A shudder ran through him. He was afraid of the crime he was about to commit, but he was even more afraid of Selma's wrath. She would never forgive him. Instead of trusting him, as she did more and more now that they were alone in Paris, she would think he had betrayed her and treat him like a stranger. That was an unbearable prospect. After all, perhaps she was right to want to leave a husband who made her so unhappy. Hadn't the Rajah locked her up for two weeks because she accepted an invitation to dance? Hadn't she nearly died as a result? It was his duty to protect her in accordance with his promise to the Sultana on her deathbed.

He gritted his teeth, and his hand grew steadier. "On 14 November," he wrote, "the Princess was delivered of a stillborn child."

There, it was done. He stared in a kind of stupor at the word that had, at a stroke, changed the course of a human destiny. From its father's point of view the child no longer existed: that single word from him, Zeynel, had just made it disappear.

When Selma had broached the subject a few days earlier Zeynel had thought at first that she was still suffering from the effects of childbirth. He soon had to face the fact that her plan was the product of mature consideration, not a passing fancy. She was afraid that the Rajah would compel them to return to India by exerting pressure through his rights on the baby.

He refused point-blank, horrified by the thought of abetting a scheme that struck him as criminal. To declare a baby dead seemed almost as abominable as killing it in reality. When she insisted, he tried to reason with her arguing that she had no money of her own; what were the three of them going to live on? Selma retorted that the balance of the proceeds from the sale of her jewellery would keep them for another six months at least. After that there would be the oil money.

"What oil money?"

"You know perfectly well, Zeynel: Sultan Abdul Hamid bought the oil wells at Mosul in Iraq – they are our family's private property. Before leaving India I had a letter from my Uncle Selim stating that the Iraqi government had agreed to pay us compensation. The war has held everything up, but it cannot last forever. We'll soon be rich, Zeynel!"

She took his hands, laughing so gaily that he did not have the heart to pour cold water on her expectations. The Iraqi government might simply annex the oil fields without paying any compensation at all. Who in the world would champion the rights of an exiled dynasty bereft of political influence?

"All right," he grumbled, "perhaps you do have some money coming to you. It still doesn't change my attitude. I'll never lend myself to such a monstrous act."

"I thought you loved me," Selma cried with tears in her eyes, "but you refuse to understand! Do you want me to be a prisoner again? Do you want my daughter to live out her life in purdah, married off at twelve to some old rajah for the sake of his money? I'll never let that happen! If you desert me, so be it: I'll stay on alone with my child. But it hurts me that you should feel your first duty is to my husband, who means nothing to you, rather than to our family. . . ."

And she turned her back on him. For days she declined to address him a word, weeping and refusing to eat. It was a form of emotional blackmail, he knew, but she was capable of making herself really ill. What would he do with the child? Seeing him waver, she changed her tactics and painted an idyllic picture of the life they would lead in a country untrammelled by the prejudices of another age. They would be like a family, the three of them.

Her implication was obvious. She was offering him an escape from the prison of his own flesh – an escape of which he had often dreamed, but which he had thought impossible until he came to Europe. Once it dawned on him that many people in France mistook him for Selma's father, or even for her husband, the world had taken on a different complexion. Suddenly he was no longer a eunuch, but a man to be treated with respect. In India, where everyone knew of his condition, he could tell that the women and young people were making fun of him behind his back. There as elsewhere, eunuchs in the grand tradition no longer existed. All that remained were a few Africans whose lack of refinement and education unfitted them to do more than guard the doors of the zenana, and Zeynel had nothing but disdain for them. In Turkey it had been another matter. The palace eunuchs were feared by the women of the harem because they had access to the master, whose confidants and advisers they often were. The Kisler Agha, or chief of the black eunuchs, was one of the empire's foremost dignitaries and sometimes wielded more power than the Sultan's ministers. Those days were gone, alas. Nothing was left of all that power and glory but the cruel mutilation that made the eunuch an object of contempt.

Finally, after agonizing for days and nights on end, Zeynel went to Selma and told her that he could not bear to see her so unhappy: he would do as she asked. He had no idea that she had written to the American, and that her suggested family of three was really intended to be a family of four. Selma had been careful not to tell him, knowing that it would be the surest way of stiffening his resistance.

The truth was, a strange idea had come to her, which first of all she had pushed aside but which gradually took root and finally possessed her completely. One day while gazing into her daughter's brown eyes, now becoming flecked with gold, she had caught herself imagining that the baby bore a resemblance to Harvey, as if its features had been moulded by her own desire that the child be his.

What if she told him that it *was* his? The little girl needed a father, and what better father could she have than Harvey? How would he ever know? The situation was so uncertain that Harvey would be unlikely to join them for several months to come. When he did, he would find himself the father of a pretty little girl, rather advanced for her age, but that was all.

Selma shivered. It was impossible – she could not lie to the man she loved. But would it be a lie? Wasn't the child far more Harvey's than Amir's? Amir was a distant, half-forgotten memory, whereas the baby inside her had blossomed under Harvey's caresses. The warmth she had felt and transmitted to it – the sunlight that had furthered its growth – was a result of Harvey's love. Had she remained in India, driven to despair by a pregnancy that bound her to an unloving husband, she felt sure the child would have been born sickly and steeped in its mother's misery, if it had not lost the will to live before ever seeing the light.

As it was, this lovely little girl was the picture of happiness – the happiness Harvey had given her. If she told him the baby was his, wouldn't she be subscribing to a truth far more profound than any that resulted from a chance occurrence in which she had not really been involved? She could not explain how, but she knew that chronology and logic were factors incompatible with what she felt in her heart of hearts to be the truth – a truth emancipated from an alien past and firmly rooted in a present that claimed her entire being. Reconciled at last in her own mind, Selma wrote to tell Harvey that she was expecting a child by him.

"Still no mail for me?"

"No, Madame, none."

It was the end of January, and Harvey still had not answered any of the four letters she had written him since the baby's birth, addressing them to his New York apartment, disguising her handwriting so as not to arouse the suspicions of a jealous wife. She knew nothing about his present circumstances. Had his divorce come through? Was he still living with Ursula? The wartime disruption of the mail might have explained why some of her letters had not arrived, but not all of them!

She was growing anxious. Now five months had passed since she had heard from Harvey. Was he too ill to write? Had something happened to him?

Fortunately she had the baby to occupy her and prevent her from brooding too much. She was adorable! She gurgled with laughter whenever she heard her mother's voice. She also cried a little – not surprisingly, since she was nearly three months old and cutting her first teeth.

"Madame?"

Selma turned. The hotel manager had accosted her just as she was getting into the elevator.

"Madame, I wonder if you could tell me how much longer you plan to stay?"

"I am not sure – another two or three months, probably."

"It's only that, well . . . I'm afraid I need your rooms."

Selma stared at him in surprise.

"But the hotel is not full! Not many tourists come to Paris these days."

"No, but . . . the fact is, your baby disturbs the other guests – several of them have left. I'm very sorry, Madame, but I must ask you to go elsewhere. I know of a family boarding house that would suit you admirably. It's on Rue Scribe, near the Opera."

Selma was taken aback. She had felt so at home here, with the garden. . . . The manager, who was not a hardhearted man, saw her look of dismay and tried to justify himself.

"We've really done everything we could, because we didn't want a nice young lady like you to have to look for other accommodation. We said nothing about your confinement, even though we never dreamed you would have the baby on the premises. If either you or the baby – heaven forbid! – had died, imagine the complications that would have entailed for us!"

Selma drew herself up.

"We might indeed have died, Monsieur, in which case I would have been *really* sorry for you! Don't worry, we will leave this afternoon. Kindly call Rue Scribe and ask if they have any vacancies."

"To be honest, I've already done so. They do have some rooms, as it happens."

"I see. Very well, prepare my bill."

"No, really, Madame." The manager shuffled his feet and looked embarrassed. "One day more or less, it doesn't matter."

"To me, Monsieur, one day more would be one day too much."

The boarding house on Rue Scribe, which went by the pretentious name "Hotel du Roy," was a third-rate establishment patronized by the provincial petite bourgeoisie and couples who rented rooms by the month while househunting. There was no lounge, just a little dining-room that served a fixed menu. When the cab pulled up and Selma got out, looking very elegant in her fur coat, the manager's wife thought she must have come to the wrong address. Then she caught sight of Zeynel carrying the baby and realized that these were the foreigners she had been told to expect.

"This way, Madame. We've reserved you the two best rooms, complete with bathrooms."

Selma gathered from the tone in which the last word was uttered that they were the only guests with access to such a luxury. She turned to Zeynel.

"I hope you're pleased," she whispered mischievously. "At least this place won't put a strain on our purse."

But Zeynel was not listening, he was too overjoyed. A moment ago, while they were making their way along the corridor, a chambermaid had complimented him on "his" baby.

The other advantage of this move was that it took them out of the orbit of the midwife who had brought the child into the world. Selma still had not registered its birth and had no intention of doing so before 15 February, a date that would deprive Amir of his paternal rights – she obviously could not have carried it for twelve months – and make Harvey's paternity seem more plausible.

She not only had no trouble adapting to her new neighbourhood but came to like it better than the more elegant, but also stuffier seventh arrondissement. Life in the capital had almost returned to normal. The theatres and cinemas were crowded, and the dance halls, after remaining closed for three months in deference to the boys at the front, had reopened in December, since there was no fighting going on anyway. The only reminders of the war were a scarcity of taxis, half of which had been requisitioned, and the introduction of days on which selling cakes, alcoholic beverages, and meat was banned. But the Parisians took that in their stride: if there was no meat, *eh bien*, couldn't one eat lobster instead! Even the sirens had stopped, apart from the usual peace-time test alert, every Thursday, at noon.

It was only at night, in the dim blue glow of the street lights, that one was really conscious of the war, and even then one got used to carrying flashlights around. Besides, the couturiers had launched a "brilliant" new fashion: hats adorned with phosphorescent flowers that discreetly advertised their wearers' presence.

People called this war "the phoney war," and no one took it seriously, least of all the journalists who helped to reinforce the prevailing mood of optimism. On 1 January 1940, *Le Matin* presented its readers with the following New Year's gift: "Morally our enemies stand condemned; politically the war is won. Now, we just have to triumph in the battlefield: we shall not fail to do so."

It seemed more and more probable, however, that Germany would not take the chance of attacking a France whose military strength was apparent from every newsreel, not to mention its ally the British Empire and its inexhaustible reserves of manpower. Selma's marriage to an Indian had entitled her to a British passport. The manager of the Hotel du Roy, having inferred from this that she was an English princess, regularly buttonholed her and asked her what Winston Churchill was up to or inquired after the health of His Majesty King George VI, who must, he felt sure, be related to her. Selma was careful not to disabuse the man and took advantage of her standing with him to extract some preferential treatment. He not only refurnished her room, which she succeeded in making almost comfortable, but allowed her to have her breakfast sent up to her room. When the other guests expressed resentment, the manager firmly retorted that he could hardly refuse these little comforts to a person of such distinction.

One of Selma's acquaintances among the long-term residents was Josyane, an actress by profession and – as she laughingly put it – "something of a witch on the side." Her talent for clairvoyance had earned her quite a reputation and her late afternoon "consultations" in one corner of the dining-room were given by arrangement with the manager, who saw them as a way of pulling in extra customers for tea or aperitifs.

Like many people born with a natural gift, Josyane despised her clairvoyance. All her ambitions were centred on the stage. She was a mine of information about the theatre and the quirks and love affairs of its leading lights. This was what endeared her to Selma, who had never lost her adolescent interest in the world of entertainment. Josyane offered to introduce her to some of her actor friends, and for the first time since the baby's birth Selma left it in Zeynel's charge. The eunuch, who thoroughly disliked Josyane, made a fuss, but Selma was used to that: he never liked it when she made new friends. Josyane took her on an all-night tour of various obscure nightspots in Montparnasse and the Latin Quarter, where the stars of tomorrow recited poetry or strummed the guitar. Though not overly impressed by their talent, Selma found it an entertaining experience. Any distraction was welcome in her present state of rising anxiety: February was drawing to a close, and there was still no news from Harvey.

For hours she would sit at her sleeping baby's side, recalling the few weeks she and Harvey had spent together. She could remember every moment of them – every word he had uttered, every smile and caress – with a precision that astonished her. What also astonished her, who had always been so lacking in confidence, was her certainty that Harvey could not have forgotten either. Even now that all appearances were against their love – if a woman friend had told her a similar story she would have felt sorry for her, convinced that she had been abandoned by her lover – even now, she never doubted Harvey for an instant. She knew that what had happened to them was different. They did not choose each other; they had been carried away by an irresistible fact of life. She could not explain the sense of fulfilment she felt; she told herself that having lived so completely, if only for a few weeks, was like having already experienced eternity, and that death itself had lost all meaning.

The baby whimpered in her cradle. Selma bent over and stroked her silky head. How could she even think of death when her existence was so essential to this little creature, this baby who bore a growing resemblance to the man she loved? The time had come to register her birth, but how? How could she justify a three-months' delay to the authorities? The problem had been preying on her mind for days.

Josyane, who noticed that she was looking worried, offered to help.

"I don't want to intrude, but if there's anything I can do. . . . I'm a Parisian born and bred. I know this city like the back of my hand."

Selma had no choice. She eventually confided in her, though without mentioning Harvey. She said she had not registered the baby at birth and only just discovered that this was a violation of French law.

"I see, so you didn't register her." Josyane eyed her sardonically. "Your reasons are your own business, but you'll have to find a midwife prepared to testify that you've only just given birth. I know one who might, but . . . she'd be running a risk, you see, because she'd lose her licence if it ever came out. It would probably cost you quite a lot. . . ." Seeing Selma hesitate, she added, "The best you can do is to go to the *mairie* with the original midwife and say you didn't know, you forgot – anything!"

"I cannot do that."

Josyane studied Selma's flushed face. She now knew all she needed to know: the innocent-looking little princess planned to falsify her baby's date of birth; that was why she could not go back to the midwife who had delivered it.

"All right, don't look so down in the mouth. I'll do my best to get you off the hook, you know that. I'll go and see the woman tomorrow."

She returned the next day, looking appalled.

"The creature's insane! She's asking the impossible – it's not worth discussing."

"How much?" Selma asked coldy.

"No, it's out of the question – far too much. She wants twenty thousand francs!"

"Twenty thousand! That is incredible!"

"I know, it's crazy, and even then she said she'd only do it as a favour to me because she knows me. You'd better not register the child at all – nobody's been asking questions, after all. Of course, if they ran a check some day – they tend to check on foreigners in wartime – you could find yourself in trouble. They might think you stole the child and take it away from you. I've heard stories –"

"No, don't!" Selma said quickly. "I'll pay. Can we go and see her tomorrow, after I've been to the bank?"

"*We*?" Josyane exclaimed. "You must be mad! She doesn't want to meet you in person, she's far too wary for that. She only accepted me as a go-between because she's known me for so long."

Rather reluctantly, Selma gave way. She suspected that Josyane had not told her the whole truth and was taking a percentage on the transaction, but she did not know what else to do.

The next day she handed Josyane the agreed sum and to calm her nerves, went for a walk with Zeynel and the baby. When she got back to the hotel Josyane had checked out. There was no forwarding address.

To Selma, the news that German U-boats had launched an all-out attack on the transatlantic supply lines between America and Britain was the best news of the year: it helped to explain why no letters had arrived from Harvey. Her spirits rose once more. The war was surely about to end. It would only be a matter of months, not a protracted affair like World War One. Young as she had been, Selma could still vividly recall the dismal wartime atmosphere in Istanbul, the hospitals overflowing with wounded soldiers, the families in mourning. Here in Paris, nobody seemed to take the latest events seriously. On the contrary, they made fun of the military weakness of the Soviet Union, which had taken more than three months to subdue little Finland, and spoke pityingly of the Wehrmacht, whose soldiers, it seemed, were starving and in rags. All the same, those very German soldiers had not only invaded Denmark but beaten the Norwegians, in spite of the French and British expeditionary forces sent to help them. . . .

Hoping to get a better idea of what was really going on, Selma listened to the radio daily and read two or three newspapers, but all reports spoke of famine raging in Germany, of growing dissatisfaction with the Nazi regime, and of a grave but unspecified illness that might soon compel Hitler to retire. As for the politicians, they never tired of proclaiming that there was no cause for concern.

So no concern was shown. It was springtime, and colourful cotton dresses and flowered hats made their reappearance. The women at the Auteuil and Longchamp horse races were as elegant as ever, and along the Seine the riverside cafés had reopened for the season.

One day, while Selma was relaxing on the sunlit terrace of the Café de la Paix with Zeynel and the baby, she suddenly felt two hands clamp themselves over her eyes.

"Guess who?" said a voice in her ear. She turned abruptly.

"Orhan!"

They fell into each other's arms with exclamations of surprise and pleasure. Selma had not seen her cousin since Beirut.

"What on earth are you doing here?" he said. "I thought you were queening it in your gilded palace in the wilds of India."

"What about you?"

"Me? I went into exile with King Zog – exile's becoming quite a habit with me. Not that I miss Albania. It's a pretty country, but a bit unsophisticated for my taste. Meantime I have been married and divorced. I divorced from the king, too! Zog settled down in the country, and as you know, the country and I are not really made for each other. Anyway, I have taken up my old job again, but on a slightly grander scale. I drive luxury cars all across Europe!"

They laughed, really glad to see one another again. Orhan turned to Zeynel, who had been watching them with a beaming smile.

"Agha! How are you? You are looking well." He caught sight of the baby and started. "Hey, what is that?"

"That," Selma proudly replied "is mine."

"Where is her papa?"

"I will tell you sometime. It's a long story."

"Secrets, secrets! That is my favourite cousin all over." Orhan glanced at his watch. "I'm sorry, I'm late for a date with a woman I'm madly in love with."

"As usual," Selma said teasingly. "That is *my* favourite cousin all over."

"Give me your telephone number – I will call you in a couple of days. I have no intention of letting you go now I have found you again." She scribbled her address on a beer mat, which he pocketed. He stroked her curls as he used to when they were teenagers and murmured, only half in jest, "The fact is, *you are* the woman I should really have married."

So saying he kissed the tip of her nose and hurried off, waving his hat as he went.

Two days later, on 10 May, the French were staggered to learn that Hitler's armies had invaded Holland, Luxembourg, and – worst of all – Belgium. Contrary to all expectations and in violation of all the rules, they had outflanked the Maginot Line and marched into a country that had proclaimed its neutrality. What was more, the cowards had deliberately launched their attack during the Whitsun holiday. Never mind, though. The French Army, supported by a few British battalions, had gone to the assistance of France's Belgian neighbours. They would soon make the Boches bite the dust.

Reports from the front remained vague for the next few days, but when Holland surrendered on 13 May the Parisians began to worry. Their fears were intensified by the sight of Belgian refugees driving through the capital in cars laden with all the belongings they could carry. The government recalled General Weygand from Beirut to head the High Command and appointed Marshal Pétain vice-president of the Council. The French hailed the victory of Verdun with relief and gratitude – the country was in good hands at last – but it did not prevent them from holding special church services, just to be on the safe side. They even filed past the relics of Saint Louis and prayed to those of Saint Genevieve, who in the fifth century, had protected Lutetia from Attila's hordes.

On 26 May, the headlines of *Le Matin* read: "Allied troops are inflicting heavy losses on the enemy. French infantrymen have lost none of their traditional qualities." Public anger was all the greater when it became known the next day that Belgium, too, had surrendered. Her traitorous king had capitulated without even warning the French and British commanders in advance! The situation was serious. Allied troops had fallen back to defend the routes to Paris against German invaders whom, by now, the capital's inhabitants suspected of being less exhausted than they had been led to believe.

At the Hotel du Roy several couples spoke of cutting short their stay and returning to the country, but the manager laughingly dissuaded them.

"Come now, there's nothing to fear. The Belgians have no red blood in their veins. The French Army is another matter!"

Tired of his bragging, Selma took Zeynel and the little girl to her room, where they devoted the entire evening to discussing possibilities. There was still time to make for Lausanne, but would it be wise? The Nazis had violated Belgium's neutrality; who could guarantee that they would not decide to invade Switzerland next? The Swiss were less able to defend themselves than the French. Selma hesitated. She had no way of gauging the relative dangers. Newspaper reports were her only source of information, but she realized to her disgust that they were totally unreliable. The fact remained that she must make up her mind, and soon.

Her worried gaze rested on the old man and the little girl, who was clinging to her knees and shouting with laughter. Their fate would depend on her decision. If only Harvey were there, or even Orhan. She did not know how to get in touch with her cousin. He had not tried to contact her, not that this surprised her. When Orhan was entangled in love's web, the world could crumble around him and he would not notice it.

She put her head in her hands. Who could advise her? Marie-Laure? Impossible! It had been ten months since she, Selma, had vanished without a trace. Marie-Laure would be terribly resentful of the fact and might take it out on her. Besides, she would be bound to ask all kinds of awkward questions about the child. No, she could not go to Marie-Laure's.

All at once she remembered Mademoiselle Rose. The French governess had written to her several times in Lebanon and later in India. She had settled down in Paris and was giving private lessons, she wrote, but none of her pupils had replaced Selma in her heart and she never gave up hope that "the little Sultana" would visit her some day. Dear Mademoiselle Rose – why had she not thought of her before? The poor dear would not be of much help – her head had always been in the clouds – but the families she worked for might know what to do.

The very next morning Selma went to Rue des Abbesses, the address Mademoiselle Rose had given in her last letter. The thought of their reunion delighted her – it would be like a glimpse of her childhood in Istanbul. She smiled to herself, recalling how the kalfas had winced at the governess's hats and her legendary social gaffes, but she was such a good soul that everyone liked her. Selma felt ashamed that she had never gone to see her after a year in Paris. She had been so taken up by her social life, and then by Harvey, and now her child, that the governess had slipped her mind entirely. To salve her conscience she went to La Marquise de Sevigné and bought the biggest box of chocolates in the store. Mademoiselle Rose had always had a sweet tooth.

She paused uncertainly outside 12, Rue des Abbesses. Could her old governess really live in this decrepit building, with its flaking plaster and peeling paintwork? She held her breath as she made her way inside past brimming rubbish bins whose stench pursued her up the filthy stairs. How could Mademoiselle Rose, who was always such a stickler for cleanliness, have ended up in this slum? She had obviously run out of money; why had she never said anything in her letters?

There were four doors on the second-floor landing. Selma chose one at random and rang the bell. It was not Mademoiselle Rose who came to the door, but a woman who knew her. Or rather, used to know her.

"Has she moved?"

"Yes, in a manner of speaking. . . . The poor dear died three months ago."

Selma thought she was about to faint.

"What did she die of?"

"Tuberculosis, starvation – everything. . . . People would not employ her any more when they found out she was sick – because of the children, you understand – so she moved here exactly a year ago. She had no work and not enough money for doctors. She got by on the few francs she'd saved. Very nice and polite, she was. I used to ask her in for Sunday lunch sometimes – she was so lonely. Still, you know how it is. One can't do much. We all have troubles of our own. . . ."

The woman had been eyeing Selma curiously as she spoke. Suddenly she smote her brow.

"Of course, I recognize you now! She kept a big photo of you in her room. So *you're* the princess she never stopped talking about. You were the apple of her eye, poor thing. . . ."

Selma burst into tears, thrust the box of chocolates into the woman's hands, and fled. She continued to sob all the way down the street. If only she had come sooner she might have saved her – she would have taken her to the finest specialists in Paris for treatment. Mademoiselle Rose might still be alive at this moment. Even if her case had been hopeless, she could at least have given her a little human warmth, a little happiness. . . .

She did not know how she got back to the hotel. Zeynel spent the afternoon drying her tears. No, he told her, it was not her fault. Everyone was careless or selfish at times. When she continued to reproach herself he picked up the little girl, who had started crying too, and forced himself to speak roughly." *She* is your responsibility now. What are we going to do? What have you decided?"

"Oh, Zeynel," she sighed, "I am worn out. Let us wait another few days. After all, everyone else is staying."

But on 3 June, when the Luftwaffe bombed Paris and sent them hurrying down to the cellar for the night, she regretted her indecision.

The next day the hotel guests from out of town packed their bags and left. There began an exodus of expensive cars from expensive neighbourhoods, the amount of baggage on board suggesting that they were bound for more than a pleasant weekend at Fontainebleau. The authorities, fearing that the enemy would find a deserted capital easy meat, redoubled their soothing communiqués and praised the courage of "the fearless people of Paris." Radio-Cité broadcast glowing accounts of the heroic resistance of the Allied forces, which were throwing back the German armies in the north. Victory was only days away.

"What did I tell you?" trumpeted the manager of the Hotel du Roy. "When I think of the yellow-bellies who scuttled off because they didn't have faith in our army!"

He refrained from adding, but everyone gathered, that he considered such people traitors as well as cowards.

His pride took a bad knock the next day, when the newspapers reported in banner headlines that the Somme front had caved in.

"Is that serious?" asked Selma, who had no idea what the Somme was but was alarmed by the looks of dismay around her.

"Serious?" sneered an elderly gentleman, eyeing her with disfavour. "My dear lady, it means that nothing stands between them and Paris."

Selma turned pale. "The Germans in Paris? But they said the army would –"

"They said! The politicians say whatever suits their book, as I know from bitter experience. I went all through the first war, Madame. To hear them talk, that was just a pleasant stroll in the park!"

In the days that followed press and radio did their best to reassure the Parisians. "Our troops are holding the enemy. Tens of thousands of men are erecting impregnable defences around the capital. Paris has nothing to fear; it will be defended at all costs." On 8 June General Weygand declared: "The enemy has sustained heavy casualties. This is the eleventh hour: stand firm!" But Paris was starting to see the first bands of soldiers in retreat. Sullen and exhausted, they claimed that they had been misled. The Germans' superiority was overwhelming, they said, all was lost.

Extra trains were run for those who wanted to leave, but most people were still undecided. To leave would mean abandoning their homes to the looters who proliferated in troubled times. Besides, where would they go? Few Parisians had second homes or friends in the country prepared to take them in, and hotels cost money. By now Selma would gladly have left the capital but for Zeynel, who was confined to bed with a severe attack of rheumatism. He begged her to go, promising that he would join her as soon as possible.

The answer was to get hold of a car, and only Marie-Laure could help with that. Swallowing her pride, Selma went to Avenue Henri-Martin, only to be told by the concierge that "*madame la comtesse*" had left Paris a week ago. On her return to the hotel Selma reassured Zeynel by pretending that Marie-Laure had laughed at her fears and sworn that Paris was in no danger: the Germans would never set foot there.

This time she had thought carefully before making a decision.

After all these months alone in the eunuch's company, she had too high a regard for his devotion to leave him behind. But for her, he might be living peacefully in India or Lebanon. On the other hand, by staying she was endangering her child. What would her mother have done in such circumstances? She would never have deserted Zeynel. Well, neither would she. If danger threatened, they would face it together.

Early on the morning of 10 June Selma was roused by a commotion in the street. She dashed out on to the balcony and looked down to see groups of people scurrying along the sidewalks. She could not hear what they were saying, but they sounded very agitated. Quickly pulling some clothes on, she left the little girl in Zeynel's room and ran downstairs. The lobby was full of fellow residents with suitcases bursting at the seams.

"The government fled during the night," they told her excitedly. "Hurry, the Boches are coming!"

A medley of voices drifted in from the street.

"Which station are you leaving from? Austerlitz? Better get a move on, the trains will be packed!"

"Me, I'm taking my bike. They say they're going to bomb the railroads!"

"Start packing, damn you!" a man shouted at his wife, who was standing in the doorway, paralyzed with fear. "I warn you, we're leaving in half an hour!"

Selma watched in amazement as cars and vans with bundles and mattresses lashed to their roofs began to stream past, heading for the Rue Royale in the hope of crossing the Seine and reaching the Porte d'Orleans and Porte d'Italie by way of the Latin Quarter. Traffic continued to build up as the hours went by, and by afternoon the streets were jammed. Parisians bent on escape enlisted anything on wheels they could find, from decrepit jalopies that broke down after a few hundred yards to overloaded handcarts hauled by exhausted men and women determined not to abandon their treasured possessions. Throughout the day police headquarters broadcast instructions: "Do not head for the railroad stations – you cannot get near them. . . . Do not take the Boulevard Saint-Michel or the Boulevard Saint-Germain. . . . Traffic in the Boulevard Henri-IV is at a standstill. . . ." The terrified people did not listen to any of it. They now had only one idea in mind: escape.

Selma watched the panic-stricken crowds from her window. When things became really critical she always kept a cool head as if fear were a luxury she could not afford. In any case, what would be the point of her joining that sea of distraught humanity with a baby of seven months and an elderly man who could hardly walk?

The next two days were a nightmare. To the consternation of many who were still reluctant to flee, General Weygand had declared Paris an open city. In other words, the capital would not be defended after all. It was to be abandoned to the victorious Boches, and the Boches, whom everyone knew of old, were bound to massacre all who had been foolish enough to remain.

But Selma and the half-dozen elderly hotel guests who had preferred to stay, either in a spirit of fatalism or for fear of dying from exhaustion on the roads, came to the conclusion that this was good news rather than bad. No defence implied surrender, and why should the Germans destroy such a magnificent city when it was being handed to them on a silver platter?

They all assembled in the little dining-room, deriving courage from each other's company, and the manager – exceptionally – opened a bottle of Armagnac. When they thanked him for keeping the hotel open, he explained that, having slaved all his life to buy the place, he had no intention of leaving it at the mercy of looters.

"I propose to defend my property," he declared, throwing out his chest, "even against the Boches. But anyway, I don't see why they should harm a peaceful hotelier."

Paris, now denuded of three quarters of its population, was strangely quiet. Selma spent the afternoon looking for some milk for the little girl. All the shops were shut, but she eventually found a grocer who sold her, for an exorbitant sum, some stale cakes and two cans of condensed milk. As she made her way back along the deserted boulevards the unwonted sound of her heels on the sidewalk startled her. All the shutters were closed, and the city seemed to have stopped breathing. The Germans were expected the next day.

All night, she sat up in her candlelit room, watching her baby sleep.

Selma woke up with a start. She must have dozed off, for the candle had gone out and sunlight was already streaming through the shutters. A low rumble filled the air. She ran to the window and peered through the slats. They were here!

A column of tanks had just rounded the Place de l'Opera, looking like gigantic beetles in the morning light. Preceded by motorcyclists and followed by armoured cars, they lumbered off toward the Place de la Concorde.

All morning she watched them go by, mesmerized by the display of serene, irresistible power. And gradually a picture emerged in her mind: a little readheaded girl clinging to her mother's skirts as she gazed through the windows of Ortaköy Palace at a squadron of massive warships gliding across the calm waters of the Bosphorus. Clamping the baby tightly in her arms, Selma went downstairs to the dining-room.

The others had clustered around the windows and were silently observing the enemy's progress. Towards noon they saw a party of Luftwaffe officers, in their impeccable grey uniforms, stride into the Grand Hotel on the far side of the Place de l'Opera.

"We're in luck," the manager growled. "If the RAF decides to drop a bomb on them we'll have a ringside seat."

Nobody replied. They all watched in despair as the red flag with the black swastika made its slow ascent of the Grand Hotel's flagpole. Behind her, Selma heard a strange noise and turned to look. The old veteran of the Great War was weeping.

CHAPTER 6

On 14 June loudspeaker vans toured the streets instructing everyone to remain indoors. "No demonstrations will be tolerated. Anyone attacking German personnel will be executed." But the very next day, when it became clear that the Parisians were too shocked by defeat to imagine any form of resistance, the ban was lifted. The army of occupation would be unable to settle in unless life returned to normal and the public services started functioning again. Bakers, shopkeepers, and restaurant owners were ordered back to work – civil servants too. "Everyone must resume his post and do his duty," decreed the French civil authorities, and it was not long before the metro, a few post offices, the banks, even the courts, started to function again as best they could.

Selma had slept little these last few nights, so when Zeynel knocked at her bedroom door on the morning of the 17 May and asked to speak with her urgently, she pulled the covers over her head and told him to go away. Undeterred, he tiptoed in with a conspiratorial air and informed her that the local government offices had reopened. Selma propped herself on one elbow and stared at him.

"You woke me up to tell me that?" she protested.

"They're in absolute chaos," he went on. "There couldn't be a better time to register the baby. Half the staff are away and the rest of them are too busy discussing the latest developments to concentrate. Now is the time to act. I will go to the *mairie* and tell them the baby was born during the night of the 14th-15th, but the midwife was so scared she vanished without making out a certificate. They will not bother to check, believe me. Quickly, Princess, give me your papers and I will bring you back a birth certificate."

Things went exactly as Zeynel had foreseen. The female clerk at the *mairie* took pity on the polite old foreign gentleman who gazed at her so imploringly. Besides, he spoke such poor French that she could not understand his explanations and was not going to waste all morning on him. She decided to dispense with a midwife's certificate. After all, circumstances were exceptional.

"Very well, if the mother's papers are all you've got, let's see them. First name, 'Selma,' wife of 'Amir, Rajah of Badalpur.'"

She carefully wrote down "Amir" in a neat, copybook hand,

mistaking it for the surname. Zeynel held his breath.

"'Rajah of Badalpur' – what's that, the father's occupation? What does 'rajah' mean?"

Zeynel hesitated. If he said it meant "prince" she would think he was pulling her leg.

"Well?" she said impatiently. "He must have a job. Is he a shopkeeper of some kind?"

"Yes," Zeynel mumbled, "that is it, a shopkeeper."

As she carefully completed the birth certificate, he felt even more disloyal to the Rajah than when he had lied to him about the child. He dreaded to think how Selma would react. To his great surprise, she found the whole thing a great joke.

"If Amir finds out he will skin you alive," she said with a chuckle. "But don't worry," she added, seeing him turn pale, "no one could possibly think the child his, not with that date and that name on the birth certificate. That is the important thing."

Selma was in high spirits. After the last few fear-fidden days, everything had finally turned out all right. She decided to leave the little girl with Zeynel and go for a walk.

She kept to the side streets so as to avoid the Place de l'Opera, now a German preserve with its new signs like "Capucine-Strasse" and "Concorde-Platz." But she soon noticed that most Parisians did not bother to take such precautions. Animated conversations were taking place around German soldiers sunbathing on café terraces. Curious to know what was being said, Selma went up to one of these groups of people. Their attention was focused on two big, blond, clean-shaven youngsters in grey field uniforms.

"You don't need to worry," said one of them, "we won't do you any harm. You were duped by the British, who dragged you into a war that was lost from the start, but it'll all be over in no time. You want to see your husbands again, mesdames? Well, the same goes for us. We can't wait to get home to our wives."

Everyone looked dumbfounded but relieved. These Germans were really pleasant. Far from being the bloodthirsty barbarians of popular belief, they were well-disciplined soldiers who, when not on duty, went sightseeing with cameras around their necks and emptied the stores of silk stockings and perfume, for which they paid cash.

The weather was good, so Selma walked on to the Jardins des Tuileries. There people were sitting chatting in the sun while not far away a German military band played Beethoven's Fifth symphony. They pretended to ignore it, but they were listening. "You've got to hand it to those bastards," Selma heard someone say, "they have a real sense of music." Marshal Pétain had just announced on the radio that all fighting must cease because an armistice was about to be signed, and although some people wept at the news, they did so more with joy than shame.

"Thank God it's over! We should never have gone to war in the first place. It was that lousy government and its lying propaganda that got us into this!"

"They told us the Germans were in rags and short of everything. Well, look at them! Have you ever seen such fine-looking troops?"

"They told us not to worry, there wasn't any danger, but when things turned sour they slunk off and left us to fend for ourselves."

Bitterness at having been misled by their own government prompted people to look with less hostility on the enemy, who carefully exploited their disenchantment. "Forsaken people of France, put your faith in the German Army!" urged posters on every wall, and Radio-Cité broadcast heartening items of information: "The German authorities are taking steps to see that Parisians suffer no shortages."

Selma walked pensively along the quiet streets. She could not help remembering another occupied city with its mourning population, men and women evading the enemy's supervision and slipping off to join a young general who had rejected the armistice and called on people to resist. Would the French find a Mustafa Kemal of their own?

On her return to the hotel she surprised the manager and his wife in the midst of an argument. They were obviously talking about her, for her arrival reduced them to silence and the woman, shrugging, disappeared towards the kitchen.

The next day, the manager sidled up to Selma.

"I hate to have to tell you this, Madame, but my wife wants me to report you to the Kommandantur."

"The Kommandantur?"

"The local German headquarters. They've announced that anyone with foreigners living on their premises must register them. The penalty for failing to do so is severe. And you're British too. . . ."

She understood. Yesterday she had been an ally; today, now that the French had surrendered and the British were fighting on, she had become an enemy.

"I told her we could keep you – that it would be easy to hide you if they came to check, but she won't hear of it. I know her, Madame. She's so scared, I wouldn't put it past her to denounce you!" Big beads of sweat were rolling down the manager's face. He avoided Selma's eyes. "You'd be wise to move out, Madame."

Selma felt as if all the blood had left her veins. She clung to the back of a chair for support.

"But . . . where can I go?"

The manager, who had been dreading a scene, was relieved. There was always a solution to other people's problems.

"Leave the centre of town, it's swarming with Boches. Try the north – try Pigalle or Clichy. You'll surely find a little hotel where they won't ask questions."

Selma moved three times in the following month.

She felt safe nowhere, trembled at every glance, saw potential informers everywhere. Although she paid twice the going rate for rooms – "You don't expect me to run a risk for nothing? I'm only doing it for the baby's sake you know" – she never knew if some cleaning woman or next-door neighbour would not eventually talk. The Germans had promised a reward to those who reported suspicious persons, and her British passport made her a prime suspect.

Her fears turned into panic when word went around that all British nationals were being arrested and sent off to camps. Assailed by visions of barbed wire, of children being parted from their mothers, she clasped the little girl to her breast. She would fight tooth and nail – she would never let them take her.

In the prevailing atmosphere of suspicion and denunciation, her beauty and bearing – the air of distinction that had so often been an asset in the past – only added to the danger of her predicament. However hard she tried to look "ordinary," people noticed her – men especially.

"Too good for me, huh?" sneered one day an unwelcome admirer whose advances she had spurned. "You wouldn't be so hoity-toity if I told the Germans who you are, would you?"

She had not taken the risk: she had sent Zeynel to settle the bill and they had left the hotel half an hour later with the baby wrapped up in a shawl.

They ended up on Rue des Martyrs, in a dilapidated rooming house recommended by someone who assured them that the landlady accepted any tenants as long as they paid in advance. Selma, seeing how bare and filthy the rooms were, could understand why. Only sheer necessity would have induced anyone to live in such a slum, particularly as the landlady, a big-bosomed French matron, had no qualms about charging as much as a decent hotel. Her lack of embarrassment was quite understandable. Her tenants paid up because the place enjoyed a safe reputation. The police, by some financially aided miracle, never set foot in it, still less the Germans, who did not care to stray into such a noisy, smelly neighbourhood. They only drove through it at night on their way to Pigalle and the Place Blanche. Seldom had the vaudeville theatres and nightclubs done better business. Sandwich men circulated with new advertisements for the Eve, the Tabarin, and the Kabarett Mayol, and all were filled to capacity with German officers and their floozies. Aside from housing large numbers of civilian and military administrators, Paris had become a German leave centre and made it a point of honour to live up to its reputation as the "*capitale des plaisirs*."

The smartest establishments such as the Monseigneur Cabaret on Rue d'Amsterdam or L'Aiglon on the Champs-Elysées, as well as luxury restaurants like Maxim's and Fouquet's, those one-time haunts of Parisian high society, were reserved for senior officers, but many celebrated French entertainers and journalists could also be seen there. By July most of them had returned: "Life does go on, and besides, art knows no frontiers" they would say.. Serge Lifar and Yvette Chauvire were dancing *Giselle* at the Opera, Maurice Chevalier and Mistinguett were scoring a big hit at the Casino de Paris, and Sacha Guitry had reopened the Theatre de la Madeleine.

Although Selma hardly ever ventured out in case some policeman took it into his head to ask for her papers, she could not resist the temptation to make an occasional foray into these chic neighbourhoods, just for the pleasure of sipping a cup of coffee surrounded by elegant, light-hearted people and forget the Rue des Martyrs for an hour or two.

One day, however, she had a terrible fright. Annabelle, an actress with whom she had dined several times in the past, walked into the tearoom where she happened to be. Annabelle saw her and looked away, but a few moments later, while passing Selma's table on the way to the powder room, she dropped a glove and bent to pick it up.

"You're crazy," she whispered. "This place is full of spies. Get out of here quick!"

If Selma had been alone she might have succumbed to the peculiar thrill she derived from courting danger, but now she could not risk it anymore. What would become of her child if she were arrested?

The little girl seemed quite unaffected by their peregrinations from hotel to hotel. Her spirits remained undampened even by the gloomy cubby-hole that was now their home. Every time Selma came in she was greeted with cries of "Mama!" and joyous gurgles that made her forget all her sorrows. She had developed unsuspected maternal instincts, and would never have dreamed that she could become so attached to this little creature. Her daughter was part of her. The physical bond between them was so strong that, when she held her in her arms and shut her eyes, it was as if the child still nestled within her – as if they were still one same flesh.

At such times her peace of mind was as absolute as her sense of belonging. She could feel, growing up inside her on the debris of her former uncertainties, a strength sufficient to enable her to take on the whole world singlehanded.

Life, Selma was discovering, was this child. This child who clung to the present, who had neither built up a past to justify her nor a future for reassurance. Would she be able to help her to avoid the mistakes she herself had made and teach her that, in the game of happiness, one can only win by accepting to lose oneself?

"You'll make our little princess ill. It is long past her feeding time!"

Zeynel was reproach personified. Since the baby's birth the eunuch had transformed himself into an authentic nursemaid. Nobody could have changed or fed it more efficiently, and Selma noted with a pang that the little girl often made more of a fuss of him than of herself.

She was late home because she had spent the whole afternoon lining up for half a litre of milk, and even then she had had to pay five times the official price. "Take it or leave it," had been the dairy-woman's curt response to her protests.

Shopkeepers were nowadays treated like royalty by Parisians ready to bow and scrape to swallow any humiliation for the sake of a bit of butter or a kilo of sugar. Almost everything was running short, as German raids on the big central market at Les Halles were a daily occurrence. Furthermore, now that France had been divided into an occupied and an unoccupied zone, the capital was cut off from many of its normal sources of supply. Ration cards were being printed and Selma, who was living on the "black market" and could not apply for one, wondered desperately how long she would be able to hold out.

She had been forced to sell her pearls when the money from the rest of her jewellery had run out. All she still possessed was the emerald ring. Tomorrow she would send Zeynel to the jeweller's on Rue Cadet. They ought to be able to live on the proceeds for another two months, but she had no idea what would become of them after that. She herself could do with very little and Zeynel did not eat much either, but the little girl? Selma could not bear the thought of her suffering. She had heard that the Swiss consulate took care of foreigners in distress, but she did not dare go there for fear that it was being watched and she would be arrested.

No word had reached her from India since the baby was born – "still-born," as far as Amir knew. Selma sometimes thought of the palace at Lucknow with all its women who used to smother her with their noisy solicitude. She was especially haunted by memories of Oujpal and the village women's welcoming smiles. Although she had no regrets, she could not repress a kind of bitter-sweet nostalgia, the kind one feels for one's adolescent years, even when they have not always been happy ones.

She wondered what had become of Amir. Now that she no longer had to protect herself against the Selma he had wanted her to be, she remembered him with a certain affection. For two years they had tried in vain to get close to one another. She had attempted to love him, this strange being who fascinated her and yet repelled something deep inside her. She now realized that he, too, had tried to understand her and curb the reflexes he had inherited from a social order in which a woman's existence was wholly subordinate to her husband's. Often they had tried to reach each other but the gap between them was too wide. Amir had made efforts to bridge it but the branches he held out had been nothing but sprigs to her. Now she could see how much she must have wounded him. Their pride, their lack of confidence in each other as well as in themselves, had blinded them to the hand that was being held out. Their worlds were too dissimilar, and their characters too much alike.

A few days later, as she was passing the counter behind which Madame Emilie presided all day long, the landlady accosted her with a suspicious frown.

"You, there! Are you Jewish?"

"No," she replied, taken aback. "Why?"

"Think yourself lucky. I reckon they're in for a rough time, the Jews. Didn't you hear what happened on the Champs-Elysées?"

And she proceeded with the relish of those who like nothing better than other people's misfortunes – not because they are enemies, simply because they are "other people" – to describe how a group of youngsters had marched down the avenue from the Etoile to the Rond-Point shouting "Death to the Yids!" and smashing the windows of every Jewish-owned store in sight. And Madame Emilie's thick lips spat out the prestigious names – Cedric, Vanina, Brunswick – as if she were reciting a list of dangerous criminals.

"That'll serve them right for making such a killing out of honest folk like us!" she concluded majestically.

Puzzled by her belligerent attitude, Selma suppressed a grimace of distaste. In Turkey, where Jews were citizens like any others, their diligence and intelligence had won them wide esteem. But the landlady's remarks were reminiscent of a line taken recently by certain newspapers that had reappeared in occupied Paris and, whether from self-interest or conviction, adapted themselves to suit the city's new masters. Selma sometimes glanced at *Le Matin*, which carried little political news but did at least announce the days on which supplies of scarce commodities such as eggs, potatoes, or coffee would be reaching the stores.

It had not escaped her that *Le Matin* had launched a fierce anti-Jewish campaign. One description of the Marais district spoke of "bearded men in long, grimy overcoats, children playing with scraps in the gutters, low foreheads, long noses, and crinkly hair, shopkeepers who inflate their prices by eighty percent. . . . Everything in the neighbourhood is Jewish," the article concluded with disgust. "How, when we claim we are promoting public hygiene, can we tolerate that repulsive stain in the heart of Paris?"

Another journalist, waxing more political, declared that the Jews were entirely responsible for France's misfortune. "In 1936 they instigated the so-called social security laws that wrecked relations between employers and employees and led to bankruptcy and unemployment."

Stores had begun to put up notices reading "Jews not admitted." These were offensive rather than effective, given that nobody was going to ask to see every customer's identity card. But the first ominous step was taken on 27 September, when the Germans ordained that all Jews should enter their names in a special register.

"They can stuff their register," Charlotte told Selma firmly. "I'm damned if I'm going!"

Charlotte, a seamstress at Maggy Rouff who rented one of Madame Emilie's rooms, was a great admirer of Selma's natural elegance. The two young women had been friends ever since the day when Charlotte, having given Selma the once-over, said, "That dress of yours – I made it!" To Selma's amazement, she kneeled down and turned back the hem. "Yes," she said, beaming with pride, "it's mine all right. The workroom superviser says there's no one to touch me when it comes to fine stitching!"

After that Selma had given Charlotte her evening gowns to sell, which she did for a good price. She had resolutely refused to take a commission, so Selma sometimes invited her for a meal and the pert young Parisian girl, with all the wit typical of her kind, regaled her with the gossip and tittle-tattle of a world she no longer inhabited.

Also Selma owed her a special debt of gratitude, now that ration cards had been introduced, for giving up her milk coupons for the baby. "Don't thank me," Charlotte had told her. "Milk makes me feel sick."

So Charlotte had decided not to register. "They'd never guess," she said. "I've got a French name. As for the rest of me, I'm a woman, thank God!" And she burst out laughing at her own little joke.

Three weeks later the Vichy government enacted a "Jewish statute" debarring Jews, "for reasons of national security," from employment as civil servants, attorneys, judges, teachers, officers of the armed forces, journalists, radio commentators, stage and screen actors, even dentists.

"I was right, wasn't I?" said Charlotte. "Not that I've any ambitions to become a minister, but it's a bit hard. I mean, have we got the plague or something?"

Madame Emilie hailed the "Jewish statute" with approval. "No doubt about it," she proclaimed from behind her counter, every inch the true Frenchwoman, "the Marshal's a great man!"

And she took advantage of the opportunity to raise the rent of the two Jewish families living on her premises. Charlotte's rent remained unchanged. Had Madame Emilie not realized that the girl was Jewish? It was rather surprising as she made it her business to know everything about her tenants. Perhaps she thought it useless to try to squeeze anything more out of a girl who barely earned enough to live on. Selma decided that she had misjudged her.

She had. A few days later two gendarmes came to arrest Charlotte. The other tenants looked on aghast as she struggled in their grip.

"You're making a mistake!" she cried. "I'm French!"

"You can explain all that down at the police station," they sneered, hustling her outside. She just had time to whisper to Selma before they thrust her into the paddy wagon.

"Watch out for the old bitch!"

Charlotte never returned, but the next day Madame Emilie was sporting a new dress. She looked quite pleased with herself.

In the days when she still had a little money left, Selma had taken to paying an occasional visit to the Lapin Agile, in Montmartre. It amused her to hear guitarists singing satirical songs and watch the carefree young Bohemian set that patronized the place, but it was mainly her memories of Harvey and their evenings together that drew her there.

Among her recent acquaintances at the Lapin Agile were some

young people who had taken her under their wing. They included Spaniards on the run from Franco, a few Czechs, and one or two Poles, all of whom had sought refuge in France and been surprised by the arrival of the Germans. Warm and easygoing, they had only one rule: discretion. Nobody asked questions in their rather nebulous world, where people came and went without explanation. Their names were obviously assumed. How did they survive? By small-scale black-marketeering, no doubt. Their resourcefulness became obvious to Selma when, after having known her for a while and decided that she was "all right," they procured her some forged ration cards and managed to get her a decent price for her long mink coat, several Hermes purses, and scores of shoes, the latter being in great demand now that leather was unobtainable.

Although they never talked politics, she noticed that often they knew of things well before other people – for instance, of the students' demonstration in front of the Arc de Triomphe, on 11 November, where they were fired at by German soldiers. Selma had once or twice overheard curious conversations that made her wonder if these frivolous young men, who seemed only interested in making a few francs and having fun, were in touch with the resistance movement that was rumoured to be in process of formation.

Sometimes the group would meet to dance in a cellar whose skylight had been bricked up to deaden the noise and prevent any light from escaping. They were flirting with danger for dancing was prohibited and, as the curfew began at midnight, they used to dance till dawn with an exuberance heightened by the knowledge that tomorrow they might not be free any more.

The first time Selma returned at dawn she found Zeynel sitting in an armchair fully dressed, not having slept a wink all night. He merely looked at her and said nothing, his most eloquent form of reproof. She sat down beside him looking contrite.

"Please try to understand, Agha. This room gives me claustrophobia. The little girl is such a joy during the day that I forget all our worries, but at night, when I have nothing to take my mind off things, I get so depressed I cannot sleep."

Zeynel took her hand and kissed it.

"Forgive me, my princess, I'm a selfish old creature. You are still so young – this existence is indeed hard to bear and you need to enjoy yourself from time to time. I would give my life to see you happy, you know that, but. . . ." His voice trembled and his eyes filled with tears . . . "the truth is I'm afraid. If anything happened to you, what would become of our little girl?"

Selma gave a reassuring laugh.

"Do not worry. I am being very careful." But she knew he was right. She went out less often and induced him to help her decorate the walls of the room and shade the light with lengths cut from her saris. The multicoloured silks made the place look rather like a gypsy encampment, but at least they cheered it up and raised her morale.

Infuriated by the landlady's spiteful comments on "all that lovely material wasted, when some people don't have anything to wear," Zeynel retorted that "the Princess" could do as she pleased with her own property. He persisted in using Selma's title even though she had urged him not to do so in case it put the rent up.

"You don't understand," he told her. "I know these people – you have to impress them or they will trample you underfoot."

He was right. The old woman not only refrained from putting their rent up in the knowledge that Selma had very little money; she handled her with kid gloves instead of making her life a misery, as she did with the other tenants. When things returned to normal, she insinuated with a meaningful smile, she was sure that Madame would remember "all the sacrifices" that had been made for her benefit. Too weary to argue, Selma gave in and promised that she would be generously rewarded. She forbore to ask what sacrifices Madame Emilie was referring to. Presumably, she found it an immense sacrifice not to insult her.

In spite of the forged ration cards food was becoming more and more of a problem. There was almost nothing to be had except on the black market, where everything was obtainable but at exorbitant prices. Selma bought the child's staple necessities under the counter and fed herself and Zeynel on Jerusalem artichokes and turnips. Even potatoes had become such a luxury that the newspapers announced consignments of them three weeks in advance. Every adult was entitled to one ounce of meat and two ounces of hard black bread a day. The sugar ration amounted to one pound a month. Coffee was just a fading memory, but the newspapers printed recipes for "delicious" substitutes made of toasted barley or acorns. As for tobacco, Zeynel, who was a heavy smoker, had to content himself with dried cornsilk.

The eunuch made a point of shopping for their tiny rations, which could only be obtained by standing in line all day. It was his job, he said, not the Princess's. Selma eventually bowed to his insistence on these habits and values from another age, sensing that their present predicament made them as essential to him as the air he breathed. What he did not tell her was that her physical condition worried him.

Selma had never been fat, but now she looked as if a puff of wind would blow her away. She had more than once felt faint in the street, and the people around her looked puzzled, never imagining that such a well-dressed lady could simply be hungry. But hunger was not the worst part. What Selma found far harder to bear was the cold. The winter of 1940 was bitter. People shivered outdoors, but they shivered indoors as well for lack of coal. Selma could not even open the windows to air her room, they were glued shut by a film of ice. One evening she found the blue-tit frozen to death in its cage. And she, who had endured everything so far, burst into tears: another little reminder of Harvey had gone. She forbade herself to imagine that it was a bad omen, but she could not help it: in the Oriental world such signs were significant.

Zeynel could not understand her grief at the loss of a bird and advised her to worry about the child instead. She was at a vulnerable age, he pointed out. So Selma took to lying in her bed fully dressed with the little girl in her arms. It appalled her to think that her daughter might fall sick. Even if she could feed her adequately by depriving herself of food, there was not much she could do about the cold, especially as Mers el Kebir had cost her her last fur coat. . . .

Great indignation had reigned among the Pétainists in July 1940 – and at that time most Parisians were Pétainists – when the RAF sank half the French fleet based in Algeria to prevent it from being captured by the Germans. Ever since then, Madame Emilie had never missed a chance to inveigh against "those treacherous English" and glare at Selma as she did. On his mistress's instructions, Zeynel would mollify the landlady with modest offerings such as handwoven shawls or strings of coloured beads, all these presents which the women of Badalpur had crafted with love for their Rani and which Selma had brought in a trunk as if they were precious soil from India. Although she winced whenever she saw Madame Emilie wearing one of these "exotic knickknacks," as she called them, Selma knew that her Indian friends would have understood.

Then had come this chilly October morning when Selma headed for the street in her otter-skin coat. Madame Emilie had complimented her on her appearance.

"I never knew *English* ladies could be so elegant," she remarked with a disingenuous smile.

Her first direct allusion to Selma's nationality had the cutting edge of a knife blade. Selma took off the fur, handed it over without a word, and went back upstairs to her room – quickly, to spare herself the landlady's hypocritical words of gratitude.

These days she went out in a woollen coat more suited to spring or fall than to such freezing temperatures. The solution was to walk fast or even run, but that she could not manage. She had been growing very weak for some time now. Occasionally, too, she felt a stabbing pain in her right side. It never lasted more than a few seconds, but the attacks had become more frequent in recent weeks. She had not mentioned them to Zeynel, who would only have become even more worried. The poor thing was in a bad enough condition already. He had lost his pot belly and was only a shadow of his former self. Selma knew she ought to consult a doctor about her recurrent pain and take whatever he prescribed, but doctors and medicines were expensive and their money had almost run out. Besides, she felt sure the pain would go if only she watched her diet a little. It was probably the poor quality oil she used for cooking.

"It isn't serious, is it, my treasure?" She hugged the baby in an access of affection. "At least you are the picture of health. You are the prettiest little girl in the world. Your mama says so and she never lies – well, almost never. Wait and see, we shall both be so happy once the war is over." She sat the child on her knees and bounced it rhythmically up and down. Screams of delight were succeeded by petulant protests when the horse grew weary and began to slow down. "Aha, so Mademoiselle has a mind of her own! All the better. I will not try to polish and refine you – I won't turn you into a fashionable young lady. You're entitled to be what you are, you don't need to justify your own existence. When I think your silly mother took twenty-nine long years to realize that. . . ."

Without Harvey would she ever have realized it? Harvey. . . .

How intensely she had at first resented his enforcing freedom on her and answering her requests for advice by telling her that any objective was worthwhile provided you lived life to the full; that attaining it mattered less than aiming for it and stumbling on the way, because failure was an incentive to self-scrutiny. He also said ideals were like hoods – they paralyzed you, prevented you from really seeing and hearing what was going on around you, and that only fools acted according to an ideal, whether borrowed or forged, because they did not have the courage to stand on their own two feet. He also talked of happiness which did not come from this or that circumstance but from our ability to live each moment as it came, for the joy or sadness of things depends on how we look at them.

"To think that it's only now that I can understand what he meant! It has taken war, poverty, and loneliness for me to find the happiness within myself. For I *am* happy. I have never loved life so much –

never, despite the fear, the hardships, has the world seemed so radiant!"

And yet ever since the death of the little bird, Selma had sensed that she would never see Harvey again. Independent of their own volition something was happening which threatened to separate them forever. Only a few weeks ago the thought would have driven her to despair; now she felt at peace with herself. Whatever happened, she knew she could face it. She was no longer her old vulnerable, tormented self; she was a woman on whom Harvey had bestowed the greatest gift of all: he had taught her to forget herself and to love.

"Oh, my treasure, my treasure!" With the child in her arms she started dancing to the lilt of a Strauss waltz coming from the radio. "You will see how sweet life can be. Now I know the secret, we shall never be unhappy again, I promise.

The little girl had put her arms around her mother's neck. She burst into laughter as Selma turned, slowly at first, then faster and faster until the colourful Indian silks on the walls sped past her eyes in a joyous fandango.

A sudden pain in her side, sharp as a dagger-thrust, sent Selma reeling. She fought for breath, tried to cry out. The child – she must not drop the child. . . . The table was only a few feet away. She tottered towards it, reached for it with one hand, clung on with all her might. An intolerable, burning sensation pervaded her. Flames, a rain of ashes. . . . She could not see anymore. She felt she was falling, plummeting into an endless void. . . .

The spirited strains of the waltz continued as the little girl lay screaming by her unconscious mother's side.

That was how Zeynel found them when he returned from shopping some time later: Selma was lying on the floor, very pale, with the terrified child, whom she had managed to save as she fell, crying with terror beside her.

CHAPTER 7

The surgeon was pacing up and down his office at the Hotel-Dieu Hospital. He eyed his hands bitterly. They enjoyed quite a reputation, those hands. Some people called them miraculous, but this time they had not been able to save a life.

He had wasted no time in getting her on to the operating table, but she was suffering from acute peritonitis and already semicomatose. For two whole hours he had cut and cleansed, ligatured and sewn, toiling away with his team of silent nurses around him. She was so young: he had to save her! And when he had finally sealed her frail abdomen he had mopped his brow and breathed a sigh of relief: his old enemy would not win this round!

But later that evening, when her temperature shot up, it became clear that septicaemia was gaining ground. Only that new drug called penicillin they were making in the United States could have saved her, but it was still unobtainable in France. He had remained powerless, watching the remorseless onset of the thing that was taking possession of the pale, emaciated body he had thought to have snatched from death.

Now it was over. It had not even lasted twenty-four hours. The infection had spread very rapidly, meeting little resistance from an organism so obviously weakened by undernourishment. The surgeon clenched his fists. He had been operating for twenty years, but every time he lost the battle with death, it tore him apart. He knew it was wrong of him, but he felt this even more strongly when a patient was young and in the full flower of her beauty, like this one, for, to his sense of failure, it added an intolerable sense of waste.

Now he must speak to her father, who had been waiting outside in the corridor ever since last night. He had smiled at the old man after the operation and said, "She'll pull through." The wrinkled face radiated gratitude, and before the surgeon knew what was happening the man was down on his knees kissing his hands and weeping with joy. Gruffly, he had helped him up and allowed him to spend a few minutes with the still unconscious patient. He had then been struck by his look of adoration. There was so much love in his face that it seemed to warm the bleak little hospital room, and the surgeon could not help reflecting that, if all human beings were capable of even a fraction of such love, war would be a thing of the past. At length he had reluctantly broken in on the father's loving contemplation and advised him to go and get some sleep. The nurses told him later that he had remained outside the door all night, sitting on the floor.

The next morning Zeynel was not allowed into the room. Doctors and nurses were busy inside. The surgeon had dropped in two or three times between operations. Every time he had met the old man's imploring gaze: "We are doing all we can," he had repeated, mustering a smile.

And now what would he tell him?

He did not need to say anything. Zeynel already knew. He had known precisely when his little girl breathed her last. A spasm had run through his body, a kind of wrenching pain, and he had sunk to the ground, hitting his head on the doorpost.

The nurse who found him there, half unconscious, sat him down and bathed his head to bring him around. Now there were things to be done, decisions to be taken. What was to become of the body? These people certainly would not have a family vault, being foreigners, so where would the corpse be buried?

None of these things was the surgeon's responsibility – the hospital administration would attend to them – but pity for the bereaved father had prompted him to prepare a few words of comfort. They went unsaid. The old man's gaze was so vacant, so infinitely remote, that words seemed out of place. The surgeon simply shook his hand and turned away.

Zeynel could remember little of what happened in the hours that followed. A woman in a white coat asked him a lot of incomprehensible questions, so he eventually handed her his wallet and told her that he just wanted his little girl buried in Muslim soil.

That afternoon two men drove up in a hearse pulled by a scrawny nag. They slid Selma's plain deal coffin into it and gestured to him to follow.

How long did he walk behind his Selma? The icy January rain soaked him to the skin, but he did not feel it. He was remembering their long walks together in the old days and her coaxing smile as she made him promise to follow her to the ends of the earth.

Finally they came to a big expanse of wasteland enclosed by dilapidated walls. For as far as the eye could see, rows of headstones protruded from the grass and low scrub: it was the Muslim cemetery at Bobigny. Zeynel could not suppress a sob at the recollection of the pretty cemeteries overlooking the Bosphorus where Selma used to love to roam.

But the imam in charge of the cemetery was growing impatient. It was late, and he wanted to recite the prayer for the dead as soon as possible, especially since the old man clearly could not afford a more elaborate ceremony – he did not even have the wherewithal for a tombstone engraved with the name of the deceased. Too bad, they would simply have to write it on a piece of wood so that the graves would not get mixed up when the grass grew again. Families did not like that. What wretchedness. . . .

Two men had dug a grave in the section reserved for women. Zeynel stared at the coffin as they lowered it on ropes into the dark pit. Why had they imprisoned his little girl in that box? She would suffocate – she had always hated confined spaces. In Islamic tradition, the body is wrapped in a white sheet and laid to rest in the soil itself, but in France they said this was not allowed.

It was almost dark when the gravediggers completed their work. The hearse had left a long time ago. Zeynel lingered on in the cemetery, among thousands of graves, alone with his Selma. How pathetic that rectangle of trodden soil seemed in comparison with the majestic marble monuments at Istanbul, which for century after century perpetuated the glory of the great sultanas! He shivered. Who would ever guess that his princess reposed in this pauper's grave? Who would remember? . . .

He stretched out on the freshly turned soil and covered his little girl with his body, trying to impart a little warmth, a little love. He was all she had left now, he would not desert her, he had promised the Sultana.

"Agha!"

Selma came running toward him across the garden, auburn curls flying in the breeze. She looked so pretty in her blue silk dress.

"Agha, take me to see the fireworks on the Bosphorus tonight!" She flung her arms around his neck and clung to him, playfully tugging his hair. "Please, Agha, you must! I want you to!"

"But it is forbidden to leave the grounds, little princess."

"What does it mean, forbidden? Oh, Agha, don't you love your Selma any more – don't you want her to be happy?"

Never able to resist her, he gave in yet again. At nightfall they strode hand in hand down the paths fragrant with mimosa and jasmine to where a gilded white caique bobbed at the water's edge.

The fireworks turned her hair to molten gold as she jumped lightly aboard. While he was settling himself at the oars, she looked at him with shining eyes.

"And now, Agha," she whispered, "we are going on a long, long journey, just the two of us.

Zeynel was roused by a tap on the shoulder. It was getting light, and the man standing over him had a puzzled frown on his face.

"You mustn't lie there, you'll catch your death."

The man helped him to his feet, brushed the earth off his clothes, and led him, shivering all over, to a small tool shed near the cemetery gate, where he poured him a big bowl of steaming coffee. He introduced himself as Ali, the caretaker.

"So, brother," he said sympathetically, sitting down beside Zeynel, "was that your woman who died?"

"My daughter," Zeynel stammered. His teeth were chattering.

"And you aren't going to give your daughter a headstone?"

Zeynel shook his head. He felt weak all of a sudden. He had not eaten a thing for three days, not since he had found Selma. . . .

Ali, with a decisive movement, cut him a hunk of bread.

"Here, eat this. If you're interested, the stonemason around the corner is a friend of mine. He could sell you a little stone cheap."

With numb fingers, Zeynel felt in his vest pocket and laboriously extracted his gold watch, his one remaining memento of his splendour at Ortaköy. He had been keeping it as a last resort, but now. . . .

"This is all I have. Would he take it?"

"Keep your watch, you'll need it. Don't worry, I'll take care of the stone. Muslims must help each other."

Overriding Zeynel's protests he hurried off. A few minutes later he returned with a small slab of white stone under his arm. Then under Zeynel's supervision, he chiselled in clumsy letters:

SELMA

13.4.1911–13.1.1941

But something was still troubling Zeynel. "They did not bury her like a Muslim," he said. "They put her in a box. Do you think we could. . . ?"

Ali's face lit up. He liked to see a real believer. Jumping up, he fetched some picks and shovels and brought a white sheet from the cemetery storeroom. It took them less than half an hour to unearth the coffin and extract the nails. Then just as Zeynel was about to lift the lid Ali discreetly retired.

"I'll leave you to it," he said. "Call me when you want to shovel the earth back."

Slowly Zeynel opened the coffin. It was the first time he had seen her since. . . . How beautiful she looked in her long white shift, so beautiful and so young, with the light auburn ringlets spread out on her shoulders. Trembling, he bent down and very gently kissed her cheek.

When he straightened up his eyes were dry. He felt suddenly drained of all emotion: this chill, silent figure was alien to him. His little girl was not there anymore. She had gone away with her laughter and gaiety, her whims and enthusiasms, her generous nature – all the things that had made the Selma he knew. She was gone. . . .

He gently wrapped the body in the white sheet and very carefully replaced it in the grave. The soil whose scent she used to love, and which now received her beauty, was welcoming her as its own. Her arms, her lips, her breasts – the whole of her perfect body – would melt into it and bloom into a thousand flowers.

It seemed to Zeynel that Selma was looking over his shoulder and smiling. This was what she would have wanted. Before long he would join her, and the three of them – he, his Sultana, and his little girl – would dwell forever in a lacework palace like that of Ortaköy, lapped by the crystalline waters of a river resembling the Bosphorus. . . .

Suddenly he caught his breath and his eyes widened in horror.

The child – he had forgotten all about the child! The little thing had been alone for three days, with no one to feed or tend her. She might already be dead. . . .

"Allah!" he cried. "Allah preserve her!"

He did not know how he got back to the hotel. He had a vague recollection of Ali stopping a hearse going back to Paris and helping him into the empty place usually reserved for the coffin. Then he had run through the streets like a madman, calling upon Allah to have mercy.

He had burst into the room to find the little girl lying on the bed with her eyes closed, very pale. Her head back and her mouth open, she was breathing with difficulty.

His cries brought a neighbour hurrying in from the room across the landing. She said he must not move the child, just raise its head and get it to drink some water, but the little girl was past drinking. In despair, Zeynel picked her up. She was frozen. Quickly he wrapped her in a bedspread and dashed downstairs past Madame Emilie, who tried to bar his path.

"Hey, you! You owe me two weeks' rent!"

He ran down the Rue des Martyrs as fast as his failing legs would carry him. On the way he stopped at several doctors' offices and hammered on the door, but to no avail: it was Sunday. Finally he accosted a gendarme, who directed him to the Swiss consulate, open every day to foreigners in trouble.

Zeynel staggered down the Rue de Grenelle, feeling close to heart failure, but he hung on: he had no right to die before he had saved Selma's child. When he lurched into the consulate, however, and a blond secretary with plump cheeks asked him what he wanted, he just had time to thrust the child into her arms before he collapsed, unable to say a word.

That afternoon Madame Naville, the consul's wife, had come in to collect a list of addresses for the next Red Cross charity sale. She took one look at the child and immediately phoned her own doctor. Then she sent for some cognac and poured Zeynel a glass. The old Muslim nearly choked and tried to spit it out, but she made him drink it up.

"It isn't alcohol," she reassured him, "it's medicine."

Fortified by the brandy and heartened by the unknown lady's kindly manner, Zeynel soon recovered. He blurted out the whole story – how his princess had died, and how her little girl had lain abandoned in a hotel bedroom for the past three days. The doctor arrived within minutes.

"Just in time!" he growled, on seeing the child's condition. And producing a big hypodermic from his bag he gave her an injection of serum. Then, very gently, he examined her.

"She is very weak. Double pneumonia, and she looks as if she has not taken any food or drink for days. . . ."

He heard a moan and turned to look at the old man slumped in an armchair.

"Don't worry, *mon brave*, we'll save her." He lowered his voice for the benefit of Madame Naville. "But she will need intensive care, and the Assistance Publique is so overstretched at the moment, with all these war orphans. . . . Unless she receives constant attention, I'm afraid – "

"I'll have her for as long as it takes, Doctor," the consul's wife broke in. "This little girl fell from the sky, so to speak. I cannot let her die."

Every day for several weeks, Zeynel came to see the child. Thanks to careful nursing and the wholesome food available at the Swiss consulate, an oasis of plenty in occupied Paris, she recovered very quickly. Before long, it was a chubby little girl who greeted the eunuch with delighted cries of "Zézél!"

He told the consul's wife everything, though he naturally omitted to mention the American episode and his letter to the Rajah. The latter had never replied, so he hoped the letter had gone astray. After the war His Highness would be able to take the child back home – that was the only possible solution now that Selma was no more. The little Princess would grow up in the zenana, get married and lead the comfortable and uncomplicated existence of a noble Indian lady. Wasn't it what Selma had tried to say on her deathbed? The eunuch recalled the young nurse who had run up to him just as he was leaving the hospital.

"Wait, Monsieur! I was with your daughter when . . . well, just before. . . . She clung to my hand and muttered something like: 'Forgive me, Amir . . . the child . . . I lied to you. . . .' Those were her last words."

Zeynel shuddered to think how anguished Selma must have felt when she realized she was going to die, leaving her child fatherless. She had done her utmost to ensure that her daugher would live in freedom, never dreaming that she herself would be gone so soon.

"My pretty princess, my poor little girl. . . ." Zeynel felt immensely weary. At the other end of the room the child was playing with her dolls. She was in safe hands now – she did not need him any more. He had done what he had to do, as well as he could. And now he, too, wanted to go and rest.

He kissed her on the forehead – gently, so as not to disturb her – and slowly walked out of the room.

He was never to be seen again.

EPILOGUE

Thus ends the story of my mother.

Not long after she died the Swiss consulate received a visit from her cousin Orham. He handed the receptionist a calling card inscribed simply: "On behalf of the dead princess."

The Rajah learned of his daughter's existence through diplomatic channels. Communications between British India and German-occupied France being cut, he was unable to have her brought to Badalpur. They did not meet until well after the war. But that is another story.

No trace was ever found of Zeynel. Did he die of grief, or was he, a foreigner among foreigners, loaded into a sealed freight car and hauled off to a concentration camp?

As for Harvey, he had not forgotten, but he discovered Selma's letters only after his wife's death. She had hidden them from him for three years.

He hurried to France immediately after the Liberation. Thereupon learning that Selma had died, he resolved to adopt her child. However, he had only just embarked on the complicated formalities when he himself died of a heart attack.

Later, much later, I wanted to understand who my mother was.

I questioned those who had known her, I consulted historical records, newspapers of the period, and scattered family archives. I lingered beside all the milestones on her road. In all these ways I tried to reconstitute the various environments in which she had lived, irrevocably changed though these now are, and to experience all that she had gone through.

And finally, in an attempt to come even closer to her, to reach her, I relied on my intuition and my imagination.

DATE DUE

GAYLORD 234			PRINTED IN U. S. A.